He made a neat stack of the model composites given him as a guideline by Kristina, and pushed it across the desk. How the hell was he to know who was the best? On the front of each glossy composite card was printed a headshot of the model, on the back three or four more carefully selected pictures, along with the model's statistics. The men all looked the same to Miles. They were nearly all handsome in a classic square-jawed, pearly-toothed, six-foot-two, forty-regular, thick-haired kind of way. And they would nearly all look ridiculous surfacing from a swamp in the Amazon. How the hell was he to choose? Was this man really out there, this fresh, manly, muscular, organic, universal, pure, virginal, versatile, sexy, butch, rugged swamp-thing? Miles longed for something more definite to work with. More than Saul Weissman's Force, at least. He closed his eyes. Maybe everything would become more clear once he began to visit the agencies.

Tim Geary became a model while at Cambridge and has worked all over the world for top designers such as Ralph Lauren. He is now a full-time writer and lives in Suffolk. *Ego* is his first novel.

Ego

Tim Geary

CORONET BOOKS
Hodder and Stoughton

Reproduced with kind permission from THE ECONO-
MIST BUSINESS TRAVELLER'S GUIDE TO JAPAN.
Copyright © 1987 and © 1990 The Economist Publi-
cations Ltd and Webster's Business Traveller's Guides
Limited

First published in paperback in 1994 by Hodder and Stoughton
A division of Hodder Headline PLC
A Coronet paperback

The right of Tim Geary to be identified as the author
of this work has been asserted by him in accordance with the
Copyright, Designs and Patents Act 1988.

10 9 8 7 6 5 4 3 2

British Library Cataloguing in Publication Data

Geary, Tim
Ego
I. Title
823.914 [F]

ISBN 0-340-61367-X

Typeset by Hewer Text Composition Services, Edinburgh
Printed and bound in Great Britain by
Cox & Wyman, Reading, Berks.

Hodder and Stoughton Ltd,
A division of Hodder Headline PLC
338 Euston Road
London NW1 3BH

For my parents.

Acknowledgments

For guiding me through the rapids I am indebted to the faultless triumvirate of Carolyn Mays, Felicity Rubinstein and Sarah Lutyens; for helping me to the river, Sara Snow, Dominic Loehnis and Samantha Weinberg. In London, Helena Frith-Powell, Matthew Conrad, Rob Haan and Phil and Philly Roberts were all invaluable; as were Wendy Hirschberg and her brother, Seth, in New York; and Iona Fergusson in Paris. But without the patience, enthusiasm and encouragement of my family: Caroline, James, Geoff, Sophie, Ronnie and Trish, this may never have been written.

1

'Let me tell you why you're here.'

With his round frame silhouetted against the dazzling blue Manhattan sky, Saul Weissman pointed a stubby finger at Miles Jensen, and looked deep into the young man's eyes. 'It's because you're not up to your balls in bullshit like the guys in advertising. If I was to tell *them* to go find a new male model for this cologne, you know what they'd do?'

Miles managed a quick shake of his head.

'They'd pick up every goddamn fashion magazine they could lay their hands on and then go choose the guy whose face appeared the most. You believe that?' Saul Weissman cracked open the shell of a pistachio and threw the pale green nut into his mouth. When he spoke again, a tiny crumb flew out with his breath. 'Those guys do not have an original brain cell between them. And you know what else?'

'Ah . . . what?'

'They're like this with the modelling agencies.' For ever using his hands while he spoke, now Weissman slapped them together as if the truth was a butterfly that he'd captured between them. He shook his catch at Miles. 'It's a joke, I tell you. A fucking conspiracy. Huh?'

Weissman opened his hands and was silent. Apparently this was his first real question.

'Yes, sir.'

'You said it.' Weissman slapped his palm down on the desk. 'So fuck 'em. Fuck, them. We're gonna go it alone on this one. *Weissmans* is gonna find an Adonis for this cologne of mine and put his face in every magazine in the world. It's gonna be like we created this guy, Milo. I want a Marilyn Monroe with a schlong, OK? All *you* gotta do is go find him.'

1

Saul Weissman sprang out of his maroon desk chair with the agility of a man half his age and a third his weight. He turned to look on to the streets of New York. With a hurried sweep of his dwarfish arm he beckoned Miles. Side by side they stood closer, it seemed, to the azure sky than to the mayhem of the streets below.

'Tell me what you see out there, Miles.'

Miles looked out. He saw Manhattan at its most glorious: the dream of his youth sanitised by fifty-three floors and resplendent in glass and concrete reality. He saw the dreams of men of previous decades piercing the sky – the desperate needle of the Empire State Building, the extravagant fishtails of the Chrysler, the arrogant phalli of the World Trade Towers. He saw a city more beautiful to his eyes than any other in the world. Beautiful because it was alive, because it challenged him as it challenged others to grab life and run with it.

'I . . .'

'Can't describe it, huh? That's it! You hit the nail but you don't know it.'

He had? The thought raced through Miles's mind that Saul Weissman might be insane. The man from the gutters of Brooklyn who'd built up a retail empire bearing his name, whose face had appeared on the cover of *Time* magazine beneath the caption 'The man who clothes the world', who'd made mincemeat of all the Ralph Laurens and Calvin Kleins of the globe, was this man certifiably mad?

'Wanna know why you can't describe it? Because New York City is infuckingdescribable. Take *that* as your challenge, Miles. You go out there and find me a male model who's . . . who's . . . beyond words.'

Could anything be beyond words for the great Saul Weissman? Somehow, Miles doubted it.

Although Weissman was by far the shorter of the two he managed to slump his short, heavy arm most of the way across Miles's shoulders. The oldest of friends. Weissman lowered his voice, became conspiratorial. 'Now, tell me where you're gonna start.'

'I suppose I may as well start right here.'

'Wrong! I want to show you something.'

Weissman moved to his desk and picked up a small photograph framed in silver. He rubbed its glass face on his suit lapel and handed it to Miles with the pride of a father displaying his firstborn. 'Take a look at that.'

As Miles studied the photograph, Saul Weissman began to rummage through the drawers of his desk, muttering and swearing to himself. Then having slammed shut all the drawers at least twice, he hammered a finger on to his desk intercom. 'Rona,' he shouted, 'I'm out of nuts. Is this some kinda joke?'

Rona's voice sounded calm and controlled. 'No.'

A bead of sweat erupted on Weissman's wide forehead. 'What did I say about the pistachio nuts, huh?'

'You said you'd ask for more when you needed them.'

'I did? Well I need them. Yesterday. Call Arty at Nuts About You. Get five pounds. Pronto. No, make it ten. OK? Now Miles, tell me what you see.'

The print was old and folded in half as if it had been carried around in a wallet for years. It looked as uncomfortable in its silver frame as the young Saul Weissman did in a suit. Though the photograph had lost its sharpness Miles could make out the buildings of Ellis Island in the background. This place, where refugees and dreamers rubbed shoulders and anglicised their names for the New World, was the first reference point for most of the rags-to-riches stories of foreigners who'd made their fortunes in New York. Miles thought it strange that Weissman, a native New Yorker, should feel sentimental about such a place.

'That's Ellis Island, isn't it?' Miles ventured. 'From Battery Park.'

'You got it! I used to go there most weekends and see all these immigrants ogling at the Statue of Liberty, blubbing their little eyes out. But you know where I was looking?'

To draw Miles in, Weissman lowered his voice from its regular shout. He laid his hands flat upon his desk, and leant towards Miles. 'As far as I could see. Further!' Saul Weissman straightened his back and swung his chair around to look towards Battery Park, apparently lost in the memory. 'Wanna know why this city's so screwed up, Miles?' he shouted.

A cough. 'Yes.'

'Because there aren't enough guys out there like me!'

Miles thought of a city full of Weissmans. A city full of short fat men in their sixties stuffing their faces with bagels, cream cheese and pistachio nuts, all at each others throats in the belief that succeeding isn't enough, you have to see the other man fail? The concept was terrifying.

Weissman himself was momentarily quiet as if he was having the same dream with a different ending. But seconds later, resembling a boxer hearing the bell, he leapt out of his chair again and began to talk with renewed vigour, pacing back and forth in front of the window. 'See Milo, it takes the same amount of guts to reach Manhattan from a Brooklyn slum as it does to get here from Poland. You with me? Brooklyn Bridge is as wide as the Atlantic. But when *I* made it to this side I never thought I'd reached the end of the road. Oh no! I could see so frigging far past the Statue of Liberty that now I've got a franchise in Moscow. See what I'm saying?'

At this Weissman spread his arms, palms upward as if he was Al Jolson at the climax of a song. 'So don't tell me you're gonna bring me back some drug-taking pretty-boy from the West Village. You're part of the *Weissmans* Empire now. We piss on horizons here. I want you over and beyond the rainbow. Go to Paris, London, fucking Peru for all I care. Just find me the right model. He's gotta be fresh, he's gotta be manly, he's gotta have bigger balls than Attila the Hun, and he's gotta have the face to make my cologne the biggest-selling cologne in the history of the world.'

Weissman found a lonely pistachio in his jacket pocket, split it and lobbed the shell into the trash can.

'So! You think you can do it?'

'I hope so.'

'Don't hope. Know. Do you *know* you can do it?'

'Um, well, yes. I know I can do it.'

'Good. Don't let me down.'

4

Weissman flipped open an antique mahogany box on his desk and took out a fat cigar. He continued from behind a great cloud of smoke. 'You'll be leaving at the end of the week. Kristina's got your details. She's taking you to Arnolfini's for lunch to run over some things. It's a nice place. Say hi to Lou the waiter. I love that guy. You met Kristina, right?'

'I think . . .'

'Been with me fifteen years. A real hard-nosed power-crazy bitch. That's why I made her my VP. Listen to what she says, Miles. She got where she is by listening to me, so some of it's got to have rubbed off by now, huh?'

Weissman laughed at this, his stomach lolloping like a water-balloon ready to burst. He buzzed through to his secretary. 'Rona, could you ask Kristina von Koeler to come in now? Thank you.' Weissman winked at Miles. 'Always be polite to your secretary, Miles. That's rule number one. You won't find a goddamn top CEO in the country who's not polite to his secretary. They can ruin you.'

Within moments, there was a knock at the door. Kristina von Koeler entered before Weissman had uttered a sound.

She was indeed the same woman Miles had met the Friday before. Blonde hair that fell past her shoulder, she must have been five-foot-eleven in her flat shoes, without an ounce of excess fat on any of the inches. When she smiled, as she did then, Miles got the impression that she was smiling because she knew something no one else did. Everything about her was well-coordinated, from the embroidered shawl draped over the softly curved shoulders of her blue Armani suit, to her own perfectly proportioned physique.

'Kristina von Koeler is from Germany, Miles. Here I am, Saul Weissman, working with a fucking Nazi.'

Kristina stared at him coldly and when she spoke, it was with the razor-sharp accent of a woman raised on a full complement of Connecticut's privileges. It was an ugly, harsh accent, owned by a beautiful woman.

'And that astute statement coming from the number one bigot in New York City. If you'd stayed at school long enough to learn anything, Saul, you might have discovered that the von in my name denotes aristocratic lineage, and most of the German aristocracy were fervently anti-Nazi.'

Weissman made a face towards Miles, his lips curved downwards. The inverted smile of a clown.

Kristina ignored him. 'What's more, I was born in the United States. In a place a damn sight nicer than Brooklyn.' She looked at Miles, and her expression changed. Without moving her head, she slithered her eyes over his body in a lascivious reconnoitre. 'Let's go!'

Weissman flashed a Cheshire Cat grin. A mouthful of golden dental work. 'What did I tell you, Miles? She's a gem. I'd give half this company to be having lunch with her, but I'm a married man. You two get to it. And Miles . . .' Weissman looked at Miles with a sternness to his expression that Miles had not witnessed before. 'That's my money you'll be spending. Don't fuck up now.'

With that, Weissman took Miles's face between his little fat hands and gave him a kiss. Smack on the lips.

Kristina was still jabbing at the elevator call-button when the doors jolted open. Miles stepped aside to let a tall man in his early twenties pass by. The man was carrying in his arms a gargantuan bag of pistachio nuts. The man had perfectly smooth, jet-black skin and an almost feminine delicacy to his features. Yet it was the brilliant white of his eyes that grabbed Miles's attention so firmly. The men looked at each other for no more than a second, but it was long enough for Miles to think he'd never seen such mesmerising eyes, eyes that exploded with life, and more than a hint of reproach.

He watched the delivery man step through to the offices, and then joined Kristina in the elevator. It began its descent.

'Did you see that guy?'

'Who?'

'The one delivering the nuts for Mr Weissman.'

'That nigger?'

Miles was taken aback. 'If that's what you want to call him.'

'I do, and I did.'

'Didn't his face strike you in any way?'

6

Kristina sighed, and looked at her watch. 'Is he famous, Miles? I don't have the time to watch television.'

'No! It was an incredible face, that's all.'

The elevator arrived in the lobby. They stepped out.

Kristina said, 'We can walk. It's only a couple of blocks from here.' She had Miles hold her large black leather bag while she put on her coat. When he handed it back, she smiled her superior smile and said, 'This is New York, Miles, not Hicksville. We're going to be seeing a lot of people on the streets. Don't try to convince me that every one is beautiful enough to be our model. You've already got the job. Allright?'

Reluctantly, Miles followed Kristina out. Already he knew: this lunch was going to be hell.

The first *Weissmans* department store opened its doors to the public on July 4th, 1972, in a depressed area in a depressed city. Midway through the seventies, Manhattan's Upper West Side was not the haven for yuppies it has since become. It could boast the magnificent Zabars delicatessen, lauded by some as the greatest store in the nation, and its luxury apartment blocks bordering the Hudson along Riverside Drive were then, as now, among the most elegant residential buildings in the world. And yet the West Side remained a poor cousin of the Upper East Side where the fabulously wealthy chose to live in extravagant serenity.

The two neighbourhoods were separated by nothing more than a mile of Central Park; but a mile was a long way in Manhattan. Just a block could separate the rich from the poor, the street dealers of drugs from the bankers and lawyers, doctors and art dealers who used the drugs behind polished apartment doors. But it wasn't the mileage that mattered – it's what it signified, for New Yorkers accessorise with their addresses. As definitive as a Chanel bag or a punk haircut, a Manhattan address revealed more about the social aspirations or achievements of its owner than anything else. And in 1972, no proud resident of the Upper East Side would have wanted an address on the socially inferior West.

When *Weissmans West Side* opened on Amsterdam Avenue, amid a thousand Independence Day banners and American flags, Weissman was thought to be taking a great risk. Most rivals laughed at his attempt to open a decent store in an indecent area. They said he'd planted his flag on quicksand.

Twenty years on, it was these critics who could be seen sinking out of view. And it was the polished heels of Saul Weissman's hand-made Italian shoes that were pressing firmly down on the crowns of his competitors' heads.

Nineteen years, eight months and a day after that grand opening, Miles Jensen walked into the sumptuous new five-floor *Weissmans* on Madison Avenue to start his first day as a member of staff. Not that you'd have guessed by looking at him. But then, Miles was supposed to assimilate, to assure shoppers that he was one of their clan and, as such, could be trusted. It was part of his job. Already Miles Jensen was blessed with a trustworthy face. In his favourite blazer he resembled an overgrown, British schoolboy with a thick crop of blond hair and a hairline low across his forehead. Miles had a small, straight nose, teeth as perfect and even as the ivories of a new Steinway and skin that glowed with a healthy redness that belied the lazy life he lived in the city. Once a rower and a squash player, now, baby-faced at twenty-nine, he'd succumbed to the comfort of urban lethargy. Comfort, that was a good word for Miles, for his naïvety of expression made those who met him think of the green lawns, white terraces and fluttering flags of the American dream.

To see Miles Jensen at twenty-nine, one would have guessed that he'd never known hardship.

Miles's job in *Weissmans* was to persuade customers to part with their money while masquerading as another shopper himself. Aware that a product appeared valuable only when it was coveted by others, Saul Weissman hired groups of men and women to wander around his stores stirring the greed and jealousy within us all. It was the kind of tactic that made him the richest shopkeeper in the world.

This is how it worked: *Weissmans* stocked a dazzling variety of goods, all under the *Weissmans* label, all guaranteed under the exclusive two-month *Weissmans* refund scheme. The guarantee made shoppers less wary of purchasing goods. It was up to the group to which Miles belonged to turn that confidence into conviction.

Dressed in a suitable manner, Miles would target a particular customer who seemed to be undecided about an item. He would sidle up beside the shopper and begin to show an interest in the same product. Making sure he was being noticed, Miles might then choose to pick it up and study it, or he might simply grab it and so declare the item to be good enough to buy without further consideration. Occasionally, Miles would stand by customers and join them in contemplation, throwing in a few encouraging observations to help them make up their mind.

Miles was still in training to be an actor, and he'd taken the job at *Weissmans* not only because he could observe people all day long, but also because he was required to lie convincingly every day.

The team worked throughout the year, moving between Manhattan stores so as not to be recognised. But it was at sale time, twice a year, that Miles had the most fun.

There's nothing like a limited demand to make people want something, and Miles was an expert at persuading shoppers during the sales to buy those items that had been left unsold throughout the season. It was *Weissmans* policy to keep only a few of these items stocked on the sale shelves at any one time. The paucity of the goods gave the impression that they were selling well. If Miles spotted a customer showing some interest in one such item, but then discarding it, he would immediately pick it up and carry it with him while surveying the other products. Now the tables were turned. Invariably the covetous shopper would stare at Miles, angry that he or she had missed out on the bargain that Miles had scooped up. Then one of two things happened. Either the shopper would ask an assistant if the store had any more of the product in stock. The assistant would go off, return with one from the many, and say, 'You're lucky, I did find one.' Or Miles would walk up beside the customer, and put down the product – say a Cashmere sweater in vile lime green, rejected throughout the season by sensible customers – in order to attend to something else. The rival shopper would pounce. Miles would turn around to find his product taken. An hour later, another vile green sweater would be vomited from the stock room, and the show would begin again.

Miles's success rate was staggeringly high. Sometimes he'd have to carry his charade right on to the cashiers' desks. Even if cashiers didn't know Miles personally, they would recognise the distinctive marks of a phony *Weissmans* credit card and carry on with the transaction, implicating themselves in the crime against the customer. It was not uncommon for Miles to have the satisfaction of seeing shoppers join him in the line clutching the same item that he was pretending to buy.

'Thanks for your advice,' they'd say. 'I just know my little girl'll love it.'

Some followed Miles to the cash tills hoping that his unsolicited conversation signified that he was looking for something more spicy than advice. Weissmans stores were crowded with lonely people shopping for company, and Miles had often been propositioned during his year at the job. Twice by women, eighteen times by men who'd wink and nod towards the Gents while plunging a hand into a trouser pocket.

When Miles caught sight of Kristina von Koeler on the Friday before his first encounter with Weissman, he'd hoped she might become the third woman that year to show some interest in him. In her late thirties, her slender body clearly well-toned beneath her immaculate clothes, Kristina was exactly the kind of older, inaccessible woman to whom Miles longed to have access.

As soon as she'd sauntered into the menswear department carrying her head on her sleek neck as it were a priceless Ming vase, Miles had known she'd be treating the staff with a beautiful woman's casual disdain. Miles had strolled towards her, browsing. Kristina had been holding the grey jacket of a woollen suit up to the light, but she'd angled her head to look past the suit to catch Miles's eye. She'd surprised him. 'My boyfriend's about the same size as you. You wouldn't try this on for me, would you?'

It was unusual for a shopper to approach Miles, and he felt himself reeling a little as the blood rose to his face. He blushed as much at the prospect of embarrassment as at the fact itself. He hated the affliction, but others found it endearing. His girlfriend Poppy said it made her feel maternal, and even Kristina seemed less cool when she handed Miles the jacket.

The jacket fitted Miles so well it could have been tailor-made for him. He'd turned for her, showed her the back, caught himself in the mirror, liked the way it looked and even thought that, had he been earning more, he'd have probably bought it himself.

'Fine,' she'd said. 'Thanks a lot. I . . . I don't suppose I could persuade you to try on the pants as well?'

That was a first for Miles, but he'd agreed, and Kristina had smiled when Miles returned wearing the trousers. 'OK.' Instantly, her manner had become brusque. 'Where's an assistant? He can fit them on you.'

'Excuse me?'

'I'm buying you this suit. I want you to wear it tomorrow when you come to meet Mr Weissman. It'll look good.' Kristina had laughed, a little vindictively. 'Oh, don't look so shocked. I can see your cheap fillings.' She'd looked about her angrily. 'Isn't there anybody who can serve me in this store?'

Then, in the manner of a petulant little girl, Kristina had stamped down her foot. 'If an assistant doesn't get here in two minutes, the floor manager's fired.' She'd smiled. 'I can do that, you see, Miles,' she'd added, extending her thin hand towards Miles. 'Kristina von Koeler. I'm Saul Weissman's Vice President. He doesn't know about the suit, but he'll appreciate it if you're wearing it for your meeting. That'll be at eleven thirty, Monday morning, on the fifty-third floor of Head Office. OK?'

'I . . .'

'Just be there, Miles. He'll explain everything. Here's my card. Now, where's a goddamn assistant?'

At last the head assistant arrived, pretending not to recognise Miles.

Kristina said, 'You probably know each other. Fit these by tomorrow. Just give my card to the manager.' She turned back to Miles. 'I'm sorry, Miles, I'm running very late. I'm not usually like this.'

'Oh! What are you usually like?'

Kristina had smiled, with closed lips.

'Who knows . . .' she'd said, resting a hand on Miles's shoulder. 'Maybe later you'll be lucky enough to find out.'

2

In the corner furthest from the door of Arnolfini's on 53rd Street there was a small table at which Saul Weissman had liked to lunch. It was to this table that the maitre d', a small Italian-American of about sixty, with strands of dyed black hair greased over his predominantly bald head, ushered Kristina and Miles with the obsequious nod of an undertaker. He held the chair for Kristina, whispered something in her ear, to which she nodded, and trotted back towards his lectern by the door.

Miles glanced around him. Arnolfini's was one of those Italian restaurants that retained a relaxed atmosphere despite the formality of its design and clientele. The noise of the busy restaurant was curiously muffled – just an occasional clink of glass, the rattle of cutlery, the crescendo of laughter coming from a table of diners sharing a joke. Somehow it sounded more like the background noise in the restaurant scene of a movie than the actual noise itself.

The majority of those lunching at Arnolfini's were business-men and women displaying no signs of appreciation for either the food or surroundings. Miles thought that to eat out in a restaurant was one of life's true luxuries. He felt a rather superior pity for those others for whom the experience had been swallowed up into the rest of their mundane professional existence. Did they think it anything but commonplace for a man dressed in a tuxedo to sweep the breadcrumbs from their crisply laundered white tablecloth? Did any of them recognise the luxury of having a chef prepare for them alone the precise meal they desired? Kristina took a breadstick from the basket of freshly baked rolls, 'How did you like Saul?' she asked.

'Can I be candid?'

'Of course.'

'I thought he was one of the most arrogant and self-satisfied men I've ever met.'

'But did you like him?'

Miles smiled. 'A lot.'

'Most people do. He's the most generous man I've ever known. Even though he's been dieting for a year, the manager still holds this table for him. He used to come here every day.'

'They must have loved him.'

'Well, you should have seen the size of the tips he left. Up to a hundred bucks. Every time. Anyway, I come here now.'

Kristina paused as the wine waiter poured a small amount of the chosen Chardonnay into her glass. She tasted it, taking her time, sniffing the aroma deeply, swilling the drink around her mouth. Miles, assuming that others knew as little about wine as he, was always embarrassed by this ritual. He relaxed when Kristina gave her approval with a brisk wave of her hand. The wine waiter left.

'To be honest, I do most of the things that Saul used to do.' Kristina took a sip of the wine. 'Except fuck his secretaries.'

'I suppose you've got your own haven't you?' said Miles, smirking.

Kristina's face hardened, as if she'd been slapped. It made her look a little like Joan Crawford. Maybe, thought Miles, the joke was too close to the truth.

'You know you're sitting here because I personally chose you.'

'Thank you!' Miles said, a little embarrassed now.

'I wasn't going to tell you this, but I considered you as our model for EDEN, but Saul didn't bite. Still, that's how he got the idea of sending you out to search.'

'Why me?'

'Most importantly because Saul works on hunches, and you're a hunch. Plus, there's no one high up in the office who can drop everything to fly around the world.'

'So why not use an outside professional?'

'Saul got his fingers burned when DPGF screwed up our last campaign.'

Miles remembered the campaign well. It showed a man in an electric chair beneath which was the caption, *You'll be shocked at our prices in* Weissmans. *Just not this much!* The press had thought it in terrible taste. *The Times* had refused to run it. Weissman, a public darling for twenty years, had been hurt by the backlash.

'So Saul's blaming the ad agencies for everything, as if this recession has nothing to do with sales. Problem was, we did so well after the ads for the *Weissman Deluxe* stores that Saul went and sank too much capital in the main store campaign. That's why it stung so hard when it backfired.'

'So now he wants to run the whole show?'

'Yes. We do.'

Miles noticed how Kristina would include herself only in policy-making decisions that had proved beneficial to the company. The buck seemed to stop somewhere other than on Kristina von Koeler's desk.

Lou, the waiter, arrived before Miles had so much as glanced at his menu.

'Why don't I order for both of us?' Kristina said. 'I know what's good here.'

'Fine with me.'

Miles returned his menu to the nodding Lou. Kristina gave their order and then leant over to take a thick file from the snakeskin briefcase by her side. She handed it to Miles. 'Everything you need to know is in there. For now it's between you, me, and a few of the brass at *Weissmans*. But not for long.'

'Am I going to be able to tell people what I'm up to?'

'You won't need to. It'll be in the press. It's a big deal for a store like *Weissmans* to license a cologne of its own, and Saul thinks that all we need do is raise the profile of the store and we'll be out of the recession.'

'That didn't work with the electric chair.'

'Granted, but he learnt his lesson. The EDEN campaign is going to be a feel-good, save-the-world kind of campaign. At first Saul wanted to get all the supermodels in one shot. You know, Wendy Radcliff, Tiziana Ferrari, Dina van Stigal, Effie Crascauldi, that black one . . .'

'Candy Hempell?'

'Right. He was thinking of dressing the models in our new Rainbow lingerie line, shoving them in a cage and suspending it from a helicopter over Fifth Avenue. Well, as you can imagine, the insurance killed that one, and anyway, the problem with these starlets is that they've become more important than the products they're selling, so we decided not to use them. So that left us with the option of either using some second-rate model which would have put across the wrong message right now, or else of running a gimmick campaign. So we figured, why not get *Weissmans* in the news by creating a brand-new supermodel of our own. A brand name supermodel if you like.'

'Why a man?'

'There aren't any male supermodels out there. Yet.'

'And you think EDEN will make this guy a star?'

'Absolutely. You see, the only real difference between a model and a supermodel is the size of their pay-cheque.'

'And how much are you paying?'

'Try to say WE, Miles. Saul likes that if you're part of the family.'

'So, how much are we paying.'

Kristina cracked a breadstick in half and crunched on the end. 'Seven.'

'I'm guessing that's hundred thousands, not just thousands.'

Kristina laughed and threw back her head. 'It's millions, Miles. Seven million dollars.'

Miles spoke slowly now, remembering why he was sitting where he was. With precision, he ran his finger around the lip of his wine glass. 'For one photograph?'

Kristina seemed immensely proud. 'One campaign, one product, seven million dollars.'

'And you were thinking of me . . .'

'We were. Went right through to a final committee meeting.

We watched you on tapes from the in-store videos. You were good at what you did, by the way.'

Miles was looking shell-shocked.

Kristina touched his hand. 'Smile. You got the runner's-up prize. Five star hotels, business class flights, chauffeur-driven limos. That's not bad.'

'No, you're right. It's just . . .'

The first course arrived, and Kristina picked up her fork. 'These calamari are the best in the city, Miles. You should eat them while they're hot.'

They didn't talk much while they ate, though Miles understood from the way Kristina spoke that the project was close to her heart. It seemed as if her future depended upon it, and with an initial investment of seven million dollars before all the costs of shooting and purchase of advertising space, it probably did. With sums like these, Miles couldn't understand why he had been chosen to search for the model. Even if it was true that he wasn't 'up to his balls in bullshit', he knew nothing about the modelling business.

Kristina tried to explain. 'This search is going to be a news item, and we think you've got a good image for it.'

'And you're sure the press will be interested?'

'Absolutely. Papers don't give a shit about hard news any more. They can't compete with CNN, so they're after entertainment and gossip, and that's what we're going to give them. And they're obsessed with anyone who's being paid a lot of money.'

'So you think a few articles in the papers are going to merit spending millions of dollars?'

'We hope so.'

'But this is the nineties! People want the truth now.'

Kristina smiled at him. 'You really don't know how the world turns, do you Miles?'

Then, to his amazement, Miles felt Kristina's hand on his knee, the fingers swirling purposefully up the inside of his thigh. Miles caught his breath. Out of his depth, he was speechless.

'Is there any area you think I haven't covered?' Kristina

said, her face revealing nothing, her hand moving inexorably closer to its target.

Miles could feel the blood rushing to his face and beginning to pump elsewhere. His heart was racing, thumping inside his ribcage, in his head, even in his throat. The muscles tightened. He swallowed audibly, and looked from side to side to see if anyone was paying attention to them. Lou, assuming that Miles was looking for him, came over to the table. Kristina kept her hand moving, tickling, caressing.

'Would you care for to see the dessert menu?' asked Lou.

Miles tried to control his breathing. He hazarded a smile. 'I . . . think we're OK for now.'

The waiter turned to go, but Kristina called him back. 'Lou, tell me what you have today?'

Miles bit his lip, took a slurp of water. Lou rubbed his flattened palms together. They moved in tiny, clammy jerks.

'We have your favourite! Tiramisu.'

'Good! Let's have some, two forks. And coffee. Miles?'

Attention again. His heart was trampolining, his whole body becoming hot. Kristina's hand was only an inch or so from the bulge in his trousers. Kristina's forefinger was teasing him with tight circles. Miles could feel the sweat beginning to break on his forehead.

'OK . . . Cappuccino.'

Kristina touched him, closer.

'No!' squealed Miles.

'No? Espresso?'

'OK, whatever. Thanks.' Kristina's fingertip moved desperately close. 'Make it decaffeinated,' Miles added.

Lou nodded and left. Immediately, Miles clapped his hand firmly down on top of Kristina's. He squeezed, hard. 'Can I ask what you're doing?'

'Proving a point.'

Then with a smile Kristina withdrew her hand, picked up her wine, and leant back in her chair. 'Why do you think your little Milo is standing to attention like that?'

Miles rubbed his forehead. He could feel the redness

burning on his face. He was so embarrassed. Turned-on, embarrassed and annoyed. 'Isn't that kind of obvious?'

'Is it?' Kristina leaned across the table so that her face was almost touching Miles's cheek. She whispered, 'Tell me, Miles. What was it that excited you? What I was doing with my hand, or what you *thought* I was going to do with it?'

'I'm very sensitive around there.'

Kristina sat upright. 'Bullshit! You had us under the sheets already. If a doctor touched you in exactly the same place you wouldn't care less. It's dead simple. It was the promise of what might come, quite literally, that got you into that rather untidy little sweat. What people *think* they're going to get, that's what really counts. And if you've got the money and the will, you can make people think whatever you want.'

Miles shook his head. He had to smile at her gall. 'Do you give everybody the same definition?'

There was a pause. Then, taking Miles completely by surprise, Kristina slipped her hand back on to his leg.

'Only when I want them to make love to me.'

Miles's mind began to reel. Only when? He couldn't believe what he'd heard! From Kristina von Koeler? He stared at her, eyes wide, face red. Maybe she was teasing him. She must be. To get his reaction, to keep control. Thinking fast, Miles decided to play it very cool. If he could. More like a rabbit caught in the headlights of a car than a man being tough, Miles didn't waver in his stare.

'Wouldn't that defeat your hype theory? If I was to get what I was promised.'

'Some arguments are worth losing,' she said, dabbing at the corner of her mouth with her napkin. 'Come on, there's fresh coffee in my office.'

Miles was sinking further into her quicksand. Again, he swallowed hard. 'What about dessert?'

Kristina stood up and pushed her chair back with her legs. 'Miles, do you know what Tiramisu means?'

'Yes, I do. Pick me up.'

'Mm. How appropriate!'

Almost without thinking, Miles grinned. 'Saul was right about you.'

Kristina licked a finger, separated a hundred dollar bill from the stack in her hand and dropped it on the table. 'That's because he knows! Let's get back before my secretary.'

Left with no choice, Miles followed Kristina out of the restaurant.

It was a few blocks back to the office. I'll get out of this somehow, he thought.

Somehow.

Up in her office with the door locked and the blinds drawn, Kristina von Koeler wasted no time. She wrapped her arms tightly around Miles and pressed her lips against his ear.

'I've watched you on the tapes, Miles. On my own. I've thought about us. You and me. About your hands on me, about you . . . inside me. Does that excite you?'

Her hair was loose and now fell dishevelled over her neck. Kristina clasped a hand around the back of Miles's head and drew their lips together. Her fingers played in the hair at the back of his neck. Miles, nervous at first, was drawn in by the eagerness of her passion, excited by the thrill of her darting tongue, intoxicated by the remarkable touch of a stranger. He felt himself giving in to his body, and he pushed his own tongue inside the sweet warm cavern of Kristina's mouth. His hands slithered with the impatience of a teenager. He slid his hand around the side of Kristina's hip and felt for the mound between her firm legs.

Kristina broke the embrace. She pushed him back towards the black leather couch. Miles's calves hit the edge and he fell backwards. Without taking her eyes from his face, Kristina knelt before him and untied his tie with impressive dexterity. Familiar territory.

Kristina's right hand reached inside Miles's shirt. She tickled her fingers over the shivering muscles of his stomach. Miles gasped. The other hand came to rest on the straining bulge within the trousers of his suit. Kristina never took her eyes from his face. 'Does little Milo like this, then?'

'I . . .'

'Does he?'

Miles's breathing was erratic. 'Yes.'

She felt for the buttons of his fly. One, two, three. She stopped as Miles met her hand with a thrust of his hips.

'Tell me, Miles. Tell me you want me.'

He felt her hand on him, the fingers wrapped around him, then, in a second, the hot breath of her mouth over him, the desperate, wet delicacy of her tongue on him. He gripped her head, moaned. Kristina looked up, her face vibrant.

'Do you want me Miles?'

Miles's breathing was heavy now, his mind spinning wildly. He nodded.

'Say it, Miles. Say it to me.'

'Yes.'

Her voice was urgent, severe.' Say it!'

'I want you.'

Immediately, Kristina stood and moved to the large closet that ran along the wall. She returned with four lengths of fabric in her hands.

Miles looked scared. 'I, I'm not sure I . . .'

Kristina grinned. 'Not you. Me. Over there, on the chair.' Kristina dropped the rope in between Miles's legs, took hold of his hand and led him to the large revolving chair that stood expectant behind her desk. 'Now, Miles, now. Just do whatever you want.'

'Hi, sweetheart, is Kristy back from lunch?'

Cindy, Kristina von Koeler's secretary, stood for Saul Weissman and said, 'Yes, but she left a note asking not to be disturbed.'

'Too bad!'

Weissman knocked on the office door, and tried the handle.

Inside Miles and Kristina glared at one another, two rats in a trap. Another knock. Miles felt sick.

'Jesus! Why didn't Cindy buzz me? Quick, press that red button there.' 'No, the other one.' Kristina was nodding

21

towards the intercom on her desk. Miles climbed off her and obliged. Kristina took a deep breath. 'Yes, Cindy, what?'

Cindy spoke with all the charm of a girl born and bred in a Long Island suburb.' It's Mr Weissman. He's here to see you.'

'Ask him to wait a moment, would you?'

Silence. Weissman didn't like waiting, but Weissman couldn't come in because Kristina was still naked and flushed and tied to her revolving chair with a knot that Miles was finding he could not undo.

'Why did you have to tie it so tight?'

'I'm not exactly used to this!'

'Jesus!'

Suddenly, detumescent now, Miles became conscious of his naked predicament. Leaving the knots, he began to conduct a frantic search for his underwear in the layers of sunlight that were slicing their way through the window blinds. He'd just found his red-spotted boxers when Cindy's drawl returned. 'Mr Weissman here, he says he wants to know what you're doing.'

Kristina wriggled. Then she snapped at Miles. 'Come and press the intercom.' Again, her tone became impressively casual. 'Please tell Mr Weissman that I'll be with him in a moment. I've just come out of meditation.'

Miles released the button and pulled on his new suit trousers. 'Meditation? You call this relaxing?'

Suddenly it was Weissman's voice that sounded through the speaker. 'Hey, Kristy, what am I running here? A fucking Ashram?'

The sound of Weissman's voice wiped the smile off Miles's face and he wasted no time putting his finger back on the intercom.

'Saul, I'm sorry. Could you come back in five minutes? I'll explain everything then.'

No reply. Miles grabbed his shirt, and fumbled with the buttons. Hadn't they invented Velcro for moments like these? Kristina struggled, a silent-movie star tied to the tracks. She shouted a whisper at Miles. 'What do you think you're doing? There are some scissors in the third drawer down. Cut this. Quick.'

'You should see yourself,' he said, unable to resist a smile.

This was not the Kristina von Koeler to which the world was accustomed. She had both legs tied to the desk, and both arms behind her back. Her black cotton underwear dangled from one leg having been torn from the constraints of the other. She had the red mark of a bite on her left breast, just below her frightened nipple, and her hair flopped untidily over her flushed brow. Her eyes were those of a newly caged cheetah, aflame with desperation.

'The scissors, Miles, or you're off this project.'

Miles found the scissors and faced Kristina. 'I'm standing here, almost fully dressed, holding in my hands your only means of escape from complete humiliation, and you're trying to blackmail me. Correct?'

'I won't be the one firing you, asshole.'

She had a point. Miles cut the fabric around her hands and feet and handed Kristina her clothes. Everything except the torn knickers. They were pushed untidily in the top drawer of her desk.

Kristina said, 'You're going to have to get in the closet.'

'But . . .'

'So you think of something!'

Miles looked about him. The office was furnished for effect, not comfort. Kristina's massive desk dominated. In front of it were two hard metal chairs, behind these a low, smoked-glass coffee table, two airline seats (First Class) and a selection of contorted wooden chairs that were designer-friendly but buttock-hostile. Apart from that, and a work of art that was, to Miles, nothing more than a mop in a bucket, the office was empty.

Dressed now, Kristina drew up the blinds. The sunlight shamed them with its brightness. As they were fifty-three floors above Madison Avenue, the windowledge was out of the question. So accepting the inevitable Miles clambered into the closet's dark space. He squeezed himself between two of

Kristina's overcoats. The door was slammed shut. Then it was yanked open. The light flew in with Miles's heavy leather shoes. The heel of one caught him high on his cheekbone, just beneath the left eye.

The closet was hardly comfortable. Pitch-black and cramped, with only enough space for Miles to squeeze himself parallel to the door, his legs bent tightly, his chin sandwiched between his knees, the discomfort was increased by the fact that he was sitting on a pair of stilettoed shoes. He heard Weissman come in and slam the door behind him. Miles pressed his ear against the side of the closet.

Weissman was growling. 'Kristy, if you want to get involved with this Hare Krishna shit, do it back home, would you? Anyway, what took you?'

'It's a little embarrassing, Saul.'

She paused. Miles wondered what she would come up with. She said, 'I was naked.'

Miles caught his breath.

'Naked? At three in the afternoon? Alone?'

'Of course. It's an intense relaxation technique. It improves concentration and productivity. I did it for the firm. You should try it.'

'Jesus! Sometimes, just sometimes, I think you're not all there Kristy? You seeing someone?'

'No. Scott stayed in LA. I thought you knew that.'

'A shrink, I mean are you seeing a shrink?'

Kristina's reply had a confessional tone to it. 'Not now, no.'

'Jesus H. Christ, Kristy. With this deal coming up? Are you crazy? Go see Hirschberg. On me. I'm not gonna have you spending ten million dollars when you're not seeing Hirschberg. Are you crazy?'

'I don't think . . .'

'Man did not come out of his cave knowing how to spend ten million dollars! Woman less so. I don't want you taking risks, OK? Look at me. OK? Promise?'

'Yes, Saul.'

'Now I came to tell you that I want Miles to find an Eve for Adam.'

'What? We can't increase costs like that.'

'Did I say we'd have to? We can cut the guy down to six, and give the girl a mil. Adam will still be the star.'

'But . . .'

'No "buts" Kristy. You know where to reach this Miles kid?'

'Yes.'

'So tell him. And keep your clothes on when you do, OK?' Weissman laughed. 'Naked meditation! Don't forget to talk to Hirschberg about that.'

Weissman touched Kristina's cheek with his palm, more in the manner of a father than a lover. 'You're hot, Kristy. You're not sick are you?'

'No. Really, no.'

'OK. That's all then. But I want you on top of that kid fast. And drop in on me later. You want to do dinner?'

'Not tonight, Saul.'

'OK then. Later.'

Miles heard Weissman leave. After a few moments, Kristina opened the closet door. 'Did you hear that?'

Miles said yes as he climbed out. He had to admit that the prospect of spending a month looking for a beautiful woman had an appealing ring to it. Already the events of the afternoon had deluded him into thinking he was sexually irresistible.

It was a delusion Kristina intended to reinforce.

'So, you heard Saul say I had to get on top of you?' Kristina slipped her hand between Miles's legs and began to massage his thigh. 'I think it's the best idea he's had for years.'

Miles twisted away. 'You're kidding,' he said.

'Oh no I'm not,' she replied.

And she wasn't, she wasn't.

Poppy White clambered on to the futon loft-bed she and Miles had shared for almost two years, and kissed the cut beneath his eye. Her lips pressed upon his skin with the delicacy of a butterfly landing on the seam of a petal.

'My poor baby.'

Miles had lied about the gash made by his shoe, of course.

He'd said he'd walked into a cupboard door because his mind had been so full of the trip.

Poor Miles! He felt like the victim, but he knew if he tried to explain to Poppy that he'd been raped, or as good as, by the most manipulative woman he'd ever met, she'd laugh, cry, then leave him. Infidelity meant just that to Poppy; an ultimate loss of faith. Six months earlier, after he'd had a mischievous fling with an actress in his class, Poppy had sworn she'd walk out on Miles if there was a next time, and he'd seen the threat as an assurance of her love and fallen for her all over again.

And now Kristina had come between them.

It was the secrecy implicit in infidelity that bothered him. He felt curiously guiltless about the deed itself. It had not taken long after the breathing had calmed and the blood had ebbed from his hardness for Miles to wish that he'd not made love to Kristina. Immediately he'd thought of Poppy – not as some ephemeral finger-wagging vision – but as the honest girl who loved him. It had been the image of her warm smile that had come to him, or, more exactly, the dimple in her cheek that would always trigger a surge of love from within him, like a magician's green stem bursting gaudily into flower.

The contrast with Kristina angered Miles. Beside the gullible innocence of Poppy he saw Kristina as some kind of supreme matador, waving the red flag of her fantastic promise without shame. This was not unperceptive. Kristina revelled in the exhaustion of her victims, using suggestive words and glances as her banderillas. And by the time she relinquished control she had no need of a sword for the kill – her bulls were only too eager to sacrifice themselves upon their own erections.

Poppy rolled on to her back beside her lover and focused on the patterned tin ceiling of their SoHo loft apartment. Miles was irritating her tonight. By now she was accustomed to his temperament, but even with the perverse rationale of his mood swings she would have expected him to have reacted to the events of the day with ebullience. How many times had he moaned to her about his unfulfilled wanderlust? How many times had he complained about the tedium of his job? Now, with his dream miraculously coming true, Miles's enthusiasm was curiously muted.

Poppy poked him in the ribs. 'Why are you being so pooey?' she said.

'I'm not. I'm reading.'

Poppy poked him again. 'I'm the one who should be upset. You're leaving me for a month.' Miles was silent. 'Can't you read that tomorrow?'

'Kristina von Koeler said . . .'

'Kristina this, Kristina that! She's the one who bought you the suit too, isn't she?'

'Yes.'

'She wants to sleep with you.'

'Don't be stupid!' Still Miles didn't look up. 'Anyway, *she* didn't have to pay for it.'

'So?'

'Poppy! She's forty; nearly.'

'All the more reason.'

Poppy flattened a hand over the page that Miles was reading. She spread out her fingers. 'Tell me what she looks like.'

'Give me a break, Poppy. I'm trying to read.'

'You're trying to be a bastard. Successfully.'

Miles, who had been lying on his side with his head propped up on one hand, twisted his neck to look at Poppy. He found it hard to meet her gaze after the events of the afternoon. He was scared she might recognise the guilt in his eyes. Yet it was not his face that was easy to read, but hers. There was nothing hard or intimidating about her features. Even her straw-coloured hair was subtle. Her nose was small and rounded, and her gentle eyes resembled those of a young animal – one of the world's cuddly creatures, a seal cub, a rabbit, a fawn. Poppy could not hurt with her eyes, neither could she hide her emotions. To look into them was to see beyond them.

Poppy's skin was slightly freckled, a feature so in keeping with her character that sometimes Miles wondered whether that was what defined her character to others. Miles saw great vulnerability in Poppy's face. He had never doubted that it would be he that wronged her, never doubted that the day would come when the kindness in her eyes would hurt more than any look of reproach.

Poppy said, 'Tell me what you're reading about then.'

'It's just about the model agencies and things. It's telling me what I've got to say to people. It's not very interesting.'

'I still don't get why you're being sent. I mean, you don't know anything about it.'

'I think it's because they knew I was an actor. I mean, she's given me all these lines I've got to say to the press. Like a puppet. Listen to this. This is under **Press Quotes**.' Miles began to read from the file. '"*It is imperative that you do not deviate from company statements without instruction from* Weissmans, New York, Inc." I had to sign this, so if I say anything that they don't like, I'll be in breach of contract and won't get paid.'

'So do as they say.'

'I'm going to. That's why I have to read this.'

'If that was a hint, it wasn't very subtle.'

Poppy sat up, and lit a cigarette. Miles, looking sideways at her, said, 'Do you have to smoke on the bed? Can't you go somewhere else?'

'Yes, sir.'

Poppy shuffled to the other end of their loft apartment and turned on the TV to watch the DEA undercover squad raid the trailer home of an illegal immigrant in South Florida suspected of having two million dollars worth of cocaine stashed away.

Half an hour later she returned to the bed. She lay next to Miles. Generosity of forgiveness had always been one of her virtues.

'Promise me something,' she said.

'What?'

Miles closed the EDEN file and lay on his back with his arms spread open. Poppy lifted herself up and into them.

'Promise me you won't sleep with any of those disgusting models.'

'What if they ask me?'

'Then tell them you have the most beautiful, wonderful, fabulous woman in the world waiting for you in New York.'

'I do? Where is she?'

'Bastard! Give me a kiss.'

And Miles did. A long, slow, wonderfully sloppy kiss. He broke, kissed her again quickly, then rolled Poppy over. Lying on top of her, Miles lifted back his head and looked into those beautiful eyes. He smiled.

'Of course!' he said. 'Of course I promise.'

3

The small, mirrored elevator that sucked Miles to the fifty-third floor of Weissmans head office travelled so fast that when he stepped from it into the reception area, he felt sure he'd left his stomach somewhere around floor thirty. It was the morning after, and he wished he was elsewhere.

Miles pushed his way through the heavy, glass doors, took a deep breath, and spoke to Cindy, the young secretary who had the dubious honour of working for Kristina von Koeler.

'She'll see you in a moment,' Cindy soon told him. 'Care to take a seat?'

'Uh, thanks.'

Miles had been worrying all morning what he'd say if Kristina tried something again, what he'd *do* if she tried something again. After an exquisite night with Poppy he'd woken feeling absolved of guilt simply because of her tenderness. It had fuelled his spirit, but he feared that his flesh might be weak. Miles smiled to himself, remembering that a computer programmed to translate that aphorism first into Russian and then back into English had confused itself into *The vodka is strong, but the meat is spoiled*. Maybe it was apt. His own meat had certainly been spoiled by Kristina's rough handling. He wouldn't let that happen again. He'd tell her straightaway. Get it out in the open. It was simple: he loved Poppy too much, and he'd made a mistake that he wouldn't be repeating; not ever.

The door to Kristina's office swung open, and she appeared dressed in a charcoal grey Calvin Klein pin-stripe suit that gloriously displayed her long, thin legs. Her jacket rippled expensively over the feminine curves of her chest. She smiled (that smile!), and firmly took hold of Miles's hand.

31

With that touch, with her soft hand taking his, Miles felt his resolve sapping out of him, like grain pouring from a split in a hessian sack.

Miles followed Kristina into the office. When she closed the door, her smile disappeared. In her high-heeled black shoes, Kristina strode behind her desk and pointed towards one of the uncomfortable metal-framed chairs. Miles sat, but she gave him no chance to speak first.

'I suppose that Saul gave you carte blanche to travel where you like, did he?'

'Yes. I think he even said I could go to Peru if I wanted.'

'Didn't he say "fucking Peru"? He thinks that's what the country's called, "fucking Peru".'

Miles thought it odd that Kristina should have made this joke without a trace of levity. Rather she seemed to be castigating him for his poor memory. Yesterday the naughty schoolgirl wanting to be spanked, today the strict headmistress. Only today, Miles didn't feel like playing her games.

'As a matter of fact . . .'

Kristina interrupted. 'It doesn't matter, you won't be going there. You'll only be going where I want you to go.'

Kristina picked up a long, slim cigarette and lit it. Miles hadn't noticed her smoking on the previous day, and it surprised him. He thought it out of character for someone who valued herself so highly.

'I don't mind telling you that I think Saul's wasting his time on this trip of yours, but as he's set on it all I can do is cut our losses. Here . . .' Kristina handed Miles his detailed itinerary. The paper cracked like a whip as she handed it to him. 'I've had all the flights and hotels booked for you. If you want to change anything contact me. OK? Questions?'

Boy, she really had learnt her stuff! Miles looked at the instructions and wondered where there was room for questions. He was to fly west around the world – from New York, to Miami, Tokyo, then to Milan, Paris and London. He then had four days to follow up any leads wherever was necessary before his return to New York.

'You don't see any point in my going to South America? Maybe Brazil? The Armani cologne model is Brazilian, isn't he?'

'Do you think we're in this to copy formulas, Miles? Because if you do, I'd better get someone else right now.'

'No, I . . .'

'Listen, I'm sending you to all the modelling centres of the world. I want you to search among the wannabes. Find me someone who's had some experience in front of a camera but hasn't had any success yet.'

'I'm getting confused here. I thought you wanted a real person. Not a model.'

'We want a brand-new face. Period. If we get someone with a little modelling experience, then so much the better. That way we'll still be able to parade him as a newcomer, and he'll have a few tricks up his sleeve. Modelling isn't just about looking cute, you know. They have to work in front of that camera.'

'Mr Weissman seemed . . .'

Again, Kristina interrupted. 'Christ, Miles! Were you listening to me? Weissman doesn't know shit about models. He knows about marketing. He needs us to feed him with the right material, then it's up to him to make this thing fly.'

'Should I be looking for a white guy?'

'Yes.'

'So why am I going to Tokyo?'

Kristina rolled her eyes. 'You don't know a thing, do you? Listen, for a start, keep an open mind. If someone is special enough I don't give a damn what shape his eyes are. Secondly, Tokyo is swimming with unsuccessful Western models. They're shipped in by the Japs because they like the fact that they're rich enough to buy whoever they want – and that means boys with round eyes. As far as we're concerned, the model's face can be on every billboard in Japan, nobody's going to know them here. It could be perfect. That's why you'll be going to Milan too. Most of this should be in the folder I gave you. You did read it, didn't you?' Miles nodded. Kristina was even checking up on his homework! 'Right then. Now, before I forget, you're going to need to sign these.' Kristina pushed towards Miles a gold American Express card and Visa card. 'We may be rich, but we're planning on staying that way, so we'll be checking every item. Business only, OK? I'll be deducting every unnecessary dollar from that overinflated pay-cheque of yours. After your behaviour yesterday I'll be making sure you haven't been . . . whoring on *Weissmans*.'

'*My* behaviour.'

'That's what I said.'

'Oh, now it figures, you found out yesterday that I like whores.'

Damn! That came out a bit strong, and he knew it.

Kristina threw her cigarette into the ashtray and strode around the desk. She stood so close to Miles that she was looking down on him when she spoke.' I have a big, big problem with cocky young men.'

No problem with young men's cocks, he thought. But he remained silent.

Kristina took a deep breath. 'However, I am willing to forgive you for yesterday.' Her eyes flickered away for a minute, then landed back on him. 'You may have misinterpreted my meaning.'

'Misinterpreted your meaning?' he laughed. 'Come on! What exactly did you mean by "Tie me up and fuck my brains out," then? That you'd like a coffee?'

She was standing beside him, staring at him. She said nothing. Miles felt his heartbeat quicken. He swallowed hard, and it sounded in his own ears like the gulp of a terrified cartoon character. He'd never known a sensation like this before. It scared and excited him. She held his stare, he had no idea for how long. If Kristina had tried to kiss him, Miles would not have resisted. His promise to Poppy meant nothing now, nothing while Kristina stood over him with the scent of her body exciting him, with her legs slightly apart, tempting him with their closeness. He nearly, so nearly, reached out to touch her. It would have been enough, and he knew it. The muscles in his arm tensed as if his body had begun to test the strength of his mind.

Yet Miles held back, then looked away. Whether he was a coward or a gentleman, he couldn't say, but when he turned his eyes back towards Kristina, she was walking back to her chair behind the desk. She sat.

For a moment, they were silent. A minute passed, maybe more. A siren sounded from the street below, and Miles focused on a jet passing over the tip of Manhattan Island. Then, calmly, as if they were in the middle of any old, mundane business meeting, Kristina spoke. 'There are, I think, some more things we need to discuss.'

So, thought Miles, the subject's dead. She wanted me to beg but I held back. He smiled.

Kristina began to talk again, straight back into her stride. 'I've made a list of the model agents you should see. Chances are that you're going to like some of them, which is OK so long as you never trust any of them. They're glorified pimps, Miles, don't forget that. Only these ones make less money than their prostitutes, so they're bitter with it. And that makes for an ugly combination. A model once told me that when she thought of her agent she thought of a chocolate-coated dog's do. They smell sweet until you prod them. I know it was crude, but it's not a bad thing to remember.'

'So you want me to work with the agencies?'

'Sure. Thing is, they'll be showing you all their top guys and girls, and I'm going to want you to look out for the new kids. They're not going to suspect anything. Most of the agents are only marginally more intelligent than the models they're representing. Some of them are stupider.'

'And if I see someone I like?'

'Call me. Always, always contact me before you make any moves. And don't be specific with the agents. Don't talk dates. Don't give anything away. When it comes to signing the contracts, I don't want an agent in sight. It'd cost us twenty per cent on top of the seven million. No way we can afford that. If they knew that, they wouldn't give us the time of day. OK?'

'OK.'

Kristina sat back in her chair and stared hard at Miles. 'Can you think of anything more we should talk about?'

Miles looked at her. Kristina began to rap her fingernails on the desk, from thumb to pinkie. Tapping out the time.

'No, not right now.'

'You know, you're tougher than you look, Miles.'

So, thought Miles, she can't see me shaking.

Kristina smiled, but to Miles she seemed to be trying to hide a look of concern. 'Who knows,' she said, 'just maybe Saul Weissman hasn't lost his magic touch after all.'

So, both of them were on his side! Saul and Kristina. Happy to entrust him with the responsibility of more than ten million dollars. After twenty-nine years, Miles felt it was time to prove his worth.

Truth was, Miles had always had an inner faith in himself. He was the Ivy League boy who'd skipped the Ivy League. The scholar who'd thrown aside his books. With proud determination he'd travelled the world deliberately avoiding the imprints of his father's footsteps. From the age of seventeen, Miles Jensen had wanted to make it up a different ladder. And now it seemed as if Saul and Kristina were giving him a chance.

Back in 1980 when he'd made the decision to skip university, Miles's arguments with his parents had been fierce. They'd wanted, desperately, for him to try for Yale, his father's old university. Miles had refused. He'd said it was merely Waspish conceit to argue that Yale prepared a man for the real world; I'm going to learn about the real world *in* the real world, he'd said. He'd travel, pick up jobs wherever he could, learn about different people, different cultures. His parents never understood. He'd never forgotten his mother saying, in the clipped British account she'd retained after twenty-three years in the States:

'You'll regret this decision, Miles. I promise you. You'll regret this for the rest of your life.'

Did he, ten years on? Sometimes, yes. Sometimes when he was among friends, contemporaries from high school who had taken the usual paths, he questioned his decision. His old buddies were confidently inhabiting a world that was alien to Miles. The world of his father's generation, the world of adulthood. Now his friends were bankers, lawyers, journalists, accountants. They talked in millions while Miles spoke of savings he'd made at A & P. They bragged of legal triumphs while he tried to interest them in a well-received audition speech. Miles had always assumed that he would be a part of this world of theirs. But when? When?

These were his misgivings. The fear that perhaps he was treating this life as a trial run, that by the time he'd learnt what he felt he needed to know it would simply be too late to do what he wanted to do. He knew that all he was striving for was the contentment of having found his calling, but it was precisely this that his friends seemed to possess.

Yet he knew of storms in their Utopias. The props of their adulthood revealed nothing of the growth inside. His friends had been transformed into staid members of an occupation. Accountants became, sometimes against the odds, cautious lovers of exactitude. Bankers became brash, proud, aggressive. The clichés seemed to be true. And now these friends could see only as far as their own defined futures. After the hardship of the first three or four years of training, all saw their mountains sloping downward, down towards rivers of gold.

After twenty-nine years Miles felt he'd only just begun the climb.

But he did dream. He dreamt that one day he would have climbed higher than them all. He'd just been waiting for a sign, and something deep within him told him that this opportunity was it.

Kristina heard the front door open, and turned her head to shout. 'I'm in the bath.'

She heard the heavy stomp of Steve Barefoot's motorcycle boots. He opened the bathroom door, and the steam rushed to envelop him.

'Hell, Kristina. You taking a sauna?' Steve lifted a half-empty bottle of champagne from the ice-filled basin. 'Or celebrating something?'

'Celebrating,' she said. 'Like it was going out of style! Want some? I do.' She hiccupped, like Audrey Hepburn. 'Some more, that is.'

A layer of bubbles coated Kristina's dripping arm as she held out her glass for the champagne. Steve Barefoot rubbed his crotch on the rim of her glass.

'I've got something besides champagne on my mind.'

'Ugh, don't. I have to drink out of this.'

'Well, do you want a . . . fill-up, or what?'

'Later, Steve. I'm relaxing now.'

Steve took Kristina's thin wrist in his fist and pumped up and down her slimy forearm. 'I'll help you relax some more. I could get in.'

Kristina pulled away and balanced the glass on the side of the bath. 'Right. Two in the bath. I'm not a teenager any more.'

Steve laughed. A real redneck belly laugh, 'No kidding, babe!'

'Watch yourself, Steve.'

Steve turned, bottle in hand, and kicked the towel rail. Kristina rolled her eyes. What a kid he was!

'Oh, great, now you're going to sulk. You've only been here thirty seconds. Try being patient. For once in your life? The way grown-ups are.'

That would hurt. She knew it would. But it would teach him for making fun of her age.

'Who knows,' said Steve, not looking towards her, 'maybe I won't feel like it later.'

'I guess there's a first for everything.'

'You said it.'

Of course, within a minute Steve relented, as he always did with Kristina. He filled her glass full, took one for himself and sat on the toilet seat. He flicked open his faithful old Zippo and lit up. He made a sharp noise inhaling. She hated that. He tried to blow smoke rings. She hated that too. Especially when he blew them in restaurants, his head back and his Adam's apple bobbing. But this time, the rings were lost in the dense bathroom steam.

Steve said, 'You're as happy as a sailor in a whorehouse. Why's that?'

Kristina held the thin-stemmed champagne glass close to her lips as she sank further into the bath. She spoke over the glass's rim. 'Because Miles is going to drive Saul crazy, that's why.'

'He still might find someone,' suggested Steve.

'It doesn't matter if he does. Everything, every fax, every call, goes through me. I get to censor everything Saul sees, so he won't be seeing any guys who are cuter than you, I promise.'

Steve look puzzled, as Steve always did. It was the way he furrowed his brow. The James Dean school of intelligence. 'I still think there's got to be an easier way. Hell, if you're like Miss Powerful, why can't you just plough right on in there and tell Mister High-and-Mighty Weissman that you've found this perfect model from Texas? Me – da daaa.'

Steve held out his arms either side of him to acknowledge the imaginary applause. Kristina took a large gulp of her champagne and turned on the hot water with her foot. 'It's a question of subtlety. I can hardly persuade Saul to part with six million dollars for a model and then show up the next day with you under my arm, now can I?'

'Why the hell not?'

'Because it wouldn't look good. Anyway, you've got to know Saul. He likes a challenge. He's got himself all excited about this wild-goose chase he's sending Miles on. I have to play along and show Miles enough so that he'll look as if he knows what he's doing. The more professional I seem now, the more Saul will trust me and the more he'll think Miles is a complete loser. *Then*, and only then, I'll tell him about you.' Kristina laughed.'Oh God, if only Saul knew you were sitting right here. He's got this dipshit flying around the world while you're sitting right under his nose.'

'Well, I'm not gonna chill until that seven million-dollar cheque is in my hands.'

'Our hands. And it's gone down to six.'

Steve stood, as if it would make a difference. 'You what?'

'He wants a girl too. We're paying her a million. I forgot to tell you.'

'Oh great. Like I lose a million, just like that.' He threw his cigarette stub into the toilet, and then spat in after it.

'Don't be gross, Steven. You lose half of a million. And you wouldn't have a dime if it wasn't for me.'

'That champagne makes you *real* nasty, you know that?'

'It makes me *real* honest. Now why don't you run along like a good little boy and get things ready.'

'Get what ready?'

'Everything. You know.'

'Shit, Kristina. Again? Can't we just do it like everyone else?'

Kristina stood suddenly, like a dolphin surging from the sea. Water splashed on to the floor. Steve looked at her perfectly toned body, evenly tanned and glistening with water and bubbles. He'd never known a woman like Kristina. Never. Even at thirty-nine she was gorgeous. He could pull the women, he knew he could. Back home in Texas there'd never been a shortage. Women lined up for a young man as handsome as he. But Kristina was unique. Smart, beautiful, enigmatic, and with the mind and experience of a high-class whore.

She was the most irresistible creature he'd ever known.

As for Kristina, she knew she wouldn't need to say a word. She stood there, dripping with promise, arms limp at her sides. Strong but vulnerable. I'm yours, her body said.

Even though you're all mine, Steve-baby. You and your three million dollars.

Steve stepped towards her and ran the neck of the bottle between Kristina's legs. She pushed him away.

'Wait! Go on and get it ready.'

Steve turned and donked the bottle back in the sink. In the bedroom he kicked off his boots, climbed on the bed, and reached up to the spring door in the ceiling.

Standing in the bath, Kristina wrapped a large towel around herself and shuddered as the sweet clinking of chains made its way to her through the steam.

4

The following morning, on the eve of Miles's departure to Miami, he was woken by a call.

'Miles? Kristina von Koeler. I've set it up for you to visit Supreme Models on Park. Do you have a pen?'

Miles groaned. 'Wait a second.'

He found a chewed pencil by the bed.

'OK, the girl you're meeting is called Basia. She's a booker at Supreme. The address is in the folder I gave you. Now, they know about EDEN, but they don't know how big it is. Keep it that way. I've told Basia about you, and I've asked her to show you around, give you a feel of what an agency's like. Don't touch any composites. If you do, they'll be pestering me every five minutes to see if we want the guy. OK?'

'What time should I go?'

'Eleven. Call me from there in case anything else comes up.'

Miles was relieved about this. He'd been nervous at the prospect of walking into an agency in Miami with the equivalent of seven million dollars in his pocket without knowing something about the modelling business. The EDEN file had provided him with some information, but not enough. He had plenty more questions to ask.

Supreme's Park Avenue offices were bigger than Miles had imagined. The only other agency he'd been in was his own, a theatrical agency run by a luvvy called Barry from a tiny two-room apartment on 46th and 9th. Miles had been twenty-two when he'd joined Barry's agency, and seven years on, Barry was still trying to sell Miles as an up-and-coming twenty-two-year old. When he did manage to send Miles on a TV commercial casting, more often than not Miles found himself called upon to act like a teenager all over again. While standing alone on an X made of tape with a video aimed at his face, a woman behind a foldaway table in a hot dark room in the West 40s would say 'and this is where your girlfriend sees your face is clear of spots.'

'Do you want the build-up to the moment?' Miles would ask.

'No, just give me a look of pride.'

Supreme couldn't have been further removed from Barry's agency. Miles stepped from the elevator into a large reception room. Framed magazine covers of Supreme's top male and female models filled the walls, and on a computer screen at the side, images of models' composites ran in a continuous sequence.

The agency took up the entire floor of a large building. Corridors ran warren-like between departments. Alongside the agents for men, women and children worked lawyers, accountants and administrators.

Miles followed the signs to the Men's Division.

The room was dominated by a large round table at which sat five agents. None seemed too interested in Miles as he walked with trepidation towards them. All five were on the phone. He waited until the girl nearest to him had finished her call.

'I'm looking for Basia,' he said. 'I've got an appointment.'

'She'll be off in a second,' the girl said, before dialling another number.

Basia, a woman in her mid-thirties with glossy, dark hair, flushed cheeks and scarlet lipstick, cupped a hand over the telephone receiver and held up a finger to let Miles know she'd be through in one minute. She then gestured towards a long couch that ran parallel to the back wall of the office. Miles nodded, and smiled. The two male agents gave Miles cursory glances. The older seemed to look him up and down, but neither greeted him.

If only you knew about the six million, thought Miles, you'd be eating out of my hand.

From where Miles sat he had a good view of the agency. Along the faces of two walls were layers of glass-fronted shelves angled to display row upon row of models' composites.

Behind him on the wall hung large prints and magazine covers of the top models in Supreme. Miles recognised all of them, but knew none by name. They were the models for some of America's top campaigns. There was even a shot for *Weissmans*.

The table at which the agents worked was littered with phones and papers, pages torn from magazines, ashtrays, Diet Coke cans, pastries, coloured pens and cigarettes. A large circular hole had been cut from the centre of the table. Within this hole, a revolving stand carried dozen of pages with models' names written at the top.

Basia was spinning the stand to remove the chart belonging to a model called John Larson. Miles thought he'd read the name in some article about the world's top models. He pushed himself up slightly on the couch to get a better view and read the words *San Francisco, Lee, $6000 p. d.* written at an angle across three days of the following week. Written in red by the side were the letters DEF.

On the phone, Basia was discussing John. She sounded exasperated. Later, Miles would learn that Basia always sounded exasperated. She assumed it encouraged pity.

'No . . . no, no way you ever said that. Nancy, how do you expect him to get from . . . yes, I know you want him there on the 30th, but he's confirmed in Paris right through the 29th . . . I never said that . . . what do you mean? . . . No, I'm John's booker. Well, I don't think Scott would have said that to you without . . . He did?'

Basia punched the hold button on her phone and glared at the man sitting at the table opposite her. 'Scott, did you talk to Nancy Silverman about John? About him going to Toronto?'

'Yeah, I told her when he was finished in Paris. So?'

'So now I've got her on the line screaming at me because you told her John would be in Toronto in the afternoon of the 29th when he won't in fact get there until the 30th.'

'Bullshit, Basia. Hold on, I want to talk to her. What line's the bitch on?'

'Three.'

Scott hit line three, all sweetness. 'Nancy, hi there, it's Scott. How you doing? So what's the problem?'

Basia turned quickly to Miles. 'I'm sorry, I've got a client screaming at me from Toronto about one of our guys. It's really a big job. But I'll be through soon.'

Scott was trying to confuse Nancy: 'Nancy, tell me something. Why would I say you could have John on the 29th when I knew perfectly well that he'd be in Paris? Why?'

Scott looked about him to see who was listening. He made a face at Basia.

The girl to Miles's left answered another line. 'Supreme. Oh hi, this is Diane. Can you hold?' She turned to Basia. 'Basia, José holding for you on line four.'

'Fucker. Tell him I'm not here.'

'José? She's stepped out for a moment. OK, hold on.' Again, she turned to Basia. 'He says he heard your voice.'

'I can't deal with him right now. Carla, did you speak to Macy's this morning?'

'Yes. They haven't decided anything.'

'How's it looking for José?'

'Not good.'

'OK, tell him we're working on it and to check in this afternoon.'

Now Scott was trying to calm Nancy down. 'Let me call Paris and see if he can get an afternoon flight on the 29th. Will that satisfy you? . . . Nancy, sweetheart, you're not shooting 'til the 30th, right? . . . So if John can get there late on the 29th it'll be OK, right? . . . He can do the fitting that night. OK? Let me call you right back.'

He threw down the phone.

Basia glared at him. 'You should have let me deal with that, Scott.'

'Excuse me, Bash. Who was the one who sent John's book to Nancy Silverman in the first place? Me. Remember? I got him the job.'

Basia ignored him and took another call as a couple of models ambled into the room, both carrying large blue portfolios. Scott turned, his expression swinging from anger to warmth along with the revolution of the chair. He held up a hand. The taller of the two, a Hispanic model of about twenty-five with thick, greased-back hair and a sharp nose, came over to the table. He grabbed Carla's shoulders and began to massage them.

'Hey, buddy!' said Scott. 'Like the haircut! When d'you get it done?'

'They did it for Versace.'

'Oh, yeah. How'd that go?'

'I think they liked me.'

'Cool. Did you guys go see J Crew this morning?'

'No one told me,' one of the two replied.

'Well, GO. You know the address, right? They've got some new model booker. She's seeing guys until twelve.'

'Do you know how many times J Crew have had me on option, man?' said the other model.

He was fair-haired, about six-one, Californian. A surfer. A breed all of its own.

Scott said, 'So you should go see this new girl. Her name's Muriel. But you've got to go like *now*, you hear? Get a cab.'

The Californian felt peeved. 'I just came from Sixth Avenue. You want to pay for the cab?'

'You want the job? If you don't go see the clients you'll never work. Anyway, I just booked you for *Details* magazine.'

The Californian laughed. 'Great. Twenty bucks!'

'It's with Tony Simson. It'll be good for your book.'

'Fuck that! Let's go man.'

'Check in later . . .'

Diane said 'Can somebody please tell me why Jason Jeffrey's book isn't back yet?'

'Check with Joseph Abboud.'

'Scott, Sarah from London. Line five,' said Mike, the second male agent, 'something about Troy.'

'I'll take that' said Basia. 'But can you talk to this guy? He's from *Weissmans*. I'm like snowed under.'

Mike stood and came over to Miles. He smiled at him.

'Hi, I'm Mike Palmer. What can I do for you?'

Mike didn't let go of Miles's hand until he'd finished talking. Mike was in his early forties, dressed smartly in khakis and a button-down Brooks Brothers shirt. His face was shadowed with a five-to-nine-on-a-Monday-morning-and-don't-you-dare-ask-me-about-it expression.

Miles introduced himself and told Mike a little about the EDEN campaign. He explained why he was there.

'I could do with a break,' said Mike. 'Let's go.'

'Is it always this crazy in here?' asked Miles.

'Unh-huh. Follow me.'

They picked up Cokes from the machine, found an empty conference room and closed the door on the madness that seemed to reign in the Men's Division of New York's number one modelling agency.

'I hope you don't mind,' Miles said. 'Apparently, Basia was doing this as a favour to Kristina at *Weissmans*, but Basia didn't look very interested in me.'

'Try working with the bitch,' Mike said. 'Now, what do you want to know? I've got about ten minutes.'

Ten minutes. To learn it all? Help!

'Well, I guess I'd better start at square one. Um, maybe you could tell me something about what you do as an agent?'

'First off, we're called bookers, because that's what we do mainly. We book jobs for our models. Basically our job is to tell the models which clients have jobs going, and tell the clients which models are available. We're the go-betweens, as it were. And even when there's not a specific job we'll send out guys to show their portfolios.'

'So the models don't actually work for you?'

'No, officially we work for them. But we don't like to think of it like that.'

'What happens, then, if I call up a booker and say that *Weissmans* is interested in one of your guys?'

'OK. First off, I say fantastic! Which one? How much?

When? What's it for? Who's shooting? Then I'd probably ask whether you needed for us to arrange for you to see the model or his portfolio, then I'd recommend some other guys with the same look, in case you change your mind about the first guy.'

'But say I'm really interested in one model. How do I find out if he's available? I got this notion that models are always flying around the world on Concorde.'

'Well, not quite. If he's in another country then I'll call up the agency who represents him in that country and see if he's already booked on those dates. If he isn't, we tell them we might want him then.'

'Will that agency be a branch of Supreme?'

'No. We've got a branch in Miami and one in LA, but not abroad.'

Mike took a swig of coke too fast and burped.

'So the agencies aren't affiliated?' said Miles.

'No, but we've got to scratch each other's backs. Way it works is that once a client has called up and expressed a strong interest in a model then we'll put what's called a first option on that guy. That means basically that you're reserving time on him, and no one else can use him on those days.'

'So the model's screwed if he's got this option and he's not wanted? Those days are wasted, are they?'

'No, not necessarily. If someone else wants to use him on the same days then that client gets a second option on the model. If *that* client wants to confirm the booking for the model, then we'd call up the client who's got the first option and say, "look, someone else is ready to confirm, blah-blah . . . we need you to decide." I mean it does happen that a client won't say no until the last minute and then the model loses another job, but not often.'

'And what happens if he's in Paris, say, and he's got a first option there too?'

'We usually work something out between the agencies.'

'So the model doesn't decide what he wants to do?'

'We like the model to think he's making the decision for

himself, but we do what we can to persuade him to take the job here.'

'Like how?'

'Like we tell him there's other jobs coming up in the city once he's here, or we tell him that the photographer is really keen to work with him, and *he's* got a big campaign coming up. Something like that.'

'Whether it's true or not.'

'Whatever. It's a job. Thing is, we only make money if the model makes money.'

'But not in another country for another agency, even if that job might be better for the model?'

'We're not a charity.'

Miles said, 'Can I ask how much commission you take?'

'This is like a visit from the IRS!'

'I'm sorry, I really don't know anything.'

'I'm kidding. Usually we take twenty per cent from the model. And then another twenty per cent from the client.'

Miles let this sink in. Forty per cent of six million dollars. That was a small fortune. No, a big fortune. No wonder Kristina wanted to avoid the agencies. Miles wondered how the hell Kristina planned to get around the agencies without alienating them for the future. She'd have to come up with something really smart. Like appearing at the last minute with a nobody from Tokyo or Moscow or Milan who didn't even have an agent.

Miles didn't think of Texas.

He glanced at his notepad. 'Um, how does it work with the models travelling? Do you ever find them jobs abroad?'

'Not unless it's a trip booked out of New York. Most models have different agencies around the world, in Milan, Paris, LA, Miami, London, maybe places like Hamburg and Madrid, you know.'

'And all of these agents are looking for work for the models all the time?'

'For the big guys, the really top guys, yeah. But mostly the model has to be in the same city as the agency so that he can go on the castings, show his book around, things like that.'

'So a model comes here, and then you arrange for him to see different advertisers and magazines in the city and hope that someone gets interested.'

'Right. Want my job?'

'I don't think I could handle it.'

'Sure you could. You just got to learn how to scare the clients into giving you more money. It's like sex – half the fun's gone if you say yes all the time.'

'Can't say I agree with you there.'

'So you'd say yes if I asked you?'

'Aah!' Miles tapped the side of the Coke can, and let out a nervous laugh. 'Maybe that'd be one of the nos.'

'I was only kidding.'

Miles stood. 'OK! Thanks for helping me out.'

'That's it?'

'I think so. Except I need to use your phone.'

'Sure, go right ahead.'

Scott rose as soon as Miles returned to the men's division. Clearly Basia had said something about the EDEN campaign when Miles was out of the room. Scott extended a hand. 'Hi, I'm Scott Farber. I'm sorry I didn't get a chance to talk to you when you came in. Do you need to see any of the guys?'

Miles said no but Scott rarely listened to that word. 'Do you want some composites?'

'Actually, I'll be coming back here later.'

'Is this a big campaign, or what?'

Miles said 'It should be in the papers soon. I'm sorry, I'm pressed for time. I'm leaving for Miami tomorrow. Could I use your phone?'

'Go ahead. You know we have a branch on Ocean Drive? Let me call Susan Rosenblaum to tell her to expect you, OK?'

'Great, thanks.'

Miles called Kristina.

She was even more curt than usual. 'Saul wants to see you,' she said.

'What about?'

'Think I'm a goddamn mind reader, Miles? Just get a cab. Now.'

Miles was nervous when he hung up. Not only did he not want to see Kristina again, but he was struck with the fear that his whole trip might have been cancelled. After all, wasn't that the way his life most often went?

At least Kristina was nowhere to be seen when Miles walked into Saul's spacious office for the second time that week. Weissman didn't get up, but stayed in his massive revolving leather desk chair, pushing himself from left to right with his small, bulldog legs. Through the windows behind him, sunlight came, splashing across the desk upon which a wide silver bowl, filled to the brim with pistachios, sat glinting by the telephone.

Saul Weissman was in a good mood.

'All psyched up, kid? Huh? Been out to buy your shit tablets and sun cream?'

'I didn't think I'd have much time for sunbathing,' Miles said.

'Hey!' Saul clapped his hands together. 'Looks like I picked me a worker. Good for you, Miles. Good for you.' Then, as if it was a reward, Weissman extended his right arm and added, 'Take a seat.'

'Thanks.'

'Still, maybe you should get some sun. I never met a man of authority who didn't have good colour to his cheeks. That's why Nixon lost it to JFK in those debates. His skin was so see-through nobody believed a fucking word he said. That's all it took. A man killed by sweat and lighting. Too goddamn pale.'

'I can lie on a beach if you want me to.'

'No, you don't have the time. I'll get Rona to arrange a sunbed session at my club. A man should have some colour to his cheeks.'

Miles noticed how pale Weissman was as he buzzed through to his secretary.

'Now,' Weissman continued, 'I got some good news for you. You been to Brazil?'

'No, sir.'

'No, sir. Nor have I. But I'm going.'

Hastily Miles said, 'I did suggest to Miss von Koeler that we should maybe take a look in Brazil. She seemed to have other ideas.'

If Weissman knew that Kristina had taken control of the whole search, he didn't seem to care. If he didn't know, Miles wondered whether he should say something. He'd like to go to Brazil, or even to 'fucking Peru.' Especially if Weissman was paying.

Weissman went on. 'Do whatever Kristy says. See, it's me that's going to Brazil, not you.'

'To look for models?'

'No! You think I'd hire a guy to do a job and then do it for him? What kind of schmuck d'ya take me for? No! I'm gonna be buying some land. For EDEN. I met this Brazilian who says he knows a guy here who knows a guy there who knows Collor. He's their President.'

'And you're going to meet him?'

'Meet him? No, but I'm gonna buy some land off of him. In the Amazon. See, these Brazilian guys can't touch it because the rest of the world's saying there's a fucking hole in the sky. Like this ozone thing's Brazil's fault. So the Brazilians are thinking "fuck it", those guys in America want to keep the Amazon for nature, those guys gotta *buy* it for nature. Guys like this Sting. Put his money where his warbling mouth is, OK? And that's what I'm gonna do.'

'You're buying a part of the rainforest?'

'Yeah!' said Weissman like a pumped-up football coach. 'Well, a tree maybe. But it's enough. You with me, Miles? Think about it. The world's gone environment crazy. We've even got this Gore guy as our next Vice President. And he's such a fucking environment nut he's gonna have us recycling our toilet paper next.' Weissman rubbed his palm over the top of his bald head and laughed. 'Anyways, so I gotta think how I can use this environment idea for *Weissmans*. It's a trend, Miles. I can't ignore that. So, what am I gonna do? I could dress my windows in jungle scenes, or, or I could run an ad with a shot of Wally the Hunted Whale, or I could do something real.'

'And buy a tree in the rainforest,' said Miles.

Weissman pointed a finger at Miles and smiled. 'Now you're thinking with me.' Weissman cracked open a nut. His first this meeting. 'But am I gonna sit on that tree, and do nothing?'

'That wouldn't be your style, sir.'

'Now you're running with me too, Miles. Of course it wouldn't. No. So you know what we're gonna do with it?' Weissman spoke slowly now as he laid out his plan. 'We are going out to shoot the campaign on my land.'

'In the Amazon?'

'In the Amazon! I'm not about to take this guy to the Plaza and shoot a cologne like EDEN in a fucking hotel ballroom, am I? With a la-di-da cigarette holder and a fucking tuxedo! Wouldn't be right. Why? Because the message is nature. Already, I got this picture in my mind of our model, a big muscular type of guy, and he's standing with the girl in the forest, and he's got her in his arms, and I want them to have this look in their eyes like they're the only two people left in the world, which, being Adam and Eve they were, right? Like it?'

'I think the idea's excellent, Mr Weissman, but have you seen the land? Are you sure everything's going to be right to shoot on it?'

'To be straight with you, Milo, I couldn't give a fuck. Once I invest in the land, the people are going think I'm like a Mother Teresa of the environment. So when I go there to shoot EDEN, these people,' Weissman jerked his thumb southwards, 'are gonna put two and two together. We'll find some tree to shoot in front of. Who says it gotta be mine?'

Weissman was having trouble extracting something from the corner of his eye. 'I'm hoping the location will give you a clear idea about the kind of Adam I want: no pencil-pushers, no fudge-bandits, no boys who look like girls. I need a guy who looks like he belongs in the Brazilian Rainforest.'

'An Indian?'

'Who knows? Maybe. But I think that *Dances with Wolves*

shit is over. You got to mix the ingredients up to appeal to everyone. Just trust yourself when you pick this guy. You religious Miles?'

Miles wasn't sure what to say. He plumped for the honest answer. 'No.'

'No! I see.' Weissman paused. 'Me neither. But I want to talk to you about the spirit.'

Oh please God, thought Miles, save me now. I'll pray later. Promise.

'Tell me something, Miles. Did you get a chance to see *Star Wars*?'

'Sure.'

'Good, because *that* was a deeply spiritual movie. It's about instinct. Luke Skywalker trusts in the Force, and it sees him through. I want you to remember that. When you go out there into the unknown looking for a model for this beautiful cologne of mine, I want my Force to be with you.'

The more serious Weissman became, the more Miles wanted to laugh. As the pressure built, Miles's face reddened.

'I'm not a stupid man, Miles. I'm aware you don't know shit about models. That's why you got to trust in your instinct. See, you know about people. We saw videos of you working in the store. You didn't know that, did you?'

Actually, he did. 'No, sir.'

'Well, I watched you, and I said to Kristina – this guy knows people. You read them right, Miles. Like me. I'm a people man. Always have been. And Kristina, she's a people woman. Together, Miles, we can make a People Triangle.' Slowly, Weissman drew a large triangle in the air with his index finger. He pointed at each of the corners. 'You, me, and Kristy. And if we keep the ideas going round this triangle, then we're gonna find the perfect guy. See, Kristina . . .' he pointed into the air again, '. . . knows what sells, I know how to sell it, and you, well you're the kind of guy we want to sell it to. That's why you gotta listen to your instinct, Miles. And if it's honest, if we can trust each other, then together we can sell this cologne to the whole goddamn world.'

Once again, Weissman drew a triangle in the air. When he spoke, it was very slowly, almost as if he was trying to hypnotise Miles. 'Me. You. Kristy, and . . .' Now Weissman picked up from the desk a tiny bottle of yellowish liquid. He held it between his forefinger and thumb and positioned it in the heart of the invisible triangle. 'EDEN!'

Without warning, Weissman flicked his wrist and spun the bottle towards Miles. Miles was lucky to catch it.

'That's EDEN, Miles. Take it with you. Take it to bed with you. Let the scent become a part of you.'

Miles opened the bottle and sniffed. Jesus, that's horrible, he thought. Really horrible.

'Go on,' said Weissman. 'Try it. Put it on.'

Miles dabbed some on his cheek. As little as he could get away with.

'Does that make things easier for you, Miles?'

Like hell. 'Yes, sir.'

'I knew it would. Wear that, and you'll start seeing faces.'

Wear this, thought Miles, and I'll be seeing Peter at the Gates.

'If you live with that beautiful scent I've produced, I guarantee you'll start seeing the kind of face you'll be looking for. Then it'll be a matter of going out and finding him. There.'

Weissman seemed all used up, like a TV evangelist who'd received word that the church had reached its daily dollar target. 'I wish you luck, Miles. Now go ask Rona about those sunbeds.'

Miles stood. 'Thank you, Mr Weissman.'

'That's OK. I'm glad we had this chance to share.'

'Um, me too.'

'The Force, Miles. It's real.'

'Thank you, Mr Weissman. I'll, I mean, I'll remember that.'

'Goodbye, Miles. I know you're gonna do me proud!'

Weissman looked back down at a sample fabric board on his desk, and Miles let himself out, quietly pulling the door closed behind him.

*   *   *

Later, his body hot from the ultraviolet rays, Miles sat at a desk in his apartment, ran a hand across his forehead and sighed. He was tired and ill at ease. So much information! So many ideas! So much energy to find two models for one horrible scent!

Yet what concerned Miles the most was that it was all up to him now, and he didn't know the first thing about what he was doing.

He made a neat stack of the model composites given him as a guideline by Kristina, and pushed it across the desk. How the hell was he to know who was the best? On the front of each glossy composite card was printed a headshot of the model, on the back three or four more carefully selected pictures, along with the model's statistics. The men all looked the same to Miles. They were nearly all handsome in a classic square-jawed, pearly-toothed, six-foot-two, forty-regular, thick-haired kind of way. And they would nearly all look ridiculous surfacing from a swamp in the Amazon. How the hell was he to choose? Was this man really out there, this fresh, manly, muscular, organic, universal, pure, virginal, versatile, sexy, butch, rugged swamp-thing? Miles longed for something more definite to work with. More than Saul Weissman's Force, at least. He closed his eyes. Maybe everything would become more clear once he began to visit the agencies.

Miles positioned the air tickets dead centre on top of the EDEN file. He'd read it from cover to cover, three times, but it hadn't helped clarify much. It contained some details about the cologne itself, the dates of the proposed shooting at the end of January 1993, the names of the agencies he was supposed to visit, and the contacts he had in various cities. But there were no real guidelines about how the model should look. Kristina, like Saul, seemed remarkably confident that Miles would live up to their expectations of him.

He turned off the desk lamp. Poppy was probably asleep by now. He'd snapped at her earlier when she'd tried to tempt him into bed. Now he wished he hadn't. Should he wake her?

His mind was too crowded for sleep. Miles climbed the stairs and crept on to their bed. Usually he liked to watch television in bed, but tonight Poppy was sound asleep, her gorgeous, delicate face denting the pillow on his side of the bed. He watched her breathe and felt a surge of love. He wanted to take her in his arms and squeeze her. Instead, he traced a finger along the curve of her lips, against her cheekbone, even across her eyes. But with her body so accustomed to the touch of his hand she did not wake.

Miles climbed down from the loft bed and returned to the other end of the apartment where their second television sat. On channel 19, with the volume low, he turned on an inane quiz show. He thought it would send him to sleep.

The show was called *Spouse Swap*. It was a variation of an old theme. There were four contestants, two couples. In the old show, husbands and wives were questioned on their knowledge of each other. For *Spouse Swap* the couples had, well, swapped spouses. For twenty-four hours. Now they were being questioned about their one-day partners by a man with a brown toupé.

The questions were of a deliberately personal nature, probing towards the big question: *had anything gone on*? Had these couples sacrificed the sanctity of marriage for the glory of televisual fame? Did Lucille know what colour underwear Ross liked to wear? Did Jaynie sleep in the nude, on the right or the left of the bed? Did Bob like coffee or tea for breakfast?

They're probably actors, thought Miles. Or the answers had been prepared in advance. Yet he kept watching, wanting to see who'd win, hoping against hope that he might be surprised. As he lay there, not able to bring himself to switch off, his mind wandered.

He began drifting, drifting to sleep. Poppy in his mind. Poppy and Saul and Kristina. A plane taking off and Poppy. A beach. Japanese men, thousands of Japanese men. A street. The toupéd man was stirring the crowd on TV. Miles's head fell heavily, too far to the side. It jolted him awake. He lifted it and began to drift again as the couple from Vermont went home with the car and the competition was won and Christ, Miles, yes, of course, that was IT. Suddenly, with open eyes, he could see what was missing from the EDEN search.

If Weissman agreed to the idea, the PR opportunities would be endless. Miles wondered if he'd be able to tell the reporter from the *Herald* he was meeting tomorrow. Probably not. Best to wait for Weissman to say yes. He surely would.

Miles flicked off the TV. This is it, he thought.

It's time for the the world to notice me.

5

November 5th, 1992. Larry Meyers woke, grasped for his watch, and whispered a foul curse to start the new day. He'd overslept, despite the noise of drilling from the road outside, and now he'd have to chase his uninspiring quarry out to the petty marshlands of La Guardia airport. Shit.

Meyers was one of the longest-serving reporters on the tabloid *New York Daily Herald*. He'd wanted to interview Miles in the city, and he'd missed his chance now. No point even calling the number he had.

Meyers let his arm drop heavily on to the bed, his scratched and battered watch squeezed between forefinger and thumb. If he'd laid it back on the bedside table, he'd have fallen asleep again, so he kept it in his hand as if to prove some rare human control of time itself.

Meyers's body ached – back, shoulders, even his feet. When he moved, his brain clunked uncomfortably against the inner sides of his skull. As far as Larry Meyers was concerned, the crisp November day beckoned like a three-day-old beefburger.

As usual, he'd drunk too much the night before. His excessive consumption of alcohol no longer incapacitated him, but it did weigh him down, slow his mind and movements. Worse though, it made him impatient and irascible. Why did he do it? He had no answers, nor did he look for them. He reserved investigation for others. Besides, Meyers maintained that self-examination was futile while the brain was constantly in the process of reinvention. He might as well ask one of the notoriously corrupt NY Police Departments to carry out a closed investigation into internal corruption.

And another thing: Larry Meyers thought that this endless

assault on his fifty-two-year-old body kept him young. It certainly kept him active. Beside him, wrapped in the billowing purple flowers of her nylon sheets, lay Brenda McCarron. The night before, Brenda had walked him from Dan Lynch's on Third, around the corner and up to her studio apartment on Fourteenth, right above the wig store where the transvestites gather. Brenda was a sultry, disappointed woman with skin that permanently looked as if it were illuminated by fluorescent light. Her lips were heavy and mottled, her eyes tired and sagged, her hands red. Yet she had a kind heart, seen only by the few, Meyers among them, to whom she chose to reveal it.

Bleary-eyed, Meyers turned towards her. She lay on her side, breathing heavily, her fleshy buttocks jutting towards him; the bloated cheeks of a medieval gargoyle. Meyers wondered whether she was dreaming of greener days in the Emerald Isle. She often spoke with the sadness of one exiled from her homeland, as if return was impossible. Meyers had met her first three years before while on a story about a homeless man whose throat had been slashed on the steps to Brenda's building. After the police had left, she, with sleeves rolled, and with an outdated neighbourliness, had washed the man's dried blood from the step, and given Larry most of the information he'd needed. She'd known the homeless man, learnt he had a brother working on Wall Street. This one fact had elevated the story from a column on page four to front page news. It had meshed well with a change in public sentiment, being a symbolic story for a self-conscious time, a Cain and Abel tale of big business against the urban poor.

Larry Meyers leant over Brenda and pulled the telephone towards him. He dialled the number of the *Herald* and asked to be connected to the new staff photographer, an English girl called Jenny Richardson. She would be waiting for Meyers in his office. He was connected, didn't bother with excuses, told her to get a car, pronto, and meet him outside the Kentucky Fried Chicken on the corner of Fourteenth and Third. 'And have someone from the office get a message to the *Weissmans* guy at the airport. Tell him

to wait in the bar near to the NorthWest Airlines desk. You
got that?'

They would catch Miles if they hurried.

Brenda woke, and rolled over – an Irish Sea wave, grey
and heavy with debris. 'What time d'ya have there, Larry?'

'Ten thirty. Just after.'

Brenda groaned, the noise turning sweet with remembrance. 'You know, that were real nice, Larry. Last night.'

'Was it? Good,' he said, sliding out of bed and sitting on
the edge to pull on his socks. He couldn't remember, not so
that he could judge one way or the other. Yes, they'd made
love, or at least they'd gone through the motions, he lying on
his back, inebriated and surprised by his ability, while she'd
moved on top, grinding, twisting, her head back, his hands
on her shoulders, a communication not with eyes and lips
and hearts, but a rhythmic, methodical, animal pestle and
mortar. He'd felt something, like a foot in a warm bath,
but the sensation was dim until the final moments when
he'd lifted his upper body and held her, his cheek pressed
against her large breasts. She had peaked once, twice? He
didn't know, but her pleasure brought him true satisfaction,
not least because he was proud of a body that had, if truth
be told, begun to fail him. Overworked, stimulated by little
besides alcohol, undernourished by meals that, on good days,
were no more than snatched slices of pizza, Meyers's body
now sagged where once he had been taut and muscular. A
man who lived for words and ideas, he surprised himself with
the nostalgia he felt for his lost physique.

Brenda rubbed her palm and fingers across his back, and
the sensation pleased him more than anything during the night
before. Though short of time, he sat still while she tickled his
back. It reminded Larry of what he'd missed in the ten years
since the death of his wife. These rare moments of tender
human contact calmed him more than anything he knew. It
was easy enough to pick up a woman willing to spread her
legs. Too easy. But this was rare.

Meyers twisted around, surprised Brenda with a kiss
rotting with beer, cigarettes and sleep.

'You're rough,' she said, touching his face.

'I'd shave if I had time.'

Meyers rubbed a hand over his thick and greying stubble.

'Sure you would!' she said.

Meyers pushed his body on to his feet and pulled on his jeans. He kicked his feet into laced shoes. With his right hand, he rearranged his balls in the jeans, and, carefully, zipped up.

'So you've taken to not wearing underwear, did ya?'

'I couldn't see them. Anyway, they're not what you'd call fresh.'

'Oh great! So you're leaving the darn things for me are ya? Some air freshener they'll make. I'd say you took 'em off you in the bed. They'll be down the bottom there.'

'I never touched them!' said Larry, thrusting his hand between the sheets and down towards the foot of the bed. 'You were the one who ripped them off me. I was falling asleep.'

'Sure you were!'

Larry's hand re-emerged with the underwear. He opened his tatty leather briefcase and shoved the underwear inside.

Brenda laughed. 'I hope to God your sandwiches aren't in there too. I hope to God for them, that is!'

'Look, I gotta run. I'll, um . . .'

Brenda rubbed at the corner of her eye. 'Forget it . . . I'll be seeing you in the bar. Won't I.'

Was this a question or a statement? Brenda tried hard to make it impossible for Meyers to tell.

'Yeah, of course, I'll see ya,' he said, and he left. Brenda listened to his footsteps, heavy on the old wooden stairs. Then there was a moment's quiet before the sound began again, though now the echo was louder for he was climbing again, clomping doggedly.

'What's the big lug forgotten now?' whispered Brenda to herself. She swung her legs out of bed and reached the door at the same time as Larry. She opened it. He smiled at her, a smile she saw so rarely.

'I never said thanks.'

Brenda was silent for a moment, though her heart was pounding. 'You never do, Larry.'

'Well, er, better late than never, I guess. So, so thanks. For putting up with me, eh? It . . . well, thanks.'

Then, with a hand raised in a half wave, he turned and set off once more. Brenda McCarron watched him leave. Almost, almost like a loving wife.

Jenny Richardson was a thin-boned, flighty English woman in her late twenties. Tony Jakes, editor of the *Herald* had poached her from an English newspaper because he'd admired the humour in her photos for years.

Jenny wasn't typical in stature for a tabloid photo-journalist, though she compensated for this with the fervency of her competitive spirit. She wanted this particular job about as much as Meyers did. Still, she liked Larry, and smiled when she saw him standing on the corner of Fourteenth and Third Avenue, looking as if he'd only just stumbled out of a bar. He was holding a cup of watery coffee and a greasy chicken leg. The *Herald* car, a maroon Cadillac saloon, pulled up gently, as only chauffeur-driven cars do. It stopped beside Meyers. He didn't seem to notice. Jenny opened the door from the inside, and called.

As he climbed in, Jenny was poised to speak, but Meyers raised a dismissive hand. 'I know! Let's go.'

'*Weissmans* faxed us a photograph of this Miles Jensen bloke so that we can pick him out,' said Jenny, handing Larry the flimsy greyish paper.

'Oh shit, will you look at this guy?' Meyers flicked the photograph with the back of his hand, his fingernails rapping against the print. 'I hope Mummy's there to hold his hand.'

'They were trying to reach him when I left.'

'Did they try the milk-shake bar?' He laughed. 'I'm, I'm sorry we missed him in town. Last night I . . .'

'I can see,' said Jenny, smiling. She pressed the button to lower the window and let in the air. Meyers was looking at her curiously. 'The chicken stinks,' Jenny lied, and leant her face towards the incoming breeze.

*　　*　　*

A message was waiting for Miles at the airport. *Call Kristina* a.s.a.p. Great, thought Miles. Weissman likes my idea. Miles had telephoned Kristina before he'd set off and explained the previous night's idea in simple, attractive terms.

He'd been mindlessly gazing at a TV show, he'd said, when the idea had come to him. Why not announce a competition for EDEN? Instead of just looking for one guy, couldn't he collect a few models from around the world and bring them to New York where the winner would be chosen? Think of the publicity, he'd said. It could be a sort of Miss World and Mr Universe combined. *Weissmans* might even get the TV stations interested. And even if Kristina and Weissman made their choice of model in advance, they could still play along with the competition and drum up media attention by parading the finalists in front of the world. Even those people who usually took no interest in the fashion world could become interested in who was going to win a contract for six million dollars.

Kristina had given the idea a frosty reception, but Miles was convinced that Weissman would agree. It gave the search some structure.

Now on the phone, Kristina sounded impatient. 'The guy from the *Herald* is on his way out. He says wait for him at the bar near the NorthWest Airlines desk, OK?'

'Yeah. Did you ask Saul for me?'

'About what?

'My idea for the competition.'

'Oh that. Yes I did. He says no-can-do, Miles. There'd be too much to deal with at this end.'

Miles closed his eyes and leant his head back in disappointment. 'Is that final?'

'Absolutely. And Miles, a word of advice. Don't bring the subject up with Saul, OK? He's not a man who likes to be told he's made a bad decision.'

Miles was about to hang up when she added, 'Oh, and don't waste much time looking for a female model. She's going to have to have a look that matches up with our Adam, and not the other way around. Keep your eyes open, that's all. Collect some composites and send them to me. OK?'

'Sure, whatever.'

Another blow. Miles felt dejected when he hung up. He'd hoped to be able to tell the reporter about the competition. It made such sense! How could Weissman have rejected the idea?

Miles had arrived at La Guardia in high spirits. The limousine driver had taken the Williamsburg to the airport, driving from the ramshackle, dated stores of Delancey across the noisy metal grids of the bridge. As they'd moved, the girders of the bridge had rhythmically blocked out the brilliant light of the sun and Miles had been reminded of old movies by the flickering contrast of light and shade. He'd envisaged himself as a star, an important man conducting important business from the back of a chauffeur-driven limousine. He'd felt invigorated by expectation, as if his future held the kind of accelerated promise given by ninety minutes in the cinema.

Miles had seen it all with crystal clarity. Success was to arrive without pain. Fast cars, orders shouted to servants down telephone wires, cocktails on the polished decks of yachts in Key West, and women, women, women. These things would follow as night follows day.

When they'd arrived at La Guardia, Miles had tipped the driver ten dollars in the mistaken belief that rich people part easily with their cash, and sauntered, head high, to the line for Business and First-Class passengers. For once, he'd not been dismayed by the sight of other passengers standing in line in front of him. So what if he had to wait? He had the covetous glances of the economy passengers to look forward to.

Yet the call had destroyed all that. To cheer himself, Miles decided to wander around the airport until Meyers arrived. He loved airports, always had. He enjoyed the conspicuousness of the private moments that occurred within them; the spectacle of men and women of all nationalities, standing side by side, laughing and crying, being exuberantly human in such grimly inhumane settings. Now Miles focused on an Indian family clustering about a departing relative. He wondered whether beneath their tears of farewell, the gripped hands and the jerky waves, was a shared suspicion that such masses of metal could fly, that perhaps one day logic would prevail and planes would come crashing from the skies with loved ones aboard.

When the Indian finally disappeared from view, Miles wandered to the bar and bought himself a freshly squeezed orange juice, courtesy of Mr Saul Weissman. He'd drunk only a mouthful of the pulpy liquid when he heard a voice.

'You Miles Jensen?'

'Yes, I am. You must be . . .?'

Meyers extended his hand. 'Larry Meyers.' Meyers jerked a thumb at Jenny. 'She's the photographer.'

Miles looked at Meyers, dressed in jeans and a crumpled, olive green jacket, and thought that with his cropped hair and unshaven, weathered face he looked much like a boxing manager in the days before managers made millions and wore Armani suits. Miles rarely spent time with people who did not care about the clothes that they wore. Even those of his friends who were proud of their inconformity tended towards a recognisable uniform of rebellion with their faded T-shirts and closets full of black.

Yet it was possible to determine something about Meyers from his perfunctory style of dress. He was straight-up. No bullshit. The story on the Weissman cologne was an unusually tame assignment for him, but he'd been given it because he was a reporter who the paper's editor, Tony Jakes, could trust, and Saul Weissman was one advertiser that Jakes didn't want to lose.

'Jenny,' Meyers grumbled, 'be a doll and get me a Bloody Mary. With enough tabasco to burn the o out of an asshole, OK?'

Miles laughed to himself when he heard Jenny ask for 'quite a bit of tabasco, please.' It was the phrase his own mother would have used.

Jenny brought the drink and left as Meyers began to fire questions at Miles without bothering to take notes or use a recorder.

'Can you tell me what kind of model you're looking for?' he asked.

'We're actually looking for a guy and a girl . . .'

'I know, but what's *Weissmans* paying her? A million?' Miles nodded. 'Peanuts. Tell me about Superman.'

Miles kept his cool. 'I – we – want to find someone who'll represent the new feeling in *Weissmans*, and that's a feeling of honesty, if you like. We in *Weissmans* want to get back to a style that's more, more organic, back to appealing to all people, whatever their nationality, whatever their colour.

Could Meyers tell that he was spitting out learned lines, that this was nothing more than another acting job? Well, this was what he'd been told to do.

He continued. 'So we're not looking for someone of any particular ethnic origin, but rather for someone whose features will appear truly universal, you could say.'

'I guess you could. Doesn't mean much though, does it?'

'Well, EDEN is going to be a fragrance that all men will feel comfortable wearing, from the President right down to the guy who picks up your garbage.'

'Which one of those guys smells the worst?' said Meyers with a smile before drinking his Bloody Mary as if it was milk.

'As I said, both will enjoy wearing EDEN. It's a unique new scent. A scent truly designed for a nineties lifestyle.'

Meyers put down his drink and took the purple cocktail parasol out of the top. He broke it in half. How many times had he heard garbage like this? Lifestyle! The only difference between nineties lifestyle and eighties lifestyle was that more guys had their heads stuffed up their asses so it didn't smell so good any more. EDEN or no EDEN. Anyway, he had a two-page release on the cologne. What Meyers needed was something personal from Miles himself. He explained this as patiently as he could given his hangover and the banality of the story. Then he asked Miles what he felt, personally, about paying some guy six million dollars for one photo?

'I think whoever I choose is going to be worth that,' Miles replied.

'Who you gonna pick? Jesus?'

'No! Just the best person to represent the fragrance.'

'OK, help me out on this one. We've got X million guys unemployed in this country – black, brown, yellow, whatever you want. Now you,' Meyers pointed the stalk of the broken cocktail parasol at Miles, 'are telling me you have to go to, where, India, Tokyo, where, and all to find a guy who'll say yes to six million dollars for a snapshot?'

As Meyers spoke, the slightest blob of white foam formed at the edge of his mouth.

'Mr Meyers, is that your name?' Meyers nodded. He was a famous man within the five boroughs of New York City, and Miles's slight amused him. Miles carried on, 'We don't *have* to do anything. We want to do this. It's Saul Weissman's decision to search for our Adam throughout the world. *Weissmans* is not a company that accepts second best.'

'Oh, that's good! Can I quote you on that? You've got to travel the world because Saul Weissman, Mr America himself, thinks United States is second best!'

Meyers was playing with Miles now. Cat and mouse. He knew the story he'd write if he wanted to stay on the right side of Jakes – he'd regurgitate Kristina's press release, add a photo, maybe spice it up a little. But he was past the days when he allowed anyone to get away with too easy an interview, especially not a smug Ivy League Sort like Jensen. Meyers saw Miles as the kind of guy who thought the world owed him a living. What really pissed him off was that the world had a nasty habit of providing.

For most of his professional life Meyers had written about, even campaigned against, the assumption of superiority among America's Wasp élite. And not even during the glory days of Reagan, when he saw his newspaper salary treble, did he ever bend in his democratic loyalties, in his utter conviction that America was destroying itself with selfishness, and that the narrow self-interests of the men in the White Office were to blame. Who knows, maybe things would change with this Clinton kid. Meantime, he'd make Miles squirm a little, threaten to screw things up in print before Miles had even reached the starting line. Problem was that Miles was holding his own better than expected. He hadn't put a foot wrong yet. And he wasn't about to.

'Do you know where I'm going today, Mr Meyers? Miami, which happens to be in the United States of America.' Miles glanced at his watch. 'And I'm going soon, so if you have any more questions about the search for our model, can I suggest you ask them now?'

'Forget it.' Meyers flipped closed the notepad. 'But we need that photo.' He looked around. 'Jenny!'

Jenny, who had been taking snapshots of unsuspecting passers-by, came to the table, inspecting the oversized flash gun on her camera as she walked. Meyers smiled at her with his yellowing teeth. 'Something simple, Chuch. Give him a magazine or something. Ask them, will you?'

Meyers pointed towards the store. He knew the owners wouldn't refuse permission to shoot there. Few ever did, hoping that, if nothing else, it would bring them some recognition among friends.

Miles was beginning to feel uneasy. He hadn't liked Meyers's tone of questioning, and now he was having to pose for some incongruous portrait. He decided to confront the journalist.

'You do know that I'm not looking for this guy in the pages of magazines, don't you Mr Meyers? Not at all. I'm going out there to search the streets. I don't want your readers to get the wrong impression.'

For the first time, Meyers let his hangover do the talking. He stood so close to Miles that Miles could smell his stale breath. 'OK, you go find me a goddamn street in here. I'd rather be on my way to Giants stadium on a day like this, but I gotta job to do, so please let me do it. I've been in this business for thirty years, so trust me – It's gonna be better for all of us if we get a picture of your beautifully rosy cheeks. Tomorrow they'll be standing in line to buy this cologne.'

'EDEN's not in the shops yet.'

'Well, it sounds like Weissman's come too early, hasn't he?'

'Meaning . . .?'

'It's a sexual term. Means that Weissman should have held on a little if he was wanting to impress Joe Public. No one's gonna remember this little baby in six months.'

Miles smiled. 'Oh yes they are.'

Meyers smiled back. 'Don't forget who's feeding them all this shit, now.'

'I won't.' Miles's smile broadened. 'Because I am.'

Jenny returned with permission from the store, and Meyers waved at Miles with the back of his hand, as if he was imitating a movie gangster giving the casual order to kill.

Jenny extended a hand to Miles. 'We haven't really met yet. Hello, I'm Jenny Richardson.'

'Nice to meet you' said Miles, meaning it. She seemed like the perfect English rose after Meyers's Manhattan bramble.

'Yes,' said Jenny. 'Um, shall we get this done?'

When Miles had finished running his hands through his hair, Jenny handed him a copy of *GQ*.

'Do you think maybe you could go and stand over there, yeah there by the light, and if you could look at the magazine as if you were studying the . . . yeah that's good, only could you maybe look like you're reading it?'

Miles was shifting his weight awkwardly from one foot to the other and holding the magazine somewhere around his upper chest. As soon as Jenny pointed the lens towards him, he seemed to forget how he'd have usually read a magazine while standing up. He said, 'I am reading it.'

Jenny took the camera away from her eye and approached Miles. She'd learnt early that the key to taking good photographs of people was to make them look and feel relaxed. 'What I meant was could you *look* like you are reading it. It doesn't matter if you are or not. Try angling the front of the magazine . . . yes, good, that's much better, and, and could you drop your shoulders a bit? Sort of breathe in and then let it all out. You look a bit unrelaxed.'

'I am a bit unrelaxed,' said Miles, imitating her in his best English accent, and looking towards the small group of people, Meyers among them, who'd gathered to watch.

Jenny kept the camera to her eye. 'Do you think you could look just a bit happier though?'

Meyers stepped in. 'Take the photo for Christ's sakes! This isn't Miss World.'

Jenny and Miles looked at one another, and as she raised her eyebrows, Miles smiled, a genuine, unselfconscious smile. Jenny pressed her finger down fast, the shutter released, and the flash fired.

Twelve hours later, the presses began to roll. That captured image of Miles displaying his perfect white teeth, was rapidly reproduced two and a half million times.

Two hours further on, Miles's face was being thrown from trucks to join the scum on the sidewalks of New York City. Beneath the photo, a celebratory story by 'award-winning' *Herald* reporter Larry Meyers proclaimed that *Weissmans* was searching the globe for an Adam and Eve couple for its EDEN cologne.

Only this time, God was being played by a handsome young man with blond hair and no white beard. A man from Chicago, Illinois who went by the name of Miles Alexander Jensen.

On the plane, amid the excitement, despite the real comfort, Miles's bubble was burst with a sudden experience that can only be described as fear. A fear not of flying, but of failure. It was a prickling insecurity that caused him to wish momentarily that none of this had happened, to wish that he was back on Madison Avenue conning harried shoppers into hasty decisions. Miles was depressed that Saul hadn't bought his competition idea, upset about the interview with Meyers, and suddenly feeling out of his depth.

The sensation made him think of Poppy as a shipwrecked sailor thinks of land – as the thing he should not have left in case he should never find it again. The acrid smoke of guilt pervaded these thoughts of her, for he was ashamed of the way he had been treating her. He assumed too much, he knew he did. Why? Because it had been Poppy who had fallen for him. Because it had been she who had, with all the determination of a native New Yorker but with none of the customary panic, orchestrated their courtship from the start.

Poppy had done what she could to tempt Miles. She'd taken him to *Tea and Sympathy* on Greenwich 'because his Mom was British'. They'd visited a store owned by a Ukrainian out in Brighton Beach because he said he liked things Russian (and because she'd have him captive on a long subway ride). She'd returned to see the movie *Jou Dou* with the confidence that he'd admire her taste and thank her. And, as a present, she had given him her own beloved copy of the poems of Anna Akhmatova because he complained about poetry he could not understand, and Poppy knew that Akhmatova would speak with simple words straight to his heart. Much like Poppy herself. Poppy showered Miles with so much affection that he began to love her for loving him and not for the person she was. Miles assumed her love, felt no need to earn it, and too often his indifference hurt her in ways invisible to him. But now as he sat with his glazed salmon steaming in front of him on the flight to Miami, he thought back to the previous few days, and was ashamed.

Poppy had been there to help him throughout, but with blinding self-obsession he'd shown no appreciation for her generosity of spirit. She had asked for nothing and nothing was what he'd given. In the race to be prepared he hadn't stopped to tell her that he would miss her, that he did love her, that he was grateful for so many things: for her simple tolerance, for her humour, for the way she had miraculously discovered so much space in the case he hadn't been able to close when he'd packed it himself. And late the night before, when Poppy had said she was going to bed and would he come because it was their last night for a month, he'd waved her off so that he could concentrate on the model composites. He hadn't bothered to join her until she had fallen asleep with the gnawing suspicion that he didn't care enough.

In the morning, Miles had been a louse. He had been panicking, and spared time only for a peck on the cheek when Poppy left for work. These are the things on which we are judged, he thought. Sure he took her flowers sometimes, or sent her a surprise card, or took her out to dinner, but these sporadic acts of romance counted for nothing when compared with the generosity of everyday kindness. If ever he went out of his way for Poppy, Miles knew he would seek gratitude, repayment. But not she. Poppy considered self-sacrifice to be implicit in true love. Miles rarely gave any thought to how lucky he was. But now, sitting bored and ripped from the comfort of custom, Miles became reflective. And it was upon the devotion of a neglected lover that he reflected with a deserved measure of reproach. As the plane jolted and creaked, Miles grasped the arms of his chair and decided that he would prove himself to his girlfriend. He would rebel against the telephone, and write long, emotive letters, saying on paper all those things he'd failed to say to her face. It was simple. She was the girl he loved, and he would tell her so.

Miles's thoughts were interrupted by the odour of an incoming air stewardess hitting his nostrils with the overpowering pungency of a magazine perfume sample. The smell belonged to Doreen. She had a name tag and a crop of facial-hair as conspicous beneath her caked foundation as the errant bristles of a paint brush lost upon a wall.

'You didn't like the salmon?'

Her voice was syrupy and lilting, such as that of a Southern beauty-pageant contestant.

'I'm not in fact very hungry. Thanks.'

'I can get you the steak. I think we still got the steak left. I'm sure we do.'

Another stewardess, older and less eager to please, held an oversized aluminium jug of coffee above her head and nudged her wide bottom between Doreen's body and Miles's face. Doreen turned to her.

'Do we got any steak left, Sandra?' she said.

'Something wrong with his fish?'

Sandra twisted around to face Miles with the impatience of a retirement-home matron. Miles was disconcerted by the way Sandra's eyes seemed to focus a little to the right of his head.

Miles said, 'Really, I don't . . .'

'I thought,' interrupted Doreen, 'that seeing as he didn't so much as touch his fish he'd maybe like the steak.' Doreen managed to impart two syllables to the final word. Stay-ak.

Sandra, the steaming pot still threatening in her hand, leant into Miles. Is this what it's like to be a baby in a cot? he wondered.

'Do you want us to get the steak or no?' she said.

'No, thank you,' Miles replied. 'The reason I did not eat the fish is because I am not hungry. I want nothing more, except for one of you to take this away. Thank you.'

Boy, did that make him feel good!

Sandra scowled some more, spun on her heel, and trotted

away. Doreen picked up his plate, looked offended, said 'You shoulda said that before,' and followed.

Miles couldn't hide his smile. He folded up his table, reclined his chair, pulled out his leg-rest, and, bored with the monotonous roar of the flight, tuned to the in-flight entertainment. Channel 4, *Everybody's Classics*. He closed his eyes. Oh, God! Vivaldi, *Four Seasons*, again.

Miles relaxed, and tried to sleep. And as Nigel Kennedy's violin tore its way through 'Autumn', Miles felt the perfumed whoosh of Doreen's pale green skirt gust across his face as she scurried back down along the aisle.

He woke to the chasm of her cleavage. Doreen was leaning over him, straightening his chair for the final descent to Miami airport. He closed his lids again, and waited for her to leave.

Miles was always nervous about landing. To distract himself, he shifted to stare out of the window at the brilliantly transformed scene below.

What a difference an hour had made! They were parallel to the coast now, the ocean shore slicing a jagged line down the land. The sea glittered under the cloudless sky, the colour of a million sparkling gems clustered beneath clear water. Sapphire and aquamarine, turquoise, lapis lazuli and beryl. Miles thought back to La Guardia's grotesque expanse of grey. Even on shore here the lawns and trees made the land look green. Man was doing what he could to smother the landscape with monotonous houses running beside sweeping drives, but even with this pattern of red-and-white-tiled roofs, kidney-shaped pools and cars, this seemed Nature's land.

As the wheels of the plane groaned down from their streamlined case, Miles's eye rested on the white trail left by a speedboat skimming over the milky-green expanse of the bay. The plane banked sharply to the side and there was now an eerie silence as it eased homeward. Miles took hold of both armrests and shut his eyes. To calm himself, he tried to imagine being in any of those places he'd rather be, beginning with the deck of that speeding boat below.

*   *   *

He was met in Miami by a chirpy smile and a clammy hand.

'Hi, I'm Beth-Ann.' Beth-Ann lifted the square of cardboard upon which she'd written Miles's name. 'I felt kinda stupid holding this thing,' she said. 'Like I was your driver or something.'

'I could see you weren't. Drivers don't usually look so happy. They've got those traffic-jam faces.'

'Oh, you! Traffic-jam faces! Mostly everyone's just smiling all the time down here. It's the weather,' she added in a half-whisper, as if sharing privileged gossip. 'It keeps our spirits up.'

Miles knew how the residents of South Florida would boast of their weather as some restaurateurs boast of air-conditioning. In the airport shop Miles could see among the postcards of flamingoes and pelicans, Art-Deco hotels and smiling *Miami Vice* actors, images of pouting, chocolate-tanned blondes, 36DD at least, sunning themselves beside drawings of exploding thermometers beneath captions proclaiming such promises as *Ouch Florida*! It's H-H-HOT!!!

The airport doors hissed open in front of Beth-Ann. Outside the air was warm and damp, and even in this concrete jungle smelled faintly of jasmine. Miles took off his jacket and rolled up his sleeves.

'Here's the car.'

'This thing?' Miles gestured towards the enormous stretch limo that was cruising towards them.

'That's our baby. At least, Mr Weissman's. We get to use it for special occasions.'

Special occasions! Miles liked that.

Inside the car, sitting at the far end of the long, burgundy seat, Beth-Ann switched on the TV. Miles slid his palm across the smooth, polished leather. 'This is the size of my first apartment!'

'Mr Weissman likes to do things in style.'

The car swung around the sharp bends of the airport. Miles thought the landscaped greenery and tubular architecture made the airport resemble an oversized gerbil's cage. A cage in which he was playing.

'Drink?' asked Beth-Ann as she swung open the polished walnut doors of the drinks cabinet.

Miles said he'd have a Coke.

'I just love this car,' Beth-Ann added. 'Only been in it twice. Miss van Koeler always takes her boyfriends around in it. Doesn't she Horacio?'

The driver slid open a small, smoked-glass panel. He spoke with a strong Hispanic accent. 'Wha' you say?'

Beth-Ann spoke more slowly than was needed. 'I said that Kristina likes to go driving with her boyfriends.'

'Wha' you talk about?'

Miles could hear Horacio's grin.

'Come on, Horacio,' Beth-Ann was speaking in the tone one would use to address a child hiding something behind his back. 'Tell us what you told Brent at the store.' Silence. 'Tell us about Kristina and the handcuffs, Horacio!!'

Miles could feel his face reddening. Beth-Ann turned to him and the grin fell from her face. She clapped her hand over her mouth, spoke fast. 'Oh, I guess I shouldn't be talking about our superiors. I'm sorry. Sometimes I just don't think enough before I speak. I do apologise. That was most impolite of me.'

Miles loved the careful, mellifluous American spoken by Southerners such as Beth-Ann. He waved a hand. The forgiveness of a powerful man. He'd wring the story out of Horacio at some other time.

'Are you from Miami, Beth-Ann?' he asked.

'Oh Lordy no. South Carolina. I came to school here and stayed on in the State. I'm store manager of *Weissmans De Luxe* on South Miami Beach.'

Miles ran his eyes over her. Dressed in her white cotton turtleneck, open denim shirt and safari shorts, Beth-Ann had the glossy-haired, ample-breasted look of healthy, white, burger-loving, middle-class suburbia. But she must have been smart too, for Kristina had herself chosen the store managers of the new De Luxe stores. They were all women, keen to get on, to make their mark without rocking the boat. The kind of women whose toughness was well hidden beneath old-fashioned homeliness. Sharks in white aprons, they had been provident choices for the *Weissmans De Luxe* stores.

'How's the store doing down here?'

'Oh it's just great. We were somewhat concerned when the Armani A/X store opened on Collins, but our sales kept holding steady. We're real happy.'

And so was Saul Weissman. In 1989, following his announcement that he was to design a range of up-market clothes, Weissman had endured a flurry of bitchy media comparisons with the highly successful Polo Ralph Lauren designs. But then came the stores themselves, and the world applauded.

Weissman had realised that there were too many potential shoppers spoiled by the retailing excesses of the eighties – the veneered shelves, the carpeted floors, the pretentious images of opulence. These were customers who frowned at the idea of shopping in the sprawling mall warehouses where Saul made his millions.

But Saul Weissman wanted their money, and he gambled to get it. He decided his stores should be radically different from any others. Out went the hunting pictures, the silver-framed photographs, the antique golf clubs neatly arranged in the shop windows. In came bold designs in metal and glass. In came fabrics of bright, confident colours – reds and yellows, purple, oranges and blues. And in came modern works of art. Here was Saul Weissman, patron of the arts, provider to the people. By opening only six stores, the first in Chicago, then others in New York, Los Angeles, Miami, London and Tokyo, Saul kept the line reasonably exclusive. But people came. They came to see the art, they came to see the stores, but most important of all, they came to buy the clothes.

At first, the high cost of insuring the art pieces caused the stores to run at a loss. Saul needed to wave his wand again, and he did that with a major, high-profile advertising campaign. One couldn't open a magazine such as *Vanity Fair* or *The Sunday Times* without seeing pages of ads. Soon they became the talk of every dinner party in all the right places.

The campaign was simple and to the point. It ran on double-page spreads. No words, just an image on each page, with the letters *WD* printed boldly at the base of one. At first the choices were uncontroversial. Dead flowers next to blossoming roses. A grainy shot of a man with hopeless wings tied to his outstretched arms beside an image of the Space Shuttle. A mud hut beside the World Trade Towers. But then the message became more daring. The jailed queen of hotels, Leona Helmsley, by the United States prosecutor. The defeated Portland Trail-Blazers next to the Chicago Bulls. And on November 5th, 1992, on the day Miles arrived in Miami, a picture of the smiling, bright-eyed President-elect, Bill Clinton, beside George Bush, who had his eyes down and a hand on his forehead.

With *WD*, it was as if Saul had again defined for the nation its mood. The Wasps had lost their sting. It was time for Americans to face a new future, and men such as Saul Weissman, refusing to be broken by recession, would be putting America first, and leading the way.

The white limousine smoothed its way past Downtown Miami's glittering cluster of steel and glass skyscrapers.

'This is actually a different city from Miami Beach. It's the commercial part of Miami. But you're staying in Miami Beach, on Ocean Drive. Right close to the store and the modelling agencies. And the beach, of course. You're staying in Maury Greenberg's hotel. Were you made aware of that already, Miles?'

'Kristina told me. Yes.'

Maury Greenberg was one of the wealthiest developers in Florida, and an old friend of Saul. He had promised Miles a suite at no cost in his Shangri-la Hotel.

They drove nearer. Past the Denny's and the used-car showrooms, awash with bunting and Old Glories. On land, the bungalows he'd admired from the sky seemed shabby. This was the dream's reality, in peeling pink paint. The bungalows had bars on their windows and trash in their yards. Scraggy dogs were sleeping in the neglected grass of the bungalow lawns. And everywhere there were wires. Telephone wires, TV wires, electricity wires, wires disconnecting people from the nature they'd come to enjoy. Wires and tarmac and rusting metal cars.

They took the MacArthur Causeway to South Beach. The road was narrow, and to the north, the bay lapped up to the lush gardens of homeowners living on the cigar-shaped Palm and Hibiscus Islands. This was the Miami Miles had expected: opulent houses, cigarette speedboats parked at jetties that ran like exclamation marks out from the smooth green grass of the lawns into the Bay of Biscayne. The city of Miami Beach sat close the other side of the bay. Miles felt a curious excitement as they approached. It was fitting that the beach should be separated from the mainland by this thin road. It made his destination seem more exclusive. As they neared, the feeling of imminent excitement increased.

'You get to see all this in the opening of *Miami Vice*. See Star Island there? Don Johnson and Melanie Griffiths live there. And Gloria Estefan. I prefer South Beach. All the restaurants and bars are right there. It's great. I mean, when I first came here there were all these old people living there, all these old Jewish people from around the country living in the hotels,' Beth-Ann scrunched up her nose like a piglet, 'but they've been renovated now, so it's just a whole lot better.'

'The old people have been renovated?'

'Oh you! No! The hotels. The old people have been moved, mostly. To homes and things. I mean, some are still there, but they don't use the beach like we do. You see them, you know, hobbling up and down. But they don't mind where they are.'

Miles doubted this, but let it pass. Miami, always a city of image, was in the process of reinventing itself once more. There was no use in arguing.

Across the causeway, and they were into Miami Beach. Miles opened his window as the car progressed down 5th towards Ocean Drive. The sea looked glorious, a shimmering expanse of dark blue and gold. Miles at once wished he could stop the car and leap into the inviting water. Coming from the wintry city he'd forgotten how seductive the sun and ocean could be.

Ocean Drive itself was separated from the beach by nothing more than a stretch of grass from which palm trees stretched finger-like high into the sky. To the left stood the ebullient Art-Deco hotels and apartments, all painted in white and pastel blues, soft pinks and yellows, celebrating icing-sugar silliness. At first sight, the buildings seemed to Miles to be curiously two-dimensional, like the painted wooden flats of a movie-set street. As if with one purposeful gust from the sea they'd fall.

The litter-free sidewalk looked no more real. Had someone screamed 'ACTION' moments before the limo had turned the corner? The people walking in front of the freshly painted buildings seemed to be performing for the benefit of an audience. They had certainly been accessorised with expertise. Models, taller than the rest, were displaying with pride their composites and portfolios. Sauntering developers, heavy with gold and tans, were jabbering dreams into cellular phones. Photographers were strolling with deliberate frowns ahead of assistants stumbling under heavy camera bags and reflectors. Frequent Rollerbladers flashed by in fluorescent Lycra suits like frisky tropical fish. A mincing man, on his pink T-shirt the words 'What a difference a **GAY** makes' was passing an old jogger wearing a striped orange jump suit, and bold, red sunglasses. A model's agent was carrying a stack of portfolios; a Cuban, lunch for four. Parked along the road Harley-Davidsons glinted, polished and loved; and an array of fifties cars were dotted along the Drive as if Detroit's decline had never occurred – a '57 Pontiac Star Chief convertible here, a 1952 Oldsmobile Classic 98 there, and, its chrome resplendent beneath the cloudless sky, a blue and white Eldorado Biarritz Convertible from 1956.

Miles had never seen such a glorious celebration of a skin-deep culture.

Beth-Ann patted his arm and pointed at a pink, white and blue building with three small round windows. 'See there? Where it says Booking Table Café? Number 728. That's the building where the chainsaw scene takes place in *Scarface*. Remember when that guy's tied up in the shower and the Columbian bad guy cuts into him and all that blood spurts everywhere? And then Al Pacino shoots the guy who tried to double-cross them? Remember that? With all the old people watching? That was right there on the street.'

Ah, the celebrity of a movie location! Still, Miles found himself staring intently. He did remember. He had even enjoyed the horror of the scene, its slimy possibility, the surprising familiarity of the sound of a chainsaw gurgling through human flesh.

'The real estate people couldn't shift it for the longest time but there's a model agency in there now, Irene-Marie. We use them sometimes. You'll be seeing them tomorrow. And . . . this,' said Beth-Ann, raising her voice when she said 'this', 'is your hotel right here.'

Miles leant across the seat and looked up at the magnificent blue, white and yellow hotel. Then Horacio opened the door, and Miles stepped out into brilliant sunshine. The breeze was cool sweeping off the Ocean. Miles put on his shades as a tall, darkly tanned man of about sixty came out of the airy hotel lobby waving a tennis racket at Miles. He was wearing pink sports shorts, and was dripping with gold. It was Maury Greenberg.

Maury spoke with a deep, sonorific voice. A voice that might have belonged to one of those narrators from movie previews that no one expects to meet in real life. 'You must be the young man Saul sent down.'

'Yes, I am. Miles Jensen.'

'Very good to meet you, Miles. Maury Greenberg.' Maury took Miles's hand in both of his and smiled like a politician. 'I got you a really beautiful room, really beautiful. It looks over the Ocean. Sound OK?'

'It sounds perfect.'

'It is. Listen, I'm out of here. Late for my game. Why don't we have dinner tonight in Miranda's?'

'Sure, where is it?' Miles asked.

'You're standing in it,' Maury replied with a laugh. 'See you at eight.'

Then he jogged and jangled his way through the wicker chairs and tables of his restaurant towards Flamingo Park, and his second game of tennis that day.

7

O ne hour later it began. The search for the model was on.

Beth-Ann, having confessed to a fear of modelling agencies, scurried away as soon as Miles reached the door of Supreme's branch on Ocean Drive. He looked up to the sky for inspiration, took a deep breath, and entered the office.

The reception area of Supreme, Miami was spacious and bright, lit from a spread of windows that faced the sea. Miles found the panorama almost impossibly perfect. It was a glittering mural, framed by two curving palms, with the coruscating sea as its backdrop. It was as magnificent a view, in its way, as that from Weissman's sky-scraping office.

Miles stepped up to the receptionist, a small girl with a wide smile, and announced that he'd come to see Susan Rosenblaum. If he could, please. Name of Jensen, Miles.

He was asked to wait. He sat on the edge of a deep, wide armchair. The office was a duplex. The agents worked on the upper level behind a shiny metal railing. Beneath them there was a spacious conference room. Susan will want to see me in there, he thought. Given the six million. The receptionist will bring coffee and the other agents will strain their ears to listen in. Something like that.

Miles looked up. The scene was similar to the one he'd encountered in New York, though the agents were, he could already see, less frenetic than their colleagues in Manhattan. Miles could hear French being spoken, and a young woman with blonde hair cut in a twenties bob rasping instructions in German, and laughing.

But for the framed images, there was not a model in sight.

A dark-haired, olive-skinned woman, overweight but rich enough to fend off ugliness, peered over the railing at Miles, and then returned to her computer. Miles hated being noticed and ignored. It made him feel self-conscious. So, wanting something to do, he flicked through a magazine. He'd never much bothered to look at male models' faces before, but now he examined each man for his suitability as Adam, just as Weissman had complained the advertising execs. would do.

Before much longer, a bald and bearded man over forty clumped down the stairs and towards Miles. The man was wearing faded grey sweat pants and an old T-shirt that might once have been yellow. Miles stood to greet him.

'Hi, I'm Tony. Susan's busy.' Tony held out his hand. 'Did you bring a book?'

'Excuse me?'

'A book, pictures, anything.'

Tony made no effort to hide the fact that he had better things to do. He looked out of the window when he finished his sentence.

'No,' said Miles. 'I . . . '

'I'm sorry, but we're really, really busy right now. Have you seen any of the other agencies?'

'Not yet. I just got here from New York.'

'Then I suggest you try to get some pictures together and maybe come back. And hit the beach, get some colour.'

Colour? What about that sunbed he'd been to? And what did he mean, pictures? Miles asked.

'Darling, if you want an agent you need pictures. Even in Miami.'

My God, he thinks I'm a model, thought Miles. Maybe Kristina was right. He couldn't wait to tell Poppy.

'I'm not a model. My name's Miles Jensen, I'm from *Weissmans*. I called yesterday. We're looking for a model for our new cologne campaign.'

Tony covered his face with his right hand and swivelled on his hips away from Miles and back again, head bent in embarrassment. He became all jittery and nervous, stumbling over his words. 'Oh, my God, I'm sorry. Really, I am so sorry.

It's been a crazy day and Thursday's the day we see new guys. You know, Miles, I looked at you and I thought you weren't exactly . . .'

'Not exactly good-looking enough?'

'Oh, heavens, no no no. You look smarter, that's all. But I'm so embarrassed!'

Miles followed Tony as he skipped up the stairs to meet Susan. She was the woman who'd dismissed him with a glance. When Tony explained, everyone at the table looked up at Miles and smiled when his eyes met theirs. Miles knew why. On the phone the day before he'd confirmed his appointment and let it be known what the size of the contract would be. Now, these agents' smiles said it all: forty per cent of six million dollars was worth kissing ass for.

Tony and Susan had some catching up to do.

'Would you care for some juice, coffee, something?'

'No, I'm fine.'

Susan dismissed Tony with her eyes. 'We could so easily have arranged a model casting for you.'

'I'd prefer just to see portfolios at this stage.'

Was that the right thing to say? He didn't know.

'You're just looking for a man?'

'For now, yeah. But it'd be great if you could get together the composites of your top girls.'

'Sure.' Susan nodded to one of the bookers who promptly stood to collect some composites for Miles. He'd never had people working for him like this before.

'Our Men's division is back here, Miles.'

Susan led him to a room at the back. She explained that the composites of those models in Miami were on one wall, those abroad on another. 'Just take your time.'

Miles looked in horror at the tens of faces staring out at him from the wall. There were so many! Where should he start? He felt hopelessly lost.

At first glance, Miles could see that here, in Supreme, the Hard Look was the most common. These were the models with faces set as stone. Their hair was tussled to perfection. Sometimes they had a woman holding them, looking up to them, but never ever overshadowing them. These were men aware and proud of their looks; men made out to be as dashing and irresistible as the heroes of romantic novels. Men who knew, with one shared, rigid look, how best to express their bubbling testosterone.

The message of these models was simple enough: I may be a model, but I am a real man, a hard man. Notice how I stare straight from my composite with eyes slightly closed and eyebrows slanting towards the bridge of my determined nose. I'm an explorer squinting at the Egyptian sun, a film star under bright studio lights, a boxer with no fear. I can talk to you with these eyes. Notice how they follow you from the page. Look deep into my stare. See how it says 'You! You'd better not fuck with me.'

Miles's heart was plummeting as he surveyed those faces. Not one of the models looked ready to step out of a swamp. Out of the gutter, maybe, but Miles's chosen model would be representing Adam, the Father of all men. It occurred to Miles that the human race would have gone the way of the tyrannosaurus had any of these models been responsible for fathering a species. Sure, we'd have evolved with slicked-back hair and high cheekbones and angry stares and attitude, but chances are the mountain goat would have come up with the wheel sooner than any of the models he could see.

Susan was soon at his side. 'Would you like to see some books?'

God, he didn't know. These faces, they didn't look as if they belonged to real people but to those mythical creatures who live in magazines and commercials. How could it conceivably be helpful to see their books?

'OK, thanks,' he said.

Susan collected the portfolios of her best models and stood looking over Miles shoulder providing him with details of which photographers had taken which shots. In response, Miles said 'no kidding' and 'it's definitely got his mark.' In truth, he couldn't have spotted their styles in a million years.

The books Miles was flicking through were crammed with

eight by ten tearsheets showing a variety of looks and poses far beyond those chosen for the standard composites. He'd seen the faces of many of the models before, and if he'd been casting for any ordinary campaign, he'd have been looking with great interest. But Weissman wanted a beginner. Miles closed the last portfolio.

'So, what do you think?' Susan asked.

'I think I've changed my mind. I'd like a casting to see some of the guys.'

Susan looked worried. 'Only Tom is in Miami right now out of those books. And he's working today and tomorrow.'

'That's no problem. In fact, I don't want to see anyone who's been working longer than two months.'

Susan looked shocked. 'Are we talking about the same campaign? Yesterday on the phone I thought you said . . .'

'That the contract would be worth six million dollars for one year.'

'And you want a nobody.'

Miles grinned. 'Nobodys have to start somewhere. Let me give you a call later when we've fixed up the casting.'

'And you really want someone just starting out?'

'Yeah. Surely it shouldn't be too hard to find someone who'll accept six million bucks for his very first job . . .'

The sunshine was crisp and luxuriant out on the sidewalk. Miles was scheduled to visit Next agency now, but suddenly he didn't feel like it. The previous night he'd hoped that everything would become clear as soon as he walked into Supreme, but the visit had caused his mind to spin even more wildly than before. How could he choose between so many? He needed time to think.

Under the green canopies of News Café, Miles took a table in the shade. He ordered a melon and carrot juice. The café was busy in mid-afternoon. Two of the tables were taken by men conducting business on cellular phones, another by an old Jewish man who, refusing to be discarded as South Beach continued its break-neck rejuvenation, sat dressed in bright yellow-checked pants and mirrored wrap-around sunglasses.

He seemed different from so many of the other old residents who were walking around with incomprehension splattered across their faces.

Across the street, a Pepsi commercial for Spanish TV was being filmed, four kids whooping it up in a spotless, white Golf convertible GTI. When passing the camera, they all held their cans in the air and, heads back, laughed. A tableaux of glinting teeth.

Wherever Miles looked, there was something to watch. And, as a backdrop to the parade of the beautiful, the ocean outshone everything. Miles relaxed, and, once he'd finished his drink, decided to accept the beach's generous invitation.

Miles had been lying on a hotel bath towel smelling of coconut for almost three hours when he took off his watch to check for a tan. The sun was retreating now behind the hotel towers, and the body worshippers had begun to slither on layers of after-sun back to cool showers and the early evening news. There were few people left around Miles on the beach, and he was revelling in the luxury of this solitude. It was one of the things he missed since he'd moved in with Poppy.

After a few minutes he decided to take a walk. A short way along, opposite a large thermometer optimistically proclaiming eighty-one degrees, Miles sat on slatted deck chair, and stared out to the horizon beyond which Weissman had told him to search. The breeze was coming easterly and cool, and he smiled into it, enjoying the sensation.

Oblivious to the neon and bustle of the Drive, a pelican flew north, low across the water. Miles watched the bird skim the sea with its surprising grace. That's what's missing on the Drive, he thought. A little grace amid the glitz.

Miles relaxed his shoulders, felt their weight for the first time in days, the tension running like perspiration from his neck, down his arms and out his fingers. He breathed in and the generous air felt good deep in his lungs. The light was falling fast on the beach, and people and objects were losing definition, fading like memories brought to life only by imagination and remembrance. Miles stayed sitting on the chair. He adored the half-light of twilight. And as he sat there calmly, himself unsure of the direction in which he was headed, Miles's mind wandered over the events of the week, drifting like a breeze on the crests and valleys of the days.

Adam, Adam, Adam, you're out there somewhere, you and your Eve. Miles thought of how right Larry Meyers had been. There was someone in the States good enough for EDEN. Ten men, a hundred, a thousand most likely – men who'd take the job for a fraction of the fee. If it was publicity Weissman was after, he could give the six million to charity, set up a fund for poor kids, have his name live on for years. The Saul Weissman Benevolent Fund. But instead they'd joined the merry-go-round. Bad money after bad, and Miles a link in the chain. Wasn't there any way Miles could make a difference? Couldn't he con them all and insist the models sign a contract offering fifty per cent of their fee to charity? The model would still pocket three million dollars. Or Miles could search for a model from among the world's poorest; change the life of someone whose life needed change. Even better: the Miles Jensen Benevolent Fund. He liked the idea of doing some good with someone else's money. Just so long as he kept hold of his own.

Miles watched while a boomerang of cloud split and reformed further along the beach. Then he stood and ambled towards the Drive. In this light, set against the stark squares and rectangles of the hotels, the palm trees looked curiously incongruous, outsiders in a city made for man. Even the golden sand beneath his feet had been imported by developers of the Drive.

Miles slumped his hands in the pockets of his trousers. In his right pocket, hidden beneath the loose dollar bills, rested the tiny bottle of scent given him by Saul. Miles took it out and smelt it once more. He winced. Ten million dollars would be spent. More, probably. Ten million dollars to persuade men to add EDEN to those accessories without which a man was only half a man. Miles grinned and turned back to the shore, the bottle still in the palm of his hand. *Wear it. Take it to bed with you. Let it become a part of you.*

Miles reached the ocean. He crouched down like a baseball pitcher before springing up and hurling the bottle. It flew high in the air, twisting and turning before plopping into the ocean, its tiny splash smothered beneath an incoming wave as Miles turned on the cool, soft sand and walked towards the Shangri-la, and dinner with the grandiloquent Maury Greenberg.

Maury was surprised; or so he said. 'That's not like Saul. I've known the guy forty years, and that's not like him.'

Maury twisted his cigar dead on the ashtray.

'Do you think I should talk to him again?'

'Let me do it.'

Maury snapped his fingers at the waitress. She was tall and beautiful and Miles hadn't been able to keep his eyes off her since she'd appeared with the charred tuna with salsa avocado. Miles preferred his women either cheap and whorish, with bright lipstick and polished nails, or simple, almost boyish, dressed, as was the waitress, in basic neutral-toned clothes. Women caught between the extremes usually failed to excite him.

The waitress had picked up on Miles's glances. They'd lingered longer after the second bottle of Fumé Blanc. She'd even responded in subtle ways. A handsome young man having dinner with the boss was worth the occasional flutter. As she approached the table now, she adjusted her waistcoat, and smiled. Miles looked up, smiled back, wished for a cigarette.

'Sweetheart,' said Maury. 'get Peter to bring me a phone. And a Perrier for me, and another Cognac for my young friend.'

'I . . .'

'It'll do you good, Miles. You need to relax.'

Miles watched the waitress go. The back view was almost as delicious as the front, her long golden hair brushed evenly down over her slim back. Proud of her curves with reason, the waitress wore a tight-fitting charcoal grey waistcoat, and black leggings over legs as slender as palm trees. The wrong side of sober now, Miles wished he could climb with his tongue to the greenery up top.

Maury, who'd been telling Miles throughout the meal how much money he'd made buying and selling property on the Drive since leaving his job at CBS in New York, was still concerning himself with Saul's dismissal of the EDEN competition idea.

'What's attractive about this proposition, Miles, is that it'll focus people's minds on a specific guy.'

Ever the salesman, now Maury Greenberg was trying to sell Miles's own idea straight back to him. Maury sat up in his chattering wicker chair and began to twist one of his oversized gold rings back and forth on his finger. Miles's eyes fell on Maury's large, deeply tanned hands. The nails were neat and clipped, as if by a manicurist, and irregular clumps of thick greying hair sprouted from his fingers. Maury was a hairy man. Hair appeared wherever it could, sweeping up from his chest through the V of his yellow silk shirt, curling this way and that through the links of his gold bracelet, shooting like prairie grass buds from within the hollow of his ears. No doubt it would cover his back too, as attractive as dead seaweed across a storm-swept beach.

'I've got two words to say to you, Miles. Human. Interest. Did you see the news tonight?'

'No, I was walking on the beach.'

'Right, you're new in town. Hey, Bobby, howya doing?'

Maury stood and shook hands with a man passing on the street. Throughout the meal, Maury's eyes had been darting left and right past Miles's head, checking out every passer-by in the busy pedestrian traffic of Ocean Drive. Whenever he'd seen a friend, an acquaintance, even a business rival, Maury's face had become more open, he'd smiled, or jabbed a finger at them, thrown a mock punch, or dismissed them with a swish of the hand and a 'ya, getouttahere.' Miles had lost count of how many people Maury had shaken hands with, or waved at, or invited to Paradise, his hotel bar, for a free drink. But he'd noticed how Maury kept a store of facial expressions to explode on his face for the few necessary seconds, before returning his focus to Miles as if there'd been no interruption at all.

As he did as soon as Bobby had passed by.

'Anyway, on the news today they had pictures of these big floods in Bangladesh and they flew these helicopters low over the water, right? Now, to me it just looks like a lake down there. I mean, I got to take *their* word for it that there's houses and stuff under the water. You know, who's to say, Miles, who's to say that they're not just showing me pictures of a lake? OK? But then, then they showed these close-ups of one kid. Just one kid.'

Maury finished his espresso in one swift movement – arm up, head back, cup down with a clink. He dabbed his lips with a napkin.

'And this kid had the water right up around his chest and he's holding on to a dead baby. Well, you know, that was it. For me. They zoomed in on this one story, and when they did that, we got the big picture. Do you see where I'm going with this? It'd be the same with your EDEN competition.'

As Maury continued he pressed his palms together, prayer-like, and moved them up and down with each new word. He spoke more slowly. 'If you could find different kinds of guys, and get different types of people identifying with those guys, then you're on to a winner. A sure winner. One hundred-and-fifty-per cent. If I was in your shoes,' he pointed at Miles, 'that's what I'd do.'

'But Mr Weissman makes the decisions. I think he's worried about the extra costs.'

'What costs? What – costs? Listen, if Saul gets this story in the news, then he can *cut* his advertising costs. They'll be buying his pages for him.'

'What about the flights, the hotels?'

'For the models? He can do deals. If you promise the PR, anyone can do deals.'

Peter, the hotel manager, arrived with a cellular phone. He was followed by the waitress, who handed Miles his

Cognac. Miles smiled at her, and felt important. Maury dialled Weissman's number and the line was soon answered.

'Hey, Saul-baby. It's the pro . . . Right . . . Well come down sometime . . . Yeah, he's right with me . . . Yeah, he's a great kid! Where'd you find him – Brooks Brothers?' Maury grinned, and winked at Miles. 'Listen, Saul-baby, about this competition for your cologne . . . You didn't? Jesus! Hold it.' Maury looked towards Miles. 'Saul says he doesn't know about any competition.'

'But Kristina said she'd talked with him.'

Maury passed on the news to Weissman, then spoke again to Miles. 'He says she didn't say nothing.'

'But . . . '

Maury raised a hand. 'Let me talk to him.'

Miles sat back as Mr Maurice Greenberg moulded Miles's virgin idea into a well-formulated plan of action. Maury spoke of international interest being raised, of press and TV coverage, even of arranging for the six finalists – yes, six would be a good number – to appear on the Trudie Love TV show. He could arrange that through his contacts.

Ten minutes later, Maury told Miles the good news. Hook, line and sinker, he said. Six guys. Saul was proud of Miles, and he'd told Maury to tell him so. Buoyed by the news, Miles talked logistics with Maury. It was early November. Miles should have found the six by the end of the month. They could be rounded up in New York by the second week of December and any guys with Christmas commitments would be forgetting them. The choice could be made before Christmas, and the shooting could still go ahead at the end of January. So long as Kristina doesn't keep trying to screw things up, Maury remarked.

'You're on the home plate now Miles,' said Maury. 'World Series, eighth inning, bases loaded. Remember: never take your eye off the ball, hit this one in the middle of the bat, and I predict it's gonna go all the way.'

8

Up the East Coast in a Manhattan apartment on Sixty-third Street and Park, Steven Barefoot heard a phone being thrown to the floor followed by the angry scream of his thirty-nine-year-old lover.

'Asshole!'

Steve groaned as he pulled back on the arms of his rowing machine. Then he shouted to Kristina, 'Whassup?'

Kristina came into the room with a newly lit cigarette in her hand. She struck a pose: legs slightly apart, one arm across her chest, the elbow of the other resting upon it. She held the cigarette in front of her lips and tapped her fingers rapidly across her chin. 'Asshole.'

'Who? Me?'

She spoke fast. 'No, not you, you jerk. Him. Mr Miles Smart-Ass Jensen.'

'What's he gone done?'

Kristina inhaled deeply on her cigarette. 'He's made me look bad in front of Saul, and he's screwed everything up. That's all! I should have known he'd do something like this.'

The seat of Steve's rowing machine clattered along its rollers. 'That was him there on the phone?'

'No, it was Saul. He tells me he's just had a call from Maury Greenberg.'

'Who he?'

'Some poxy real estate salesman in Florida who wanted to know why Saul didn't like Miles's competition idea. I mean I said to Miles this morning, *don't* bring it up with Saul, *do not* bring it up with Saul.'

'He didn't. I thought this Murray guy called.'

'Don't try to get smart with me, Rancher. It's the same

97

thing. Anyway, Saul knows about it now, and he's at *my* throat for saying no without asking him. Saul thinks it's a great idea.'

Steve stopped rowing and picked up the bottle of mineral water beside him. He drank and burped. 'So what the hell does that mean?'

'It means we're up Shit Creek.'

'Can't you still hide the good guys from Saul?'

'You're a dipshit, Steve. You know that? How can we have an international competition for a cologne featuring a bunch of ugly bastards? The way I had it set up before, I could have kept all the model entries a secret within the company. But now Saul wants the models' faces splashed across the papers. He's even talking about getting them on TV.' She inhaled twice; blew the smoke to the side. Like Bette Davis. 'And you want to know the worst thing? Worst thing is that as far as the goddamn company's concerned, it *is* a good idea. So of course Saul wants to know why *I* didn't like it. He probably wants to know why I didn't think of it too.'

'So what we gonna do now?'

'God knows. I'm going to have to get you into the competition, I know that much.'

'You think you can do that?'

'Should be able to. I'm still Saul's eyes and ears. Problem is that I'm going to look stupid if we don't pick good models.'

'I'd be good,' said Steve, rowing again.

Kristina walked past him to the window and looked down on to the street. 'You'd be OK. But what are we going to do? Have you and then five hunchbacks? Did your brain get that far yet?'

'You're not being very pleasant tonight,' said Steve.

Kristina didn't turn around. 'I don't feel it.'

'Does that mean you don't want to have sex?'

'What a charmer you are, Steve. Yes. And I mean yes I don't. Not yes I do.'

'I'm going out then.'

Kristina swung around to Steve, looking as if he'd just slapped her. 'Where to?'

Steve stood, lifted his tank top over his head, and used it to rub the sweat from his armpits. 'I don't know. A bar someplace.'

'You can't.'

'Oh, no?' He handed the top to Kristina. 'Then stop me.'

Kristina sighed as if the world was coming to an end, then, with head down, she raised her eyes to him. 'I need you here, Stevey.'

'Like hell you do,' Steve said. 'Like hell you do.'

After the call to Weissman, Miles and Maury talked a while, drank some more, and discussed Miles's options. Miles had found an invaluable friend and ally in Maury, and felt none of his customary embarrassment when Maury hugged him goodnight in the lobby of the Shangri-la Hotel. The gorgeous waitress was watching.

'Have you known Mr Greenberg long?'

'Oh, long enough,' said Miles, casually.

'I haven't seen you around, have I? Are you staying here?'

'Yeah, but only for three nights. I'm from New York.'

She smiled at him, sweetly. Miles couldn't remember ever having seen such polished, lickable skin.

'Would you like to come along to a party at Zio Luigi's? We're all going to Nubar after, and then . . . who knows?'

Miles was silent for a moment. What was he worried about? He was alone in Miami, he was supposed to be scouting for models, he was in a great mood, why shouldn't he go? So what if he thought the waitress to be irresistibly sexy in the way that only those women who don't try can be? There was no crime in allowing his eyes to slither down her body. He could trust himself not to do the wrong thing.

Probably.

'OK, that sounds good. I should be looking around the clubs, anyway.'

The waitress seemed pleased. 'Good. I'm Sandy.'

Miles waited at the bar for Sandy to change. The barman,

having seen Miles with Weissman, offered him a Stolichinaya and tonic on the house.

'Thanks,' Miles said, 'and go easy on the tonic!'

The barman was a young man who, with his greased-back hair and rich hazel eyes seemed to Miles to be yet another model. But then, nearly all of South Beach's barmen, waiters and waitresses looked like models. A desire to be discovered seemed a prerequisite for the job.

Miles sat on a stool and nibbled around the edge of a cheddar cheese biscuit goldfish – fins, torso, then head. He sucked at the salt on his fingertips, and took another. 'What's, er, what's Sandy like?' he asked the barman.

The barman rolled a beer mat along the bar. 'Sandy. She's cool. She's trying to be a model. Comes from Philly originally. Goes out with a friend of mine, as a matter of fact. Tony, the barman at Nubar.'

'Oh,' said Miles.

It was an 'oh' any actor playing the role of Miles would have struggled with. An 'oh' layered with sentiment, spoken casually enough, but heavy with absurd disappointment that Miles's noble decision not to take Sandy to his bed had already been made for him by another.

'Hang on!' The barman slapped his palm against his bronzed and furrowed forehead. 'What am I saying? They split. Just this last weekend.'

Miles said 'Oh,' again. This time, the *oh* was as in 'hope.'

Sandy joined them before Miles had finished his drink, so he swallowed the vodka in one. He left five bucks on the bar, and followed Sandy out.

'You look nice,' he said.

Sandy had changed into old Levis, black suede boots and a white shirt. Her jacket and tits were loose. She'd added a little eyeliner, but nothing else. Miles felt his heart somersault once more when she touched his hand.

It was a Caribbean cocktail of an evening, indulgent and promising. The ocean breeze was cool against Miles's flushed cheeks, the strip bright with the childish promise of neon. They walked fast through the crowds, the alcohol racing around his body. Throughout the day, Miles had been deriding those people parading up and down Ocean Drive to the beat of the pop being vomited from the sidewalk café speakers. Miles knew that at home, in front of bed and bathroom mirrors, these men and women had styled themselves for the Ocean Drive Show. Once on display they'd chosen a speed to walk, an expression to hold, an attitude to possess, from the hand-in-pocket amble past the News Café, to the uppity stride in front of the Clevelander's cheap masses.

Now, though, it was Miles himself who longed to be admired as he strutted beside his gorgeous companion. The audience was seated at tables on the sidewalk. He tried to make it obvious that Sandy was his, but the flow of people in the strait between the tables and the valet-parked sports cars was so strong that Miles soon tired of the endless collisions and fell in behind Sandy. Now her role was as a mobile lighthouse in the sea of people.

Miles needed her. The vodka hadn't done him any good – not sloshed like that on top of the Californian wine, the Cognac and caffeine. Of course, as yet another victim of alcoholic self-deception, Miles thought it not he but the world that was behaving strangely, performing out of sync. People were conspiring against him. One minute they'd be ten feet away, the next they'd have rushed up to his face. Even the chairs were against him – an arm here, a leg there, always obstructing his path. Now suddenly a car talked to him, making his heart skip a beat. He collided with a chair as the computer voice droned on: *Protected by Viper. Stand Back. Protected by Viper. Stand Back. Prote* . . .

Sandy turned around. 'Oh God,' she said, glancing at the Porsche, 'that's just so LA!' Then she looked up at Miles. 'Are you OK? You look kinda sickly.'

'Me good.'

'What?'

'I'm fine.'

'Let's get off Ocean. You can get a coffee, if you'd like.'

They stopped on Collins Avenue at a Cuban café with a

counter facing the street. Miles drank down the tiny cup of bitter, grainy coffee, and a glass of water. He asked for another glass.

'Ever seen how models never actually drink in sports ads?' he said, misgauging the volume of his voice. 'Look, like this.' With pantomime exaggeration, Miles threw back his head and drank so fast that the water splashed out of his mouth and down his chin. Finished, he wiped the back of his hand across his lips in slow motion, then grinned at Sandy. He turned profile.

'I'm a model. I don't drink like that,' said Sandy without humour. 'Come on.'

One block off Ocean Drive, and they could have been in any run-down Hispanic neighbourhood. Here and there impressive Art-Deco buildings reminded them of the Drive, but walking briskly in the comparative emptiness of Collins Miles felt as if they'd left the real show behind. He began to feel more drunk, a sure sign that he was sobering up.

Up on to Washington, and the party at Zio Luigi's was about to break up. At a long table strewn with the mullock of a drawn-out dinner, Miles saw yet more composites corporealised. Had he begun to see things? Or was this city truly peopled by the beautiful? Miles felt belittled. Sandy took his arm, as if they'd been friends for years. Suddenly he imagined her naked and curled around his body.

'That's Rosa over there,' she said. She gestured towards a woman with shoulder-length brown hair and a friendly, laughing face. The candles of Rosa's birthday cake were being relit for the benefit of those with cameras. 'She's thirty today. She runs a model agency right around the corner.'

'A men's agency?'

'No, both. I'm with them.'

'Where are the women, then?' asked Miles.

'Rosa likes men. See that guy at the end? He's a really famous model. Troy Turnbull. Let me quickly say hello to Rosa. Hang on.'

Miles focused on Troy Turnbull. He'd seen Troy's image countless times before, most recently hung framed on the wall of Supreme in New York. It was the largest print behind the booking table. Miles was surprised to see how perfect Troy appeared in the flesh. The model had a severely angled face, such as that which might have been sculpted by an apprentice yet to learn how to add sentiment to the features of his work. He moved slowly, as if being photographed at a low shutter-speed in bad light. His hair was cut short and gelled to perfection, and he smiled often with an expanse of glistening teeth. He wore a sheen of light brown stubble, and a sleek, black Agnès B turtleneck beneath his Valentino jacket. His skin looked healthy and well-toned, as if he pulled faces before a mirror each day to exercise his assets.

Beside Troy were three women, two agents and a young Puerto Rican model called Cheyenne. Coked to the eyeballs, Cheyenne was loud, like an episode of *Sesame Street*. She couldn't keep still. Everything she was doing she was doing to excess. While Troy thought he looked suave moving in slow motion, Cheyenne twisted and turned as if a swarm of wasps had chosen her tiny black dress for a nest. Often she would flip back her head and snort with laughter, like Woody Woodpecker, her long and luxurious curly hair splashing the air behind. Whenever Cheyenne wasn't pinching and poking Troy, who remained unamused, she was firing water from a plastic water gun at the models surrounding Rosa. Miles wondered if Cheyenne could possibly be right for Eve. Cheyenne's was a breezy appeal, a truly enigmatic mixture of childishness and grace.

To the left of Troy sat two older women. They had about their expressions the undeniable weariness common among model agents. Sometimes they smiled, and lit cigarettes.

Miles, beginning to feel uneasy standing alone among strangers, looked towards Sandy, who'd been whispering into Rosa's ear. Sandy picked up on his glance, waved him over, and introduced him to Rosa.

'Did you just have some pictures in British *GQ*?' Rosa asked in her sultry, hoarse voice.

Miles thrust his hands into his trouser pockets and kicked at a beer bottle top on the floor. He didn't like the attention of the men sitting around Rosa. He felt as if they were judging him. A tickle of sweat troubled his armpit.

'No, I'm not a model.'

'Oh! So what do you do?'

'I'm scouting for *Weissmans*. We've got a new cologne campaign coming out.'

'Oh that's you? You were in Supreme today.'

'Small town!'

Rosa stood, realising herself to be in the presence of a prospective client. She touched Miles's hand. 'You better believe it, honey. So when are you coming in to see us?'

'I can come tomorrow.'

'Fabulous! You looking for a girl too?'

'Eventually, yes.'

Rosa turned to Sandy. She put an arm around her. 'Trying to get lucky, are we sugar?'

'Go fuck yourself, Rosa,' said Sandy through her smile.

'She's a darling, isn't she? Oh, Miles, have you met Troy?' Miles said he hadn't. 'You have to! Are you coming to Nubar?'

Sandy said that they were.

They lost half the party en route. Troy had wanted to go home, but after Rosa had had a professional word with him, he'd tagged along, po-faced. The remainder of the group gathered again in front of ten Harleys, and behind the semicircle of people pushing towards the looping, red velvet ropes in front of the door of Nubar. Heavy rock music rolled like storm clouds from behind the curtained door.

'Is this just a bar?' Miles asked Rosa.

'Yeah, it's new.'

'Why the ropes, then?'

'Sweetheart,' said Rosa, 'this is Miami Beach. Don't ask stupid questions.'

'I thought . . .'

'Honey, it looks fabulous if you can get a crowd outside. And it makes us feel better when we get inside. I got to go talk to Billy. He's one of the owners,' she said over her shoulder.

Of course, Billy was only too happy to please the owner of one of South Beach's agencies, and the others waiting, Hispanics mainly, opened a reluctant passage for Rosa and the group. Inside, the place was brimming. The group split further. Three of Rosa's male models set off in a pack to shop for discounts – girls on introductory offers, women past their sell-by date, perhaps even a multipack of three. The rest of the party moved to the end of the thirty-foot bar for drinks on Billy. Left were Rosa and Sandy, Troy, Miles, Cheyenne, and two other models, an Englishman called Rob, and Glurg, a Scandinavian.

Rob cornered Cheyenne, and bought her a Sex on the Beach; in the hope. Rosa stood with Troy, a perk of her job. Sandy and Miles were lumbered with Glurg. The music inside the bar was frustratingly loud. Hard rock, it came from vast speakers hung at an angle from the ceiling. Miles could barely hear what Glurg was saying in his undulating Scandinavian voice. Not that he cared much. Glurg was about as interesting as a television test card. 'Miami is much hotter than Stockholm,' Glurg was shouting. 'And the beer is more cheap too. A beer like this in Stockholm is six times as much as here. You have been to Sweden?'

What had Glurg said? Miles thought it best to look up and nod. Glurg seemed pleased. 'You liked it?'

Miles nodded again. And looked up. He had to look up at Glurg, because Glurg was about six foot five. He was as blond as the sun, and had some obvious molar planets dotted about his face. He smiled a lot, and kept running his thin fingers through his straight, boyish haircut. Glurg had arrived that morning from Paris, and, in his understated Swedish way, was trying to be one of the in-crowd in South Beach's hottest new bar. But it was hard, because Glurg was whiter than white bread: in the way he moved his heavy, round shoulders; in the way he dressed in last year's clothes, with a starchy new baseball cap and white T-shirt tucked into black Levis that ran down to his Timberland boots; in the way he drank his beer, crisply, wiping at the corner of his mouth with a knuckle, as would any boy accustomed to drinking at his mother's dining-room table.

And Glurg looked younger than his twenty-two years. He had no beard to speak of, and his lips were full and red. Miles tried to place Glurg's look among the composites he'd seen, and decided he belonged to the clean-cut, catalogue crowd who only undressed for *Tweeds*, *J Crew* bathing trunks, and the occasional *Bloomingdales* underwear shot. Glurg was not the type to be photographed being kissed by adoring women, especially not when half-naked in an Amazonian swamp. Sandy put a hand on Miles's shoulder. 'Let's go up the other end.'

They made excuses to Glurg, but were stopped on their way by Rosa and Troy. When Troy spoke, his voice sounded as if it was low on batteries. 'I hear you're scouting for *Weissmans*.'

'That's right.'

'Have you had a chance to see one of my books yet?'

'No, I'd like to,' Miles lied, knowing that Troy was about as new and fresh-faced as the Michelin man.

'Here.' Troy reached inside his brown leather shoulder bag and took out a folder, the size of a slim hardback novel.' This is my personal portfolio. I had it bound in leather when I was in Italy. Take a look.'

Miles did as he was told. He was still quite drunk, though the wave of vodka-induced nausea had passed, and he flicked through Troy's book with as much interest as if it had been the insider's guide to astrophysics. Past the magazine covers and the international ads that Miles couldn't help recognising; past the shots by Weber and Gianni, Meisel, Watson, Nadir and Ferri. It was truly a fantastic collection of images, printed proof that lit-right, dressed well, and photographed with imagination, Troy's characterless face assumed characteristics perfect for each market. But Miles couldn't have cared less. He handed the book back to Troy with a flick of his wrist and a casual word of thanks. A thanks but no-thanks.

Troy, accustomed to adulation but aware of the six million dollars, swallowed his pride, and tried harder. 'I've got a whole load of pictures coming out in *Mondo Uomo* soon.'

Miles had no idea what *Mondo Uomo* was but managed to say that he looked forward to seeing them. Then he and Sandy said goodbye, and that they'd see him soon. Troy looked discouraged, knocked back his mineral water and immediately headed for the door, home, and another fifty push-ups before a night alone in bed.

Miles and Sandy nosed their way through the people. The bar was rectangular in shape, the walls constructed of exposed brick blocks in a statement of unashamed nineties inverted chic. Though Miles couldn't see faces clearly in the dim light of the bar, he could see enough. After a day on the Drive and in Supreme his standards had already been raised. Normal people no longer impressed him. Among the mixture of Hispanic locals, older Europeans, gay men from around the country, and kids on a night out from the University of Miami, he saw not one face that he thought even worthy of a second look. He turned to Sandy and shouted above the din. 'I want to get out of here. You?'

Miles was bored with being jostled by people carrying beer bottles and plastic cups of cheap liquor.

Sandy looked worried. 'I got to talk to someone.'

'Who? Rosa?'

'No, him. The barman. He's my ex.'

Sandy pointed to a man wearing jeans, cowboy boots, and a snakeskin waistcoat over his bare, hairy chest. The man, Tony, was standing on the bar, moving his hips in time with the music, courting attention. As Miles turned to look, Tony arched his spine backwards, held a high-necked bottle at arm's length above his head, and poured a stream of clear liquor into his open mouth. A cheer rose above the music. Suddenly Tony straightened, cheeks bulging, and flipped open a Zippo lighter with his right hand. He brought it towards his mouth then blew out a wide sheet of flame high above the bar. There were more cheers.

'His party trick!' said Sandy, as if she'd seen it a thousand times before.

'Is she always his assistant?' asked Miles pointing towards Cheyenne who'd climbed up beside Tony. In her right hand she was holding the liquor bottle high above her head. Her left hand was placed on her hip. Slowly, Cheyenne began to walk the length of the bar, swivelling her hips, blowing kisses to the crowd. At the end she pivoted before advancing on Tony, her lips pouting, her eyes radiant, her left arm pointing to the surface of the bar in front of him. The crowd bellowed its approval as Cheyenne mouthed the word *down*. Obediently, Tony fell to his knees. Cheyenne reached him. She slapped one hand on Tony's shoulder, and jutted out her arse as she lifted the bottle and poured the liquid into his gaping mouth.

It happened very fast. In one move, Tony flicked the Zippo, lit the liquid and stood to blow the flame above the people. Only Cheyenne couldn't stop her performance. As she threw back her head, Tony ignited the alcohol. The flame embraced Cheyenne's combed and curly locks in its ascendancy. There was a crackle of frazzling strands. Thinking fast, a barmaid slopped a bucketful of icy water over Cheyenne's burning hair. Cheyenne stood frozen. About her was the gruesome scent of smouldering hair. The music was thumping on, but the crowd had quietened. Tony, who'd leapt off the bar as soon as Cheyenne had become a Roman candle, climbed back up and took the shivering girl in his arms. He kissed her gently on the forehead.

Rosa hung her head in her hands. 'Jesus Christ,' she said. 'That girl's supposed to be working tomorrow.'

'A date up in smoke,' joked Rob.

Sandy turned away. 'Let's get the hell outta here,' she said.

She and Miles left, and strolled towards a sandwich bar.

'Cheyenne's only fourteen, you know,' said Sandy. 'Rosa says she'll be a big star one day. If she can keep off the coke.'

'And if her hair grows back in time,' said Miles.

'I guess you've got to feel sorry for her.'

'Yes,' said Miles.

'It can't be good to burn your hair like that.'

108

'No,' said Miles.

They looked at one another. Sandy started it with a quivering of the muscles around her lips. But Miles was the first to laugh out loud. Soon they were laughing so hard they couldn't breathe properly. Sandy fell into Miles's arms.

'Let's forget the sandwiches,' she said.

They walked to the beach and kicked off their shoes. The sand felt warm beneath their feet. They sat close to the gently swishing waves. Miles made a pancake of sand, and threw it into the dark ocean.

They were silent with their thoughts. In a world without rites, Miles would have followed his urge to embrace Sandy then, to take her delicate face in his hands and press kisses upon it. He wanted to feel the exquisite form of her mouth against his, to taste her tongue, to feel the smooth skin of her naked body against his cheeks. But the moment, the moments, passed. He wondered what Sandy was thinking, whether she was waiting for him. When he turned to look, she smiled at him and, surprising himself with his courage, Miles lifted a hand and stroked her cheek. 'You're . . . incredibly beautiful. Did you know that?' he said.

Sandy looked down. 'Hmm! I'm not a very successful model.'

Miles took away his hand. 'You should be.'

'Thanks.' A pause, then: 'Miles, do you . . .'

'What?'

'No, forget it.'

'Tell me.'

'Really, nothing.'

They were silent. Then Miles said, 'I do then.'

'What?'

'I do whatever you were going to ask me.'

Sandy laughed. 'I was actually going to ask if you have a girlfriend.'

'Um, yeah, I do. We've been going out for about two years. She's really sweet.'

'Oh right.'

Miles wished he hadn't told her now. 'It's kind of weird being, you know, alone like this with someone else.'

'What's weird about it?'

'I don't know . . . I mean, I wrote this letter to my girlfriend right here on the beach today, and I was thinking she was, you know, everything, and then . . .'

'What?'

'And then here I am back on the beach and she's not even in my mind. Well, she is in my mind. I guess I kind of wish she wasn't . . .' He scratched at his forearm, and looked out at the tiny lights of a cruiser leaving for the Caribbean. Then he turned to see Sandy staring at him as if she could understand the stranger beside her by the profile of his face. Miles wanted to kiss her, wanted to be naked with her. He leant forward, and she did not move, and their lips were almost touching when Sandy touched Miles on his cheek, gently restraining him with the pressure of her hand.

They sat on the beach for a while longer, but the tension had gone, and Miles had begun to feel tired and drunk again. When he found Sandy a cab, the two shook hands, as if a kiss would have been dangerous. Miles was filled with a mixture of pride and regret as he walked to the hotel. It was better that he was alone. And yet it was so much worse. He decided to ring Poppy, see if he could persuade her to talk dirty to him.

Undressed in bed he dialled their number in Manhattan. After twenty rings (five more and I'll hang up) Miles clicked down the receiver and laid his head on the pillow. Where was she? She never went out late. Not on a Thursday night. He called again; twice. Nothing. Miles pictured her in another man's bed. He felt helpless, and it made him angry. He wished now that he'd tried to persuade Sandy. Maybe she'd have been in his bed if he hadn't mentioned Poppy. Damn! Damn! Next time, he thought, next time I'll keep my stupid mouth shut. After all, it's not every day you can prove to yourself that you're free.

9

In a dream, the phone rang. Miles ran to it, and fell downstairs. He woke with a start. The phone was still ringing, and as the sun met his eyes it seemed to pierce deep, pain shooting through his pupils as if the flimsy curtains held within them a lens to amplify the rays.

In fumbling for the receiver Miles knocked over a glass, and swore. He heard the sound of a sunny voice.

'Hi, it's Beth-Ann. Where were you?'

'Uuuuh?'

'For breakfast,' she said.

Miles pushed himself up in bed, and winced at the pain in his head. It felt as if someone was standing beside him gleefully practising swings with a mallet at his head. Head up? No you don't! *Bam*. Turn to the side? *Bam*. Eyes open? Double *Bam*, a blow to each socket.

'I'm coming,' he said. 'Hang on.'

Beth-Ann was more amused than annoyed. 'It's ten thirty, Miles. I left an hour ago. You missed your appointments at Next and Irene-Marie.'

'Poor Irene,' Miles croaked.

Miles sat up and looked for his tube of headache pills. Beth-Ann was bubbling on, like a pan of boiling water. 'And Dawn Woodcock from the *Miami Herald* is coming to the hotel in, uh-oh, half an hour.'

'Just what I need!'

'Are you OK? Miles? You don't sound too great.'

'I was . . . I was working late.'

'Oh, you devil you!'

'Mmm, I wish! Listen, Beth-Ann, I'm going to skip the agencies. I'm going crazy looking at cardboard. I really need

111

to see these guys for real. You think you could help me out with a casting tomorrow?'

'Oh, sure. That'd be a pleasure.'

'Say ten o'clock. Up here. Room 51.'

'I'll be there.'

Miles sat motionless for twenty minutes before the pills filtered some relief to his skull. Then he turned the TV on to a local morning show, its volume low. A fleshy TV chef was preparing salmon and crab fishcakes.

'. . . Just make sure the fish is tightly knit together, or you're going to get a lot of those unhealthy fats being absorbed, and we don't want that, do we?'

After the cakes came ads for lawyers and limousines, and then the local news update, with Kitty Peters. Kitty looked damned serious.

'Our top story today: Fernando Padrillas, the Florida city youth who captured national headlines with his legal battle against the Best Burger chain, has had his case rejected at Dade County Courthouse. Shane Diamond is in Downtown Miami, and has the story.

A short, bearded man in a cheap suit appeared on screen standing at an angle to the camera. Behind him were the steps of the courthouse. Shane spoke into his microphone with all the sincerity his small frame could muster. It sounded to Miles as if Shane had too much saliva in his mouth.

We all remember the night of August 19th, the night when a hurricane came and tore our calm to pieces. But for some, that night will live as a nightmare long after most of our memories have gone, blown with the wind. Fernando Padrillas is one such young man.

'Friends and neighbours remember his father Frank as

a kind man, a good neighbour, a man who went out of his way to help others. On August the 19th, when most of us were in hiding from the terrible force of Hurricane Andrew, that kindness was to cost Frank Padrillas his life, and Fernando, his father.'

Miles watched as photographs of a smiling, contented Frank Padrillas came up on the screen, along with video of the storm in Florida City, and a shot of the Padrillas' wrecked home. He heard how Frank had died. Battling against the storm, trying to visit the house of an elderly neighbour, he'd been almost decapitated by a billboard sheered from its frame by the wind. The billboard belonged to Best Burger. Fernando believed they should pay for his father's death. The court thought otherwise.

Interviewed in front of a new Mobile Home, bought with cash from Frank's life insurance policy, Fernando announced he would appeal against the decision. For as long as it took.

Fernando towered over the nodding reporter.

'Why they make the billboard there? It was too close to the houses. Before the Andrew, I saw it move in the wind. Like this. It's big business. Big business. I want the justice. For me, and for my father.'

Miles watched, mesmerised. The story, that was nothing new. A variation of an old theme. For once, the small man was probably wrong. As a gesture of goodwill, Best Burger had paid Fernando's legal costs and offered him and his mother a year's free supply of the Best Burger Big One. Onions extra.

No, it was not the story that made Miles sit up and ignore his clumping headache. It was Fernando Padrillas himself.

Fernando's appeal was unmistakable. He was a strong man, about twenty-two, Miles guessed. He had broad muscular shoulders and a face that remained masculine despite its angular refinement. His hair was thick, and parted in the

113

centre, falling casually each side of his forehead. His eyes were dark and strong. Yet it was the way that Fernando moved that caught Miles's eye. Even as a man, Miles could see that Fernando was sexy. That was the word for it: sexy. In the way that a rolling ocean wave is sexy. And just as Sandy was beautiful without needing to try, Fernando had no need to flaunt his strength. It was apparent in the language of his body, in the way he moved his arms and shoulders as he talked, in the way he twisted and turned his head as he surveyed the wrecked neighbourhood where once his family had lived.

Fernando Padrillas moved as if he was being watched by a crowd of beautiful women. Even in his suit, Fernando dripped with the most marketable appeal the world has ever known. Simply put, Fernando Padrillas oozed sex.

Miles lifted the telephone receiver to his ear, and punched 153 for the front desk.

'Mr Greenberg, please. It's Miles Jensen.'

He was connected. Maury sounded breathless.

'I'm doing twenty on my exercise bike,' he explained.

'Maury, do you have any influence at Channel 7?'

'I know people. What's up?'

'I'd like to track down a guy called Fernando Padrillas. He was just on *Seven Sees* news. He's the guy who's been trying to sue Best Burger.'

'Found a cat's tooth in his quarter-pounder, right?'

'No, his dad got killed by a piece of a billboard.'

'Oh, shit, yeah! I remember. And he's a great-looking kid, am I right?'

'Something like that.'

'OK, I think there's something I can do. Call me in fifteen.'

Then Miles put a call through to Beth-Ann and asked her to have Horacio ready with the car in case he should need it. Next he rang through to all the agencies listed in his file and surprised them by announcing that instead of paying them a visit he was to have a casting for models the next day, and that only those guys with three months' experience, or less, were welcome. To a person, the bookers all promised some great new faces.

Then he called Maury.

'Good news. This Fernando kid lives with his mum in Sunshine State Mobile Home Park in Florida City. He's training to be an engineer. I got the exact address written down here.'

'You found him? Just like that?'

'Let's just say that the South Beach Police Athletic League were very grateful for my contribution last month. Incidentally, he's got a clean record.'

'Thanks! I suppose I can't tell him I got the address from Channel 7, then.'

'Miles, you're gonna show up on the kid's door and wave six million dollars in his face. You think he's gonna give a fuck how you got there?'

'I guess not.'

'You guess right.'

Horacio collected Miles in Saul's dinosaur of a car as soon as Miles had finished an easy interview. The reporter, Dawn, had been suitably impressed by the size of the EDEN contract. She'd said the story would run in the Sunday edition. Miles advised her to keep in touch.

'Who knows,' he said, smiling and feeling important, 'if you call Saturday night, you may get a world scoop!'

Miles sat up front as he and Horacio left for the short ride south to Florida City.

'So,' he said after a while, 'you can tell me now.'

'Huh?'

'About Kristina von Koeler and her boyfriends.'

Horacio waved a dismissive hand. 'I don' see much.'

'Is there much to see?'

Horacio laughed, 'By the soun' o' it, yeah.'

Miles looked out of the window to his right. 'What about the handcuffs?' he said.

Horacio was hesitant. 'You don' say I tol' you.'

'I promise.'

''Cause I lose my job, man, she say tha' to me.'

'I promise, Horacio.'

'OK, OK. Kristina, she ask me to drive her, you know,

aroun' an' aroun', just a drive, dri'. An' she ha' a big guy in
the back, this black guy, he from South Beetch gym. So, I
driving and I hear some noises, you know? Ugh, eee, oooh,
aaah, like this. So after maybe one half-hour, this guy, he
knock on the window here . . .' With his knuckle, Horacio
tapped on the sliding tinted window behind his head '. . . and
he say to me, "take me to the hardware store, man. Fast."
So I go to store on Washington, and when I stop I ge' out
real quick to open door for him, because I wann' take a look,
yeah? And, man, there she is! No clothe. No fucking clothe'.
And she ha' her hand tied with the handcuff on the bar at the
top where is the curtain for the window, you know?'

Horacio was laughing as he paused to turn his neck before
making an awkward right turn. 'The fucker lost the key for the
handcuffs, man. I found it later behind the seat. You believe
this? He had to buy this big, what-you-call, cutter from the
store. So, Kristina she give me two 'undred dollar cash say
I no tell no one.'

'Was that the only time?' Miles asked.

'Why you wan' know this, man? You got something, like,
goin' with her?'

'No, of course not. It's . . . amusing, that's all.'

'Well,' Horacio said, taking a hand off the wheel and
turning it, palm up, towards Miles, 'there been others,
sure. She like the car, you know. She like the man in
the car.'

'I've got this feeling that Kristina likes her men everywhere.'

'Maybe! Maybe!' laughed Horacio.

The limo turned right along a small street littered with
trash. Three kids, not yet in their teens, ran away from the
Lincoln they were hoping to steal. Horacio turned through
the gates of Sunshine State Park. The arch under which they
drove was leaning precariously, and eight of the letters were
missing from the nameplate. *Sun hi e tate ark M bile Hom We
ome*, it read.

'Nice place!' said Miles.

The massive car looked absurd in the park, but Miles

wanted Fernando to understand that this was to be a serious offer.

They found the Padrillas home with ease. Miles took a step up to the peach-coloured door. He knocked, and then heard a woman's voice from inside.

'Si?'

'Hello, I'm looking for Fernando Padrillas. Is he there?'

Miles could hear Spanish being spoken. Next door, an old man without teeth curled open his net curtains and stared. Then Fernando spoke. 'I'm not giving interview.'

'That's not why I'm here. Look!'

From his pocket Miles took a copy of the article that had appeared about him in the *New York Herald*. He slid it under the door. 'My name's Miles Jensen. That's me in the photograph. Read it.'

Miles looked around him while he waited. Almost three months after Hurricane Andrew, the park still looked bedraggled, like a war zone occupied by an uncaring invading force. To the north, Miles could see more than one mobile home, immobile now, lying deserted, turned on its side. Another stood without a roof, the living area waterlogged and redundant. The remains of a large fire in the centre of the park could be seen. Lying in a ring around the hardened grey and black ash were the charred remnants of people's lives – magazines, sheets of plywood, broken lamps, a child's cot, a mattress, half-burned and stained, its bent springs rusting from the rain.

Around the perimeter of the park, the jagged trunks of trees stood like broken pencils. Nothing green existed at a height of more than ten feet, and the only birds Miles could see were circling high in the sky above. Sunshine State Park was a joyless and depressing place. The kind of place to make one angry with the world.

Miles had been waiting for about three minutes by the time Fernando opened the door. Fernando's mother stood behind him, a short woman with a kind face and soft eyes. She wiped her hands with care on her apron before she shook Miles's outstretched hand. Fernando stood combing his hair.

'You for real, man?' he said.

Miles pointed at the car. 'You think I'd drive out here in this thing if I wasn't?'

Fernando looked at his mother, who shrugged. They both looked back at Miles.

'So?' said Fernando. 'What you want with me?'

'I saw you on TV this morning. I'm sorry about that court decision, by the way.'

Fernando shrugged, looked away.

'Well, as I say, I saw you and I thought immediately that you might be the kind of person we're looking for.'

'To be model?'

'Yes.'

Fernando began to laugh. He handed the article back almost pushing it into Miles's face. 'You fucking kidding me, man? You fucking joking, right?'

Fernando's mother slapped his arm with her hand.

'Fernando!'

Fernando held his arm, and screwed up his face in a mock grimace. But he was still laughing. 'I'm no fucking model.'

'I know you're not. Not yet.'

'Go to South Beach, man,' Fernando pointed north towards Miami, 'that's where they hang out. In Warsaw.'

Miles had heard that Warsaw was South Beach's most popular and notorious gay club.

'I've just come from South Beach,' Miles said. 'They know about it there. In fact, last night one of the world's top models was almost begging for this job.'

Fernando smoothed back his hair with both hands. Maybe it wouldn't be so bad, he thought. At least his girlfriend would be impressed.

'What would I have to do?'

'If I chose you then we'll fly you to New York in December, take a few photographs, something like that, and then choose an outright winner. Maybe even you.'

'Then?'

'Then? Well, then we'd fly you to Brazil in January where we're going to take the photographs.'

'Is that it?'

'Pretty much. Oh, and we pay you six million dollars.'

Even though Fernando and his mother had read the article, Miles was glad to see that they looked at him in astonishment.

'What's the catch, man?'

'No catch. Except you've got to beat the other guys in the competition, and I haven't even found them yet. I'm looking now. That's why I'm here. I'm hoping you might be the first.'

'I don't know. Sound too good, you know?'

'Listen, Fernando. At least let me take some shots of you and send them to my boss.'

'OK, man. Why no, huh? Six million dollars, that'd be good, uh Mama?'

Fernando turned to his mother, and she smiled at them both. But the smile soon fell away, weighed down by the sadness in her face. She turned. Who was Miles but another man arriving in a shiny car, full of promises? Too many men in suits had knocked at their door since her husband had died. They never came inside, never waited for an answer when they asked how she was, never talked of anything but what miracles they could perform. And what had they brought, these lawyers, detectives, welfare workers? What? False hope, promises to be broken, lies. Nothing more. None had brought any good to her, nor to Fernando. He'd grown up, sure he had. He was a good boy, looked after her well, since then. Stopped with the drugs. But they took him in, these men. Made him want to fight. She knew why. She knew he was fighting for her.

Saturday morning. A glorious, breezy day. Out on the sun-kissed streets Miles no longer felt the need to question Miami. It was all true. The sky was permanently blue, the streets cleaned themselves, the people were perfect.

South Beach was the paradise that everybody claimed it to be.

Ocean Drive was surprisingly peaceful at eight forty-five

that morning, but for the noise coming from the juddering engines of production vans parked in the streets adjacent to the Ocean. Inside these monsters, air-conditioners and coffee pots, hair dryers and irons were working at full power. This was the most intense time of the day for the behind-the-scene players in the fashion game. The hairstylists were busy straightening curly hair, curling straight hair, undoing the dos of those models who'd wasted their time by a mirror before work. Make-up artists were smoothing foundation over spotted skin, painting black eye-bags pink, twisting the morning's sleep from the corner of a model's eye, struggling always against the gravity of early morning expressions. Relegated to the back of the vans, clothes stylists and their assistants were choosing and adjusting the clothes for the day, turning up pant legs, pinning jackets and dresses, coordinating colours with models' tans and bloodshot eyes. The models themselves were hiding behind newspapers with muffins and coffee, or sitting looking sullen while others worked hard to make them look their best. Every morning of the season, these scenes would be played out in the vans, parked, as they were, along the sidewalk of this most sunny location.

Miles fought his way through a crowd of Japanese on a golf tour of South Florida, and chose a cafe where breakfast was $1.99 for two eggs, orange juice and toast. A good deal? Not with coffee at $2.50 a cup. He sat at a table on the sidewalk with the sun in his eyes and the beach as his view. Two tables away a fashion shoot had already begun. An older model, a lithesome man in his late forties with neatly trimmed grey hair, and tight, young-looking skin, was turning in time with the camera's clicking shutter. The model wore no shoes, his pants had been pinned up above his ankles, and, behind him, his jacket was a jungle of safety-pins and clips. The model's shirt was at least a size too big in the neck, so a wad of tissue paper had been jammed into the collar at the back, out of the view of the camera. The coffee he sipped at was cold.

The model had been asked by the photographer, a tall German with deep-set features and small, round glasses, to act as if in deep conversation with an imaginary person. The model obliged, a frown now, a grin then, before a quizzical tilt of the head and a casual gesture with the back of his hand towards the headlines of the *New York Times*. His expression followed the movement of his hand. Look, my friend, as the hand opened out, did you read this here? and the fingers tapped the article. He got into a rhythm of this until the film ended and the assistant reloaded the camera and the German said: 'And now we doing something else?'

Miles watched, impressed. The model was a consummate professional, an actor probably, with twenty excuses as to why he'd turned to modelling. The real reason was the money, of course. Nothing else.

A female stylist was repeatedly running into shot to adjust the knot of the model's tie, much to the annoyance of the impatient photographer. The tie was clearly the product being sold. All around it everything was perfect. The shirt was creaseless, pulled flat by the model in a nifty move that required him to slip a hand inside the fly of his pants to yank down the shirt. The lapels of the jacket had been carefully pressed and taped to the suit body. To keep it in place with just half-an-inch showing to the world, the cuff of the shirt had also been taped to the inside of the jacket sleeve. And on the model's head there wasn't a hair out of place.

The shot was finished when the poached eggs arrived. The crew had retreated, photographer and assistant to scout for the next location, the rest back to the van. Miles was feeling on top of the world. In an hour, Miami's rising stars would be coming to his room in the Shangri-la. To see him, Miles Jensen, a man with the power to make someone very rich, and very happy.

Already, Miles was confident that Fernando was a good choice. Before Horacio had driven Miles away, Miles had taken a video of Fernando to send back to New York. He had bought the camera on his *Weissmans* card from the Happy Day Mall near to Florida City. He'd filmed Fernando stripped down to his jeans, and catching a football thrown to him by Horacio. Fernando had performed better than Miles could have hoped. His athletic body looked natural and well-toned, and his manner in front of the camera was relaxed and confident. As far as Miles was concerned, he'd already found his Adam.

He turned back to look out to sea. Time for another coffee, then it was back to work; if sitting behind a table looking at models and their portfolios could ever be considered work.

Four hours on Miles rested his elbows on the hotel room table and let his face fall into the nest made by his open palms. His voice was muffled when he spoke through the crack between his hands. 'Tell me it's over, Beth-Ann. I don't want to look.'

Beth-Ann looked up and down the long hotel corridor before closing the door to the bedroom and turning the key.

'That seems to be the last of them,' she said cheerily.

'Thank God. What time is it?'

'Two forty, just after.'

'How? How is it possible?'

Miles stood and arched his spine, his hands on his hips, the thumbs meeting at the small of his back. 'You know, it wasn't like I didn't tell the agencies. Three months' experience or less, I said, and they send me every model in South Florida. Could you believe that guy, the one who drove from, where was it . . .?'

'Palm Beach?'

'Right! I mean the things some people will do . . .'

'. . . for six million dollars!'

'Well! Lucky I didn't ask to see the women too. How many do you think showed up anyway?'

'About twenty. And then there was that waitress from the restaurant downstairs. Sandy. I sent her away.'

Miles's heart seemed to rise and fall at the same time. 'You did? She's about the only person I wouldn't have minded seeing. She's a friend.'

'She shoulda said that.'

'Mmm.' Miles picked up his wallet and looked for his cash inside. 'Are you hungry?'

'You bet. As a matter of fact, my like totally favourite

Cuban restaurant's around the corner on Collins. Chicken, black beans, fried plantain and rice for $4.25. It's for when you're starving.'

'It's for now,' said Miles.

Miles closed the door on the one hundred and twenty-two composites that had been given to him that morning. Brandishing their books, the models had come in droves. Some had played it cool, some eager, some had even brought their girlfriends, offering a double act.

'You got to see us work together, dude. It's raw.'

Those models that Miles had met previously spoke to him as if he was an old friend. From Rosa's party came Frank, Tim and John. They'd been angry with Rosa for failing to tell them about Miles that night. She'd been working so hard on her beloved Troy. The same old story. Now, the lads were all chummy, trying to make amends for failing to notice Miles the first time around.

'Awesome what happened to Cheyenne! You heard that she's like bald now!'

'Yeah, like fucking Sinead O'Connor, man.'

'You shoulda come with us later, we coulda shown you around.'

Most of the models brought an attitude in with them, one that corresponded with the look in their books. Which came first, the attitude or the look? Miles couldn't tell. Those models just starting out, the only ones Miles had requested to see, tended to be the quietest. He put that down to nervousness.

Some models had arrived loud and sweating, dressed in exercise clothes, and all pumped up from the gym. Perhaps they'd heard that Miles was looking for a muscular model. A few tried to be sophisticated. They came tarted up in designer clothes and shades. Valentino and Ray-ban; Armani with Cutler and Gross. The most successful models were the tattiest and most offhand, confident enough of the images within their portfolios not to need to look exquisite themselves.

Yet they all had one crucial thing in common. They were all wrong for Adam.

Unless he met someone that night, Miles was going to be leaving Miami for Tokyo with only one model down, and five still to go.

Miss Kristina von Koeler never liked to go into work on Saturdays. But this, this was important. The video of Fernando had arrived, sent up by Miles the night before. Kristina needed to see it before Saul returned to the city from his house in East Hampton.

Kristina fed the tape into the machine. Usually, she enjoyed watching videos of young men in the privacy of her office, but now she was nervous. What would she do if Fernando was clearly more handsome than Steve? More than anything, Kristina wanted her fifty per cent share of Steve's six million dollars. There'd been a time recently when she'd expected the wealth that her marriage to Scott Cornwell would have brought. They'd been engaged for three months when he'd left for a two-week trip to LA and stayed there, making it clear he didn't want her to follow. With Scott's millions Kristina could have purchased those things she needed if she was to become the complete woman she longed to be. Now he was gone, her EDEN ploy was all she had left. It *had* to work. She had her eye on an apartment in Sutton Place, and there was a brand-new Mercedes convertible sports car that was perfect for her, and a trip to the Couture shows in Paris was long past due.

Kristina would go to any lengths to secure the money she dreamed of. Whatever the cost to others.

An image flickered on to the screen. A foot, some grass, the sky, then a figure running for a football. He was well-built, she could see that immediately. Very well-built. Oh, look at the power of a body like that. The potential of a man like that!

A black screen, then Fernando close up turning profile, grinning to the camera then winking at it before running and leaping for a ball sent far wide by Horacio. Fernando was strong and quick and caught the ball at a lunge before falling hard on to the balding grass of the park. She heard Miles's beckoning voice, breathy and distorted so close to the microphone, and then Fernando returned, and the lens was moved lecherously across his taut and tanned chest. Kristina grinned.

'He's Hispanic,' she whispered. 'That's beautiful.'

Kristina watched until the tape was through, then she rewound it, locked the door, and settled back to enjoy the video as only Kristina von Koeler knew how.

Sandy was working at Miranda's Veranda on Miles's last night. She avoided his eyes at first, but he waited for her on her route back to the kitchen, and agreed to a quick break. Miles thought that Sandy was looking more delicious than any of the carefully prepared plates she was running from the kitchen.

'I hear you came to my casting.'

'I came to say hi.' Sandy looked about her. 'Can you step behind here with me a minute?' They stood behind a pillar, and Sandy took out a cigarette. Miles lit it for her. 'Thanks. They don't like me smoking.'

'I was . . . wondering what you were doing. Tonight,' said Miles. 'After.'

'I'm meeting someone.'

'Oh OK. I didn't think you, I mean I was just, you know, I don't know what I'll be doing really, I was maybe going to have a drink here or something.'

In response, Sandy inhaled and blew a smoke ring.

'You didn't leave a composite for me,' he said.

'For you or for *Weissmans*?'

'Which answer will get me a drink?'

'I should get back,' Sandy said.

'Really? Um, what time are you going out?'

'As soon as I'm through.'

'Oh right. 'Miles opened his diary and wrote something down. He ripped out the page. 'That's my number in New York. If you ever come up. We could have that drink then. I'd . . . I'd like that.'

'Thanks. Listen Miles, I've got to go.'

'OK. It was nice meeting you.'

He held out a hand.

'You too,' Sandy replied squeezing his hand and leaving Miles thinking, if only for a second, that he'd never wanted any girl so much in the whole of his adult life.

10

In Los Angeles, Miles changed planes after a six a.m. flight from Miami. He'd promised to call Kristina once Weissman had seen the Fernando tape. Nothing had been signed yet. If Weissman disapproved, Miles knew he'd be back where he'd begun.

In Manhattan, Kristina was in a wonderful mood.

'Fernando was great. Really great. But Saul said he wanted a word with you.'

Just one word from Weissman? That'd be a first.

Weissman shouted through the speaker-phone in Kristina's office. Even three thousand miles away, Miles had to hold the phone a few inches from his ear.

'Hey, how's LA looking?'

Miles explained that he was only there for a couple of hours.

'Two hours? Jesus. Two hours. That's a long time in LA. A long time.'

'You don't like this city, Mr Weissman?'

'Hey, does the Pope eat bacon? I mean . . . yah, forget it. No. That's the simple answer. En-Oh. I hate it. Too many airheads. Anyway, listen kid, good work in Miami. But go easy on the ethnic shit, would you? Read the Bible on the plane. Check out Genesis. I do not, do not, think that Adam was Hispanic. I mean, it's OK for PR, for the contest, don't get me wrong. The way I see it, Miles, we can milk these minorities as much as we want. But we gotta pick someone in the end, you know? You gotta find me someone I could use. Remember: EDEN's a strong, fresh, nineties scent. We can't have a spic. Wouldn't look right. It's a cologne, Milo, not a mouthwash.'

127

Miles took his orders, hung up. So, they liked Fernando. Enough for the contest, not enough for the six million. That worried Miles, and made him feel guilty. Fernando would be dreaming of the dollars, no question. At first, Miles had been standing on the outside, amused by the games being played by Saul and Kristina. But now he was involved. What would it do to a dreamer such as Fernando to have his dreams toyed with like this? Miles had let Dawn at the *Miami Herald* know about Fernando, and a photo of him had already appeared in the local press. The national press would come next, then CNN – Elsa Clinch and her crowd. Miles feared that as soon as Fernando lost the contest he'd be dropped like an astronaut admitting to vertigo, and from his experiences as a failed actor Miles knew how much more difficult it is to cope with the roller-coaster of dreams and disappointments than with the everyday toil of stomping foot after foot.

Miles stayed by the phone, staring at a nun in the booth opposite who was indelicately scratching herself beneath her habit. Shouldn't he call Fernando, tell him right now that there was no hope? But then what? No doubt Miles would lose his job, get flown home, give up on his own dream. Quite simply, Saul and Kristina would crucify him.

So he changed his mind, telephoned Poppy, left a message on the machine and went to the bar in search of a beer. In the end, he was thinking, it's only us. And we have to look after ourselves . . .

The flight from Los Angeles to Tokyo's Narita airport left at eleven fifty-two in the morning, a mere twelve minutes late. It was direct to Japan, eleven hours in the air, scheduled to arrive at four thirty on the afternoon of the following day. Flying over the International Date Line, the passengers of TA flight 312 were to lose twelve hours in half a second. The thought unnerved Miles. Twelve hours, stolen in broad daylight. Oh, he'd get them back in untidy three- or four-hour packages, but when? Perhaps they'd arrive on a day he wished could be shorter – when he felt sick, on a painful anniversary, in some loathsome city. It wasn't a good deal. And what if he was never to fly back around the world, east to west, to reclaim the hours? He would die in deficit.

For this one flight, Miles was flying in the luxury of First Class. His wide seat was as comfortable as a good armchair. No one was pushing at his elbows nor stealing his precious leg-room, no one was disturbing him with a reading light while he was trying to sleep nor questioning him about his life. It was more comfortable than most of the places he frequented on the ground. Best of all, Miles had a gaggle of air stewardesses who'd arrive at the press of a button.

They even came without being called. Working, no doubt, on the premise that if you get the Fat Cats tanked up on booze then they'll sleep soundly for most of the flight, the stewardesses regularly pressed drinks into their passengers' hands. Doubles, trebles, bottles; whatever it took. Miles had resisted at first (he'd read the in-flight article on dehydration and jet lag) but he'd given into the champagne. It was the idea of it that tempted him. To drink Moët et Chandon in First Class at thirty-five thousand feet was proof enough that he'd arrived. All the while, Miles had been encouraged in his endeavour by a young stewardess called Alice who'd seemed to want him drunk.

They'd been airborne for about two hours when, with an undeniably tempting smile, Alice appeared to empty the remainder of a bottle of Moët into Miles's glass.

'I . . . ehm . . . I'm not sure I need that,' Miles said as he watched her pour.

'We don't *need* many things, do we? We don't *need* most of the things we *like*.'

What was she? A philosopher? A philosopheress? Miles took a sip.

'In fact, sir, if you don't mind my saying so, you don't need to be in First Class. Do you? Our Economy passengers, for instance. They'll make it to Tokyo. Won't they now? It's what you want that counts.'

'Mm. Maybe.'

'I mean, sir, you don't *need* to be told that you're a very handsome man.'

In an instant, Miles could feel his face reddening. 'I . . . no, there's no need to say that.'

'But you are.'

'Um, thanks.'

He drank some more, and Alice plumped her pert little bottom on the arm rest next to him. 'Mind if I perch?'

'No. Go ahead.'

Alice leant into him. 'They're kind of stuffy, most of them up here. I like things to be a little looser.'

Alice placed a hand on Miles's shoulder. Her bright red nails dripped on to the lapel of his jacket like the wax from a gaudy candle. Was it, Miles wondered, happening all over again? A week ago he'd never been seduced by women. Not like this. Not overtly. Now it seemed to be happening for the second time in seven days. Seduced by an air hostess! It was a porn reader's dream, right down to the garish lipstick and the dyed blonde hair. He remembered Maury Greenberg quoting Tony Montana: 'first the money, then the power, then the women. In that order.'

'Do you mind my asking if this is business or pleasure?'

'You mean talking to you?' said Miles, loosened by the alcohol. 'Business.'

Alice laughed, louder and longer than the joke deserved. Very slightly, she tightened the grip on his shoulder. 'No-o-o. Tokyo.'

'Now that really is business. I'm a model scout.'

Miles had picked up that self-description in Miami. He liked its pithy authority. 'I'm looking for a model for a new cologne,' he added.

'Not for *Weissmans*?'

Miles almost spilled his drink. He twisted his neck right around to Alice. 'You know about it? My God! How?'

'I read it in the *LA Times*. In the "News from New York" section. What exactly do you have to do?'

'I have to find the two models who'd look best for the cologne, that's all,' said Miles.

'Oh. You think I'd be in with a chance?'

'I . . .'

'Or would you need to see more?'

Suddenly, without warning, Alice leant down and pressed her lips so close to Miles's ear that the warm whispers of her breath sent a shiver down his spine. 'You can meet me during the first movie. In the scene when de Niro comes on. Come to the back of the plane. The end bathroom.'

Then, after a quick look left and right, she took something from her pocket and deftly pressed it into Miles's hand. She squeezed his fingers shut around her gift. 'And I'll want those back.'

Then she stood and gracefully walked away towards the front of the plane. Miles watched her go, his mouth literally hanging open. This doesn't happen, he thought, not in real life. Especially not with women called Alice. Yet the proof was in his hands. Though Miles knew what he was holding, he could not bring himself to look. Yet there was something exciting about the truth. For a few moments more, Miles kept his hand clenched tight.

There were another twenty minutes to go before the movie began. Miles was sure he'd know what to do by then. He'd have cleared his mind enough to know whether to return to Alice her scrumpled, warm lace underwear, or whether to forget her offer, and hide her gift in the oddly suggestive elasticated seat-pocket in front; for someone else to find.

When the wheels of the plane finally skidded to a halt on Runway 3 of Tokyo's Narita airport, Miles's head hurt so much it felt as if someone was drilling a hole into his skull from the tender base of his neck. He wasn't sure why. It could have been the champagne. It might have been the lack of sleep. .

But it was probably the incident with Alice.

He'd resolved to go and meet her. On a plane once from Jamaica he and Poppy had so nearly become members of the mile-high club after she'd emboldened him under a blanket. Since then he'd regretted their cowardice. Why there should be glamour attached to making love in the discomfort of a cramped toilet at thirty-five thousand feet, Miles couldn't say. Yet the idea appealed to him as it did to others. Alice held appeal for him too. She was at the other end of the spectrum from Sandy. She was a particular kind of Venus – a Venus flytrap, tempting suckers with her meretricious loveliness. In the half-hour it took for Miles to decide, he'd determined that this was an opportunity he just shouldn't pass up.

Alice had been waiting outside the toilet when he'd walked there through the darkened plane. Most passengers had remained undisturbed in sleep. Others had been concentrating on the movie. The de Niro scene. Alice had smiled when Miles arrived, said nothing, shot a glance down the aisle, and taken his hand to lead him into the tiny cubicle. Without words they'd kissed fleetingly, touched each other, and then Alice had hitched up her skirt and sat up on the metal washbasin, one foot on the toilet seat, the other on a small trash-basket she'd moved for the purpose. Head back, legs apart, her neatly clipped pubic triangle pouting in perfect symmetry, she'd become a living centrefold open just for him. Seeing Miles's excitement, Alice had wasted no time in undoing Miles's belt. Miles's trousers had fallen as his penis bounced up with a flourish. Alice had tapped it with her finger, like a music teacher setting a metronome in motion. Then she'd looked at him and smiled. 'You know what to do,' she'd said.

And he did. But he didn't do it.

Suddenly, and without knowing why, Miles had lost his nerve. Was it the thought of Poppy? Perhaps. Or was it that the way in which Alice had positioned her trimmed and deodorised vagina in the tiny space of the toilet revealed indubitable practice at the routine? Confronted with the reality of his fantastic image, he hadn't cared for what he'd seen. In an instant, Alice's availability had become her downfall. Once given what he wanted, Miles no longer wanted it any more. Still hard, excited even, Miles had zipped up, muttered some kind of apology and scurried away. A frightened rat.

Once back in his seat, Miles had translated his disgust into moral rectitude. The incident was surely confirmation of the cleanliness of his soul.

Never for one instant did it occur to him that there might be more to being good than simply not being bad.

11

Ask anyone. Miki Katanabe was not usually late. So as she skipped across the perfectly polished tiles of Narita airport to the place where Miles stood waiting, she felt terrified, as she had done on the day when, aged thirteen, she'd been hauled in front of the headmaster for smoking in the break.

The fear was the same. What kind of person would Mr Jensen think she was? What if he complained to someone in New York? It was terrible, really it was.

She was breathless when she reached Miles. 'Oh, Mr Jensen-san. *Sumimasen*. Excuse me. Excuse me.'

Miki bowed slightly as she spoke, the tiny jerks of a nervous bird drinking from a pond. 'I am sorry I am late. Please forgive me.' She patted her chest with her hand, and lifted her eyeballs to the ceiling. 'My name is Katanabe, Miki. Oh, I'm sorry, other way! Miki Katanabe.'

Miles smiled warmly. 'Hello, it's nice to meet you.'

He didn't offer his hand. He'd been told it wasn't customary. 'You're only a couple of minutes late,' he reassured her. 'Don't worry at all.'

Miki began to bow and nod again, relief spreading through her muscles like a rainbow of oil across water. 'Thank you, thank you. You were looking so very angry!'

'Probably my headache,' said Miles.

Miki looked devastated. Was she the cause? She waved her tiny arms. 'Here we have car and driver waiting. OK? We go? Driver has good pills for the head.'

Miki wanted to carry Miles's heavy suitcase. He wouldn't let her. Instead she trotted with him as they walked to the exit, seemingly unsure of whether she should walk in front, behind, or beside him.

Later, Miles would reflect on how typical Miki was of this generation of Japanese. She was small, if taller than her parents and their friends. Her English was adequate, careful. She never risked difficult grammar or vocabulary for fear of making a mistake. She was dressed immaculately, as if she'd copied her entire outfit from a page in American *Vogue*. She wore a navy-blue, linen trouser suit with a bright, white cotton shirt, and a Hermes scarf wrapped a little too tightly around her neck. Her shoes were from Ralph Lauren, her bag from Chanel. To Miles, she seemed a sweet child wrapped in adult's clothing, a shy schoolgirl playing the efficient business-woman. She was perfectly mannered at all times, as if she had studied some minor character from a BBC period drama series, and was now living the part. Even her make-up had been applied perfectly, as if painted on by a professional.

In these aspects of her character, Miki was like her country. She'd imported all the ingredients from the West. It was the right recipe she was yet to find.

Once they were in the car, a dour machine with a Spartan interior, Miki handed Miles a fax that had arrived from Kristina. In Kristina's looping, confident handwriting, it read:

Miles, hope First Class was good enough for you. You'd better prove yourself to be a good investment!
Don't forget these things . . .
1 Models in Japan are usually small. We don't want anyone under six foot.
2 Miki Katanabe can arrange a *Weissmans* shoot if she has to. If we call it a test we won't have to pay the models.
3 Remember the PR aspect at all times. Find me some-one with an interesting history. In that, Fernando was OK. If not rags to riches, then riches to riches. It sells as well. Aristocracy is a bonus. Saul's new line is that if Adam was from bad stock, then we're all screwed.
4 Tokyo is expensive. Eat noodles, not steak.
Keep us posted, Kristina.

Miles folded the paper and put it in his pocket. He couldn't understand Kristina. If she was so jealous of him being on the trip, why hadn't she come herself? It didn't make sense. She wanted to make all the decisions, and yet it was he, not she, riding in the back of this car into the monstrously ugly concrete jungle of Japan's capital city with a squeaky and nervous young woman playing with her earrings by his side.

It was a little past seven by the time Miles had checked into his room at the impressive Akasaka King Hotel in central Tokyo. His bags had been carried to his room by a tiny man wearing white gloves. Miles kicked off his shoes and lay back on the bed, propped up by all the pillows he could find.

Miles loved hotels. He never merely treated them as places to sleep for the night. He used them for all they were worth. He wrote letters on hotel paper, drank from his minibar, ordered room service, used four towels after he'd showered, took long baths under thousands of bubbles, watched TV from his bed, ordered adult movies at $7.95, asked the front desk to wake him in the morning, had his shoes cleaned and a paper brought in with his breakfast. He had the thermostat set to the ideal temperature, stole the soap and the sewing kit and the notepad, sometimes the towels, once even the robe, and he made love, as often as he could, across the fresh and crisply inviting laundered sheets.

The way Miles saw it, hotels are designed for sexual activity. He could hardly remember a hotel room in which he hadn't indulged in sex of some kind. Even when he had been alone.

Miki had arranged a dinner for Miles with the heads of the three top agencies in the city. Given the choice, he'd have stayed in, but he was bulldozed by Miki's efficiency. 'We go Shabu-Shabu, yes?' she'd said. He'd agreed, ignorant of what he was accepting. Shabu-shabu could have been some obscure Japanese act of sexual deviancy. Then again, with the prim Miss Katanabe in mind, Miles thought probably not.

Miles showered, then unpacked his guidebook. He looked

for the chapter on Manners and Conversation, and began to read.

> If bowed at, bow back, (it told him) with the depth and intensity of the host's bow.

Naked, and with the book in his hand, Miles stood in front of the full-length mirror.

> The arms should be kept fairly straight with palms flat against the thighs. The eyes are lowered, as well as the upper body.

Miles kept his eyes up to see how he looked. Too stupid to try this in public, was his verdict. He climbed on to the bed and read on.

> Male displays of camaraderie such as back-slapping, vigorous handshakes, and arm-touching, should be avoided. Eye contact should not be insisted upon. It may be considered impolite and an infringement on personal space.

The book went so far as to advise Miles that when conversing, he should take a position a little further from your host than normal.

Miles hoped he'd remember enough when the time came. He didn't mind having a guidebook for behaviour. In fact, he thought he might buy one for America. Perhaps somewhere there was a publication to advise him on how to react if a powerful and alluring woman should again place her hand on his leg during a respectable lunch in the heart of New York City.

Miki and Miles arrived for dinner a minute after eight thirty. The three agents with whom they were dining were already waiting by the door. Waiting for the boss to arrive before sitting down. Miles liked that. When they met him, they shook his hand and thrust business cards at him. A demure hostess, dressed in a blood-red silk kimono, smiled at Miles with her lips closed, and, clopping in wooden sandals, ushered them to their table. The restaurant was crowded but quiet. Three New Yorkers would have made as much noise as all the diners in this restaurant, thought Miles.

Beyond the tables of the first room was a traditional Japanese eating area behind *shoji*, the paper screens. Tatami matting covered the floor. In the centre of the room there was a low, rectangular, dark wooden table. Six slim green mats were positioned symmetrically on the tatami.

'No chairs, right?'

'It's Japanese way,' said Joe, speaking rapidly. 'I don't like it. I like to sit at table. With knife and fok!'

Joe Fujimoto was the thirty-one-year-old owner and head booker of Tokyo's Mr Man agency in the fashionable suburb of Omotesando. Dressed less formally then the others, he wore white jeans, a denim shirt and an American flying jacket. He reminded Miles of a French teenager trying to emulate an American man of the fifties. Joe sat himself to Miles's right, and immediately touched him on the arm. So much for my personal space, thought Miles.

'When I go to New York everybody take me to Japanese restaurant,' said Joe. 'But I don't like the Japanese food. I like burger.'

Miles laughed. The other two agents seemed to regard Joe with disgust. Yuki and Taka, the head bookers of Spring and Al agencies respectively, were older than Joe, but Miles could sense a wider chasm than that of the years. They sat quietly, stern-faced, as Joe monopolised the conversation with his celebratory opinions on all things American.

Five years before, Joe had taken over Mr Man agency when it had been teetering on the brink of collapse. Since then he'd transformed it into the second most successful agency in Japan, overtaking Taka along the way.

Ironically, he'd trained as a booker under Yuki at Spring. They'd never cared for one other. There'd been a simple and blatant clash of personalities. Yuki Mitukoshi was forty-five years old. She was an inflexible professional, neither liked nor understood outside Japan. She rarely smiled, even when happy. She wasn't prone to displays of enthusiasm, even when meeting models she thought perfect for her agency. She preferred to keep her cards tight to her chest and so was regarded with trepidation by the bookers in other countries where gushing was the norm. Yet where it counted, where the money was made and the deals were closed among the clients in Japan, Yuki was trusted and respected to provide the best and most appropriate models for any job. Clients knew that Yuki Mitukoshi never told lies. At times, she was in danger of giving model agents a good name.

By contrast, Joe Fujimoto was a flamboyant man, and a daring agent. He worked by pushing clients to their limits with unreasonable demands, and then backing down to give the impression of a concession. His was the Turkish carpet dealer's approach to business. He knew his price, started much higher, then haggled down to the sum he'd hoped for at the start. And once he'd closed a deal Joe liked to say 'OK, but you're robbing me.' He'd heard the expression once in a made-for-TV American film.

Miki turned to Miles as he sat cross-legged in front of the table. Already, his thigh muscles were beginning to ache.

'How do you like Japan?' she asked nervously.

'It's interesting, but I've only been here for four hours!'

Joe cut in with the vocal tempo of a DJ on speed.'Your first time?' Miles nodded in assent. 'Oh my God. I have to take you to some place I know in the city.' Joe leant right into Miles, and whispered, 'the Soaphouse!' Joe giggled and gave Miles a light punch on the arm. To cement their friendship. To get nearer to that forty per cent. 'I have so-o-o many, many friends. They come back to visit me only to go to places I show them. When you come to see my agency we talk with many, many model who tell you same. Really. I have the best guy model in Japan now.'

Yuki watched Joe with dismay. She found it deplorable that he'd chosen to throw aside the traditional way of doing business in Japan in favour of this modern, aggressive style. She remembered how once, when he'd still been working at

Spring, Joe had shown her a collection of video tapes he'd brought back from the US entitled *How to be tough but tender in business*. Had he watched only the first half? Joe was about as tender as the Japanese had been in Peking. Yet if Yuki had been honest with herself, she would have admitted that her dislike of Joe came in no small part from her jealousy of his great success.

On the table in front of Miles, a large iron pot of steaming broth was being heated by a raging gas flame. Arranged in an exquisite pattern on a plate before him was an assortment of thinly sliced beef and vegetables. As Miles studied the delicate array of reds and greens, the purple of the aubergine and the tiny sheaf of bamboo shoots, he thought his plate looked like a work of art. So he just looked at it.

Taka took control. 'You must pick up meat with chopstick and you put in water and then it cooks. Also the vegetable.'

Quick! Miles tried to remember what the guidebook had said about chopsticks. There'd been something about never pointing them at anyone, nor leaving them crossed. And he must never stick them vertically in the rice. But wasn't there something else?

'You leave meat in water very short time,' said Taka, 'and take out and you eat with one of sauces. Like this.'

Taka flipped one of the dark red strips of beef into the pot. In seconds it turned a tempting dark brown. Expertly, Taka fished it out, swished it through a rich soy-based sauce and handed it to Miles. The beef melted on Miles's tongue, more succulent than any meat he remembered having eaten. He smiled and with his mouth still full, nodded in approval.

'*Oishii, ne?*' said Taka. It's good, isn't it?

'It's great,' said Miles.

The butterflies in Miki's stomach fluttered up into a smile. Jensen-san was happy! Now she could eat.

Joe filled Miles's glass with Sapporo beer, until it almost overflowed. 'In Japan, we fill always the glass of other people with beer. You must never fill own glass.'

'What if no one fills your glass?' asked Miles.

Joe, Taka and Miki smiled.

141

Joe spoke, 'They will. Always. It is old understanding between Japanese people.'

Yuki glanced across at Joe. Understanding! What did he know of the word? Shamelessly, Joe had broken the understanding that existed between agencies of a daily rate for models below which they could not, *could not*, be offered to clients. Sure it was a monopoly of a sort, but the agents knew that once the ball of cheap rates was set rolling, it would be impossible to stop. The clients would begin bargaining for lower and lower rates.

It was Joe Fujimoto, a man who had worked hard to carry that ball to the top of its hill, who was responsible for giving it such a hard push down.

Joe's face was bright red when he held up the beer bottle to offer Miles another glass. Miles declined.

They had finished the exquisite meal, and Miles was enjoying his green tea. By now he'd made his apologies, uncrossed his aching legs, and stretched them underneath the table. Miles hadn't even had a chance to advise the agents on the type of model he was looking for. Whenever he'd tried to bring up EDEN and the search, the conversation had been changed. Maybe this was their way. He'd have to look it up. But anyway, after his trip to Miami Miles had learned that agents don't listen to clients. They nod and smile and say 'oh sure!' and then they go and show you their favourite models anyway. The ones they discovered snorting coke in the bathroom of a bar. The ones they were fucking, or wanting to fuck. The ones in desperate need of a job. If by some happy coincidence, one of these models should be suitable for the client, then the agent would congratulate himself on a job well done.

Outside, they said their goodbyes. Miles nervously prepared himself to bow. He let his hand fall to his thighs, the palms flat. He reminded himself not to look up. Taka and Yuki stepped forward and in turn shook Miles's hand. Then Joe slapped him heartily on the back.

'I'll catch you later,' Joe said as the cab drew up to take Miles and Miki back to his Akasaka Hotel.

And that was that.

Once in the cab, Miles turned to Miki to ask her something that had been bothering him all evening. 'Miki, Japan is a country with a long and great history, right?'

'Yes.'

'And now it has the most efficient and envied economy in the world, yeah?'

Miki laughed in agreement.

'So why the hell do you have to import hundreds of Western models? Why can't you just use Japanese models?'

'We have models from Japan . . .'

'So use them.'

'They are not as elegant as you are.'

Was she blushing? He thought so. He couldn't tell. Miki's face was lit by the glare of neon advertisement lights that blistered the darkness either side of the street. Yellow, orange, red, splashing across the back seat as the car crawled its way in the ten p.m. jam of traffic.

'That's it? You think we're better looking?'

'It's very complicated, Jensen-san.'

Miles wanted an answer, and he was boss. 'Yes?'

'Oh! Everybody thinks Japan always like this. Always like Sony and Toyota and Matsushita. Big corporation and electronic. But in before World War Two we were much smaller, more like farming country. Many, many people thought the Emperor Hirohito he was the God. He sat on a big white horse, and the people did not look at his face. We thought because he was God we would win the war. But after Nagasaki and Hiroshima we think there were many, many problem in Japanese style of old thinking. Because we lost, and Hirohito says he is not God now. We have very much respect for America and England because they win war against us. We were saying that it must be good in America and England. And then the American come in with money and many thing from your country that we do not have in Japan. Refrigerator and air conditioner and televisions. Many thing. So we want these things and we start to make them. But little piece inside us say that because all America have these thing then America is a luxury country. Always we see America as luxury country. So this is why. When we use the Western model for advertisement we are saying that the product is very luxury. Like in America? You understand?'

'That's crazy, Miki. I've seen ads for incredible Japanese computer products with pictures of dumb-looking Americans. It doesn't make sense. I think you should send all Japanese people on a plane to see what America is really like. We'll probably have Japanese models on our New York billboards soon.'

Miki thought this hysterically funny. She was still giggling as the cab swung into the driveway of the hotel. It stopped, and Miles put his hand on the door to open it.

'No! Cabs in Tokyo have doors that open automatic.'

'See! You don't get that in America.'

Miki spoke in Japanese to the driver, and the door flew open. 'It is very, very difficult to get taxi late at night in Japan, so I sorry I stay with this one. I will see you tomorrow, Jensen-san. At hotel, OK? Thank you for coming to dinner with me. I had a nice time.'

'Me too, Miki. Me too.'

Forgetting, Miles put his hand on the door just as the driver slammed it shut. Then he watched as Miki turned and waved at him through the small oval of the rear-seat window.

12

W ith a towel around his waist, a cigarette hanging from his mouth, and a cup of sweet black coffee steaming by his side, Jeff Gifford looked at his reflection and grinned.

'Fuckin' A!'

He opened the mirrored door of the bathroom cupboard and began to rummage through the pills and razors, the moisturiser, face scrub and bronzers, the acne creams and the One Touch spot concealer make-up. Past the Vitamins A, B, C, D, E, the multivitamins and the zinc, the iron tablets, cod liver oil and garlic, the protein powders, condoms, spermicide, lubricant, nose-hair clippers and bubble gum. There, balanced at the back, tucked in behind the cotton balls, was the large tube of bright yellow, hard-fix hair gel for which Jeff had been searching. He took it out and squeezed. Nothing. He put the tube on the floor and stamped on it. Nothing. He hurled it against the mildewy, grey tiles of the shower. Nothing.

With fist clenched, Jeff thumped open the tiny bathroom window, took aim, and lobbed the tube of gel into the neat stone and evergreen garden of his ageing, hostile neighbours.

'For Pearl Harbor!' he shouted.

Less accurate than the Japanese, he missed the pond, and the empty tube skidded across their patterned stone terrace, and on to a patch of much-loved moss. 'Shit!'

Jeff knew he could get some gel off his Brazilian roommate. Marching through their small shared living room, he kicked over an old wooden chair before entering the other bedroom.

The room was dark and musty. It smelt of French cigarettes and sports socks, lung-ripened alcohol and sex. Two figures lay sleeping in the single bed, their bodies wrapped around one other. Jeff took a guess and kicked one with the heel of his unshod foot, in the manner of a narcotics agent breaking down a door.

'Shithead. Fabio. Fucker. Fuckhead.'

A kick with every expletive.

Fabio Nirao lifted his head. The girl, whoever she was this time, pulled up the torn and unwashed sheet to hide her face, and let out a faint whimper that Jeff thought he recognised. Perhaps it just reminded him of his little sister from the days when he'd enjoyed cramming his soiled underwear into her mouth.

Fabio spoke without looking up. His voice was deep and resonant. It should have belonged to someone much older than he. It was a voice to command authority.

'Always. Always you wake me,' groaned Fabio. 'Why?'

'I need some gel, bro.'

'What?'

'Your hair gel, man. I need it. Where is it?'

Fabio was silent, contemplating the inanity of the request. Then he said, 'In my bag.'

Jeff kicked him again, laughing. 'Where's your bag, Fab-man?'

Fabio sat up in bed and spoke in an angry, tired drawl. 'Hey, stop to kicking me. Or I won't give you nothing!'

Jeff grinned gormlessly at his roommate, and thought that he looked rough, even for Fabio. His thick lips were swollen and dry. His eyes were half-closed. He had two days growth on his beard. His heavy, dark brown hair had lost its familiar lustre and the dark bags under his eyes showed through his sallow skin.

Jeff knew why. He had left Fabio in Fantasia, Tokyo's most popular nightclub, at three in the morning. Fabio, drunk already, had said he was only warming up. God knows how much more cheap Japanese whisky he'd consumed since then. And after all that he'd brought another girl home with him. A naïve American, probably. A sweet sixteen-year-old hoping to strike it lucky in love, and ending up just getting laid.

Ego

Hedonism ruled Fabio Nirao's life. At twenty, confident, handsome, and with an endless supply of attractive women in Tokyo, he was not going to let morality get in the way of pleasure. That would come later; perhaps.

'Look in my black bag. Over there,' he said.

Jeff took the bag and tipped it upside down on the chair. He found the gel and spun it in the air. 'Thanks, bro.'

Jeff flicked on a light switch and stood in front of an old and cracked mirror fixed to the back of Fabio's closet door. He squeezed a massive dollop of the gel into his hand. 'You know, Fabio, it stinks in here, man. You should open a window or something.'

'I'm going back to sleep.'

'Joe said he wants us at the agency at one. To see this guy from New York.'

'Who care?'

'Word on the street says they're paying ten million dollars. That's who cares.'

'So they choose some big model. John Larson, Eamon, Troy, someone like that.'

Fabio let his head sink back on to the pillow, and began to caress the girl under the sheets. First things first.

'Fabio, man, I'm telling you. Joe says they're looking for a new face. Six new faces. For a competition in New York. I'm telling you, dude.' Jeff combed the gel through his wavy blond hair. 'Listen, Fab-man, I heard they want a girl too. Maybe the creature from under the sheets can come along.' He laughed, a raucous laugh. 'Hey, so long as she doesn't have four legs, man.'

A girl's voice came from the pillow beside Fabio. 'Fuck off, Jeff.'

Jeff was silent. He stopped working on his hair. With the comb in one hand, and with the other hand cupped over his hair, Jeff resembled Elvis, or an actor from *West Side Story*, posing before launching into song. The song would have been about lost love and betrayal. Could it be? Not with him! My Jodie? Not with him! Oh no, no.

Jeff scrunched up his face. 'Jodie, s'that you?'

'Fuck off, Jeff.'

Jeff, stunned, was silent. He'd split up with Jodie Barrerra only two days before. She'd always feigned disgust at Fabio's reputation as the Tokyo Casanova, but now . . . Now she was in bed with him?

'Oh, for Christ's sake guys!'

Jeff hurled the tube of gel at the bed. It hit Jodie, above the ear – the only part of her that was visible.

'Fuck off, Jeff,' she said again, her vocabulary exhausted.

Jeff stood at the end of the bed, unsure of how to act. 'Thanks, guys. Really, thanks a lot.' Neither of the lovers stirred. 'Hey, Jodie,' whined Jeff, 'don't bother coming to the casting. They don't like hookers.'

Fabio sat up violently, awake now. He pointed towards the door. 'Get out my room, OK. Just get out. Let it be.' Fabio had a habit of speaking in Beatles' song lyrics. It was how he'd first learned his English in Brazil.

Jeff took an aggressive stance. Feet slightly apart, upper body jutting forward; an angry cockerel with one tuft of hair standing on end. 'You're in big shit, Fab. Big fucking shit!'

Beneath the covers the lovers were getting busy. Jeff gritted his teeth, turned and left. On his way out, he slammed the door.

As usual, this was his most eloquent mode of expression.

As Jeff was slamming the door, and Fabio was urging Jodie's limp hand towards his crotch, Miles was standing in A1 agency in front of yet another wall plastered with models' faces. Beside him, Taka Kidani was tense. Taka kept removing his tiny round glasses and wiping them on his red and blue striped tie before pushing them back up his nose with the middle finger of his right hand.

Miles had been in Taka's agency for an hour, meeting those models who weren't working, looking at the books of those who were. Now he was contemplating his choices. Taka's agency represented at least forty men and women flown in from all over the world to lend the Japanese their desired sense of luxury. Taka was about to discover if any of them were in with a chance of the six-million-dollar prize.

Taka wasn't confident. Having been an agent for twelve years he could sense when a client was not satisfied with his choices. Still, in this business there was always hope. With good reason Taka suspected that there were times when clients carried the composites home with them only to choose the model from a random shuffle of the cards.

Already that morning, Miles had been to see Yuki at Spring. She'd been quietly confident when he'd arrived. She knew she was the best agent in Japan, just as she knew that she represented the top models. The fact that only two models were available to see Miles was a measure of her success. All the rest were working.

Miles had been warned that Yuki's models were all experienced professionals of a standard to be found in the major European cities, yet he'd visited Spring in the distant hope that he'd find someone unusual and distinctive. Instead he found that Yuki had played it dead safe with the market. She hired for Japan, not *Weissmans*, and in not one of the books that Miles studied did he find a model suitable for Adam. He hadn't even bothered to pick up any composites. There was no use in playing games with Yuki.

She'd seen him to the door. 'Thank you for coming,' she said. 'I think I know what you are wanting and this agency is not right for you. We have only the experienced model.'

'I was told that agents were never that honest, Yuki.'

'Aaah. Client trust Spring. I had before one guy who maybe you like, but he is in Europe now.'

'Could you give me his name?'

'Chester. Chester Hunt. He is American. Different from many Americans. He is more like you. He came here to Japan before anywhere else to stay with someone. He is very, very natural looking. I think he has rich family.'

'I know about him. I didn't know he was a model. His dad's a famous politician in the States.'

'*Hai.*' Yes.

'Do you know maybe how I can reach him?'

'I think he is with Ugly People agency in Milan.'

'Great, well I'm going to see them.'

Yuki paused, glanced at the floor and seemed to be looking for the courage to say something. 'Maybe I have one idea of man here in Japan.'

'Who is he?'

'He is friend of Chester. But . . .' audibly, she sucked her breath in. She shook her head, clearly trying to decide whether to tell Miles about this model. 'I don't know. I will call you at the Akasaka King.'

'I'd appreciate that. You know I'm only here for three days, don't you?'

'*Hai*.'

With this, she shook Miles's hand, bowed at the diminutive Miki, and said goodbye.

In A1 agency, Miles was having more luck, though he'd just surprised Taka by showing an interest in only those models with the fewest pictures in their portfolios. Deliberately, Taka had kept these portfolios away from Miles. Miles had insisted. And to Taka's amazement, when Miles left the agency, he did so carrying with him the composites of the three most frequently unemployed models in the agency.

Miles and Miki took the stammering elevator down from Taka's office. The air was surprisingly fresh for such a polluted city, and Miles suggested that he and Miki should walk to Mr Man's. Miles needed a walk to help him think. He was depressed by what he'd seen, or, more to the point, what he'd failed to see. Sure, there were some great faces among the many he'd looked at, but they all belonged to the successful models. Saul Weissman had been adamant about his desire for a new face. Simply put, all the best models were ruled out. Neither could Miles choose a local resident as he had in Miami. So where could he look? Outside of the fashion business, the majority of the Westerners in Tokyo were teachers, bankers and diplomats. Miles doubted he would find any suitable or willing model among their number.

As Miles and Miki walked amid the thunderous traffic, the alarming thought struck Miles that perhaps his quest was impossible. Could Kristina be wrong? Miles had been told that in the mid-eighties the modelling industry had boomed, and that there was always fresh blood in every agency. Now, in this recession, the young hopefuls were being rejected right from the start, sent back to their high schools and colleges, to their apprentice jobs and parents. These days the agencies were full with the old-timers. If a model had a proven record he or she became a safe bet for most jobs. It was a hopeless time for a search such as this.

Of course, there was no shortage of beautiful people out there in the world, but most of them were hiding in beautiful places. Only the rich and privileged can afford not to sell their looks, so perhaps in them lay Miles's greatest hope. Miles felt that if he could ferret his way into their world in Europe, he might be able to find the perfect model for EDEN. Surely, considered Miles, someone could be tempted from his French château or English country mansion by the glorious scent of six million dollars. Greed runs no less thick in blood that's blue. If Miles was very lucky, he might find some man to balance out Fernando, his only model so far, a poor Cuban immigrant living with a widowed mother in a trailer home in suburban Miami.

'Fernando. Fernando. Telephone!'

Fernando Padrillas shuffled on bare feet to the phone, rubbing his eyes as he went. He took the receiver from his mother. '*Si*?'

'Hi, Fernando. How are you?'

'Who this?'

'You don't know me. My name's Rosa Bertaum. I run Rosa's Models in Miami Beach. Maybe you've heard of us.'

'No.'

'No problem. We are in fact one of the biggest and most respected agencies in Florida.'

'I'm no' a model. I'm doing the *Weissmans* competition, that's it.'

'I thought maybe you'd like to drop by the agency so we could run through some ideas.'

'I'm no' a model.'

'What if we sent a car out to pick you up? You can come

151

by, and if you don't like what you see then all you've wasted is an hour or so. How does that sound? Only it looks to me like you could work really well here in Miami.'

'I don't know.'

'In fact there's a casting come through today I'd love for you to go on. It's for a job paying – what's that Swiss client paying, Za? – paying $1500 a day, Fernando.'

'For one day?'

'You got it.'

'OK. I'll come in. To see, nothing more.'

'Great. We can get a car to you in an hour. Look forward to meeting you. Ask for Rosa.'

'OK.'

'Bye.'

Fernando hung up, and went to tell his mother the news.

The guidebook that Miles had brought with him to Japan described Omote-Sando Boulevard as being Parisian in character and though Miles thought this to be an insult to Paris, it was indeed because of the European feel of the street that Joe Fujimoto had moved Mr Man here in the spring of 1991. It was certainly a pleasant street by the standards of an unpleasant city, for birds could be heard singing vibrantly from the trees that grew thick down the Boulevard. Outside of its splendid parks Tokyo was not a green city, and this brief stretch of foliage did something to help lift Miles's sagging spirits.

Drowning the birdsong, a man dressed as a clown was skipping outside a garish McDonald's singing in Japanese the name of his restaurant sliced into a coleslaw of syllables. 'Mac-U-don-A-lid-O!' Instinctively, Miles looked away. Now he knew what had been in the bomb. A million spores of America's uncultured culture had landed on Hiroshima, and they'd been germinating ever since.

Miles preferred the other side of the street. There was the beautifully laid-out branch of the Shu-Uemura make-up store, its interior purely black and white, precise and inviting. A little further down, they passed an old two-storey building covered in a flowering vine and from inside of which could be heard the commanding shouts and falling bodies of a martial arts school. Close to that, a store for tourists was crammed with Japanese artifacts – flawless lacquerware bowls, vases and trays, delicate dolls, cultured pearls, brightly decorated kimonos, woven fabrics, swords, paintings and porcelain.

Five minutes further up the street, Miles caught sight of Mr Man agency. Joe had chosen to locate Mr Man on the first floor of a modern three-storey building. The front of the agency was a stretch of pure glass, like that of a shop window, and for most of the day there were spectators enjoying this rare insight into the workings of an international model agency.

A few of the models had fans, one even a fan club. These fans, teenage girls mostly, would congregate after school at a coffee shop across the street. With customary bravado, Joe had surprised the previous owners of this café by offering them a sum for their establishment well above the market rate. Unaware of Joe's plans for Mr Man, they'd sold up. Within three months, thanks to the busloads of schoolgirls hoping to catch a glimpse of their favourite male models, the coffee shop had tripled its profits.

Now it was the turn of Miles and Miki to look through the window. Inside, he could see the models waiting for him. Impatient high schoolers waiting for teacher. There were about thirty men in all, and half as many women. The boys were all keeping themselves busy – crowding around the booking table, peering out of the window, preening themselves in the reflection of the glass, shadow-boxing, criticising their rivals' portfolios, making illicit international phone calls, annoying the agents trying to work, rearranging their clothes, scratching their balls. It was far removed from the average Japanese office in which all the employees went about their business with quiet diligence, taking care not to disturb their co-workers, concentrating on nothing more than their task at hand. Only a month before, on a TV chat show, a right-wing traditionalist had cited Mr Man as being a bad influence on the young that gathered to watch. For his pains, Joe Fujimoto had sent the old man his promised case of Scotch whisky.

Miles looked at Miki. 'Well, then,' he said, 'let's go into the lion's den.'

Jodie Barrerra had always wondered, and now at last she knew. As she dug her fingers into Fabio's back and cried out, he released himself, and his body lurched in orgasm for the second time that morning. They lay still for a while, Jodie stroking her lips across the dark skin of Fabio's thick neck. He relaxed his shoulders and rolled on to his back, leaving one hand draped across Jodie's flat white stomach.

'So that's why.'

'Why what?'

'Why all the girls in the agency want you,' she said.

'Most of them had me.'

'Ugh, don't!'

'You're the best, Jodie. You know I'll be true.'

'Right, Fabio. Sounds like a new line.'

'It is.' Fabio laughed. 'First time anyone say that to you!'

'Hey, Fabio. Is it true about the condoms? That you had like, five hundred sent to you from Brazil?'

'Who told you?'

'Everyone.'

'You seen the Japanese ones?'

Fabio lifted his hand from her stomach. Jodie had noticed his hands the night before. They were thick, incredibly powerful. The hands of a workman, or a sculptor. Or a lover like Fabio. He waggled his little finger. 'They like this. Maybe smaller, I swear. Once a Japanese girl screamed when she saw me!'

'I would have too. Probably. If the light had been on. You're like an elephant.'

Fabio grinned. 'Am I?'

'You know you are.'

Jodie punched him lightly on his muscular shoulder. 'Am I! You just wanted to hear me say it.'

'I don't want to hear nothing. I want to do it.' Fabio moved his hand down and between her legs.

'No, Fabio. You're completely crazy. We just – Fabio, *no*. I have to get to a casting. I thought, oh, I thought you

had, no, to see someone, stop! from New York. Fabio. Fa
–!'

But Fabio Nirao wasn't in the mood to listen. He rolled
on top of Jodie once more and swallowed her protest in the
cavern of his mouth.

Joe Fujimoto cast his eyes around the room, then walked over
to talk to Jeff. 'Fabio is no working today. Where is he?'

'Don't ask me, man,' Jeff said. 'Haven't seen him.'

'Did he know about casting?'

'Hey, you think I'm his mother, Joe? How the fuck you
expect me to know?'

'Relax buddy. Have you seen the *Weissmans* guy yet?'

'No. I'm next.'

Jeff glanced across at Miles who was sitting at a table in the
far corner, looking at the book of an Irishman called Gerry.
Jeff wasn't worried about Gerry. He looked like shit anyway
– pale skin, dark eyes, a weird angular face, no way was he
right for a cologne campaign. He didn't even work out. Not
like Jeff himself. Jeff spent at least an hour every day in the
gym. He'd been kinda skinny once, but not now. Now he
longed for the chance to show off his new muscles. Yeah,
man, he felt good about this job. Only the other day that cute
girl Donna had read out his stars to him. Now is the time for
effort to be rewarded, they'd said. Now indeed. Rewarded
with six million dollars.

Miles handed Gerry his book, and thanked him. Jeff was
quick to move in before Alain, a Frenchman he despised with
all his heart.

'Hi, I'm Jeff.'

'Good to meet you, Jeff. You're American, right?' said
Miles.

'Yeah, from Chicago.'

Miles looked up from the first page of Jeff's book. 'Oh,
yeah? Me too.'

Jeff said a silent prayer. Fuckin' A, thank you God! This is
my lucky day. Thing was always to try to find a connection
with the client. That was the only way they remembered you

from among all the hundreds of faces they saw. Now God had given him a fellow Chicagoan.

Turning the pages of Jeff's portfolio, Miles stopped on a shot of Jeff wearing a bandanna on his head, Calvin underwear on his butt, and holding the ultimate nineties accessory in his right arm – a baby, black no less.

'That shot was taken in Milan. Marco Benedicce. I love it.'

Miles asked, 'Have you been modelling long?'

Jeff knew what to say. 'No, I'm kinda starting out, you know. I was going to go into the Marines, but I met this dude from Click in New York who really liked me, and all, but he said I should go to Milan to get some shots, and then I ended up coming here pretty soon after.'

'Have you ever worked in New York?'

'No, they're still waiting for the Jeff Gifford phenomenon, man.'

Jeff laughed, to show he was joking. Even though he wasn't.

Miles flicked through the rest of the book. The copy on the Japanese tear sheets amused him. It was written in a bizarre pidgin English and splurged across the magazine pages. On a photograph of Jeff dressed in loud-checked pants and lounging in thirties glasses on a golf buggy heavy with antique clubs was written, 'Now, We should answer golfing color exact, The beginnings of all, When We have to do with you.' On another, a shot of Jeff in yellow socks, purple shorts, a printed shirt displaying a selection of fruits, and a floppy, flowery hat were the words, 'Yes, Yes Colorful way of Showing mmm Sensuous color.' On reaching the last page, Miles returned to the Italian baby shot, the best shot of Jeff's body.

This was a good sign for Jeff. He knew when a client was thinking hard about using him for a job. It was something one learnt early as a model. There had, it was true, been times when he'd been fooled – sometimes a client would decide he liked Jeff on the first page of his book, and then flick speedily through the rest. Yet usually Jeff could tell, and when a client spent time looking at Jeff with the baby, that almost always meant they liked him.

Miles turned to Miki. 'You think we could arrange a test for Jeff on Thursday?'

'*Hai, hai,*' said Miki nodding enthusiastically.

Miles looked up at Jeff, who could hardly contain his elation. 'Are you working Thursday?' he asked

Jeff shouted for Joe, and asked him if there were any jobs or options on him for Thursday. Joe went to the booking table to look at the charts. He rejoined Miles. 'No, Jeff's free. He's a great kid, huh? I saw Jeff in Milan. I said this guy big model one day. So I bring him to Tokyo real quickly.'

'I'd like an option on him on Thursday. We'll talk about it when I've seen the rest of the guys, OK?'

Miles was feeling in control now. He was becoming accustomed to the jargon, and he was no longer surprised if people ran when he called. He was finding too that the more authoritative he became, the more seriously he was taken. He felt born to this!

For another three-quarters of an hour Miles looked at the portfolios of these men from around the Western world. The models had come from Holland and Italy, France, Australia, England and Germany, America, Brazil, Scotland, Ireland and Spain. There were none from Africa, Eastern Europe or the Far East. In Spring he'd seen an Indian but the model's mother was British, and he'd grown up with her outside London. Joe had three Japanese models on his books, tall guys who looked as Western as they could while still remaining Japanese. Miles hadn't been shown their books. At the end of his hour and a half visit to Mr Man, Miles felt he'd seen as broad a spectrum of models' faces as he was likely to see anywhere in the world. Joe Fujimoto had done his homework, and he knew it.

'So, my friend, what do you think? Pretty good guys?'

'They're great, Joe. I took some cards.'

Miles waved a few composites at Joe.

'That's all you taking? Come on!'

'I've got to go around the world yet, Joe.'

'Client know best! So, what's happening Thursday?'

'I'll let you know. It's probably going to be just a test. No fee!'

'No problem, man. I got some other very good guy you didn't see. They're in the show. You're coming, right?'

'What show?'

'You don't know about the big fashion show? Man! I have like thirty guys in it. It's at the Olympic stadium. Just here in Yoyogi. It's going on TV. Big show. You see maybe forty guys from my agency. Maybe more than one hundred model in whole show.'

Miles turned to Miki. 'Did you know about this?'

'No, *sumimasen*. Sorry.'

'Sorry's not good enough, Miki. I'm only here five days. You're supposed to know about things like this. I can't afford to just, just miss out on seeing a hundred models, can I?'

Joe would like the way he was talking to her.

'I am sorry. I will try.'

'Don't worry, man,' said Joe. He put an arm around Miles's shoulder. 'I have ticket for all bookers. I give you one. We can go together. You can meet here at seven, OK?'

'You're sure? Don't the bookers want the tickets?'

'Hey, man, don't worry. You're my new friend!'

13

It was something that Yuki would never have done; but then, Joe Fujimoto credited himself with more expansive talents. He was the guardian of his boys while they were in Japan, a big brother who liked to ingratiate himself by being bad. At his naughtiest, Joe would lead his clique of models (the favoured usually prating Californians or Frenchmen) into the seediest parts of Tokyo, up deep into Shinjuku and the tight vaginas of simpering Japanese girls. Now, tame by comparison, he was escorting Miles to a place to which agents were rarely welcome: backstage before a fashion show. A security guard in a jacket so small that it seemed to push his body fluid into his flushed, cherubic cheeks, signalled the direction Joe should take, advising him to follow the signs.

The show was in celebration of cotton. In America, they called it 'The Fabric of Our Lives', and celebrated it with two-minute, feel-good commercials of cotton-picking heroes and happy fathers back-lit by dusty sunsets of gold. In Tokyo they took it no less seriously. The show was being filmed for TV in the massive national stadium in Yoyogi Park, built to house an Olympic swimming pool. Appearing were various Japanese media stars, and more than eighty male and female models, Westerners all save for a lone six-foot Japanese man, Masahiro. He was one of a tiny group of Japanese models that worked well thanks to the Caucasian features of its members. In the same way that the most successful black models in the States had light skin and unthreatening blue eyes, so Masahiro and his friends were hired because they barely resembled the rest of their race.

Miles followed Joe through a warren of concrete tunnels.

159

On a balcony overlooking the changing area behind the stage, six male models were gathered and giggling. Joe slapped one on the back, and kept his hand on the model's neck. 'François, guy. How you doing?'

François didn't turn around. 'OK, Joe. Look here!'

François nodded at their spectacle. They were thirty feet up. Beneath them was the changing area for the models. Each model had a collapsible rail upon which hung the outfits he or she would be wearing on the catwalk. The men were divided from the women by a length of white fabric (cotton, of course) stretched taut between two poles. Looking from the balcony, the division meant nothing. As Joe and Miles joined them, the boys were ogling bare breasts and thighs and vocalising criticisms with their brash machismo.

A Cockney called Dave with a middle-weight boxer's frame pointed towards a forky Spanish girl struggling off balance with a pair of tights. Miles thought she was beautiful. She had a powerful nose and a dark, gypsy look. Her hair was thick and wavy and the colour of dark chocolate. It tumbled on to her shoulders.

Dave was less enthusiastic. 'That girl there,' he said, 'has got these tits like pancakes, right? But her nipples are rock hard. Like fucking horse pellets.'

'Like what?' said Joe.

'The things you feed horses with mate. They're like, what, one inch long, and really hard.' He laughed. 'You can get your teeth right round 'em. She sounded like a fucking 'orse when I did that, and all.'

Dave began to imitate an excited mare, then drew hard on his cigarette.

'You never had her,' said another, English also.

'Fucking did. Last week.'

'She'd never have you. She's married.'

'Is she? Fuck me.'

'No thanks, mate.'

'I think the guy's through here,' said Joe.

He and Miles moved towards the cigarette smoke and the noise. They entered soon a drab, rectangular, windowless room lit by institutional fluorescent, and filled with foldaway chairs and trestle tables. Models crowded the tables, babbling. They were gathered in groups defined by age and race and language and trendiness and sex and sexuality. But more than this, Miles could see how the models in each group tended to resemble one another.

The men seemed especially loyal to their cliques. The dark, brooding masculine men, all in T-shirts and sweats with their muscles on display and their cheeks glowing from the gym, were bunched away from the slimmer, more sophisticated guys whose high cheekbones and long faces were almost feminine in their appeal. Even those with short haircuts huddled away from those with long. It was very chicken and egg, this. Had their looks or their characters come first? After a while, Miles decided that the groups were evidence of nothing but simple narcissism. In this world, the models would say, I will judge you on your looks. You look just like me, and as I love myself, so I will love you too.

Joe said, 'There's Jeff. You like him, no? Let's go.'

Miles followed with canine obedience.

Jeff and the models were gazing into the small oval mirrors that stood in rows along the tables, and checking themselves out as they spoke. They were talking oranges, and water.

'Like I wonder sometimes if all the oranges are gonna like run out, man. Know what I mean?'

'I hear you, bro. It's like juice is all over. Airplanes, restaurants . . .'

'Yeah – look at McDonalds, Dennys, Burger Kings, Hiltons – you name it. They all got juice.'

'My uncle grows oranges in Florida.'

'Shit! Like that's gonna do it, right? Bruce's uncle saves the world! Who is he? Mr Tropicana?'

'No, but he grows a lot.'

'Probably they'll start using powdered shit soon.'

'D'ya hear that they invented powdered water?'

'Get outta here.'

'Swear to God. Powdered water.'

'So you mean they can fly it to Africa and places? Somalia and shit.'

'Guess so.'

'That's stupid, how d'ya make it?'

'Duh! It's like milk powder!'

'You need water for that, dipshit.'

'Well, I guess like you need less water or something.'

'Maybe they'll start using those rain machines, man. They make rain. They could ship those to Africa.'

'Maybe.'

Jeff noticed Miles, and stood. 'Hey, good to see you.'

'Likewise,' lied Miles.

'Take a pew, man. Take a pew.'

Miles sat and put his camera amid the rubbish on the table behind him. The table was covered with the usual paraphernalia of a model's mobile life. Upon it, black knapsacks had spilled note-pads and bandannas, Walkmans and bananas, tapes, tatty bestsellers, vitamins, backgammon sets, bottles and bottles of mineral water, make-up, Marlboros and magazines. Here as well, styrofoam cups were scattered around – crushed, torn at, branded with lipstick or half-filled as ashtrays with a grey soup of chewing-gum wrappers and bloated cigarette butts.

Jeff wanted to know from Miles what the story was for Thursday, how big the EDEN campaign was going to be, if it was true they were looking for a new face, if he should shave before the shoot because he was trying to sprout this goatee, if the big campaign would interrupt his contract and if he'd make it to Chicago for Christmas. So what if stupid people said Chicago was provincial? He loved it, always had.

Miles nodded and gave away what details he could, though Jeff didn't seem to listen for answers before asking the next question. Jeff was clearly excited. He seemed to be making plans already.

'Everything's in its early stages now,' said Miles. 'And there'll probably be about three of you on Thursday's shoot.'

Jeff was dismayed. He'd thought he was to be tested alone. 'Oh! Who?'

Miles was saved by an announcement from one of the organisers. The Japanese official was dwarfed by the models standing around him, so he stood on a chair and shouted. 'All models go change to first outfit. Any models need hair doing, do now. OK? I mean now. Make-up too. All other next door. And please do very very good. This is big show. Many people here. Big TV . . .'

'Let's go sit at front,' said Joe.

As Miles stood, he deliberately looked to his side to inspect his reflection in the mirror. And as he followed Joe through the models and towards the auditorium, Miles ran both hands back through his hair, and slightly, very slightly, sucked in his cheeks.

Twenty minutes on, it began. The show was as lavish as a Broadway production. The Olympic swimming pool had been covered by boards upon which a massive catwalk stretched out into the auditorium. TV cameras had been positioned neatly along its edge, and suspended also from the ceiling. Hundreds of lights, shining in bunches through differing coloured filters, were directed at the stage. Each side of the stage was a unit of twelve-foot-high speakers surrounding a large screen. Beside this, an array of coloured laser beams flashed high into the curved concrete roof of the stadium. The music echoed. Miles could feel the waves of sound pummelling his chest.

The show began with acrobatics. A troupe of Japanese gymnasts dressed in pink and orange and green, leapt and somersaulted and did bizarre things with and to their bodies amid the manufactured smoke. Suddenly the music stopped, the acrobats leapt to the ground, and pointed their arms towards the stage entrance.

The lights faded, and there was a planned silence before the music began its reverberating crescendo of suspense, film-score style. Trained over years, the audience knew to get excited. Instantly, the stage was flooded with brilliant white light as the first female model stepped on to the catwalk, and posed. The lasers ejaculated, the crowd was hushed, and

Miles watched as one by one they came, the squabbling teen-agers from backstage miraculously transformed into objects of desire.

Miles's eyes were particularly drawn to one girl who seemed to be walking with more assurance and grace than the rest. Surprised, he saw it was the Spanish girl – Pancake chest. Yet as he watched her advance down the catwalk his mind was far from the callous comments of before, for now, despite himself, he found himself quite in awe of her. That she knew how to use the catwalk was not surprising – most girls did. They were all walking with their hips and keeping their eyes focused and stopping at the end of the catwalk to peer around and pose and pivot and pose again before returning back to the top. That was standard, taught once, remembered always. But the Spanish girl was anything but standard. She seemed to have an aura that many of the others lacked. Now it no longer mattered to Miles that he knew how she and the others were backstage, in their agencies, in the clubs, living their lives. They were merely average people falling short of expectations. But up here on display they shone uncommonly. Up here they represented something beyond flesh and bones. This Spanish girl had been so ungainly then, as bare-breasted she'd tripped with one leg in her tights. Now she looked complete, as if this was the only place where she belonged. The catwalk was her courtroom, and the jury was on her side. She looked majestic and desirable and powerful because she was beautiful in a place where nothing more was required.

When she reached the end of the catwalk, she looked out and straight into Miles's eyes. He felt the blood burn in his face, and right then he knew he would have given himself to her, as a slave, as a lover, as anything she'd want him to be. Miles's eyes followed her back up the catwalk. She seemed to be making more of an effort now that the attention was on others. She'd spiced up her walk, was swinging her hips, moving her head, then stopping, just for a moment, so that some eyes would be drawn to this change in her pace. Then she was gone, and Miles watched with glazed eyes as the other girls shimmied by.

Thirty came and went. Then a change of music and lights and mood before the men. The first to appear was Thierry, a vulgar Frenchman with Spring whose book Miles had seen earlier that day. To the music of Mungo Jerry, Thierry swaggered at quite a speed, followed at five-second-intervals by a succession of men most of whose faces Miles now recognised.

Most, but not all.

There was one male model who Miles could not remember having seen. He was tall, with olive skin and an irreverent, appealing smile. He walked down the catwalk in a completely different manner from the others. The Spanish girl had been more glorious than the rest because she was more beautiful. With this man, it was not his beauty that set him apart, but his arrogance. It was making him the star of the show.

The other men were walking in the only way they knew how. Unable to celebrate their beauty as the women did, unable to mince or swivel, the men sauntered casually, ambled coolly, imitating Brando in *On the Waterfront* or Jesus on the Lake of Galilee. They walked as if nothing and nobody could touch them. It was all sex and confidence and manly strength. They came down the catwalk more like the minders of a president than the president himself. All but this one model. He was campaigning from start to finish. Fuck these clothes, his demeanour proclaimed, I'm here all for myself.

He didn't march steely-eyed, he walked, like a drunken man on a spring day who's just learnt of a large inheritance. Occasionally, he would stop to blow a kiss into the crowd, or he'd twirl in a full circle without breaking his movement forward, or else he'd do what most of the cool, tough men would never ever dare: he'd grin.

'Joe,' said Miles, excitedly, 'who's he? Do you know?'

'Of course, I know! He with my agency. From Brazil. His name is Fabio Nirao.'

*   *   *

The show was dragging on with too many models and outfits when Joe and Miles ducked backstage once more.

The scene was greatly changed. The dressers were working diligently now, handing the models their outfits to wear. If there was a quick change, the dressers, silent always, would have to keep their cool. In rehearsal, if there'd been one, a routine would have been worked out with the model. The dresser would take off one shirt from the model, then hand him another, buttoned, before undoing his belt for the trousers to be slipped off, along with the socks, then maybe she'd get a quick glimpse of a dangling cock as she knelt to roll on virgin socks and hitch up new trousers while the model looped a knotted tie over his head then tucked in the shirt while he stamped his foot into shoes and had his laces tied. A break in the chain – a mislaid sock, a belt not looped in the pants in advance, a shirt missing cuff-links, a pair of boots too narrow for his calves – and panic would set in. Other dressers would arrive to help, a spaghetti of fingers fumbling over the model. Then the cry would come from the entrance to the stage, the model's name relayed through the crowd like a bucket of water to fire. Often the model would arrive up the ramp, flustered and untidy for a last-minute comb from the attendant hairstylist and a fluff of powder from make-up before being counted, three-two-one GO, on to the stage and into the glare and the sea of eyes, eyes, eyes.

Now Miles could see the skill. Once on the catwalk, the models rarely betrayed the panic backstage. Neither did they take their backstage attitudes on to the runway. Waiting in order for their turn, the men walked a fine line between machismo and future employment. To care about hair and clothes and beauty was considered a sin by all but the gays and the Americans, so the real men made sure they cracked jokes about each other, ruffled up their hair, maybe dared to untuck a shirt to look more cool and in control. Only in the seconds before walking into the lights did they conform and agree with reluctance to go through with the performance, for the sake, you see mate, of the money.

Joe and Miles stayed backstage until the end of the show, when a cheer went up from the models, and the young Japanese dressers had their cheeks kissed and their hearts broken.

Miles waited for Joe on the street. There was to be a party in a nearby bar, and Miles wanted to go. Amid the swarm of black-haired heads surging from the auditorium, Miles was surprised to see a face he recognised. It was Yuki, and she almost smiled when she saw him. She came over.

'I talked to Chester's friend,' she said.

'Oh great. And?'

'He say you go there eleven tomorrow. OK?'

'Sounds great. Who is he?'

Yuki took a slip of paper from her bag and handed it to Miles. Upon it was written an address and a name. Miles was to meet a Spencer Kemble-Finch. The address – Number 1, Ichibancho, Chiyoda-ku. The location of the British Embassy.

'Does he work at the Embassy?'

Yuki shook her head vehemently. 'He is son of British Ambassador.'

'Really?' The idea of snaring a member of the élite excited Miles. 'And he's a model?'

Again, Yuki shook her head.

'But you think he could be?'

Yuki nodded, and murmured '*hng*.'

'Is he with you? With Spring?'

He hoped not. To find another Adam without an agency would be perfect. Yuki explained: 'Once he came in with Chester Hunt and I said no because he had no picture. So, I do not represent him.'

'Well, this is very kind of you, then, Yuki. Thanks.'

'*Do itashimasshitae.*' Don't mention it.

They were joined by Joe and a throng of models, male and female. Yuki made a quick excuse, and left.

'Talking with enemy!' said Joe.

'Don't worry, Joe. I won't be using a Spring model. I can promise you that.'

Joe smiled, said 'Good,' and the herd trotted off to the bar.

Designed by a Californian, furbished by an Italian and used by a race on top of the world, the Bar Beyond was the most extravagant drinking hole Miles had ever set foot in.

It was triangular in shape. The simple, heavy steel door opened in the centre of the shortest wall, opposite the point of the triangle. To the left, the bar stretched thirty feet or more. It was constructed of thick, greenish glass, swimming inside the hollow of which was a spectacular collection of brilliantly coloured tropical fish. The tank was lit within by strong white lights. Bright rays scattered and splashed coruscating across the surrounding walls.

The floor was slated, the roof glass, the walls raw concrete. Behind the bar, six clipped and uniformed barmen took supplies from bottles lined, as if art exhibits, along the glass shelves attached to the length of the wall. The eight shelves reached to within inches of the base of the gallery above.

There were two areas to sit. On the ground level, phallic, mushroom-shaped stools sprouted in front of the fish-tank bar. Jutting out from the facing wall were thick, rectangular granite slabs about four feet from the ground. They were supported at the end by a vertical plate of dented, blackened iron secured to the floor. Generic chrome and black leather bar stools surrounded these tables.

Up two curved and shining metal staircases, positioned one each side of the entrance, and held from the ceiling by steel suspension wires, was the balcony. Serviced by yet more tailored male waiters, it was only wide enough for a table and four chairs. Hanging out from all three walls, it was a perfect place from which to observe the scene below.

The tables were metal with legs that were insectile in shape: thick where they met the body of the table, then curved and tapering nervously to the floor. In the gallery, the chairs were stark and utilitarian, though they'd been padded for comfort. Dim, thin lights hung down like studio microphones towards the centre of each table. Even up in the gallery the light shimmered from the watery bar below.

On the lower level, in the tightest corner of the bar, there stood a vertical bank of television screens, eight in all, displaying not the American diet of football and music videos, but eight diverse images of underwater life. They had been programmed so that, at times, a manta ray would swim angelically through all eight screens, from top to bottom, and back up again.

That night, because the bar had been reserved for three hours for the party, a video of the Cotton Show delivered by bike before many of the guests had arrived, ran in the four middle screens.

From his table with the Mr Man models on the balcony, Miles had been watching out for the Spanish beauty. After an hour, and too many Jack Daniel's, Miles saw his opportunity, and hurried down the spiral staircase. The Spanish woman was alone at the bar. Miles approached her.

'Can I buy you a drink? Maybe?'

'They're free,' the woman replied, looking past his face and over his shoulder as she spoke.

'Right, so they are. Can I *order* you one then?'

'I already did that.'

'Right.' Miles smiled, though he didn't much feel like smiling. 'Just me then!'

He ordered another whiskey. The woman turned her back on the bar and rested her elbows upon it. She seemed to be searching in the throng for a friend. Close up now, Miles could see how enticing were her eyes, rich and brown under long, thick lashes. She'd painted a dark line around her slightly down-turned lips.

The barman gave the girl her drink. It looked like vodka or gin. She seemed about to move away.

'I saw you in the show,' Miles said quickly.

'Want a medal?'

She took a sip from her drink, removed the lime and threw the bright semicircle in her mouth, chewing it without wincing at the sourness. Still she did not look at Miles.

He persevered. 'I mean I noticed you. More than I noticed the others. That's, that's my job, to notice models. See, I'm scouting for . . .'

The girl turned to him and a faint grin turned the curve of her mouth. That's all you need with these people. thought Miles. Tell them your pockets are lined with gold and they'll give you all you desire.

The girl opened her luscious mouth. 'I'm married,' she said. Then, with a wave of her fingers, added 'Bye!'

Damn. The bitch! Of course, now Miles *really* wanted her. He felt his face turning red. If he tried to stop it, he knew it would only get worse. He longed for something witty to say.

The barman slid Miles's bourbon over the fishtank. Miles took a gulp. A male model, his bare shoulders incongruous here, tried to nudge his way through. Miles stood his ground. The girl hadn't moved away yet. Perhaps that was a good sign. He wasn't well practised at this. He drank some more.

Suddenly, he said, 'I'm not a breast man myself.'

The girl turned, a look of intense anger on her face.

'What did you say?'

She gave him an exaggerated blink.

'I . . . nothing.'

'No. What did you say?'

She was looking straight at him now. Miles downed his drink, winced and wiped away a tear. 'I said . . . I said that, I'm not . . .' He took a deep breath. 'I said I'm not the best man. At this.'

'No, you didn't.' She seemed to know. 'You know you didn't. You said "I'm not a breast man."'

Miles held up his empty glass, and shrugged his shoulders. 'Whiskey.' He pointed into his open mouth, and grunted 'Unh,' as if he'd bitten his tongue. 'Twists up your tongue!'

'Twists up your brain, more like.'

'Don't you think it untwists your brain. You know? Let's you, let's you . . .' he scratched his head, 'say things.'

She was silent. She took a long drink from her vodka. He

was sure it was vodka now. He could smell. She turned and put her glass on the bar.

'You . . .'

Oh Christ, thought Miles. I don't like her tone.

'You're like that fish there.'

Repressing a smile, the girl pointed towards a grotesque, muddy-brown fish about six inches long. It had a harvest of whiskers and a blunted, snub snout. With alarming stupidity it insisted on ramming its head into a barnacled rock in the tank. Ssshh-tomp, reverse, Ssshh-tomp, reverse, Ssshh-tomp!

'It's kind of ugly,' Miles said.

'Uh-huh.'

'It's kind of stupid too.'

'Uh-huh.'

'Persistent fucker, though.'

'Seems so.'

Then, as if on cue, a gloriously coloured fish, its fluorescent green body speckled with bright oranges and reds, darted by, and then somehow stopped dead before jetting up to the surface beneath their glasses. Miles took a chance. 'You remind me of this one here. It's got beautiful eyes.'

The Spanish girl peered into the tank. Then she turned to Miles, stuck two fingers into her open mouth and made a retching noise.' Sick, really. Sick!'

'It was a compliment,' whined Miles.

She looked down, and then spoke very quietly, so that Miles could only just hear what she'd said, which was, 'I preferred the comment about my tits.'

'You did?'

'At least that was honest. Wasn't it?'

'It just kind of slipped out. I, I didn't actually mean to say it.'

She took a handful of rice crackers and threw them in her mouth. She chewed noisily. 'You're not very good at this, you know?' she said, more conciliatory now. She leant on the bar, and focused on something deep down in the tank. 'Well,' Miles explained, 'I'm as good as married too.'

'I envy her!'

'Seriously. I wanted to talk to you because, well, I wanted to . . . talk to you. That doesn't mean I want to sleep with you. Necessarily.'

'Necessarily?'

'God, this is like some kind of trial. OK, the facts, Madam Judge. I saw you in the show. I thought you saw me. At least you looked at me. So when I saw you here I thought I'd say hello. I thought you might be interested to know that it's my job to find a female model for a cologne campaign who's going to be paid one million dollars. Maybe that's not enough for an audience with you. I don't know what else you want me to do. I could try standing on my head, I guess.'

She held up her hand. 'No, you're doing fine. Well, better!'

'Good. I'm Miles, by the way.'

'Jack,' she said, shaking his hand.

Her hand was surprisingly cold.

'Jack?'

'It's a long story.'

'It doesn't sound very Spanish.'

'How did you know I was Spanish?'

'I guessed,' he lied. 'Your complexion. Your accent. Though your English is perfect.'

'I live in London.'

'Oh.'

'With my husband.' She paused. 'What did you say you did? I can see you're not a model.'

'You can?' Miles ran his fingers through his hair and sounded disappointed. 'I'm, I'm scouting for a couple of models for a new cologne that *Weissmans* is bringing out.'

'Classy!'

'You'd be surprised. There's a competition. We're paying the guy six million dollars.'

'Jesus! You shouldn't be looking here,' she said. 'Go to Europe.'

'I am. I . . .'

Then, without warning, Miles was slapped so hard on his back that he fell forward, and spilled his drink. When he twisted his neck around, he saw Jeff Gifford.

'Hey! Party on, dude! I want you to meet my roommate. Fabio, here's the man responsible for my early retirement.'

Miles shook Fabio's wide hand. Fabio stood dressed in ripped jeans, a grey T, and biker boots. He had a cigarette in one hand, a girl in the other. He looked much like a young Marlon Brando, only more handsome. It was the attitude that was the same. Miles stood to judge Fabio's heigh better. Over six foot, thought Miles. That should do.

'I saw you in the show,' said Miles.

'That's his big chat-up line,' Jack interrupted.

Miles paid no attention. 'You were walking down that catwalk as if you owned it.'

Fabio shrugged his broad shoulders, and thrust out his thick bottom lip. 'There's nowhere you can be that isn't where you're meant to be.'

Miles looked quizzical.

'Beatles!' Jeff whispered into Miles's ear.

'Let's tequila,' said Fabio.

The model under Fabio's arm was whining. 'Not again, Fabby!' She kissed him. 'Let's go.'

'But life is very short, my sweet.'

'I think tequila's a great idea,' said Jack.

Jeff ordered. '*Sumimasen*. Five shots-u.'

They all drank, and sucked on their limes. After all the bourbon drunk with the boys on the balcony, Miles was beginning to see treble. Still, he joined them all in another as they revelled in their stupidity.

Jet-lagged, excited and drunk, Miles ordered yet one more round. Jack smiled at him, and it was worth every hangover he'd ever had. It made him feel bold. 'I think you're beautiful,' he slurred in Jack's direction. 'You want to have lunch with me tomorrow?'

To his amazement, she said yes, OK, if it was on him. She wrote her number on a napkin, and thrust it in his trouser pocket.

'Good,' said Miles.

He tried to say something else, but the words didn't come out, so instead he asked Jeff for a cigarette. When he lit the wrong end, the others laughed. Miles was beginning to feel too sick to join in. He belched, nervously, and then began to yawn. He was starting to feel sick. Another yawn, and a risky belch. Thankfully, Miles wasn't too drunk to know it was time to leave.

'It's been a long day,' he said. 'I'm going.'

'Get some sleep there, bro.' laughed Jeff. 'See you Thursday.'

On his way out, Miles turned back to Jack, and held his thumb to his ear and his little finger in front of his mouth in the shape of a phone receiver. 'Tomorrow,' he mouthed as he walked into someone. Jack nodded, Miles waved, and then he stumbled out.

He found a cab after a long walk during which he collided with two mopeds, stationary, an old woman, as good as stationary, and a letter box. It took a while to persuade a cab to stop. In the meantime, Miles had joined the other drunken men tripping and lurching their way to the last trains leaving from the bustling station at Shibuya. Under the flare of gigantic neons, steamy heaps of vomit had marked like beacons the trail to the trains. Miles had almost taken a train himself, almost joined these married Japanese workers in their routine of work, work, drink, vomit, work, and get to know the wife and kids at weekends, but on the platform he'd remembered where he was, and tripped back on to the street.

The cab only stopped for Miles when he remembered to hold up two fingers to the driver as a promise to pay twice the metered fare. It was a trick gleaned from the guidebook, and in the state Miles was in, fifty-five dollars didn't seem so much for a fifteen-minute ride back to his Akasaka home.

The light in his hotel bathroom was fitted with a dimmer switch. Miles thought he looked best with the bulb burning low. From his jacket pocket, he took a cigarette given him by Jeff. He lit it, filled a glass with water, and leant back on the towel rail. The spotless mirror reflected his upper body back to him, and he raised his glass in a toast. He drew deep on his cigarette, but, not really a smoker, he didn't inhale and when he opened his mouth the undiluted cloud obscured his face. He waved it away, turned a little to the side, ran his hand through his hair, and muttered, 'Yeah, yeah well I was going to be a model, sure, but . . . nah! Not my scene.'

Miles shook his head at his reflection. 'I had . . . other goals.' He let the cigarette hang from his mouth, and turned his head left and right in the soft light before sweeping his hair back over his ears, and winking at himself. 'Let's do lunch . . . right, call me! Well, time for bed. Want to come?'

Miles raised his eyebrows, and slurped down the water. He drank another glassful quickly before he twisted and hurled the cigarette towards the toilet bowl; a second baseman going for a double play. It missed hopelessly, thudded against the wall and fell smouldering on to the bathroom tiles. Miles bent down to pick it up, and as he did so, the vomit came in a crescendo of bilious heat, cool water followed by a hot splurge of stinging whiskey and tequila. It tried to escape through his nose, and he winced and retched again and cursed his stupidity as he clung to the cool polished toilet bowl and fell to his knees.

He knelt for God knows how long, dribbling and moaning like a baby and thanking the Japanese for their scrupulous hygiene. Then he stood and risked another glass of water before feeling his way, like a blind man, back to the sanctum of his wide, cool bed. Miles fell face down on the cover, and never made it beneath the sheets.

14

'*Irrasshimasae.*'

In a loud, squeaky voice, a purple-uniformed Japanese woman wearing a pill-box hat welcomed Miles into the Akasaka King elevator.

'Lobby,' he murmured. 'Please.'

She bowed towards the control panel, not towards Miles, and when they had plummeted too fast for his delicate stomach, she bowed again and announced in Japanese that they'd arrived. At least, that's what he thought she was saying, and not 'you look as if you're about to throw up again, you stupid bastard.'

In the hotel lobby, the staff were bowing at him and welcoming him to the new day. He wished they'd all quietly fuck off and stop staring. He knew quite well, thank you, that he'd looked better before.

The short journey in the thick Tokyo traffic took half an hour, and cost a small fortune, but Miles was just in time. An alert uniformed guard hopped from his hut as Miles stepped from the cab.

'I'm here to see Spencer Kemble-Finch.'

In broken English, the guard told Miles how to find the ambassador's residence. 'Look for Lolls-Loyce car,' was the last detail he gave.

The British Embassy compound was remarkably calm and spacious, set, as it was, in the heart of that teeming city. The houses stood upright and alone, like Britons, and to his left as he walked Miles saw a tennis court for the first time since his arrival in Japan. Birds were singing. Miles considered the value of this space alone in an area so close to the Imperial Palace. Typical England, he thought. Despite

177

its tenuous history in Japan, the country probably felt it deserved such voluminous surroundings. Stupid bastards still had this notion that the world respected them.

Around another corner, and Miles saw the Rolls parked in between the severe stone columns of the residence's porch. Miles nervously pressed the bell beneath the well-polished brass plate, and waited. Footsteps echoed across the stone floor within the hall, and the handsome door was opened by a gruff Japanese man in his mid-fifties. He was almost completely bald, and he had a round, gawping kind of face, such as that of a carp out of water. He gave Miles an unwelcoming, suspicious look, his bulbous eyes twisting wearily in their sockets as he gazed. He opened his mouth before any sound came out. 'Yes?'

Miles was about to reply when he heard a voice coming from behind the butler. 'That's OK, Tetsu. I think he's here to see me.'

A tall, athletically built man arrived after his own voice, and held out a hand. 'Are you Miles?'

'Yes.'

'How do you do? I'm Spencer. Come in.'

Miles recognised the absolute confidence and charm of the well-bred. That was the thing about the English – they possessed an air of superiority that was confirmed with every movement they made, every vowel they formed with their lips, every history-soaked vein in their skin. The butler sniffed and ambled away. Spencer shouted to his back. 'Be a good man and fetch us a couple of Kirins, would you Tetsu? We'll be in the living room.'

Miles studied his host as Spencer led him through the grand, pillared hallway of the ambassador's residence. He'd known what to expect. He'd had a mental picture of Spencer ever since he'd learnt of their meeting. He'd imagined a man tall and thin, with fair, straight hair pushed casually back, and roughly parted in the centre. He'd seen a pale face, with clear skin, a pointed, slightly upturned nose and rather feminine lips. He'd imagined Spencer would be wearing corduroy trousers, green, with heavy leather brogues and a double-cuffed shirt, maybe in light blue to match his eyes. His cardigan would have a leather patch on the right elbow, his teeth would not be perfect. He would smile often, and Miles would feel at ease. The image had remained so strong that Miles had never questioned it.

He was, then, a little surprised by the Englishman's appearance. Spencer had dark brown hair, straight and parted in the middle. His rich suntan exaggerated the whiteness of his teeth and eyes. Miles could tell at once that Spencer was a sportsman who kept his large frame trim through exercise. His forearms were thick and muscular. He had hazel eyes and fairly short, thick eyebrows. He used his smile to great effect, knowing, as he did, that it changed his entire aspect – his eyes narrowed softly, and deep dimples cut shadows into his healthy cheeks.

He wore a large, loose heavyweight rugby shirt, its sleeves different colours from the body, its collar white. In place of the imagined cords, Spencer wore faded sweat pants. No socks, no shoes, and large hairy toes. Spencer was unshaven when he met Miles, and his eyes were still puffy from sleep. Miles was becoming accustomed to meeting only people who took an absurd amount of care over their dress and appearance. Perhaps, wondered Miles, if Spencer had known the size of the EDEN contract, he'd have made more of an effort. Yet even dressed as he was, the man had an elegance and air of authority that Miles found curiously compelling.

Spencer led the way into a relatively small living room with French doors that opened on to an expanse of tended green lawn. It was all very English and cosy.

'I hope Tetsu wasn't rude. He likes to run rather a grand house, I'm afraid. Still, shouldn't complain. He does bloody well! Sort of taught himself how one runs an English house. He was a bloody marvel when the Royals came.' Spencer slumped into a chintz sofa, feet up. 'Can't say he bothered much when the PM was here, though. He didn't like the man. He can be a ghastly snob at times.'

'Your Prime Minister?'

'God, no. Tetsu. Doesn't like Americans much either. Sorry!'

'I'm half-English.'

'You are? Oh good. I'll have to tell him.'

They were silent, and Miles shifted in his chair, as if he wasn't sure how he should be sitting. Spencer was picking at the hard skin around his big toe.

'I told Tetsu to get us some beer. I didn't even ask you. Would you have preferred something else?'

'I'd better. I'm suffering a little from last night!'

'You should have a Coke. It's bloody marvellous. Coke and aspirin.'

Spencer lifted himself up and pressed a button that rang a bell in the kitchen. Tetsu emerged with the bottles and glasses on a silver tray. Spencer asked for the Coke, and sat back down with the bottle of beer.

'So, how's that reprobate Chester?'

'Chester?'

'I thought you two were friends. Chester Hunt.'

'No, not at all.'

Miles explained how Yuki had thought of Spencer when Chester's name had come up. Miles then told Spencer about the campaign, the model search, and, of course, the six million dollars. Would Spencer be interested?

'You are aware, I hope, that I'm not a model,' he said.

'Yeah. That's good news, in fact.'

'If I were to, and I don't know what you're thinking, but if I were to be a competitor, would that make me in some way obligated to the company?'

'To *Weissmans*? Oh no. Not unless you won, of course.'

'I'm not sure my father would be too pleased.'

'Is that a problem?'

'Well, he wants me to get a job. He has done ever since I left the army. I'm only just back from wind-surfing in Australia, you see. He doesn't think it's much of a life for a twenty-six-year-old.'

'He wouldn't complain if you made six million bucks.'

'No. No, I suppose he wouldn't.'

Spencer didn't seem too sure.

'We're having a test shoot tomorrow,' Miles told him. 'Could you at least make it to that?'

'I suppose so.'

Miles hid a smile. It always amused him to see how hard the English tried to hide their emotions. Spencer was behaving now as if the prospect of earning six million dollars came his way every day of the week.

'You know, there are lots of guys who'd leap at this chance,' said Miles, a little patronisingly.

'Sorry! I am grateful that you're asking me. It's a bit odd, that's all. I never thought of myself as the modelling type.'

'This whole campaign is a little different. The six finalists are going to be high profile, so the more, you know, presentable you are, the better. I don't want to choose just regular models.'

'You'd prefer an ambassador's son.'

'That kind of thing, yeah. But still I think you'd look good for this, whoever you were.'

Spencer looked uncomfortable with the praise. Miles remembered having heard once that the two things the English are taught not to take from strangers are sweets and compliments. Spencer seemed no exception.

'OK. Well, I've got your number,' said Miles. 'I guess my assistant, Miki, will call you later with the details for tomorrow.'

Before Miles left, they chatted a while about England, and Miles's family there. Miles asked Spencer how he knew Chester Hunt.

'He and my sister had a . . . thing.'

'A thing?'

'They used to fuck a lot,' he explained. 'All day in fact. She's swanning around Paris now. You should call her.'

Suddenly, Miles remembered Jack. He asked if he could use the phone.

'Go ahead. Keep it local, would you? We don't want the British taxpayers getting upset.'

Miles and Jack arranged to meet at one thirty in a sushi bar close to her home. Miles took copious instructions, and hung up a little flushed. Spencer guessed why. 'Ah, but have you seen the filly in daylight?'

Miles replied with a grin. 'Not yet. But I don't expect to be disappointed there!'

He wasn't. Jack arrived looking as if she'd just stepped off a Paris runway. True, she was wearing Black Frys shades to hide the shadow beneath her eyes – out all night in a club called Barrocco, she'd told Miles on the phone – but she looked immaculate otherwise. She wore a cream silk shirt and a suede waistcoat beneath her Irish tweed jacket. A printed silk scarf around her neck kept out the cold.

'You look great,' Miles said.

'I look like my grandmother,' Jack replied.

The restaurant served raw fish on rice, sushi, and raw fish without rice, sashimi, and not a lot else. Some soup, perhaps, and some fermented beans, but when Miles tasted that particular Japanese delicacy he thought it shared the texture and taste of the bacterial grunge found wedged in the toe of a well-worn summer sneaker.

No question, Jack was overdressed for this joint. The locals seemed to be using it as a fast-food café, and a few eyebrows were raised as she and Miles found places around the bar. For his part, Miles was feeling an almost childish excitement as they prepared to eat. Not only was he having lunch with the woman who'd laid siege on his soul the previous night, he was doing so in a restaurant the like of which he'd never laid eyes upon before.

It was fast food with a difference. The diners sat on stools around an exposed area within which five chefs prepared the fish with staggering speed and precision. There were no menus. A conveyor belt snaked its way along the edge of the table carrying the fish on a ceaseless electronic river of temptation. The chefs stocked the belt with a mouth-watering assortment of fish: tuna, octopus, roe, hake, whitefish, scallop, shrimp, yellowtail, the roe of sea-urchin, on and on. Whenever a type of fish ran short, it was replaced by one of the chefs, sometimes at the behest of a grumbling client who'd waited too long for his favourite dish, like a passenger impatient for a suitcase on an airport's carousel.

Miles watched the dexterous movements of the chefs. In seconds, they'd take a lump of cooked rice, mould it into a tiny brick, add some wasabi – the bright green Japanese horseradish that gives the sushi its kick – and then cover it with a strip of glistening raw fish, newly cut from one of the hefty slabs bought fresh that morning from Tskiji fish market. Once made, the sushi was arranged in the centre of a plate to be put on the belt.

Miles and Jack both helped themselves. Jack showed Miles how to flip the sushi over into the soy sauce without saturating the rice, and poured him a cup of tea from the spouts that curved up in front of the conveyor belt.

'Fish seems to be our thing,' said Miles.

She nodded, chewing. 'You know, they usually serve sushi in Bar Beyond. They cut it up on top of the fish tank. Don't you think that's cruel?'

'Not really. Fish only have five-second memories.'

'So that's worse! Every five seconds they have to live through death for the first time. They never get the chance to get used to it.'

Jack snatched another plate from the belt; scallop.

'It's hard to know what to choose,' said Miles.

'Just go for whatever looks good. It's usually worth it.'

Miles glanced at her, and smiled at the irony Jack was missing. They ate and drank tea, and were quiet a while, more like friends than strangers. Jack took another plate of the dark, red tuna.

'Mmm, Mmmm, Mmmmm,' she hummed, her mouth full. 'This is absolutely incredible. Try it.'

There didn't seem to be any tuna on its way, so Jack stripped her fish from the rice, (it'll taste better) and fed it to him. Miles leant towards her and opened his mouth. He closed his lips greedily around the smooth wood of the chopsticks. The fish felt warm and tender against his tongue. It was soft and succulent as ripened avocado. Miles wanted to savour it. He pressed the tuna against the roof of his mouth, and ran his tongue over the fish's fleshy smoothness. Jack smiled at Miles's enjoyment. The tuna had a delicate taste, faintly but pleasantly metallic, and only slightly suggestive of the sea from which it had so recently come.

The restaurant itself was filled with an odd mixture of Japanese men and women, all of whom would occasionally stare at the foreigners in their midst. Whether they were suspicious or amused, Miles couldn't tell. A couple of school children, dressed in blue and white uniforms and with their leather satchels strapped on to their backs, came in for three plates each. Their faces were round and ruddy and cheerful. When they smiled, their eyes seemed to close perfectly shut. To reach the counter, they had to lift their elbows oddly high, like chickens flapping clipped wings. Beside them sat two builders, their hair cut short and spiked. They ate fast, and smiled often at shared jokes. Three baby-faced businessmen in shiny, Italian designer suits came in with identical maroon briefcases, sat and ate without words. They smoked together after the meal and looked remarkably similar to the schoolboys with their satchels. A woman in traditional silk wore a high wig and had fourteen plates stacked in front of her. She ate with her body bent over the food, her expression pained but determined, as if this was a penance for a private crime.

Suddenly, Miles said: 'I'm going to suggest you for the EDEN campaign.'

He reminded her of how impressive she'd seemed on the catwalk. Jack tried to explain.

'Tokyo is nothing, Miles. Nobody important is watching, the money is so-so, everything is worse than in Europe and the States, but still there's this, this feeling you get when you come on to the catwalk. I don't know if you've ever been watched like that. You're under the lights, the cameras are flashing, and suddenly you don't know anything except what you're doing right that minute.'

Jack put her palms up against her temples, blinkering her eyes. 'It's like you start to believe that you *really are* beautiful, you know? Because if you don't, you're going to feel stupid up there, and the audience will notice. So every step you take you feel more – I don't know how to say it – more grand, more beautiful. I don't even remember seeing you because there was nothing coming into my head, it's all going out, out. This is a problem for models because after the show is finished, you don't always remember that it's over. See?'

Jack smiled at him. She clenched her fists and shook them in frustration. 'Aaaaah! I wish I was talking in my Spanish. It is hard to explain. See, once you have this feeling that everyone is loving you, and looking at you, then you don't forget it. Sometimes in Tokyo I walk along the streets in the same way that I walk on the catwalk, and I think everyone is looking. It makes me feel good. It's really like a drug. Especially when you start to believe that your looks are all that you have. It's not easy to get off the drug.'

'Come on, Jack! You know there's much more to you than that.'

She touched his hand. 'I think I like you, Miles. You're not so sure of yourself.'

'Meaning?'

'I don't think you realise that you are handsome.'

He blushed. 'So,' he said. 'Let's go.'

They counted the plates in front of them, and paid for that many. The cashier didn't doubt their honesty.

As Miles had a couple of hours to kill before his scheduled meeting with Miki, he accompanied Jack to the *Comme Des Garçons* shop in Aoyama. A friend of hers, she said, could get her big discounts.

Miles was in awe of the clothes so neatly displayed in the austere head store of the world's greatest designer. He'd never been able to afford designer clothes, so he'd never paid much attention to them, but as he stood now in a navy-blue suit with white cotton stitching he wondered if he'd ever been dressed so well. He thought the style suited him. 'I think I need a haircut,' he said, studying his hair when he stood before the mirror to look at the suit.

When, laden, they left half an hour later, Miles resolved

never to let Poppy know how much his suit and shirts had cost.

In the models' apartment the phone was ringing.

'*Yo, Moshi-Mosh*!'

'Jeff?'

'Hey, Joe. What's happening, brother?'

'I got your details for tomorrow.'

Jeff let go his penis and picked up a pen. 'Shoot.'

'Seven a.m., Roppongi crossing.'

'Oh, man! You're kidding me! Seven? For a test?'

'For six million dollar, Jeff.'

'I guess so!'

'Tell Fabio too.'

'What?'

'Tell Fabio. He's going with you.'

'He wasn't at the casting! Why's Fabio coming?'

'Miles like him.'

'Shit man! Shit. I should'n' of introduced him. Shit! That was stupid.'

'Miles saw Fabio in the show.'

'Still, I should'n' of done that. Who else is going?'

'Some guy called Spencer, or something. He's not model.'

'Hey, dude! Like I'm scared.' Jeff, flaccid now, laughed and zipped up. 'Like some bozo off the street's really going get this campaign.'

'Don't be late, then.'

'I'm never late, Joey-Jo-Jo. Hey, man, when we going to do the Soaphouse again?'

'If you get this job, we'll go every night 'til Christmas.'

'Now you're talking, man. Now you're talking.'

They hung up. Jeff was really pissed that Fabio was coming on the shoot. Fabio always got it too easy – women, money, happiness. All three came to him too goddamn easy.

Hungry, Jeff fixed himself another bowl of Kinokuniya Muesli. He was worried now. He wondered whether it had been a mistake to buy that $1000 video camera from Akihabara. No, damn it! He could afford it. He *still* felt good.

It was all in his stars. Miles liked him. Miles had even gone and sat with him before the show. Yeah, no problem.

Jeff began to build mountains in his mind with the money. Six million dollars, man. How many Harleys was that? Shit! He wanted a Jag, a black XJS. Move to LA with his Jag, and six mil. Get out of this shit, do some acting, get a place on the beach. Some big fucking pad with a pool and shit. Get some Cali. babe with big tits, and blow-job lips.

He felt a stirring beneath his shorts again.

Maybe he'd *forget* to tell Fabio about the shoot. But, no. Joe would never believe him. Rather, he'd just have to whip Fabio's Brazilian ass in front of the camera. Prove who was better. Jeff felt right for this job. Better than he'd felt for years. It was in his stars. He just knew it!

He was going to be rich.

15

At seven fifteen the following morning, Miles slunk down in his minibus seat and thought, So this is glamour?

The minibus was inching its way out of Tokyo on an elevated highway in dense traffic under low November clouds. Miles thought he'd never seen such a grey, depressing place as this. Lives were being lived in the boxed apartments that bordered these roads. It would all fall apart soon, he'd heard. Not the roads, but the system that kept them jammed for eight hours a day while workers lived crowded by the kerbs. By Western standards, these workers were wealthy. Here in Japan they ploughed their savings back into bulging industries, and continued to live badly for the good of a nation. It couldn't last for long. The guilt was seeping away from greed, and the me generation was growing up fast.

Miki interrupted his thoughts with the loud rustle of a 7–11 bag. 'Sandwich?'

'Why not.'

Miki handed Miles a tiny, cold, crustless egg sandwich suffocated under layers of plastic.

'Are there any rice balls in there, Miki?' Jeff called out from the back.

Jeff was given his triangular rice ball. Fish wrapped in rice wrapped in seaweed wrapped in cellophane.

Behind Jeff and Spencer in the back of the bus, Fabio was sleeping, and the photographer's assistant was staring out of the window, his Walkman emitting a repetitive din that sounded like glass being smashed in the distance.

The bus was designed for the Japanese, so there wasn't much room for the Westerner's legs. All the Japanese but Miki were soundly sleeping. The photographer in the front, the hairstylist in the middle, Miki's assistant rolled mouse-like by Fabio in a corner in the back.

Miki herself was as well-dressed and alert as ever. Perhaps, thought Miles, she's not human at all. Rather, she's a new Japanese invention. A living Barbie for the nineties. Android Barbie, with brain cells and a bedtime of ten. Miss Barbie Style and Efficiency, she could be called. Real hair, real Asian eyelids, lifelike emotions, available in a variety of designs. Perhaps if Miles pricked her, she'd fuse and rebel, rip off her Hermès scarf, bare her breasts, shoot up some drugs, chill out.

Miles drank a hot, sweet milky coffee out of a can bought steaming from a machine at the gas station. Jeff searched through his bag and found a tape and leant across to the driver, who was playing Schubert.

'Thanks man.'

The driver slid Jeff's tape into the unit, and the bus continued to the calming sound of Jim Morrison giving his all as Jeff Gifford beat out 'The Best of the Doors' with his fingers on the imitation leather of the van's front seat.

They arrived at ten and parked in a field. Those who hadn't slept had managed to slump into a kind of comatose boredom kept uncomfortable by the squashing of limbs into the cramped spaces. They climbed out of the van, stretched, groaned, and looked for places to pee.

'Where's this great mountain?' Miles enquired.

Miki pointed beyond the wooded field in front that swept up into the mist in front of them. 'Behind cloud.'

'You're joking. We came all this way for some grass?'

Miki laughed. Miles felt like hitting her. He didn't quite know why he'd agreed to this. If Kristina hadn't insisted on a professional shoot, Miles would have been satisfied with a few snapshots in his hotel bedroom. Yet here they all were, in the middle of Japan, halfway up a mountain in the clouds. 'What's wrong with the park in Tokyo? That's green!'

'Photographer like it here,' Miki replied, pointing at the photographer who, far from being concerned about the fog, was helping his assistant to erect a metal rail from which he was about to hang a hessian backdrop. Miles was incredulous.

'They're shooting against an old sack! They're not even going to use the field? This is crazy. They could have used my hotel room. That's got brown walls for God's sake.'

'I go ask.'

'It's kind of late now, Miki.'

Miki skipped off to talk to Naomichi-San, the photographer. She returned looking satisfied. 'He say the light is very, very beautiful here.'

'Beautiful? It's about to piss with rain.'

'I'm sorry, Miles-San.'

'It's not your fault, Miki. But perhaps you could get things moving a little. It's like we're here on a picnic.'

'You are hungry?' Miki asked enthusiastically.

'No. Wanting to get moving.'

'Oh! We do hair first.'

Katoh, the hairstylist, had set up a chair in the field, and was giving Jeff an intense head massage.

Miles looked in the van. Spencer was struggling with something stubborn in his nostril, and reading Tom Clancy. Fabio hadn't woken up yet. The driver was attempting to construct an origami flower from the flat seaweed coating of his rice ball. He raised an eyebrow at Miles when Miles looked in. Miles thought he'd try the photographer.

'Naomichi-San. Everything OK here?'

'OK.'

The photographer was a man in his early thirties. He had long hair tied in a ponytail at the back, crooked teeth crammed into a small mouth, and long, feminine fingers. He wore black. Black Doc Martens, black Levis, black-T, black cardigan, black Yohji Yamamoto jacket, tiny round black sunglasses, and, of course, black hair. He looked at Miles, sucked in the air through his teeth, almost said something, then laughed and waved with his hand in front of his face.

'Clouds,' said Miles, pointing up and putting on a glum face.

Naomichi smiled some more and waved his hand in front of his face, as if indicating a bad smell.

'Maybe – you, – take –, sunglasses off?' Miles suggested.

Naomichi nodded and smiled warmly, and then turned to help the assistant who was losing his balance as one leg of the heavy backdrop stand began to sink into the mud. Giving up, Miles joined the hairstylist who had begun to work on Jeff's hair.

'How many shots we got, you know?' asked Jeff.

'You'll have to ask Miki. We're going to do whatever we need. I don't know too much about it.'

'Man, I've been to this place like five times with Naomichi. Isn't that right, Katoh?'

Katoh, a young and enthusiastic Japanese man who'd spent a year in a salon in London, laughed. 'Right!' he said, vigorously brushing Jeff's thick blond hair.

Somehow, it took another hour and a half to prepare it all. Fabio had been woken to have his hair done, and was flirting with Miki's diminutive assistant, Keiko. Even in the cold, he was shirtless, tweaking at the hairs around his nipples in some private joke. Keiko was laughing as she pressed the clothes on an ironing board at the back of the van. The bizarre contraption she used was hissing and gurgling like a horny octopus, but it got the job done, and all the clothes were made perfectly creaseless.

While Fabio had his hair done, Spencer quizzed Jeff about what they'd have to do. Jeff was a willing teacher. 'There's like a few basic rules, OK? Don't look right into the camera unless the photographer wants you to. Look like to the side somewhere. And always focus on something. Like this.'

Jeff stood facing Spencer, but his face was angled a fraction to the left. He set his eyes fast on some distant object. Instantly, his whole face had assumed a different character. The muscles around his lips twitched slightly as he flexed his mouth into a smirk. There was a new tautness to his cheeks, as if they knew they were being looked at, as if his face had taken on a character of its own.

He broke the pose, turned. 'OK, you got that? You got

to be conscious of like even what the hairs in your nose are doing, right, and then once you've gotten like a mental feel of how your face is, you got to remember feeling, like *exactly* how your muscles were. Then you can do different things but keep coming back to that one look. It's easy.'

Jeff broke into a deliberate, model's laugh – face vibrant, eyes smiling, teeth glinting, head back. Miles thought Jeff did this well. He looked happy. It was in the language of his body too. Jeff's shoulders had relaxed when he laughed.

'Then there's like different ways to stand, right? Hey Miki,' he shouted, 'what we wearing first?'

'Suit.'

'OK, suits man. They're real easy. I like to put one hand in the pants' pocket, then you twist your body away from the camera, and turn your head back towards the lens.'

'Do I look at the camera?'

'Whatever. Way I like to do suits is to be laid-back, you know? I mean 'cos if you're wearing a fucking suit already you don't need to be real formal. You just got to play around out there. Gotta be zany and crazy for the Japs . . . Hey, Miki. I'm *Baka-ne*?' Aren't I the crazy one? he was asking. He pulled a face, as he would have done to amuse a five-year-old-child.

Miles had seen how the models often treated the Japanese in this way. Grown people resorting to the humour of young children when attempts at adult communication failed. The Japanese didn't seem to mind.

Miki had the models change into their suits. They were going to shoot an in-store, point-of-purchase advertisement for which the models would usually have been paid $1500 or more. Today, because this was a trial run for a six-million-dollar job, they were working for free.

Miki had had to cut the shirtsleeves near the shoulder to make them hang far enough to be visible beyond the jacket sleeves, but apart from this the clothes fitted well. Dressed and shoeless, the models were gathered together in front of the light brown backdrop. They stood in a row staring at the photographer. Spencer looked older and more content now he was dressed in a charcoal pinstripe suit. He could have been an exalted surgeon, or a lawyer. Fabio resembled a crooked Latin American politician, and Jeff, well Jeff had suddenly assumed the appearance of a trainee vacuum-cleaner salesman. Out of his jeans and boots, and with his wide, pumped-up shoulders squeezed tight into the jacket of a suit, Jeff's neck seemed shrunken and his head looked as if it no longer belonged to the body beneath. Miles had noticed this phenomenon before while working in *Weissmans*. Some people looked stupid in suits. It was as simple as that.

Still, Miles wasn't after a Suit Man for Adam. He hadn't forgotten Saul's words on the subject. *I'm not gonna shoot a cologne like EDEN in a fucking hotel ballroom, am I?*, he'd said. So long as Jeff stayed in the swamp, he was doing just fine.

To take the shot, Naomichi, the photographer, arranged the models in a semicircle. Miles wandered across the road to survey the scene.

They were in a verdant valley, reminiscent to Miles of Vermont. The grass was lush and thick and here the hills sloped gently, at the base of the mountain above. He sat on a small rock. The air was delicate, the calm broken only by the repeated whir of the camera motor. When Miles breathed in, it was as if the thin oxygen was percolated at once through his lungs into all the cells of his body. He felt high. What a week it had been! Only seven days ago he'd been leaving for Miami, so unsure of what he'd achieve. Now there was a fashion shoot taking place because of him. He was responsible for this, for eight people working beneath Mount Fuji on a cool November afternoon.

Later, in the Tokyo *Weissmans* in Shibuya, thousands would pass these photographs without a second glance. Perhaps a few would stop. Maybe a young girl would notice one shot and wish to meet the model because she liked the look of his smile as the sublime Mount Fuji light fell slanting across his chiselled face.

Miles wandered back to the van, catching his reflection in the van window. He ran his fingers through his hair.

'You want I cut it?' said Katoh.

'You think it needs cutting?'

'Sure. I give you great cut.'

'OK. Why not? Thanks.'

When Katoh was finished, Miles inspected his new look. His face seemed longer and more angular now that some length and thickness had been taken from the hair at the back and sides. It had been styled long on the top, cut for a centre parting for the first time since Miles was ten. Now it seemed as if Miles cared about his hair. Jeff, who cared about little else, was impressed.

'Looks great, man. I guess you never tried modelling?'

'No. I've been acting in New York, though.'

'Yeah? That's cool. I want to act in LA.'

Before they left, Miles had Naomichi-San take some shots of Jeff, Spencer and Fabio without their shirts on. Bare-topped and goose-bumped in the November cold, the three were asked to copy Bruce Weber poses for the camera while Miles shot video to send to New York.

As he looked on, Miles congratulated himself. Any one of the models could make a good Adam. They compared well with Fernando. All three had impressive bodies. Jeff sported the chunkiest – a slab of meat of which he was inordinately proud. While Miki had been worrying about the cold and Fabio had been navigating Keiko's hands to the knot beneath the skin of his bare shoulders, Jeff had been sweating chin-ups on the branch of a nearby tree. Only when he'd felt sufficiently pumped had he joined the others for the shot.

Yet there was something that disturbed Miles about Jeff. Maybe he was too perfect. While Spencer and Fabio posed as men confident of their allure, Jeff stood as a bodybuilder proud of his achievement. There was hardly a bone out of place, not a skin cell that wasn't glowing nor a lustrous hair growing where it shouldn't. True enough in the polaroid that Naomichi had peeled for Miles, Jeff's body seemed superb. Yet wasn't he exactly the kind of model Miles had always despised? Jeff could hardly be anything *but* a model. A movie star, perhaps, or a local TV station's weatherman, or maybe, once he'd aged sufficiently, a minor politician, but if Jeff walked into a house dressed in a plumber's overalls, he wouldn't be trusted. His perfection made others suspicious and sneering. Men looking like Jeff only wore plumber's overalls in order to remove them to the monotonous beat of a porn-movie soundtrack.

Miles was more impressed with Spencer. He'd expected coyness, but Spencer seemed remarkably at ease showing off his pectorals. Miles hadn't guessed why, but the truth was that the Englishman was more comfortable celebrating his own beauty than he had been advertising *Weissmans* ugliness. Spencer Kemble-Finch was unequivocally proud of the man he was, just so long as he wasn't seen to be wearing the synthetic clothes favoured by another class of man.

Half-naked now, he stood rigid but handsome, his hands cupped behind his back. Spencer reminded Miles of his own maternal grandfather, a gifted sportsman in the twenties. Photographs of him hung in the living room of Miles's parents' home. Miles recognised a shared stance that he thought peculiarly English. Theirs was the assuredness that came from a place in England's long and proud history. Spencer was happy and proud to be British. A rugger-playing, ex-army son of a distinguished servant of Her Majesty the Queen, he wasn't about to pout like the American nor slouch like the Brazilian.

But Fabio's slouch was in no way lazy. He possessed a compelling vitality. It was plain to see that Fabio celebrated life with an energy that was rare to find. He certainly loved being bare-chested, it being halfway to his favourite state of dress. And he moved with a fluidity that came from a lack of tension within. Fabio did not suffer from the tautness of self-doubt. As Miles framed Fabio's hairless chest in the video's view-finder, he thought how much Fabio was like Fernando Padrillas. They both shared smooth, olive-toned skin and upper bodies that were naturally heavy and muscular. And in both, self-confidence bred magnetism, not arrogance. Yet Fabio could boast a sensitivity to his features that was missing in Fernando. Miles wondered whether it came from

Fabio's thick, sensuous lips. Further traces of femininity could be found in his gentle eyes and long eyelashes, but he was neither less attractive nor masculine for having them. He was in all respects a man – in his movements, in his strength, in the way he talked and walked and laughed.

Soon, the shoot was finished, and the crew joined the brooding driver back in the van. They set off for the city. Once again, the Japanese fell asleep almost immediately.

Less nervous now, even Miki nodded off, as if human.

Jeff had sat himself next to Miles, and was lying about all the clients in the States who were desperate to use him on his return. Ralph Lauren had been asking about him, he said. And Banana Republic. He'd have to decide who'd be good for him.

Miles, tired, didn't care. 'It's been a long day, hasn't it?' he hinted.

'This is nothing. The Japs make you work like dogs.'

Jeff then proceeded to tell Miles about the rigours of a male model's life in Japan. Only the other day, he said, he'd had to get up at four thirty to catch the subway to the train to the airport to Osaka. Once there, he'd discovered he was modelling work overalls for electricians and chefs. Fifty in one day, an incessant routine of studio poses for a group of people none of whom could speak English. At four they'd finished, and he'd left in a cab to the plane to the train to the subway. He'd got home at ten p.m., he said.

Miles looked at Jeff and wondered why it was that the Japanese thought that this young man from Chicago was better than any of their race at providing an image to sell white aprons to chefs hidden from the public's view over steaming pots of soggy white rice.

16

Mexican, they'd decided. Spencer knew of one, Chimi-changas, close to the Akasaka King, and they agreed to meet there at nine. None of the Japanese had wanted to join them, so for dinner it was to be Miles, Spencer, Jeff, Fabio and any women they could persuade to come along.

Before leaving the hotel, Miles Fed-Exed the day's video to Kristina along with his opinions on each of the three models. He promised to continue the search that night.

Chimichangas was a short walk from the hotel. Everything within it seemed to have been imported from Mexico except the waiters. But even they, in their wide sombreros and with their bushy moustaches, looked uncannily like the real thing. They blended in well. Miles had stepped from a noisy Japanese street into a serene Mexican world, with terracotta tiles on the floor and natural red and orange stucco walls. Images of Mexican revolutionaries and presidents jostled for space on the walls beside striped authentic tapestries. The tables were made of an uneven grainy wood, the tall chipped sideboards painted a distinctive faded pale blue.

Miles had persuaded Jack to join the party, Spencer was there, and Joe Fujimoto had appeared with Fabio and Jeff. They'd brought with them a tall, blonde, French model called Anne, and an American, Tiffany. There was a tension to Tiffany's face that made it seem as if she was on the verge of tears. She had long jet-black hair, and narrow features. She was wearing an old, shiny brown leather coat that she refused to take off. If she was beautiful, it was because she was vulnerable.

Jack told Miles she liked his new haircut. It made him feel good. 'But now you look like a model,' she added.

That made him feel even better. Tiffany sat beside Miles.
'How old d'ya think I am?'
'I don't know. Nineteen, twenty.'
'Some think I'm even older.'
'Do they?'
'But I'm just sixteen now. Last Monday.'
'Happy Birthday last Monday, then.'
'Thanks.'
Tiffany raised her bottle of Corona, and drank.
'Originally I'm from Dallas, but I moved. Dallas is so like, you know, smalltown that I just went and packed my things and moved up north and now I'm living in Seattle. Have you been there Mike?'
'It's Miles. And no, I haven't.'
'It's really great except for the rain which can be a bummer but there's like this energy in the city now with the music and all, and my boyfriend is a bass guitarist and I'm so totally in love, like I had no clue at all it was possible to be in love like this 'cos I'd only been out with guys in Texas before. I tell ya I cried for days and days when I came here because he is the, *the* most incredible guy I ever met. He's a guitarist but he's more than that, I mean he's a true artist, you know, I mean when he plays metal he gets so into it with the chords and the music and all that he's screaming and crying out loud when he's playing it's incredible to watch. My mum's not happy because he's forty-three now but he's like a kid even though he's so mature. It's hard to explain.'
Tiffany took a breath.
'Kevin – that's his name – was like one of the first guys in the whole Seattle scene. I mean his band was there before Nirvana and he says Kurt Cobain's like a complete asshole but I think that's because Kevin's totally against drugs. He hardly does any because he was like so into Jim Morrisson and drugs completely screwed that guy up. I don't know if you saw the movie of *The Doors* but I think that Jim Morrisson if he'd lived, would've been maybe the greatest artist of the twentieth century. Seriously. His poetry is so beautiful it makes you cry, like really, really cry tears because he talks

the music of the soul. That's one of Kevin's expressions. Kevin's a poet too. I can't wait to see him again. He said he wanted an open relationship with me being away for so long, but I'm going to trust him. Do you think I should? . . . I'm sorry, I forgot your name.'

'Me? Oh, Miles.'

'Well, you think I should trust him?'

'Who?'

'Kevin.'

'Yes.'

'Why?'

'Er, he's a poet.'

'Damn right he is.'

Tiffany suddenly became glassy-eyed. 'But I'm gonna leave him if he fucks around.'

They ate their Mexican food the way Mexican food should be eaten – with their brains addled on alcohol. They'd downed eight beers and four pitchers of frozen margaritas by the time the food arrived. Everyone but Jack, who like the good model she was, was having a salad, had forgotten what they'd ordered, but since it was all the same food – beef, beans, flour, sour cream, and avocado – mashed up in different ways in order to add length to the menu, it didn't much matter. Tiffany was ravenous, she'd said, which was a relief because she couldn't talk with her mouth full. Joe was soon drunk and had begun to hiccup. Spencer and Jack were getting on famously, talking about Fulham in London, and flirting without shame. Miles felt curiously jealous, as he had done when he'd heard about Sandy's boyfriend in Miami.

Jeff was trying to get Miles to tell him if he'd been chosen for the competition, and Fabio was touching Anne underneath the table.

'To where do we go later?' asked Anne.

'Stupid question,' said Fabio, planting a thick kiss on Anne's lips. They both smiled, knowingly.

Jesus, thought Miles. He makes it look so easy. Is that all you do? Just kiss and say it? *'Don't be stupid you're coming home with me tonight?'* Wasn't Fabio right? Wasn't what he said what everyone wanted to hear? Let's quit the bullshit and head straight for the bed, or the kitchen, or the living-room floor, or even the back of the cab if we really can't wait? Who needs reserve? Who needs to feel guilty about being – alive?

Joe disturbed Miles's thoughts. 'When we go to club, you need this.'

Joe took a Mr Man composite from his case. It belonged to a model called Tony G. who, in his headshot photograph, looked uncannily similar to Miles.

'Why?'

'To go to clubs,' said Fabio. 'You get in free with composite.'

'Do they know this guy?'

'No, no,' slurred Joe. 'He left two year ago.'

The cheque arrived, and was handed to Joe. Joe pointed to Miles. No one else paid any attention. Mentally, Miles converted it to dollars. Eight people, $535 dollars, without a tip. In Benny's Burritos in New York, it would have cost $150. But what could Miles do? No one was thinking twice about paying, so he handed over his card, and prayed that Kristina would be kind.

The waiter returned and Miles signed. No one thanked him.

'OK, guys,' said Joe. 'Let's Roppongi.'

Roppongi was a neighbourhood in Tokyo that stayed open all night. One visit and the tourist threw away any misconceptions he might have had about the Japanese as a race. Unless, of course, he came expecting to find a happy, fun-loving, loud, drunken group of people. At night they crowded the sidewalks of Roppongi. The main street was given over to pleasure, lit as an amusement arcade by neons from bars and clubs. It was to Roppongi that the *gaijin*, the outside people, flocked to party with the Japanese. And it was to Roppongi, and a club called Fantasia, that Miles was taken then.

The club was behind an unlit black door down a dark side street. Opposite the entrance, a model was lying drunk and curled in his overcoat. A girl was beside him, smoking.

'Is he OK?' Miles asked.

'Sure,' she said. 'It's only Dave.'

Jeff laughed, and tapped a foot against Dave's leg.

'Stop lying in the gutter stinking of piss, bloke.' There was a grunt from the prostrate figure. 'He's from London,' added Jeff, as if that was explanation enough.

Upon entering Fantasia all, except Joe, were given tickets for food and drink. This was one of the ways models fed themselves in Japan. Tired of noodles, unable to cook, they'd eat greasy chicken wings, pizza and ice cream in the clubs, courtesy of the club owners. The logic was that free food was an easy way to tempt models, and that models were an easy way to tempt Japanese clubbers.

Fantasia was crowded with models, and a few Japanese. The natives were mainly sitting at tables in the club's mirrored alcoves. At most of the tables a man sat resting his arms either side of him on the back of the curved, red seats. The men had red faces and grey shiny suits, loosened ties and younger women. They were ignored by the Western models. The models weren't allowed to use drink tickets if they sat at the tables, so this was where the clubs made their money, charging exorbitant sums for bottles to be brought.

Joe Fujimoto had decided to take a table, and ordered champagne all round. On the way in Jeff had found some friends by the bar and was telling them about EDEN. Fabio and Anne had moved on to the dance floor, and were wrapped in each other's arms, dancing slowly to the Shamen's frenetic song 'Ebeneezer Goode'. Jack, Spencer, Miles, Joe and Tiffany sat at the table.

'Good Tokyo Man,' said Joe, lifting his glass in a toast towards Miles. Then Joe leant back, lit a cigarette, and within an instant he too had adopted the gormless manner and blank expression of the other Alcove Lords in the club. Miles realised then that every one of these men was stultifyingly drunk. Like victims of shock, they were existing in their own worlds. They could do nothing but sit and smile and attempt to make sense of the world of the sober. Their arms were up on the seats for support, cigarettes were held limply, burning slowly down to their filters.

In most respects, Fantasia was an unremarkable place, with a small wooden dance floor, red seats, mirrors and a disco ball. Its one distinctive feature was that it displayed not only music videos on the screens in every corner, but sometimes scenes from within the club itself. Two cameras, one each end of the room, recorded the play of the clubbers. It was a model's paradise, the reason for the club's great success. In London, the camera would have been focused on the most absurd. In Tokyo, it sought the best dancers, the slickest clothes, the gorgeous among the beautiful.

Miles enjoyed the show on the screens. He'd never been much of a clubber himself, and the screens made it easy to judge others without being judged himself. In fact, most of the people in the club seemed to be watching the screens instead of participating themselves, as if acknowledging the 'look don't touch' ethos of the new decade.

Tiffany didn't agree. As 'Pearl Jam' spread from the speakers she sprang to her feet. She stood by the table, her body swaying with the music. 'Man, I love this song. Want to dance, Mick?'

'I'm Miles.'

'You want to?'

He hesitated. She looked as if she might cry. He said, 'Why not?'

Tiffany jumped onto the dance floor. By the time Miles reached her, she seemed to have forgotten he was coming. She was dancing in front of the mirror, throwing her body from side to side, her head always moving in the opposite direction to her hips. A male model moved beside her, he too looking in the mirror as he danced. Miles began to jig behind Tiffany, like Gene Pitney, but she ignored him so he shuffled his way in between her and the mirror, and tried to incorporate his wave into his dance. 'Hi!'

'Love this song, man,' said Tiffany, beginning an almost epileptic series of convulsions. A space was clearing around them now, as if they were finalists in a fifties high school dance. Only here, dancers were moving away because of the danger from Tiffany's boots. Suddenly, she grabbed Miles's shoulders and began to rub herself on to him. Tiffany was still wearing her long leather coat. and as she bent her knees to gyrate down Miles's body, her coat rode up her thighs revealing her bare legs. Desperately, Miles was trying to move in time with her, but Tiffany was so unpredictable that whenever Miles felt he was loosening up into her groove she'd begin something else. It was as if she was dancing to a different song in her head. After a couple of horrendous minutes, he gave up. 'I'm going back.'

'Don't you love this song?'

At the table, Spencer and Jack could hardly breathe from laughing. 'We enjoyed the show,' said Spencer pointing up at the screen which still showed Tiffany dancing. 'I think you need a glass of bubbly.'

'I think you need lessons,' said Jack.

Spencer thought this very funny. He touched Jack's hand as he laughed.

'You try it,' said Miles.

'Want to?' Spencer asked Jack.

As they stood to dance, Miles said 'I meant with Tiffany,' but they ignored him.

Miles sat. 'Shit!'

'Happy Tokyo Man,' repeated Joe, raising his glass.

'Right!'

Fabio swaggered up to the table with Anne. He had a double whiskey in his hand. 'Get on down,' he laughed.

Jeff was quick behind. He didn't want for Fabio and Miles to become too friendly. Not that he was worried. Fabio had been his usual arrogant self all day. Jeff was sure that Miles liked him more.

'Is there any champagne left there?' Jeff asked.

Miles lifted the bottle out of the ice bucket. It was empty. Jeff nudged Joe. 'Hey, Joe, Joe, man.'

'Uh?'

'Drinks-wa, Dude. The fizzy shit, man.'

'OK.'

Joe waved his arm in the air and the waiter arrived with a full bottle of Taittinger.

Tiffany, appearing as if from nowhere, swooped.

'Yeah!'

In a second she'd climbed on to the table with the bottle and was drinking it while dancing for the crowds.

'Go for it girl,' shouted Jeff.

Miles heard a few other voices, American mainly, from the crowd. The camera moved on to Tiffany, and the performance flickered on to all screens. There was, however, one angle the cameras weren't getting. The angle that the inebriated Joe Fujimoto desired, so half-leaning, and half falling forward, he tried to peep up Tiffany's long, leather coat.

She noticed. 'Hey asshole!'

Tiffany lifted the champagne bottle and brought it hard down on to the top of Joe's head. He slumped on to the table.

The screens switched back to the music video.

'You kill him!' screamed Anne.

'I didn't hit him hard,' protested Tiffany.

She jumped down, landing on Jeff's foot. Miles picked up Joe's head and slapped his cheeks. Joe didn't respond. He looked white and lifeless.

It was Spencer who took control. He kicked away the table and checked to see that Joe's tongue was where it should be. He felt his pulse. He felt for breath. 'The man's fine. What happened? Did he pass out?'

'Tiffany hit him with the bottle.'

'Bloody child! Bring me some water.'

A bottle was handed from the table beside them, and Spencer poured it over Joe's head. Joe opened his eyes.

'Bloody fool drank too much,' said Spencer. 'That's all. Fujimoto-san. *O-genki desu ka?*' Are you OK?

The crowd had seen the blow on the screens and were gathering around the table. Those who'd seen what had happened were exaggerating details for those who hadn't. Someone had seen Joe's hand up her dress. Someone else had heard that Joe and Tiffany were lovers. Here was a story to be told in every Japanese studio and agency and location for weeks, months, maybe years to come. And Tiffany was the temporary starlet.

'Anyone know where the man lives?' Spencer asked.

'Yeah. In Hiroo.'

'All right. I'll take him home. Jeff, you come with me and show me the way. Jack, do you need a lift?'

Miles willed her to say no. She didn't.

Outside, Spencer managed to find a cab. He gave directions to the driver in Japanese.

Miles said he'd contact them all before he left on Saturday morning. The four remaining watched the cab go. Fabio and Anne, Miles and Tiffany.

'Well,' said Miles. 'How do you top that?'

'With a little help from your friends!' said Fabio, squeezing Anne. He then held out a hand to Miles. 'We are going. I hope maybe I see you again.'

'You're going just like that?'

Fabio nodded.

'OK. Thanks anyway, Fabio. You looked good today. We'll . . . we'll let you know about it as soon as we can.'

'It's nothing to get hung about.'

Anne kissed Miles on both cheeks, and, with a glance towards Tiffany, winked at him. As they walked away, Fabio turned around and, with a laugh, said, 'Good luck, man.'

Miles turned to Tiffany. 'Where do you live?'

She was silent, but her bottom lip had begun to quiver faintly.

'Are you all right?'

Suddenly, standing there on a bright and busy sidewalk, Tiffany began to howl with tears. She flung her arms around Miles and pressed her head into his neck. Her nose was wet beneath his ear.

'What's wrong?' he whispered.

She didn't answer. Her lanky frame shook as she coughed tears into the cosy nest between Miles's neck and shoulder. His arms around her, Miles patted the warm leather of her coat. 'Why don't we walk back to my hotel room, and I'll get you some tea or something. OK? Come on, it's freezing out here.'

Tiffany swallowed and looked up at him. Already her thick, black eyeliner had streaked down her face, and in the harsh light she looked sickly and lost. Miles was surprised by the sudden compassion he felt for her. He could see that she longed for just this, a shoulder to cry upon. Miles put an arm around her, and together they walked without speaking. For once he didn't care what the people thought as they stared. Tiffany's howls began to recede into the occasional gurgling sob and before many minutes they were inside Miles's pleasant hotel room. Tiffany wiped at her eyes.

'The bathroom's through there. Why don't you take off your coat?' She sniffed and shook her head and dived into the bathroom. 'I'll get some tea, all right?' Miles shouted through the closed door. Tiffany whimpered in agreement. Miles kicked off his shoes and sat on the bed. He rang for the tea. Tiffany emerged.

'Better?'

'Yeah.'

Tiffany did look much better. She'd washed her face and combed back her hair and stopped crying. She looked younger without the stern lines of her black make-up.

'Get comfortable. Are you sure you don't want to take that coat off?'

Tiffany looked down and rubbed at her eye. 'Do you got a robe or something?'

Miles collected a thick white robe from the back of the bathroom door. He held it out to Tiffany. She turned away from him, and let the coat flop to the carpet. She'd been wearing nothing underneath it but the tiniest black bra and panties. From the back, her body looked fragile. Her skin was pale, apparently thin, punctuated with moles. Miles felt the first unwelcome stirrings of lust. He sat back on the bed. Tiffany sat in the armchair. She sighed, and it sounded as if she was releasing the accumulated tension of weeks.

'Do you have any spliff?' she asked.

'No, sorry.'

'You don't think I hurt him do you?'

'Joe? He probably won't even remember.'

'Yes he will. Everyone's going to talk about it. You can't do anything here without everybody talking about it. I hate it.'

'It was his fault.'

'He won't think like that. I've probably screwed everything up now. And things were just picking up for me.'

Noiselessly, like snow on snow, Tiffany began to cry again. But now she wanted to talk. She spoke through incessant sniffles, breaking sentences to swallow or lick her upper lip or blow her nose or wipe at her cheek with the palm of her hand.

'It's like . . . you know I wish I hadn't come to Japan. Fucking Joe came to Seattle on some stupid shoot or scout or something, I don't know, and I was working waitressing in this bar . . . and, and he was talking to me all like how I was going make all this money out here and shit and be a big star, and all, and, and he seemed like such a nice guy. I mean in Texas I'd always been real bullied at school and stuff . . . I mean just names, but like scrawny and skinny and No Tits Tiffany and even my mum always said I was like real ugly because I didn't have big tits or nothing, you know? And, and . . . well, then I met my boyfriend Kevin but he's a fucking asshole drug-taking bastard and I thought I'd get away from it all if I was . . . here, you know . . . like really prove something to them all, and, and make some money so I could like do what I wanted, go to New York or something and then and then when I get here and Joe's all like . . . oh, yes you can do this and you can do that and you look like Tania Fern and all these other trendy models and then I was thinking that he really meant it, you know, like he could do that and it's just not . . . it's just not been like that . . .'

The sobs came stronger now, but after a while Tiffany blew her nose and carried on. 'Like it's not my fault. It's his. I mean, I've been here like five weeks now and I've only been doing these stupid fucking, fucking magazine jobs that . . . that don't pay any money and these stupid photographers go out and buy Italian *Vogue* and American *Elle* and things and they say do this, do that, like I'm supposed to be Kristen McMenemy or someone, you know? But then they never got the guts to use me for the advertising jobs, and Joe's saying he's not gonna give me my guarantee unless I do more work.'

'He has to, doesn't he?'

'Maybe, but he fucks you over and make you pay for all these things in the apartment and composites and taxes and visas and all these things that how was I supposed to know about? He says it always comes out of the guarantee. And then there's this girl, Juana, and she's nice but she's working every day and it makes me feel like so ugly when they don't want to use me for the pictures like it's worse than not modelling at all to be here and be like away from home and still . . . still get no work. Like every day we drive around and see clients and shit and usually they look at my book and they look at me and then they . . . pick one of the other girls. I didn't even get to do the big Cotton Show like everyone else. And now Joe's talking about sending me to Osaka, and I don't want to go there, no way.'

A knock on the door. A muffled voice. 'Loom service.'

Miles took the tray and tipped the waiter. He offered a cup to Tiffany.

'Thanks.'

She picked at the crest on the robe, and then looked about her. 'It's a nice room this.'

'Yeah, it's good. Sugar?'

'Mm, four. Make 'em heaped, would ya?'

'Four?'

'Trying to put on some weight. Joe says I'm too skinny. Like you got all these girls killing themselves – throwing up and shit – to lose weight and here's me trying to put it on.' She laughed a little, and Miles smiled. 'I wanted to hit that fucker Joe for the longest time.' Tiffany laughed harder, sniffing as she did. 'I bet he sends me back home now. I'd be glad. Take a holiday, something. See my dog. I got the cutest little dog.'

'What kind?'

'Yorkshire terrier. I call him Crunchy 'cos he's always

crunching his teeth on something or other.' She laughed.
'They're from England originally.'

'Yes. I know.'

'You got a TV?'

'Yes, in that cabinet.'

'With movies?'

'I think so.'

'Can we watch one?'

'Sure. If there's something on.'

'They got the porn movies here but it's all fuzzy over the pubic hairs. D'ya see that yet?'

'No.'

'Well they do. Fucking hypocrites. They all sit on the subway and read these nasty comics with violent rapes and virgins and little girls – real bad sex, but then they don't even allow them to show any pubic hair. It's weird.'

Miles, who'd been looking at the hotel movie guide, said 'They're showing *Wayne's World* in ten minutes.'

'They are? Oh, great. Let's watch that.'

Miles programmed the channel. 'Why don't you come up here on the bed?'

They made a bank of pillows and turned off the lights and watched the movie, and Tiffany laughed as if she'd never cried. Or as if she'd never laughed. Miles strongly believed in the balance of life. For every smile, a frown, for every low, a high. And if you don't reach the extremes, then you haven't learnt how to live.

When the movie ended, he asked, 'Do you want to sleep here?'

Tiffany didn't reply, but picked at a button on the sleeve of her leather coat.

'It's a big bed,' he said. 'Just sleep. There's even a whole hotel washbag you can have. Toothbrush and everything.'

'It's kind of hard to get a cab now,' she said, softly.

'Decision made then. You want to use the bathroom?'

'No, you go ahead.'

Miles washed and undressed and returned in his boxer shorts to find Tiffany curled up with the light off on her side of the bed. Miles switched out the bathroom light and climbed in beside her. He lay straight and still and wondered whether Jack had gone home with Spencer. He wasn't sure if he wished Jack was here beside him now.

Tiffany spoke without moving. He imagined her eyes open. 'You wanna lie spoons?'

'Um, OK.'

She reached out with her thin arm and pulled him and gripped his hand. She tucked Miles's arm up between her small breasts. Miles kept his distance, but she shuffled her hips back until his knees were bent right into hers and their bodies were touching from chest to toe. She liked this, to be wrapped in him, to feel the warmth of another. Miles's body was firm. And he had strong hands. She wondered if he could feel the beat of her heart through his palm.

Tiffany's body was thin and bony and her hair smelled of smoke but her skin felt soft and good next to his. Miles bit his inside lip as he felt himself harden in his shorts. He lay still and silent and hoped she wouldn't feel his erection angled against her backside.

'What's that doing?' she said, after a while.

He heard a smile.

'Saying hello, I guess. Sorry!'

'That's OK.' She felt for him with a her hand, and squeezed him once.' It wouldn't have felt right if you didn't get one of those,' she said. 'Makes me feel nice.'

'I might have been gay,' he said.

'I knew you weren't, silly.' They were quiet for a minute or two. 'Is it allright if we, you know, sleep?'

'Of course it is,' Miles replied, and almost at once he felt his head heavy on the pillow as, at a little past four thirty on the morning of Friday, November 13, he relaxed and began to drift to sleep.

17

A phone was ringing. Miles groaned. He kept being woken by phones ringing too early. He wished he'd taken it off the hook. He tried to ignore it but curiosity triumphed.

'Hello?'

'Hey, it's me.'

Poppy!

'Hi.'

'Don't sound too happy!'

'You woke me.'

'Maybe I worked it out wrong. What's the time there?'

'I don't know. Hang on . . . it's eleven.'

'Why are you still in bed then?'

'Late night.'

'Who with?'

'People.'

'Girl people?'

'All kinds of people.'

'Are you alone now?'

'Of course.'

'Promise me.'

'Poppy! I promise.'

'Say, *If I'm not alone I hope I die in a plane crash.*'

'No.'

'Why not?'

'Because.'

'Because you've got someone there.'

'No, because I don't like saying things like that.'

'You always do that to me.'

'I don't mind *you* saying things like that.'

'Thanks. Tell me you love me then.'

'Mmm. I do.'

'Say it out loud.'

'I love you.'

'Say it five times.'

'I love you. I love you. I love you. I love you.'

'That was only four.'

'I love you. That's five.'

'I got your letter. Thanks. It was great.'

'Good.'

'I'd send you one but you're never in one place long enough.'

'No.'

Tiffany climbed out of bed and headed towards the bathroom. Miles put a finger to his mouth. Tiffany nodded, and collided with the bathroom door. It clonked shut.

'What was that?' asked Poppy.

'Just me.'

'Oh. So. Are you having a good time?'

'It's OK.'

'I saw you in the *Herald*.'

'Oh.'

She imitated his grunt, 'Oh.'

Miles tried: 'What time is it in New York?'

'Nine p.m. So what's tomorrow looking like?'

'I haven't opened the curtains yet.'

'What's Japan like?'

'Nice.'

'Oh great. Now I know. Listen, why don't you call me sometime when you're awake. We're wasting our phone bill.'

'Mmm.'

'Love you.'

Silly voice time.

'Me loves you too,' he said.

'That's better.'

'Bye, then.'

'Bye.'

Neither one hung up.

'This is stupid,' she said.

'OK. One, two, three. Bye.'

'Bye.'

More silence.

'Real bye this time.'

'OK. Real bye.'

'Bye.'

Miles hung up.

'Finished?' asked Tiffany from the bathroom.

'Yeah,' said Miles.

Tiffany came back wearing the bathrobe and holding her hands to her face. 'Don't look at me, don't look at me, don't look at me.'

'Why?'

'I look like shit.'

'Who cares?'

'Me. And so will the clients. I've got to get to my castings.'

'Let's get some breakfast,' said Miles.

Too late for breakfast in the room, they had what the Japanese call Hot Kohi in a coffee shop in Roppongi. In the daylight it's an untidy, ugly place. They passed the spot where Tiffany had stood crying. It seemed an age ago. A fantasy, almost.

When they parted, Miles told Tiffany not to worry about Joe. He said he'd have a word with him, sort him out, put him right, that sort of thing. Miles felt like a big brother. Tiffany kissed him, and she said he'd been great, and, awkwardly, they wished each other good luck.

'Have a nice life,' she said, before turning and leaving in her long brown coat. He smiled.

It was his last day in Tokyo. He didn't have much to do. Spencer had invited him to the embassy for a game of tennis, but he didn't feel like it.

Back in the hotel room, Miles called and explained.

'Well, I'm not sure I'm up to it, either,' said Spencer.

'How was Joe?'

'A little sore, but fine.'

'Did you go home straight after?'

'Jeff did, thank God. Jack and I went for a drink in Shibuya.'

'To Bar Beyond?'

'Yes. How did you know?'

'Wild guess.'

'Jack told me I reminded her of one of the fish. Ow!'

'Spencer?'

'Sorry, Jack just pinched me. Ow, get off. Get off!'

'Oh, she's there is she? Could you tell her . . . tell her hi.'

Spencer did so.' She says 'hi' back.'

'Right. I'll . . . then . . . we'll be in contact soon.'

'You're jetting off to Paris, are you?'

'Yep.'

'Let me give you my sister's number.'

Miles took Georgina Kemble-Finch's number, and said goodbye to Spencer. He wondered if they'd ever meet again. Suddenly he thought how he'd hate it if he was responsible for Spencer earning six million dollars.

Miles had only half a day left in Tokyo. In the next hour he had to meet a couple of journalists covering the search in Japan. The rest of the day he spent as a tourist. He rode the subway and was impressed by its cleanliness and punctuality. He took an elevator to the top of the Tokyo tower, and once up there wondered why he'd bothered to get a better view of such an ugly city. He watched rows of grown men and women playing Pachinko, a mindless, vertical pinball game. He went shopping in Ginza and ate sushi once more for his lunch, bought from a shop that opened onto the street. The assistant neatly laid out his six pieces in a wooden box and then wrapped the box for him. Miles unwrapped it in front of the Meiji shrine in Yoyogi Park, and felt he was experiencing Japan.

Later, in Shibuya, he bought himself a grey suit from Agnes B, and a shirt and top from Yohji Yamamoto. Miles was beginning to feel so much more comfortable in designer clothes. He felt it was important for him to look his best, even if the suit did cost as much as his hard-earned monthly salary.

* * *

Joe had insisted ('You won't regret it. You and me. No stupid model girl'), so Miles had said yes. They were going to a Soaphouse.

On his way through the hotel lobby, Miles was handed a fax from Kristina in New York. It was her response to the video. She'd made her choice between the models.

Two names out of the three.

Miles found in his diary the telephone numbers for the models' apartment, and for the British Embassy. He decided to call as soon as he could. After all, he thought, it would be too cruel to keep the guys waiting for the news.

The following morning Miki saw Miles off with a gift-wrapped present and a handshake and a giggly squeal when he gave her a peck on the cheek. Waving at the gate, Miles was surprised by the depth of his sadness. He'd anticipated Japan to be a harsh and hectic country, yet for the most part he'd revelled in its joys, and already looked forward to his return.

Of course, he was leaving on a high. After a Yakitori dinner in a Shinjuku back street crowded with tiny, smoke-filled barbecues, Joe had treated Miles to the promised session in a Soaphouse. Miles's three 'attendants' had lathered his entire body, finding about him erogenous zones that had never featured before. Miles wondered what the blissful, mind-bending torture would have done to his fantasies. Where now would he imagine tongues? And how would Poppy take to licking the back of his knee? He'd never imagined his first experience with prostitutes (however high-class) would take him to such heights of sexual pleasure.

In the 747, the memory made him erect. His hormones were on overdrive. He thought how greedy they were. Once stirred up they grew teeth and nibbled away at sexual restraint as if demented Pacmen. Miles would think he was doing well, hide a while, focus on mortality, read, pinch himself, but they'd always get him in the end with electric assaults on his crotch. Now they were making Miles wish Alice was serving on the flight. Having been dumped by Kristina in Economy class, Miles was smarting from the lack of attention paid him by the cabin crew. Not one of the stewardesses had given him a second glance, and 'Ice with that?' was the closest any had come to affection. Oh, a frisky steward had winked at Miles, but none of the women had shown interest.

Miles thought the movie might cheer him a little. It was a slick tale about fire-fighters, starring a couple of big names, and a mass of special effects. But watching it on the plane's tiny screen, the image broken by heads, it was about as much fun as if Miles had been treated to a live methylated spirits-and-matchbox reconstruction of *The Towering Inferno*. Usually he could sit through any tripe for hours.

Now, surprisingly, Miles turned away from the movie and closed his eyes in the hope he might grab some sleep as the plane roared monotonously back west towards Milan, and a whole new continent to search.

Jeff Gifford's Tokyo apartment smelt of cabbage and cigarettes.

'Yo bro Fab-ee-o, what ya cooking?'

Jeff slammed the door behind him and stole a stick of celery.

'Vegetable with the noodle soup. You want?'

'Nah. Got to take a shower, then I'm going out with that Bibi bitch from Denmark. D'she call?'

'No. Joe called. Before, ten minutes.'

'What's he want?'

With the celery cigar-like in his mouth, Jeff peeled off his sweaty tank top and looked at his reflection in the window. Then he bent and touched the ground between his toes with the tip of the celery before crunching some more.

'Maybe he wants to come out on a double date. With Tiffany.' Fabio didn't laugh at the joke. 'Hey dude, smile! You got a problem? Are you lonely? Missing Mummy?'

Jeff tickled Fabio under the chin.

'Joe heard from *Weissmans*,' Fabio said, evenly.

'Oh, shit! So that's the problem. Well at least you can root for me, bro. When is it? It'll be cool being in New York at Christmas, even if I don't win.'

'That's why Joe call. You cannot win. They want only me and the English guy going.'

Jeff rubbed his top across his forehead, and took another bottle of water from out of the fridge. He grinned. 'You're fucking kidding me. I know you, asshole. You haven't heard nothing. They wouldn'a had time yet anyway. Clients never decide like that. Anyway, Miles liked me.'

'Call Joe. He tells you.'

'I'm not going to call him. I'm not going to play your stupid games.'

Jeff took off his cross-trainers and threw one at a beer can sitting on top of the TV. It missed. His sweat-pants he hurled towards his bed. 'OK, I'm gonna call him. But only to prove that you're a lying asshole, man. I know it's not true.'

In their apartment there was a free-standing payphone, painted once in psychedelic colours by a gay Swedish model. It swallowed ten-yen pieces. The models had found a way to make it regurgitate them too. Jeff stabbed a broken knife into the coin slot, angled the phone above his head, and shook. The money showered on him. He dialled Joe at the agency.

Fabio chopped the carrots into thick chunks and added them to the stock. Then the potato. The noodles would go in later.

He heard Jeff hang up.

'I told you!' Fabio said, as kindly as he could.

He looked across at Jeff who was sitting almost naked by the phone, a hand still on the receiver.

'Jeff?'

'I know what you're gonna say, Fabio. Don't bother.'

'I am going to say "sorry".'

'Yeah right! Bet it hurts you real bad.'

Jeff had his back to Fabio now and was bending down by his bed, rummaging through the clothes on the floor. 'Where's my towel, Fabio? What d'ya do with my fucking towel?'

'I didn't see it.'

'You're always using my things, man.'

'I didn't see it.'

'Like you drank all that beer I bought.'

'I get some more.'

'Right. Next month, asshole.'

'Hey, be cool.'

'What'd ya fucking do?' Jeff screamed. 'Suck his fucking cock? Did you fucking swallow for him?'

Fabio came out of the kitchen and pushed Jeff hard up against the wall, his hands on Jeff's shoulders. 'I didn't do anything. OK? Grow up! Try to see it my way!'

Jeff lifted his arms up fast and pushed Fabio away. He swung out a punch, and it caught Fabio in the neck. Fabio hit back. His fist glanced across Jeff's face, below the eye. As Jeff put a finger to his face to check for blood, Fabio grabbed Jeff's shoulders and threw him hard to the side and on to the floor by the bed. He didn't want to fight; not over this.

'It's not my fault about it. OK?' said Fabio. 'OK?' He returned to cooking his soup. 'There's no time for fussing and fighting, my friend. We can work it out.'

Jeff lay on the floor. His face was throbbing. He laid a cool hand over his face, and closed his eyes.

Why Fabio? he wondered. Why? Why? Why? Why? Why? Of all people. My roommate. What does he have that I don't? And why was I so stupid as to introduce them in the bar. Stupid, stupid, stupid. I hate this place! I hate modelling and I hate this place . . .

Jeff brought a hand to the tenderness around his eye. If it turned black, he knew he'd lose even more jobs. Fuck Fabio! Fuck him! Why did it always go his way?

In the bathroom, Jeff inspected his eye in the mirror. It wasn't too bad, just a little red beneath the eye. Jeff kept on staring at himself in the glass, as if by staring deep into his own reflection he'd discover something he hadn't known before. And as he stared his eyes welled with tears and he began to hate what he saw. He wasn't any different from the rest. He wasn't good-looking. He wasn't going to win anything. Every time it happened like this. Every goddamn time. The clients liked him, and he'd get excited and then they'd pick someone else, some lazy, lucky, cock-sucking prick like Fabio Nirao.

Jeff let his head fall forward onto the mirror. With clenched fist, he began to beat the glass. 'Fuck them all, man. Fuck them all. It's not fair. It's just not fucking FAIR.'

The mirror cracked. Jeff wiped at his nose. The crack dissected the reflection of his face. He turned away, stripped off his underwear, and climbed into the shower. He twisted the fierce spray on to his face, and the water mixed with his fresh tears, and then the tears became angry sobs and his body shook and the strength spluttered from him until he let his knees bend and he fell sitting in the tub with the water beating mercilessly down on the back of his bowed and aching head.

In New York City, in a Greek diner on Lexington Avenue and 64th Street, Kristina von Koeler watched her man chomp ravenously into a bloody, half-pound burger. Despite giving into Steve's filthy choice of restaurant, Kristina was in a particularly good mood. Miles Jensen was playing into her hands, and he didn't even know it. Even amid the greasy smoke of Aristotle's, Kristina could smell the money. She was that close. Three million dollars, three million dollars, three, million, dollars!

'Strange, but I almost feel sorry for him,' she said.

Steve Barefoot swallowed a mouthful of burger. Kristina could see it travel down his gullet. He looked up. 'Who? That Jeff what-his-name guy? Nah, fuck him.'

'Oh, he's fucked all right. But if he's feeling sorry for himself now, just wait until he sees your face on those EDEN posters. He is going to lose his mind.' She laughed. 'He'll probably come to New York and kill Miles Jensen.'

'Did you bring me Jeff's composite to see?'

'Yes, I did. Take a look.'

Kristina retrieved Jeff's composite from her bag and slid it across the table.

'Oh my God! That is really weird, Kristina. I don't like that. That's weird.'

Kristina took the composite back, looked at it, and then up at Steve. 'Apart from those twins who made it so big I have never, in twenty years in the business, seen two models who look so alike. It's even more amazing when you see the video from Japan.'

'Did Saul Weissman see this?'

'Yes, after me, of course. I took it into him, and I said, "Bad news, Saul. Miles Jensen's found this great looking guy called Jeff, but I've heard he's a big-time drug user." Well, maybe you don't know this but Saul's like completely, and I mean completely, anti-drugs. So, of course, he says that no way can we use Jeff, but – wait for it – we should get Miles to look for someone exactly like him.'

'You serious?'

Kristina nodded, her excitement making her look younger than her thirty-nine years. 'Absolutely. I nearly, so nearly, said that I had someone in mind, but I didn't. Because I've come out with something a whole lot smarter.'

'Which is?'

'London. That's where you're going to be discovered.'

'By Miles? Are you crazy?'

'No!' Kristina shook her head. 'Because you'll be discovered by me.'

'What?'

'You and I are going to Europe next weekend. And that's where we're going to meet for the very first time.'

'What about Miles Jensen?'

'Oh, he'll be there,' she said airily.

'Have you lost your mind?'

Kristina sucked long and hard on her diet Coke. 'Miles *has* to be there. He's going to be our witness when you walk through the door. And he's not going to be able to say he doesn't like you because I'm the boss. See?'

'But what if he finds someone first?'

'Steve, you don't seem to get it. Every call, every photograph, every everything comes through me on its way to Saul. Miles hasn't even got Saul's number. I'm going to let Miles find me two more guys before he goes to London. And

222

when he gets there he's going to meet me and we're going to search for that one last face together. Miles won't have a clue that you're waiting to walk through the door. But when you do, you'll become our sixth guy, and poor little Miles will be getting on the first plane back to the sales floor. And the beauty of it is that it doesn't matter who Miles finds in Italy and France because Saul's got it in his head that he's just desperate for a guy who looks like Jeff. Imagine how happy he'll be when I show up with you.'

Steve allowed himself a smile. 'You think it's that easy? I mean, that does sound good.'

'It's not good,' said Kristina. 'It's perfect. And it's going to keep getting better and better and better.'

18

It was an altogether different kind of hotel room. Miles's bedroom in Japan could, except for the green tea and the kimono, have been a room in any decent hotel anywhere in the world. This room could have been nowhere but in Europe.

Miles lay down on the small double bed with his fingers knitted behind his head. He looked up at the ceiling. The wooden fan lay still. An ornate, flowery cornice ran boldly between wall and ceiling, in places its cream-coloured paint chipped and flaking. It was a small, unspectacular room. The shuttered window had no view across the city of Milan. Opposite him in the narrow street, a balconied bedroom might have offered some attraction, but it had been uninhabited since his arrival, and a white cotton bedspread, undented and smooth, was nothing to salivate over.

Here in Milan there was no Miki to spoil and guide Miles. He sat up on the bed and opened his diary. When he'd called Spencer in Tokyo to tell him the news about the competition, Spencer had come up with a number for his friend Chester Hunt in Milan. It was this number that Miles now found, and dialled.

Chester Hunt's reputation preceded him. As the son of a famous Senator he'd been in the public eye since birth. Blond-haired, blue-eyed, many had seen Chester dressed in a suit applauding his father at campaign rallies while most boys his age were playing Cowboys and Injuns. It had seemed almost as if childhood was an inconvenience for the young Chester. To the public, the boy seemed intelligent and purposeful; an immature facsimile of his father. Few doubted that he would follow in the family footsteps and become a politician himself. Being perceived as a future politician was half the battle won already. And if he kept his looks, then that was the other half. All he'd need then would be a constituency, and a temporary cause.

At Groton, Chester had been an A student. At Harvard, third in his first year. At twenty-one, he'd dropped out. The press had swooped. Longing for reasons for his U-turn, they'd scoured Chester's past for problems. His survival in a car crash that had killed his mother and only sister six years earlier was cited as the true cause of the action, but beyond this the press found no academic difficulties, no abuses of substances or people, not even a consolatory hint of homosexuality.

Chester drifted for a while after leaving Harvard. Occasionally his name would appear in a Manhattan tabloid's gossip column, but the press soon lost interest in the sterility of Chester's record. To their further dismay, there seemed no visible rift in the Hunt family. Though Senator Tristan Hunt was far from pleased with his son, he was not going to let Chester's selfish meanderings interfere with his own re-election hopes. So the Senator from North Carolina had kept on smiling, smiling, smiling.

In private, it was a different story. As a long-time politician he believed in patience and compromise. It was an uncustomary mistake. Within six months, Chester had run to Paris, and the start of a new kind of life. AFD, he called it. Away from Dad.

The phone rang with its unfamiliar tone. A man answered. '*Sì?*'

Miles cleared his throat, and reddened in the privacy of his hotel room. He'd been practising his Italian. 'Ah, *buona sera. Posso parlare con* Chester Hunt.'

'Sure. Chester! Phone.'

A pause. A voice.

'Chester?'

'Speaking.'

'You don't know me,' Miles began, 'but I'm a friend of Spencer Kemble-Finch . . .'

As Miles ran through his story for Chester, it seemed as

if this had been his life for years. It no longer struck him as peculiar to refer to himself as a model scout, to explain that six million dollars was to be paid, to disclose that this was what he did. The trip to Miami the week before seemed like distant training. Miles was sure of his ground now and confident that he understood the EDEN image.

He knew the face he was looking for, and he had a gut feeling that Chester might just be the man.

'Where are you staying, Miles?'

'By the Piazza Duca D'Aosta.'

'OK, why don't I come round? We can have a beer or something. In about half an hour?'

'Sounds good.'

They took a table beside a potted orange tree in the airy hotel lobby, and drank Peroni beer.

Chester had changed. Rock star had replaced fledgling politician. Not that Chester could escape from the boundaries of his upbringing. He'd advanced towards Miles with his palm open and held up in a half-wave, and when he'd shaken Miles's hand he'd smiled widely and said 'Good to meet you,' as if he'd meant it. Yet Chester was trying to shake off his past. He'd grown his hair long, an inch past the shoulder. It was thick and blond, and he'd parted it on the left side of his face so that the bulk of it swept up and down to the right. Chester had a wide forehead, and a hairline high upon it that kept him from seeming too feminine.

But his great strength came from his eyes. They were sharp and brilliantly blue, eyes that had truly stopped people across a crowded space, made them look again and forget for a second what they'd been doing. Chester's eyes shone from the shadows of deep sockets above which were thick, gently curved, long eyebrows. His nose was not perfect, his lips were full. Miles was noticing a pattern here. Models seemed to have thicker lips than most men. It made them more sensuous, more sexy, more kissable. And ultimately more feminine.

When Miles asked Chester how long he'd been modelling,

Chester explained that he'd moved to Paris to concentrate on his drawing and painting. He'd always wanted to be an artist, he said, and he'd found it impossible beneath the shadow of his father. In Paris he'd rented a studio in the Montparnasse, and there he'd met up with an inspirational teacher. On his course, funded by the City of Paris, Chester met Spencer's sister, Georgina, and at once they'd fallen for one another. Chester explained. 'You know, it never bothered me that it was a merely visual attraction for Georgina. I get so angry with people who try to deny this. I mean, I want to know what you've got to go on at first *besides* physical attraction. I think it's exciting to see someone beautiful. And it goes on being exciting. Who's to say you need more than that?'

'Chester,' said Miles, 'you're talking like a model. You can't have a relationship based only on looks.'

'Yeah you can, because what's so great about people is that what's inside them actually shows on the outside. Sure that's an Oprah Winfreyism, but you just need to take a look at someone like Rembrandt to see what I mean. That guy gives a part of himself away in his self-portraits. They're like a whole autobiography. Or what about that, what's it called, that Bathsheba of his? You know it? There's this girl reading a letter, OK, from David, I think, and there's so much happening in her face. It's this incredible, extraordinarily private moment of hers, and Rembrandt's given that to us with one image. You walk away feeling as if you understand Bathsheba as a person. Go look at it sometime. And the thing is, you haven't even seen her moving, you haven't seen the way that she laughs or smiles or plays with her hair or anything. So when in real life you get all those things as well, then you can pretty much understand the whole person just by looking at them.'

Chester swept his hand over the tablecloth as if brushing crumbs on to his lap. 'It's not a coincidence, Miles, that bad people look bad. That's coming from inside. And then there are all these beautiful people you know right away you wouldn't want to touch with a bargepole. See? That's what I'm saying. You can't separate the external from the internal.'

'OK, what about Jeffrey Dahmer? He's clean-cut, respectable-looking.'

'Miles, give me a break. One, he's out to lunch, simply not with us, and, two, I bet you if you'd met him before you'd have figured out there was something odd going on.' Chester paused. 'What? What are you looking at?'

'I'm figuring you out,' said Miles. 'Looking at you, I'd say that you're of average intelligence, quite sensitive, you like the colour blue, prefer fish to meat, you're a rebellious Democrat who enjoys visiting the dentist but you're angry with the world about something right now, and that, in a nutshell, you're confused, fucked-up, morally perverse and on the verge of insanity.'

'There you go,' laughed Chester. 'I told you it worked.'

'So what about you and Georgina?'

'We split up. She's a bitch.'

'Ah, so you misjudged her.'

'No! I needed a bitch in my life.'

'So you went to Tokyo with Georgina when you still liked her?'

'That's right. And I'd already done a few editorial pictures in Paris with this stylist friend of mine, and Yuki said I could join Spring and it just went from there.'

'How far did it go?'

'I went back to the States after Tokyo and I didn't try anything there, and then I came straight here. I'm not one of these guys who's ashamed of modelling. I get jobs because I look great. Hey, big deal, you know? And it's fun. Like I'm doing this test job out by Lake Como tomorrow that'll be great. What are you doing?'

'I don't know.'

'Come along, why don't you? I'll call my friend, Michel.'

'What do you usually call him?'

'Do you want to come or not?'

'Sure.'

'Great, I'll see what I can do.'

Paolo Carsagna's seventeenth-century palazzo sat on a hill

overlooking the south-western finger of the spindly Lake Como. It was an enchanting place to live. The villa was built by Paolo's predecessors when in the service of the Duke of Milan, and it had remained in the hands of the Carsagna family ever since. Its beauty, many said, came from its simplicity. The symmetry of its classic Romanesque design evoked an easy sense of beauty, a gift to the soul demanding no effort from the eye. Few had looked upon the bleached facade of the villa without feeling an inner sense of peace.

It was Gary Dartford who pointed out the villa as Paolo's home. Gary was the photographer's assistant. A twenty-six-year-old Londoner, he was tall and untidy and industrious. He had wild, curly, dirty-blond hair and a large, happy face. He dressed to suit his character in baggy, blue cotton sweat pants, battered Nike sneakers, a purple T-shirt and a heavy black leather jacket.

'I wouldn't half mind living here,' he said.

Through the fog of the smoke of a fat joint, the five people in the car looked up in awe.

'What does this guy do?'

'He sells shoes,' Gary replied.

Gary drove up the steep slope to the villa as he'd driven the whole way from Milan, fast and carelessly, one hand on the wheel, the other on a bottle of beer.

The French photographer, Michel Forgat, was unpacking a metal camera case from the back of his Citroën when Gary's car crunched noisily to a halt on the stony drive at the back of the Carsagna villa. He wore small, round glasses that he took off to clean before approaching his assistant's car, 'Gary, you are idiot driver! Go take this inside. Who are you?'

Miles held out his hand. 'Miles Jensen. I think Chester told you . . .'

Chester joined them. He gave Michel a hug. 'Miles is the guy I rang you about, Michel.'

'*D'accord*. Where's the girls?'

Michel saw the two models climb out of the car: Petra, a German and a Dutch girl called Lottie. Smoking grass had made pinpricks of the pupils of Lottie's cornflower-blue eyes.

'*Ciao, bellisima,*' said Michel. 'Come inside. All the others are here.'

They passed through a narrow opening in the sixteenth-century stone wall into a serene formal garden of hedges and lawn and weathered statuary. In the centre was a deep, murky green pool. It was unrippled and reflected not only the clouds above but the stone balustrade that surrounded it. Petra smiled into it. She splashed at her reflection with her hand, and then stood and stubbed out her cigarette in one of the urns that stood on top of each corner of the balustrade.

'I'm hungry. Shall we look for food?' she said to Lottie.

Michel led them through the villa, through room upon room filled with glorious antiques. Frescoes were painted on many of the walls, floral studies mainly, some faded badly. The floors were of richly polished wood and their footsteps echoed in the high-ceilinged rooms as they walked, as if they could hear the footsteps of inhabitants of the past.

'Wouldn't this be a great place for a party?' said Lottie.

They reached a smaller room at the far end of the house. It was much more cosy than the others. Rugs covered the floorboards, and there was a large fire burning. The room smelled of cinnamon. As soon as they entered, Paolo stood and welcomed them. Michel introduced Chester and Gary, Petra and Lottie. He ignored Miles.

Paolo was too conscientious a host to do the same. The skin of his hand was smooth. 'And you are?'

'Miles Jensen, sir. This is a beautiful house.'

'Thank you. You are a model?'

'No. I'm a . . . I'm a professional observer.'

'You are the same as me, then. Come in. We have plenty of the food and wine.'

Paolo Carsagna was as smooth as a greased snake. He was in his mid-forties. His grey hair was cut short and his tan was impeccable and even. His skin bore the effects of a multitude of paid hands. He smiled often, and smoked slowly. All his movements were as slow and deliberate as his speech. Paolo was the kind of man who dealt with every situation with a smile of arrogant charm. He trusted implicitly in his power to succeed. There was a story told about Paolo among the workers of the factory where Carsagna shoes were made. Once a man brandishing a sawn-off shotgun had burst in upon the offices, demanding money. Paolo, hearing the commotion, had entered the room, and, upon seeing the gun, smiled, taken out a packet of cigarettes and offered one to the attacker before suggesting that the man should come into his office for a drink. Paolo, they said, had carried the gun. After the police had left, Paolo had fired it into a tree that later died of its wounds.

There were two others in the room, models both. A girl from England called Kelly and an Italian man called, for some reason, Funk. Kelly was waiflike, Funk butch and dark, with thick greased-back hair and stubble. He wore a Versace printed silk shirt. He and Kelly were drunk.

Paolo had an arm over Lottie's shoulder. '*Allora*, Lottie, *desidera?*' Paolo pointed at the plates of food laid out on the long pine table. 'This is prosciutto *crudo*. Really, it's wonderful. And here, I love this, this is some salami *con funghi e carciofini sott'olio*, with, er, the mushroom and artichoke. And please you must have this *insalata di mare*. It comes from my favourite restaurant in Milan, and I love it.'

'I'm a vegan,' snapped Lottie. Paolo looked quizzical. 'I don't eat any meat or fish or eggs.'

'*Benissimo*, darling, then you must try this. 'Paolo lifted up a plate filled with brightly coloured vegetables, cooked and soaked in olive oil. 'This is only the red pepper, and the onion and aubergine and tomato and potato.'

'Maybe I'll have this.'

'Please try. Would you like some champagne?'

Kelly called from the sofa on which she was sprawled. 'I'll have some more champagne, Paolo.'

'Of course. *Subito*.'

With glass filled, Miles cornered Chester. 'What are you shooting here?' he asked.

'Shoes, I think. I don't know, and I don't care.'

'Are you being paid?'

'No, but it's worth it just to get out of Milan. Once you've been here a while you'll do anything to get out of the city at weekends. Besides, I like getting drunk on someone else's champagne.' Chester emptied his glass and helped himself to another. 'It tastes better.'

Paolo was standing by Lottie. She picked up a photograph in a beautiful silver frame. 'Who's this?'

'My wife and children. Beautiful, no? I love them, very much.'

'Are they here?'

'No. She like Rome. Let me show you instead my garden. See through here how your eye follows down to the statue.'

Paolo greased an arm about Lottie's waist and led her to the pane. 'Every vista in my garden is designed to create a sense of harmony and proportion. It is, if you like, an image of man at the centre of the Universe. I love to be a part of beautiful things like this.' He turned his face to her. 'And like you.'

'Paolo, man is nowhere even close to the centre of my universe. Excuse me.'

Paolo looked a little shocked as Lottie untangled herself from his arm and took a chair next to Petra. Lottie took a sip of Petra's champagne.

A cook entered, brandishing a large bowl of steaming fresh pasta. She thumped it on the table. Paolo applauded. 'Mangare, tutti.'

And that's what they did. Only Gary Dartford worked, as assistants always do. He'd been told by Michel to set up lights in one of the bedrooms, and to check the cameras, and to label the film and to arrange the shelves in the background of the shot, and to dust, if dusting was required.

The others ate and drank more than they needed which, apparently, was the whole idea. Petra and Lottie were sharing one sofa, throwing grapes into each other's mouths, enjoying the accepted decadence this involved. Michel was looking at the models through a frame he'd made with his fingers to decide how they'd look on film. Paolo had given up on Lottie and was on the sofa leaning over Kelly. He was talking about the difference between Italian and British leather shoes.

'It is the same as the character of the people. The British

shoes are very, what is the word, very – sturdy. They will last well in the bad weather. They are very dependable and,' he smiled, 'predictable. Our Italian shoes are more soft, more sophisticated, more delicate. Your foot is a very important part of your body. It must be very much cared for. Italian shoes care about the feet. British shoes care about the rain.'

'I left my boyfriend when he bought a pair of Italian shoes.'

'He should have bought Carsagna shoes.'

'He should have bought DMs.'

Gary came back to announce that the set was ready, so the party moved into the bedroom. Michel wanted them half-naked. He'd got this idea, he said with a Frenchman's absurd seriousness, that all the people should be on the bed together, thus linking their minds and their bodies as a way of showing the humanity of all people.

In English, thought Miles, they'd call it an orgy.

Paolo seemed prepared for one. He'd set himself up in the corner. He had a large smooth silver tray on his knee upon which he was cutting and dispensing lines of cocaine. Paolo concentrated intently on slicing and arranging the powder with a razor. He liked to make each line perfectly straight and even. Abandoning lire, Paolo preferred to snort through a rolled hundred-dollar bill.

The models' poses had begun simply enough with Chester shirtless in jeans, elbow on knee, hand on chin, sitting on the edge of the bed gazing out, while Kelly, kneeling behind him, draped her arms over his shoulders and pressed her lips into his hair. This was a common enough kind of pose, the image based on the suggestion of imminent sexual union. Images such as this were sold as sepia print posters in subway stations the world over, and bought by teenagers imagining models as people with a past and a future and a place in their beds for their fans.

As the afternoon matured, so did the poses. Liberated by champagne and cocaine the models didn't need Michel's encouragement. With the natural light faded, and the tungsten bulbs giving the room the atmosphere of a movie set, the models lost themselves in a guiltless world halfway between reality and illusion. Chester lay propped up with pillows, Petra under one arm, Lottie under the other.

'Kelly,' said Michel. 'You have lipstick?'

Kelly brought it, and Michel asked Chester to put it on. He did so, and now, lit from above so that the light cast a dark shadow beneath his cheekbones, Chester's face seemed more feminine than Petra's. Michel asked Petra and Chester to kiss.

They kissed for the camera as if no one was there. When Chester put a hand to Petra's face, Michel asked him to move it, but they didn't break the kiss. Michel told Lottie to smooth her fingers through Chester's fine hair. At the corner of the bed, Kelly was sitting on Funk, and trying to kiss him too, but he didn't seem too interested while the lens was pointed elsewhere.

For his part, Michel was enjoying himself. He loved coming to Paolo's. The models always loosened up. 'Petra, that's beautiful. Oh yes. Lottie, keep like this. Lottie look more happy, please. Yes, beautiful, beautiful.'

Miles leant on a fresco at the back of the room, a vine spiralling wildly from the top of his head. He didn't think he could do this. For him true kissing, by reason of its being the most conscious sexual act, was more intimate and private than anything else. Miles had made love to women he hadn't wanted to kiss, but he'd never kissed a woman with whom he hadn't made love.

To Miles's left, Paolo was dark in his corner as the bright lights shone on the bed. Yet his actions were unmistakable. With his right hand lost beneath his black cashmere turtleneck sweater, Paolo was masturbating. Miles looked away, but high and drunk, he registered no surprise.

Lottie shrieked suddenly, and sat up. Angrily, she spoke to Michel in French. 'Michel, if you want two women kissing, then why don't you do that? Why have Chester and Petra if you want two girls?'

'Hey, Lottie, ssshh. I'll get you in the shot soon.'

'That's not my problem, Michel. My problem is you want obviously two women kissing but you've got a man and a woman kissing.'

'Two women kissing is boring, Lottie. Boring like Madonna. You stupid. This is exciting for me. This is asking a question. Is one man? Is one woman? Look at the polaroids. Two women is boring.'

'Oh yeah?'

Leaning across Chester's bare chest, Lottie took Petra's head in her hands and kissed her. Petra put out a hand and stroked Lottie's long blonde hair.

'*Magnifico*,' said Paolo, quietly.

Michel climbed on to the bed for a new angle, and the sound of the shutter fired up the girls. Trapped beneath their bodies, Chester leant his head back. The girls moved up the bed so that their heads now rested on the base of Chester's thick neck.

'Good. Tongues, Petra, Lottie. Let me see your tongues,' urged Michel.

Lottie was almost licking Petra's face now as Michel shot with his finger held down on the shutter. The high-speed clicking was turning them on. Another film finished, and Michel climbed off and handed the camera to Gary. Lottie and Petra slowed their kissing, but they didn't stop.

'Girls' said Chester, looking more nervous now the play was over, 'we're finished.'

Petra and Lottie kissed on.

'They like each other, I think,' said Michel, laughing. 'I think by tonight they will be lovers!'

Lottie looked up at him and grinned. 'You didn't know?'

'Eh?'

'Petra *is* my lover, asshole.' Lottie laughed. 'Poor little Michel! We know why you brought us here.'

Michel turned away and asked for the loaded camera from Gary. He spoke to Lottie with his back turned. 'You're here for the photographs, you stupid! This is only professional.'

'Oh, yeah?'

236

'Go, now, please. I want now to take pictures of the others.'

Lottie and Petra sauntered out of the room, hand in hand. Chester joined Miles by the wall. He buttoned up his denim shirt.

'Let's go see what we can find in this place,' he said.

He picked up a bottle of champagne as they left. Across the cobbled courtyard stood a modern building with a vaulted roof. It looked like an indoor sports centre, and smelled of chlorine. Chester flicked up a bank of lights. He leant down at the edge of the large, oval swimming pool.

'Great, it's heated. Come on!' Quickly, Chester stripped naked and jumped in. 'Come on, Miles.'

Miles, checked there was no one around and then, laying his clothes neatly folded at the edge of the pool, dived in and joined Chester, who was treading water at the pool's deep end.

'I'll race you to the end,' said Chester.

Chester won easily. He splashed water across Miles's face, and leapt up to dunk him under before swimming to the side to fetch the champagne. With the bottle raised above his head, he brought it back to Miles, who drank while he paddled furiously with his spare hand. Miles handed the bottle back to Chester.

'This is the life, eh?' said Chester. 'I love being naked in the water. Except it makes me feel horny.'

Tiring, they swam to the edge of the pool and supported themselves at its edge. They'd finished half of the bottle. 'So, how does this competition thing work, Miles?'

'I don't know the details yet. My job's to find six guys to go to New York.'

'How many do you have now?'

'Three.'

'Including me?'

'Not yet.'

'OK. I'll race you again. If I win, you include me.'

'But I haven't been to the agencies in Milan yet.'

'Pah! You know what you'll find? The world's greatest

selection of dweebs. No hopers, wannabes, dumb fucks from
Idaho. Or fags like our friend Funk here.'

'He's a fag?'

'Sure he is. Michel didn't want competition for the girls.'

'So he didn't know they were gay?'

'Are you kidding? No! None of us did. So, what you say?
Swim it?'

'This is for six million dollars, Chester.'

'I'll give you two seconds.'

'Two full seconds?'

'One, one thousand, two, one thousand. Like that.'

'And if you lose?'

'I lose.' Chester took a long swig of champagne and
grinned.' But if I win . . .'

They shook hands, and counted down from three.

Chester watched Miles go, and soon he was after him,
swimming as if his life counted on it. He swam breaststroke,
always his fastest. His heart was pummelling inside his chest.
Miles was halfway now, swimming faster than before. Chester
swallowed a mouthful of water, but he pushed on. Head down,
up, breathe, stroke. His arms were hurting. *Come on, body.
Six million dollars. Come on. That's it!* Now he was closing
in on Miles, up beside his ankles with fifteen feet to go.
Miles wasn't giving in. Chester pushed harder, his shoulders
screaming. Miles was too close to the end. *Slow down, damn
you, slow down!* Chester found an extra strength and lunged
forward to the bar at the end. He touched, his fingers grazing
the mosaic tiles at the end. He looked across. Miles looked
back, smiling.

'Two seconds,' Miles said, breathlessly. 'You can put that
in your impoverished artist's memoirs.' He pushed himself
out of the water, and shook his hair.' The two seconds that
cost me six million dollars. I like it.'

Chester was out of the pool and up beside him. 'One more
time. No handicap.'

'Sorry. They were your conditions.'

'Come on, Miles.'

Chester grabbed Miles's body, and tried to push him in.

Miles secured his footing, and they were naked and wrestling when the door opened. It was Funk.

'I come too,' he said with a smile.

'Un-unh. Not me,' said Miles. Hurriedly, he grabbed his clothes and hid his nakedness from Funk. Funk stripped, dived in, and swam underwater to Chester, slowing as he approached.

Miles dressed, and left. He found Gary back in the house, lying on the bed smoking grass. Gary held the joint towards Miles. Miles shook his head.

'Where's everybody?'

'Michel and Paolo and Kelly went off to some bedroom, and Petra and Lottie are making out in the kitchen.'

Miles sat on the edge of the bed, and let his head hang back as he looked up at the ceiling. 'It's a little crazy here.'

'It's Milan, mate. Get used to it. These models get so bored they'd do anything for a change. Beats dancing for dollars.'

'What's that?'

'There's all these clubs around Milan that the models get paid to go to. Some geezer gives them fifty quid to pull in the crowds. They've got this thing about models here. They've got this idea that most models are Americans and that all Americans are movie stars.'

'This goes on a lot?'

'All the time. They get paid for what they look like. It's the same thing as modelling clothes really. They get a free ride, free drinks, maybe a blow job out the back from some girl who thinks he's the one doing her a favour.'

'Sounds the same as . . .'

'Well, you know what they say. The only difference between a model and a prostitute is the way you spell it. Dead right, too. Now, I've got to pack up. As soon as Paolo and Michel have given one to Kelly, Michel's going to want to leave.'

'I'll take this case down for you.'

'Cheers.'

Miles lifted the weighty lights into the car. Then he returned to the swimming pool. The water was calm. On the tiles to the left of the pool, a trail of watery footsteps led through an arched corridor. Miles followed. He heard something behind a small wooden door. It sounded like a moan. Miles pushed open the door. Inside the sauna stood Chester, naked still, his hands on Funk's head, his hair straggling wet over his face. He smiled broadly at Miles.

'Join the party. Funk'll do you too. He'd like to.'

Funk said nothing. Naked also, he was kneeling in front of Chester, one hand around his own hardness, the other on Chester's. His mouth was too full for words. He didn't turn around, but continued with the sure motion of his head.

'You should do this, Miles. It's great,' said Chester, but Miles had already mumbled an apology, turned, and begun to walk as fast as he could from the pool, wondering as he went whether Georgina Kemble-Finch had known.

Gary alone hadn't been drinking, so he drove. Chester sat in the front, smiling mysteriously. Lottie was asleep on Petra in the back, and Miles sat staring out of the window. He was restless. He wasn't used to so much coke. He thought his jaw might be moving from side to side, so he leant his face on his upturned hand. He couldn't sleep. Gary was singing badly out of time with Van Morrison.

Miles was worried about Chester. He knew how good Chester could look, that he modelled well, and that he'd be great for boosting the exposure of the competition; but he was a long-haired, bisexual, drug-taking college dropout. Not exactly Weissman's type! Still, maybe none of that would show in public. Not unless someone came forward and talked to the press. A journalist such as Larry Meyers could have a field day with Chester Hunt. Senator Tristan Hunt was the kind of rich Republican who journalists like Meyers loved to hate. To discredit his son would be to damage the Senator. The reasons wouldn't matter, but they would hurt *Weissmans* and the competition. Miles was surprised he cared. Was this what they called company loyalty?

He decided he'd wait a day or two before calling Kristina.

See who was in Milan. He had a full day coming up in the agencies, and he might find his model there.

If he didn't, then Chester Hunt would have lost his swimming race, but won the chance to earn six million dollars for just a few days' work.

19

In the hot and happy city of Miami Beach there's a logic to the abundance of beautiful people. Without its models and film stars and well-tanned rich, Miami Beach would crumble once more. Another city would be crowned the Casablanca of the nineties, and the media machine would crank itself up again and dance along with its barrowloads of superlatives. Miami Beach belongs to the beautiful, and its models are the most beautiful of all. It might even be said that the city belongs to them.

The same was not true of Milan. Few in Italy's second largest city would care if the models moved on. The city itself would not change or crumble. The splendid Gothic buttresses would not crash from the sides of a Duomo that has stood its ground since 1386, La Scala would not fall silent to the enriching arias of Verdi and Tchaikovsky, Mozart and Puccini. Not even the designers, Milan's modern-day stars, would move their glittering boutiques from the Quadrilatero D'Oro. Milan doesn't need its models like the models need Milan.

Miles had spent Tuesday morning leafing through the portfolios in Milan's top modelling agencies. He liked the agents he met, their endless enthusiasm and their semiserious tantrums. He liked the way Italians lived, a Catholic race not concerned with scoring points for an afterlife.

As Milan was the model capital of the world, the Italian agencies were larger and more international than those Miles had visited in Miami and Tokyo. Yet the jargon he could hear was the same, as were the booking tables and charts, ringing phones and composites. If he did notice a difference, it was in the numbers of models spending their days hanging-out in the Milanese agencies, hoping that a client or a friend might surprise them, and walk through the door. For most models, Gary had explained to Miles, waiting is all they have to do when they're not drinking or fucking, eating, working-out or sleeping, most often in that order.

For these models, the real world existed elsewhere. The models mixed with the North Italian city like oil with water. They came for one reason alone: to work. In New York or London most models had full lives – apartments, pets, lovers, hobbies, friends, a past. In Milan they had modelling, and nothing else. The business became their life and alone determined happiness. If they got a job, they were high. If they got a good response at a casting, their spirits were lifted. If they got no work, then the earth might as well have split open under their feet.

In a cafe on the elegant Via Vincenzo Monte, Miles ordered a foccaccia sandwich with mozarella, tomato and prosciutto, and a cappuccino. It was chilly outside, with a dull cover of clouds spread low over the city. Still, he wanted to watch the world go by. That, he supposed, was what one was supposed to do in Europe. And if he was lucky, he might even spot a face in the crowd.

Indeed, there was quite a traffic on the sidewalks of the Via Vincenzo Monte. Opposite Miles in a bar, a group of young Italian men were lounging with beers and cigarettes, their scooters leaning lazily in front. The men were dressed fastidiously in polished leather shoes, neat pants, and smooth, natural-toned sweaters worn under checked, tweed jackets. Their hair was combed into place, as if by Mamma. Miles watched as one of the men stood in the path of a couple of leggy female models who were walking arm-in-arm in the shade of the trees. Miles couldn't hear what was said, but the girls soon joined the men at their table.

A noise distracted Miles. He looked to his right and saw a herd of male models approaching the cafe. They were doing the model walk. It required having one hand on a portfolio, the fatter, the better. The other hand had to swing. The walk was usually brisk, the speed of people with places to go. It was also bold and heavy and chests had to be stuck out as if to protect the face should the ambulatory beauty collide with an unexpected wall. Models liked to walk in a line across the pavement, so that others, and not they, would have to step aside.

Miles couldn't guess the origin of the walk. It was a curious mix of effeminacy and machismo, a cross between the charge of a Congo mountain gorilla and the prance of a San Francisco drag queen. The models passed, loudly. Miles dismissed them all as candidates for Adam. He was becoming dejected by his failure in the city so far. Milan had been the most likely place to find a suitable beginner, but the market in models seemed as divided here as anywhere. The best worked, the rest did not. If only, he thought, I could find a star of the future. Failing that, he knew he'd have to be satisfied with Chester Hunt.

In truth, everything was going Chester's way. Miles didn't have much energy or enthusiasm for the search today. He blamed the cocaine from the day before. That's why he'd stopped using it in New York; because it made him feel as if the drug had not manufactured energy but borrowed it from the days ahead. Now, as always, it was a bad loan. After paying off the interest, he never had anything left to help him through the present.

The afternoon was no better for Miles than the morning had been. In desperation, he arranged appointments to meet with four satisfactory models the following day, but among them he thought none matched Fabio or Fernando, Spencer or even Chester. Miles's task now was to find men to equal those already chosen.

After a few more useless forays into the agencies, Miles called it a day and took a tram back to his hotel. He bought a ticket and had it punched in the machine even though Chester had told him never to bother.

Miles had promised to meet a couple of agents in a club called Hollywood that night. He desperately needed a kip first. He didn't much feel like going out. No energy. If only, he thought as the tram rattled through the misty streets, I could lay my hands on a delicious little gram of good old Charlie C.

*   *   *

At ten a.m. the following morning, two of the models Miles had arranged to meet arrived at I Spy agency fresh, or otherwise, from the gym. Miles was polite and looked at their books and, to humour them both, asked them questions about themselves, but they disappointed him. They were superfit and as handsome as department-store mannequins, but if Kristina and Weissman hadn't liked Jeff, then they wouldn't like these two. Miles was being faced with the same problems in Milan he'd encountered elsewhere. The best models were all too experienced for this campaign. He was seeing instead a procession of hopeless wannabes.

By now, Miles had sent a large number of female composites to Kristina in New York. He was even more confused by the women than he was by the men. He'd been littered with composites of the latest, the hottest, the best girls, the ones who were wowing audiences on the catwalks in Milan and Paris, and those breaking ground in the magazines. Yet Miles couldn't get it. Half of these girls simply weren't beautiful. Here he was being told that the ideal Eve had to be five foot seven with a bony chest, Bambi eyes, ironed hair and a prepubescent, vacant look. Miles liked his women to be women, not anorexic orphans. If they took one of these girls to the Amazon, he thought, even the piranhas would turn her down. By now, he was glad that the task of choosing Eve had fallen at Kristina's feet.

Miles made no great discoveries during the morning, and was thankful of the break that lunch in Chester's apartment would bring. Miles had accepted the invitation to give himself an opportunity to judge Chester one more time.

He arrived at the ugly, post-war complex close to Porto Genova a little after one. When he buzzed up, Chester shouted down the stairwell. 'Follow the bolognese! Third floor.'

Chester welcomed Miles at the door, who almost stepped on a plate of cheese omelette as he entered the models' dank apartment.

'Don't worry,' said Chester. 'It's yesterday's.'

Chester took it to the kitchen and threw the plate in the sink. The old egg sank before resurfacing.

'Sorry about the mess,' he said. 'A couple of guys really went to Nam here last night.'

'What?'

'They lost it. It happens in Milan sometimes.'

Miles could see what Chester meant. The living room was a war zone, the smart-bombs having targeted the closets, the trash-can, the sink and the bookshelf. Miles trod warily towards the window and an old, striped mattress upon which were threadbare sheets, a stained blanket, a pillow missing its case, two full ashtrays, an empty bottle of wine, a football, a hard-core porn magazine called Mr SuperSex, a carton of Winston cigarettes, cassettes, a Walkman held together with frayed grey masking tape, a selection of men's fashion magazines torn apart for pictures, some rolling-papers, a bowl half-filled with the morning's sodden cornflakes, and then the clothes – socks, skid-marked underwear, inside-out jeans, a pair of black leather trousers and some greying sneakers.

'Grant sleeps there,' explained Chester, returning from the kitchen. 'He's an animal. And Christian and Paul sleep next door.'

'They sound well-suited.'

'They're not gay.'

'I meant . . .' Miles waved a hand. 'Forget it.'

'Wanna beer?'

'Sure.'

The apartment front door opened when Chester left for the kitchen. It was Christian, one of Chester's roommates. Miles thought that Christian wasn't nearly as bad-looking as Chester had earlier suggested. He was nineteen, with straight fair hair, and a round, healthy face. He wore blue jeans, a white Tee, muscles and a tan. Apparently, in the previous summer Chris had been used for a national campaign in America, half-naked by a lake with a golden retriever draped content on his shoulders, its legs flopping on to Christian's hairless chest. After this, Christian's agency in New York had prophesied great things but when no jobs had come up in the city his booker had told Christian what bookers tell anyone not working: go to Milan, do editorial, prove yourself there. Then come back with editorial tearsheets. The money jobs, they'd vowed, would follow. Yet the problem for Christian, as for too many others, was that the jobs weren't arriving even in Milan.

Chester returned with the beer. 'Hey, Chris! The agency called. You got a booking.'

'Oh, yeah?' Christian threw down his leather knapsack. 'Who with?'

'Armani. They want you for the show.'

Christian's face lit up. He punched the air. 'No way, man. That's like the best news in years. No fucking way!'

Chester grinned. 'You're right – there's no way. But the agency do want you to call.'

Christian looked as if he might burst into tears.' You know you're an asshole sometimes, Chester.'

'Only sometimes?'

Christian ignored him, and dialled his agency. Chester fished out a half-finished joint from one of the ashtrays and lit it. He took a toke, held his breath, and handed it to Miles. 'I'd better go check the pasta,' he said, taking with him the broken curtain rod he was using as a spoon.

Christian was soon off the phone. Miles, who was leaning on the window sill relishing the grass, asked him if it was good news.

'Nah. I got an underwear fitting with Lucca.'

'What?'

'I try on their new underwear lines for them.'

Chester shouted from the kitchen. 'They only pick the boys with the cute buns.'

'Fuck off, man. I don't see you getting too many campaigns.'

'You wait. Why do you think Miles is here?'

Christian looked once again at Miles. Miles was getting used to being eyed up by models. Christian's look wasn't in any way lascivious, but it was wholly judgmental. He looked at Miles's clothes – the regular Levis, the plaid green Ralph

Lauren shirt, the deck shoes – and he looked at his face, at his haircut, at the way he was standing. Here, there was no shame in judging a book by its cover.

'You'd never use Chester, would you?'

'Only if we get desperate,' joked Miles, handing over the joint. Then, out of curiosity, he said, 'Can I see your book?'

Christian's portfolio was pitifully short of pictures, but in all of them he looked just like the kind of boy you'd hope your daughter would bring home. Miles knew that the quietly handsome look wasn't enough these days. 'I hear you haven't been too lucky,' Miles said.

'There's nothing going on in Milan right now. It's terrible.'

'So why stay?'

'I need the tears, and all the best magazines are down here. So all the young photographers are here too.'

'But if there isn't any work . . .'

'Something should come up.'

Miles had met too many young models like Christian since he'd arrived in Italy. That morning he'd heard about one model who'd taken to sleeping rough in the parks and the train station because he couldn't afford the flight back to the States. He stayed alive through eating free at Hollywood nightclub, acting as bait for the paying customers.

Chester brought the food, the plates like wounded jellyfish – a sloop of tomato sauce over spaghetti, the strands of which hung limply in a fringe over the side, the whole slippery and wet on the plate. They ate noisily, like Japanese. Christian and Chester talked about the dearth of modelling jobs, allies really in their quest for employment. Miles was getting the impression that a model's life resembled the sex life of a married adult – long periods of frustration punctuated by the occasional bout of good fortune and satisfaction.

'What are you doing this afternoon, Chris?' asked Chester.

'I got a casting with Donna Carlinni, then I'm going to shoot some pool.'

When Christian had gone, and Chester had thrown the plates in the sink (I'll wash them Friday), Chester joined Miles on the couch. 'How's the great model search going?'

'It's coming on.'

'I hope I didn't ruin my chances on Sunday.'

'With the swimming race?'

'No. Later. With Funk.'

Miles said nothing, not knowing what to say.

'If you hung around you'd find out that blow jobs are Milan's number one currency. It's how half the models get booked. Especially some of the big campaigns. Give good head and you can buy yourself anything.'

'So what was Funk buying?'

Chester laughed. 'That was charity work.'

Unamused, Miles drew in deeply on the spliff.

'Hey, man, what's the big deal? A mouth's a mouth, isn't it? If that's what Funk wanted, hell . . . Besides, everyone knows that gays give the best blow-jobs. Men know what men like. You should try it sometime. You might be surprised.'

'It's not my taste.'

'How do you know? If you just closed your eyes . . .'

Chester rested a hand on Miles's thigh. Miles stood up immediately.' No . . . thanks. But no.'

Chester leant back on the sofa and smiled. 'You should try enjoying yourself some more. You're the kind of guy who's always holding back. Everything's conditional – I'd have done this *if*, I'd do that *if*. You know?'

Miles put on his coat. He shook his head, a little irked at Chester's perception. 'Chester, you've known me two days.'

'I've known you all my life, man! You're exactly like I used to be. Jesus, do you think I'd have let another guy anywhere near my dick when I was at Harvard?'

Miles coloured.' I don't know why you think your . . . blossoming sexuality has got anything to do with me.'

'It's an example. I'm just saying, you know – I'm not gay. I'm just living well. I'm just happy.'

Miles collected together his things from the mess of the apartment. He looked around the room. 'Forgive me for not envying you.' He looked at his watch. 'Listen, I've got to get to Industria studio. Thanks for lunch.'

'When can you let me know about the competition?'

'I thought we swam for it.'

'Are you being serious?'

'I'm a serious kind of guy. You said so yourself. Bye, Chester. Good luck.'

Chester came to the door. He shouted at Miles as Miles skipped down the stairs. There was a note of desperation in his voice. 'Listen, Miles. I didn't mean anything by all that. I was . . . I'm sorry, OK? Miles?'

Halfway down the stairs, Miles turned, looked up and smiled. 'Too late, Chester,' he said, and then, remembering Tiffany, he added, 'Have a good life,' before scuttling out of view wearing a faintly malicious grin.

Tuesday afternoon, and the phone in Kristina's Manhattan office was ringing. In front of her on the desk was a fax from Milan. It was of a blond, long-haired young man sitting on the edge of a bed. His ear lobe was being nibbled by a topless female model. Hoping for an impartial judgment, Miles had sent no further details. Now he was at the other end of the ringing line, sitting with a beer in his Milanese hotel room. When Kristina answered, he said, 'Do you like him?'

'He's great. Great eyes.'

'And his hair? What does Mr Weissman think?'

'The hair's fine.'

Truth was, Weissman didn't yet know about Chester. Kristina had no doubts that when Weissman *did* see Chester's hair, he'd hate it, and that suited her scheme just fine.

'Who is this guy?' she said. 'He looks familiar.'

'I'll give you a clue. His dad's a politician.'

'He's not a Kennedy!'

'Nope. Here's another clue. North Carolina.'

'Oh my God. Senator Hunt's kid, what's-his-name.'

'Chester.'

'That's right. I should have remembered a stupid name like that.'

'Should I tell him yes?'

'Absolutely.'

Now that Kristina was confident about Steve, she was even happy that *Weissmans* could get some useful publicity out of Chester. Working like this for the firm almost felt like the old days.

'Did you see anyone else in Milan?' she asked.

'No.'

'No problem. Chester's a good choice.'

'Thanks! I'll call him right now. Anything else?'

'No. Try and find me someone high profile in Paris. Someone else like Chester would be great.'

'I'll try.'

'And Miles, make sure you only get one model in Paris. It'd be better for PR if we chose the last guy in London.'

As soon as Kristina had hung up, she went to see Weissman. She found him scrabbling about his desk like a thief.

'Sweetheart, my Danish grew legs! Can you see it?'

Kristina found the brown paper bag in Weissman's overcoat pocket. She passed it to him.

'Fantastic! Where would I be without you?'

'Still on your diet, probably.'

'Exactly!' he said, as he lovingly extracted the gargantuan raisin Danish from its bag. 'You know what that slave-mistress, my dear wife, gave me for breakfast? Herbal tea. Grapefruit. Miss Becky's Bran Delight, and toast with no-fat no-sugar jelly. Now, how can a man work on that? Man needs sugar. So, what's this problem?'

'I'm afraid that's exactly what it is. Our wonder boy, after four cushy days in Milan, has only been able to come up with *one* face. This one.'

Kristina flicked the fax of Chester across the table. Weissman looked long and hard. He took a mammoth bite of his Danish. He chewed, and Kristina waited for the fireworks. The vision of Saul Weissman when he chose to explode was truly something to behold.

'Long hair, huh?'

'I know. And he doesn't want it cut.'

Ssshtdunk! Weissman slapped his palm on to his desk.

'Of course he doesn't want it cut. Haven't you seen what's happening out there? Long hair's the new thing, Kristy. I love this guy. Where's he from?'

'He's American.'

'Good.'

'He's Senator Hunt's son.'

'Even better.'

Kristina tried again. 'I read somewhere that he dropped out of college. Harvard.'

'So? I never made it to college. Kristy, sweetheart, where's the problem? This is a beautiful choice. An inspired choice. Just think of the press. In fact, I'm gonna call Tony Jakes at the *Herald* right this minute. Why don't you have someone put a package together of the names and faces of the guys chosen so far, including this Hunt kid. OK?'

'I'll have Cindy do it.'

Kristina walked to the door, then, conscious of the drama, swung around to her boss.' I'm just so sorry that Miles failed to find someone more like Jeff, that's all.'

'You told him that's what we want?'

'Yes,' she lied.

'So, he's still got Paris and London. You worry too much. You need to relax. Are you getting laid these days?'

'I . . .'

'I'm sorry,' said Weissman, surrendering with the handkerchief he'd just used to wipe the crumbs from his mouth.' I shouldn't have asked. But GET LAID. It's better than that voodoo yoga you were up to. OK? Now, I got a call to make. I'll speak to you later.' Weissman buzzed through to his secretary, Rona. 'Get Tony Jakes for me, would you? I got a ball here that could do with a push.'

Tony Jakes was a walnut of a man. Fifty-four, four foot six, hard, irascible, he'd been the editor of the the *New York Daily Herald* for eight years. It was he who'd earned the gratitude of millions of New Yorkers by turning the fortunes of the paper around. Right from the start, Tony had believed that if you want to sell a paper, you don't tell the public what to read, you ask them. It didn't take a genius to understand the reply, and into the *Herald* came sex, violence, gossip, and at least two pages a day devoted to the personal lives of the nation's TV stars.

Yet back in his native England, Tony Jakes had had a deservedly high reputation as a serious, committed journalist. He hadn't lost his taste for hard news stories since. So, along with the gossipmongers and agony aunts, the *Herald* employed a core of dedicated investigative journalists. The stories they chose, it must be said, veered towards the sensational – serial killers, racist attacks, terrorism, abortion rights, mafia corruption – but they never lingered on the lurid. The paper was mindful of the causes and implications of each story it ran. And on no less than five occasions since Jakes had taken over, items in the paper had led to police arrests. It was rumoured in the city that there was a price on Jakes's head for his part in the trial and arrest of the Mafia boss Tony Fratacci. When Jakes heard, he'd responded with a four-word headline: **Come And Get Me**.

Jakes was sitting on the edge of his desk when Larry Meyers entered the editor's office. Jakes gestured towards the door. Meyers turned back to shut it. He was usually in and out of Jakes's office in under a minute, but now he guessed something must have come up.

'Found anything new on the Brooklyn story, Larry?'

'Some kid says that Jerome was taunting the others. The kid told it to me like Jerome had it coming.'

Meyers, whose 'Racism on Our Streets' series had won him a Pulitzer two years before, had been writing a story on a black kid called Jerome Williams who'd been beaten up by some Italian kids in Brooklyn. The beating had seemed motiveless, and this was one of Meyers's favourite themes: violence and hatred, he believed, were basic instincts that had to be lived with. They only became damaging to the moral fibre of a nation when the people ceased to be shocked by them, or when the violence became senseless. Now his Jerome story was taking on a new slant. Callous though it sounded, maybe Jerome had asked for what he got.

Jakes took the pen he was sucking on out of his mouth. 'I had a feeling about this, Larry. It was all too, I don't know . . . too perfect. You think it was a setup?'

'Did you see that kid? He's lucky to be alive. If he asked for it, he was stupid, not canny.'

'Yeah, well, if there was a good reason why they set on him, let's let the story die.'

'I figured as much. Was there something else?'

'Yes. I've just got off the hooter with Saul Weissman and he was talking about his cologne competition . . .'

Meyers held up a warning palm. 'Tony, don't tell me . . .'

'It won't take you long. Think of it as a break.'

'Tony, do me a favour here. I'm right in the middle of something. I don't need a break, for Christ's sakes. And when I do I'm gonna go to the fucking Caribbean, OK? Get a staffer to do it. Why me? What about whats-her-face, the cute one – Celia. She could do it.'

'I know she could, but Weissman wants you. And you can still go on working on the discrimination story.'

Meyers could hardly believe what he'd heard. He let it show. 'Who the fuck's running this paper? Saul Weissman?'

'No, I am. But Saul Weissman said, in no uncertain terms, that he looked forward to reaching the public through a series of double-page ads in the New Year and . . .'

'Tony, is this you? Are you OK?'

'Listen to me for five seconds. It's not so bad. One, it's the kind of story that Joe Public likes . . .'

'And you got fifty guys could write it . . .'

'Two, beside Saul being a good friend of the paper he's a good friend of our beloved proprietor, and three, I think that someone like you could bring the story to life.'

'Jesus Christ, Tony. What's there to bring to life?'

'I can think of things.' As Jakes spoke, he slapped out the points with the back of his right hand on the palm of his left. 'No store has ever done anything like this, no store has ever paid anything like this, nobody else has got the guts to spend money like this during a recession like this, and no one else is guaranteeing us revenue like this. Added to which, we're going to have great-looking photos beside every story, one of which will be about Senator Hunt's kid. He's become one of the finalists. Look.'

Tony Jakes handed over the photo of Chester with Kelly taken in Milan by Michel Forgat. Meyers let out a half-laugh through his nose. 'Which is the girl?'

'I'd like you to get a reaction from Senator Hunt.'

'He'll be pissed. I could write that. Senator Hunt was mightily pissed to learn of his son's sudden sex change.'

'Will you do this for me, Larry?'

'Tony, you know these guys here, they go from club to club, you can only find them in the chic restaurants. I'm gonna have to get into that world. That hurts me. Do you have any idea how much a bourbon costs in these places?'

Jakes was laughing. 'We can manage a few free dinners, Larry. If that's all it's going to take.'

20

The message from Kristina had been clear enough. Miles had to find only one competitor in Paris; someone with a high profile. Another Chester Hunt, perhaps, or a Spencer Kemble-Finch. Miles thought that maybe one of those brutish, young French actors would do well, fresh from looking angry in the latest succulent French movie. Who better than a Frenchman to play Adam? wondered Miles. Only a Frenchman would have the absolute conviction that he'd engender the perfect species.

Miles had been in Paris for a full day by the time he met up with Georgina Kemble-Finch. He'd traipsed from agency to agency – Glamour, Bananas, Best One – leaving each with handfuls of composites that later he'd sifted through and, mostly, discarded. In Paris, Miles had found his reputation preceding him. In the fashion business, gossip came second only to money. Now, whenever Miles entered a Parisian agency he was greeted with an immediate and enthusiastic reception. Owners would take him by the arm and lead him into their treasure troves.

The nervousness that had once accompanied Miles into the modelling agencies had now been replaced by a sense of self-importance. And he no longer had to argue with the agents who'd become aware that *Weissmans* was serious in its quest for a newcomer. It was what half the world's top models were bitching about. And although the Parisian agents couldn't wholly resist the temptation to push their biggest stars, Miles was no longer being presented with the flotsam of the middle ranks. Instead, he was shown the beginners, those the agents liked to call the 'faces of tomorrow'.

The faces of tomorrow looked remarkably similar to the

faces of today, only younger, less jaded, more desperate to become rich. Many, Miles was pleased to see, had grown their hair long. That was encouraging as far as his choice of Chester was concerned. In Milan he'd heard complaints from models that long-haired bikers and musicians and grunge aficionados were stealing the professional models' jobs. Doing in Europe what Marky Mark was doing with Calvin Klein underwear in the States. In Paris, it seemed that the models were growing their hair to claim their jobs.

The other new breed was more curious. They were an offshoot of the feminine waifs. These men were feeble, androgynous, disinterested in building bodies. Rebels against fashion, the French agents called them. Miles was as confused about these male models who weren't real men as he was by the female models who weren't real women. This latest fad, this throwback to the seventies or sixties or some such decade, made no sense to him. In New York, he'd heard, some women had taken to impersonating male female impersonators to imbue themselves with enough credibility for entry into the city's most happening clubs.

Miles arrived at the small bistro in the rue des Francs-Bourgeois that Georgina had described as her 'favourite haunt', and searched for her. She'd said that she had long hair and would be wearing a chunky woollen turtleneck, and no make-up.

'I'll be the one with red lipstick, then,' Miles had joked.

Miles couldn't see her, and joined the line on his own. At ten to one, the restaurant was full. Miles had always interpreted this kind of scene as the true Paris. Every major city had its landmarks, its Eiffel Tower, its Notre Dame, its Louvre, and tourists were drawn to them in search of the familiar seen in books, on postcards, and in movies. Miles had wondered if the day might come when identikit cities would be built in America's open spaces. A Paris could be built in Arizona; Berlin in Wyoming; London in Texas, close to the old London Bridge. Or Europe's capitals could be condensed, and bunched together in gargantuan theme parks. The attractions without the grime, traffic and noise.

Miles smiled at the thought, and looked out to the street for Georgina. He knew his scorn of the masses was hypocritical, for ten years before he too had been to see the sights. Now, though, it was to places such as this restaurant that he liked to come. In Manhattan, tasteless turkey sandwiches were grabbed by workers on the move and the make, eaten with diet sodas at office desks with the rye bread crumbling in their busy hands. As he looked about himself at the thirty or so Parisians dining in the restaurant, Miles could not detect concern on any of their faces for anything but their meal, and their partners. It was a simple question of priorities. Lunch was an event in Paris, and one of the reasons for living, and that was a belief that Miles was happy to share. Especially when the *pommes d'allumettes* looked so divine.

Miles had allowed two couples to move in front of him by the time Georgina arrived. She was late, a discourtesy that always bothered him. However, Miles didn't let his annoyance show as he shook her hand, and listened to her excuses. She was less attractive than Spencer, with a chin that seemed a size too large, as if a mistake had been made in assembly. Yet she had an endearing smile, and a hearty, English face.

They sat soon, and ordered from the set menu, warm goat's cheese salad first, then for Miles the steak frite, for Georgina the veal stew. And, of course, a carafe of house red. They spoke much of Chester. Georgina surprised Miles by her affection for him. Behind the hedonism, she claimed, Chester concealed crippling self-doubt and loathing. 'I've never known anyone who tries so hard to be happy,' she said, 'who ends up being so sad. And he's one of those models who has to keep telling you how great the job is, but who'd never want a son of his own to do it.'

'Basically, you're telling me he's confused,' said Miles.

'He's so confused, in fact, that he even talked about going to fight in Bosnia. He thinks that everyone should have something they care about more than themselves.'

'That's just twenty-something angst isn't it? You can't really knock him for that.'

'But the problem with Chester is that he cares about things

259

for such a short space of time. I mean, what about the painting? I'm still in the class where we met, and look what he's doing . . . He seems to keep taking steps backwards from responsibility. He's just like Spencer, in fact. Maybe you're attracted by immature men, Miles.'

'Not at all. I just thought Spencer might look good.'

'Daddy's having an epileptic fit over it. I think the thought of having a male model for a son might send him to an early grave. He's very motivated. Spencer's been sort of going off the rails since the army.'

'With six million dollars he could buy the railroad for himself!'

Over coffee, Georgina asked Miles if he was going to Tiziana Ferrari's party.

'What party?'

All that Miles knew was that Tiziana Ferrari was one of the most beautiful women in the world, and a genuine supermodel. He'd never dreamed of attending a party of hers. 'She's having a launch party at La Piscine Bleue tonight. She's got this beauty contract, and I can't think of any better place to go if you want to see people. *Everyone's* going to be there.'

Miles knew about the La Piscine Bleue club from a previous trip to Paris. It had been fabulously trendy then, and crowded with male and female models. He was surprised it was still so popular in a city in which clubs lasted as long as virgins in a brothel.

'It's not exactly original, but there you are,' said Georgina. 'Tiziana's been a friend ever since Daddy was Ambassador in Rome. I know her whole family. I'm sure I can get you on the guest list.'

'Wouldn't it be easier if we went together? Maybe?'

Miles knew from experience that it was never easy getting into La Piscine Bleue. Georgina thought a while, but then agreed, and they fixed a time and a place to meet before parting for the afternoon, Georgina back to her studio, Miles for a quick walk around the Marais, and to the few agencies he still had left to see.

*　　*　　*

'I'll just be coming to Rosa's agency to take a look,' Fernando Padrillas had said the first time he'd talked with the Miami agency. 'Nothing more.' He didn't mind joining a competition for which the prize was so high, but he wasn't about to become a full-time model. He wasn't the type, whatever anyone else might think.

It had taken Rosa ten minutes to persuade Fernando to change his mind. As soon as he'd walked through the door, she'd begun to sing his praises, and before long they'd been talking money; lots of it. Rosa knew all the right things to say, and she'd urged Fernando to strike while the iron was hot. She knew of photographers who'd be able to take some great test shots. The agency would lend the cash for these until Fernando got his first job, and handle everything else. All Fernando would have to do would be to show his face around Miami Beach a little, and get to know the photographers and clients. And as soon as the clients knew that he was up for a six-million-dollar campaign, the jobs would start to pour in. She was sure. 'In this business,' she'd promised,' it only takes one person liking you to start an avalanche. And you, Fernando, couldn't have dreamed up a more beautiful start.'

Rosa's had even found him a job on his first day. It wasn't much, a promotional pamphlet for a new gay club on Washington Avenue, but it had earned him $200, a sum that had almost covered his initial fees.

And now, on the day that Miles met Georgina in Paris, Fernando could be seen smiling for his first ever major catalogue booking. Sometimes the photographer wanted a more serious look, but Fernando couldn't wipe the grin off his face. Last week he'd taken his beautiful girlfriend to the beach, kissed her and gone home. Now, he was taking an even more beautiful girl to the beach, kissing her, and going home with fifteen hundred dollars for his pains.

Fernando Padrillas could hardly believe his luck. He closed his eyes and turned his face to the glorious sun.

Oh, Papa, he thought, if only you could see me now.

Miles looked at his watch again, and then out into the deserted square in front of the Pompidou Centre. Georgina, damn her, was late, and Miles was beginning to care.

He'd eaten well, too well, with an agent from Glamour in the China Club before returning to his hotel in the rue des Beaux Arts to change. Back there he'd dressed in his dark blue Comme Des Garçons suit with a brand-new white Agnes B shirt, and no tie. He'd looked at himself and wondered if Chester was right. Miles's new elation showed in his face. He felt at last he'd begun to walk the same way that the world was turning, only now he was walking faster than the globe, so soon he'd climb to the top, to where he belonged. And as he'd studied his reflection in the hotel mirror, Miles had seen a man who looked as rich, handsome and important on the outside as he felt in every cell of his body. The future had arrived, and it smelt gloriously sweet. Starting tonight, Miles was sure, great things would happen.

Forty minutes on and still waiting in the Café Clemenceau, Miles wasn't so sure. Where was Georgina? The Café Clemenceau was one of those places that needed to be bustling, or else it felt cold and sterile. Its design was stark, black and white and mirrored. At midnight, it was almost empty.

The waiter's shoes clicked crisply across the tiled floor. Miles ordered another coffee, and self-consciously lit a cigarette. The only other table was occupied by three gay men, two a kissing couple, the other a man of about thirty with an almost shaven head, and large watery eyes. For the past half-hour he'd been keenly staring at Miles. Miles had tried to appear amused by his own company, but he'd not been able to resist the occasional glance across the room to see if he was still being observed. He suspected it was the wrong thing to do. There he was, all dolled-up and handsome with his hair slicked back and a glow in his cheeks, offering furtive glances to an interested stranger. He hoped he wasn't giving off messages in a gay language of signs. Was this, Miles wondered, how it felt to be a beautiful woman? Through no fault of his own, Miles felt threatened by the aggressive sexuality of the man. After another peek at his watch, Miles decided that Georgina had stood him up. By now she was bound to be at the party. He decided to go there alone, in the hope that his name had been added to the list for the party of one of the most beautiful women in the world.

It was a short enough walk, but Miles's heart sank when he saw at least a hundred people outside the club, smothering the entrance in their desperation to get inside. Amused on the other side of the street, photographers waited, the orange lights of their flashguns ticking in anticipation. One swung his heavy lens around to Miles as Miles sauntered up to the group, but thought better of it and lowered the camera again. Ignored by all, Miles joined the back of the crowd. He thrust his hands into his pockets and tried to look as if that was where he was happy to be. In truth he was wondering how the hell he was going to get inside.

The focus of the crowd's attention was a bovine blonde called Julia who was standing in a long overcoat at the top of the stairs, a clipboard in her hand. In this space, standing beneath the turn-of-the-century façade in front of a curtained door, Julia was all-powerful. Beside her were her heavies, three beefcakes in tight, light grey suits, bouncers who looked as if they could stop a car advancing at forty miles an hour. Everyone else in the crowd was acting as if they were Julia's best friend. They were calling out her name, smiling, explaining why they alone should be admitted. Sometimes it worked. For the first ten minutes, Miles just stood there, cold and hopeful of seeing someone he knew from the agencies; of seeing Georgina. When nobody came, he held his hand high up in the air, and waved. Julia looked straight at him. He hoped she'd notice the suit. He was no ordinary punter.

'Je suis un ami de Tiziana!'

Julia's smile was condescending.' *Tout le monde dit la même chose.'*

'Mais, c'est vrai, madame.'

'Nom?'

'Oui,' he assured her.

'Non! *Nom*, name.'

'Miles Jensen.'

Julia ran a finger down the names on her list. Miles edged forward, his heart palpitating. *Please! My name should be there. Don't leave me with these hopeless people.* Julia turned another page. Miles pushed further forward. Then she looked at him, shook a finger, and looked away. *That's it?* thought Miles. *That was my chance?* The whole idea of being desperate to be somewhere he didn't belong was anathematic to him. Yet getting into the club had suddenly become the only thing that mattered. Forget wars, famines, debts, lovers, venereal diseases; admission was everything.

The truly beautiful had no problem, nor did the recognisably rich or connected. As the minutes passed, Miles's jealousy of these people grew along with his hatred for Julia. How dare she? Didn't she know how much his suit had cost? Wasn't he as handsome as a model? Sure, there were some other models around him, but they were dressed in jeans and leather jackets. What could they expect? Miles was so much more like those who were rolling up in cars, and rolling in in seconds. They really pissed Miles off. Who the hell were these old, bejewelled men striding in front of their bimbettes, parting the crowd as if they had Moses's tricks up their sleeves? Miles couldn't part the people to get forward an inch. He was beginning to wish he hadn't come at all.

Behind him, there was a sudden flurry of activity as the photographers surrounded the open door of a chauffeur-driven car. Everyone turned to look. Miles, responding to the exploding flash guns, looked to see who'd arrived. He recognised at once the sultry faces of two of the most photographed women in the world, the supermodels Dina van Stigal and Wendy Radcliff. There was no question that they were fabulously beautiful, no question that, in black, in Versace and Alaïa, they were overwhelmingly desirable. But there was something more: they were world-famous. Their celebrity set them apart, gave them a distance from the common person as if they belonged not here on a street in Paris, but in an altogether higher world inhabited only by other celebrities from movies, royal families and print.

The bouncers stepped down to clear a path even though one

had opened in reverence. The crowd fell silent. Julia unhooked the rope, and received a kiss from both women in thanks. They've probably never been refused entry anywhere, Miles thought. He wished they could know how it felt. When Julia turned back towards the crowd, she was smirking with the favour of the fabulous. Miles clenched his teeth. *Bitch!* He'd been waiting half-an-hour now, stuck on the street like a complete idiot, just to be allowed to enter a room full of poseurs, minor celebrities and models. Who'd even want this, let alone queue for it? Damn Georgina!

Miles was thinking of leaving when he was surprised by a tap on his shoulder. He looked around and up at a face he'd thought he'd never be happy to see again.

'Glurg! My God, what are you doing here?'

'Coming to the party with my agent. I am back from Miami.'

'Evidently.'

Glurg looked a whole lot better than he had done before, as if he'd spent the weeks turning like a chicken in a French rotisserie. In contrast with his darkly tanned skin, Glurg's eyes and teeth were a brilliant white. Miles decided he'd ask for a composite to send to Kristina.

'Troy Turnbull is here in Paris too,' said Glurg.

'Really? I can't wait!'

Pushing up behind Glurg was a scorpion of a woman called Catherine, an agent Miles had met the day before. They smiled, both wanting something from the other. Miles's need was more pressing.

'You need to be coming in 'ere with me?'

'Please. I should have been on the list.'

'No problem.'

It wasn't. After one gesture from Catherine, Miles was relieved to be inside. Julia had ignored his passing scowl. Once in, Miles was surprised that now he wished for those left outside to be refused admission to the club.

The open bar, Glurg said, lasted until one, and as it was a quarter to, he and Miles went straight upstairs. Having visited La Piscine Bleue before, Miles knew his way around. The dance floor was downstairs. Upstairs, it was much more quiet.

The barman, noticing the hunk that was Glurg's outstretched arm, served them fast. Two vodka-tonics each, and two beers to keep them happy.

'It's very good here, isn't it?' said Glurg.

Miles looked about him. Upstairs there was no music, so the large room had more the feeling of a bar than a club. It was here that the clubbers retreated to from the noise and mayhem of the dance floor downstairs. They came, some sweaty and breathless, to pick up a drink and perhaps a partner for the night. Though bodies moved little, eyes were frenetic. There wasn't much to do upstairs but watch. Unless, of course, you were one of the few *being* watched. Members of a club as exclusive and impenetrable as any in the world, these were the few in possession of the most coveted gift of them all: beauty. Beyond La Piscine Bleue, something more was required. Here in Clubland, it was the most beautiful who were deified, and duly worshipped.

Sitting at a table to Miles's left, Wendy Radcliff was one such Queen Bee, surrounded by devotees. Wendy had this knack of looking and acting as if she was alone, though she knew she was being lusted after. And Miles was lusting along with the others. Too many TV shows and magazine articles had hammered in the point that Wendy was one of the world's great beauties for Miles to think anything different, but Wendy's great appeal, Miles decided, came from the fact that she so nearly looked ordinary. She could almost have been the girl next door, the girl the guys had actually had. This made their dreams seem tantalisingly close. Yet with Wendy, everything was more refined – the gentle curve of her jawbone, the precise symmetry of her eyes and lips, even her crisply neat nostrils. If Rodin had sculpted the perfect American homecoming queen turned beautiful woman, he could have modelled his work on Wendy.

A man in a green flying jacket carrying a bottle of beer stopped in front of Miles, and interrupted his thoughts.

'Hi. How are you?'

Miles didn't know whose hand he was shaking. 'Ehm, good, thanks.'

'How's the search?'

'Good, thanks.'

'You should have said something when you came into Supreme.'

Now Miles remembered Scott Farber from Supreme agency in New York. Georgina had been right. This party was like a Thanksgiving for the fashion community, and the whole family had come.

'I was under orders.'

'From Kristina, no doubt. The biggest bitch in the business. Anyway, buddy, come see us in the agency. We've got some great guys. I got to talk to Miss Wendy here.'

Miles said to Glurg, 'Let's look downstairs.'

They descended into the depths, where the music thumped into their bellies. Years before its conversion to a club, this was where the swimming pool had been, and still the pool's blue tiles cling in even lines along the walls.

In the space where Glurg and Miles entered, there were tables and chairs set in alcoves around the walls. It would have been almost grubby were it not for the people inside. The velvet of the red seats was worn and tatty, and the gilt had chipped from the chairs. But the people, ah, the people, they looked as if they'd all been newly painted by artists intent on perfection. It made Miles feel good to be a part of this crowd. Unsure of how to act, he reached in his pocket for a cigarette, a Gauloise from a packet he'd bought that day from a gruff old lady in the *tabac* by the hotel. He lit it and coughed and looked around, hoping to see Georgina.

In front of Miles, male models had gathered. They were grouped together in a circle, blocking the passage to the dance floor so as to be as conspicuous as possible. Miles knew that they were models because they'd all dressed down while those less sure of themselves had dressed up. For these models, black biker boots, jeans and T-shirts were *de rigueur*. Variations came, it's true, with the jackets, some heavy leather, some crumpled cotton in the *Miami Vice* look, while others chose to wear nothing but their musculature. Three of them wore red bandannas, none wore clothes that distracted from their physical selves. When they met, they appeared to mirror each other's movements – a broad arc of the arm, the meshing of fingers, a hand through the hair, much as a cat will use its paw to merge the scent of a human with its own. Miles and Glurg pushed by the group.

The dance floor downstairs at La Piscine Bleue dissected the two seating areas, and beside it was a brightly lit bar, surrounded by video screens, at which Glurg and Miles stopped for another drink. The music was loud, so they stood silent, and watched the dancers. Most of the models were dancing with other models. Right in front of them, though, a goddess of a girl was dancing with a man who could, if he hadn't been so singularly unattractive, have been her father. The girl herself was sublime. She had long, straight, centre-parted hair, and stunning tear-drop eyes. Her mouth was wide and thin-lipped. She'd painted herself with only the lightest suggestion of lipstick. Looking like Cher, only younger and more beautiful, the girl's face would have been a plastic surgeon's dream. She was dancing vigorously, yet she was neither flushed nor sweating. By contrast, her ageing companion boasted of his efforts with swamps of perspiration across his black silk shirt. Greying hairs were matted to his forehead like bugs on flypaper. From what Miles could gather, a lack of sweat was part of the model's total beauty package, a vital remove from the common person. The girl looked as if ice wouldn't melt in her cleavage. Miles could imagine her filing her nails while her companion heaved and grunted above her as he struggled towards orgasm.

Suddenly, Miles noticed Georgina. She was sitting at a table in the furthest corner, away from the dance floor. Beside her sat Tiziana Ferrari herself, radiant in the simplest of clothes. She was wearing a tight black dress that swooped confidently down in a wide U to her cleavage. Tiziana had always been the supermodel whose look Miles had liked the most. He even knew her statistics from an article he'd once read – 34–24–35 – served up in five foot ten inches of curvaceous perfection.

He'd dreamt about her once. A simple, *Boys' Own* sex dream in which Tiziana had ridden him in ecstasy, her glinting long hair swishing wildly about as she moved. As a result, Poppy had left for work late but happy.

Miles ran his fingers through his hair, lit another cigarette, told Glurg he'd be back soon, picked up his drink, and strode towards the table. Georgina waved. Miles had decided not to look at Tiziana until he was introduced. No point in looking desperate, he thought, especially with the other four people at the table gazing up at him. His hand was shaking a little, and he thought maybe he'd gone red.

'You made it,' said Georgina.

'Yes. Um . . . you didn't.' Miles laughed. 'To the Café Clemenceau.'

Georgina, rather dramatically, slapped a hand on her forehead. 'Don't tell me you didn't get the message I left at the hotel.'

Miles shook his head. He wished he could say 'I don't believe you left a message, you lying bitch.' Instead what he said was: ''Fraid not.'

'Aaah!' screamed Georgina. 'Stupid bloody French. You can't trust them.'

'Don't worry, I didn't stay long. I had a coffee and was out of there. I guessed something was up.'

'And you got in here all right?'

'Oh sure. Almost immediately.'

'Good. Join us for a drink. Do you know Tiziana?'

Miles's head snapped around to where he'd been longing to look. Tiziana almost smiled at him. 'Have you been dancing?' she said.

Miles was taken aback. 'Oh, um, sure! If you want.'

Someone laughed. It echoed in Miles's head.

'No, I said *have you been dancing*. You're red.'

'Oh. I . . . I'm sorry, yes. I have. It's hot!'

Hot, and getting hotter.

'Eaghch. How could you?' Tiziana said. 'It's so crowded.'

'Oh, you know . . .'

Miles shrugged his shoulders and shifted on his feet. The muscles of his face struggled their way to a smile.

'Do you want to sit down?' Tiziana asked.

She picked up her drink as if to move across. Miles's heart skipped a beat. Would he like to sit? Next to Tiziana? And with the whole club watching? And in his new suit and haircut? Of course he would. For once in his life, here was a dream coming true.

'You can sit here,' she said. 'I'd better show my face upstairs.'

'Oh, are you going?' Miles said, cheerily.

'Mm. See you later, Georgie.'

Tiziana's dress was short and revealing, and Miles followed her backside out of view.

'Don't stare, it's rude,' laughed an American sitting beside Georgina.

'Calvin taught Tiziana how to walk,' Georgina said. 'He taught them all!'

'Not exactly! I teach girls how to walk on the runway. Not in La Pissoir as I call this place.'

'But, Calvin,' protested Georgina, 'if you teach a girl how to look sexy and elegant while she's on the catwalk, she's hardly going to start walking like a whore in the real world.'

'Excuse me, Miss Thing,' Calvin said, clicking his fingers. 'My whole life is dedicated to teaching them *how* to walk like whores. That's the whole point!'

Calvin laughed again. His perfect white teeth glinted purple in the fluorescent light from the dance floor. Calvin's skin was a dark black, his face round and cheerful. He'd cut his hair short, and wore a dark blue reefer jacket still buttoned with its bright gold buttons. Georgina's attention, however, was on Miles's new suit.

'You look nice,' she said.

'Very eighties,' joked Calvin.

'I'm beating the trend, Calvin,' said Miles. 'You watch! There'll be this big eighties revival soon. Penniless clubbers will be power-dressing.'

A sound came from Calvin's neighbour, like Mick Jagger talking in his sleep. 'The ayees a gouh nah sowel, maaan.'

'Excuse me?'

'Nah soul, I said. The ayees.'

Calvin translated. 'Eamon thinks he's got more soul than a whole decade.'

Eamon lifted his lip, and gave Calvin a sidelong glance. Eamon was a model from London's East end, one of the world's most highly paid. He had fleshy, bright red lips and a mop of greasy black hair. Miles had seen him three-quarters naked in some pop video. Maybe one of Madonna's. Right up there with the trend, Eamon was wearing a tight, bright red shirt that boasted an albatross of a collar. Its double cuffs were hanging down over his hands, so that every time he wanted to pick up his beer he had to lift up his arm and shake the cuff down. His jewellery jangled as he did so. On top of the shirt he wore a fitted grey pinstripe waistcoat. His trousers were tight and high-waisted, black too. His fingers were heavy with rings, but his seedy drug-dealer image was spoiled by his pumped-up pectorals and perfect skin, his lip gloss and mascara. The make-up was most probably from a new line for men that Eamon was about to launch himself.

Eamon mumbled some other insult in Calvin's direction before twisting his body back to the black girl beside him.

Suddenly Georgina squealed, stood, and leapt out over Miles. She ran to embrace a young man who'd just sidled up to the table.

'Giovanni!'

The man kissed Georgina on both cheeks, and spun her around. The sailor and his girl.

'Who's he?' Miles asked Calvin.

'Tiziana's brother. Isn't he *the most gorgeous*?'

Miles had read about Giovanni Ferrari. He was one of those so-called playboys beloved by gossip columnists the world over. Though not an actual European prince, he had, at thirty, the looks, wealth, hobbies, breeding and immorality of one. Much of his notoriety came from being Tiziana's brother, but he'd built up a reputation in Europe as being an astute dealer in nineteenth-century art, and in New York as being an astute collector of beautiful women. His affair with Effie Crascauldi, the Swiss milk-chocolate bombshell of the supermodel circuit, had been followed with Rottweiler determination. In the previous season, Giovanni had turned his attention to the glamorous sport of Formula One powerboat racing. He'd finished low in the rankings, but many spoke of his daring and promise. Thousands of women the world over would have given arms, eyes, teeth to be in Georgina's shoes.

Georgina held Giovanni's arm tightly as she introduced him to the others at the table. 'I had a crush on Giovanni for the first twenty years of my life,' she said.

'Why did you stop now, darling?' Giovanni said.

His voice was deep, his accent lilting and strongly Italian.

'Who's saying I did? Now sit down and have some champagne.'

'The champagne of this club? No! Do not be disgusting to me! I have some Scotch.'

He lifted the glass and drank. The ice chinked.

'Oh, G., you see Miles over there? You'll never believe what he's done with Spencer *and* my old boyfriend Chester.'

As Georgina regaled Giovanni with exaggerated details about the EDEN campaign, Miles studied the Italian. His hair was light brown, and thick. It waved over his neck and halfway over his ears. His nose was narrow, its bridge kinked slightly. A million words had been written about this endearing imperfection in his sister Tiziana, but the familial gene had moulded first her elder brother's features. Giovanni's eyes, set in deep sockets beneath strong, noble eyebrows, did not sparkle as Tiziana's. Rather, their questioning sadness added an air of sensitivity to Giovanni's face. There was a depth to his aspect that the other models lacked; a sense of the past. If Giovanni was an antique of exquisite, polished mahogany, then the other models were as poor modern reproductions.

In stature, Giovanni was tall and broad. He liked to stand erect, yet he did not appear tense. If anything, he was disarmingly at ease with himself and the world. It could perhaps have been seen as a fault in Giovanni

Ferrari that he was so conscious of his proximity to perfection.

That Giovanni would make an exemplary competitor, Miles doubted not at all. The risk, rather, was that Giovanni would transform the competition into a one-horse race. He had everything the other finalists possessed and more, for Giovanni had the devastating confidence that comes from being born an aristocrat. If Giovanni agrees to compete, thought Miles, then the prize is as good as his.

Miles adopted the most casual tone that he could. 'Giovanni, would you be interested in coming to New York?'

The slim cigarette bobbed up and down in Giovanni's mouth as he replied. 'I love to go to New York. Each year I come four or five times.'

'I come four or five times a night,' screamed Calvin.

'I meant for the EDEN competition,' Miles said.

Giovanni lowered his solid silver cigarette lighter, and he spoke slowly. 'Me? To model? Please, are you crazy?'

'This isn't any old modelling job. This is for . . .'

Giovanni took the cigarette from his mouth and shook his hand at Miles. 'Please, my friend, I do not know you, but do not be insulting to me like this. A model!'

'Something wrong with models?' mumbled Eamon.

'Many things,' Giovanni said, lighting his cigarette now and giving Eamonn a drop-dead smile. 'Many things.'

'It's not easy being a model, you know,' said Eamon.

'I do know.' Giovanni smiled, and looked about at his audience. 'That is one of the problems.'

'Yeah, so what else do you have a problem with?'

'I don't like to be the image of a model. It is not good for a man to be thinking he is too beautiful.'

Giovanni rubbed the silver lighter on his lapel, and smoothed it into his pocket before adjusting his silk Armani tie.

Eamon protested. 'It's not the model who says he's beautiful. It's other people.'

'Please!' Giovanni held his hand up in the air, as if giving the order to a dog to sit. 'No argument. I am Italian, and I am a man.' Giovanni looked at Miles. 'Do you think you are the first person to ask me to be model? I am all my life now with models and agents and photographers and people who think I must be, be . . . discovered. Always I say same – no! What reason do I have now to say yes?'

'I can think of six million reasons,' Miles said smugly.

Giovanni looked at Georgina with an expression that seemed to be saying *Who cares about six million dollars?*

'It's only going to be one picture,' insisted Miles.

'Oh, of course, one picture, then maybe one more and before the photograph we have the competition in New York. No? That will be a circus, my friend. A circus like was in Rome with the Christians and the lions.'

Giovanni drank from his glass and looked past Miles to indicate that the conversation was as good as over.

'I never saw you as the type to be terrified of publicity,' said Miles, emboldened by the alcohol.

Giovanni was losing his temper now. Always it was the same with the Americans! They were born not to listen! 'I am choosing my own publicity,' he said. 'Why would I want to waste my time to be like Tiziana and going to *Weissmans* store to promote this cologne? No.' He brought his palm down on to the table. 'This is not my life.'

Miles had no reply. If Giovanni didn't want to compete, then there was no way that Miles could force him. At least, none that he could think of now.

La Piscine Bleue was more crowded with handsome men than any place Miles had ever been in his life. Why then, he thought to himself after an hour of wandering through the club, can I find no one for Adam?

His greatest problem continued to be that the best-looking men tended to be models with successful careers, thus counting themselves out of the final. Men such as Troy Turnbull, who Miles had run into on the stairs. Troy had greeted Miles as if they'd been high-school buddies, before boring him with details about his new spread in the men's section of British *Vogue*. Miles had made excuses, and escaped. Yet he'd seen no one else. There was Glurg, of course, but now he looked second-rate beside Giovanni. In fact, everyone did.

Downstairs, Miles leant back against one of the pillars by the dance floor. Giovanni was dancing with his sister. They were the stars of the floor, attracting twice as much attention as everyone else, with half as much effort. Miles stared at Giovanni as the Italian swayed with his sister. He seemed so perfect! If only there was a way . . .

Suddenly Miles felt a hand on his arm. It was Georgina. 'Come and dance with me,' she shouted above the music.

Miles smiled politely, but turned her down.

'Spoilsport!'

'Can I get you a drink, though?'

'Oh, lovely. Champagne, please.'

Miles pushed his way to the bar and returned with a glass.

'Thanks! It's a miracle I'm not dancing naked on the tables actually,' Georgina said, taking a swig. 'I get very naughty when I'm drunk and Giovanni's been pouring this stuff down my throat.'

'You two seem pretty close.'

'We've known each other for years.' She laughed. 'I could tell you things about G. you wouldn't believe.'

'Oh yeah? Like what?'

Georgina tapped Miles on his nose. 'Like I'm not telling you, nosey parker.'

To his left, Miles saw a couple stand to leave the club. 'Do you want to grab that table?' he said. 'And I'll get us a bottle.'

'At last,' Georgina smiled, 'my prince has come!'

They talked and drank until almost two more bottles had gone and the whole world seemed a joke. Once, Georgina tried to stand, but she fell back into her chair. This, too, they found hysterically funny. At least, Georgina did. Miles laughed along because he thought that was the smart thing to do. Just as it had been smart to keep filling Georgina's glass while he drank little himself, just as it would be smart to start asking questions before she lost her mind. He leant across the table and offered Georgina a cigarette.

'I don't smoke,' she said, taking one. She took hold of his hand as he held out his lighter. 'I've got a boyfriend, you know.'

'Yes, you told me at lunch.'

'But he's, he's away. Somewhere. Don't know really. Lausanne, I think.'

'Oh, right!'

'He wants to be a psychiatrist.'

'Does he?'

'Yeah. Don't know who'd ever go to see a French psychiatrist, though.' She laughed. 'Far as I can see the French are all bonkers. Would you?'

'What?'

'Miles! Ever go to a shrink.'

'I . . . no, I mean, I don't think so.'

'No.' Georgina sipped at her drink, bringing her head to her glass. 'I wouldn't either. Tiziana does. She told me.'

'Well, I guess it's not easy being a supermodel all the time.'

'You're right. Ten thousand dollars a day is very difficult to live with. Actually, that's got nothing to do with it. She's been going for years.'

'How come?'

'Family stuff, you know.'

'Like what?' asked Miles, tipping the last of the champagne into Georgina's glass.

'Promise you won't tell anyone.'

'I promise.'

Georgina giggled, and leant forward in her chair. She took Miles's head in the palm of her hand and pulled him forward so their heads were almost touching. 'Well, I was staying with them once,' she whispered, 'when I walked into the bedroom. And that's how I first found out.'

Half an hour on and Georgina was seeing double.

'Why don't we get you a cab?' Miles suggested.

'Are you coming with me?'

'I think I'd better hang around here a while,' said Miles. 'But I'll see you out.'

Luckily there were plenty of cabs waiting by the door, and within minutes Miles was back downstairs. He too was tired, and a little drunk. But he was also excited, as he had been ever since Georgina spilled the beans about the Ferraris.

Miles searched the floor for Giovanni. Had he gone? Miles hoped not. But then he saw Giovanni shouldering his way to the bar. Miles pushed forward, and reached the bar first. He pretended to be surprised.

'Oh hi! Can I buy you a drink?'

'*Grazie*.' Giovanni took a folded silk handkerchief from his pocket and briskly wiped the slight perspiration from the sides of his nose. He smiled. 'However, my friend, I do not change my mind about your competition because of one Scottish whisky!'

'I wasn't expecting you to.' Miles paid the barman and passed the double Scotch to Giovanni. 'Are you racing your boat next year?'

'Of course. I hope my father will again sponsor me.'

Aldo Ferrari, Giovanni's father, built not cars but buildings. He owned Italy's largest building company. Estimates of the size of his wealth varied, yet no one disputed the fact that Aldo was an enormously rich man who had a lifestyle to match his bank account.

'This was for him a very bad year.'

Miles and most of the world were aware that Aldo had been hit not only by the recession in the construction industry, but also by the political and financial scandals that had been rocking Italy's ruling élite.

'Can't you raise the money elsewhere?'

'I don't know. I will see.'

'I can think of an easy way, Giovanni. You know, there are going to be only six guys in this competition . . .'

Giovanni shook his head and made a tutting noise.

'Please,' continued Miles, 'just let me finish. I've chosen four men so far, and you'd beat them all, hands down.'

Giovanni seemed pleased by the compliment. Miles continued. 'What I'm saying is that unless we find someone absolutely incredible in London, I think the EDEN contract would be yours.'

'Is that your promise?' Giovanni asked, looking down and rattling the ice in his glass as he spoke.

'No, it's an opinion. I can only influence the decision, I can't make it. But I know the other models. I *chose* them. I mean, don't you think you're better-looking than Spencer Kemble-Finch? Or Chester?'

Impeccably discreet, Giovanni offered no response to the question, asking, instead, one of his own. 'It will be six million dollars for only one campaign?'

'Yeah. It's a massive PR stunt, and the model happens to be at the right end of it.'

Giovanni drew in hard on his cigarette and stared deep into Miles's eyes. Miles waited, his heart thumping. Giovanni was a fish who swam in rapid waters. A catch such as he would be quite some achievement, and Miles knew it.

Giovanni tilted back his head and drained his glass of whisky. 'I decide,' he said, talking around a cube of ice in his mouth. Giovanni spat the cube into his empty glass. 'I say "no". There are some things a man should not do!'

'And you never do those things.'

'Of course not!'

Miles looked down at his glass. 'That's not what I heard.'

Giovanni smiled. 'They write many stupid things in the American papers. You should not believe them.'

'I don't. But I didn't read this. Not yet, at least.'

'I never liked the riddles. What didn't you read?'

'How you like to sleep with one of the world's top female models.'

Giovanni, whose face had been creased with concern, let out a burst of laughter and put his arm around Miles's shoulder. 'I think you are the last person in the world to hear about me and Effie,' he said. 'I have been seeing her for more than two month now.'

Miles took a step away from Giovanni and looked him in

the eye. 'I was talking about someone a lot closer to home,' he said. Then he drained his glass and put it down on the bar. 'I'll be here for a little while longer,' he said, 'if you suddenly change your mind.'

With that, Miles walked away leaving Giovanni feeling more ill at ease than he'd ever felt before.

21

Miles woke with a start and turned the light on and off to see the time. It was five thirty on Friday, November 20th. The sounds of a strange city, carrying far in the thin air of dawn, disturbed him; a car horn, a yapping dog, a man coughing then his guttural spit and the diminishing slaps of footsteps. Miles yanked at the tube-like pillow of the bed but it remained uncomfortable so he abandoned it and slid his feet down into the cold corner of the sheets. He rubbed his feet together, the nail of his big toe scratching his sole. Then he brought the blankets over his head, and tried to find comfort in the unfamiliar contours of the mattress.

But he couldn't sleep while the cogs of his mind were spinning. Had Miles merely been excited about Giovanni's ultimate acquiescence in La Piscine Bleue, he'd have probably drifted to sleep with self-congratulatory images of himself returning to New York with the prize. Instead he felt ashamed. The tactics he'd used had been despicable. That Miles knew he'd never have told the press about Giovanni's relationship with Tiziana helped little. The truth was simple. Miles had blackmailed Giovanni, and he had no excuses for that.

Of course, it would all seem so different if Giovanni was to win, and truly Miles thought he would. Weissman couldn't but recognise the advantages of a spokesman of Giovanni's temperament and skill, and there was little doubt that the Italian was perfect for the job. What's more, Giovanni had the charisma of a natural leader of men. The concern was that Weissman would reject Giovanni as being too famous. Though Giovanni had never modelled, his face had been in every tabloid newspaper in New York. Miles thought of the others – Fernando, Fabio, Spencer and Chester. Chester, it was true, brought with him a ready-made image; but the others Weissman could do with as he wished. Hadn't that been his aim all along? To create a male supermodel out of a nobody? The problem with Giovanni might be that he'd outshine the cologne itself.

Miles curled himself into a ball. Had he made a terrible mistake? Would Giovanni's reputation as a playboy be his downfall as Adam? Would Giovanni be dragged by the media through the mud, and all for nothing? It shouldn't have mattered to Miles whether Giovanni had said yes or no. But it did, and Miles knew why – because it reflected well on him; because he'd get a slap on the back and perhaps a hefty bonus from the great Saul Weissman; because, by netting Giovanni Ferrari, Miles was proving to Weissman, to Kristina, to Poppy, and to the world, that he was a man whose time had finally come.

Five hours on, Miles took breakfast in his room with the croissant flakes falling onto the creased and crested sheets of the bed. Though he'd slept, he'd woken feeling guilty still. For some reason he kept thinking of his mother, of how horrified she'd have been had she known of his actions. Miles had always imagined that it had been from her that he'd inherited his values, as if her Englishness lent them substance. She had had such pride in beliefs forged over the generations. And wasn't Miles being disloyal to those now?

He climbed out of bed, took his jacket from the chair by the window. On the street, a man was running with an orange crate loaded with sticks of bread, whistling as he moved. Miles looked back to his jacket and found the card upon which he'd written Giovanni's home number. Miles returned to the bed, and dialled.

'Pronto.'

'Giovanni?

'Si?

'It's Miles Jensen.' There was a long silence before Miles continued. 'I . . . I've been thinking and I've decided I . . . I probably shouldn't have done what I did.' Again he waited for a response; none came. 'I thought that we could maybe meet somewhere and talk about the whole thing. Giovanni?'

'Si?'

'Do you have any time? I mean, I . . . I still think you should enter the competition.'

'I have been thinking also.'

'And?'

'And I will tell you when we meet. You know the Café Flore?'

'Yeah.'

'Then if you agree I will see you there at twelve.'

The State Senator for North Carolina was, as might have been expected, a fine-looking man. He had a wide face, thick grey hair, wrinkles carved deep into his skin, and an athletic frame. He'd been a quarterback at Harvard in the forties and a keen sportsman ever since. Senator Tristan Hunt was a man to command authority, and one of the most powerful and respected Senators in the land.

His youngest son, Chester, had been to him once the source of great pride. That there'd been fierce battles between them had never much worried him. The death of the Senator's wife, Chester's mother Susanne, in a car accident in West Virginia in 1984 that had also taken the life of Chester's sister Chelsea, had put immense pressure on Tristan's relationship with his son, but the Senator had expected that time would prove more useful than coddling affection in healing their rift. Chester was a good student, always had been, and with his intent focus showed no signs of running off the tracks. In time, the Senator thought, when Chester was running for political office, they would be allies, and no resentment could then remain.

When Chester dropped out of Harvard, this Senator, renowned in the nation for his political foresight, was taken completely by surprise. He reacted with shock and anger and an almost complete lack of understanding. Until his son came to his senses, he didn't want to be involved. He insisted on being kept informed of Chester's whereabouts, but there was to be no direct communication between them.

When Jake, the Senator's secretary, handed his employer a photograph of Chester half-naked on a bed in Milan, along with the news that Larry Meyers from the *New York Herald* had been on the line, the Senator acted with his customary truculence. He tore the photograph to pieces, then threw them in the trash before returning to the Committee recommendations on homosexuals serving in the armed forces. He didn't lift his head as Jake told him all about the *Weissmans* EDEN campaign.

'The papers want to know how you feel about Chester's inclusion in the competition,' concluded Jake.

Jake was an eager man, fresh from college and with a future clearly mapped out goal by goal.

'Tell them he's a grown child and he can do what he likes with his life,' the Senator answered gruffly.

'Sir, we have the debate next week on State nursery-school funding. Aren't you speaking about the decline of the nuclear family?'

'Well, I've got my proof,' snapped Tristan. 'The Hunts go atomic. The Hiroshima Hunts. Now let me get on.'

'Sir . . .'

'Jake, it's the Democrats who waste their time with ideals. Most of us have too much sense.'

'Sir, I thought you always said that the truth is less important than . . .'

'All right Jake, do this for me: tell the *Herald*'s distinguished political commentator that Senator Hunt is as confident now as he ever was that his son will continue to excel in whatever field he chooses for himself, and that Mr Saul Weissman is a pillar of the national community and an example to Americans black, white, brown, green, Jewish, Catholic, Hindu and Mormon. Get the drift?'

'Thank you.'

'And if you have the good fortune to speak with my son please inform him that if he tries to put so much as one foot in this country while his hair is down to his waist, I will – personally – see to it that he is deported.'

'Yes, sir.'

'And excluded for ever from a trust fund he can hardly do without.'

Once, in the days when Paris had truly been at the cutting edge of art and intellectualism, Café de la Flore was one of those places where the cutters congregated. Opposite the church of St-Germain-des-Prés, the oldest in Paris, and across the boulevard from Les Deux Magots, another celebrated café with a literary prize all of its own, the Café de la Flore had somehow managed to retain an air of superiority and exclusivity despite its inclusion in most guidebooks to the city. It was, perhaps, because the prices were so high that the majority of tourists passed it by. It may also have been that Parisians were notoriously xenophobic in their desire to keep the best places for themselves, and waiters thought nothing of scaring aliens away.

In a corner of the café, surrounded by perfectly polished mirrors that spread high all around, sat Giovanni Ferrari, looking about as Parisian as it was possible for an Italian to look. As it was warm inside Flore he'd removed three layers and sat in a navy cashmere turtleneck, a cigarette in hand, a beer on the table. Frenchmen loved to coordinate their layers. In winter, they'd wear long coats over jackets over waistcoats over shirts over visible T-shirts, none too thick so as to stifle, all easily removable to attain that perfect temperature for themselves. Giovanni rose when Miles approached. There was an awkward moment, but then he extended a hand. Miles shook it. 'Would you like a drink?'

'I'll take a beer too, I think.'

They sat with Stella Artois, and Gauloises, blatantly ignoring the new government ban on smoking in restaurants. Sitting opposite Giovanni at their wooden table, Miles could see the outside street reflected in the mirror.

Miles spoke: 'I want to say that I'd never have, you know,

gone through with what I said. I must have been drunk last night.'

'Is that not the excuse of a coward?'

'I meant . . .'

Giovanni raised a palm and smiled. 'You think I care what you say about this? It is a total stupid! No one can believe something like this.'

No one? wondered Miles. *I did; still do.*

'But I was talking to Tiziana and she say that this, this campaign is a good idea for me. Many people think this is a good idea.'

'And you?'

'You think I will win the six million dollar?'

'Probably.'

'I think you will help me win.'

Miles laughed. 'What is this? An offer I can't refuse? Either I make you win or I get a visit from the mafia?'

'No, please! I think you do not know how to do business, my friend.'

'Well, I . . .'

'This is not a movie! I am saying that if you make sure I win, then of course I will repay you.'

Miles looked about him as if they were planning a crime. 'I can't make promises.'

'I know. But you said to me I win unless you find someone who is more better in London. So it is simple, no? You choose in London a model who is *not* good.'

Miles took a moment, and then said: 'And you'd make it worth my while.'

'Si.'

'How much worth it?'

As he waited for Giovanni's reply, Miles thought about the proposition. At La Piscine Bleue, Miles thought he'd stumbled across Giovanni's greatest fear, the fear of having his relationship with Tiziana exposed. Now he thought that this wasn't it at all. Rather, it was the thought of losing the competition to a bunch of nobodys that worried Giovanni the most. He was too accustomed to being judged the winner.

He wanted to enter the competition only if his victory could be assured.

Miles could see his own mistake now. Repeatedly, he'd told Giovanni that it would be Saul Weissman who'd choose the winner, thus making himself appear less valuable. If Miles wanted a decent percentage of the money, he'd have to convince Giovanni of his worth.

Still, Miles's position was strong. So confident was he that Giovanni would win anyway he knew he could make unjustifiable claims now about his influence with Weissman. If Giovanni lost, then life would carry on as before. But if he won and paid up, oh, the bliss of it! Twenty per cent, the sum an agent would take anyway, was already more than a million dollars. A million dollars! If Miles played his cards right when they were back in New York, if he acted his heart out to Giovanni, he could probably convince him that he was fighting a battle with Weissman on Giovanni's behalf. The fiercer the fighting, the more Miles seemed to be putting his career on the line, the more he'd be worth. It struck him now that it would be better to negotiate a price closer to the time when the decision would be made.

'If I win the six million,' said Giovanni, 'I will give you five hundred thousand dollar cash.'

Miles tried to look absolutely calm while he felt like dancing around the café. He finished his beer, and took his time. Then he spoke, as if they were playing a game with Monopoly money. 'For the five hundred,' he replied, 'I promise I'll choose someone in London who can't win. But later, if I have to put my ass on the line for you, I think I'll be worth a little bit more that that? Don't you?'

Giovanni shrugged his shoulders. 'Let us talk again,' he said, 'when I see how bad your British man will be.'

In New York City, Steve Barefoot sat on his canvas ex-army bag and counted on his fingers how many pairs of underpants he'd packed for London. One-two-three! Kristina was in the kitchen, a space almost unknown to her. She poured herself a Snapple Lemon Ice Tea and took two aspirin, as she always liked to do before boarding an international flight.

Steve called to her from the bedroom. 'Is it cold in London now?'

'No, it's hotter than Florida.'

'It is? I don't need this jacket, then. Do I?'

Kristina swept into the room. As she talked to Steve, she took one more jacket – simple, black, Armani – from her closet and folded it into her groaning, Louis Vuitton case. 'I can't conceive how the temperature in London, which is cold, of course, could possibly be a problem to you. You wear the same filthy clothes everyday anyway.'

'I won't when I'm a millionaire.'

Steve spoke the word with relish in five syllables; Mil-lee-on-ay-err. It was more than a word to him; it was a concept to which he'd become accustomed. He'd already been out spending money which he didn't really have. He'd found two thousand dollars in an envelope in the back of a drawer in Kristina's apartment, and he'd bought himself a whole bunch of things with that: some $800 cowboy boots, a brown leather jacket, twenty-five CDs, and a cheap gold pendant for Kristina from Canal Street. In *Weissmans* a cute girl had appeared from nowhere and told him that she had the very same portable CD player that he was looking at, and it worked like a dream. Steve had bought it, and it had gone into the suitcase along with the other things he was hiding until the EDEN contract was his. Shit, when the six million dollars came in, Kristina wouldn't care about a piddling $2000. They could burn that amount and not even notice it. That's right, he thought, he'd actually have money to burn.

Kristina asked Steve for help in closing her case. He looked at it in wonder. 'How long you planning on staying in London? A year?'

'Did you pack the handcuffs?'

'No. And I'm not going to. In London, England, you and I are going to make love in the proper way.'

'Just get the cuffs.' Steve shook his head, stood his ground.

'Oh, God! I'll get them then.' She came back. 'Don't forget who's paying for this trip.'

'I am, in the end. This pretty little face of mine,' he said with a smile. 'This is a joint venture, which does make me wonder why I'll be travelling in the cheap seats of a cheap airline while you'll be up there in fancy Business class.'

'We musn't be seen together. Not at all. Not until after Monday. What if someone saw us on the plane? It would ruin everything.'

'You know, you must have some kind of crazy mind to think up all this shit.'

'Well, thank God I haven't left it up to you. Now the car's coming in a minute. Do you have everything?'

'Sure do.'

Steve picked up his small bag. 'Good. You can carry my cases for me then,' she said.

Steve saluted. 'Yes, ma'am. Anything you say.'

The music was so loud that Miles could hardly hear Georgina asking him if he was leaving.

'Yeah, I am.'

They were in a nightclub called Queen on the Champs-Élysées. Named appropriately, it had once been a gay club, but had since been invaded by straight men and women. It happened all over the world. Energetic in their pursuit of a good time, gays would establish a club which soon would become the hottest place in town. Then, patting itself on the back, the hetero community would discover it, and invade.

Dina van Stigal and Wendy Radcliff were in Queen that Friday night, along with Giovanni and Effie. Wendy had been one of the first to come to the club where she could dance and relax without a hundred men around her, longing to take her to bed. It was a novel sensation. In gay clubs, the supermodels could show off their clothes, make-up, hairstyles and boyfriends without constant sexual threat. Now though, Queen was becoming like every other club, and the girls were being forced to spend most of their time at tables on one of the upper levels.

Miles was at one of these tables, with Georgina, Effie and Giovanni. Georgina had been bad company for all but herself. On mescaline, she'd been babbling about colours and painting and how nobody loved her.

Giovanni and Miles were getting on well. The prospect of outsmarting the system had smoothed out their earlier problems, and they were becoming friends. Giovanni's supermodel girlfriend, Effie, was big-boned and blonde and very beautiful, but she hadn't been paying much attention to Miles. Still, he'd been thrilled enough just to be seen there. It didn't matter what the people were actually like.

Miles hadn't yet told Giovanni about his conversation with Kristina. After their meeting in Café de la Flore, after they'd shaken hands and parted as friends, Miles had returned to the hotel to call her. She'd been less excited about Giovanni than Miles had hoped, but she'd told Miles to confirm him all the same. Then Kristina had broken the news about London. She was coming to help Miles search for the final model.

The mere thought of Kristina joining him in London had removed from Miles his invigorating sense of power and responsibility. But worse, much worse than this, was the fear that now, under Kristina's supervision, he might have to choose a model for Adam more suitable than Giovanni.

Miles took a cab back to his hotel. He much preferred Paris by night. Driving towards the Louvre, with the city's architectural highlights illuminated on each side of the Seine, Miles found no distractions to steal the glory from the sights, from the bridges and the Louvre itself, from the Palais de la Justice, Sacré-Coeur and the Eiffel Tower. He gazed out in awe. For the first time he too was thinking like a Parisian, seeing a city of dreams the ugly problems of which were hidden in the darkness. The jumbled claustrophobia of Paris had disappeared and in the end the city had won, as the city always does.

Paris had found itself yet another lover.

Sitting in underpants, with cigarettes and bourbon, was how

Larry Meyers liked to work. Staying true to the image, he'd until recently remained loyal to his clackety old typewriter, but Jakes had bought him a word processor, and it was at this, in his 47th street apartment, that Meyers sat reading over his freshly typed article.

Once they thought he was dead, but they said they could rebuild him.

Then he died again.

Now, he's back. Back in a new guise. Back as a modern-day hero. Butch, manly, healthy and strong, a Six-Million-Dollar-Man for the nineties is coming to our town soon.

We've got Saul Weissman to thank for it. Seems like we keep thanking Saul Weissman for making this city a better place to live in. We thanked him for building a garden in Bedford-Stuyvesant. We thanked him for showing the Russians the good side of our way of doing things. We thanked him for keeping his prices down and his standards high. And we're thanking him again. You might think that there's nothing commendable about paying a male model six million dollars to have his photograph taken for EDEN, the new Weissmans cologne.

But you'd be wrong.

Saul Weissman's got the guts to say 'to hell with this recession.' Saul Weissman is believing in America. If Bill Clinton remembers he's got men like Saul Weissman running our businesses, men like Saul Weissman who only yesterday was called an 'example to all Americans' by Republican Senator Tristan Hunt, then the President's going to believe that Yes, We Can Rebuild This Country.

Saul Weissman's been searching the globe for his six men. So far, he's found five. Why these men? Out of the millions?

It isn't hard to see.

For twenty-two year-old Fernando Padrillas, the visit from Weissmans came out of the blue when his world seemed hopeless and grey. Last year, Fernando's father died in a freak accident. He was decapitated by a Best Burger billboard during Hurricane Andrew. Says Fernando: 'We were left with nothing. No home, no family, nothing except the clothes on our backs.' But Fernando and his mother found the courage to fight. He took Best Burger to court.

On the day his appeal was rejected, a man from Weissmans appeared.

Fernando: 'He came in a limousine and said "Do you want six million dollars?" I said, 'Yes, of course!'

Already Fernando is causing a storm of his own on the shores of fashionable Florida. He's put his Degree in Engineering on hold while he struts and poses for some of the world's top photographers. Photographers like Italian, Aldo Tocca: 'Fernando has raw energy. He is not afraid to be a man.'

Owner of his new modelling agency, Rosa Bertaum, says: 'Fernando's got what it takes to go all the way.' And Fernando? He's staying philosophical: 'this is God's way of saying sorry for the pain. I am keeping my fingers crossed that they give the campaign to me.'

If he gets the six million, Fernando says he'll buy a new home for his mother, and 'the best lawyer in the world to help me fight my case.'

The other finalists had better watch out. Fernando Padrillas is one hell of a fighter.

Spencer Kemble-Finch sounds like a butler in a TV sitcom, but he's the one who's getting served upon. As British as London Fog and Roast Beef, the twenty-six year-old was a Captain in the Life Guards Regiment, protectors of the Queen of England. But rebellious Spencer, grandson of the Lord who owns London's fashionable King's Road, gave it all up for a life of leisure and surfing in sunny Sydney, Australia.

A spokesman at his old regiment said, 'He was a good soldier.' Closer friends say he couldn't take the pace of army life. Like Queen's son Prince Edward before him, Spencer dropped out. Spencer will be coming to New York from Tokyo where his father is Ambassador. Yesterday the Ambassador's secretary was the model of British discretion. 'I know nothing about the competition,' she said.

But Spencer wants to be a model of another sort. 'I'm very flattered to be included,' he said. Asked about his chances of victory, he said, 'May the best man win!'

Keep your chin up, Spencer, but make sure it's your best side!

Also chosen in Tokyo in Japan, the black sheep of the final is Brazilian Fabio Nirao. And although Fabio is only twenty years old he's anything but wet behind the ears. Known as the Tokyo Casanova, he's been breaking hearts all over Japan with his tanned, muscular body and his winning smile. Irresistible is the word that most women use.

His agent Joe Fujimoto phrased it differently: 'Fabio is sexy. He is the big model of tomorrow.' Since being chosen for the competition, says America-loving Joe, 'Fabio has become Japan's top model,' working for up to six thousand dollars a day.

Dedicated to his diet of beer and cigarettes, Wild One Fabio, who many liken to a young Marlon Brando, is likely to break as many hearts in America when he arrives for the competition. 'I'll make it there like I make it anywhere,' says the self-confident young model.

American Chester Hunt, the twenty-two-year-old son of Senator Tristan Hunt of North Carolina has always found his way into the national spotlight, and now he's done it again. Once tipped as his father's natural successor, Chester, whose mother and sister died eight years ago in a tragic automobile accident, has since become a long-haired wandering rebel. Now he's found his cause. Chester dropped out of Harvard not to pursue a career in politics, but to become a fashion model.

'I've always been a visual person,' he says. 'I'm proud of what I do.'

And the Senator? Sources close to him claim he's deeply disturbed about his son's behaviour and has threatened to cut him off without a dime. Yesterday he was putting a brave face on a rift that is becoming wider by the day. 'I am sure he will do well,' the Senator said.

Chester is even more confident, saying, 'I'm the look of the nineties.' What is that look? See for yourself. It was taken by famous French photographer Michel Forgat. 'Chester is very natural model.' he told me yesterday from his exclusive Paris studio. And what does he think of the long hair? 'It's very sexy for a man to discover his feminine side,' Michel says. 'In the end, it makes him more of a man.'

I wonder if Senator Hunt would agree.

Yesterday in Paris, Giovanni Ferrari, brother of supermodel Tiziana Ferrari, became the latest addition to the impressive field of competitors. Thirty-year-old Giovanni is no stranger to the Herald. *His much-publicised affair with Bavarian beauty Effie Crascauldi has survived rumours that's she's seeing Heavy Metal star Machete Flower, and now Milanese art dealer Giovanni is looking forward to another season of the exclusive and glamorous sport of the playboys – speed powerboat racing.*

Our own Style Queen, Cynthia G. said she was 'shocked and amazed' by Giovanni's inclusion. 'He doesn't like to be photographed,' Cynthia told me. But she could understand why Weissmans would want him. 'He's a fairy-tale Prince come to life – tall, dark, handsome and well-mannered.' As a final word of warning to the others, she added, 'I've looked at them all, and Giovanni must be the favourite.'

Will Giovanni, a man born with a golden spoon in his mouth, walk away with the prize? Or will it be one of the others? We will have to wait and see.

This weekend in London, England, Saul Weissman's Scout About the Globe, Miles Jensen, will choose the final entrant. Then the competition comes to New York.

An appearance on the Trudie Love show has been promised.

Ego

The winner and the new Six Million-Dollar Man will be announced at a glittering party to be held by Saul Weissman at Grand Central Station. And the Herald *will be there, keeping you informed every step of the way.*

The morning in Paris was bright and blustery. People were keeping themselves to themselves more than usual, rounding corners with their heads down and their hands thrust deep in their pockets. Miles was taking a walk before breakfast, feeling depressed about returning to New York. What would he do back home? He couldn't slip back into his previous style of life, not after this. Even to the outside world, he was different: new hairstyle, new clothes, new friends. And inside he knew he'd changed. His ambition was out of its lengthy hibernation. He couldn't go back to the shop floor at *Weissmans* as if this adventure had been nothing more than a holiday. No, he'd lived and played with the most beautiful in the world. He'd visited the place that most people only dream of reaching, and fallen in love with it.

The idea of becoming a model had been sown by an agent's mistake in Miami. Now in Paris the seed was germinating. Acting wasn't the answer. Miles felt he'd learnt that much. He'd been stupid. Twenty-eight was too old to be able to make it big. It wasn't the same in modelling. There was a big market for models of his age. They made safety-razor and car advertisements. They hugged their fathers beside misty rivers, back-lit by sunsets of gold. They held babies and loved them in the new nineties dawn. They gripped bunches of flowers behind their backs for independent women in business suits who'd rediscovered a love of chilvary. This was the age for the all-round men – new fathers, sportsmen, lovers. It was only the thought of a new kind of life that saved Miles's spirit from sinking too low. A new kind of life, and a brand new dream.

22

T wo days later, on a damp Monday morning in Kensington, Miles's depression had deepened. He blamed his weekend in London.

His mood had begun the moment he'd arrived at Heathrow. It had never struck him before how a place as internationally generic as an airport terminal could define the character of a nation. But then from his trip around the world he remembered the stark, run-down, seventies warehouses of Africa, the cramped bustle of Hong Kong, and then the visually imaginative Charles de Gaulle in Paris. He loved its cavernous tunnels, its walls of rough and pitted concrete, its airy glass heart. You could love it, or hate it, but they were damned if you were going to ignore it; and you couldn't get more French than that. And Heathrow? Well, its brilliantly characterless, odourless and dull spaces were, to Miles, solidly evocative of the England of today.

He wished it didn't have to be that way. He'd visited his mother's family on several occasions in his youth and developed a potent love of England. He could remember days when he'd argued its merits to his classmates. He could remember the pride he'd felt knowing that white America was born of a seed carried from England. He could remember sunshine. But recently, as now, the country seemed smothered in cloud. Miles was not surprised that London lacked the brilliant skyscrapers of American architecture. He thought they would have seemed out of place in a nation that no longer searched for the sun. England, too, remembered sunshine in its past, and from what Miles could tell, it considered the memory enough.

These thoughts were running through Miles's mind as he

walked to his meeting with Kristina in Models Too agency. He was walking because the tube had broken down somewhere west of South Ken, and the traffic was slithering through the drizzle like an injured slug.

He gazed at the *Independent* as he walked, its headlines considering the ethics of allowing a soccer fan to die. The fan was in a coma known as a Persistent Vegetative State, kept alive by a Life-Support Machine. Isn't that England's story? Miles wondered. The country wasn't really functioning any more. It was simply *existing*, being kept alive by a once glorious past. And without that, what would the country be? Another Greece, perhaps, remembered only for its attraction to foreign tourists.

Before long, he arrived at the agency. He was thumbing through a collection of composites and eavesdropping on a young female booker explaining to a hopeful model on the phone that, sorry, the agency already had two black models, when Kristina swanned in late, calm and composed.

'My, my! Look at you,' she said, her tone soft as steel.

'What?'

'Look at you! The hair. The clothes. You look odd.'

Miles felt the blood flushing his face for the first time in days. The booker at the table had only known Miles as he appeared now. Miles preferred that. Already, a part of him was embarrassed with the man he'd so recently been. Trust Kristina to be the first to stir up the past.

'When did you arrive?' he asked.

'Saturday. I've been seeing some old friends.'

In fact, the only old friend she'd been seeing was Steve – beneath her, on top of her, to the side of her, in the shower with her, inside her. Once on Saturday she'd dashed out on a solo shopping spree to Harrods and Harvey Nichols leaving Steve in front of Grandstand, but they'd stayed in bed for the rest of the time. Steve knew nothing of London except that the cabs were different, and milk was about the only foodstuff delivered.

That morning, before she'd left for the agency, Kristina

had made Steve promise that he'd follow her soon in a cab to the agency.

'Stop worrying, would ya?' he'd said.

Twenty minutes after she'd arrived at Models Too, that's precisely what Kristina was doing. Miles was, unfortunately, impressing her with his brisk efficiency in rejecting models. Now, he was threatening to leave – and still there was no sign of Steve.

Miles asked Kristina to join him out of earshot of the booker. 'There's no model here as good as the ones we've got.'

Kristina shook her head. 'I'd like another look.'

'Trust me,' he said. 'I know.'

Kristina took a step back and snorted a laugh through her nose. 'And you think I don't?'

'I . . .'

Miles didn't have to answer. At that moment, a man pushed his way through the door with all the confidence of a movie cowboy entering a saloon after a victorious duel on dusty Main Street.

Miles looked up in shock. 'I don't believe it! Jeff Gifford!' The man stared at Miles. 'I'm sorry,' Miles said. 'I thought you were someone else.'

'That's OK.'

Steve brushed past Kristina without a glance in her direction. He introduced himself to the booker, Tania, and said that he was new in town and looking for an agency.

Miles whispered to Kristina. 'It's incredible. Did you see the pictures of Jeff Gifford from Tokyo? This guy, I mean, I mean he could be his identical twin brother.'

Kristina pretended to study Steve for the very first time. 'He does have a great body.'

'Maybe, but you and Mr Weissman didn't like Jeff.'

'We liked his look, it was Jeff we had a problem with. I heard bad things about him in New York. But this guy . . . this guy could be just what we're after.'

Alarm bells began to ring in Miles's mind. If Kristina liked this model, and if Kristina knew what Weissman wanted, and if Kristina decided that this was what it was, then suddenly the chances of Giovanni becoming Adam looked bleak. 'I don't know, Kristina,' Miles whispered. 'Isn't he a bit, I don't know, plastic and stupid looking?'

'Who cares? He's sexy.'

'I wouldn't know about that, I . . .'

Kristina swung around, took hold of Miles's arm with a tight grip, and led him into the quiet corridor, out by the photocopier machines. 'No, Miles, you wouldn't know. You don't know a thing about sexiness. Steve here . . .'

'Who?'

'Steve . . .'

A look of momentary panic swept across Kristina's face.

'He's called Steve,' she said quickly. 'I heard him say his name. It's Steve.'

'Oh, right.'

'Yes. I was about to say that he'd be the only sexy competitor. Your lot . . .'

'My lot?'

Damn her! No way could she criticise his models like this. Hadn't she approved them all? He raised his voice in anger. 'Why agree to them if you didn't like them?'

Kristina spoke in a quiet, cool, dismissive tone.' We weren't exactly inundated with models from you, were we? Tell me, exactly how many options did we have from Miami?'

Miles opened his mouth in shock.

'Fernando? Fernando Padrillas isn't sexy to you? That guy hasn't got anything *but* sex appeal.'

'Whatever, Miles. It's too late. The sooner you get back to that shop floor, the better it'll be for EDEN.'

'I'm not going back there.'

'Oh, I see. You've done the flights, now you want a cruise on *Weissmans*? Am I right?'

Miles clenched his teeth.

'Miles, there's simply nothing left for you to do. We've got our six guys, now you can go back to work.'

Miles stared at her, his heart thumping. This was worse than he'd feared. At least he'd expected to be working with the models until the end of the competition. Surely Weissman wouldn't agree to this. What about the EDEN triangle? Who'd ever heard of a two-sided triangle? And what did Kristina mean by 'We've got the six'? Was this Steve guy definitely in? What would that do to his chances of making a million out of Giovanni? By now there were so many bells ringing in his head that Miles couldn't hear himself think.

'There's a plane that leaves first thing tomorrow morning,' said Kristina. 'I'll be booking you on it. I'll tell Saul about Steve. If Mr Weissman wants to see you tomorrow, you won't need to go to work until Thursday.'

To stop himself shaking, Miles took out his pen and played with it as he spoke. 'I'm sorry, Kristina, but I was under the impression that we were choosing these models as a team. This, what's his name . . . this Steve, I mean, he's the first guy you've seen in London.'

'I don't *need* to see any more. He's perfect. If you can't see that, I don't know why we sent you at all.'

'I didn't ask to go.'

'Are you complaining?'

'No, but I don't know where you get . . .'

At that moment, Steve emerged from the Men's division. He looked Kristina in the eye, but there wasn't a flicker of recognition as he turned and moved up the stairs, two steps at a time. Kristina glanced across at Miles, and waited until Steve was nearing the top. Then she called after him.

'Stop!' Steve turned. 'Excuse me. Do you think we could have a word?'

Steve Barefoot paused a second, then slowly descended the stairs, the jubilant sound of cash tills ringing in his ears.

There'd been a crash on the M4. For a while, Miles had sat with the taxi immobile and expensive, convinced that he'd miss his plane. So when the staff at the check-in told him he'd make the eleven a.m. flight from Heathrow to JFK only if he ran, he did so.

He arrived sweating and flustered and didn't even notice her when he handed the stewardess his boarding card.

'7G, sir, is through on your right.'

Miles looked up. 'It's you!' he exclaimed. Then, more mildly,' Er, hello. I was on the LA-Tokyo flight.'

Alice looked at Miles.' 7G is through to your right. Kindly take your seat.'

I know she remembers me. She must. There can't have been that many in between. Can there?

Miles took his seat next to a Middle-Eastern man wearing a grey suit, a white shirt with no collar, dark sunglasses and a Walkman. The man had short dark hair and skin that bore the cratered ravages of adolescent acne. Despite himself, Miles's first thought was that the man was a terrorist. Miles sat and reached for his seat belt. The terrorist was sitting on it. Miles twisted to him. Quietly, he said, 'Excuse me.'

The terrorist did not turn. He was staring ahead at the back of the seat in front. Miles wondered if the man was contemplating his imminent explosion. Miles couldn't tell if the terrorist's eyes were open or closed beneath the blackened shades, but the tinny din coming from the Walkman suggested that he was deaf to Miles's request. Miles tugged gently on the strap. Nothing. Then Alice appeared.

'Please fasten your seat belt, sir.'

'I . . . he's sitting on it.'

Alice leant over Miles and took hold of the man's arm and shook it. She talked loudly. Miles caught a glimpse of Alice's breasts, and wondered why he'd run scared from her. The man moved his buttocks, but said nothing. Miles took hold of the warm metal buckle of the strap, and fastened up. He lifted his head.

'Thanks,' he said. 'I . . . '

But Alice was already gone.

Kristina von Koeler reached orgasm on the carpeted floor of room 36 in the exclusive Byron Hotel without the assistance of handcuffs, collars, chains or leather straps. Steve hadn't even been asked to boss her about. And now, as he lay on top of her, his weight on his shoulders, his punctured inner-tube of a penis slithering out from the darkness, Steve wondered whether perhaps, possibly, maybe, Kristina von Koeler was in love with him. He bent his thick, muscular neck down and kissed her sweetly on her open lips.

All day in London they'd been as happy as kids at Christmas. For the first time since they'd met, Kristina had been relaxed holding Steve's hand in public. And they'd been shopping together, she emerging from the changing rooms in Joseph and Jaspar Conran and Harvey Nichols and Browns, wearing tight, expensive dresses and skirts and wondering how she looked. For once, she'd revelled in the public attention of her much younger man. As if to reward him, she'd then taken Steve to buy some clothes on her credit card, clothes she knew Sam Weissman would admire when he met him.

Kristina had no doubts in her mind. She had, at times, been nervous that Miles was doing too well, but now that Steve was in the final, she could persuade Saul to choose him without any problems. After all this time the money was almost in her hands. She felt happier than she had in years. She knew she was beautiful and smart and well-off, but now she was going to be rich. Real rich. Irresistibly rich. For ever and a day rich. And wouldn't her female wealth attract even more, male wealth?

The thought was so good that it made her feel hot. Eagerly she pushed her tongue into Steve's mouth. *Think what the money could bring.* She could feel him hardening once more. *Freedom. Freedom and acceptance.* Steve sighed as she felt him with her hand. *A return of pride to the von Koeler name.*

Suddenly with a moan he was inside her again. Kristina closed her eyes and basked in a bath of hundred-dollar bills. She moved her hips, imagining George Washington beneath her buttocks. They were kissing frenetically now, teeth clashing, tongues fighting. Kristina screamed in joy imagining each thrust of his cock to be worth a hundred thousand dollars. Counting as he moved, her body juddered free on the thirtieth stroke as her mind was filled with the image of three million single dollar bills fluttering like doves down from the heavens above.

* * *

They were smooth at 35,000 feet when Miles saw his chance. So far, Alice had been ignoring him. She was working First Class with Julie, and Miles was in Business. Too small a fry, no doubt; and he'd rejected her once already. Now, though, she was walking along the aisle with a jug of juice in her hand. Miles stuck out his hand.

'Could I have some of that, please?'

'I'll be right back with a glass – Miles.'

She returned; he said, 'I thought for a moment you didn't recognise me.'

'Will that be all?'

Miles laid his hand over the sharp rim of his plastic cup so that she wouldn't see him shaking. 'I was wondering if there was a,' he coughed, 'a De Niro scene today. Or not.'

'I believe the movie on this flight is *Honey I blew up the kid*. Robert De Niro's not in that.'

'No, I mean. Last time, you said I could . . . meet with you during the De Niro scene.'

Miles brought his hand to his face and nervously rubbed at his eyebrow.

'He's not in this film.'

'Right, I see. I guess I shouldn't have missed him the first time it was playing.'

'Will that be all, sir?'

Alice left Miles embarrassed, but not ashamed. For the whole of the next hour, he thought of her. The image he had of her, with her legs splayed in a V for him, was almost palpable, almost odorant. It excited him more now than it had then. When the movie began, Miles searched in the quietened aisles for her. She didn't come. After half an hour, he went to search up front. He found Alice sitting with two others in the stewardesses' galley.

'Could I have some coffee? Please.'

Alice didn't reply at once. He thought he saw her glance briefly at his impatient bulge.

'I'll bring it in a moment.'

Miles returned to his seat and waited. He was excited now. Kristina had been right. It *was* the expectation of fulfilment that was most exciting. Now the waiting hurt. Alice was taking so long. But then she emerged through the First Class curtain and there was no coffee in her hand and she was moving with a spry step and as she passed she glanced at Miles and he recognised the glint in her eye. The invitation. He waited, let a man in a suit pass before him, and then followed Alice towards the back.

Yes, yes, yes, yes, yes! This was how life should be lived. The bull's horns in my hands.

The man in front of Miles was walking slowly. Miles wanted to push past him. Miles wondered if Alice would have again removed her underwear. He hoped so.

And then, quite suddenly, it struck him. The man in front, the man in the pinstripe suit, the man who must have been forty plus, had come from First Class! And they had toilets of their own . . .

She wants revenge on me! She's chosen this man to get revenge. How could she have? LOOK AT HIM.

Yet there the man was, clearly following Alice. They reached the last block of seats, the part of the plane most like a seedy bar, where the sallow-skinned smokers and drinkers always gathered in groups. Excusing himself, Miles pushed his way through the gap where the stewardesses were relaxing, and turned up the far aisle. He'd hoped to overtake the besuited man here, but the cut had cost him vital seconds, and ahead now a large woman was reaching for something from her overhead compartment. Desperately, Miles glanced towards Alice, but the man in the suit had already reached her, and they were talking and she was flicking strands of hair off her forehead in that way she had. The man was overweight. He had a double chin and a smug, pasty face.

He's stretching, getting himself warmed up. He's done this before. He knows Alice. He knows the routine.

Miles reached the end of the plane, and looked out of the window. Opposite, the man was still talking to Alice. At least they hadn't gone inside yet. Perhaps there wasn't a toilet free. Unless she was talking dirty to him, getting him hot. Miles nibbled on the cuticle around his nail.

Come on then, get it over with.

Miles was still as horny as hell. He looked down at the undulating expanse of the Atlantic below. Then he turned back. To his astonishment, the man was walking away, stretching the muscles in his shoulders as he went. Miles waited a couple of seconds, and then walked across to Alice. The corners of her mouth flickered upwards. Silently, immediately, she and Miles entered the cubicle at the end.

'I knew it when I saw you,' Alice said as she bent down to remove, deftly, her underpants and tights. From behind her as she bent down, Miles began to fondle Alice's plump breasts. He pushed his crotch into her buttocks and thrust forward his hips.

Alice continued to talk very matter-of-factly. 'You guys are all the same. Second time around, you think it's all your idea. It's a control thing.'

'Ssshhh!'

Miles unzipped himself. Alice turned to face him. With her foot, she shoved aside the trash-can so she could climb up into place. Her eyelids flickered down to him. 'You look pretty keen.'

'Turn around,' he replied.

Miles firmly took hold of Alice by the waist and twirled her about as if she was his tango dancing partner. He was breathing heavily, desperate for contact. As Alice bent forward, Miles lifted her skirt with one hand and took hold of himself with the other. He probed. When he felt Alice's hot wet sliver, he plunged. He thrust. Once, twice, and then he came. Alice lifted her head up to watch the contortions of Miles's face reflected in the mirror. Then he quickly withdrew, and straightened his back. He pulled a paper towel from the slit in the wall. He held it out. 'Do you . . .?'

Without speaking, Alice took the towel.

'That's never happened before,' said Miles.

Alice hardly looked sympathetic. They were silent as Miles tidied himself up.

'Um, do you want me to go back to my seat first?'

Alice stared at him. Miles looked past her into the mirror, swept his hair to one side, and grimaced at the redness of his cheeks and neck.

'I am still here, you know,' said Alice.

'What?'

Alice reached for Miles's hand and fed it to the hungry mouth between her legs. Then she let it go, and closed her eyes. Miles looked into the face of this woman he did not know. The slippery touch of his own emission disgusted him. Silently, rapidly, Miles removed his hand, turned, unlocked the door and lurched out.

A young boy of about five stepped keenly forward to enter the toilet.

'Uh, no. Don't,' said Miles. 'My wife's in there and she's, she's not well.'

'My daddy's a doctor,' the boy said in an arid English accent.

'Really? Oh, well, she's fine, I mean she's getting better.'

'My daddy is a doctor.'

'I know. You told me.'

The little boy started running back along the aisle. Thank God, thought Miles. Then the boy stopped and tugged at his father's sleeve. 'Daddy, Daddy. There's a woman and she's sick.'

A kind-looking man in his early fifties turned in his seat and looked around. Miles reached them.

'Is there a problem? I'm a doctor.'

'Oh no . . .'

'Yes, Daddy. He said. The woman's sick in the loo,' said the boy.

'My wife was sick,' explained Miles, colouring. 'But she's fine. Thank you.'

The doctor nodded.

When, a few minutes later, the doctor noticed Alice scampering past, smoothing down the wrinkles in the skirt of her mauve uniform, a wry, knowing smile flickered across his thin lips, and he was momentarily distracted from his somewhat tedious book.

23

Two overlapping hearts and a toothy grin drawn in red on their blackboard; bills stacked and opened; three *New Yorkers*; a letter from his mother; a message on the answering machine from the great Saul Weissman. These were the things that Miles Jensen found when he returned to his Tribeca apartment after nineteen days away. Nineteen days! Was that all it had been?

At the other end of the loft, a note taped on to the TV from Poppy said 'Call me. I love you.' Miles swung his suitcase up on to the loft bed, and then immediately lifted the telephone receiver. As he waited for Rona to connect him to Weissman, Miles could smell the oddly metallic tinge of Alice's odour lingering on the fingers of his unwashed hand. He pressed the fingertips against his nostrils.

An unmistakable voice. 'The wanderer returns. Miles, how ya doing, buddy?'

'Pretty good, Mr Weissman.'

'Didn't I tell you to call me Saul? Huh? Call me Saul.'

'Yes, sir.'

'*Yes, sir*! How d'ya like that? Call me Saul: "Yes, sir!" So, you want to come in and see me kid? Talk about those great guys you found?'

'Sure.'

Miles grinned. He knew Kristina was wrong when she'd castigated him for picking a bunch of losers. They were winners, all of them, with Giovanni the top of the heap. Miles hoped he might find a way to make Weissman feel the same. He had to act fast, he knew it. Before Kristina came back the following day.

'Do you mind if I take a shower first?' Miles asked.

'We're gonna be talking, not making out, Milo,' laughed Weissman.

'I'll come straight in, then.'

'Take a shower. Take a shower. Come by at two. Kristy's coming back a day early, sometime around lunch. She says she's found our man. You think she's right?' Miles was silent. 'Is that a no, Miles?'

'Could we talk about that when I come around?'

In the shower, Miles worried about Kristina's early return. He'd hoped he might have had time to find an alternative to Steve before she returned from London, but now the only option was to discredit Steve so that Giovanni could come to the fore. He wasn't sure how. What he did fear was that Kristina would push Steve for the job as he was the only model chosen by her.

After his shower, Miles changed his new suit in favour of the *Weissmans* suit Kristina had bought him three weeks before. He shaved, spread some of Poppy's gel on his hair, collected his notes and composites, and headed for the door.

It was a magnificent Manhattan winter's day. Swimming-pool skies, sharp, glassy air. Miles wanted to walk to Weissman, to help clear his mind.

He slanted across Washington Square. Beneath the arch, six people stood on a stage. A group was listening to a black feminist writer reciting a poem on female circumcision titled 'The slice/Of her life'. Miles listened for a while, and was handed a leaflet financed by the Black Sisters Against Everyday Slavery. He folded it and put it in his jacket pocket and continued on his way. Up on Sixth Avenue and Eighth Street a man was selling incense and books on Black Awareness, beside paraphernalia from Spike Lee's Malcolm X film. Miles hadn't dried his hair properly (he never did, Poppy said, he always left it wet at the back), and his head was getting cold, so he bought a Malcolm X baseball cap. A Wasp in a grey suit joining a fad.

He ducked into Balducci's because they sold their food as Art, and a visit always cheered him up. It smelt of fresh sawdust and garlic and roasted chicken and orange and newly baked cookies and coffee beans. He bought a carton of goat's cheese salad for himself, the best in the city, and then a half-pound of pistachios for Mr Weissman. Saul. Miles hoped Weissman wouldn't be stuck on his brand from Nuts About You. How many pounds had he had delivered when Miles had been there? Miles smiled, and, as he did so, the idea struck him. Of course! EDEN, Adam, the first man in the world. Of course, Miles!

Miles quickly looked at his watch, threw down his basket of food and raced out of the door for a cab. If he got to Weissman before Kristina, then he was still in with a chance of selling the idea to Weissman – and clearing the way for Giovanni to win.

All he'd need was for Saul Weissman to bite at the bait.

'You're looking just absolutely gorgeous today, Miss van Koeler,' said Cindy, chewing on a chunk of apple.

'I bought it in London.' Kristina was wearing a grey Joseph suit. 'Messages?'

'They're on your desk. And Mr Weissman just called. He wants to see you.'

'Damn! OK, I'll drop in on him.'

Kristina took the elevator one floor up to Saul's office. He was waiting with the door open, a wide smile on his face.

'Kristy. How was London?'

'Excellent. Thank you, Saul.'

'I haven't liked the city since the 1960s, myself. It's got no balls any more. Did you find any balls there, huh?' Weissman laughed at his joke. 'You're looking beautiful, if I may say so.'

'Saul, I wonder if we could get on. I came here straight from the airport. I was hoping to get home.'

'Fine, but I got some incredible news for you first.' Weissman seemed truly excited about something. The last time she could remember him like this was when he'd surprised her with the keys to a brand new Porsche. His enthusiasm was infectious. Maybe he'd bought her another car.' Or he was going to announce a bonus in her salary for the good work done in London. Either way, Weissman was always at his most lovable when he was being generous.

'You want to see what I got to show you, Kristy?'

Kristina smiled. 'Sure.'

Weissman pressed the buzzer on his desk. 'Rona, sweetheart, show them in, would you?'

Them? Kristina hoped to God Saul hadn't bought her some stupid parrots similar to his own. She turned to look as into the room came Miles and a young black man who she recognised from somewhere. He was striking looking. A fairly small head, hair cropped very short, piercing eyes, a thin nose, high cheekbones, and beautifully smooth dark skin.

'Miles you know. But this, this is Reuben. Reuben works at Nuts About You. He's been bringing me pistachios for – how long is it?'

Reuben shifted his weight from one leg to another. 'Two years.'

So that's where I saw him, thought Kristina. In the elevator, on that first day with Miles.

And he's fancied the nigger ever since.

Weissman put his arm around Reuben's shoulders, and led him towards Kristina, as if Reuben himself was to be his gift to her. Thoughts of slave-trading came to her.

Weissman patted Reuben on the upper chest. 'For two years this boy has kept me alive. But familiarity breeds blindness. It took Miles here to show me the obvious.'

Kristina stood. There was something she didn't like about what she was hearing; not at all. 'So?' she said, warily.

'You tell her, Miles. You tell her.'

Miles was so excited that there was a nervous flutter to his voice. He spoke through his smile. 'Reuben is joining the competition.'

There was a loud silence. What Kristina wanted to say was that not in her lifetime would a nigger be chosen for a *Weissmans* cologne. Instead, she took a deep breath, and said, as calmly as she could, 'Oh.' A slight cough. 'In whose place?'

'In the last place.'

Kristina jumped on this. 'Which *last place*, Saul? All the places are filled now.'

'In place of the last guy. This American you picked up in London.'

'Steve Barefoot?' Kristina said, her voice a little shaky now. 'Instead of Steve Barefoot? No way, Saul. No.'

'Why not?'

'You just can't. You can't. You just can't.'

Kristina was visibly shaking. She lifted her hand to her forehead before turning and striding to the window. Miles could see her shoulders rise and fall as she breathed in to control herself. Then, in a calm voice, she said, 'Saul. May we speak alone?'

Weissman thrust forward his bottom lip and lifted his eyes to the ceiling. *Don't ask me!*

'OK,' he said. 'Reuben, why don't you go back to work now. Here,' Weissman took out a silver money clip, and peeled off two one hundred dollar bills. 'That's one for you, and one for Arty for letting you go. OK? Miles, you can wait outside for us.'

Miles said goodbye to Reuben and waited with Rona. He wished to God he could be inside with Saul. He couldn't sit still for worry. He stood and went out into the lobby and pressed the elevator button. He returned. *Damn Kristina! She was such a slippery bitch. God knows what she's saying.* Miles remembered Kristina's comments about Reuben the first time she'd seen him. He knew she wouldn't like him, added to which she seemed to have developed this sudden fondness for Steve. *She probably wants him in her bed.* He remembered the way she'd been gazing at Steve in London, undressing him with her eyes. Miles tapped his pen on to the palm of his hand until Rona looked up with a scowl on her face. He stopped. Rona scared him.

Five minutes later, Weissman opened his door. He made a gloomy face, and beckoned Miles inside. Miles sat in the chair beside Kristina. She'd calmed down but she didn't turn to look at Miles. Weissman sat at his desk and leaned forward on his elbows. He looked more serious now than at any time since Miles had met him.

'Kristina says we'd be making a terrible mistake. Kristy says that if we run this competition with six white guys, then no one's gonna stand up and say "hey, where's the black man?" But if we have a black model and we don't give him the contract, you with me? – well then, we'd be opening ourselves up to criticism.'

Miles intervened. 'No, I disagree. I think . . .'

Facing Saul, Kristina darted a finger at Miles. 'He's pissed off because *he* wasn't the one who discovered Steve. That's all. It's unbelievably petty.'

'That's not true,' Miles objected. 'My reason is the same one I gave Saul earlier.'

Kristina seemed to wince when Miles called Weissman by his first name.

'Which was . . .?' prompted Weissman.

Miles crossed his legs and took a long breath. This was it, a moment that could alter his financial future. 'Simply because racism is the biggest single issue in this country. It certainly is in the city. Not just black/white, but all the races. It doesn't matter whether you're talking about schools or crime or the hospitals or transportation, everything these days comes back to the race issue. Now, the whole structure is constantly shifting, and in place of the Irish . . .'

Kristina, looking at Saul, said, 'What is this? Some kind of sociology lesson?' She turned in her chair to face Miles. 'Don't try and be smart with us. You don't know shit about selling. This is nothing but a game for you. You're back to your job on the floor tomorrow, but I've got to *sell* EDEN. Now, how do you think we're going to manage that using a fucking nigger?'

Weissman slammed his hand on the desk. 'Don't use that word in my office, all right? Never. Now, Miles, please go on. One of us was listening.'

'Kristina,' said Miles, 'I'm not saying we have to use Reuben for the final shots. What I *am* saying is that if we include a black model in the competition we'll be making the statement that *Weissmans* is a store for the future.'

'I like that idea, Milo. A store for the future. I like that.'

'I mean,' continued Miles, encouraged now, 'it'll be the same with Bill Clinton's Cabinet. That'll be PR too. He could pick fifty middle-aged Wasps to fill the Cabinet posts, but he knows this country needs to be united. People need to believe that they're being represented. So he's going to choose people of every race and sex because it *looks* good. That's what matters, and I think that's the way *Weissmans* has got to look. We've got to look as if we care. We've got to look as if this is a store for all people, whatever their colour or religion or sex. A store for the future. A store for the whole of America.'

Suddenly, a tear bulged in the corner of Saul Weissman's eye. He bounced from his chair without speaking, came over to Miles and leant over to embrace him. 'That, Miles,' he said in a voice breaking with emotion, 'was beautiful. Fucking beautiful.'

Kristina looked at them both. Saul, she knew, would never in a million years change his mind after a gesture such as that. The embrace had been a Mafia Don's kiss. She'd lost the battle.

But they'd only just begun the war. 'OK, we'll use him.' Miles grinned from ear to ear. 'But not in place of Steve who's by far the best-looking guy we've got.'

Suddenly, it all seemed so simple! If they ditched one of Steve's real rivals and replaced him with a no-hope nigger, Steve's chances of success would be even higher. 'What about ditching this Giovanni guy? He's the wrong image for the campaign.'

Weissman shrugged. 'Miles?'

'Bad move. Very bad move,' Miles said, shaking his head.

'Why?' wondered Weissman.

'Why?'

It looked to Miles as if Weissman was nodding back in slow motion. Miles couldn't think why. Hadn't he wondered himself whether Giovanni's playboy image could damage the innocence of the Adam idea?

'Why?' Miles said again, playing for time now. 'I'll tell you why, Saul. Um, can you tell me why you built a store in Moscow?'

Weissman threw up his arms in apparent desperation. 'Now what kind of question's that? Why do you think? Because I've got vision, because my horizon's the whole goddamn world. That's why.'

Miles smiled. 'Exactly,' he said. 'And that's why you've got to appeal to the whole world with EDEN. Look, we've got guys in the competition with whom people of all nations can associate.' Miles counted out the competitors on his fingers. 'Reuben for the blacks, Fernando for the Hispanics, Chester for the American whites, Giovanni for the South Europeans, Spencer for the North Europeans, and Fabio for South America. Now which of these continents can we afford to lose?'

Weissman paused, and then said, 'You're right! None of them.'

'Are you trying to tell me,' complained Kristina, 'that Spencer character is more beautiful than my Steve? I mean, than Steve.'

'No, I . . .'

This time Weissman butted in for his say. 'Kristina, I don't think you've been listening. It's not that simple. Miles here has pointed out that we can make a positive statement with this competition. You see? He's absolutely right.'

Kristina was getting agitated again.' But Saul, I . . .'

Weissman raised his hand and stood up as if he was the foreman of a jury that had reached its verdict.' There is one more reason why we have to dump Steve. He's the only model who's not appeared in the newspapers, and I don't want to start screwing around with these guys in public. The same goes for you two. This thing's got to be played fair: no preferences, no games. We've got our six guys, now let's figure out who's best for the job. You understand?'

'Absolutely,' said Miles.

Kristina stared at Saul. Miles thought he could even see her nostrils flare. 'Saul. I really think we're making a mistake. Of all the models, Steve should be in the competition.'

Weissman sat down. He took out a pistachio nut and in the silence all three heard the snap as he cracked it open. Weissman brought the nut to his mouth. He chewed, swallowed, and then spoke in a masterful crescendo, from the soft voice of a priest in the confession box to the rumble of a World Wrestling Federation commentator. 'For the woman who didn't even *tell* me about this competition, the woman who thought the whole competition was a lousy idea, you have got a lot of fucking nerve TELLING ME HOW TO RUN IT! NOW GET OUT!'

Kristina's chair crashed back on the floor as she stood, swivelled and flew out of the room. The door smashed shut behind her, bringing a framed photograph of Saul Weissman shaking Jimmy Carter's hand crashing down to the floor.

The world's top retailer breathed in deeply. Miles was still and nervous. Then, very slowly, Weissman stood, picked up the glinting silver bowl of pistachio nuts, and carried it around the desk.

'Go on,' he said, 'take as many as you want.'

Steve Barefoot couldn't remember ever having felt better. Here he was returning to New York City an international man of the world. He couldn't wait to tell the folks back home. It wouldn't be long now, not long before he'd fly into Dallas airport rich as an oilman. First thing, he'd buy himself a ranch.

Oh yes, sweet Mary, life would surely be fine.

The stretch limousine he'd hired at the airport to take him into town double-parked on 63rd Street. Steve tipped the driver fifty dollars, and said 'Have a nice day now,' as if he meant it.

Kristina had said she'd be home. Steve hoped she'd be in the bath or shower and he could creep in, and they'd make love normal-like, as they had in London. That's what he'd remember about their trip – that they'd screwed as a man and woman should, nothing kinky or weird.

Steve fumbled with his key, and listened for sound within the apartment. He heard nothing, and when he opened the door, he found the lights were off.

'Kristina? You home?' Steve kicked closed the door. 'Kristina? Where you at?'

Kristina's shoes were on the polished hardwood floor. Her bag was on the table. Even her keys were there. Maybe she's sleeping, thought Steve. I'll go climb on in beside her, wake her up with a nice fondle. He pulled off his boots and tiptoed into the bedroom. That's weird, he thought. A slanted rectangle of orange light lit the lower half of Kristina's torso. She was fully clothed, sprawled at an angle on the covers. Steve turned on the light in the corridor, and opened wide the door.

'Kristina?'

His eyes adjusted to the light. On the bedside table he saw a smoky-brown tube of prescription pills capless by the lamp. He ran over and turned on the light. Sleeping pills! He shook the tube. It was empty. Beside Kristina on the bed, a glass was tipped on its side. Steve shook Kristina's limp body. 'Kristina? It's me. Kristina! Wake up, sweetheart.'

Steve's own heart was thudding wildly in his chest as he felt for the pulse of hers. She was still alive.

'Oh God? Thank you, God!'

Steve slapped at Kristina's cheeks, but she didn't respond. He sniffed at the glass. Vodka!

'Oh, no! Oh God no! Oh, Jesus, Kristina!'

Tears began to course down Steve's face. Running, tripping next door, Steve grabbed the phone and dialled 911. He spoke through tears. 'Hello, this is an emergency. Help me. I need me an ambulance NOW. I think my girlfriend's going to die.'

The nerve endings in Miles Jensen's fingers were tingling with excitement as he knocked on his own apartment door. He heard Poppy's light footsteps within.

'Who is it?'

Miles faked a Chinese accent. 'Derrivvree.'

Poppy didn't open the door. 'I didn't order anything.'

'Derrivvree.'

'How did you get into the building?'

He shifted into Brooklynese. 'Lady, I got a delivery. A Miss Poppy somebody. That you, or what?'

Miles counted the locks. One, two, three. He held the wide spread of flowers in front of his face. Under each arm he was sandwiching a bottle of fine champagne. Poppy was quiet for a second.

'Miles, it's you. Oh, look . . .'

Poppy took the flowers, rescued the champagne and kissed him once on the lips. He clasped her around the waist and walked her backwards into the apartment, his lips against hers, and closed the door with the back of his foot. Poppy took the flowers to the basin and unravelled the crinkling plastic. 'Oh, babe! Look at these! They're beautiful. Thanks.'

'They're because I didn't call.'

'Hmm! What happened to you? I saw you had time for a shower.'

'There was a sudden emergency at *Weissmans*.'

'Oh! Is it sorted?'

'You bet. You want champagne?'

'Stupid question.'

As Miles was opening the champagne, Poppy studied him. He looked different. It wasn't just the haircut, or the colour to his cheeks. It was the liveliness of his face that was new. It made her a little uneasy. 'You had a haircut.'

'I know. Like it?'

'I think so.'

'I think it makes my face look better. It kind of brings out my cheekbones.'

'Since when have you been worried about cheekbones?'

'Since always. Here . . .'

They took their glasses to the other end of the apartment. 'So, tell me all about it,' said Poppy.

Miles slumped into the sofa and looked all around. 'You know, we need to do something to this place. Don't you think it's, I don't know . . . drab?'

'No, it's fine. I want to hear about your trip. Were you a good boy when you were away?'

'Poppy,' Miles said, putting down his glass and pulling her towards him. 'Now, you know me!'

Steve stood by Kristina's bed, his head hanging low. Kristina, propped up in bed with pillows behind her back, was wearily massaging her temples.

'Never, never have I been so humiliated. I wake up to find half of Lennox Hill hospital standing around me.'

Steve drew in on his cigarette and spat out an imaginary fleck of tobacco. 'Well, fine Kristina. I'll leave you next time.'

'That was the whole fucking idea. Jesus, I open my eyes and it feels like a sixties orgy.'

'I said I'm sorry. Hell, I thought you were going to die.'

'From *three* pills?'

'How was I to know that? You weren't moving any.'

'It's called sleeping.'

Steve lifted his canvas bag and shook it empty on to the bed. The last object to fall out was a tiny model of a red double-decker London bus. Steve quickly hid it in his pocket. He spoke quietly. 'I was really scared.'

Kristina stared at him. His eyes were red.

'You've been crying.'

Steve turned from her and folded a shirt into the closet. 'You try sitting with someone you think's gonna die.'

Despite herself, Kristina felt a sudden gust of love for this oafish, beautiful rancher from Texas. 'Oh! Come here. Come sit by me.'

She opened her arms, maternally. Steve joined her on the bed, but instead he took her in his arms, and they lay quiet for a few moments with their thoughts.

'Stevey?'

'Yeah.'

'I got some bad news.' He waited. 'Saul . . . Saul's chosen someone else for the competition.'

Steve didn't believe her. This simply wasn't the way Kristina imparted news of this nature. Kristina never kept her fangs and venom hidden if she had an enemy to bite.

320

'You're having me on.'

Kristina shook her head by his shoulder, and a shiver of fear swept through his body. He sat up and looked into her oddly expressionless face. 'What do you mean?'

'Saul's chosen a black model. Miles put him up to it, and now Saul's set on it.'

'What are you saying, Kristina? Are you telling me that's it? Are you saying I can't win?'

Kristina pushed herself up on one arm and looked at Steve in the face. Then she leant forward and gave him a fleshy kiss on the lips. She trickled her fingertips across Steve's strong cheeks. 'Of course you're going to win,' she whispered. 'EDEN's mine. It's always been mine. Do you think I'd ever give up as quickly as that?'

'So what are we going to do? I mean, how can I win if I'm not even in the competition? Kristina?'

Kristina's hand snaked its way inside Steve's heavy denim shirt. 'I don't know how yet, but I promise you, Steve: we're going to win that campaign even if we have to kill someone to get it.'

24

Wednesday morning, November 25th, and Miles Jensen woke up with a body that felt heavy as lead. Poppy was up and showering and Miles felt as if he'd slipped back during the night into the tedious groove of his life before the search. Their daily routine had begun. When Poppy finished the shower, Miles would take over the bathroom, have a piss of varying accuracy, take a shower, and shave to the noise of Poppy drying her hair. Then she'd come back to the bathroom to finish her make-up and complain about the steam. A banana, a peck on the cheek, a hurried chat about choices for the evening, and then they'd go their separate ways. Miles had found comfort in the regularity of this. Now he wanted something else. He wanted breakfast in bed and the liberating ignorance that comes with an unplanned day.

The rot in his mind had begun the night before. Then, Miles had been aware of his physical and emotional reserve while making love to Poppy. He'd been faintly bored by the greedy rush to orgasm that had been their sexual reunion; bored because his mind had been preoccupied with the competition. Saul Weissman's vindication of Miles's success had, it was true, been deeply gratifying; but, Miles thought, Poppy's interest in the EDEN campaign, and, more importantly, Miles's part in it, had been annoyingly slight. It was almost as if Miles resented Poppy for not caring as much as he did himself. Poppy may have been more interested had Miles shared with her the facts about Giovanni, but Miles feared that she might spread the news. Furthermore, the money had nothing to do with Poppy. Miles had no idea how much his life might change once the cash was in his palm.

Miles heard the handle of the bathroom door thud open

against the crumbling plaster of the wall. Poppy swore at it, as she did at least three times a week. When the steam caused the wood to swell, the door needed a kick to open it, and all too often Poppy's kick was too ferocious. It had used to make Miles smile. Now, he didn't even stir. There were more important concerns.

Kristina had been unequivocal in her instructions. Miles was, she'd stated, expected back at his job at the Madison Avenue branch of *Weissmans*. The idea of being cooped up all day in the store sickened Miles. It was a reversal of his fortunes. His hope lay with Weissman. In the excitement of the previous afternoon, Miles had forgotten to ask Weissman about the future. Miles hoped that Weissman might give him an administrative position of some sort. Ideally, Miles thought he should be put in charge of the PR for the competition.

That was it, then. He'd go into work, show off his new style, tell his colleagues some secrets about the supermodels, and then put the call through to Weissman. An hour back at work, he thought, now that won't kill me.

Kristina knew something was up from the smirk on her secretary's face. But it was not until she opened the door to her office that she understood, for she found it filled with the scent and colours of fifty spectacular bunches of flowers. Someone had really gone to town on her. The flowers seemed too exotic to have been bought during winter in Manhattan. Kristina recognised some – ginger lillies, birds of paradise, heliconia, delphiniums, larkspur, phlox and gerbera. Most would have been enthralled by such a display, but Kristina's first thought was one of despair. Clearly Steve had gone crazy and ordered these before he'd heard the bad news! Yet when she stepped forward and saw the envelope on her desk, Kristina recognised the capital letters of Saul's chunky hand-writing, and a great smile spread across her face. Inside the card there was one word: *Sorry*. Something fell out. A cheque? No. A doctor's appointment card. My treat, Saul had written on it, an appointment with Dr Hirschberg the psychiatrist. That afternoon.

Kristina shook her head. Long ago she'd given up resisting Saul on this. At least the two hundred-dollar chat with the doctor gave her the chance to relax for forty minutes. It was always Hirschberg who did the talking.

Kristina picked a solitary pink rose from the garden in her office, and took it to Weissman. It matched the bright pink of his shirt.

'Am I forgiven?' he asked.

'For shouting, yes.' She kissed him. 'For Reuben, no. I'm hoping you've reconsidered.'

'That Miles kid made a lot of sense to me, Kristy.'

Kristina wasn't surprised. She knew how Weissman was. The flowers had not been sent as admission of an error, but to safeguard Kristina's loyalty. If ever Weissman did screw up, he'd go into hiding. Defeat had never rested easily on the small man's shoulders.

Right now, he thought he was sitting on a winner.

'We got to get moving on the details of this competition. What you got for me?'

Kristina flipped open her Ralph Lauren Filofax. 'The models are flying in on Sunday 6th, in the evening. Maury Greenberg's squared up that deal with Sy Green at the Midas Hotel, so that's where they'll be staying. The more often the models mention the hotel in the press and on TV, the cheaper it's going to be. Maury did well. Now, I've scheduled the first press conference Monday morning.'

'Where?'

'In the Midas lobby.'

'No. Fix it up in a store – make it *Weissmans West Side*. Get them to doll it up real nice for Christmas.'

'I'll do that. The rest of Monday the models will set-tle in, then Tuesday they'll come in here to meet you properly.'

'Not together, Kristy.'

'No, one by one. Then on Wednesday Maury Greenberg's fixed up that Trudie Love show which Matt Skolaski says they'll air Friday the 11th. Meantime Bruce Stone's going to be taking test shots of all the models. We booked him

for Thursday and Friday. He says we'll see the prints
Friday night.'

'How much?'

'Twenty grand for the two days.'

Kristina had fought hard with Weissman to have the brilliant
Bruce Stone as the EDEN photographer. He was an almost
maniacal workaholic, a lean, lanky, hard-bitten, parsimonious
Scot who'd built up a reputation for never failing to produce
images on the inspired side of competent. Weissman himself
had favoured the New York-based Sam Emsiel, a more daring
and innovative creator of images, but Kristina had warned
Weissman that Emsiel's price would be too high, and that
his artistic vision would be at odds with Weissman's own.

However, Kristina's real reason had been that Stone was
renowned for preferring to shoot heavily muscled men such
as Steve, and, as the photographer was to be consulted on
the choice for Adam, so Kristina had hoped Stone would be
a useful ally. Steve Barefoot was precisely the type of model
Bruce Stone preferred to shoot.

'The party's all fixed up for the evening of Monday 14th in
Grand Central. I'll get a list to you.'

'OK.' A buzz from Rona. 'Yes, sweetheart?'

'Miles Jensen on the line.'

'OK, put him through.'

In the staff canteen at *Weissmans* Madison Avenue store,
Miles was feeling pretty damn good about life. All morning
he'd been exaggerating details about his friendship with the
supermodels, and now, leaning on the wall to his side, chewing
a toothpick, he was about to talk to the great Saul Weissman
himself. He'd even felt a twinge of sadness as he'd told his
colleagues that this would be the last day at work. A twinge;
nothing more.

'Saul,' said Miles, loud enough so that Roseanne at the
table nearest him could hear, 'Good morning.'

'Hiya, kid. Out of bed yet?'

Miles smiled. 'I'm at work, back at the Madison store.'

'You are? Jesus, what the hell for?'

'Kristina told me to come back,' said Miles with relish.

Miles almost wondered whether Kristina would survive the week in the company she was making so many mistakes. Weissman wouldn't like his golden boy to be treated like this.

'Hold it,' said Weissman. Kristy, Miles says you told him to go back to the store. Did you?'

'Yes, I don't see what else he's got to do around here now he's found the models.'

Weissman held up his hand to her, and paused. Kristina was none too pleased with him at the moment, and the last thing he wanted was to alienate her yet more. He decided what to do. Reconnecting himself with Miles, Weissman said 'Thanks for checking in, kid. We're going over the details now. Everything's looking good. Call us soon.'

In the office, Kristina listened with obvious contentment. But a rush of panic was sweeping through Miles. He turned around so that the others in the canteen couldn't see him. 'What would you like me to do, then?' he asked.

'Oh, didn't I just say? We'll call you. Do your thing for now, and be there if we need you.'

'You mean . . . here?'

'Sounds like a good place to me. What's the store like today? Is it overflowing with Christmas shoppers?'

'Oh, it's quiet, but Saul, I thought . . .'

'Quiet? Three weeks before Christmas. That's not good. Not good at all. Get them buying my products or we won't have any money left for this cologne, allright?'

'Sure, I . . .'

'Miles, don't let me keep you. Let's talk later,'

'Well, I . . .'

'Good. We'll be in touch.' Weissman put down the receiver. 'He's a smart kid, Kristy. Really smart. Now, where the hell were we?'

Seven miserable, grey days on and it was a dejected Miles Jensen who pushed the elevator button to take him up to the fourth floor of *Weissmans*, Madison Avenue. Every night, morose and angry with the world, Miles had returned to his apartment, expecting at first, hoping in the end, to hear a message from Weissman's office. Nothing had come, and even the air had begun to feel heavy.

Miles couldn't believe what had happened. At first he'd persuaded himself that Weissman had been humouring Kristina, keeping her happy for a day or two. Now he thought otherwise. An invitation had arrived to a party to be held in the waiting room of Grand Central Station on Monday, December 14th at which, it stated, the EDEN models would be announced. That was the only contact he'd had with the office in the past week. If Kristina had expected to see him, Miles thought, then the invitation would not have been sent.

Giovanni had called twice. Miles had played along, saying that he'd been in regular meetings with Weissman, and that everything was looking fine. Giovanni had been excited at the news that a token coloured man had been chosen to fill the sixth place, and he'd congratulated Miles on that. As far as Miles knew, Giovanni would win. But then, Miles didn't know very much any more, except, of course, that he was unhappy, and out of love with the world.

Back home, away from the drudgery of the store, life was no better. Although Poppy had tried to be her usual comforting self, her compassion was tempered by a disdain for Miles's churlish self-pity. He was yearning for an indulgent happiness in which she had played no part, and Miles could not hide from Poppy the truth that he'd enjoyed an intoxicating liberation on his excursion from New York. Poppy saw the issue in simple terms: Miles had had a taste of the good life and was no longer satisfied with his apartment, his neighbourhood, his friends, his clothes, even, it seemed, himself. And although he denied it when asked, it was only natural for Poppy to assume that she too was included among those things that her lover now considered repugnant.

Poppy herself couldn't understand the complexity of Miles's depression, because Miles wouldn't speak of it. In his endless telling and retelling of incidents and impressions from his trip around the world, Miles was concealing his deep dissatisfaction, his belief that God had reneged on His commitment to Miles's future. It was not the clubs of Miami, the Soaphouse in Tokyo, the villas of Italy or the restaurants in Paris that Miles missed, but the sense of responsibility and hope that had accompanied him in those places.

On Thursday, December 3rd, Miles had been assigned the eighth floor. Reproduction antique furniture. It was a thankless task, and Miles's sullen slouch betrayed the heaviness of his heart. A woman in her thirties was standing inspecting a de luxe fake walnut television cabinet boasting fine genuine brass knobs. Made for a hundred dollars, it retailed at five. Miles could not imagine wanting it in any home of his.

'That's a lovely piece,' he said. 'My wife bought one last month.'

The woman was tall, and had a somewhat twisted expression, as if she'd been born with the sourness of a lemon in her mouth. She sighed, and seemed genuinely happy to have someone with whom to share her indecision. She had a surprisingly gentle voice. 'You don't think it's pricey?'

'No, not at all.'

'You don't sound very convinced.'

As the lady stared at the cabinet, she seemed to be thinking of something else. Then she turned back to Miles, who was pretending to be inspecting a set of burgundy leather armchairs. 'Have we met?'

'Er, no. I mean I don't think so.'

'Oh, excuse me!'

Miles drifted away. A couple of minutes later, the woman returned. 'Aren't you the man who's been going around the world for the store?'

'No. You must be mistaken. I work in Insurance.'

'Are you sure?'

'Of course.'

'Oh, I'm sorry.'

She trotted away once more, but she left Miles thinking. If his cover was blown, then he couldn't do his job, and through no fault of his own. Only one person was responsible.

Miles almost ran to the phone. There was a long, anxious wait before Rona connected him to their boss. When Miles told his story, he added the lie that the same thing had happened three times during the week. 'I'm worried, sir, that I could do harm to the reputation of *Weissmans*.'

'Damn right you could,' Weissman replied. 'You'd better get outta there. Swing by the office at two, and we'll see if we can't fix something up.'

'See this isn't like me, Kristina. I never was a city person, never.'

Steve Barefoot's face was illuminated by the bright light of the refrigerator. He squatted in front of the open door and surveyed the almost empty shelves. Finding nothing that appealed, Steve opened the freezer and took out a tub of Ben and Jerry's Rum and Raisin ice cream. With his spoon he burrowed deep beneath the jagged surface to find the nearest raisin.

Steve spoke through a mouthful of ice cream. 'I'm cooped up here like a goddamn battery hen. You don't want us seen out anywhere, I got to keep my head down, I can't go into the modelling agencies . . . nothing. I mean, shit, if things don't go right now, I've as good as wasted two months of my life, haven't I? I coulda been doing no end of things back home, couldn't I? Kristina? You listening to me?'

Kristina was lying in her black and pink Lycra gym-wear, with an lemon iced tea, looking up at the ceiling. 'I can't think with you moaning like that.'

'It's OK for you. You got people to talk to all day. I'm like a goddamn battery hen or something.'

'So you said.'

Steve lifted Kristina's legs and sat himself at the other end of the couch. She ignored him as he made his swift way towards the bottom of the tub of ice cream. 'At least tell me what you're thinking. Maybe I can help some.'

'Highly likely, Steve.'

'Try me.'

Kristina sighed. 'Well, now that Saul's got Miles back under

330

his wing, I'm thinking that maybe there's a way to kill two birds with one stone.'

'Like how?'

'Well, one of the models has to drop out of the competition for you to get in. Think how much better it'd be if he dropped out because of something Miles did. Then we could get rid of two problems at once.'

'Why you so worried about Miles? I got a much better idea.'

Kristina extricated herself from Steve's arm, and stood. As she bent down to touch her toes, she said, 'I don't think riding down Fifth Avenue with a lasso in your hand is going to do much good.'

'Don't try to be funny. Why don't we try to figure out some way to get shot of *two* models at one time? It'll look like rivalry, see? I mean, say this black dude Reuben beats up one of the other guys, beats his face in real bad or something. Then neither of them'll have a chance. See?'

'Fine, but how do we make them do it?'

'I don't know. We could think of something.'

Kristina found a cigarette, and lit it. 'Amazingly enough, that's not bad. Only forget about Reuben and Fernando. We'd need to stir it up with the other four.'

Kristina stood silent, smoking, thinking. Then she turned to her young lover. 'You know, maybe,' she said, 'just maybe you're not as stupid as you look.'

Steve grinned. 'I'm as horny as I look, though.'

Steve lifted his arms and pulled Kristina back on to the couch. He kissed her, his mouth cold and sticky from the ice cream. 'And I got no end of ideas about how to deal with that.'

Miles was late for Sunday brunch, but Saul Weissman didn't mind. They were meeting in a retro-fifties diner on the Upper East Side – the kind of unimaginative, cosy place that played with its prices in the belief that all things were better in the old days, even a chocolate milk shake. The staff, a motley bunch of snide college dropouts, had been forced to cut their hair and wear their smiles as befitted the fifties idyll. Regularly, they took their resentment out on the customers suffering enough in the easy familiarity of the Lexington Avenue Original Take Five Diner.

Sandwiched in between a 3-D Mets montage and a humourless Protestant couple eating oat bran, sat Saul Weissman. A fairy-tale ogre surrounded by food. The table was one of those tiny chrome-edged, grey-pink formica numbers designed so that one's cutlery would always skim, lemming-like, off the side. It could barely contain the assortment of dishes Weissman had ordered. In front of him was a double order of the Take Five Wicked Wondrous Sunday Brunch – four eggs, two poached, two fried, easy over; a heap of hash browns; two muffins, one banana nut, one chocolate chip; a side of French toast with syrup; bacon; toast with jelly; coffee; one orange juice, one grapefruit; and, as an extra, a strawberry-raspberry double-thick milk shake.

'I ordered for you,' said Weissman. 'But seeing as you never showed, I figured I shouldn't waste it.'

Miles was eight minutes late. He sat and studied the menu. It was printed on cardboard, coloured pink and cut into the shape of a fifties Chevvy Convertible.

'Actually, Saul, I'm not too hungry.'

'Are you crazy? Brunch is one of life's great pleasures. It's like lunch, except it's breakfast so you can still have lunch at lunchtime but not feel guilty. My wife's cooking me this big Sunday lunch because she thinks I'm in the office all morning.' A look of panic froze Weissman's face. 'Oh, no. What if she calls the office?'

'You'd think of something.'

'You're right, I would. So, you know what you want?'

Miles's mind scrambled at the smorgasbord of breakfasts on offer. 'I'm going to get the Alpine Delight, I think.'

'Jesus, what are you? A bird? A fucking chicken?'

'It's all I want.'

'Suit yourself.'

It had been three days since Miles's two o'clock meeting with Weissman. In a moment of nothing-to-lose courage,

Miles had suggested that he himself would be the ideal person to look after the models while they were in New York. In a second, Weissman had agreed.

Miles was aware that his position as the liaison between the models and the Weissman office would make an excellent impression on Giovanni. Miles also guessed that the job would be easy enough. All the arrangements had previously been made by Kristina and her staff, from the bookings in the ultra-modern Midas Hotel in the centre of Manhattan, to the times of the interviews, television appearances, press conferences and shoots. There would be problems, there always were, but Miles envisaged eight smooth days towards Giovanni's victory, and his own new-found wealth.

Weissman sucked a dollop of shake through his thick, stripy straw, and looked across at Miles.

'Girls,' he said.

'Sir?'

'Have you seen the female models Kristy picked out?'

'No, I haven't been in on those decisions.'

'I don't much like them. They're too Waspy. They all look like Kristy did when she joined me in '76. Ice Women.'

Miles looked up from the grape he was peeling. 'I don't think Kristina would be too happy if I got involved.'

Not only did Miles not care too much about the future Eve, he also found female photogenicism hard to fathom. Women were either beautiful to him, or they weren't. He found it hard to recognise faces that would only appeal to others.

'If we had the time and the money, I'd send you scouting again. You did a beautiful job with the men.'

'Thank you.'

Weissman picked up a triangle of toast and swept it around his yoke-stained plate. 'Pity you didn't do so good with the women. You were supposed to be looking for an Eve as well.'

'Kristina told me not to spend time looking for the women.' Weissman didn't respond. 'The day I left. The same day she turned down the competition idea.'

Whenever he could, Miles liked to remind Saul of that decision Kristina had made.

'Did you at least see any models who you thought would be good?'

'Well, sure. A few. I sent the composites.'

'Were you attracted to these women?'

'Yeah. I mean . . . sure.'

'You're my guinea pig here, Milo. If you like the girl, then chances are the EDEN buyer's gonna like her. So, let's get these models to New York for me to see.'

'Just like that?'

'Yes, *just like that*. What? You think I built up this company by taking days to make a simple decision? No! I'm trusting you. Now, let's see how many we need.'

Weissman cleared a space on his plate, and counted out the female models with cold hash browns. Immediately, he pushed one to the side. 'There's one girl on Kristina's list who's like the Queen of Ice Women. I want to keep her. She's German. Andrea something or other. Then there's this black chick who's something really special. Helima. She's worked for us before. She's from, I don't know, Ethiopia or somewhere.' Weissman sucked on his milk shake. 'If I liked chocolate, I'd go for Helima. No question. And we gotta have a black girl now we've got Reuben. So. There's two. Now, I need a waif.'

'A what?'

'One of those little girly models everyone's going so crazy about. They're English mainly. What's her name, that little one . . .'

'Oh, you mean Tania Fern?'

'Right! Get me one of those. Make sure you get one of the real ones: no tits, no hips, no sex appeal, no colour, no style, dodgy complexion, and long, straight, greasy hair. OK? If you can't get an English girl, try the Lower East Side. You know what, Milo? How about that? How about a homeless person? That could work great with the press.'

'A real homeless person?'

'No, someone with a Park Avenue penthouse who likes sleeping rough! Yes, of course a real homeless person.'

'You're kidding.'

'No, I'm not. They got everything, and we wouldn't have to fly a model over. Will you do that for me?'

'Um.'

'Good. Failing that, call London. That's where these waif things come from.' Weissman shoved across another brown, greasy potato. 'That's three then. Now let's get three from you. Try and match them up in your mind with the guys.'

'I'll see what I can do.'

'No. Do what you can do. Now, when are the boys arriving?'

'Tonight.'

'And they're all staying in the Midas?'

'No. Only Fernando, Spencer and Fabio. Giovanni's staying in his sister's apartment, Chester's got a family place, and Reuben's staying at home.'

'OK.' Weissman leant back and spread his arms across the top of the seat. 'Now tell me, who do you think's gonna be our Adam?'

Keep your cards close to your chest, Milo. Don't give anything away.

'They're a good bunch of guys, Saul. I couldn't really say.'

'You gotta have a favourite. That's only natural.'

'No, really. I mean, I guess if had to choose right this minute, I'd say, *maybe* Giovanni Ferrari has the edge.'

'Yeah? Why?'

'He's the most natural. You can tell that he's always had it good. He's got this air about him that sets him apart from the others.'

'I'll bear that in mind. It's good to see that you care, Miles. Very good. I'm glad you're back on the team.'

'Thanks.'

'You know what? When we're through with this I'm gonna offer you a position in the company. Would you like that?'

Miles reddened. Was it what he wanted? He looked back at his boss. He wished he could answer with the truth, and say, 'All you've got to do is hand the cash to Giovanni

Ferrari, and I'm never going to work in your office again; or any.'

Instead, Miles nodded, and said 'Yes, Saul. I'd like that very much.'

25

'Now where the fuck is Father Christmas?'
Bob Brandt, the *Weissmans West Side* store manager, blinked back at Saul Weissman. 'I'll find out.'

'Do that. What's the point of having a frigging grotto if we got no Santa to put in it?'

'I don't know, sir.'

'There isn't one, numbskull. Now find him.'

As Bob Brandt skipped away, Weissman cast a critical eye over the Christmas decorations on the first floor of his flagship store. Aside from for the glittery gold and silver reindeer hanging by wires from the ceiling above, he thought everything looked good. A festive Garden of EDEN had been built within the Cosmetics Department. Tanned and alert mannequins of Adam and Eve were wearing original *Weissmans* plaid flannel shirts, red woollen gloves, and pointed hats. Styrofoam snow lay thick on the floor. The snake was a stuffed sausage of non-laddering tights, covered in red and green velvet. The red bulbs of its eyes flickered in time with the Christmas jingles.

In front of the scene was a long table with chairs for Weissman, Miles and the models. Weissman looked at his watch. It was two minutes to nine. Weissman loved Monday mornings. He'd always been at his most energetic at the start of the week. Over the years, personal assistants had quit for just this reason alone.

In Bob Brandt's office on the eighth floor, the models had gathered. This was the first time they'd all been together, and they were circling one another with suspicion, but without hostility – more like dogs on the verge of mating. What united all but Fernando was a desire to seem uncompetitive and calm.

Fabio was succeeding better than the rest, sitting as he was in the corner of the room with his eyes closed. And it was not until he heard the punchy tone of Saul Weissman's voice that he snapped himself from his slumber. Weissman was standing in the centre of the room.

'You're all great-looking guys,' he began, 'and I'm truly sorry that only one of you's gonna win. Still, I hope you'll enjoy yourselves while you're in New York. If you need anything,' Weissman jerked a thumb at Miles, 'Miles is the man you gotta ask. He's got my credit card, so go easy on him, OK? Now we're gonna be going out there to answer a few questions for the press, so maybe you can hold any questions you personally might have until after that. But let me remind you guys that you're gonna be media property for a week, so try to act nice, OK? Show yourselves in your best light. Personally, I don't give a monkey's tit if you make assholes of every one of yourselves. I don't care if you go out there and badmouth me or *Weissmans* or this beautiful cologne. But remember that I'm listening, and I'm watching, and if you screw up, if you do anything I don't like, then you, are, not, going, to, win the six million dollars. Period. This is a fair contest. You all come in here with an equal chance of winning, and an equal chance of screwing up.'

Miles caught Giovanni's eye, and tried to smile without smiling. Reuben turned his face to look out of the window. Fernando grinned and looked around at the surly expressions of the other competitors.

'Looking at you guys now, I can't say who's gonna win. So it's gonna be up to you to impress me. And the guy who does that the most is gonna win. OK? Now, I wish you good luck.'

The reporters were gathered and waiting for the EDEN finalists. Philly Griff was there from Channel 6, along with Larry Meyers, and a surprisingly large international collection of press journalists and photographers. Both men from Associated Press and Reuters had come.

Weissman led the models in, introduced them, and took his seat in the middle of the table. The cameras flashed.

'If this many of you had shown up when I opened this store nearly twenty years ago, I'd be a rich man by now.'

That got the ripple of laughter Weissman had hoped it would. 'Now, as you know, I'm not gonna launch EDEN until the spring, but you'll find in your Press Package that I've included, as an early Christmas gift, a small bottle of the fragrance. No doubt you'll agree that it's got a truly fantastic aroma.'

A few of the assembled people opened their bottles, and Miles was convinced he could see them wince. Weissman didn't notice.

'It's a woody fragrance that officially they call *Fougère Aromatic*. You'll be getting a full list of its ingredients later, but I did wanna say now that *Weissmans* did not use any natural animal products. *Weissmans* is a store that's dedicated to the environment, and I'm proud to reveal today,' Weissman paused to make sure of the attention he desired, 'that to coincide with their launch of EDEN, *Weissmans* has recently purchased from the Brazilian Government some land in the Amazonian Rainforest on the promise that we'll keep the land as nature intended it.'

For the next ten minutes, Weissman did what Weissman did best: he talked. In effusive terms he sang the praises of his six finalists. He called them his *Weissmans* Dream Team. He took up where Miles had left off, and explained that the competitors were from all walks of life, and that *Weissmans* was symbolically embracing the world. *Weissmans*, he added, 'is a store for tomorrow as well as for today.' Then, with a sweep of his arm, he opened the floor for questions.

Meyers was first. He wanted to know how the winner was going to be chosen.

'One thing's for sure,' Weissman insisted, 'they're not gonna be parading up Fifth in bathing suits. This isn't Miss World! What we're doing is having the wonderful Bruce Stone take some test shots of the guys, and we'll be moving from there. I'm hoping one of these guys is gonna, you know, shine from the pictures.'

'Where are the women?' someone said.

'They'll be here Wednesday,' Weissman replied. 'That treat's in store.'

A voice from the back. 'Giovanni, you have any plans to marry Effie Crascauldi?'

Giovanni smiled gently. 'This is my private life.'

'So you don't deny it.'

Giovanni adjusted his tie and looked away from the journalist. 'We have not decided anything like this.'

Trina Conrad from the *Star*: 'Mr Weissman, you have a Brazilian in the final.'

Weissman glanced down the table. 'Fabio, yes.'

'Will he be receiving preferential treatment because of this new association with Brazil?'

'No way. This is a fair contest.'

Meyers again: 'Chester, what does your dad think?'

Chester swept back his long hair and looked unamused. 'He's a busy man. I'm sure he's got other concerns.'

'So he's not interested?'

'He's a busy man.'

'Did you leave America on bad terms with your dad?'

'No.'

'Why did you drop out of Harvard?'

'I felt a need to branch out.'

'Have you given up the idea of a career in politics?'

Chester laughed. 'I'm too young to have given up anything.'

'Does that include drugs?'

Chester glanced across at Weissman and made a face that said 'Don't blame me.' Then he looked back at Meyers. 'I think we should keep the discussion focused on the competition, don't you?'

'That's what I'm doing,' said Meyers. 'I'm wondering if you think your fame puts you at an advantage.'

'I'd imagine the reverse.'

'I heard you were involved with the sister of one of the other competitors, is that right?'

'Excuse me, but if you know, why are you asking?'

Miles interjected. 'Mr Meyers, I chose all the competitors

on merit alone. I met Spencer in Tokyo, and Chester in Milan. Their friendship was incidental.'

Meyers let it go. Anyway, Trina Conrad from the *Star* wanted to ask all the competitors in turn how they'd spend the money were they to win.

Spencer, at the far end of the table, responded first. 'I'm sure I wouldn't do anything too rash. Six million dollars can be frittered away. I'd probably invite suggestions as to where I should invest. I don't really know. I suppose I'd like to buy a house in the English countryside, too. For my part, I haven't given it too much thought. Um, yup.'

Next to him sat Reuben. He didn't look at Trina when he answered the question, but drew interlocking squares with his biro on the notepad in front of him. Reuben talked in a slow, deliberate voice as if he was taking care to think before the words came out. 'I guess I'd take a good look around in this city and see if I couldn't use some of the money.' He did look up now, and his bright eyes locked with Trina's. She felt faintly embarrassed by their intensity. 'I'm involved in three garden projects in the city, you know, like volunteer garden programmes that I think, I *hope*, bring real joy and happiness and . . . and a sense of peace to those depressed communities. I'd definitely give to those, buy others. And I'd . . . I'd use the money to help in the struggle of the black man to find his feet in a society that keeps pulling away the rug.' He laughed. 'I mean, I don't think six million dollars is gonna go far, but it'd help some. That's it, I guess.'

Reuben looked at Chester to his left. Again, Chester tossed back his hair. He seemed undecided on what to say now. Then it came to him. He smiled, stood, and made out as if he was leaving. 'I may as well go home now,' he laughed. 'Reuben's probably won right out with that speech.' Chester sat and patted Reuben on the back. 'Smart!' He turned to the journalists. 'I feel the same as Reuben. I'd give all the money to the homeless.' He paused. 'I hope Mr Weissman heard that!'

'Yeah! But I don't believe it.'

Chester feigned disappointment. 'Seriously, though, I don't

think money can help in finding out who you are. It wouldn't help me become a better artist. I'm sure if I did win I'd give some money away, but I'd also buy something I didn't much need. An Aston Martin, or something. I mean, you only live once, right? There's no point being too pious.'

On the other side of Miles and Weissman, Giovanni leant forward on his elbows. 'For me, the answer is very simple. I am the racer of the speed powerboat. I would be use the money for this. It is the true answer.'

Giovanni leant back, and seeing his cue, Fernando talked quickly and more loudly than the others. 'This whole thing, you know, it's like a dream coming true for me. So I don't go to bed every night thinking I want to buy *this*, or I want to buy *that*. No! I'm thinking, heh, you know, maybe I can win, maybe I can do some good thing for my life. You know, like get a start. My mother, she's living in bad mobile home after my father was killed. I'd do good thing for her, and I'd like to pay for expensive lawyer to fight for me against the Best Burger chain for the killing of my father. So . . . sure I'm hoping I win the money, but I'm not all the time thinking like this.'

Fabio was the last. Miles had forgotten how heavily accented Fabio's voice was, and how much worse was his command of English. His message, by contrast, was clear to understand. 'Money can't buy me love,' he said, to laughter. 'If I win the six million dollars I will go to my country Brazil and buy a beautiful house and I hope I will marry a beautiful woman. This is what I want in my life.'

He grinned. Trina Conrad, forty-four, divorced, the wrong side of svelte, too smart for most men, decided she would happily fly with Fabio to Ipanema beach, and stay with him for ever. She envied Fabio for not forgetting what it was to be happy.

Weissman looked around. 'Anything else?'

A young man lifted his notepad. He worked for the *Herald*'s main rival, the *New York Daily Mail*. Tall, thin, English, and unusually personable for a reporter, his name was Kevin Post. Larry Meyers considered him both a friend and a dangerous rival. 'I was wondering whether Giovanni will be visiting any of Tony Fratacci's family while he's here.'

Giovanni shrugged his shoulders and shook his head. 'I don't know the name.'

'In the recent scandals in Italy hasn't your father been implicated with the Mafia in the construction business?' Giovanni's smile was designed to cut Kevin to the quick, but it passed right through the reporter. 'And haven't there been links made to the Mafia in New York and to Tony Fratacci's family in particular?'

'My father is a successful man. The people are always jealous, always wanting to . . . to pull down him in some way. This is not a problem for my father or for me. I am not interested in rumours.'

Yet in the back of the room, someone was. Every piece of information she could use against these six men she was storing in her brain. Kristina may have looked passive enough, but her mind was hard at work. Steve should be there, she thought. Not Reuben with his phoney liberal views and promises to change the world. She despised weak men such as he. Men who wouldn't confess to their desires. *Reuben's the same as the rest. He wants a big house. A phallic car. Those shiny suits black men wear. The second he discovers what money can bring he'll be screwing every nigger on the block to get his hands on more.*

You can live with your dreams, Reuben. I'm going to act on mine.

Kristina's eye travelled down the line of finalists. Who would be sacrificed to make way for Steve? The upright and haughty Spencer didn't trouble Kristina. She was sure Weissman wouldn't approve of him. Reuben? Wasn't he like something unpleasant stuck to the sole of her shoe? Chester, she had to admit, had some style. He'd mixed the new look – the sneering, long-haired anti-fashion grunge – with his own long-established elegance. Chester was wearing a ribbed white vest beneath a shirt open to display an odd, claw-like chunk of silver jewellery that hung on a thin, black lace. If someone were to put the notion into Weissman's head that his Adam should be up with the times, then Chester would doubtless be a danger.

Then there was Giovanni. Smooth, confident Giovanni. His obvious disdain for all about him drew Kristina in. That excited her. Already she longed for *him* to want *her*. He was a challenge, and a danger. Perhaps he'd have to be the sacrificial lamb. Fernando was to Giovanni's left. Naïve and excitable where Giovanni was calm and resilient, Kristina knew Fernando was no danger. And at the table's end sat Fabio, relaxed, composed, disarmingly sexual. Kristina swore at Miles under her breath. These models were all that Weissman could have hoped for. Kristina knew it was going to take all her resourcefulness to make sure that Steve would beat them all. He had to! The millions were rightfully hers, and not one of these imposters at the table was going to steal them from her.

Kristina looked about her at the scene in the flagship *Weissmans* store: a winter's EDEN, a bank of photographers, and a gaggle of journalists scribbling conjecture: useless, hopeless conjecture.

If only they knew. There's only going to be one winner, and he isn't even here . . .

The big party, it had been announced, would be held in the former main waiting room at Grand Central Station, but that was not why Miles was sauntering around the terminal at lunchtime on Monday, December 7th, a week before the event. At the party, the winners of the most talked about modelling campaign of the year would be announced. A man and a woman and two contracts worth a total of seven million dollars.

The female model was to receive a million dollars. In front of Miles, on the vaulted ramp leading down to the IRT and the ladies' bathroom and changing rooms, Miles was scanning the faces of the homeless women to see if he could find just that winner. It was a perverse duty he was carrying out for his boss. Who did Weissman expect Miles to find? A Wendy Radcliff down and out? A Candy

Hempel begging for a dollar? Maybe in some mythical past when beauty wasn't valued so highly the beautiful might have been here; not today. Weissman had cited the sad case of Gia Carangi, the supermodel and prostitute who'd made $100,000 a year before her self-destruction with drugs and, ultimately, AIDS.

'There might be another Gia down there,' Weissman had said. 'You never know.'

No, Miles didn't know. He'd guessed, though, and as he walked up and down the ramp, he saw faces that reflected nothing but wan sadness. He stood outside the public bathroom, appalled by the stench, ashamed to be judging these homeless women on their looks as if the same rules applied to all, as if they had a chance, or a choice. He cast his eye around, but wrapped in tattered seventies cast-offs, ironically and ludicrously fashionable in their thrift-store styles, none of the women came even close to being suitable.

Miles took some polaroids for the sake of it, handed out a few dollars and was happy to be out on the streets and away from the claustrophobic depression of below. He was going to the Bowery to look around there, just for Saul. And if he failed there, as he suspected he would, he'd put a call through to London and request from an agency a top model who might resemble a bag lady from the streets of New York.

At six that evening, Kristina, Miles and Weissman gathered in the office where it had all begun. Miles was nervous, not about the meeting, but about Giovanni and Kristina.

After the press conference, Kristina had beckoned Giovanni aside and asked him to join her for dinner. She hadn't said why. So far, Miles had signed nothing with Giovanni. Their deal was based on nothing more than trust. Kristina had the power to ruin everything now.

Giovanni himself had tried to put Miles at ease. Following the choice of Reuben as the sixth man, Giovanni seemed truly confident in Miles's ability to help him win the campaign. What's more, Giovanni didn't seem too troubled by the quality of his rivals. Fabio, he said, was a threat. But no one else.

To Miles's surprise, Weissman echoed Giovanni's feeling. 'So far I like the Brazilian kid. He reminds me of how I was at that age.'

Miles couldn't imagine the resemblance, but if Weissman did, that spelled trouble.

'You're right, Saul,' said Kristina. 'I think he's got what we're looking for.'

Kristina too? This was terrible. Miles had assumed that Giovanni would make an immediate and favourable impression on Weissman and Kristina.

Weissman resumed. 'Fabio's what I wanted, Miles. He's a real man. There's something about some of the others that makes me uneasy, you know? That English guy. Spinster Kemble-Finch. Is he a dick-licker, or what?'

'Spencer? I don't think so.'

'Sounds like one. And what about Fernando talking about Best Burger when we're discussing my beautiful cologne? People put things together. I don't want the public thinking burgers when they smell my cologne.' Weissman took a swig of Coke from the can on his desk, and then leant back. He rattled his fingernails on the surface of the can. 'And another thing? What is it between these kids and their dads. I mean I had Chester, Giovanni *and* Fernando spending half the frigging conference talking about their fathers.'

'I'll ask them not to, Saul.'

'Do that. Now, I want us to have a six p.m. meeting every day. I don't want secrets, I don't want back-stage manœuvrings.' Weissman struggled his mouth around the long word. 'Miles, how you doing on those women?'

Miles leant forward and tossed the photos of the homeless women on to Weissman's desk. 'They're the best I could come up with. I looked around Astor Place and Second Avenue and the Bowery too, but nothing.'

'OK. We tried. Did you find someone else?'

'Yeah I called Models Too in London, and they suggested this girl. She's called Jessica Warren.'

Miles gave both Kristina and Weissman a copy of the fax

sent by Models Too. It showed a girl wearing an old, frayed camisole. Her stare into the camera was uncompromisingly stark. Her scraggy hair looked wet. She wore no make-up. Her nose was large, her eyelids red, there was a suggestion of acne underneath her sallow skin. Her arms were twig thin, her chest almost completely flat. The lighting was harsh, mid-morning daylight.

'They say she's doing really well. She's been working for *The Face* in London.'

'She looks like she was dug up yesterday. I like that. You think she's pale enough, Kristy?'

'Saul, if you want her, bring her over. It's obviously out of my hands.'

'We're sharing hands on this, Kristy. And I think we need one of these waif things. Miles, tell them we'll pay any job cancellation fees she's got, but don't suggest it unless they got ants in their pants. Who else you got?'

'I've got Jack Linda flying in from London, and . . .'

'Who? Jack? What is this shit?'

'Jack's the Spanish girl I met in Japan.'

'Tell her if she wants in on this competition she's got to change her name.'

'But . . .'

'No buts. Tell her to add a goddamn i; or an ie. What's wrong with Jackie? Jack's a man's name.'

'OK, I'll tell her.'

'Who else?'

'I'm trying to contact this girl in Miami.' He handed Weissman Sandy's composite. 'Maury Greenberg said he'd help me find her. She works for him. And then I'm going to be talking to Giovanni about Tiziana tomorrow, unless Kristina wants to ask him herself. You're seeing him tonight, aren't you?' he said, turning to her.

Kristina, who'd been sitting listening in what Miles considered to be a remarkably relaxed manner, hesitated before answering.

'Is that right, Kristy?'

'I'm having a bite to eat with Giovanni. I felt that as

Miles has met all the finalists, and you're interviewing them tomorrow, then I should get to know them too.'

Weissman drummed his fingers on the desk. Then he said, 'I don't like it. Go tonight, but quit there, OK? I don't want to stir things up. Why don't we have a party on Wednesday night to celebrate the Trudie Love show or something? OK? You can meet the guys properly there.'

'Whatever you say, Saul,' said Kristina.

It alarmed Miles that Kristina was being so pliant. Weissman stood and grinned and came over and kissed Kristina's hand.

'Whatever you say, Saul!' he repeated. 'Now that, sweetheart, is music to my ears.'

Poppy was standing by the door with that look on her face.

'Who's Sandy?'

Miles took off his jacket and threw it on a chair. He felt his intestines tangling. 'She's a model from Miami. Why? Did she call?'

'Yes.'

Miles twisted the cap from a Rolling Rock beer and found the trash can at twenty feet. 'What she say?'

'She says call her. She said you have her number.'

Miles walked to the other end of the apartment and picked up the phone. Poppy opened the fridge. 'Yes, I will have a beer, thanks.'

Miles made out that he hadn't heard. He dialled the number in Miami he'd been trying without success for two days. Poppy, noticing how he hadn't had to look the number up, came to peer at a magazine, and to listen.

Miles sat on the edge of the sofa bouncing a tennis ball as he talked. 'Hey, how are you? . . . I know, isn't it great? Yeah, Wednesday morning if you can . . . Yeah, that was Poppy.'

Miles walked with the portable phone to the other end of the apartment and pretended to look for something to snack on. Poppy could barely hear now. 'I can fax the flight times to your agency tomorrow . . . Until after the announcement on Monday . . . I know, it's like serious money!' Miles lowered his voice. 'It could even have been worth that night on the beach!' He laughed. 'Right . . . yeah, well Rosa said you were trying to get lucky. I think I should be getting some agent's fees here . . . You will?' Miles blushed. 'That'd be nice.' Feeling guilty, Miles walked back to Poppy, deciding to show he had nothing to hide. 'Great. Be in touch if you don't get the information . . . No problem. I know, me too . . . see you then . . . yeah, will do . . . bye.'

Miles hung up and tried to look uninterested.

'You've gone all red,' said Poppy.

'No I haven't.'

'Your neck's all blotchy. Like after we've had sex.'

Miles didn't answer. He loosened the strap of his watch. After a couple of minutes, he said, 'What were you thinking of doing tonight?'

'Miles! We're going to Stefan and Jen's for dinner.'

'Oh shit! I've made this plan to go out with a couple of the guys.'

'So unmake it.'

'I can't. They went to the gym, then they're coming straight down. I was going to ask you to come along.'

Poppy turned the page of her magazine. 'Were you? When?'

'Now. I mean when I got home.'

Poppy didn't raise her eyes. 'Well I'm going to Stefan and Jen's,' she said, disapproval leadening her tone, 'And so should you.'

'But we see them all the time.'

'So! They're our best friends. Anyway, they're more fun than a bunch of models.'

'How can you say that when you haven't met them?'

'I've seen them.'

'So! That doesn't mean anything.'

'If you're a model, it means everything.'

'Fine! Do what you like.'

'I will.'

Miles went to look through his closet for something to wear. He pulled out his Yohji Yamamoto black top, the new Stüssy jacket, and his Malcolm X cap. He began to undress to take a shower.

'Did you go out with this girl in Miami?'

'What?'

'Did you go out with Sandy or whatever she's called?'

Miles continued to undress. 'With a whole lot of other people, yeah. And when I got back to the hotel at about two I tried calling but you weren't in.'

'Don't try to turn this around.'

'I'm not. I'm just wondering where you were.'

'I can't remember. I think I stayed uptown with Daisy one night.'

'You think! Right.'

Miles kicked away his underwear, and wrapped a towel around his waist. He moved towards the bathroom. Poppy shouted after him. 'Don't try to accuse me of something just because you're feeling guilty about this girl.'

Miles thudded back on bare feet. 'What have I got to feel guilty about, Poppy? Unh? Poppy? What?'

'Something, or you wouldn't have gotten so uppity.'

'Jesus, you're acting like some jealous teenager.'

Poppy snapped shut her magazine. 'Jealous? Of what?'

'God knows. That I'm meeting new people, I guess. That I'm doing something important, that . . .'

'Important! Give me a break, Miles.'

They were silent, and the novelty of self-destruction tasted oddly sweet to both of them. They stared at one another, motionless both, each waiting for movement from the other. It was Poppy who broke the stare. She switched on *A Current Affair*. Miles strode back towards the bathroom.

Again, Poppy called after him. 'If you think what you're doing's important, Miles, then you've got pretty fucked-up principles.'

Miles stood still at the other end of the loft. 'At least I'm really doing something with my life.'

'Hey! We'll hang the Nobel Prize behind the TV, shall we?'

'Fuck you, Poppy!'

'It'd make a change.'

Under the soothing hot jets of water, Miles calmed, and

began to regret his words. Wasn't it the truth that riled? That had made him shout? No, he hadn't been unfaithful, but he'd committed the crime in his mind. He'd wanted Sandy. In fact, he wanted Sandy still.

Dripping and spongy after his long shower, Miles stepped out of the bathroom. 'Poppy?' The apartment seemed deserted. 'Poppy?' Miles slopped his way to the end of the loft. He called again, but Poppy had left. 'Shit!' Miles picked up the phone and dialled their friends' number.

On the second ring he thought again and shivering from the sudden, wet cold, he briskly hung up and hurried back to the steamy warmth of the bathroom.

26

Tuesday, December 8th; Larry Meyers always took the subway first thing in the morning. He was too impatient a man to tolerate early traffic, and anyway, he claimed that all his best ideas came to him on the trains. Always brutal in his passions, Meyers detested those New Yorkers who derided the subway system. They were the scared of New York because their neighbours were strangers and ignorance is like the dark.

Meyers took the subway to 110th Street and Lexington Avenue. It had been too long since he'd been to Spanish Harlem. It was to Meyers's credit that he regularly visited all parts of the city he wrote about. Today he'd taken the subway a stop too far so that he could walk back down to 101st Street and his scheduled interview with the most unlikely EDEN competitor.

It was a bitter day. The temperature had slid forty degrees in twelve hours and now the wind was funnelling up from the south, cutting sharp into Meyers's skin. He loved this, to be purified and intoxicated at once with the chill slicing through to the bone.

Close to the subway exit men and women, like heaps of tossed-out blankets, huddled with knees bent under their chins sharing none of Larry's joy. They lined the sidewalk over the subway grids and beneath the noisy pink and yellow bunting that stretched optimistically from the store. Head down, Meyers walked by on concrete littered with crack vials and syringes. No hand came out for money or food, neither did he stop to offer it. This city's grotesquely human in its contrasts, Meyers thought. Somewhere not so far away he'd crossed a divide, and now he was in a place unrecognisable to most of the residents living only a quarter of a mile downtown. A neighbourhood of burnt-out buildings. A neighbourhood under siege from the menaces of crack cocaine. A neighbourhood that had lost its young and its old and was left only with the tolerant and weary. Meyers's mind worked with the fatalistic clichés of his tabloid press, but for once even his words could not exaggerate the truth, and he walked briskly on with a heavy heart.

The warm aroma of freshly baked bread sweetened his thoughts two blocks south. In the window, a pink Mickey Mouse cake, beside it, another baked to be Bart Simpson. Past a billboard for Lotto – *All you Need's a Dollar and a Dream* – and an intimidating huddle of youths, their baseball caps turned backwards, their arms lost inside oversized clothes, and soon Meyers was at 101st Street. It was a surprisingly beautiful block in parts serene and tree-lined, much different in atmosphere from the discord through which Meyers had so recently passed.

Reuben King opened the door wearing sweat pants, thick woollen socks, and an old sweater. He stood back to let Meyers inside. 'I'm the door on the left.'

Reuben lived in a studio, lodging with a family who occupied the rest of the house. The room smelled of coffee, and there was an open fire burning feebly. Reuben's wide Ikea bed was unmade, and occupied by a woman who sat up when Meyers came in. She was naked beneath the sheets.

Reuben ran a hand through his short hair, and laughed. 'We slept too late. This is Marcie. Marcie, Mr Meyers.'

'Larry, please,' protested Meyers.

Reuben poured Meyers a coffee without asking and gestured towards a stool by the fire.

'This is a nice block.'

'Yeah, we think so too. We're hoping the developers don't get their hands on it. The prices around here are going crazy and some of the people who've lived here all their lives are getting forced out. That's bad for a community like this.'

Reuben sat on the foot of the bed and took Marcie's foot in his hands.

'Sounds like a whole 'nother story,' said Meyers, 'but I've got to get to Brooklyn, so I'll keep this short and sweet if I can.' He lifted a sheet of paper. 'I got some basic notes on you from *Weissmans*, like how you got chosen and so on. Now I'm correct in saying your father wasn't around much, and your mother's in Georgia, and that you're twenty-four.'

'Yeah.'

'Now your father was . . .'

'Man, you want to know about the competition, that's cool. But I'm not talking about my dad. Or my mother. You got what you need there.'

'OK, but you were making out that you were interested in the community, now is that because you have regrets about your own family life?'

'Well, sure, I had some things to come to terms with, but I'm healing fast. I've let those regrets work their way through me so I've come to terms with my anger. It's not anger any more.'

'You have the look of someone who's quite angry.'

Reuben laughed. 'I do?'

'It's those eyes he's got,' Marcie said. 'They're real nasty.'

Marcie lifted herself up in the bed and kissed Reuben on the neck. Without looking, he gently put a hand to her cheek, and spoke to Meyers. 'I guess I am angry, somewhere deep down. It's like how much longer is this shit gonna go on, you know? Like it don't matter what's in the law, what's on the statute book if people are gonna go on thinking of the black man the way they do.' Reuben suddenly seemed awake and animated now. 'You know what I'd like more than anything, more than this crazy six million dollars, more than a big car and everything. I'd like all white men to become black men, just for a day.'

Marcie interrupted. 'Yeah, but only for a day. Otherwise they could like it too much!'

Reuben smiled at his idea. 'Just for a day so's they could understand what it's like to walk into a job interview or to some expensive New York restaurant – or, no, wait, we

355

could send 'em way upstate New York. You hear what I'm saying, Larry?'

'If everyone turned black they'd be the majority.'

'OK they'd take turns, like jury duty or something. I mean, the way I see it is that the constitutional fight's won already. We gotta move on.'

'And you think the best way to move on is to stand up and shout?'

'Could be. I mean, I mean I'm not going to *change* people's minds. I don't think you can do that. But you can create an environment, a way of speaking and thinking and looking at the world that accepts the black man as an equal to the white man, and then kids will grow up and they'll think, shit, what was that racism all about? You know I spend a lot of my time on these three garden projects – there's one just up here past 118th – and I get to thinking when I'm there that this world we're in is like a garden, with all different kinds of flowers and vegetables. But then you got the weeds, and they're in every garden, and every year you try to cut 'em down, but they come right on up again. But if you get down to the roots and clear the soil, then the beautiful things can grow. That's what we got to do with society. We got to clear out the perennial weeds. Clear it and start again.'

'I see you got a map of Africa behind your bed. You think of yourself as African?'

Again, Reuben laughed. 'No, no, not at all. I'm an American. I don't even want to be an African-American. I just want to be an American.'

'So why's it there?'

'It looks good,' said Marcie.

'Actually, I was involved for a time with MAP.'

'Remind me . . .'

'The Movement for African Peoples.'

'Dr Gardner's movement?'

'That's right. He's a good man, but I think he's gone too far with this Ice Man/Sun Man argument. You know, he says like that our whole civilisation came from the black men of Egypt, and that the white man, the European Ice Man, has since then acted in a hostile manner to the black Sun Man. I used to believe all that, but now I think it's divisive. What we got to do is settle down and prove ourselves. We're a minority, and we're proud to be a minority, but that means we gotta fit in with the majority and beat them at their own game.'

'This is heavy stuff for a guy who works in a peanut store.'

Reuben burst out laughing, and he answered the point with a broad smile on his face. 'Hey, Jimmy Carter made it to President, didn't he? I mean, I kinda fell into that job. I don't intend to stay there, but most of the time I'm sitting down there in the store reading or thinking things out, and it's close to Kennedy College where I take night classes, so it's cool. It's not a career. I wanna be a writer one day.'

'Oh, yeah? So being in this competition hasn't changed your ideas about your career? What about modelling?'

'No way. I mean I'm only in the line-up because they wanted a black man. You know what, Larry? Don't write that.'

'You don't think you'll win then?'

'No way.'

'Would you like to?'

'I wouldn't say no to six million bucks. I could do a lot of good.'

'You mean you were being serious about giving to charity?'

'Yeah. Look, it's like another one of those things that man can't seem to get a grip of. I mean, it's the oldest cliché in the book to say that money doesn't bring happiness. But still we don't get it into our heads. I read a survey once that said it all. They asked these different groups of people how much more money they thought they'd need to be comfortably rich, right? Now the guys out there on the street say like twenty dollars a day. More. The ones making thirty thousand a year said they needed forty thousand. The guys making eighty thousand said they needed a hundred thousand. Whatever anyone had, they wanted more. I mean, even the ones on 250,000 dollars a year said they wanted more than 300,000. People just don't get it, and it makes me wonder what's wrong with us that we can't understand something so simple. It's like God forgot that part of our brains or something. But personally, I'm happy. I'd give up fighting if I had too much money, and then what?'

'Give it to me,' said Marcie.

'Marcie's already gone and made a list of the things she's gonna buying if I win.'

'You'd better believe it.'

Meyers looked up from his notepad. 'That's all very noble, Reuben, but I walked down from 110th, and I didn't see much celebration of poverty.'

'Maybe not, but you go take a walk down to where the rich folks live. Like five minutes down from here. You know you're there because you hit all these hypertension clinics and psychiatrists' offices and pet shops. The Upper East Side's like one big pet shop because everyone's so fucked up they can't have like normal relationships with normal people. They all got their doctors and their doggies.'

Meyers smiled. 'Point taken.' He then ran his eye down his notepad, and stood. 'I got plenty here to go on. Thanks for giving me your time.' He held out a hand. 'I'll probably see you again.'

'This'll be in the papers tomorrow, or what?'

'Should be tomorrow, yup.'

Reuben laughed. 'This is totally crazy. I mean one minute I'm like a nobody nigger delivering peanuts, and the next I'm in the *Daily Herald*, and on TV.'

'Oh, I meant to ask, what do you think of all that?'

'What do I think? I think it's a dream. A big, weird, crazy mother-fucker of a dream.'

While Meyers and Reuben were chatting over coffee, the elevator up to the fifty-third floor of *Weissmans New York* was doing things to Miles's stomach that he didn't like at all. He had another lousy hangover. It felt and sounded as if the IRT was careering through his gut, and any moment now express train would be careering out of his throat. It made him yawn, and feel dizzy.

It was Fabio's fault. He'd been the one who'd bought those last two pitchers of margaritas in El Teddy's, and it was then that the real damage had been done. The drink had tasted too much like the lemonade Miles's grandmother had used to make. It was unfair, like feeding a kid M&M's packed with nitroglycerine.

Miles shuffled past Rona and found Weissman in one of his coltish, fidgety moods. He had a lollipop in his mouth. 'You sick? You look sick.'

'Self-inflicted, I'm afraid, Saul,' Miles said casually.

Weissman pointed the lollipop. 'Don't do that again. Not while you're working for me. You hear?'

Miles studied Weissman's face for clues to the seriousness of this admonition. Weissman wasn't smiling. 'You see the papers?'

'Er, no.'

'You should have read the papers. That's what I pay you for.' Weissman moved to his desk, and picked up one of the tabloids. 'It's all bullshit. I mean what kind of headline's this' *Mafia Playboy says no to wedding plans.*' And look: *My father, Best Burger, and me*! And now this Reuben guy's being called some kind of black hero. *Black competitor dreams of building city gardens of Eden.* Now what did I say? Didn't I tell you to find me models who weren't gonna bring along all this extra baggage? Huh?'

Miles was more bold with Weissman these days. He took a step forwards. 'Don't you think the press is always going to look for something spectacular?'

'No. Not if there's nothing there to find.'

Weissman sat, said 'Jesus!' and put the lollipop back in his mouth. Miles shifted uneasily from foot to foot. Weissman swivelled his chair to look out of the window.

'I got the fucked-up son of an asshole politician, the smarmy son of a Mafia boss, a Spic who's using my cologne to fight his court battles, a faggot Brit who's lost his head somewhere way up his ass, a new frigging Malcolm X, and a Brazilian kid who . . .'

Weissman paused, and when he turned around, his demeanour seemed to have softened. This man's a kid, thought Miles. He goes from tears to laughter in seconds.

'You know what, Miles? I *like* Fabio. He's straight-up. He's got balls. I like him more and more.'

Miles was still standing, or swaying, and speechless. He was in no state to defend either Giovanni or the other models. Anyway, it wouldn't have been wise to fight with Weissman in this mood. He was a bull who'd seen red. 'Cat got your tongue, Milo?'

No, but the roof of his mouth had. He unstuck it. Gcluck. 'No.'

'Yuk!' said Weissman, throwing the lollipop in the bin and grimacing as if his taste buds had instantly sparked into action. 'I hate cherry. Now there was something . . . Oh yes! We have a development. The producers of the Trudie Love show are gonna air the show live. They want a live telephone vote thing during the show. Great, huh?'

Miles nodded, though he felt like shaking his head. It wasn't great at all. Miles was worried how Giovanni would come across to the TV audience. Miles feared that Fernando and Fabio would sweep the board. Fabio was becoming a bigger threat with every minute.

'Thing is, they wanna do it Thursday now so we're gonna try to get Bruce Stone to shoot tomorrow. I need you to arrange that with the guys – who goes when, and so on. How many of the girls have we got by tomorrow?'

'Five. Sandy, Jack, Andrea, Jessica, Helima.'

'OK this is what I want you to do. Go to Stone at the studio, tell him which of the men he'll be shooting tomorrow, and then have him choose the girls to go with them.' Miles nodded. 'And don't forget we got that party tomorrow night. I want the girls there too.'

'Yes, sir.'

'OK Go, get outta here. And Miles . . .'

'Yes?'

'Try cashews. They'll soak up that stomach acid.' He waved. 'I'll see you at six.'

Mr Steven Barefoot, of Texas, was beginning to lose his mind. He was a man of action, a man at home on the back of a horse teaching city folk how to ride and herd and lasso bullocks. A man who liked to be in control. One of the top three dude ranchers, and responsible at times for up to fifteen paying guests, he'd been too satisfied to dream. Until Kristina. From the moment she'd given herself to him in the stables, she tied up with riding tack and teased with the horsewhip, Steve had been hers. 'Imagine having enough money to buy this place ten times over,' she'd whispered.

Well, he had imagined, and believed. And given everything up for a promise of eternal happiness, forgetting with his greed that it was something he already had.

Now in New York, time was running out fast. Steve couldn't understand Kristina's confidence. She'd come back from her dinner with Giovanni Ferrari sparkling with excitement. Everything, she'd told him, was back on track. He should just wait and see.

God, how Steve hoped so. He'd even taken to praying again, though something inside warned him that God didn't take kindly to requests such as his.

It was ten to six, and Weissman was throwing darts. The board was a gift from his English silk tie manufacturer, and though Weissman had forgotten how to score, he liked to play when his mind was in a spin. As it was now.

All day he'd been interviewing the finalists. He'd hoped that a clear favourite would emerge, but now he hadn't a clue. 'OK,' he said out loud,' if this hits the bull's-eye, then . . . then . . . Chester's gonna win.'

He let the dart fly.

Chester's attitude had impressed Weissman. The Senator's son had sounded truly excited by the prospect of working with the great Bruce Stone on the campaign. The six million hadn't seemed to be the issue. Chester was a wealthy kid already. His passion to win sprang from elsewhere. The hair Weissman had his doubts about, however fashionable it was, but he knew that Chester could make a fine All-American Adam.

The dart thought otherwise. It seemed to be on target until the last moment when it hit the metal ring surrounding the bull, and bounced back to the floor. Weissman smiled. So close . . .

He thought of the others. What about Fabio? There was so much that Weissman liked about the Brazilian, and yet Fabio was slovenly, unmotivated, almost too casual. He'd breezed into the interview late and grinning, and it had annoyed Weissman, not simply because he expected greater respect, but because Fabio's charm and assuredness had made Saul feel unusually niggardly and punctilious.

Weissman let fly a dart, aiming at treble twenty. It missed the board completely. See! That was the thing about Fabio! He disrupted your best intentions. You hated him for his cockiness, his arrogance, his luxurious beauty, his devil-may-care chauvinism, and yet you ended up wanting to *be* him. And wasn't that the whole purpose of advertising?

Weissman stepped forward and twisted from the board those darts that had made it. Their brittle Union Jack flights put him in mind of Spencer. Spencer had arrived punctually in a pin-striped suit with his hair slicked back. When he'd shaken Weissman's hand he'd spoken of his pleasure at being a finalist with such sourness that Weissman had found the message impossible to believe. Spencer tried hard enough, he said all the right things, and he was extremely handsome, but the composite parts failed in Weissman's mind to form a satisfying whole. He was like a barking guard dog with nowhere to protect. Perhaps, Weissman thought, Spencer only belonged in a uniform defending his little nation.

Weissman steadied himself and began to throw again. A twenty. Very nice. He was getting better. Soon he'd be able to hold his head up when he played in an English pub. Boy! Another twenty, and that one skimming the wire around the treble. Two more, and I'll give Fernando the campaign, he thought. The first sank in beautifully. Weissman lined up the second with his eye. He rocked his hand on his wrist, and then let go the dart. It missed hopelessly, hitting the six. Something inside had told him it would.

Weissman laughed at himself again. Perhaps it'd be for the best not to have a Hispanic Adam. Still, with each passing day Weissman's approval of Fernando grew. Who knew how he might feel by Monday. He'd already had a U-turn in attitude over Fernando's court case. During the interview, Fernando had spoken so movingly about his father's death that Weissman had ended up putting a call through to his own lawyer, Seth Jacobson, to see if Seth could help out with Fernando's case against Best Burger. Somehow, he felt it was the least he could do.

Could he do anything for Reuben? He rather wished he could. He'd found Reuben to be surprisingly articulate and self-effacing. And there was a disarming quality to his expression that stayed in the mind after Reuben had left the room. An impression of fortitude. A handsomeness deeper than the skin. Damn it! He didn't know. He was getting all wound up on his own ideas. Reuben was a good-looking kid. They were all good-looking kids. He chucked the dart at the board without care.

The dart thudded dead centre into the bull.

Weissman laughed, and sat back down at his desk to wait for Kristina and Miles. His desk was the right place from which to consider Giovanni. The Italian had smoothed his way into the office to shake Weissman's hand as if he was negotiating for the merchandising of a *Weissmans* line across Europe. Clearly, Giovanni was treating the competition as a business enterprise. He would doubtless make the most sophisticated and mature spokesman if he became Adam, yet the latent philanthropist within Weissman shied away from plumping for Giovanni. The Italian was already so rich and well-established. Sure he'd make a wonderful Adam, but would the message be right?

The message, Weissman knew, had to be spot-on. A lot of money was at stake. Too much? Weissman rubbed his forehead and wondered. The clock ticked to six. So many sixes! Wasn't that a bad sign? Six million bucks, six men to choose from, and six days left to go. Maybe there's a devil at work here, thought Weissman. Maybe he'll help me make my choice. He smiled at the thought as there was a knock at the door. A figure entered.

'Oh, hi there, Kristy. It's you.'

If he hadn't rolled over, then he wouldn't have known. And if he hadn't known then he wouldn't have cared. And if he hadn't cared he might have slept and woken fresh for the most important photograph of his life. But it wasn't to be, for at a little past midnight on the morning of Wednesday, December 9th, Spencer Kemble-Finch altered his position on the stiff, laundered pillow of his hotel bed, and felt it. Close to the end of his nose, on the left-hand side. Like a dagger in the dark, Spencer knew what was before him. It felt like his demise, for his nose had sprouted a spot.

In panic, Spencer threw back the covers and trotted into the tiny, precise hotel bathroom. He turned the dinner switch up to full. A kind smoked mirror covered all of one wall. Dressed in his flannel pyjamas, (striped, drawstring, Jermyn Street) Spencer angled his head so that the sharp overhead light fell on the left face of the nose. And there it was, an unmistakable bump that had appeared in the last couple of hours and which doubled, trebled, quadrupled in size as he stared. Spencer leant right into the mirror, and with forefinger and thumb, he gingerly pressed down the skin either side of the bump. There was no escaping the truth, the pulsating red truth, surrounded by a white halo of infection.

Spencer wondered what the hell to do. He thought he struck a rather pathetic figure in front of the mirror, at once distressed and listless. What *could* he do but scour his face with soap, as he did, avoid the mirror, as he tried, and drink three glasses of water before returning to bed? It might be gone in the morning, he thought. Spots can come and go. He remembered that from his adolescence.

Back in bed Spencer tried to sleep but beneath his eyelids psychedelic flashbulbs were exploding. He opened his eyes to the loud and unyielding darkness. Oh God no – Bruce Stone! Spencer had been terrified enough before the spot, but now – Stone was one of the world's top photographers. He was accustomed to photographing the most beautiful in the world. Now an acne-ridden amateur was about to walk through the studio door. What would all the people think? In the callousness of dark, Spencer imagined a studio crowded with trendy people, fashion people, TV people, model people, journalist people, curious people. And they'd be standing there and pointing at his nose and wondering why he didn't know how to pose or smile or turn to the side with his hand in his pocket as Jeff had tried to teach. From the moment he'd been told about the photo shoot, Spencer had been nervous. Now his unease was truly turning nightmarish.

Spencer eased himself into a new position in bed. Just forget about it, he told himself. It'll be better in the morning. He forced himself to think about Jack, and their night together in Tokyo. She was arriving in New York later that day. Spencer wondered if he'd sleep with her again, if she'd urge him on as she knelt with her elbows on the bed, praying like the good Catholic girl she was that he'd enter once more from behind. Spencer clasped a cool hand over his penis. It quivered but fell limp like a ham actor dying on stage. His body, he decided, was intent on nurturing the spot.

With palpitating heart Spencer gingerly felt for it again. Damn, still there! Outside, a loud screech of wheels, a car horn and someone shouting 'mother-fucking asshole'. Don't they ever go to bed here? he wondered. Then it hit him. Of course they don't! Not in the never-sleeping city.

So *even the shops would be open*!

Spencer jumped out of bed, heaved his jeans and a sweater over his pyjamas, then socks, shoes and a hand through his scraggly hair.

He found the bustle of the hotel lobby oddly reassuring, like when, as a child, he'd been rescued from the night and carried downstairs to meet the grown-ups. Now people were still drinking at the bar and living normal lives outside the torturous chamber of his room. And no one was staring at his nose.

Spencer approached a young porter whose face, ironically enough, was pitted with acne scars. Spencer asked where he might find a 24-hour chemist.

'Surely, sir. There's a *Love* drug store only four blocks north on Broadway.'

'Thank you very much.'

'Glad to be of assistance.'

It was bloody freezing outside. At the end of the block a cloud of steam was rushing wildly out of a striped funnel that jutted from the road. Spencer passed a black man in a bright waterproof jacket. He was staring grimly in front, clapping his gloved hands together, beating out the slow rhythm of the icy night in a muffled thud. Spencer crossed the road from him, and jogged on to Broadway. The streets were dotted with isolated figures. As Spencer's mind was laden with images of urban violence he ran a crooked line towards the drugstore, crossing the road whenever he neared a man. Yellow cabs were juddering fast and noisily over squares of steel in the street. With the freezing wind sneaking down Spencer's neck, he upped his tempo for the last one and a half blocks.

It was warm and quiet inside the *Love* store. In the store's globular fish-eye mirror, Spencer studied his face. He thought he could see the spot. Finding the skin creams he chose a type for *Non-oily adult skin that breaks out infrequently*. The extra-strength variety. The manufacturers no longer found profit with regular strength in a market overloaded with expectation.

He ran back, the air like shards of glass in his lungs.

In the bathroom, he followed the instructions. *Rinse affected area. Apply lotion sparingly to affected area. Leave affected area overnight*. He wished his nose could have been featuring in a TV cookery show. *And here's one we did earlier, and just look how nice* . . . But no. There was no escape from the waiting. For a moment, Spencer watched his reflection in the mirror, as if something would happen at once. He saw the lotion dry white, then . . . nothing. He returned to bed, jittery with apprehension about the day ahead. It was twelve minutes past one.

The seconds, the minutes, the hours sped by like a stalactite forming. Two a.m. passed; two-thirty; three. By three-thirty-eight, Spencer was getting truly frustrated. He revisited the bathroom to inspect his nose. The tiny bump was covered in a flaky, white coat. He washed it off. Little had changed underneath. Back in bed he applied another coat of lotion, hoping that he hadn't disturbed the ongoing chemical effect. Soon, hating the horrible, clammy darkness, Spencer turned on the radio. The relief of another voice talking in his head brought on the sleep, and at twenty minutes past four he drifted from consciousness into a dream where he was happy, and somewhere else.

27

Wednesday, December 9th, 9.29 a.m. Hester Street, Lower Manhattan.

'There he is! Look! He's with someone. See him?' said Alvarez.

Detective Brian Reilly turned with a wry smile. 'He's only the other side of the street!'

Diego Alvarez had only been in the force for three years. His keenness and enthusiasm amused his partner. Reilly had joined the NYPD twenty-nine years before, and he'd stopped getting kicks out of the job sometime in the mid-seventies when the black and white had turned grey. To Reilly, there was bad, and there was not so bad, and most people dithered in between; cops excluded. They were on the wrong side all the time. They just chose a different form of expression.

Reilly and Alvarez had been working on the Fratacci case for five months. The family had lain low for a while after Tony's arrest and conviction, but Tony's skittish young brother, Johnny, had soon enough stepped into the vacuum, and business had begun once more. The scale was smaller, but they were taking bigger risks, and no one doubted that Johnny had been responsible for the murder of Sal 'Slim' Alfredi outside his suburban Queen's home at the end of July. Alfredi had made a move on some Fratacci construction contracts after Tony's demise. The family hadn't been amused. Word was that Alfredi would have backed down, no problem, but Johnny was new to the power game, and killing was still where it was at.

The unit tracking Fratacci hadn't got hold of the hard evidence yet, but they were picking up pieces day by day, and Reilly figured that Fratacci better revel in his freedom while it lasted, because it wouldn't last for long.

Reilly and Alvarez were sitting behind the tinted windows of a lime green Oldsmobile at the end of Hester Street when they saw Johnny Fratacci step from the door of the IVA social club. He was wearing his favourite grey cashmere coat with the black velvet collar, and he ducked down into his Lincoln without so much as a glance about him. His companion, a man, shortish, stocky, balding, clearly Italian, closed the door for Johnny, and climbed in on the opposite side.

'We know him?' said Alvarez.

'Nah. Looks like, ah, like some heavy from Jersey. Look at that jacket. It's got no shine.'

Reilly started the engine of the police car and eased it out in pursuit.

Johnny had a big, moated place out in the unlikely town of Far Hills in New Jersey. Reilly feared that Johnny was headed there. The detective didn't feel like driving the turnpike again. Out and back for nothing. Still, they'd reached that stage in the case where they were searching for anything juicy to book Fratacci on. It had become like Capone and the tax fraud – once they got hold of Fratacci they weren't going to let him go. Last thing they wanted was another slippery bastard like Gotti.

Detective Reilly was surprised when Johnny's car stayed east and swept steadily through midtown up First Avenue.

'I'll bet you he's taking the Queensboro Bridge,' said Alvarez.

'Twenty bucks says he doesn't.'

'Make it ten.'

'Chicken.'

The car slowed on the approach to the bridge, but then passed it. It turned into Sutton Place, and then left on to Riverview Place. Reilly had to be careful here. They could easily be seen. He pulled up so that Alvarez could use the 500mm lens.

Johnny was greeted at the door by a young man. He introduced his associate. Reilly whistled as Alvarez fired off the shutter, thirty frames at least by the time the door was closed.

'Look's like Johnny's necking with the big boys here. Could be something. You recognise the guy at the door?'

'No clues.'

'OK. Take down the address and we'll call a scan. Then reach into your back pocket, find that skimpy wallet of yours, and just behind your girl with the big bazoobies you'll find a ten-dollar bill that now belongs to me.'

Bruce Stone's magnificent daylight studio occupied the top floor of a five-storey cast-iron building in Manhattan's lower West Village. With its hardwood floors, its high tin ceiling and its wall of windows through which the generous western light could gush, it was a studio that made other photographers green with envy. On a summer evening when the streets and studios to the west were shrouded in shadow, the sun across the Hudson painted these white walls a luxurious and flattering orange. Thanks to the studio's location, Bruce Stone had all his soft-lighting provided by a benevolent God.

At nine thirty on Wednesday morning. Chester Hunt, relaxed after a comfortable night in his father's grand Fifth Avenue apartment, walked through the studio's door, tossed back his hair, and took a look around. At a table opposite sat Bruce Stone himself. He was a tall man, balding in the most attractive manner. His hair was evenly grey, as it had been since his mid-twenties. Shaped in a widow's peak, he wore it long over his ears, but above the collar. Stone resembled not so much an ageing rock star, but the rock star's manager who'd wisely invested his money instead of snorting it up his nose or shooting it through his veins. Though Stone's skin was leathery and wrinkled, making him look older than his fifty-three years, he still looked healthy. His eyes were dark blue and gentle, his accent a jumbled haggis of East Coast American and Borders Scottish.

Stone was flicking through the portfolio of a leggy Brazilian model who he was considering for a swimwear catalogue to be shot the following week in LA. She looked nervous, no doubt having heard of Stone's reputation as a surly and difficult man. She was looking not at him but at a large platter of muffins and croissants and pastries such as could have been found in almost any studio in the city. Throughout the morning, the food would be picked at, blueberries stolen, icing discarded by thinning girls, croissants left too long under the drying heat of the lights. And then at half past twelve the same caterers would arrive with chicken and fish and salad for lunch, and clear away the battle zone that had been breakfast.

Chester threw down his knapsack. To his right he could see Bruce Stone's three diligent photographic assistants setting up the lights and unpacking the rolls of film.

The Brazilian girl left, and Chester advanced to introduce himself to Stone. The photographer almost smiled.

'They're doing hair and make-up over there,' he said. 'They might want to do something to you.'

At the opposite end of the studio from the assistants, the make-up artist was already at work on the face of the female model. Someone else, who Chester assumed was the hairstylist, was lying on a couch with his cowboy boots up and his eyes closed. Chester joined them.

The make-up artist introduced herself as Catherine. Catherine was French and one of the world's leading make-up artists, famous for her short temper and even shorter stature. Whenever she was working on set she had to stand on her make-up box to reach the models' faces. Yet Catherine was large in reputation. She'd made up the faces of Candy and Wendy, Tiziana and Effie. And it had been she who'd cut Dina's long hair four years before, a snip that had rocketed the model up to the big league, and life as a superperson.

Now Catherine was standing with a sponge, applying foundation to the model who'd been chosen as Chester's partner. It was Jack Linda.

'Oh, you're Jack! Spencer told me about you.'

'Nice things, I hope.'

'Spencer always says nice things.'

Catherine stamped her foot. 'Sweetie, I cannot be doing this with you talking.'

'Sorry!'

Jack had been delighted when she'd seen Catherine arrive at the studio. The two had worked once before, for Amica in Europe, and Jack was aware that if anybody could cope with the tired face she'd picked up on the flight from Japan, it was Catherine.

The Frenchwoman spoke to Chester. 'Why don't you get Brock to do something to your hair, mm?'

Brock, the hairstylist, opened one eye, and beckoned Chester towards him. He held out a hand. 'I'm Brock.'

Brock looked like he'd had a rough night. His own dark shoulder-length hair was tangled. His eyelids were struggling. His skin looked pale and sodden. Of all the relatives in the fashion family it was the hairstylists who behaved the worst. While the working models were tucked up in bed nurturing their beauty with bottled water and face creams, and the make-up artists were tending to their kids or taking yoga classes in empty dance studios on the Upper West Side, while the photographers' assistants slumped with Mexican take-outs in front of Bergman, Kurosawa and Chabrol, and the photographers dined out with hopeless tarts sporting silicone breasts and attitude, the hairstylists, the bad boys, usually men, usually gay, were out in clothes tight to their contours, babbling gossip, searching out straight men to tempt from the narrow, defining excess. They had the connections without the responsibility. At nine a.m. they didn't have to focus a lens or line an eye, nor did they need to look healthy and happy. They just had to be conscious enough to perform a job they learnt in a year. Brock himself was only just the right side of consciousness. But he did manage to stand and run his fingers through Chester's hair.

'You're fine. Maybe I'll run a brush through it later,' he said in a voice that sounded as if he'd been gargling with carpet tacks. Then he leant in and whispered, 'The cheapskates are only paying a thou.'

Jack was soon made up, and Brock ran his fingers through her hair as he'd run his fingers through Chester's. A thousand dollars worth of skill and creativity.

It was now that this shoot differed from most since there was no product to sell, and no clothes for Chester and Jack to change into. In fact, Stone wanted both topless. Jack was hesitant at first – she'd always thought her breasts too flat – but couldn't say no; not with Stone; not with a million bucks at stake. So, both wearing jeans and nothing else, the two models stepped on to the brightly lit set.

The assistants had laid white sheets and large wooden boxes for the models to sit on. Stone had Chester stand to the side of the boxes. Jack was told to sit and wrap her arms around Spencer's waist, her cheek pressed against his hip. Stone looked through his lens for the first time that day, and then turned quickly to his first assistant, Rob. 'Jesus! What have you two being doing with these lights? Chester looks like he's been in a brawl at Ibrox Park.' He stood and walked away. 'You should be able to light a simple shot like this without my help.'

Temperance was one of the cardinal virtues that every assistant had to learn. Stone had instructed Rob to light the model sitting down. Now that he'd decided to have Chester stand it was obvious that the lighting would be wrong. Simply, Stone was to blame. Rob wished he could tell him so. Instead, he apologised, and redirected the light. The assistants who travelled the furthest were always those who never answered back.

Stone returned. 'OK. Better.'

As Stone framed the image once more, Chester stared back into the grey mirrors of the 150mm lens. There was a moment's quiet before the first picture was taken. And then Chester heard the first heavy snap of the shutter, and it was to him as the starting pistol of a race. This now was his Olympic hundred metres – the one moment for which he'd been training. He stared intently into the lens. It was the centre of his universe. The studio didn't exist; the hairstylists, the assistants, the make-up artist, the walls, the city, they no longer existed. Around the cool sphere of the lens they blurred into one. The lens was everything. Six million dollars were hidden in its hollow darkness, waiting for Chester to reach inside. He needed to capture that one perfect moment when the camera mirrors would open and record something beyond his features. Stone could not create this alone. Chester had to speak through his eyes, he had to reveal himself through his face, he had to give it all to the lens. He took his eyes from the lens, and burnt them into a chair by the door. He felt it now. He flexed the muscles of his face into his favourite expression, and gorged on the focus of the camera. He was becoming lost in the image, living for the image alone.

'Chester,' Bruce Stone said, 'you look like you're on acid.'

Chester blinked. 'I do?'

'Yes. You're getting this glassy look in your eyes.'

'I am?'

Rob handed Stone a newly loaded camera. The 120 film he used had only twelve frames per roll, so changing the film was a task that had to be carried out with hasty precision. Once the right mood had been established the last thing Stone wanted was for it all to be lost while an incompetent assistant fumbled with the film. During the shooting it was the second assistant's duty to load the cameras and check that there was no dust behind the lens, that the aperture and exposure settings were correct, and that the film had wound through. If something went wrong, the wrath of the crew fell up him alone.

'Jack, nice,' said Stone. 'Maybe press your cheek close on to his skin. Imagine he's about to go away somewhere and you don't want him to go. Really hold on tight. Chester, the position's good. I'm getting a nice shape, but remember to try to look as if you're with us.'

'He's probably dreaming of the money,' said Brock.

'Right, Chester, don't dream of the money.'

Photographers usually repeat the jokes made by hair-stylists. Since he'd begun modelling, Chester couldn't remember a photographer making a joke of his own.

Stone began again. Shooting as he was with the flash heads, he had to wait a second between each shot for the flash to fire again. It had always annoyed Stone that on television and in movies, photographers were always seen moving around their models saying 'Lovely' and 'Beautiful' while their cameras clicked with the rapidity of AK 47s. Stone worked from a tripod. He talked rarely while he shot. He always made slight adjustments between frames. He was a professional creating art.

Brock took Catherine aside. 'Can you believe this? He's ripping off Patrick's Calvin Klein shots. Isn't he? I mean look at the way she's holding Chester.'

'Bruce always shoots this way.'

'Yeah, but still . . . I mean, *look*! They're both half-naked. Jack's got like *no* bosom to speak of, I mean, what's Bruce doing?' Catherine didn't respond. 'But Chester's divine. He's got this furry hair going down his navel that's to die for. It's all blond and bushy.'

Bruce Stone shouted. 'Brock! Jack's hair, can you sweep it back on one side away from Chester?'

Brock sauntered in. He resented having to do what he was being paid to do. He only ever wanted to get out of bed for a *Vogue* cover.

It didn't take much time for Stone to finish the shot. Chester had tried to heat things up between Jack and himself. Once, he'd hazarded a hand close to her breasts. Stone hadn't wanted that. In this shot, the woman was an accessory, and nothing more.

Meanwhile, as Chester and Jack dressed, Spencer Kemble-Finch was walking around the block trying to muster up the courage to take the elevator into Stone's studio. He'd been inside the elevator once, but he'd slipped back out before the doors closed. Back with his fear to the streets.

Time was really against Spencer. Yet the whole idea of walking into Stone's studio to model, to model for Christ's sakes, with this thing on the end of his nose was beyond terrible. Twice during the night he'd applied more cream. And when he'd got up and to looked in the mirror, he'd found the cream had burnt a scarlet circle the size of a penny on the end of his nose. In absolute panic he'd done the one thing he'd known he shouldn't. He'd squeezed. He'd squeezed as if his life depended on it. A tiny speck of clear fluid had encouraged him, and he'd squeezed even more. After ten minutes his nose had become a battle zone. Spencer's fingernails had cut two tiny perfect semicircles in the skin, and a layer of skin, softened by the shower, had peeled off. When he inspected it again, he'd thought he would lose his mind.

It had taken an hour and two mini bottles of Scotch for him to regain his composure. Hope lay, he'd thought, only in the pharmacy. So back in the *Love* store he'd purchased, on recommendation, some hypoallergenic blemish concealer. This act itself had taken some weight off his mind. Carefully he'd rubbed the dull pink cream on to the whole of his nose. Then it had been time to go.

Walking in the wind back to Stone's building, Spencer again turned the corner, and then immediately spun on his heel and hid. Outside the building Chester was standing with, of all people, *Jack*! He couldn't face seeing her too, so he waited, peering like a criminal around the corner, until they left in a cab. Then, breathing in deeply, he set off, more scared than he'd ever been in his life.

In his trouser pocket, Spencer's fingers were crossed as he walked with a pattering heart into the darkened studio. Stone approached with a slight smile. 'You must be Spencer.'

'Yes,' he said, his voice shaky.

'I'm Bruce Stone.'

Stone introduced Spencer to the others. Spencer was glad to see how few people were there. They were intimidating still, but he could live with this. And, most importantly, with the curtains drawn it was blissfully dark.

Another female model had arrived, the South Ethiopian of whom Weissman had spoken with such praise. Her name was Helima and she had one of the most delicately beautiful faces Spencer had ever seen. Her cheekbones were pencil-thin, as was her strong, curving jawbone. It seemed as if with the slightest knock, they would break. Her lips too, were narrow, and they curled in a little when she smiled, as she did when she held out her hand to Spencer. Her hand was remarkably bony, her fingers long. Her eyes were the shape of almonds.

'Sit here,' said Brock, 'while I do your hair.'

He hasn't said anything about the nose, thought Spencer. Not yet. Brock flattened a palm on the top of Spencer's head, and, looking into the reflection in the mirror, said 'You been modelling long? I don't think I've seen your face before.'

'No, this is my second time, well, you know, second shoot, that's what I meant. I did my first in Japan.'

'You live there or something?'

'My father's the ambassador.'

'Oh, excuse me!'

Ten minutes later, Brock and Catherine swapped models.

'Sweetie, you want to go to bathroom and wash your face? You have some cream or something on your nose.'

'I do? Oh.' Spencer scratched at the back of his neck. 'I hit my nose on a tennis ball, I mean a tennis ball hit me and I thought in case there was no one here I'd, it'd be better to, to, you know, make it better.'

'No problem. If you wash, then I will do something.'

Beneath the tap the red reappeared. Spencer looked at the window and contemplated escape. He'd never have to see any of them again. He could catch a flight back to London, and forget it all. But he steeled himself and returned to the studio. When he passed Stone, Spencer scratched an imaginary itch on the bridge of his nose. There was nothing he could do with Catherine.

'*Eeeaah! Je comprends, chéri. Tant pis*. Never mind, we can do.'

And then Spencer watched as Catherine magically sponged the redness away. Second by second, he felt as if the weight of the World Trade Towers was being lifted from his shoulders. *So this is how they always look so perfect*, Spencer thought, unaware that he alone out of the six needed make-up applied to his face.

When, twenty minutes on, Catherine had finished with Spencer, he stripped down, glanced at himself in the mirror and wondered for a second whether Helima might fancy him now that he was back to his rather fanciable self.

*   *   *

It was late in the afternoon, and on the phone, Giovanni Ferrari was acting innocent.

'So,' said Miles, 'you're never going to tell me what you and Kristina got up to at dinner.'

'I told you, my friend. Nothing.'

'You didn't go back to her office after?'

'No.'

'She didn't try to cook up some deal with you?'

'No.'

'OK.' Miles looked at his watch. 'You know who Bruce Stone's shooting right now? Fabio.'

'So?'

'So I hope they're not getting on too well.'

'My friend, I say before to you – you should not be too worry about Fabio.'

'Oh no? Come join me in one of my meetings with Weissman and Kristina. They're both salivating over the guy. I'm going to have to work really hard to make sure they choose you.'

'It is only Wednesday. Many thing may happen,' said Giovanni.

'They'd better. Listen, I've told Weissman that Tiziana has agreed to enter, is that right?'

Tiziana Ferrari was Miles's new trump card. The super-model had agreed to join the competition. Privately, her offer was conditional. If Giovanni won, as he expected to, then she would model. If he didn't, then she would withdraw.

'She can arrive Friday afternoon, only.'

'That's fine so long as she confirms as a competitor.'

'She will.'

At that moment, Poppy came into the apartment. Miles told Giovanni that he had to go. Poppy came and sat opposite Miles and rubbed the palms of her hands wearily over her face. With the deliberate dullness of his stare, Miles knew he was being provocative. He began to chew at a matchstick. He and Poppy were silent.

Then Miles said,' So where did you go last night?'

'To Stef and Jen's. I told you.'

'I got out of the shower and you'd just disappeared.'

'You were being an asshole.'

Miles concentrated on picking something from under his nail with the match. 'So are you going to come tonight, or what?'

Poppy let out a half-laugh. 'That's nice.'

'What?'

'The way you said that.'

A pause. Miles lit a cigarette and blew the smoke towards Poppy. 'Should I be on my knees?'

'Don't be a jerk.'

'What then?' he said, knowing.

'"Are you going to come tonight or what?" is not a very nice way of asking. Do you want me to come?'

'It's up to you. Don't come if you don't want to.'

'I never said I didn't want to.'

'OK.' He stood. 'So come.'

'Not if you don't want me to.'

'Jesus, Poppy, when did I . . .'

'You *sounded* as if you didn't want me to.'

Miles raised his hands. 'I'm sorry I sounded like I sounded, OK.? I'll try again.'

'Not if you don't mean it,' she said.

'Christ! What's *wrong* with you? I have to go to the party because it's my job right now. I asked you along, and now you're making a fucking scene about it. Just say yes or no. It's your life.'

'It's *our* life, Miles.'

'See, you're doing it again.'

'Well maybe it makes a difference to me if you want me there or not.'

'I don't want you there if you're going to mope around feeling jealous.'

Suddenly, Poppy was shouting. 'How many times do I have to tell you that I'm NOT JEALOUS, Miles? Get it into your stupid head. I'm, not, jealous! If any one is, you are. *You're* the one who doesn't want *me* to come.'

'Oh really? Why?'

'I can think of reasons.'

'Such as?'

'How about because you're kind of keen to keep that world to yourself, because it's going to lose its glamour when I step in, because you won't be able to flirt with your Sandy or God knows who else, because you're probably embarrassed by the way I look and dress, because I notice you haven't even thought of stopping me yet . . .'

Miles took his cigarette from his mouth. He paused, deliberately. 'Have you finished?'

Poppy stared at him, and she searched his face for kindness. She found nothing there; nothing more than the hollow dullness of his stare. A tear bulged in Poppy's left eye, and then escaped briskly down her cheek. She wiped it. Miles said nothing. They listened to each other breathing, unsure why they were doing this to each other. Then, quietly, Poppy said, 'I'm not coming while you're like this.'

Miles stood at once, said 'Suit yourself,' and set off towards the bathroom for a shower feeling curiously light-headed and victorious.

28

B ruce Stone was enjoying himself for the first time that day. 'Very good, Fabio. Give me more of that.'

Fabio and Sandy were in front of him on the set sitting on the floor. They were working beautifully together. Sometimes that just happened. Two models who'd never met one another before would communicate with the intuition of longtime lovers and the chemistry would be captured on film.

Stone suspected that Fabio was the one who merited the praise. He had a way of seducing those around him with an uncalculating charm. Stone had noticed this before among Brazilians. When he himself had visited the country for an Italian *Elle* shoot, he'd been moved by the pure humanity of the people. Stone remembered how when travelling on buses, standing women would refuse his quaint and chivalrous offers of a seat, but instead, without words, dump their sleepy children on his lap with the simple trust that comes from being unspoiled humans together. Fabio exuded warmth and humanity, and because he lived this way all the time, it made him irresistibly attractive as a man.

Fabio was dressed in faded black jeans, out of which the elastic of his underwear brimmed, as froth on black stout. Fabio's hair was cropped short, and thanks to Japanese sunbeds, his body was darkly tanned. His chest was hairless, his pectorals boldly defined by shadow. Stone had removed the set boxes. Fabio was sitting upright his arms, making a triangle behind him with the floor and his torso. His legs pointed straight to camera. Sandy was to his left, her left leg flat on the sheet, her knee against the small of his back. She, too, was looking into the camera lens, her head tilted against Fabio's and her chin resting on his muscular, round shoulder.

Her left arm was draped across his lower chest, the tips of her fingers on the elastic of his underwear.

Stone was shooting faster than he had all day. He had no doubts about this shot, and few about his own choice for the EDEN models. He was right there, and with a woman whose beauty was the perfect contrast.

After fifteen more rolls of film, Stone called it a day. He'd worked longer and later than planned, and already the model's party in Rudy's Fish and Grill was beginning.

Fabio beckoned Sandy aside. 'You will come now to the party with me?'

'I have to go back to the hotel first.'

He touched her on the arm and didn't waver in his stare. 'Do you want I come too?'

Sandy hesitated, then she looked up at him. 'Let's meet up at the party, shall we? There's not much time.'

'OK,' smiled Fabio, 'I like to have much time.'

Sandy, flushed, dressed and ran for a cab. Catherine and Brock cleared up and left. Bruce Stone poured out a large Scotch for himself and one for Fabio. 'Are you going to be hanging around in New York?' he asked.

'We will see about the competition.'

'Well, listen, whatever happens with that I've got some work coming up that I'd be very interested in using you for. Who are you with in the city?'

'I have no agent.'

'OK. Let me give Scott a call at Supreme. I think he's the best in the city. You can go in and see him.'

'Oh, great. Thank you.'

'It's my pleasure. I only hope we get to do this campaign together.'

'You hope, I hope, maybe it come true,' said Fabio and then, with a grin, he finished his whisky in one.

It was dark and bitterly cold on the street, but Kristina had told Fabio that he should walk, and she'd drawn a simple map to Rudy's Fish and Grill. Make sure you don't get it confused with the Black Hole, Stone had warned. 'That's a gay bar about three blocks down from Rudy's.'

Fabio had left feeling exhilarated for the first time since he'd arrived in New York. Though he believed that people too concerned with the future never leave time to revel in the present, he was beginning to dream about what could be. It was all going his way, and shooting with Bruce Stone had been an exciting taste of the the big time.

The city was quiet where Fabio was walking. He took Varick Street up to Leroy, and then passed a pretty, vine-covered cluster of mid-century brownstones. Following Kristina's map Fabio turned right up Hudson Street past some crowded, homely restaurants. It was eight p.m.. Fabio liked New York. He liked its variety and pulse, and he was as thrilled as every other first-time visitor by its sheer, magnificent, heart-lifting beauty.

From Morton Street he took a right on to Washington. It was darker here and but for a woman walking her dog, the street was almost empty. Across from Fabio, a dull grey Lincoln saloon, its windows tinted back, was moving slowly. Fabio wondered if it had been following him. A moment's nervousness came and went. He speeded up. Don't worry, he told himself. He checked again on the map. Only four blocks to go. He thought he could pick out the lights of Rudy's.

Ahead, a cab squeaked to a stop outside a bar. A man wearing black leather trousers and jacket, and with a handlebar moustache, climbed out. Fabio hadn't a drop of prejudice in his body, but he'd never understood the attraction men felt for other men. He smiled to himself as the man hopped into the Black Hole bar.

And then it happened. The Lincoln stopped suddenly across the street. Three men wearing hooded sweat shirts and cotton balaclavas leapt out and surged at Fabio. Fabio turned and immediately began to run, but one of the men was on to him already. He grabbed Fabio's jacket and yanked Fabio back. The attacker was built like a bulldog. He hurled Fabio against the concrete wall. Fabio yelled out as the skin was ripped from his cheek. He threw a desperate punch which landed hard in his attacker's gut. The man reeled backwards. Fabio ducked to his right and tried to run but from behind him one of the other men twisted an arm around Fabio's neck and squeezed. Fabio gasped for breath. Terrified now, his eyes searching frantically for another figure on the street, Fabio took hold of the man's sleeve with both hands and tried to release the grip. He kicked back with his leg, but now the other two had joined in the attack. They kicked the backs of Fabio's legs and brought him to his knees.

Suddenly a hand was on Fabio's hair, pulling his head back. Fabio opened his eyes. In front of him stood one of the three, his feet balanced and apart. In his hands he clenched a baseball bat. The man lifted it back and above his shoulders.

'Nooooo . . .'

Fabio wrenched his neck to the side. The polished wood came down hard and shattered his right cheekbone with a crushing blow. Fabio screamed again. Through the ocean of sound in his head, Fabio heard another voice now, screaming from behind, then footsteps.

'Hey, fuckers. Stop! Get off him. Help. Someone help. Call the cops.'

The attacker had no time. He brought the bat back half way and put the weight of his body into the swing. It landed at the base of Fabio's nose. The bone cracked, and his teeth snapped like biscuit wafers.

The man shouted as he hit, 'FAAAAGGGGGOOOOOTTT.'

Then he ran.

Fabio slumped on to the sidewalk, vomiting out the blood from his mouth. He lay, his torn cheek bleeding on to the concrete. He heard the screaming of wheels, then bottles smashing, footsteps, voices, a siren; and then . . . nothing.

In the bustle of Rudy's Fish and Grill, Saul Weissman was being introduced to five of his six female finalists. Helima he knew from before. He thought her the most beautiful black woman he'd ever set eyes upon, a view shared by many others who'd met her. Sandy he was impressed with. He talked to her about Miami, and about his old friend, Maury.

Jack introduced herself as Jackie under Miles's firm instruction. Kristina's choice, the ice-cool German model Andrea, gripped Weissman's hand as if she was trying to crack a walnut between her fingers. She didn't smile. She was half an inch under six foot. She had cropped, reddy-brown hair, piercing dark eyes and a mole on her right cheek. Andrea said her grandmother lived above the *Weissmans* store in Hamburg, and swore by it, even though she is right-wing and know you are Jewish, It was told as a joke, but Weissman didn't get it. There were limits. He moved on and left Kristina explaining to Andrea how once, in Germany, her family had been rich.

Jessica Warren was the thin English girl whose portrait had been faxed from London. She hadn't grown any, nor had her hair been washed, but Weissman found her to be more appealing in the flesh. Her soul hadn't been bleached from her by an unsympathetic photographer waging a public battle against beauty. It was to Jessica that Miles was talking when Weissman came and put his arm around Miles's shoulder.

'Excuse me, sweetheart. I need him for a moment.'

Weissman turned Miles around and walked him to the corner of the restaurant, by the scrap-metal coat rack, and the front entrance.

'Where the fuck is Fabio? He's more than an hour late and I got the photographers waiting to take the group photo.'

Miles took a swig of his Becks. 'I don't know where he is.'

Weissman prodded Miles in the chest. 'Don't be so cocky. You *should* know. It's your job to make sure all the models are here. Did you try the hotel yet?'

Miles stood straighter, made sure he sounded more serious. 'Yes, no reply. And I tried Stone's studio. They say he left more than an hour ago. Maybe he's got lost.'

'You didn't give him the address?'

'Yes I did. I've run out of places to look.'

Then, as if inspired, Miles saw a golden opportunity. 'Saul,' he began, 'I've got to be honest about Fabio. I think I made a mistake choosing him.'

'Nah. The kid looks great. And I already heard from what's-her-name . . . Sandy . . . that Stone loved him. Really loved him.'

Miles had heard that too. That's why it was past time to knock Fabio down.

'It's not his look, it's his attitude. He was late for the shoot in Tokyo, he was late getting ready for the press conference, and now he's late coming here. He's got this totally laid-back attitude to the whole thing. It's as if he couldn't care.' Now Miles launched into an out-and-out lie. He looked deep into Weissman's eyes. 'He even said to me that he thought the whole competition was ridiculous, and that you should choose him right away.'

Weissman paused for a second. Then he said: 'Oh yeah? He said that did he? Well – fuck him.' Weissman swore so loudly that half of the group turned around. Weissman continued more softly, but the anger was as clear to detect. 'No way am I going to give six million dollars to a screwing, lazy schmuck like him. He doesn't deserve it.'

As Kristina came to complete their triangle, Miles's stomach flipped over in excitement. Miles was sure that Giovanni was Weissman's second choice. Weissman continued.

'You know what I'm gonna do? I'm gonna go ahead with this photo, Fabio or no Fabio.' He clapped his hands together, and raised his voice. 'Before we get too tanked up, folks, maybe you could do some posing for me, yeah? We got a couple of photographers here from the press. Maybe we could all put down our drinks and our cigarettes and do what they want. It shouldn't take long.'

Miles and Kristina were left alone as Weissman and the models grouped together for a photograph. She took a swig of her Absolut and soda. 'Did you hear about Fernando?'

'No. What about him?'

'Saul's lawyers got on to his case, and now Fernando's settled out of court on the condition that he doesn't mention Best Burger on the Trudie Love show tomorrow, or ever, in fact. He's got to make a public statement exonerating the chain.'

'You're kidding.'

'Yes, Miles, I am. I thought it would be an uproariously funny thing to say that to you.'

'You're not kidding! How much did he get?'

'I don't know. I heard $500,000.'

'Jesus! You're kidding.'

'Say that again,' she smiled, coldly 'and I'll throw this in your face.'

'That's weird, though. Fernando's been acting quiet all evening.'

'Maybe he doesn't think half a million's enough for a father.'

At dinner Miles sat at one end of the table, Helima to his left, Fernando to his right. Poppy had chosen not to come. The stupid thing was that he *had* wanted her to, sort of. He'd wanted her to come and see his new friends. He'd wanted her to come and witness his new authority and prestige. He'd wanted her to be impressed. Then he'd imagined her somehow, well, disappearing. With a headache, perhaps, or a sudden attack of debilitating nausea. Then when he'd get home she'd apologise for having left, and he'd forgive her, and she'd tell him how wonderful he was, and they'd make love for hours without getting bored.

The reality was less soothing. While Helima was being chatted up by a zealous Chester, Miles turned to Fernando. 'I heard about the settlement. That's incredible.'

'Mm.'

'You're not happy?'

'It's cool. I telephone to my mother.' He smiled. 'I told her "don't go to work tomorrow, Mama. You don't have to go to work." You know what she say? She say "I don't got nothing to do if I don't go to work." She work in this chemical factory and she wants to go there tomorrow. It's crazy!'

'It probably hasn't sunk in yet.'

'I think she don't believe this to be true.' Fernando was playing with his unfinished food in front of him. 'I don't think she feel anything is true any more. Like this – me, here. You know?' Fernando pushed his plate away, and reached into his pocket. He took out a battered gold lighter. He showed it to Miles. 'I carry this for the good luck. It was of my father. He had this when he died.' Fernando stared at the lighter. He turned it over and studied it as if he'd never seen it before.

Then he looked at Miles. 'It's strange, because it is when I am happy that I become sad!'

Fernando began to pick at the wood of the table with his fork. 'You don't think when someone is alive . . . you don't think one day . . .' Fernando sighed and looked up to the heavens. 'Agh! I don't know how to say this. I mean, my father he was like just *there*, you know? All the time. So I didn't talk to him or I didn't say thing to him. He was . . . there. And then when he was kill I came into the house, after, you know, and I feel like calling to him. It's true. It's like I couldn't believe . . .' Fernando paused, 'it's like I couldn't believe, you know? I mean I was saying in my head "he's dead, he's not here you stupid," but there was some part inside that wouldn't believe what the other part was saying. You understand? I mean like you watch the TV and they say "it's beautiful weather tomorrow" or like "the Dolphins win the football" and you think "oh, Papa will be happy!"'

Helima said, 'Can you pass the salt.'

Fernando did so without looking at her. Miles made a face at her and she turned away. She immediately told Chester that there was something the matter with Fernando. Chester leaned forward to have a look.

Fernando was playing with the lighter. He laid it in the centre of his palm and stroked it with a finger as if it was a dying animal. 'Maybe you will think I crazy but I was hoping . . .' Fernando screwed up his eyes, but still a tear was squeezed out. He wiped it quickly away, and laughed at himself. 'I mean look now I have this money, but it's like they say, "here, here's your money instead of your father." Always, I was thinking it would feel better if I could win in the court but now it feel . . . worse. I mean they give me more money than I was ever dream about, but they take away something too. I don't know what they take . . . something, something now is not here that I have before.'

Miles said, 'I think it's like anything. Fighting's the easy part. But now you don't have anyone to blame. You don't have an enemy to stand up to and say, "Look, you're responsible." That's not easy, but it had to happen one day, and it's much better that it happens with you getting this money than with you getting nothing. Isn't it?'

'Maybe. But now I have to be silent. It's like I do a deal with my father's memory. I sell it for the money.'

'That's crazy! Think of what he'd have wanted.'

Fernando was about to reply when Weissman slapped a hand on his shoulder. 'Hey kid. I found out they got a TV back there. You want to come watch the fight?'

'Oh! OK, sure.'

Weissman was a devoted boxing fan. He'd almost cancelled the dinner when he'd remembered that it would clash with the WBC heavyweight fight from Las Vegas, but he'd found a solution now. Weissman had discovered that Fernando had always been a fan. Fernando reckoned that the underdog, the Briton James T.Book would come out strong in the first few rounds, and, if he could land a series of heavy punches, would win the fight by the fifth against the current champion, Moses 'Madman' Mantissa. Weissman disagreed.

'Miles, you coming?' Weissman said.

'Er, no, I don't think so. I've got a call to make.'

At the phone, Miles called Poppy, but when the machine picked up he put down the receiver, ran his fingers through his hair, and made his way to the chair Weissman had vacated beside the beautiful Sandy.

Larry Meyers looked at his clock. Eleven ten, and outside it was snowing. He put aside his book and picked up the ringing phone. He hoped it wasn't Brenda McCarron. He simply didn't feel like sharing his soul tonight. It had been battered enough during the long day in Brooklyn. 'Yeah?'

'Larry? It's Bill.'

Bill Padham was a fellow journalist on the *Herald*. His slow, nasal pattern of speech had once infuriated Meyers. By now, he didn't even notice it. Bill continued. 'We got something come in on a gay bashing in the West Village.'

'Oh, shit, Bill. I did that story weeks ago.'

'Wait. One of the fudge bandits at this Black Hole bar says he recognised the kid from the papers. He says he's one of the *Weissmans* models.'

Right away, Meyers's mind began to spin. He hadn't been

an investigative journalist this long to accept facts as he heard them. This was no random attack, he thought. Not if it was on one of the finalists. Either the guy had been recognised, which in Manhattan was reason enough to beat the shit out of someone or it was an attack planned to take the competitor out of the final.

'Where is he, St Vincent's?'

'Yeah. They took him there about an hour ago.'

'State?'

'He's alive.'

'How bad was it?'

'I don't know. All I heard was someone tried to hit a home run with the kid's face. One of the guys from the Black Hole bar stayed with the guy at the hospital.'

'Cute! OK, thanks, I'll get down there right away.'

Half an hour on, Larry Meyers was surrounded by the squeaks and smells of thick, warm leather. The Black Hole is a small, single-room gay bar tight with men who share similar tastes in clothing, facial hair, and sexual appetite. It's an unremarkable place – a simple wooden bar, sawdust on the floor, a few homely pine tables, dim, smoky lighting, hubbling chitchat. Behind the bar there's a depressing cluster of photographs of smiling men, regulars once, dead now from AIDS. The centre-piece of the bar is a sculpture made by the bar's Italian owner, Roberto. It's a two-foot tall penis erected with fusilli pasta.

Meyers found the piece distracting, and turned away from it as he asked the questions. He was talking to four men, all in their early forties, all leather-clad and stern-faced: Peter, Joel, Michael and Art.

'Who heard them shouting?' asked Meyers, pencil in hand.

'Bobby heard the kid,' Joel replied.

'Has Bobby gone home?'

'He went to St Vincent's.'

'But you heard the men screaming faggot?'

'That was what they said. Definitely.'

'And queer,' said another.

'And queer,' repeated Joel.' They said faggot and queer.'

'Who was the one who thought he recognised him?'

'That was Bobby too. He says he saw him in the *Weissmans* cologne thing. He said he remembered him because he was the cutest. He said he was from Mexico, I think.'

'Nooo. Brazil,' said Peter.

'That'd be Fabio,' said Meyers.

Art agreed. 'Uh-huh, that's what he said. Fabio.'

'Is this kind of attack common around here?'

'It's been getting worse. The more we die, the more they hate us.'

'Here, here, Peter,' said Joel.

Larry had written a whole series dealing with attacks on gays about a year before. He'd left his investigations with the impression that most attacks occurred through the unhappy coincidence of the wrong person being in the wrong street at the wrong time. Though brutal and vicious, most attacks appeared spontaneous. This was what troubled Meyers about the attack on Fabio. Meyers scented premeditation.

'Did anyone see the guys' faces?'

'No,' said Joel. 'They were wearing those horrible masks with holes in them.'

'You know, like in *Silence of the Lambs*, 'Michael explained. 'But I saw their car had a Jersey plate. I got a couple of the numbers which I gave to the police.'

Meyers ran a hand through his thinning hair. 'I'm getting the feeling that this was an unusual type of attack.'

'Oh no. It's been going on for years.'

'But how often do people jump from cars to attack you?'

They all seemed to say that it had happened before. Meyers considered the facts. Maybe Fabio really had been the victim of a gay-bashing. Why not? He'd been only thirty yards from a notorious gay bar. Meyers decided to check up the facts with Bobby at the hospital. Apparently, he knew the most.

Meyers passed the usual assortment of drunks and druggies in the hospital's Emergency waiting room. Upstairs, he met with Bobby who'd chosen to stay at the hospital until Fabio came to.

'He's in the operating theatre now.'

'How bad?'

'We don't know. He lost some teeth, and his eye looks terrible, but that's all I know.'

'Can I buy you a coffee?'

'Love one.'

They sat with plastic mugs.

'It makes you so angry. I mean, what had this guy done to them? Bastards! I mean, he doesn't even *look* gay.'

'His face or his clothes?'

'His clothes. There isn't such a thing as a gay face, Mr Meyers. But he was dressed pretty much the same as the bastards who attacked him.'

'Which was?'

'Oh, you know – jeans, boots, work jackets. That guy they beat up had one of those sandy-coloured canvasy jackets on. You know the ones. They've got a dark collar on them.'

That this had been an anti-homosexual act of violence, Bobby had no doubt. His was a mentality born of persisting persecution. Yet from what he'd said then, and went on to say later, Bobby found it hard to understand why Fabio should have been singled out. He couldn't, he said, have been less provocative in his appearance.

As Meyers talked to Bobby in the small hours of Thursday morning, his convictions crystallised. He was sure that Fabio had been the victim of a planned attack. The why was easy enough. The whom would be more difficult to fathom. The scent of pursuit excited Meyers. Had it been the models themselves who'd attacked Fabio? Or had some hit-men been hired? Would Fabio be the only one, or was this the beginning of a kind of Agatha Christie depletion? Or could Meyers have got it all wrong, in which case he should be writing the story on an unimportant page, a two-line snip saying 'Homosexual beaten by man wielding baseball bat. Police appeal for help'? It was upon this that Meyers focused his happily employed mind as he left St Vincent's for the walk across town, to Brenda and a quick drink in her bar.

29

The news was passed from Weissman to Kristina on the morning of Thursday the 10th. She was talking to him with one hand on the receiver while she applied lipstick with the other. Something bold today: Wild Strawberry.

'Of course we can, Saul. There must be someone to take Fabio's place. This is New York! . . . Right, I'll be there in twenty minutes.'

In the room next door, Steve was still snoozing, his gawky, morning-face turned towards the door. He'd spread out in the luxury of Kristina's king-sized bed. Kristina entered the bedroom and clapped her thin, elegant hands. 'Hey, Sleepy-head. Wake up.' Steve didn't raise his head from the pillow. 'That was Saul. Fabio Nirao's been hurt.'

Steve pushed himself up on one arm. 'Hurt how?'

Kristina's tone was apathetic. 'Apparently he was beaten up visiting some gay bar in the West Village. Anyway, his face won't be recovering any time soon and Saul wants six competitors to appear on the Trudie Love show today.'

'And he's only got five.'

'Einstein!' Kristina sat on the edge of the bed and asked Steve to fix the clasp of her necklace. 'But we know where the sixth is, don't we?'

Steve took his hands away from Kristina's neck. 'You had something to do with this, didn't you?'

Kristina turned and played with the hairs on Steve's chest. He was warm, like fresh bread from an oven. 'What kind of person do you think I am, Steve?'

A smile broke across Steve's lips. 'Oh, I know that youda done this if you could. I'm just asking if you *did* do it. I won't let on. I promise.' Steve reached out for her with his strong, hair-covered arms.

Kristina stood and pulled at the hem of her navy-blue jacket. 'This jacket's been pressed.'

'Was that a yes or a no?'

'Don't be ridiculous. I'd never do anything like that. Not that I'm crying over it. Now all I've got to do is to talk to Saul and get you into the competition. He's already at the office panicking, and I gave Miles the morning off.'

'That was convenient.'

Kristina was studying herself in the mirror that was her second-best friend. 'It was lucky! Now, listen carefully. The Trudie Love show begins at two, but the producer will want you all there at twelve thirty, so be here, showered, shaved and ready for my call.'

Steve threw back the covers. He was naked. 'I'm ready for you now. See?'

She turned to him. 'Ugh, put it away. Try to be serious for once. Now, tell me where you've been staying.'

'Here with you.'

Kristina sighed. 'Come one, Steve, I don't have the time. We went through all this yesterday.'

'Oh, right. I am staying on St Mark's Place with a friend. He's called Chip. His walls are painted blue. He has a plant in the . . .'

'It's not a joke, Steve. This is our big day. You can't screw up on me now. Saul must never, ever know about us. You and I met in London, and we haven't seen each other since. We're strangers. OK?'

'That may be right,' said Steve, laughing and exaggerating his Southern drawl as Kristina walked to the door. 'But you and my pecker are the best of friends!'

Saul Weissman was sitting on the floor surrounded by agency books when Kristina joined him in his office. Every agency in the city produced and distributed books containing photographs of all their models so that clients could avoid the tedious process of casting. Weissman never liked to work this way. Now he had no choice, and the books from Zoli and Click, Wilhemina, Omars and Supreme littered the space around him.

'You know, Kristy, Miles did a great job. Twenty minutes I've been looking at these, and already I'm losing it.'

Kristina joined him on the floor. For about fifteen minutes she stayed silent. Then she snapped shut the Click model book. 'Hey, Saul, I've had a great idea. Remember Steve Barefoot? The guy I found in London? What about him?'

'Is he in New York?'

'Could be. I've got a number somewhere.'

'He'd be good if we could track him down. See if you can't get him in here a.s.a.p. for me to meet him.' Kristina could hardly contain herself from running to the door. If he was dressed, Steve could make it to the building in fifteen minutes. And although Weissman hadn't met Steve yet, she was convinced he'd like him as he'd liked Jeff from Tokyo. She was at Weissman's door when he surprised her by saying, 'Meantime, I'll see how Miles is doing.'

'What? I thought he was busy this morning.'

'Yeah, but when I heard about Fabio, I told him to go into Supreme just to take on look around there.'

'But, Saul, we won't have to worry if Steve Barefoot's still in New York.'

'Maybe, maybe not. All I do know is that we're running out of time.'

The detective sergeant, Meyers heard, was on to it, even though the evidence was scanty. They were using what they had: numbers from a Jersey car plate that would be run through a computer; loose descriptions of age and height; a claim by one witness that the attacker had had a foreign accent, possibly European. The sergeant was not, however, too taken with Larry Meyers's theory that rival competitors in the EDEN campaign could be involved. 'Sounds like the plot of a bad movie,' he said.

As far as the NYPD was concerned, this was nothing more than another anti-fag attack. 'There are even voices,' stated one cop 'who say the boy had it coming. It's not AIDS. It is all this fucked-up liberal shit making out that it's some kind of crime to be a normal white guy.'

Meyers was keeping a more open mind. He'd called Reuben after his visit to the police, and heard from him that all the finalists had been in the restaurant at the time Fabio was attacked. Fabio, Reuben explained, had been on a shoot in Bruce Stone's studio and had never shown up to the dinner.

'Did any of you get any feeling that Fabio might win?' asked Meyers.

'No. It's pretty open, I'd say.'

'And you didn't notice any hostility towards him?'

'No, he was one of the most popular guys.'

'OK, Reuben. Thanks. And good luck on the show.'

Meyers planned to go to the Trudie Love studio to talk to the models. The police weren't bothering to pursue that line of enquiry. Meyers figured that if he got no clues from the contestants, then he would drop it too. However tempting it was to find a motive, Meyers knew that in New York City, two and two hardly ever made four.

Meyers called in at St Vincent's on the way to the TV studio on the Upper West Side. Fabio didn't look too pretty. He was lying with his torso angled up in bed, an IV drip in his arm. The left side of his face was covered in swabs, and one eye was swollen and closed. His top lip had been smashed apart and was stitched up on both sides. It too was grotesquely swollen. Fabio was asleep. Meyers asked the nurse where he might find a surgeon who'd know about Fabio's condition. She said that Dr Milsner knew, but shouldn't be disturbed.

'Don't worry, sweetheart. He knows me.'

As a city reporter for twenty-nine years, Meyers knew many of the doctors in the major city hospitals. By chance, Ian Milsner had been a good friend since Meyers had written a controversial piece about the hopeless AIDS drug, AZT. Off the record, Milsner had said that he'd lost all faith in it. Of all the opinions he'd heard, it was Milsner's that had struck the truest nerve with Meyers. Milsner had trusted Meyers since then.

They caught sight of one another in a corridor on the seventh floor. Meyers explained why he was interested in the case, and asked how bad Fabio was.

'It could have been worse. He had a bad blow to the zygomatic arch . . .'

'The?'

'The cheekbone. He had a nasty blowout fracture which basically means that the muscles around the eye are under a lot of pressure, and unless they're untrapped then the eye can get set in a fixed position. Say, looking down all the time.'

'That's going to happen?'

'No, not now. Our resident facial surgeon, Wilbert Ark, came in. He does a good job. So Fabio's bone's been elevated and repaired.'

'But he could have been blinded?'

Ian smiled. He knew Larry's game. 'Say that if you want, Larry, but there was no damage to the optic nerve.'

'His mouth looked pretty beat up.'

'There's a lot of swelling, of course. I think he lost about eight teeth, and he's got some tooth embedded in the gum. His lip should heal OK but it went right through at the point of impact. We stitched that up.'

'Is he going to be scarred?'

'Difficult to say. Let's say he won't be working as a model for some time.'

Meyers shook his head. The cheekbones and the smile. Like crushing a pianist's hands. Meyers was suspicious.

'I feel sorry for the kid, you know.'

Ian Milsner raised an eyebrow. 'You're feeling sorry for someone?' He placed a hand on Meyers shoulder. 'Now isn't that a first, Larry?'

Fabio has woken. By his bed, there was a large bouquet of flowers.

'Who the flowers from?'

Fabio shook his head. Meyers read the card. *From Bobby and all the boys at the Black Hole*. 'That's nice of them,' said Meyers. 'Real nice. Did you know them before?' Fabio shook his head. 'So you weren't going in there?'

Fabio lifted his hand and waved it furiously.

'You were just walking up to the restaurant and then these guys jumped from a car and attacked you, right?'

'Ay 'ollowed 'ee.'

'They followed you?' Fabio nodded. 'For how long?' Fabio shrugged his shoulders. 'Say three blocks?' Fabio nodded. 'Or more?' Fabio shook his head. 'I guess maybe they were waiting for the street to clear. Can you think of anyone who'd have wanted to hurt you?' Fabio shook his head. 'OK. Listen, do you need me to contact anyone, or has that been taken care of?'

'OK,' Fabio murmured. He tried a smile. His eyes softened.

'I always said that a mugging should be included in every trip to New York. At least you can tell the folks that you saw the city like a native.'

'Hanks!'

'I gotta get moving. I'm sure you'll be out of here soon. I'm sorry about this, though. It's . . . it's bad luck.' When Fabio raised his eyebrows, Meyers studied the model's bruised and battered face and found that not a trace of anger could be seen.

In Kristina's Upper East Side apartment, Steve Barefoot was struggling with his hair. He'd fallen asleep after Kristina had left. Her phone call had woken him up.

'Get up, get dressed, and get down here NOW.'

The dressing had been easy. His outfit, replete with Stetson and string tie, had been chosen already. It was his hair that was causing the problem. Just before leaving, Steve had squeezed on to his palm a dollop of Kristina's hair gel, and rubbed it in. Except it hadn't rubbed in. The thick, gooey, orange substance had simply cemented the strands together. So he'd had to wash it out, and he'd dried his hair with the dryer on high, and the result had been a storm-swept jungle of frizz. So it had been back to the water, and a smaller amount of gel, and the whole process had taken a ludicrously long time, and he'd left to meet the man who was to make him a millionaire with his hair looking worse than it had ten minutes before.

In the *Weissmans* building, Kristina was still thumbing through the agency model books to keep Weissman happy. Her mind was elsewhere. Steve was taking too long and Kristina didn't underestimate Miles's ability to ruin her plans.

Weissman seemed to read her mind. 'I'm gonna give Milo another call. See if he's found anyone.'

'Really?' Kristina said calmly. 'You don't think we should wait until he calls?'

'Wait? What for? Sweetheart, we got less than three hours to find us a model. I'm not gonna sit on my ass getting piles.' He pressed his buzzer. 'Rona, honey, get me Supreme.' The connection with Miles was quickly made. 'So, what's it looking like, kid?'

Miles, standing once again in the Men's division of Supreme, New York, said he thought it looked pretty good. In front of him, three bookers were collecting together the composites of their most suitable models. Having as good as ignored him the month before, now they were bending over backwards to help him out. Basia was drooling over Miles as if he was a celebrity.

'We should find someone.'

'OK, kid. Listen, we got that Steve you met in London coming over here any minute. If we don't hear from you soon, we'll be signing him up.'

'I'll see what I can do.'

Miles hung up concerned. He imagined that Kristina would like nothing more than to reintroduce the model that Miles had been responsible for dismissing. He joined the bookers. Scott was talking about the previous night's world heavyweight fight. Fernando had predicted accurately. Against all the odds, the underdog, James T. Book, had caused a sensation by winning with a third-round k.o. But Miles's thoughts weren't with the fight itself. He was thinking about why it was such hot news. If the favourite, Moses Mantissa, had won, the news would never have made the front page. Yet the star had fallen. What if, Miles wondered, he could find a star to fill Fabio's place? Then, when Giovanni won, his status would be immediately elevated. At the moment, the line-up included no successful

models. To have one of the top guys as a sacrificial lamb would
certainly boost publicity. Miles walked over to study the wall
of composites. He went straight for the composite of a familiar
face and picked it up.

'Scott, is this guy in the city?'

'Yeah, you're lucky, buddy.'

'Perfect! Can I use your phone?'

30

She wasn't religious; not in the strict sense of the word. Yet Mrs Jeanette Flighty was a woman who believed in Fate. And Fate, she told people, had not been kind to her. Born in 1948 into an unhappy Pennsylvanian family, Jeanette claimed that she'd never known an hour when she hadn't dreamt of the big time. Then Fate had stood in her way, taking when it appeared the portly two hundred and eighteen-pound shape of the TV megastar, Miss Trudie Love.

Trudie, the bitch, looked exactly like Jeanette. She looked like her, she talked like her, she even moved like her. The only difference that mattered was that Trudie Love was a household name all over America, and few had ever heard of Jeanette Flighty. One day, Jeanette thought to herself each morning, Trudie Love will worship the ground I walk on, and I won't even give her the time of day.

As Miles Jensen sat in the front row of the studio from which the Trudie Love show was to be broadcast, he studied Jeanette, and guessed not at the resentment in her heart. She was a short, round woman in her mid-forties. Her features were essentially down-to-earth and kind, yet there was an edge to them as might have shown on the face of a kindly grandmother convicted of murdering a child. Jeanette's eyes were close together as if pushed nearer the bridge of her nose by the plumpness of her cheeks. In truth, she was a plain and average woman in all respects other than her striking similarity to the ebullient, adored and irreverent Miss Trudie Love.

The set, as everybody commented to their neighbour, was smaller than it looked on TV. The audience numbered a hundred and fifty, and sat on portable plastic chairs uncomfortable enough to ensure that their occupants remained upright and awake throughout the broadcast. The set was designed to resemble a living room. A coffee table, a vase of fresh flowers, a glass dish of shiny honey-dip doughnuts, a backdrop of flowered wallpaper, and framed paintings of rural scenes. There was even a window looking out on to a yard. Until they came to the studio and saw walls made of plywood, many viewers swore that this was Trudie's home, situated somewhere in the Catskills.

There were three cameras, one at each side, and one dividing the audience in the middle. The cameras looked oddly archaic and cumbersome, as if left over from the early days of television. Everything else was slick and modern. Trudie had an armchair the size of a small car. Her guests sat on two sofas by the coffee table. The whole studio was brightly lit, and hot. Miles and the audience had a brief, tantalising glimpse of Trudie as she entered the studio to go backstage, but now her lookalike was holding court, warming the audience up, as she'd been hired to do for the previous four years.

Jeanette stood with an oversized microphone in her right hand. In her left, she held a half-eaten doughnut, stolen from the dish on the table. She was trying her hardest to be funny. 'Did you guys have lunch yet?' Silence. 'Helloa!' Jeanette tapped the end of her microphone. 'Anyone at home? I said did you guys HAVE LUNCH YET?'

A few members of the audience laughed nervously and said yes.

'I can't hear you!'

This time, they said yes more loudly.

'I had lunch early, so I'm having a snack.'

Jeanette took a large bite and chewed obviously. A woman at the back laughed; elsewhere, the silence was leaden with self-consciousness. Jeanette soldiered on, seemingly nonplussed. 'I'm one of those people who can get through a whole cake in one sitting by eating tiny portions at a time. Do you do that? I mean you think, oh, I'll just have a teeny sliver of that, and then you think, oh, well, seeing as I only had the teeniest sliver, there'll be no harm in having another teeny sliver, so I'll keep cutting and eating and thinking, well this much can't hurt me, until I've finished the whole darn thing!'

This, Miles was surprised to hear, did get a few more laughs. Jeanette, meanwhile, was finishing her doughnut and walking to and fro in front of the audience. 'I mean I always try to lose weight, but I do it the wrong way! Like sex! I heard that sex helps you lose weight. The more you have, the thinner you are, right? Now, let's see . . .' Jeanette placed a fist on her right hip and surveyed the audience. She pointed to a tiny, anorexic twig of a thing. 'Are you married, madam?'

'No,' replied the woman.

'No! Of course not! Two years of marriage and you look like me. So you're not married but you're looking?'

'Kind of.'

'Taking them out on test drives, right? Uh-oh, nice chassis, shame about the carburettor, right? Nought to sixty in ten seconds, then they have a cigarette, right? No, but like I said, the more you do it, the thinner you get . . . unless, of course, your husband's like mine. You know what his favourite movie is? Huh? You know?' Jeanette looked around, then she lowered her head and clasped a bejewelled hand to her forehead. '*9½ Weeks*,' she said. 'That's right! Every night Bob drags me to the goddamn refrigerator! And it's not ice cubes and grapes with Bob. Oh, no. He's feeding me chicken legs and Hershey bars. I'm the exception. I'm this size *because* I'm sex crazy and married to a man who can't get it up unless he's feeding me a tub of Choc Choc Chip ice cream. It's hell, let me tell you.'

Applause now. Jeanette knew she'd won them over. She quickly glanced at her watch. 'I've got to go before Trudie sees me. She's jealous because I'm the funny one. But because we're going out live today I want you to do something very hard. I want you to laugh at Trudie's jokes.' Jeanette held up a palm. 'I know, it won't be easy, but try. Nice and loud. Think of one of my jokes if you have to. Trudie always does – '

Applause, laughter, and then Trudie came on set, clapping. Jeanette gritted her teeth when the sound of the applause trebled.

'Jeanette Flighty, ladies and gentleman. Give her a hand – she needs three to get all that food in!'

Jeanette threw Trudie a mock punch, and then walked off, hating, hating, hating. Trudie took over, and explained how the show would work. 'We've got these beautiful men coming on, so try to restrain yourselves, ladies. It's live so we're going to be running through it exactly as you usually see it on TV. So please, no flash photography. If you want me, take me now.'

Trudie stood in the sultry pose of a glamour model, lips pouting, cleavage forward. The audience loved it, and the cameras clicked. America hadn't quite decided why it loved Trudie Love. She was fat, but not what you'd call cuddly. She welcomed guests with an archaic God-fearing, mid-American, Tupperware friendliness, but rarely missed with the barbed put-down. She pandered completely to newsworthy fads and fashions, but stayed the right side of sensationalist. She encouraged people to cry on her show, but often castigated them when they did. She promoted racial harmony, but implicitly preached something else. She was over-the-top, in love with herself, politically incorrect and watched by more viewers than watched any other daytime chat-show host. She was Trudie Love, and she was a sensation.

'Now, people, when the cameras are turned on you, try to look happy. I know that Jeanette – bitch – ' she whispered breathily into the mike, 'has put you in a bad mood, but I'm here, allright . . . ALLRIGHT?'

Trudie lifted both hands in the air, evangelically, and the crowd applauded. Miles joined in.

'Allright! Thank you for coming. Enjoy the show, it's going to be great.'

During the next ten minutes, Matt Skolaski, the assistant producer, coached the audience on when they'd be asked to applaud, laugh and look happy. There was an obvious ripple of nervousness as the crowd came close to its moment of fame.

Soon, Matt raised a hand, and silence fell. Trudie, freshly made-up, came and stood in front of the camera. Behind her stood Reuben, Fernando, Giovanni, Chester and Spencer. Matt counted down the audience, it obediently focused on one camera, and then the scream went up: 'We Love Trudie Love, Live from New York.'

Applause, cut to Trudie.

'In the studio today, six of the hunkiest, sexiest, most beautiful men in the world. Let me tell you, if sex appeal could be measured in calories, these guys would look like me. Don't go away, we'll be right back with the *Weissmans* wonder boys.'

Trudie fell back into the arms of the models as the station went to commercials. They were taken offstage as Trudie sat in her chair and was miked up. Matt Skolaski and an assistant sat at the base of the camera into which Trudie was to talk. In their hands they held large cardboard cue-cards on which were written questions and comments to help Trudie through the show. In the seconds before the show was back on air, a make-up girl rushed on and dripped eyedrops into Trudie's eyes. Then Matt's assistant counted down, three-two-one, applause. Trudie held her hands in the air.

'Don't stop, don't stop. Hi, there, we're back and what – a – show – we – have. Next Monday, one of my six guests is going to become the most highly paid male model in the world with a cologne contract for *Weissmans* worth, wait for it now . . . Six, Million, Dollars. I'm lucky enough to have them here with me, and you're going to be lucky enough to be able to call into the number of your screen and cast your vote. I have no idea how anyone's going to be able to choose because they're all, and I mean *all*, divine and let me introduce them to you one by one, they are – Fernando Padrillas, Chester Hunt, Spencer Kemble-Finch, Giovanni Ferrari and Reuben King.'

As Trudie read out their names, the audience applauded with enthusiasm. The models came on and sat on the sofas. Trudie swooned and patted her chest. She avoided the body-mike with care.

'Help, help, is there a doctor in the house? My blood pressure . . .' Trudie fanned her face with her sheaf of notes. 'Guys, before I ask you how you came to be involved with this, let me tell the audience some tragic news.' Trudie moulded her face into a sorrowful, pained expression. 'Last night one of the finalists, a sweet young man from Brazil, became the victim of New York street crime.' As Trudie spoke a photo of an unblemished Fabio was shown. He was horribly attacked in Greenwich Village and is now lying in St Vincent's hospital . . . do we have a picture of him today?' Trudie asked, looking beyond camera.

A photo of Fabio's disfigured face, taken in the hospital only an hour before, came up on the screen. The audience gasped. Larry Meyers, sitting at the back of the audience, surveyed the faces of the models for a reaction. All winced dutifully.

'My heart,' said Trudie, 'goes out to him, as I'm sure yours does too. Fabio, if you're watching. Get well soon.'

Applause. The models joined in. Trudie counted to three before looking happy again. 'But this morning *Weissmans* chose a replacement. Before I introduce him to the world for the first time, just you take a look at this.'

On to the screen came a commercial for a brand of multivitamins. In it, an Olympic god of a man spun around with a giant, discus-shaped vitamin pill in his hand. He released it, and the camera panned in on his glorious looks. The cropped blond hair, the thin nose, the sharp cheekbone, the statuesque profile. Miles smiled and looked down the line to where Kristina sat, ashen-faced. Around her, the audience was clapping.

'Here he is. The sixth finalist and probably the number one male model in the world, Mr Troy Turnbull.'

To adulatory applause, Troy walked out slowly, his hair sculpted in place, his cheeks glowing in terracotta-red perfection, his brilliant teeth glinting in the lights. He acknowledged the audience with a half-wave before lifting Trudie's hand to kiss. Then he took his seat beside Reuben. He shook Reuben's hand.

Ego

In Kristina's apartment on the other side of town, Steve Barefoot watched with glassy eyes. He was spread out over the bed, his head hanging over the edge. His body felt limp and battered. His mouth hung open as he gazed. Anger hadn't hit him yet because he didn't know with whom to be angry. By the time he'd arrived at Weissman's office, his chance had already gone. Kristina had met Steve at the elevator door, and broken the news that Weissman had chosen Troy Turnbull because he wanted to prove that the competition included the best in the world. It was Miles's fault. In a state of obvious shock, Kristina had told Steve to return to the apartment, and wait for her.

There now, Steve poured himself another whisky. He held the bottle up to the window. Ooops, half gone! On the TV, Troy was telling the audience how he'd been whisked from the middle of a shoot to appear on the show.

'Bastard,' shouted Steve. 'Bastard.'

The whisky stung the back of his throat. Trudie was encouraging the viewers to dial in and vote for their favourite model. Steve drained his glass. I know what I'll do, he thought. I'll call up, vote two hundred times for a loser like Reuben. That'd show them. That's what I'll do. He put on his jacket.

Why'm I getting dressed? I'm not going anywhere. Am I? I'm not going anywhere. So why? I don't know. So why did I put my jacket on? I'm not going . . . or am I? Hey, maybe I will. Maybe that's just what I'll do. Maybe . . .

Steve slammed the front door on his way out. Then he came back in and picked up the polaroid photos of himself and Kristina making love on the bed. Chains and all. Laughing, he left the apartment again.

Now this, he thought *will really show 'em good*!

Matt Skolaski was about as happy as an associate producer could be in the middle of a live TV show. Everything was going well. The models were behaving, the audience was responding, and Trudie Love was performing magnificently. Trudie had a knack of appearing to be in awe of her guests (at times for their courage against tragic adversity, at others for their sheer beautiful talent) while nudging never more than a toe over the slippery edge of her TV star's pedestal. Most observers agreed that it was this quality that had taken Trudie to the top, and kept her there. She was Mrs Middle America. Hers was an over-the-garden-fence curiosity brought to national television. Trudie's approach rarely varied. Look at me, she said, I'm fat and over forty and unthreatening, and you can tell me all.

In the first segment of the show, Trudie had asked each of the models to tell their story in turn. Chester was the only one of the six who admitted to having had a desire to model. Trudie had then introduced the five female finalists. Weissman had been concerned that the women were getting too little publicity, and he'd arranged for Andrea and Sandy, Jack, Helima and Jessica to be sitting in the front row of the audience, between Miles and Kristina. Tiziana was still on a trip in the Caribbean.

Trudie had heaved herself up from her chair and carried a microphone over to the women. First off she'd asked Andrea to stand beside her. Andrea was as tall, thin and strikingly beautiful as Trudie was short, fat and average. Trudie had made a face to the audience that displayed gut-wrenching envy. *You are better than I*. Nothing more had been needed for the girls to relax, and talk. The producers, however, had only given the girls five minutes, a minute each to introduce themselves and say how lucky they were. It was the men the show was about, and soon enough Trudie was smiling into camera and announcing that after the break she was going to ask all the men what they thought about when they looked in the mirror each morning.

During the break, Trudie was pampered and powdered. As Spencer was sweating a little, the make-up girl powdered him too. The attention of the audience and the other models made Spencer sweat a lot. No sooner had the girl powdered his nose than a drip dribbled down from his temple.

'One minute!' screamed the producer's assistant.

Spencer felt as if the whole world was watching.

'Are you OK?' asked the smiley make-up girl. 'I know it gets hot under these lights. Try to relax.' Then she raised her voice. 'Quick, bring me towels.'

Try to relax! Spencer's heart was throbbing so loudly now he wondered whether the clip-on mike would pick it up. His ribcage was like a jungle drum beating a signal of panic. And what about his nose? What if he sweated so much the concealer came off? Though the spot had chosen not to come to anything, Spencer's military-style attack on it had left a hideous red patch.

'Thirty seconds.'

The make-up girl gave Spencer a tissue to use when the cameras weren't on him.

Trudie leant across. 'I always used to be like that.'

'But you're somewhat larger,' said Spencer, regretting it immediately.

Trudie scowled before she turned from him and smiled at camera. 'We're back, you're on Love, and we're live. Now you guys, are any of you going to tell me that you *don't* like the way you look? Fernando?'

Fernando grinned and ran a hand over his smoothed hair. He blushed very slightly. 'Oh, I'm OK. I mean I get the girl! It's nice to look good. I don't think I'm incredible or nothing, but I look good. It help in life.'

Chester was sitting cross-legged and composed. He seemed experienced at this beside the jittery Fernando. He brushed a hair from his face. 'I like the way I look, and I like other people to like the way I look. It's a crime for a man to say that, but it's true. I mean there's this weird thing that male models have to go through, you know? One minute we're being gloated over in the magazines, and the next we're being criticised for trying to look our best. I mean, something's wrong there.'

Troy leaned forward. As usual, he talked very slowly, in his deep voice. 'I think it depends on when you use your gift. There's nothing wrong with using your looks professionally. The problem comes when models go around thinking that they're fantastic because they look good.'

'But they are,' said Chester with enthusiasm.' That's my

point. It *is* important what people look like. It makes a difference to our lives.'

'Rubbish,' said Spencer. 'We don't want the world to be run by a bunch of bloody models.'

'You tell him, Spencer,' Trudie said, with an unfathomable degree of mockery.

'Reuben, how about you?' asked Trudie.

'Well, Trudie,' began Reuben with a smile. 'It doesn't matter what you're like inside if you're a black person. People still got bad ideas about you because of your skin.'

Applause from the audience. Though she'd been advised to become more liberal, this time Trudie felt it'd be too much to join in. But she did nod with the semblance of sincerity. Then she looked towards Giovanni, Giovanni had been quiet throughout, doing no more than was required of him. He was leaning back on the sofa, legs crossed. He was dressed immaculately in cashmere and tweed.

'I'm happy with who I am. This is the only important thing in the life. To be very happy as the person you are.'

Enjoying the sound of its own hands, the audience applauded again. Trudie held her hands out in front of her, and tapped them together. Then she said, 'OK, but that's a bit like Donald Trump saying we should all get by on the money we've got. I mean, look at you. You're beautiful, you're rich, you have the girlfriend that most of the men in the world would like,' Trudie turned to the audience, 'Effie Crascauldi, isn't that right, guys? I mean, Giovanni, you're the most perfect guy I've ever met. Please, MARRY ME!!'

Giovanni continued as if he hadn't heard the last three words. 'It is not like Donald Trump. He could give his money away. What could I do? I cannot be different. I am born this way. What I have on the outside does not make me happy inside.'

'No, but it helps, honey. Believe me, it helps.' Trudie made another face of envy towards the audience and patted the spare tyres around her stomach. 'Spencer, what about you?'

Trudie leant forward, chin resting on hand, brow furrowed.

Spencer was tense. His armpits were a soggy oven of unease. An Englishman to the core, Spencer had developed a breezy charm to call upon, as a method actor digs down for past pain, whenever it was needed. Had Spencer encountered Trudie Love filling a corner of a cocktail party, he would have lit her cigarette, flattered her with a perfected inflection of his head (eyebrows raised, body immobile from neck down) and asked her about her youth, her children, her country. No one witnessing a performance such as that would have guessed that, to Spencer, an appearance on national TV would be tantamount to torture. Yet he was indeed sweating terror. This was the Englishman's greatest fear: he was being questioned about his vanity, and worse still, his emotions. He rubbed together his palms and quickly mopped his brow. 'Well, naturally one would be . . .'

'Hold it, sweetheart,' said Trudie, still smarting from Spencer's comment about her size. 'This is going out live to Nebraska. What d'ya mean *one* would?'

'Oh, I mean, I suppose *I* would be foolish not to regard my um, my external appearance in the, in the best possible light, though I agree with the gentleman on the end . . .'

'Troy.'

Spencer seemed to find the name difficult to say, as if it was obscene. 'Yes . . . Troy . . . that it is rather the way that one uses one's natural benefits that's important. One . . . or at least *I* found I could command a greater respect from my men because of my demeanour.'

'Men? Don't tell me you manage the Chippendales!'

The laughter irked Spencer. 'No. I was until recently an officer in the British Army.'

Trudie tilted her head as if she was impressed, but then she said, 'Oh, you'll be able to star in the sequel: An officer and a male model.'

'It'll be worth it if I win.'

'Good point.' Trudie asked. 'What about that? I mean, shouldn't you guys be tearing each other's eyes out? You all seem to get along so well.'

413

Maybe they *have* been tearing their eyes out, Larry Meyers thought. Or smashing each other's teeth in.

Troy spoke first. 'I've only met these guys for two minutes, but I know what this business is usually like. It's rarely personal. Clients look through hundreds of books for each job. You can't point a finger and say, "he's the guy I gotta beat."'

'But this is different,' said Trudie. 'You can see your rivals. It's gonna have to be one of you guys. Chester, what do you feel about suddenly having to compete against a model like Troy Turnbull?'

Chester looked hard at Troy. 'He looks OK, I guess.' The audience laughed. 'But seriously, every modelling job I've ever got has been because I'm the right look for the product. It's not a question of who's the best-looking, you know? That's too hard to judge. If they want a guy with long hair, then they'll choose me. If they want a different look, then maybe they'll choose Reuben.'

Reuben laughed. Trudie blurted in, 'What's so funny?'

'I'm not gonna sit here and say that Saul Weissman's not gonna choose me, but all you got to do is open a men's magazine and count the number of black models and you'll see my chances.'

'You think they're discriminated against?'

'Sure they are. I mean, the only reason that they use white rap artists for ads is so they can reach the black market without using black models.'

Matt Skolaski was running a finger from side to side across his neck. *Cut this, let's move on. This isn't Donahue on racism, this is Trudie on gossip.*

Trudie turned to Fernando, whose reply was more in line. 'We're all happy to be competing, you know? I mean, this is my first time in New York, and we're staying in the Midas Hotel which is beautiful.' He slapped a hand against the back of his neck. 'I'm going aroun' with my head looking up all the time. You know?'

Trudie said, 'We'll see if we can't get someone to come and massage Fernando's neck during the break.' Following orders the audience began to applaud, the camera pulled back, and Trudie added. 'And we're going to talk to Renata about what *numbers* might mean for the six finalists. So don't you go away!'

They were back on air, and Spencer was shifting about in his chair as if about to receive an enema of acid. Reuben was chewing on a match. Chester was playing with the pendant about his neck. Fernando had lifted a foot on to his knee, and Troy was arranging his profile towards the camera.

'OK,' said Trudie, 'let's face it. This modelling business has got a pretty dicey reputation hasn't it? Are any of you guys worried about that?'

It was Chester who spoke. 'We're back to the issue of how society sees men. Like it's becoming OK for men to look good. Men's grooming and fashion and style are becoming as important as women's. I mean, look, one of us is going to be paid six times as much for a campaign as the woman. That's something new. I think we're going to have male supermodels soon. I wouldn't mind being one!'

'I don't know,' said Trudie. 'I think the women in the audience want character before they want looks.' Most of the women applauded. 'Now my cute little producer's telling me that the phone lines are jammed, so keep trying, and before I give you *those* numbers, I'm going to talk to our wonderful numerologist, Renata, who's sitting in a studio in LA.'

Trudie walked over to the satellite screen. Renata sat in LA with a montage of the Hollywood hills behind her. She was in her mid-fifties. She had a permanent smile fixed to her face, copied, perhaps, from the President. Her grey hair was tied in a prim bun. She had narrow eyes, and stretched skin.

'Good morning, Renata. How is LA today?'

'Good morning, sweetheart. Oh, it's beautiful here, absolutely beautiful.'

Trudie looked down at the cue-card held by her feet.

'Now you've been looking at the men's names. What have you come up with?'

'Well, I want to run through them all one by one. Now,

Fernando. His major talent number is a value 5 which means he's an enthusiastic, versatile man. The first letter *F* shows strong family and community bonds. He is a protector, but he's also something of a gambler. He has an electric and magnetic personality.'

Cut to Fernando, who seemed pleased enough with the judgment.

'Moving along, we have Spencer. He's a number 2, which means that he's very patient, very diplomatic. First letter *S* shows public-service ambitions riding high.'

Trudie interrupted. 'His father is British ambassador in Japan, Renata.'

The audience applauded.

'Well, there you are. Spencer's surely a wonderful communicator, but he must be wary of being proud and aloof. He's something of a perfectionist, Trudie. So watch out.'

Spencer's look spoke volumes of disdain.

'Now Chester is very interesting,' Renata continued. 'A number 6 makes him a showman. He likes the opulent, good life.'

'Is she right, Chester?' said Trudie.

'Could be!'

'Chester will burn the candle at both ends to get that life. He's very energetic, and very emotional. He has the kind of character a politician would need.'

'Now you're not just saying this because of Senator Hunt, Renata?'

Renata screwed up her eyes and shook her head. 'Oh no, not at all. This is all from the numbers. He's a giver to the community at large. And I must add that all names beginning with C have the strong point of self-expression and imagination. OK? Now, Reuben, Reuben, Reuben. He's an 11, which is the number of upliftment and humanity. The *R* is important here. It shows that he's a selfless man. Reuben is greatly concerned about brotherly love and I expect he will be a zealous crusader for personal beliefs, alrighty? Many Reubens become welfare workers and the such. Now Giovanni is a number 1 character which makes him a courageous, leader type. The Strong Point of the first letter *G* is that he's very *private*, so don't you be surprised, Trudie, if he doesn't give much away. The last letter *I* is also interesting, because it shows that misplaced sympathy might weaken his personality.'

'You hear that, Giovanni?' said Trudie, turning. 'Don't fall in love with the wrong person.'

Giovanni tilted his head a fraction to the side, as if to say that he didn't need a numerologist to tell him that.

'Exactly,' said Renata. 'Now, finally, I've had to work out Troy's chart quickly . . .'

'Let me just interrupt, Renata. Now, you're not just guessing here, are you? There's a system to all this.'

'Oh, Trudie, absolutely, absolutely. I mean, we are all our first name. For Troy, I add up the value numbers of each letter – so 2 plus 9 plus 6 plus 7 makes 24, and then I reduce the double number to a single, so 2 plus 4 which gives him the major talent number 6, so he's like Chester in that he's quite a showy man, but he has a sense of responsibility for his family and community. The *T* . . .'

'Renata, honey, I'd love to go on, but my producer's telling me we're right out of time. Quickly before you go, pick a winner.'

Miles hadn't been told this would be happening, and he didn't like it at all.

'I would have to say that the numbers favour . . . Chester.'

Chester grinned, the audience made faces at one another and Trudie thanked Renata, who had just a second to plug her book before the satellite cut off.

Sitting in her seat at the other end of the female finalists to Miles, Kristina von Koeler wondered about this endorsement of Chester. Saul was watching. One by one, she studied the men on the set. Maybe there was still time to salvage her dream. Steve was history now. In the three days until Monday's decision, maybe she could persuade Chester to do a deal with her. OK, so it wouldn't be for three million, but maybe one, or even two – enough, at least, to put her up where she knew she belonged. His only great rival was

Giovanni, and he was no threat while she knew what she knew. In fact, Kristina thought she might send a short note to the Italian suggesting that he might do well to drop out before it was too late.

Trudie was talking to Chester. 'So Renata chose you. Do you think she's right?'

'I wouldn't like to predict.'

'Chester wouldn't,' Trudie remarked, 'but you out there would, and in about ten minutes I'm going to tell you who you, in your thousands I have to say, have been voting for. Join us after the break for that, and much more.'

During the break, the boys were looking nervous. Although the real decision was three days away, whatever happened now was bound to influence the outcome. Like a campaigning politician, Weissman had been reiterating his dedication to the people. This was to be the People's cologne. What they said mattered. Now they were speaking in their thousands.

As Matt Skolaski counted down on his fingers the seconds for the final segment of the show, a chorus of nervy coughs preceded the return to broadcast. Then applause, and Trudie. 'Hello, hello, it's Love, Love, Love. And do I love my guests! Now, I have to ask you all something: for years we've had the top girls, right? I don't know about you, but I'm getting *sick* of Dina and Candy and Wendy and all that crowd. Do you think it's the turn of the men? Are we all going to be talking about Chester and Troy and Fernando?'

'I hope so,' said Fernando. 'I hope.'

Troy said, 'There's not the same market for men as there is for women. Men don't shop so much, there aren't as many men's magazines, there's just not the same exposure. There's never going to be a big demand.'

'I'm sure it won't happen in England,' Spencer volunteered. 'You'll have sporting heroes and so forth, but not models.'

Giovanni said, 'Perhaps it is like this more in Europe. I don't think to be model is very good for the image of the man. It is all right in the culture and in the heart of the people for a woman to think about the beauty. It is not so important for the man.'

'What about you, Reuben?' Trudie said.

'Look, I already knew Troy Turnbull's name, and I'm not even interested in fashion. I think it's going to happen. Why not? I mean, maybe not to a black guy, but it'll happen.'

'Candy made it,' said Chester. 'And she's black.'

'OK. Maybe,' said Reuben, smiling. He didn't want to come across as being too bitter. Marcie had warned him about that.

Chester was the last to speak. 'Sure it'll happen, because it's what society wants. See, look at this city. It's so boring these days, right? I mean, all those guys who had their good time in the sixties are standing up and preaching to us, like don't do drugs, don't drink, go work out don't hang out, drink water not wine, you know, all this bullshit.'

Off camera, Trudie was handed the vote results.

'It's like the only thing that matters any more is being healthy. But inside, people still want to be wild and crazy. They want to have a good time and *that's* what they think models have. They think models are beautiful and healthy *and* decadent, and that's the perfect nineties combo. So sure it's the perfect time for male supermodels.'

Trudie nodded and looked at the audience. 'And the critics say my show's mindless, right?' Laughter. 'Well I hope they're tuned in now to hear such articulate guests.' Applause. 'OK, guys. You've been fabulous, really, fabulous, but now it's the moment of truth. On this piece of paper I have the results of the thousands of viewers' votes that have come in in the last hour. OK then – ready? This is in the order . . .'

Suddenly there was a loud noise from the back. A man was shouting. He sounded drunk. 'Is my name there? Where's my name, Tru? Is my name there?'

Kristina swung her head around in horror. Trudie allowed only a moment's alarm to trouble her features before she spoke into the camera above the shouts of the man. 'We're going quickly to commercials, but make sure you stay right there on the edge of your seats . . .'

The station went to commercials. Trudie looked at Matt

Skolaski. 'Now who,' she said quietly, 'the fucking Christ is that?'

She didn't wait long to find out.

'My name should be there, Trudie. Steve Barefoot's goddamn name should be there,' Steve said, swaying closer to the set. 'Is it?'

A security man grabbed Steve, but Steve swung around and shoved him hard away. The guard landed in the lap of a lady from Tucson, Arizona. The audience gasped. Was he dangerous? Did he have a gun? Were they about to witness something they could dine out on for years? The models were asking each other if anyone knew Steve. Matt Skolaski was getting nervous. With his headphone like a noose around his neck he shouted, 'We've got forty-five seconds. Someone get him out, and I mean NOW.'

Three other security men arrived. Though Steve was strong, they were managing to drag him outside. He was shouting, 'She said I was going to win! I was going to get the six million. Krist . . .'

And then Steve was out of the studio. Just in time for the countdown back to air.

In his fifty-third floor office, Saul Weissman was staring at his TV wondering what the hell was going on. God dammit! This wasn't good; not at all. First Fabio, and then this. Somewhere soon, heads were gonna have to roll.

On the screen, a woman Weissman's age was stirring a muddy laxative. 'She should eat nuts,' he murmured.

Trudie Love once again filled the screen. 'Welcome back. Now the phone lines are closed, and I truly have some fascinating results.'

The screen went blue. In white lettering, the name of Spencer Kemble-Finch appeared; beside it, his score. Trudie explained. 'Now remember, these are the percentages of calls for each model, not the actual number they got. So, here we go: we have Spencer with 2%, Troy with 7%, Giovanni, he got 15%, Fernando was next on 22%, Chester Hunt, Renata's choice, has 25% and the man most of you want to see as the EDEN cologne model is . . . Reuben

King with 29% of your votes.' Trudie's figure returned to the screen. Then a shot of Reuben smiling. In the background, the show's theme music had already begun to play.

'That's it, we're all out of time. Thanks to my guests, to Renata, and to you at home. Tomorrow meet the man who still lives with the woman who, wait for it, sucked, out, his, eyeballs with a vacuum-cleaner hose. That's right. See you then, Love loves you all! Bye-zee-bye.'

Weissman stared at the credits, and then said out loud, 'So Miles? Look what you've got us into now . . .'

31

W hen Trudie Love shook, as she was shaking now, the vibrations could be heard in the studios three floors below. She was standing in her office, legs apart, hands on hips, her nostrils flaring in the direction of Dick Whelps, Head of Security at Channel 6. Matt Skolaski stood behind. 'It had to be during a live show, didn't it? Any normal show wouldn't do. Oh, no! You had to let him on in the middle of my first live show in three fucking YEARS!'

Dick Whelps took a step back. Trudie swung around to face Matt Skolaski. She poked him violently in the chest, before smoothing away a trickle of sweat with the back of her hand. 'What did I say? I said I'm not going to do a screwing live show with six morons. Don't work with children, they tell you. AND YOU GIVE ME SIX SCREWING MODELS! I knew something like this would happen. I knew it. It's a wonder that bitch Renata didn't predict it.'

Angrily, Trudie twisted to face Dick, yanked her hair up into a messy bun, made a grotesque face, and mimicked Renata's nasal voice. '"Let me tell you, Trudie, your security man has got three numbers on the underside of his cock – 666. Now that means he's a complete DIPSHIT!"' Trudie, as herself again, looked Dick Whelps straight in the eye. 'The way I see it, sugar-pie, is that your number is zero. Zero for the quantity of brain cells functioning in your head, and zero for the number of days you've got left in this job.'

Matt spoke up. 'Trudie, two things . . .'

'Don't start your Ivy League boy lecturing on me, Matthew. I don't need that while half the States is laughing at me. Oprah's probably opening the champagne right this minute.'

'Trudie, please. For a start, the show went well . . .'

'Until Einstein here,' Trudie yanked a thumb at Dick Whelps,' invited half of Bellevue in to join the party.'

Matt remained composed. 'As I said, the show looked good, the *Weissmans* models did fine, *they* weren't responsible for what happened, and this guy only got inside because he showed a card from Kristina von Koeler. Isn't that right?'

Dick hazarded a step forward. 'Like he said: the guy showed this card, one of my guys took him upstairs, he's sitting happy as Larry in the hospitality suite watching the show, and then he goes and makes this dumb move. We wasn't to know.'

Trudie shook her head in disbelief. She unwrapped an indigestion tablet as she spoke. '*Wasn't* you smart enough to smell the whisky? Or to have seen that he was drunk? Or maybe you have to be totally SENSELESS to get a job on security here.'

Trudie heaved a great sigh and chewed on her indigestion tablet.

Matt touched her on the arm. 'Why don't I take you to see the tape? You can hardly hear the guy.'

'Really? Are you sure?'

'Absolutely.'

Trudie rearranged her hair with both hands.

'You're not just saying that?'

'No.'

'But how did I look? Did I look OK? I tried to look OK.'

'You looked as fabulous,' Matt's eyes flickered to Dick Whelp's face and back again, 'as you always do.'

Kristina had come to her decision in the closing seconds of the show. She wouldn't glance at Steve if she saw him. Let him say what he liked. She would deny it all.

As her cab rocketed – these Haitian drivers! – through Central Park, Kristina decided that she'd covered the tracks of her relationship well enough. Steve's ticket to London had been paid for in cash, as had his cheap room. It had been easy to keep him hidden from the discreet staff of the Byron Hotel. In New York, she and Steve had rarely been out together.

She didn't have a doorman, and on top of all this, Miles Jensen had been in London to witness her first meeting with Steve. She thought she was safe enough and after Steve's deranged appearance on national TV there was little question that the scales of sanity were heavily weighed against him. Let Steve say what he liked. No one would believe him now.

The cab turned up Madison. It was mid-afternoon on Thursday, and Kristina knew that if she was going to strike a deal with Chester Hunt, she didn't have much time. She wondered how to approach him. With Steve, the process had been gradual. With Chester, Kristina knew she'd have to find another way.

She called for Steve as she opened the door of her apartment. There was no reply.

The bedroom reeked of whisky. At the end of the bed, the bottle had spilled. Stepping over the stain (Conchita was coming tomorrow) Kristina telephoned and asked for an emergency locksmith to come to the apartment at once. Then, standing on tiptoe on the bed, she opened the cupboard above the closet and heaved at Steve's case. It wouldn't budge. Kristina pulled at it hard, and as it slid out the weight of it tore at her fingers and shoulders. She let it thud to the floor. On her knees beside it, she looked inside. Kristina saw the assortment of presents Steve had bought himself – the cowboy boots, the CDs, the disc player, a cheap, gold woman's necklace. Where the hell had Steve found the money for all this? He'd arrived penniless. He hadn't earned anything. He didn't even have a credit card. He only had the money she lent him. Then it struck her. What about the $2000 she'd saved from her trip to Paris? Kristina pulled open the drawer. The hotel envelope was inside, but the $2000 was gone.

'Asshole! Damn stupid asshole.'

Kristina slid open the closet door. It clattered on its rollers. She tore out Steve's clothes, sending the hangers jangling to the floor. All of Steve's possessions she shoved into his case. Anything that wouldn't fit would go straight out the window. There wasn't much. His filthy jeans, the leather jacket, the boots he wasn't wearing. His spare Zippo. A photograph of his 'folks back home.' His condoms – no, might as well keep those, she thought. Briskly, Kristina flipped through the CDs and took out those she thought she might listen to. The Discman she'd keep and take with her to the gym. The boots Steve could sell to buy a flight back to Texas, away from New York, and out, for ever, from her life.

The Love that was Trudie led to a fair amount of hate. After the show, the models had the day to themselves. Reuben, riding high, went back to college. Chester and Fernando went, once again, to work out.

Troy had a Bloomingdales shoot to return to in a studio in Chelsea. Miles had gloated at the expression on Troy's face as Trudie had announced the viewer votes. On hearing of his paltry eight per cent, Troy had, of course, smiled. A glinting, perfect, Oscar-loser's smile that had hidden not an ounce of the disappointment inside.

Spencer had handled it much better. With his haughty smirk he'd dismissed his two per cent vote as being something wholly inconsequential. Something very un-British. Spencer had, of course, the double advantage of being from a race well-practised both at losing, and at hiding all emotions at all times from all people.

Giovanni hid nothing. He stormed off the set as soon as the show was over. Miles followed. He caught up with Giovanni waiting for a cab on the street. In the rain, Giovanni lifted his jacket over his head. He turned the tent towards Miles when Miles ran up beside him.

'Something wrong?' asked Miles.

Miles had noticed that when Giovanni was angry, his Italian accent was more pronounced. 'This, this game show, it was pre-cise-ly what I was not to want. In Paris, in La Piscine, did I not told you, Miles?'

'You should have got into it more.'

A cab pulled up.

'Tcha! I am not the performing chicken.'

Giovanni bent into the cab.

'Are you going by Weissman's office?' Miles asked.

'I am going to my home. To Sutton Place.'

'Can't we swing by the office?'

Giovanni nodded, and Miles joined him. After Miles gave the directions, they were both silent. Raindrops hammered in fierce gusts across the windshield. With a squeaking handkerchief, Giovanni rubbed clear an oval window through the steam. He looked out.

'Listen,' said Miles, 'that's the worst over, I promise. Tomorrow, you and Tiziana have got your test with Bruce Stone, then there's that brief store appearance on Sunday, and then on Monday it's all over.'

Giovanni kept staring out.' Over, or beginning?'

'Beginning,' Miles urged.

'Maybe for Reuben.'

'Don't tell me that's what's worrying you. God, Weissman probably wasn't even watching the show. Anyway, as I've told you before, Reuben and Fernando are not threats to you, Troy never had a hope . . .'

'And Chester . . .?'

'Chester hasn't got anyone on his side. You have.'

'Ah! My saviour.'

Miles twisted in his seat.' Yes, Giovanni. I think I might be. Fabio might be gone, but Chester's still a big threat. Weissman's always been against you for some reason, and Kristina probably hasn't exactly been singing your praises. You know, you really need me to argue for you.'

'And it is in your interest to do this.'

Miles hesitated a second before plunging in.' Maybe, but I think my support's worth more than what you're offering. I'm putting my ass on the line for you.'

'No! You are doing it for yourself, but you are also becoming greedy. You are wanting all my money.'

'No I'm not. Just twice as much as I'm getting. And in writing so that you don't back out.'

'I don't like people who cannot trust me.'

'Giovanni,' Miles said with a smile,' what do you expect from me? You're Italian! You guys only make agreements to break them.'

The cab was nearing Weissman's office.

'I think maybe you are bluffing to me,' said Giovanni. 'If Chester win, you will get nothing.'

'And you won't get the six million. So who's taking the biggest gamble? I'm going in there right now, Giovanni. I can say whatever I like. If you turn me down, who knows . . .'

Giovanni looked at his hands, and picked something from under his thumbnail. 'All right, my friend. I say $750,000.'

'One million,' said Miles, his heart beating wildly.

'But never any more!'

They shook hands, and Miles stepped on to the street feeling like a character from *The Godfather 3*.

Matt Skolaski was standing over Steve, one hand on his hip. 'You, Steve, are one lucky guy.'

Steve didn't feel lucky; he felt sick. When the security men had bustled him into a tiny storage room in the Channel 6 building, he'd almost thrown up over their shoes. A black coffee and a stern talking-to hadn't made him feel any better.

'Trudie's not pressing charges,' Matt continued, 'nor is the station. So all you've got to do is get out of here before anyone changes their mind.'

Steve offered a half-hearted nod, lifted himself to his feet, and followed Matt out of the room. Steve ran his fingertips along the edge of the wall as he walked. As they descended in the elevator, he belched nervously, and tried to focus on the control panel. Matt escorted Steve into the rain before returning to the room upstairs, where Trudie was admiring herself on the tape.

Steve walked like a blind man off the sidewalk and into West 55th Street. A car honked, and swerved from him, soaking Steve's pants as it passed. Steve stumbled back, and lost his footing. From the cover of an adjacent building, a man in an old raincoat came over and lifted Steve to his feet.

'You need some help there?'

'I'm, ah, yeah.'

'Why don't we get some coffee,' the man said.

'OK, what . . .' said Steve.

What else did he have to do?

'Good,' said the man as he guided Steve back on to the sidewalk and towards a coffee shop he liked at the corner of the block.

Miles was looking at Bruce Stone's prints of Spencer, Fabio and Chester when Kristina entered Weissman's office, flustered and late.

'Fabio looked just great in these,' said Weissman, shaking his head. 'Just great. I feel terrible for the kid.'

'Is that all you feel terrible about, Saul?' snapped Kristina, not sitting down.

Miles raised his eyes to look at her. By now, he recognised Kristina's war tone.

'Shouldn't we be feeling terrible that exactly, exactly what I said *would* happen *has* happened?'

'And what's that?'

'Reuben winning on Trudie Love. Can you imagine the outcry now when he doesn't win the EDEN contract? His face is already splashed all over the newspapers. I mean, did you read that interview with Larry Meyers? And then he had to launch himself into that . . . that *tirade* against the fashion industry on the show. I said he'd stir things up. He might as well be called Rodney King, mightn't he?'

'Afternoon, Kristy,' Weissman said. 'Are you through?'

Kristina breathed in deeply, and slumped herself into a chair. Weissman carried on. 'What do you think we were discussing, huh? The rain? No! We were talking about the show. Miles was telling me that the results proved him right.'

'Makes a change.'

'He was saying that Reuben's victory proves we were smart to include him. And Fernando. Now we got every Black and Hispanic thinking *Weissmans* is the store for them. It's everything we ever wanted. End of story. So let's move on. What's happening with Fabio? If I go see him, can we get a photographer down at the hospital?'

Kristina nodded, dissatisfied that she hadn't drawn blood over Reuben's success.

'Good. Make sure the press knows we're treating him good. And buy him something from me. Get a package from Nuts about You.' He waved a hand. 'Something . . . Now, Miles, who's shooting with Stone tomorrow?'

'Reuben, Fernando, Giovanni, and Troy if he can.'

'Make sure they all get there. What else?' Weissman tapped his pen on the desk. 'Oh, right, Kristy, I was showing Miles these prints Stone did Tuesday. I want the press to have one. Which do you think?'

Kristina took them from Miles. She whisked through. 'Simple. It can't be Fabio, it can't be Spencer, so make it Chester.'

'Yeah? Really? You think? With all that hair?'

'*All that hair* is what people like these days.'

Weissman lifted both palms up in surrender. 'Yeah, maybe. Miles, you do that.'

'I'll do it,' said Kristina.' Wonderboy hasn't been editing pictures as long as I have.'

'Work it out yourselves. One more thing, sweetheart. Miles tell me that the guy shouting on Trudie Love was Steve Barefoot.'

'Yes. I think it may have been him.'

'It was him,' said Miles. 'And he got into the building flashing around a business card of yours.'

Miles was surprised that Kristina looked so shocked.

'He did? God! Well, I guess, I must have given him one in London. I thought we were going to use him then.'

'Seems like he thought so too,' Miles said.

Miles had been suspicious about Steve and Kristina ever since her outburst over Steve's exclusion. Never had he guessed at the depth of her involvement, but neither had it taken too much imagination to cast them as lovers after their meeting in London.

'He's from Texas,' Kristina said. 'Let's hope he goes back.'

'If he causes any more trouble, I'm gonna send him,' joked Weissman.

Kristina looked into her employer's eyes and wondered

how bad Steve would have to be for Saul to keep to
his word.

Larry Meyers was on to something, and he knew it.

He was sitting now in a cab on East 63rd Street, waiting for
Steve to come down from Kristina's apartment. The rain was
pattering an incessant tune on the glistening roof of the yellow
cab. The driver, a woman, was reading the *Herald*. Meyers
smiled when she turned the page on to his interview with
Reuben. Days had been when he'd have got a real kick out of
seeing his words in print. Back then he'd cut his articles out,
sent some home, pasted them in a scrapbook. Those were
the days he'd get so upset with editors for tearing his words
apart that he'd call up his friends to explain. 'So what?' they'd
say. 'It reads fine,' and soon Meyers realised that it was only
he who cared. 'Larry,' they'd tell him, 'am I boring you with
the problems in my life?'

Meyers peered out of the window. It wasn't a doorman
building, so he'd have to check with the neighbours to
corroborate Steve's story. Pity. That'd take time. Steve
hadn't been making too much sense in the coffee shop,
mumbling and sniffling into his cup, but the story he'd told
was good. Very good. Steve had shown Meyers the polaroid
of himself making love to Kristina, and Steve had brought
Meyers back to the apartment to show him 'the chains and
things'.

Steve had promised that Kristina would be in the office but
had run up alone, 'just to be sure.'

So what the hell's he up to? Meyers wondered. The meter
clicked up another quarter. Meyers leant forward. 'Lady, d'ya
like that article?' Yvonne, her name was.

'You read it?'

'I wrote it,' said Meyers.

She turned around, and he was pleased that she looked
impressed. Yet before she could answer, there was a tap
on the window. Steve was standing on the street, his
eyes glazed. Meyers opened the door. The suitcase was
at Steve's feet.

'I couldn't get in,' he said, 'Look.'

Steve handed Meyers the note Kristina had left. *Locks have been changed*, it read, *so don't even think about it. If you're here when I come back tonight, I'll have you arrested for stealing my $2000. K.*

'What's this about the two thousand bucks, Steve?'

'I borrowed it. I didn't think it would mean nothing when we got the six million, see? I mean, how could it of?'

'You know where you're gonna go?'

'No.'

'OK. Get in. The paper can set you up someplace.'

In the cab, Meyers turned to the distraught-looking Steve and, to cheer him up, said, 'If you ask me, Kristina von Koeler's just made the biggest mistake of her life.'

Five thirty p.m., and it was time for Miles to lie.

'Hi, babes. It's me.'

In her Legal Aid office, Poppy White lifted her shoulder to cradle the telephone receiver against her face. She and Miles hadn't spoken since he'd left for the party the night before. At one time, midway through the evening, Poppy had dressed (simple, she'd thought – jacket and jeans) having decided that Miles had no right to ruin her life. She would go to the restaurant because she wanted to. Then the phone had rung and she'd heard the noise of a party when the machine had picked up. But he hadn't bothered to leave a message. So Poppy had lost her resolve, and undressed, and decided that it wouldn't be right to go chasing after him when he was being so callous.

She'd half-expected Miles to return home repentant, as he had many times before. Repentant, perhaps, because he knew sex usually followed forgiveness; but no matter, for their physical union was the ultimate expression of themselves and they always rediscovered their love.

But it never happened.

Poppy had been woken by Miles's return, and she'd waited for his whisper. It hadn't come, neither had he slithered his hand deftly between her breasts, nor pressed his body warm against hers. Silently, he'd slipped into sleep beside Poppy, leaving a desperate gap between.

In the morning, they hadn't exchanged a word.

'You left very quickly this morning,' Miles said. 'I'd have liked to have seen you.'

'Would you?'

'Oh don't start, Poppy. Of course I would.'

'Hmm. Did you have a nice time last night?'

'It was OK. Did you hear about Fabio?'

'Who?'

It was too easy for Miles to forget that the EDEN campaign was not at the centre of Poppy White's life. 'He was one of the models. He got mugged. We had to draft Troy Turnbull in at the last minute.'

'I've heard of him.'

'Who hasn't? Did you see him on Trudie Love?'

'Miles! I was working.'

'Oh, right . . . Um, listen, babes, I know I said we'd go to that movie tonight, but . . . but I can't. Sorry.' Silence. 'Poppy?'

'Why not?'

'I have to go out with Saul Weissman.'

'Oh.' Another pause. 'When did you find that out?'

Once told, the lie spread as fluently as bacteria in a warm, damp space. 'About ten minutes ago.'

'Couldn't you have said you were busy for once?'

'No, it's important. Anyway, we were only going to a movie . . .'

'A movie *with me*, Miles. Something, anything *with me*.'

'Come on, Poppy. What do you want me to do? You think I want to work late?'

Poppy sighed. She knew that there were only ever losers in arguments such as this.

'So what time do you think you'll be back?'

'I don't know. It depends. Late maybe. I don't know.'

'Don't wake me if I'm asleep, OK?'

'OK.'

They hung up. His excitement smothered the shame. He dialled another number.

'Hey, it's Miles! . . . No, we had nothing going on . . . just me, then . . . great, so let's make it just after eight.'

With a tired Waldorf salad and a cranberry juice for company, Kristina sat at her desk early that Thursday evening scouring the pages of fashion magazines for models who looked like Chester. On the desk in front of her were pages of long-haired men, torn mostly from European magazines such as Britain's *The Face* and Italy's *L'Uomo Vogue*. Few of the American men's magazines had dared to make use of the new message yet. Part of a perversely Conservative culture, they rarely did until after the fashion had become old and tired elsewhere. The journeys made by fashion styles were often bizarre. The Americans would end up importing ideas from British designers who'd been inspired by styles on the American streets.

Kristina's real task would be to find Chester's Achilles heel. She'd noticed how Chester always appeared testy when his father's name was mentioned. If Kristina could think of a way to involve Senator Hunt, or even to threaten his involvement, then perhaps she could persuade Chester to make a deal with her.

On the top of a blank sheet of paper she wrote: CHESTER, SENATOR HUNT, ME. Below on the page, $6,000,000. As she was drawing a box around the sum, there was a knock at the door.

'Who is it?'

'Stan Maychick, Security.'

Stan Maychick, dressed in uniform, took off his hat as he entered the office. Kristina admired his muscular, tall body.

'Apologies to disturb you, but have you seen anyone you didn't, like, recognise on the floor here?'

'No, why?'

Stan shuffled on his feet. 'There was some guy running down the emergency stairs. I picked him up on the hallway video on the 52nd.'

'He wasn't black was he?'

'Yeah. You saw something?'

'I had this salad delivered about ten minutes ago.'

'Maybe that was it. I'm sorry to've trouble you.'

A flicker of a come-hither smile creased Kristina's cheeks. Stan Maychick paused for a moment, and their eyes met. He wondered if he understood this silent language. Kristina stared back, but then returned to her work. She heard the door click shut.

Chester, Chester, Chester how can you be mine? The son of a Senator. A public figure. What do you fear the most? That's all she needed to know. What – did – Chester – fear?

Kristina lay on the couch, unzipped her pants, closed her eyes, and slid her fingers beneath the elastic of her knickers.

There had to be a way. Chester. Six million bucks. Only four days to go. Stan Maychick. She wondered where Steve was. She'd have liked him there then. Him and his expert mouth. She hoped to God he'd kept it shut since the show. She didn't want anyone else to know what she'd got up to, what *they'd* got up to. Chester must have secrets too, she thought. It was Kristina's nature to wonder about the hidden proclivities of almost everyone whose hand she took, but to learn of Chester's darker side could prove useful beyond measure. Was there a way she could find out? Or better still, could she entice Chester into *committing* an act he'd then wish to keep secret? Maybe she could send a rent boy to his apartment, wait and see from there. Or else, or else . . . No, she couldn't. And yet . . .

Kristina was soon out of the office, and taking the elevator to the basement. She found Stan Maychick seated in front of a bank of black and white video screens. He was reading a magazine. He stood, surprised, when she rapped her knuckle on the open door.

'Did you catch him?' she asked.

'Nah. As I said, I guess it was some delivery guy.' Stan seemed unable to look Kristina directly in the eye when he talked.

'These screens,' Kristina said, pointing, 'can you see everything on them?'

'There's cameras all around on a rotation. Like this one,' he gestured towards the screen on the bottom left, 'shows the lobby. But no one's there now because it's getting . . . late. Still, to be honest with you, I don't, like, sit staring at the screens. You know, I look every half-hour or so. That kind of thing. I usually got better things going through my mind.'

Stan gave Kristina a look: a definite look – the head to the side a little, eyes half-closed, tongue squeezed between upper and lower teeth.

'Are they taped?' said Kristina

'Oh, yeah, on a continuous reel. It tapes over itself every coupla hours, but you can always stop it if you want to see something again.'

Kristina nearly smiled. 'I've been working in this building for eighteen years and I've never been down here before.'

'Surprises,' Stan suggested, 'are always nice.'

'You think so?' Kristina said, turning away. 'Oh, I wouldn't be so sure.'

'I'm gonna talk to my editor,' Meyers said to Steve. 'See what we can do. I'll see you later.'

Meyers gave Brenda McCarron's hand a squeeze of thanks (and promise) before turning and leaving her apartment. He'd been spending more time there recently. Aware of the folly of making demands upon him, Brenda let Meyers come and go whenever he pleased. They never spoke of the future, nor did they share a life beyond the apartment and the bar. Brenda wasn't even sure whether there were other women. She knew one thing only: that this was the way it had to be. Meyers was a man who, through knowledge, had lost faith in his fellow beings. Trust could only be built slowly, and the choices had to be his.

Steve and Brenda listened to the heavy thump of Meyers descending. Steve shifted awkwardly on the edge of Brenda's tatty couch. 'You sure you don't mind me being here?' he asked.

'Now why should I mind?' said Brenda. 'I t'ink it's terrible what that girl's gone and done to you. Terrible. Just a note on the suitcase there, you say?'

'That's all. Sounds like she never wants to see me again.'

'And a good t'ing too, Steven. I say get shot of her. There's no forgiving a t'ing like that. No, none at all. Now, what'd you like for me to be getting you to eat?'

Steve put a hand on his stomach and groaned. He'd eaten nothing but a square of toast all day. There'd been no time for breakfast, rushing, as he had, for his appointment with Weissman. Lunch had been half a bottle of whisky.

'I don't feel hungry, thanks.'

'I'll get you something any road.'

Brenda yanked at the sticky door to her fridge. She grimaced at the barrenness of its shelves. 'It'll have to be eggs. I'll rustle up a cheese omelette for the both of us.'

'I . . .'

'Now stop it! You'll only get yourself more miserable on an empty stomach there.'

More miserable, wondered Steve, how could I be? Kristina's brutality was almost too hard to believe. Images of the affair kept flashing through his mind – the seduction in the stable, the time in his Texan bed when she'd persuaded him to join her in New York, the jacuzzi in Dallas, the trip to London. Steve tried to recall whether the words 'I love you' had ever crossed Kristina's lips. Often enough she'd needed him, she'd wanted him, she'd even longed for him; but he doubted now she'd ever loved him, and he hated himself for his blindness.

With his world turned upside down, Steve couldn't remove from his mind an image of himself running fast, treading air, surging nowhere. He'd travelled so high with his dreams that now the ground seemed lost from view. Only Meyers and Brenda seemed good and kind and true, and only one thought fuelled his heart: the rock that Steve would cling to, the rock that would steady him and bring him back to earth would be the rock of revenge; and, with the help of Meyers and the *Herald*, Steve was going to hurl it with all his might at the woman he wished he'd never, ever met.

32

M iles stepped into the lobby of the Midas Hotel at five minutes to eight, and glanced around. Belying its suggestive name, the Midas was not resplendent with cheap glitter. Neither did it share with most American hotel lobbies the smoky glass mirrors, the plastic pot plants, the dribbling fountains, nor the check-in desk of imitation marble staffed by permanent smiles. Instead the designer, a Frenchman, had done what he could to make the interior resemble anything but a hotel.

In the centre of the room was a tall Perspex column encrusted with multicoloured fluorescent lights. Spreading from the light-sculpture, tables and chairs were set in a circular recess. This, the Midas bar, had for the last year been a popular place among New Yorkers not staying at the hotel. There were few fashionable places in the East 40s, and the bar was open twenty-four hours a day. The allure had dulled, but the bar was never empty of the Bridge-and-Tunnel crowd chasing trends a year out of time.

On the street level, the reception desk was almost hidden to the right of the large steel door. The staff were dressed in black jeans and white shirts. They were of all races, all young and beautiful and eager and hard to distinguish from the hotel patrons. To the left of the entrance was a small sushi bar, into which visitors could peer through a plain and solid glass wall. At the far wall, opposite the entrance, pastel-coloured sofas provided quiet places to sit. A few tables were reserved for board games. Chess, backgammon, draughts.

The lobby of the Midas had been designed to cater for a new, dull decade. The stimulation was purely visual. Though crowded, it never buzzed with excitement. People slouched with ten-dollar drinks, watching and waiting for something to happen to somebody else.

Miles rebelled with action. After checking himself out in the Gents downstairs (in more ways than one, for at the back of each urinal was a mirror that exaggerated its genital reflection) he took the elevator up to the sixth floor, and knocked on the door of Sandy's room. He heard her moving inside, and then the brush of her nose against the door as she looked out through the peephole. She unlocked the door.

'Hi, Miles. Sorry! I was just on my way.'

Sandy looked far from ready. Her hair was wet from the shower, and the buttons of her white shirt were undone beneath her breasts. Miles caught a glimpse of her smooth skin above the waistband of her black jeans. He could almost feel its silkiness.

'Come in. I'll just finish drying my hair, OK?'

Sandy returned to the bathroom as Miles followed the corridor into a small, compact room. It was efficiently designed, to Miles's taste, as if by a Swede or a German. Light came from a low oval window opposite the door, and from spotlights hollowed in the ceiling. The large bed was part of a built-in unit behind which was an elaborate panel of switches needed to operate everything from the TV that rested on a wall bracket eight feet up in the corner, to a **Do Not Disturb** light that shone in the corridor outside. There was a trim desk, the chair of which slid neatly into grooves cut in the underside of the desk. Stationery was kept in glass compartments on the wall. There was one armchair, green, boxy. Miles sat on its edge.

Sandy, Miles concluded, could not have been expecting him up now, or later. Her belongings were scattered over the bed. Miles was oddly excited by the scene. It was familiar enough – a pair of blue jeans, heaved inside out and left on the floor, some eyeliner in front of the mirror, a bra draped over the back of the chair, panties on the yellow bedspread, a book left on a pillow, spread open like a sunbathing butterfly. Yet Miles felt as if he'd walked in upon a private moment, and in doing so had become intimate and involved with Sandy. She'd obviously just been reading the book. The pillow behind where her body must have been leaning was creased and dented. He leant forward and touched it. Still warm! Her warmth! Had she been naked? In underwear? What matter, she'd been alone, in her own space, and now he was here too. He felt light-headed and – dare he even think it – in love?

The asthmatic whine of the hair dryer stopped suddenly. Sandy re-entered the room. 'You want a drink from the minibar? It's on you guys anyway.'

'Still trying to be my waitress, are you?'

'Don't be a jerk, Miles. You want something, or do you want to buy me a beer for fifty bucks downstairs?'

'I think it's nicer here, don't you?'

They had a beer each. Sandy sat back where he'd pictured her, the pillows behind her back. Miles moved to the bed and sat cutting an angle across the bottom corner, looking towards the double-glazed window. He leant back on his right arm. Sandy was lying with her bare feet towards him. They were clean and soft and Miles longed to take them in his hands. Instead he picked at the label on his bottle.

'Why didn't your girlfriend want to join us?'

'Poppy? She's busy.'

'Did you ever tell her about Miami?'

'What about it?'

'I was wondering if she knew about our walk on the beach.'

'No, I mean, there wasn't much to tell. Not in the end. Was there?'

Miles ran a hand through his hair and looked out through the window. The rain had stopped, but the clouds were thick and menacing. Their gorged bellies were splashed with pink, orange and yellow from the brilliant lights of Times Square.

'Miles?' He turned to her. 'That night, did you . . .?'

'What?'

Sandy looked down. 'No, forget it.'

She took a swig of beer. Miles followed. They were silent. A heated argument could be heard from a neighbouring room. Miles was tempted to press his ear against the wall, but then the voices stopped, and were followed by commercials.

'It's nice not to hurry out,' Sandy said. 'I've been walking around the city ever since Trudie Love. My feet are like really sore.'

'Are they?'

Miles lifted a hand and rested it on the ankle of Sandy's right leg. He moved his thumb back and forth very gently and tried to look bored. To show that he meant nothing by it. He could feel the thump of his pulse in his neck.

'Do you know about reflexology?' he asked her.

'No, I had a chart once showing which areas on your foot like relate to which organs. I tried it but it didn't work. They say there's even one for the sex organs.'

'There is? Tell me where? Is it here?'

Gently, Miles tickled Sandy on the underside of her foot. She shrieked, and yanked her foot back. Miles grabbed it and tickled some more. 'No, stop it! Miles, stop it! I'm ticklish.'

'No kidding!'

Miles leapt up on the bed and, straddling Sandy on all fours, began to tickle her stomach. She twisted and squirmed like a fish out of sea.

'No . . .' She was half-laughing, half-angry now. 'No, Miles, stop it. I hate it. Pleeease. Stop it. Stop it.'

Oh, to be this close!

Sandy lifted herself up and pushed Miles. He sat back, taking the weight in his own thighs.

You've been here before, Miles. This close, with only one barrier left to cross. So cross it.

In the six weeks since their night in Miami, Miles had lived the fantasy to its conclusion countless times. The way he'd seen it since, they'd kissed on the beach without words, and the kiss had enveloped them, and become the sexual act. Details of Sandy undressing, details of her nakedness, were never conjured up in his mind. Merely the image of their writhing union. Now, Miles was a little disturbed by the solidity of his fantasy. Understanding could only be found by venturing into the unknown. He leant in for a kiss.

Suddenly, a sharp knock at the door. Miles and Sandy looked towards it, as if guilty. The knock came again. Then a voice. 'Sandy? It's Jack. Sandy?'

Miles moved as fast as an adulterer, lifting himself from Sandy. She swung her legs off the bed and shuffled towards the door. Miles flattened a hand over his hair and adopted a casual pose, one leg slung over the chair's arm, face relaxed. He reached for Sandy's copy of the *Herald* and opened it on his lap, though the excitement had ebbed. Miles heard Jack speak.

'Hi, Sandy, sorry, but Spencer's not here, is he?'

'No. I haven't seen him.'

'We were supposed to have a drink. He's not in his room. I thought maybe I heard some noises in here.'

Jack tried to peer into the room. The bathroom wall hid Miles from her view.

'It was just the TV.'

Jack saw the TV turned off.

'What are you doing tonight?' Jack asked.

'I'm going to meet a friend for dinner and I'm running late.'

'Oh, I'm sorry. If you see Spencer, can you tell him to call my room? I think maybe he's not happy after the show.'

'No problem. And I'll see you tomorrow, yeah?'

Sandy closed the door. Miles waited for her to return, hoping she might give a sign that what they'd almost had could easily be. She sat opposite him on the bed.

'That was Jack.'

'I know. I heard.'

Damn it, Miles! Say something! Do something!

He looked at Sandy, at her graceful neck, at the luscious smoothness of her skin, and thought that he'd never been so close to such a complete woman. He longed now to possess her, to know she could be his.

Sandy bent down to look for her boots. 'Let's go!'

Miles stood. Out of habit he felt for his wallet in his back pocket. Normality again!

'How does Japanese sound to you? EAT's near here.'

'Whatever you want, Miles. I'm easy.'

With her boots on, Sandy stood from the bed. Miles walked ahead of her down the narrow corridor. His feet felt heavy. He opened the door. As Sandy came towards him, Miles saw that the collar of her jacket was tucked under itself. He let go the handle and the door clonked shut with a heavy sound, as if they were in a safe. A place where no one could reach them.

'Your collar's all screwy,' he said.

Sandy stopped close beside him. The back of his hand tingled as it brushed against her neck. Miles turned back the collar and smoothed it flat. Neither moved. His heartbeat quickened.

And then he touched her.

He lifted his hand and stroked her cheek. The thrill turned his stomach. Sandy leant her face into the warm cup of his hand and closed her eyes. Her lips rested on his fingertips. Miles lifted his other hand to Sandy's face, and then cautiously brushed his lips against her cheek. Slowly, Sandy turned her mouth to his until their lips touched. For a few seconds they were still like this as if, for once, defeating time. But soon, with the typical impatience of a man, Miles broke the spell and lightly skimmed his tongue on the underside of Sandy's upper lip. She lifted her limp arms and wrapped them around his back and pulled his body towards her. Miles plunged his tongue inside her mouth. When she met it with hers nothing, nothing existed for them but the rapture of this kiss.

In time, Miles moved forward his hips to share with Sandy the hard proof of his longing. She moved against him in willing return, and the thrill made Miles catch his breath and break the kiss and lean his head back as if looking up to give thanks. Sandy kissed the base of his neck, and he lowered his head, and when their lips met again, they met more fiercely than before as if speaking without words of the weeks of their desire.

For minutes they abandoned themselves to each other before Miles lifted Sandy to the bed. He supported himself on his elbows above her. They did not move too fast but kissed as only new lovers can, while their love has yet to be shared. No thoughts of Poppy came to Miles's mind; no shame nor regret. Only the glorious thrill of Sandy's touch.

He undressed her while still clothed himself. Her naked body lay stretched out for him, and he worshipped it, exploring its secrets with his lips and tongue. He kissed her mouth, her face, her gossamer eyelids, her tender neck, her breasts. He lingered on her nipples, exciting himself with their response to him. He traced his fingertips down her slender torso, following them with his tongue over the smoothest shadows of her stomach. Then his hands were beneath her, and she lifted herself to him and slowly, so slowly he lowered his tongue to kiss the vulnerable flesh of her inner self turned inside out.

Sandy sighed as she felt the electricity of his tongue, but soon she clasped her hands around his head and pleaded for him to undress and join her. Miles stood, stripped, and the first exhilarating touch of their nakedness was as a light filling the darkness within them both. They lay, indulging in the wholeness of this pleasure, happy to be patient as they kissed. And then, after a while, Miles lifted himself on one arm and while staring into Sandy's urgent, naked face, he entered her.

The pleasure sounded from their lungs in unison, but their sensations were separate until slowly again they kissed and savoured the delicacy of their union. And when Sandy bent her knees and lifted her legs and clasped them around Miles's back he felt wrapped and squeezed in her skin, as if their ribs were locked in a wishbone. They began to move together, and the fire that had been lit in their minds spread fast through their bodies – crackling, shooting from head to toe, engulfing them and then, and then it burst from them with the flames of absolute joy as they climaxed together, truly together so for a second they existed in a place somewhere outside themselves, the wishbone splitting dead centre when they broke and breathed as one.

They lay silently, their bodies speaking with the heaviness of their breath. And then Miles suddenly laughed, as if his body itself was laughing, and he kissed Sandy's flushed cheek and felt for her hand to hold beneath the covers.

He did not think of Poppy waiting at home, and he felt no shame.

Tony Jakes, Meyers often said, moved like a pissed-off hippo. Meyers had seen the brisk, determined walk, the quick snap of the head, the belligerent stance in other tabloid editors. It was a graceless motion born of a war against time. Now Jakes was leaning with one hand flat on his desk, and the other rapidly flicking aside the photographs he didn't want for the front page of Friday's *Daily Herald*. Eventually, Jakes jabbed his finger on one of Fabio Nirao in his hospital bed, wearing an *I Love New York* baseball cap. His face was in sharp focus, horrible and swollen. The IV drip bordered the frame, flowers filled the other side.

'Where's that "before" picture of Fabio?'

Will Haverson handed it to Jakes. The headshot, of Fabio smiling, had been taken from his Japanese composite. Fabio looked particularly friendly; as if he wouldn't harm a flea.

'That's great. Let's put "Welcome to" across the top, the two photos in the centre, and then "New York" underneath. OK? And Larry's story on pages four and five.' Will Haverson nodded, and left Meyers alone with Tony Jakes. Jakes sat. 'Larry, I want to wait on the *Weissmans* VP story.'

'But . . .'

Jakes held up his hand. 'It's not gonna go away. You can put your friend in a hotel on us, get the whole story, and we'll run it when the competition's over. You say Saul Weissman doesn't even know about it?'

'No, that was Kristina's whole idea.'

'Right, so I don't want to sit at Saul Weissman's table next Monday night after my paper's implied that his whole competition was rigged.'

'But it won't be news after the result, will it? It'll just be a cheap story about an old broad who likes to get tied up.'

'Larry, I've made my decision.'

'I think you're wrong.'

'An editor's prerogative, wouldn't you say?' Meyers turned to go. 'But heh,' added Jakes. 'I did tell you the *Weissmans* story wouldn't be so bad, didn't I?'

Meyers smiled. 'You know what, Tony? I hate your fat guts.'

'Night-night, Larry. I'll see you tomorrow.'

At first, Miles thought he was dreaming. Sandy had been featuring in his dreams lately, so it was hard to believe that the voice was truly hers. He opened his eyes, and she smiled at him, and laid a hand on his shoulder. She was on the telephone.

'You think it was because of the Trudie Love show?'

She was sitting up in bed. Miles rolled on to the snug warm pillow of her lower belly. He kissed the skin. Sandy tapped him on the back and pointed at the phone. It concerns you, her gesture said.

'Jack, there's nothing you can do. Don't worry, Yeah, I'll see you in the morning. Bye! That,' Sandy said, pulling at a lone black hair on Miles's shoulder, 'was Jack.' Sandy yanked at the hair. 'She rang to say that her lover-boy Spencer has gone.'

'Gone where?'

'To England.'

Miles sat up. 'You're kidding me.'

'No. He just left. Jack got a letter. Apparently they had something going on between them.'

'Yeah, I know they did. That was my fault.'

'Miles, it's all your fault.'

He laughed. It was true. Fabio, he and Sandy, Spencer and Jack, Giovanni. He'd stirred all the pots. It was no wonder that lids were beginning to fly off.

Miles looked at the time. Damn! It was almost midnight. He and Sandy had ended up ordering room service and dining in bed. Acting the illicit couple mindful of time. Then they'd made love again and it had been as exquisite as the time before. When they'd fallen asleep, their bodies had curled in the shape of a smile, and in their peace they'd slept too long.

'I've really got to go now.'

'Back to the wife?'

'Don't! Please don't.'

Miles swung his legs out of bed and walked to the bathroom, the muscled tautness of his buttocks pleasing Sandy.

In the shower, Miles thought of Poppy. The relaxing warmth of the water drained from him his courage. Where would she be? In bed? Awake? Waiting for the key in the door? He hoped she'd be sleeping. He didn't want to face her tonight. He certainly had no desire to make love to her. No desire! The truth was that simple. She had not acted wrongly, she had not changed, she had been nothing but gentle. And he had no desire for her.

Back in the bedroom, Sandy was powder-dry and tempting when Miles, dripping still, bent down to kiss her. Her tongue was sweet, and he felt a hand part the towel and find its target. Miles stood away.

'I've got to go, really.'

'How's it going . . . choosing?'

'It's fine.'

'I hope you're fighting for me.'

'Yeah, of course.'

''Cause we could have a lot of fun with a million dollars, couldn't we?'

'I thought we had a lot of fun without it.'

Miles finished dressing, his mind already outside the room. Sandy's lingering farewell kiss annoyed him.

He took a cab. Inside it smelled of stale cigarettes and unclean bodies. Miles's washed skin felt spongy and warm and vulnerable; like that of a new-born babe. How would he cope if Poppy suspected? He wished only to sleep. She probably wouldn't think twice. If he walked in there believing in his lie, then Poppy would believe in it too. There was the answer. He hoped.

When the cab pulled up outside the apartment, Miles was dismayed to see that the lights were burning strong and that, at a quarter to one, Poppy was still awake. He breathed in the freezing air, braced himself, and began the arduous climb to their fourth-floor loft apartment.

Home in his father's palatial Upper East Side apartment, Chester Hunt lifted a bottle of mineral water from the fridge and took it through to the living room to watch TV. The room was expensively decorated in the style of an English drawing room, with fine antique furniture, and stretched silk on the walls. Chester liked it for it had been his mother's before she'd married, and much within it reminded him of her.

Tonight, he was back from a great time at Nell's nightclub with Fernando, Jessica and a tab of E. He felt unusually happy. It would have been nice to have found someone with whom to share his mood, and his gargantuan bed – male or female, no matter – but, then again, it didn't feel so bad to be alone. Such times had been few and far between since Chester had quit Harvard. His incessant quest for the good time was a symptom of his continuing flight from himself. Contentment, Chester found, came only when he forgot he was alone.

His mother watched him as he turned on to Channel 35. A silver-framed photograph of her stood on the baby grand piano. It was a black and white portrait, formal and stylised. It made her look, as is so often true of images of that period, serene, angelic almost. She was sitting in half-profile, a simple diamond necklace caressing the skin of her bare neck. Her hair was tied up at the back. A half-smile, with lips closed, imparted an air of benevolence to her face. Chester moved his eyes from the TV on to the portrait. He'd inherited her soft eyes, her fair hair, her nose. The rest, the violent cheekbones, the wide forehead, had come from his father.

Chester picked up the portrait and ran his fingers over the glass. It was warm; peculiarly so. Perhaps this is where she lives, he thought, with her skin warming the glass. *Is it? Are you watching, Mother? Tell me then, will I win?*

She must have been my age when they took this, thought Chester. He wondered what had been going on behind her eyes. What had she imagined? Too short a life playing political wife with Tristan Hunt? Two kids? Death with a steering wheel puncturing her lungs? No. Rather Chester imagined that his mother had thought, as did he, that one day something would happen to make it all worthwhile. For her, maybe it would be a husband, a child, money, a move to a new house. That she'd have passed old goals and felt no better would not have damaged her hope. She, as her son after, must have believed that happiness would exist in some place that actually could be reached.

On the television a naked woman was pissing into the open mouth of a man. A number came up on the screen – 970-something. Chester flicked it off. He took his water out on to the terrace. It was cold, and the clouds hung low so that the buildings further downtown disappeared eerily into their cover, like headless people. Manhattan had taken on the aspect of a dream city. A Babel reaching the heavens. It appeared unchaotic and calm from the haven of that Fifth Avenue balcony; the type of place where Chester might find his particular happiness. He laughed at himself. So much for his new found elation! One look at a picture of his mother and it was gone again. He peered over the edge of the balcony, tempted, as ever. The phone rang. He walked to it.

'Hello?'

'Chester? It's Kristina von Koeler. I'm sorry to call you so late, but I was wondering if you'd have dinner with me tomorrow night?'

'I . . . er, sure.'

'I want to talk to you about an idea of mine.'

'Which is?'

'Why don't I tell you then.'

'OK. When, where?'

'How about Arnolfini's at nine? It's close to my office.'

'Sure. I know where it is.'

'Oh and Chester, can we keep this between ourselves?'

'OK. I can do that.'

After the call, Chester flopped on to the sofa, and smiled. With the mind of a politician's son he was already trying to decode the messages behind Kristina's move. He couldn't imagine what she might want from him, besides money of course, but of one thing he was convinced: Kristina von Koeler had called because she was sure that he, Chester, was going to win the six million dollars. And as he lay flat on the sofa staring up above, Chester Hunt began to think so too.

Poppy was at the far end of the loft watching TV when Miles came in. 'Hi!' he said, 'what are you watching?'

Poppy neither replied nor turned to greet him. Miles took a deep breath and walked up to join her. 'Hi, babes! Anything exciting happen when I was gone?'

Still Poppy didn't turn. Instead she pulled her knees up beneath her chin and focused on the television. She's annoyed about last night, thought Miles. That and me not making it to the movies tonight. He glanced at the box. Dick van Dyke! Poppy hated Dick van Dyke. 'What are you watching?' he foolishly said again.

'Guess.'

Miles eased off his tie and walked into their closet. He called over his shoulder. 'I kind of meant *why* are you watching that. I thought you hated it.' Poppy was silent. Miles returned to her. 'Have I done something wrong?'

Slowly Poppy turned her head to look at him. 'I don't know. Have you?'

Miles sat on the arm of the sofa and took off his watch. 'No. You're not being very friendly, that's all.'

'Oh.'

'Oh! Well thanks for sharing that. I'm going to bed.'

He headed for the bathroom, turned his head to find her looking at him. Then she said, 'An English guy called Spencer called you.'

'Shit! Did he?'

Miles knew how angry Weissman would be if he found out that Spencer had called and failed to make contact.

'He said it was urgent. I told him you were at the office with Saul Weissman.'

'Really? We . . . we went out to dinner.'

'Where'd'ya go?'

'Oh, an Italian place near there. I think it's called Arnolfini's.'

'You think?'

'Yeah! What difference does it make?'

She turned her face away. Miles stood staring at the back of her head for a moment before escaping to the warm security of the bathroom. He couldn't figure out what was wrong with Poppy. Best let her calm down, he thought. I'll take a shower and maybe she'll go to bed.

Under the jets of water he lifted his floppy red member. It looked so feeble and incapable of sin now; like a scrubbed street urchin in an old British movie. The crime was apparent only after closer inspection. Poppy, thought Miles, simply musn't be allowed to look.

Still, the worst was over. So long as he didn't slip on the lie. It was simple enough. *I met Weissman at the office. We drank a beer. We dined at Arnolfini's. I had whitebait, veal, cappuccino. I cabbed it home. End of story.*

Out of the bathroom Miles was glad to find that Poppy had gone to bed. He joined her, deciding against a kiss. He wondered whether Sandy was sleeping. It was hard to be apart having recently been so close. The bed on his side was cold, but he didn't move to Poppy. Beside him, she was lying utterly still. Too still, thought Miles, for her to be sleeping. He felt like saying something, but he couldn't think of anything to say that wouldn't be a lie.

It was she who broke the silence. 'Miles?'

'Mmn?'

'Was it raining tonight?'

God, the relief . . . He felt like breaking into song. Sweet Poppy! 'No. It's cold though. The wind's strong.'

Poppy was turned from him, speaking without lifting her head from the pillow. 'When did you go to dinner?'

'Ah, about eight thirty, I guess. Why?'

'I just wondered.'

They lay silent. With his eyes, Miles tried to follow the pattern of the tin ceiling, lit from outside by the street's yellow glow. He lost its trace in the shadow. A break in the chain. He closed his eyes.

Suddenly Poppy sat up, the swiftness of her movement

startling Miles in the dark. She turned on the light, and Miles blinked at its brilliance. When he'd adjusted his eyes, the room seemed smaller. Poppy, simply, looked tired and white. Miles thought for a second how much less beautiful she was than Sandy.

'He rang me back later. From the airport.'

Miles lifted his hand and touched Poppy's arm. 'Who babes?'

'Spencer whatever he's called. He rang me back after he'd spoken to Saul Weissman.'

Miles could feel himself shaking inside; the tremors before an earthquake. 'So?'

'Saul Weissman said he didn't know where you were.'

Now Miles could feel the shock burst on his face. His heart crumpled, though not with shame or guilt or remorse, but with a sudden self-pity that he may have been caught. 'He must have called Saul before I got there,' Miles said.

'He called at ten thirty!'

Miles sat up. 'He couldn't have done. We went to dinner. I had veal, and then cappuccino.'

'What?'

'I mean that's what I had for dinner. I'm just telling you. Spencer's completely crazy, I promise. I mean, he quit the whole competition tonight to go to England.'

'So?'

'So I can't believe you'd believe him instead of me!'

'Because he wouldn't have had any reason to lie to me.'

'Nor would I, babes. I don't know why you're being so weird. It's not like you at all. I'd tell you to call Saul or the restaurant if it wasn't so late. I don't know what else I can do to make you believe me.'

'You can tell me something.'

'What?'

'Tell me why your hair was wet when you came in.'

Without thinking, Miles reached up to the back of his hair and felt the wet strands where he often failed to dry properly. 'I just had a shower.'

'Don't be a jerk, Miles. I said when you came in.'

Miles looked into her eyes. Then he reached out for Poppy's hand. She tensed up, held it back. 'I don't know. Was it? It probably just looked that way.'

Poppy was silent. A minute passed, more maybe. Miles could tell that she didn't believe him. He wished she would just turn out the light, let him go back to sleep. For him, the horror of the moment was that there was no escape. They were in bed. The night was young, and he feared that she might eventually learn the truth in the hours to come.

'This is stupid,' he said. 'If you won't believe me, I don't know what I can do.'

'Just tell me the truth, Miles. Please. I don't think that's asking too much, is it?'

Miles felt as if his heart might explode. Why did she have to find out? Suddenly he felt a hatred for Spencer. The idiot was to blame. And why had Weissman been in his office so late? Poppy continued to search Miles's face for an answer. She showed no intention of returning to sleep. Miles longed to find an escape, but Poppy's eyes had assumed an alien brittleness. The windows of her soul. He guessed that she knew, and he sighed and rubbing his eyes, he tried to look everywhere but into her face until he'd steeled himself to lift his face to the woman with whom he had shared the last two years of his life.

'Poppy,' he said. 'Do you have a cigarette I can have?'

33

Almost all the three hundred passengers on the Virgin Atlantic flight back to London were asleep as the plane eased evenly through the black sky. Spencer was wide awake, watching the movie on the tiny screen in the back of the seat in front. He had a headache, and wasn't listening. At times, tiny noises pierced the guttural monotone of the engines as the sounds of cinematic climax escaped from those headsets being used. What had he done? It was so unlike him to run from a fight, and yet he'd been playing a game the rules of which he'd never been taught. He couldn't have won. He knew it. The humiliation would have continued. That was what he'd despised. Hadn't those horrible, shallow people understood that his life had never revolved around his appearance? He'd been a bloody officer in the Life Guards, and, yes, that *did* mean something. A lot. He considered himself a thoroughbred tossed in a stable of mules. He had more history and breeding in his foreskin than that lot had in the whole of their bodies.

But what he'd hated most of all had been his damn, bloody powerlessness. He'd always considered himself to be the type of chap who could assess a situation, and then act upon it. But with this modelling lark there was nothing you could do but just stand there and let them point their grubby, arse-wiping fingers at you. Powerless! It was truly a relief to be shot of it, and them.

Not that he'd ever before thought of himself as a man to quit, but he accepted he'd made an error, and the most noble thing was to get the hell out with some dignity still intact. His father, Spencer knew, had been right. The EDEN competition had been beneath him. He'd been drafted in to give the whole damned thing a good name, and a bit of class, and he should never have agreed to go. But the worst thing was that he'd tried to be a male model and failed. It was awful!

Spencer Kemble-Finch shut tight his eyes and prayed to God that never again would he have to sink so low.

It was all running smoothly in Bruce Stone's magnificent studio on the afternoon of Friday, December 11th. The lighting hadn't been changed, and the routine that comes with a two-day shoot had been well-established. On set, surrounded by the lights, with Brock and Catherine looking on, were Jessica Warren and Fernando. The jazz of Hank Mobley was filling the broad space with its joy, and at the far end of the studio Giovanni Ferrari was quizzing Miles on why he looked so tired.

'I had a bad night with my girlfriend,' Miles explained. 'Very bad! She . . . er . . . she found out about something I didn't want her to, and then she kept me up all night talking about it.'

Giovanni blew across the top of his coffee. 'You make mistake! It is much better for the relationship if you never tell the truth.'

'But then if they find out it's even worse. Women always say that it's the lying that hurts the most.'

Giovanni smiled. 'They say this because of the pride, and because they do not want you to feel important. You should listen to me. If you tell the lie all the time, then they never think of asking the truth.'

'Well, it's too late now. I told her everything.'

'Then you are the fool!' Miles looked away. 'Do you love her?' Giovanni asked.

'Yeah. I mean . . . probably. It's hard to tell when you live with someone.'

Again, the confident smile. 'No, my friend, it is never hard to tell. You will know when you are in love.'

'Then I guess I am.'

'OK. So now you must be the romantic with all the romantic things. She will forgive you very soon. And if she does not, then it is better that you will not be together.'

'You're sounding like an agony aunt.'

'I am Italian, and Italian men understand the love.'

Miles laughed, and glanced down, noticing as he did a collection of colour polaroids that was on the table beside him. They'd been taken by the assistants to test the composition of each picture before Stone went to film. Any details missed by the naked eye, from the lighting to the hair and make-up, from untidy creases in the clothes to loose electrical wires in the background, showed up in the polaroids. Usually they allowed the photographer to explain the shot to the artistic director who'd explain the shot to the client who'd complain and, most often, be ignored. Sometimes they were shown to the model. This morning, however, they'd been taken just for Stone.

A few of the polaroids showed Reuben with Andrea, the German model. The striking contrast between them had favoured Reuben. His face looked powerful, almost menacing. The Ice Woman Andrea seemed lessened beside him. Miles was impressed.

Giovanni took the polaroid from Miles. 'Reuben could be good model.'

'He *is* a good model. But it's his bad luck that you're around.'

Giovanni was about to answer when the studio door opened, and Tiziana breezed in. Everyone immediately stopped what they were doing, and looked at her. Looking exquisitely beautiful, her immaculate skin tanned and still vibrant with the Caribbean sun, she walked over to Giovanni swivelling her hips as if not twenty, but twenty thousand eyes were upon her. Then, having kissed her brother, she tilted her head and smiled at Stone, and opened wide her arms for him to approach. Miles thought that such vaunting attitude would have seemed sadly narcissistic in most women, yet Tiziana's beauty was so celebrated and complete that for her to ignore it would, he thought, have seemed churlish. This acceptance of her beauty made her seem more beautiful still. She shook Miles by the hand, and her touch alone excited him.

Catherine skipped over to give Tiziana a kiss. Catherine

had only met the supermodel once, but that was considered enough to claim deep friendship in fashion's great big dysfunctional family.

Stone apologised and returned to his camera. 'OK, you two, just half a roll more. Fernando, try holding Jessica out in front of you. Like . . . maybe like a caveman bringing home his supper.'

'Thanks!' said Jessica.

'Who's the girl?' Tiziana asked.

'A new British star,' said Giovanni.

'I wonder what she wants to be when she grows up.'

'A rocket scientist?' suggested Miles.

'I meant a man or a woman.'

'Be nice,' Giovanni said. The older brother.

'Yes! Well, at least I don't have to be worried about any competition.'

Miles felt sorry for Jessica. He seemed to be the only one there who liked her. She was brash, funny, frequently obscene. She'd taken off her shirt to reveal her small, upward-turning breasts even before Stone had asked her to. Was it because Jessica was English that Miles liked her so? He knew how many misconceptions existed about English girls. In America they were thought to be prim and proper and sweet, wearing wild flowers in their hair and guarding their virginity until marriage, maybe longer. The pretty and proper films exported by England – the BBC period dramas, the Merchant Ivory novel adaptations, the twee comedies – were partly to blame, but so too was America with its eagerness to snap up the clichés, to label, simplify, believe.

Tiziana sat at the table and sighed. She addressed her brother in Italian. 'You should be grateful that I'm doing this for you, G. I am so tired!'

Giovanni asked her why.

'This time last week I was in Vienna. Then I had to go to Paris for just one photograph for an article about the supermodels, then I had a two-day job in Las Vegas with Steven, then a day shooting *Vogue* in New York, and in St Barts we had to get up at six every morning.'

'Tough life!'

'You try to live on a plane.'

'Well, you can relax most of the weekend.'

'I hope so.' Then she said in English,' I need something to drink. Does Bruce have carrot juice?'

'I can get some from the deli, if you'd like,' said Miles, happy to serve.

'Yes, please.'

'Small or large?'

'Darling,' Tiziana smiled as she tapped on the base of her cigarette box. 'Stupid question!'

By the time Miles had returned with the juice, Fernando and Jessica were gone. Stone had liked Fernando almost as much as he'd liked Fabio. That surprised Miles, and he hoped Weissman wouldn't find out. Giovanni, who hadn't needed anything done to his hair or his face, was chatting with Stone now, so Miles let them be. The friendlier they became, the better. Tiziana was getting a face massage from Catherine. She told Miles to leave the carrot juice on the side.

Miles went to look out of the window. God he really was tired. Everything was coming together at once – the final, Sandy, the void beyond Monday, Poppy. Poppy! Though Miles had succumbed in the end, the truth he'd told had been garnished with lies. He'd sworn by the 'yes I fucked her but I didn't *make love* to her' distinction, but Poppy hadn't seemed too impressed. Miles had tried to explain how he'd dropped in at the hotel to check on the models, how Sandy had been upset about something, how innocently in her room they'd drunk too much before Sandy, naked beneath her robe, had advanced on him with a kiss and a suggestion he was too much of a man to resist. Poppy had listened with a jilted lover's punishing insistence for detail, but her eyes had betrayed her suspicions. His infidelity, she claimed, had been on the cards since his return from abroad. When Miles had begun to object, Poppy had turned from him to sleep.

A whoop of laughter. Miles glanced up at the set. Tiziana was topless now, and being tickled by her brother. Miles wandered down to watch, picking up a muffin as he went, feeling a little self-conscious in their presence. Yet as he watched Tiziana and Giovanni establish their pose, his unease soon gave way to excitement. This pairing was perfect! She, Eve, born of Adam. Their likeness extended far beyond their facial features to the colouring of their skin, the slender shape of their necks, to their hands. Tiziana's hands, flowering from the thin stem of her arms, seemed larger now she was half-naked. As she sat beside Giovanni she lifted one hand to obscure the lower part of her left breast. It was the perfect gesture, the type of instinctive pose that elevated women such as she to the status of supermodels. She knew that to cover the whole bosom would seem coy, embarrassed. Instead, the slight covering of her breasts hit the right note of innocent yet sexual enticement; Eve discovering her nakedness, proud and ashamed at once. Everyone was silent. Only the clonk of the shutter could be heard, the whir of the camera motor, the high-pitched beep of the flashlights recharged. There was an understanding among them that this was the best shot of the six, and, for once, something worthwhile was being captured on film.

Giovanni himself was masterful in front of the lens, and absolutely at ease. While Tiziana was sitting, looking at him, her face in half-profile, the taut tendons of her neck slicing a dark shadow from the lights, Giovanni was staring deeply into the camera lens. His head was tilted slightly to his sister, as if he was listening to her. His expression, too, was perfect. He was looking quizzical, slightly defensive, unsure of what had become of his rib . . . Miles thought back to the moment he'd met Giovanni, to the tactics he'd employed in Paris to persuade him to come, to all that had led to this. He saw the couple now, and imagined them in Brazil the following month. The final image would probably be not far removed from this. It would be printed in the world's top magazines. He, Miles Jensen, was responsible, and it made him feel proud.

Miles could hardly wait to show a polaroid to Weissman and Kristina. His excitement was such that he forgot all about Poppy as, stealing a polaroid as he went, Miles slipped from the studio, ignored the elevator and skipped down the stairs towards the daily meeting at Weissman's, two joyous steps at a time.

For a woman who never had much to say, Dora Barefoot, Steve's mother, always took a long time getting off the phone. It was as if she expected a nugget of priceless information to be saved for the dying seconds of each conversation.

From the way she spoke, it sounded as if she'd never been north of the Mason-Dixon line. 'There must be something else, Steven.'

'No, Ma. Nothing.'

'Oh! I'm sure *I* had something to say . . .'

Steve flicked on the hotel television to ESPN, the sports channel. It was doing a profile of Kirby Puckett. Steve turned up the volume.

'. . . are there people there with you?'

'No, Ma, I told you. I'm here alone. It's the TV.'

'Do you have to watch television while we're on the telephone, Steven?'

'I'm listening to you.'

'I suppose one of these days you'll tell us what you're getting yourself up to in New York.'

'You'll know.' Steve laughed. 'Hey, you might even see me in the papers.'

'Now don't you joke with me.' He imagined her shaking her head, wagging her finger.' You know we're worried about you.'

There was a knock at the door.

'Listen, Ma. Someone's here to see me. I gotta go.'

'Call us soon, you hear?'

Another knock.

'I hear ya loud and clear. Bye.'

'Love you!'

Steve pushed the receiver into its cradle, and stood to open the door. It was Larry Meyers. He stepped in and looked around the hotel room for which the *Herald* was paying.

'Like the place, Steve?'

'It's great, Mr Meyers. How long can I stay?'

'A couple more days. We don't be running your story till Tuesday. But I'd like a few more facts from you now, and then there's a photographer calling later. A cute English girl.'

'Can't wait!'

Meyers sat at the table, and took out his pad. 'So you were telling me about your trip with Kristina to London . . .

Chances are that if Kristina von Koeler had known about Meyers and Steve, she'd have packed her bags and moved out of New York. But Kristina thought that it was Steve who'd escaped. His suitcase had promptly been collected from outside her building, and there'd been no word from him today. Kristina prayed that by now Steve was back with his cattle and folks.

Kristina looked towards the door of Arnolfini's and wondered why Chester was late. Sipping on her Kir, she thought back to the meeting with Miles and Saul. Miles had burst in with the giggly breathlessness of a schoolboy, brandishing the polaroid of Giovanni to show to his boss. Weissman had been dangerously impressed, and it had taken a fair amount of sourness from Kristina to calm him down. She'd claimed that the Italians were 'way too eighties', and that the veneer of good breeding and wealth was no longer what was required. If *Weissmans* wanted the future, there was only one way to look: towards Chester Hunt. Weissman had said he'd give it some serious thought.

It was Friday night, and Kristina had three more days to make him change his mind.

A gust of cold air, and Chester came in from the street. He waved at Kristina. He was, she thought, looking his best. Since the Trudie Love show he'd not only spent hours pumping his muscles in the gym, sweating out the toxins in readiness for the next intake, he'd also been twice to the sun-tanning salon. He took Kristina's hand, apologised for being late, and asked for champagne.

They spoke of the cold weather and the speed with which Christmas was coming before Kristina said, 'Why don't I order for both of us? I know what's good here.'

462

'I think I know what I want better than you do,' said Chester. 'Thanks all the same.'

The small talk continued into the pasta. And then, after almost an hour, Kristina made her offer: for her services in securing Chester victory in the competition, she thought she was worth thirty per cent of the six million. Almost two million bucks. Chester could take it, or leave it. But if he left it there was no way he could win. 'It's simple. Either you win over four million dollars and the chance to become one of the most talked-about models in the world, or you don't get a thing. What do you say?'

Chester, who throughout had listened in silence, could no longer suppress his grin. 'You must rate my chances pretty highly.' He leant forward on his elbows with his wine glass cradled between his hands. 'In fact, if you didn't think I was going to win, you'd have approached someone else. Wouldn't you? What about Giovanni?'

'He can't win.'

'Oh no? Why?'

'I know things. I can't tell you what, but I know things.'

Chester laughed. 'You shouldn't have told me that. Who else would I have to worry about except him?'

'Fernando, Reuben and Troy.'

Chester smiled. 'Right!'

Kristina's face suddenly hardened, and she leant into Chester and lowered her voice. 'Believe me, Chester. You haven't got a hope without me. I could ruin you.'

Another burst of laughter erupted from Chester. 'What, by Monday night?'

'By midnight if I wanted.'

Chester responded to her seriousness. 'Do you know how I see this now? I think that between them, Saul Weissman and Miles have chosen me, and now you're desperately trying to get in on the act. Did you happen to notice that it was *my* photo in the papers this morning?'

'Of course. I chose it.'

'Whatever, Kristina. Thanks for dinner, but my answer's no. I think I'm going to win, and I'm sure that's why you're here. If you'd asked me two weeks ago things may have been different, but no-can-do now.'

And so it began: her alternative plan. Her plan to trap Chester into agreeing to her scheme. Beneath the table, the scene of previous crimes, Kristina pressed her leg against Chester's, and said, 'Fine. Let's forget the competition, shall we? Can't it just be us having dinner?'

Chester studied her face for a second before smiling, lowering a hand to Kristina's leg, and saying. 'That suits me just fine.'

And now Poppy was leaving. Without plates being thrown or insults hurled, Poppy had told Miles as soon as he'd walked in that she was moving out. For the past hour he'd been scurrying after her as she collected her things, but no amount of pleading promises had shaken her resolve.

'I'm not saying it's final, Miles, but I've got to have space to think this through.'

'I'll give you space, babes. I won't pressure you. Please don't go now. I've got so much else going on, I don't need this as well.'

She continued to sift through her clothes. 'Oh, sorry if I interfere with your life! Maybe you should have thought about that before you got into her bed.' She threw a shirt into her case. 'Or did you do it on the floor?'

'Please, Poppy! How many times do I have to tell you: I *wasn't* thinking. That was the whole point. She was flirting with me, and then I made a stupid mistake *without* thinking. I accept that I did a bad thing.'

Now she looked at him. 'That's big of you, Miles. I accept it too. That's why I'm going.'

'No, babes, please. Please!' He took her in his arms now, his voice was shaking with emotion. 'It won't happen again, I promise. Ever. It isn't as if there was anything between me and her. It was all physical. I told you.'

Poppy broke free. 'I know you did, but you don't get it: *I didn't believe you*. If you'd fucked anyone other than a model, you know, I maybe, maybe would have thought you were

464

telling the truth. But you've been a complete model groupie since you got back from your trip, like the sun shines out of their asses. Christ, Miles, you even want to *be* one now. And then you expect me to believe you when you turn around and say this model forced herself on you! I mean I can really picture you trying to fight her off.'

'What are you talking about "I've been like a model groupie"? I've been doing my fucking job! I don't think I deserve such a hard time for doing that.'

'OK, Miles. You're a saint, and I'm a complete bitch for moving out. Is that better? You came back from the trip and you've been wonderful to me ever since, and then you were raped by this disgusting model and I'm just too stupid to understand. Is that better?'

'Don't be dumb, Poppy. But maybe you haven't realised how stressful this whole thing's been. I'm sorry if things have changed, but maybe if you'd taken more of an interest in the guys then you'd understand.'

'Forget it, Miles.' She closed her suitcase, the fasteners clicking loudly in the silence. 'We'll talk about it later.'

After she'd gone the silence of the apartment seemed horrendous to Miles, and he fell on his bed and cried with self-pity at the sickening injustice of it all.

Kristina's plan was unfurling as she'd hoped.

Her performance in Arnolfini's had been quite masterful. Slowly, surely, she'd shed her aggression and become a coy, flirtatious teenager desperate to be kissed, scared to move too fast, palpably shivering beneath the skin. Chester had grown in confidence with every moment, believing she was offering herself to him. It had never occurred to Chester as he'd tried to seduce Kristina that it was she who was in control, never occurred to him that she'd come to the office because she'd known he would follow, never occurred to him that now, seated at her desk, Kristina was wearily rubbing her neck for she guessed he needed encouragement if her ploy had a chance to succeed. But why should it have occurred to him? Chester could never have known what Kristina had in her mind.

'Where does it hurt?'

'Here.'

Chester laid his broad hands on Kristina's shoulders, and began to massage her neck with his thumbs. The desk lamp was the only light on in the office, and in the shadow cast on the wall it seemed as if he was strangling her as he kneaded his hands on her skin. Kristina groaned, the tone taunting and sexual. Relaxing the muscles in her neck, she let Chester feel the weight of her head in his hands.

'Does that feel good?' he asked.

'Mmm. Keep going.'

'I can feel like a zillion knots here. Why don't you lie down?'

Chester pulled the cushions from the couch and arranged them on the floor. Kristina lay on them, face down. Chester knelt beside her. The office was quiet but for the occasional sigh of pleasure as Chester worked down Kristina's spine, pushing in, pulling the tension out.

'Would it be easier if I took my shirt off.'

He was hesitant; surprisingly so. 'OK, yeah.'

Kristina sat up, and lifted off her blouse. She wore no bra. Chester looked a little frightened when he saw her naked breasts. She lay flat again. Chester pushed in with his thumbs at the base of Kristina's spine.

'Ow! It hurts there.'

'Here?'

With his fingers spread out across the cheeks of her buttocks, Chester gently kneaded around the bone. Slightly at first, then with greater urgency, Kristina began to rotate her hips. There could be no mistaking the sexual nature of her gyrations, and after a couple of minutes Chester succumbed and slid his hand over her buttocks and down towards the heart of her desire. Kristina lifted herself to meet his hand until he found her, through the skirt, through her underwear. Suddenly, Kristina turned over. She could see his excitement.

She whispered to him. 'Chester. I hear you're a bad boy.' Chester smiled, and tossed back his long hair. 'Do you want to be bad? With me?' Chester smoothed a hand up Kristina's leg. 'Do you like fantasies, Chester?'

Chester lunged forward and kissed Kristina. His mouth was hot and eager. She broke the kiss, and leant her mouth to his ear. Her heart was thudding desperately. She whispered: 'Chester, I want to be raped.'

Chester lifted his head. 'What?'

Kristina spoke fast, breathlessly: 'Not here, not like this. Somewhere else. I want it like the real thing. You can gag me, handcuff me, anything. Any way you want, Chester. Any way you want. Will you do that for me?'

He swallowed. 'Where?'

Kristina grinned with her mouth open. She leant back and closed her eyes. He kissed her again, and she felt for him through his pants. He sighed in pleasure.

'Somewhere . . . dangerous. Not in here.'

'I'm not going outside. No way.'

'No. In the building. We can do it in the stairwell. Please. I want it to be real. It wouldn't be real in here.' Kristina stood and went to her desk. She put her shirt back on and took from the drawer some handcuffs, rope and a length of *Weissmans* fabric. Chester was still on his knees. She handed them to him.

'Whoa! You do this all the time?'

'No. Never like this. Promise me you'll play along. I want you to treat me real bad, Chester. I want to know what it's like. Just once. I want to feel it just once.'

Chester's voice was shaking from nervous excitement.

'This is weird, Kristina.'

Again she felt for him, weakening his reserve. 'Just once,' she pleaded. 'I saw some old pipes out there in the stairs. Do it there. Tie me there.'

'Is there anyone around?'

Kristina shook her head. Chester looked about him in the office, undecided. Kristina slid a hand through his fly. They kissed, locked hands. She felt for the strip of fabric, and took it back from his hand. Turning her back to him, she threaded the gag into her mouth, and flipped the ends over her shoulders. As Chester stood behind her, knotting the gag at the back of her head, Kristina felt him with her hand. When the gag was tied Chester leant forward and felt for her breasts. Suddenly, Kristina lifted her elbow and brought it hard back into his chest. Chester swore, and when she turned around it wasn't a game any more. She lifted her arm and slapped Chester's face hard.

'Bitch!'

Chester flung his arms around her and carried her out of the door. She was kicking now, making noises through the gag. Chester pushed her through the EXIT door into the cold concrete stairwell. It was quiet, dimly lit. The pipes ran down one corner. Chester threw Kristina against them. She grunted, twisted around, as if to run. Chester swung her back. He pushed his body against hers and lifted her arms above her head. Though Kristina was struggling Chester was much stronger. Her screaming was turning him on. He leant his body against Kristina's, lifted her hands above her head and cuffed them high in front of her, to a bracket against the wall. Kristina was madly trying to kick him with her heel. She was trying to turn her face from the pipe, screaming through the gag. What was she saying? Haagh, Haaaahh. It was almost a cry.

Chester pushed his face up against her ear. He bit at the lobe. 'Are you hot? Is that it? Uh? Feeling hot? Because you like it like this, do you? You're too old and past it to get it any other way, are you Kristina? Over the hill, right?'

Chester held her legs and tied them apart with the rope. Then, with one tug, he ripped at her $2000 dollar skirt. He tore it away. Now she was all his. He was driven now. It had become real. He'd have her where she wouldn't want him. Using all his strength, Chester ripped away Kristina's tights and underwear. He released himself through the fly of his pants. For a moment he stroked the taut cheeks of her buttocks before feeling with his fingers for her luscious wetness, and then back to the sweet tight hole of his choice.

Kristina made an odd, groaning sound as he pushed his finger inside. He withdrew, took a step forward, and lunged.

A noise again, as if from her belly, pain or pleasure indistinguishable. Chester couldn't stop himself now. He was forcing himself deeper, violently so. He wished he could see her face, see her eyes, see if she believed in this too. Wasn't it what she wanted? He was calling out, 'You like this? Do you? Is this what you wanted?' His strokes were getting fiercer now. Kristina was keeping her muscles so tight. It was madly, wildly intense. Chester felt stronger than he ever had before. More of a man. He longed for it to last, longed for it to end, longed for it to last, longed . . . but suddenly the end was upon him. He gripped Kristina around the waist and thrust hard inside. A spasm, a glorious half-second, and then he screamed so loudly with the release that he didn't hear the EXIT door slam open.

The first Chester knew was that someone – a man – was behind him with his hands on Chester's shoulders. It was Stan Maychick, the security guard. Stan pulled Chester back and threw him against the wall. Chester tripped, fell sideways down the stairs. Two steps at a time. He lifted Chester, and swung him against the wall. Chester was shouting. 'Stop. It's not what you think. Please. Stop.'

Stan shouted back 'Shut up. Shut the fuck up.'

They heard the elevator doors opening. 'Down here,' Stan screamed. 'In the stairwell.'

Two policemen appeared. One came down the stairs. Violently, he cuffed Chester's hands behind his back. Stan Maychick bounded up to Kristina.

'It's not what you think,' screamed Chester. 'Please.'

'Where's the key to these cuffs?' asked the officer by Kristina.

'They're in my pocket,' gasped Chester. 'Please, she'll tell you. It was all her fucking idea. Look at the cuffs. They're padded, for Christ's sake. This is her *thing*. She asked me to do it.'

Stan was talking to the policeman. 'That's not how it looked on the camera.'

It was then that Chester noticed the video camera directed at the corner where Kristina was still tied. He hung his head in disbelief. Kristina groaned as the gag came away. Stan Maychick had undone the ropes at her feet, her buttocks not escaping his gluttonous eyes. Once the policeman had freed her hands he turned Kristina around. She was shaking, crying. Her hands were to her face. Then she dropped them to cover her nakedness. Chester looked up in horror. The right side of Kristina's face was red, a bright, horrible red. The officer touched the middle pipe. Quickly, he pulled his hand away. 'Shit that's hot!'

Chester's mind was swimming in panic. What had he done? The outside pipes had been cold. He couldn't have known. It was all her fault. It had all been her idea.

'She wanted it,' he pleaded. Tears were beginning to stream down his face. 'I swear to God. She asked for it. Kristina, FOR GOD'S SAKE TELL THEM. PLEASE.'

Chester darted his head around desperately. He found no sympathy in the eyes of any of them. The walls were closing in on him. He gasped for breath. Kristina turned from him.

'Let me go to my office,' she said in a hushed voice. The officer took her elbow. She turned through the door. Chester broke free and tried to run up the stairs towards her. He tripped, was pulled back.

'You can't do this to me. Jesus Christ. Please no. Kristina, please. Oh God NO. Kristina. PLEEEAAAASSSSE . . .'

Virginia Snyder had been Senator Tristan Hunt's private secretary for thirteen years, and his lover for ten. The affair had predated the death of Tristan's wife by two full years. A secret then, it was common knowledge now, and it was Virginia who picked up the phone early on that Saturday morning in December.

Her voice was croaky when she spoke. 'Hold on.' Virginia coughed, demure even now. She switched on the bedside lamp. 'Tris . . . Tristan . . . It's Chester.'

Tristan rolled over in bed. 'What's the time?'

'Twenty after one.'

'Tell Chester from me that if he wants to talk, he'll have to call at a more reasonable hour.'

Virginia passed on the news, and listened to Chester. Tristan had rolled back to go to sleep. Virginia shook him. 'Tris, he's been arrested. In New York.'

'Good. He could do with a night in jail. Tell him I'll see to it in the morning.'

Virginia relayed the response to Chester, then listened. She cupped a hand over the phone. 'Tris, I think you have to speak to him. He's very upset.'

'He hasn't called me in a year, and now this,' he said as he reluctantly took the receiver from Virginia's hand. 'Chester?'

Virginia watched her lover as he pulled himself up in the bed. It was staggering how quickly this strong, dignified man could look haggard and weak. It was to Virginia like watching a nature film in which a time-delayed camera had recorded decay, for Tristan's face seemed to skip the years in a second. She'd seen this expression in him once before. When the Senator had been told of the death of his wife, it was Virginia who'd been sharing his bed. She slid a hand behind the Senator's neck and felt for the soft warm curls at its nape.

'Jesus, Chester, the Senate hearings are around the corner . . . No, of course I care about you. But I've got rather more to lose . . . no . . . well frankly it *is* a little hard for me to believe that . . . Let me call Jim Woolard . . .' The Senator screwed his eyes tightly shut, and pinched at the bridge of his nose. 'No . . . Chester, calm down. That won't happen . . . Now listen very carefully. Don't say anything to anyone. Whatever happens I don't want . . . Oh, no, don't tell me that . . . Jesus!' Tristan Hunt leant his head back and stared at the ceiling. On the bedspread, his fist was clenched tight. Suddenly he was shouting, 'Then whose fault was it, Chester? Something like this was waiting to happen! Ever since Mom you've been wanting to discredit me haven't you, Chester? Chester?' Tristan Hunt let his head fall into his hands. 'Shit! He hung up on me.'

'What's happened? Tristan? Darling?'

His voice was hoarse.' Chester's been arrested for rape. He's trying to sell me some ludicrous theory about her blackmailing him.'

'Don't you believe him?'

The Senator said nothing. After so long in politics, the truth no longer came easily to him.

Virginia spoke again. 'What are you going to do, darling?'

'I'll stand by him. Anything else would look terrible. Apparently the press are on to it already.' He closed his eyes. 'Damn him, Ginny! Damn him, damn him!'

The phone rang again. Tristan grabbed at it.

'Chester?'

But it wasn't his son. The Senator's face hardened, and he clicked off the phone. 'The vultures,' he said, 'think they can smell a corpse.'

34

T he silence of Kristina's apartment seemed horribly loud to her that morning. The familiar seemed foreign. Had someone been in the bathroom? It looked different. The protracted nightmare had blurred her recent reality. It was shortly after five.

Kristina stood before her bathroom mirror and traced a groove with a finger through the thick cream on her face. The police medics, those cloying nurses who'd assumed that it was the rape that troubled her, had decided that there'd be no permanent scar. The skin, they'd purred, might be red for a while, but physically and emotionally they were sure the scars would heal. *Feeling better now?*

Stupid fucking bitches! How could they heal the scar of three million dollars lost? Didn't they know how much worse were their sterile swabs and smear-tests than the rape had been itself? How much less she welcomed the nail-scrubbed touch of their cool fingers? How the degradation of describing the ordeal rankled? '*No*, no oral sex:' '*no*, anal sex is not a part of my usual behaviour;' '*no*, there was never any fear when we entered the building alone.' How could there have been fear, she'd wanted to say, since I took him there to have him rape me?

That confession had tickled the underside of her skin: *I asked for it because I never thought you police would be called. I asked for it so I could threaten Chester with this criminal ordeal. I asked for it because I thought he'd offer me any amount to keep my mouth shut, to keep the security tapes winding on and erasing their evidence. Yes, the guard was always a risk, but I thought he would add to the pressure, see? See? Make a deal, Chester, or the*

473

guard'll call the cops. Make a deal, Chester. Make me rich.

But the confession had never come. She'd planned to talk to Chester as soon as she was dressed, but the police had taken him to the precinct station house before she'd had a chance. And then in the station reason had deserted her. She should have confessed before the questions and tests, before she had to endure her torment at the hands of the police. Yet her mind had been with EDEN, with the loss, with the breakdown of a plan she'd conceived and nurtured. *Pay him six million dollars, Saul, because I can always get a chunk of the cake* . . . Suddenly the tomorrows were gone. No more schemes. No hope. Nothing. And Reason lost in that vacuum of despair.

Yes, officer, he raped me! Yes, I'll put my legs in the stirrups. No! His fluids only. No! No other men. No! Not for two days. Feel? How do I feel? Ask me in a while. It's only just now sinking in.

Saul Weissman had always been a vociferous watcher of television. His running commentary on all things from movies ('Don't tell me you didn't know she was cheating you on the side!') to current affairs ('Go in there with the guns and show 'em who's boss') had once irked his long-suffering wife, Patty, but she'd learnt to close her ears to him then, and whenever else Saul was ranting about things inconsequential. When people asked Patty why her marriage had lasted so long, she used to smile and simply say 'Earplugs'.

But this morning it was different. This morning she recognised the concern in her husband's voice and ran to him in the kitchen where he stood with coffee in his hand. The television was turned to CNN, a picture of Chester at the top of the screen. Saul Weissman gestured for his wife to keep quiet as he turned up the volume on the set.

Bernard Shaw, CNN anchorman, flawless as ever, was talking.

'This just in from New York: Following his arrest late last

night under suspicion of rape, Chester Hunt, the son of Republican Senator Tristan Hunt, has been released on bail following his speedy arraignment this morning. Shannon Seal has more.'

The voice of Shannon was heard over recorded pictures of Chester stepping into the street, shielding his face and then running with a police escort to a waiting car.

Looking angry and bewildered as he came face to face with reporters for the first time since his arrest, twenty-two year-old Chester Hunt refused to comment as he was escorted by his lawyers to a nearby car.

The footage now was of the limousine speeding away, pursued by desperate photographers.

'Chester Hunt, in New York as one of the six finalists for a competition to find a model for a *Weissmans* cologne was charged at ten thirty-five this morning with rape in the first degree, a felony that carries a maximum penalty of twenty-five years imprisonment. He was released on bail of $200,000.'

Then Shannon, a primped poodle of a reporter sporting rock-solid hair, could be seen live, looking at a large microphone as if she wanted to sit on it. She was outside the Manhattan Central Courts building at 100 Centre Street. Her microphone was growling with the wind whipping up from the tip of the island below.

'Though they are sparse, a few more details of the incident have been filtering through to us. The victim, believed to be in her late thirties, was apparently burnt about the face during her gruesome ordeal. It has now been confirmed that the incident took place in the Weissman Corporation head office on Fifth Avenue.'

'Can you believe this, Patty? I don't believe it.'

'The victim is not suffering from any serious injuries, and was released by police doctors in this morning's early hours. Chester Hunt's father, Senator Tristan Hunt of North Carolina, has flown to New York from Washington to be with his son.'

From the studio, Bernard, looking troubled, asked:

'Are we to suppose that this incident comes under the heading of a Date Rape?

'Bernie, it certainly seems that way. Chester and the victim were known to have dined together in an Italian restaurant before the alleged rape.'

'Shannon, thank you. We will, of course, be keeping you abreast of any developments in this story.

Now, most people wouldn't associate igloos with New Mexico, but an Inuet . . .'

Weissman hit the mute button. He felt that odd mixture of excitement and disgust that follows shocking news.

'What was this Chester boy like?' asked Patty.

'He was like this, obviously. A dangerous beast. But he had us all fooled. I was even thinking of choosing him. Can you imagine that, Patty? I have to call Kristy.'

It rang twice before her machine picked up. Saul spoke: 'Kristina, did you hear the news? Where are you? Call me.' Then he hung up, and went to his study to get Miles Jensen's home number.

Souls, they say, are offered a momentary glimpse of the body they've departed as an answer, perhaps, to the riddle of identity. *See? This was you, look how wrong you were.* Now Kristina, lying awake after a fitful and unsatisfying sleep, considered it prescient to be hearing her own voice on the answering machine proclaiming repeatedly 'Sorry, I'm not here right now.' It was true. She didn't feel a part of the world to which she'd belonged twelve hours before. Weissman's voice was puncturing the tense, quiet space of the apartment 'Did you hear the news?' *Of course, Saul! I am the news.*

Kristina had, she thought, two options now. She could dress, apply thick make-up to the branding on her cheek, cab it to the precinct, and confess all. That would be the answer if that would be the end of it. Yet she was fearful of the life to come. It was not a spiritual heaven or hell that troubled Kristina. Rather, it was the hell on earth that would surely follow any confession she might make.

As it stood, Kristina's name would not be revealed by the press. Yet, if she dropped the charges, she'd be a carcass for the media. They would tear her apart, eat her alive, destroy it all. She would become the thing that they made her. The notion was yet more horrible than the truth. In the simplest of rape cases there was always a hidden yet implicit belief that the victim has got what she deserved, the legacy of a world made by man. Kristina could hardly bear to think what would be made of her, a woman led by greed and ruled by the basest of sexual urges who'd *pleaded* to be raped. She would be a villain to all women.

No, the confession was not an option. Her mistake had been made in the confusion of the arrest and now there was no turning back. That was plain to see. No – turning – back.

Her identity could remain a secret to all but those closest to her. She would be praised for her bravery in the ordeal. She would not be fired from *Weissmans*. History would know only one truth, and no court in any land could discover the other. If she believed it herself, she could deceive the world. His word against hers.

This, Your Honour, is what happened: I went to the office to get something – keys. We'd had dinner. He was a nice man. Younger. Strong. He flattered me. In the office, he put his hands on me. I am thirty-nine. It felt good to be massaged by his hands. Until he hit me. He dragged me outside. He handcuffed me to the pipes. I was burnt. See, here, the scar.

The man, this animal before you, he . . . raped me. Look into your heart, Your Honour. Examine your mind. Could anything else be true?

Reuben King and his girlfriend Marcie were crouched on the floor, racing cockroaches.

'Let's make it best of three.'

Marcie was laughing, 'No way, Reuben. You said that if your roach won you were going to win the competition, and if mine won, you weren't going to get shit.'

'Yeah,' Reuben answered, 'but like in my head I knew, I *knew* yours was going to win. See? I gave you ihe best one. Because I'm nice.' Marcie hit him over the head with a pillow.

'Best of three,' he said.

The roach racecourse was simple enough. It was constructed of tape boxes turned on their sides on the floor. The track was four inches wide, blocked at one end. A plastic roach 'motel', filled with poison, marked the winning post at the other. There were three curving tunnels leading to the feast. Reuben had for long doubted the efficacy of these contraptions. He suspected that at least one in every three-pack acted as fast food for the roaches. You put the trap down, the roaches fed and multiplied, you went out and bought more traps. A manufacturer's dream.

Neither of the cockroaches had been tempted that Sunday morning. Reuben's roach hadn't made it halfway down the track before turning back for home.

Once again he swept them both back to the starting line, and once again Reuben's roach hardly moved. Marcie's, shinier, more determined, was sprinting for home.

'Yours is the black brother,' laughed Marcie, 'and he ain't getting nowhere.'

'But he's got new, hidden tactics, see?' said Reuben, picking up his shoe, and slamming it down on Marcie's roach. The champion splattered crunchily, just short of the line.

'Eeouuughh. That's not fair.'

'I know, but I'm going to win now.'

Reuben's roach stopped momentarily to sniff the gunge that had been its rival before crawling past the finish.

'OK. That's one all. Now for the decider.'

This time Reuben's roach ran unchallenged into the poison trap.

'Ha! It's gonna die now.' Marcie said. 'See? Everyone gets what they deserve in the end.'

'I deserve a kiss,' Reuben said, flinging his arms around Marcie's shoulders and pushing her back on to the bed. He fell on top of her. Her tongue was warm. He rolled to the side. 'I thought I'd go see Fabio in hospital today. He's got no family or nothing. You want to come?'

'I don't know him.'

'That's no problem.'

'What are you gonna do later?' Marcie said, her voice tinged with petulance.

'I've got to run by the new garden. We're gonna move some stuff around. And there's a talk at Kennedy by Doc. Gardner I thought I might look in on. On Afrocentricity.'

Marcie touched Reuben on his almost hairless leg. She tickled a finger of her hand up to his warm mound of cotton. She liked to feel his dick through his Y-fronts. Its shy, heavy promise.

'Why do you have to be so good all the time?' she asked feeling him with her thumb as if testing the ripeness of an avocado in her palm.

'Who knows, Marcie? Who knows?' Reuben lifted himself off the bed. 'I guess 'cause it feels better in the end.'

He pulled a sweat shirt down over his head. His right arm missed the sleeve, and for a moment he punched the chest hopelessly before his head popped out.

'I wonder what you'd be like if you won,' said Marcie. She leant her chin on her hands at the end of the bed.

'The same,' smiled Reuben. 'Only richer.'

'Miles, you sound like shit!'

'Sorry, Saul.'

'Did I wake you? Haven't you heard the news?'

'No, what news?'

Weissman told Miles what CNN had told him.

'Christ! Do we know who was raped yet?' Miles asked, sitting up in bed now.

'No. No clues. And I can't get through to Kristy.'

'How do you think this'll affect the competition?'

'That's up to us. We gotta ride a fine line. We want EDEN to be mentioned as many times as possible, but we gotta wash our hands of Chester. You with me? What I don't want, Milo, is for my product to be associated with what Chester did. I mean, "Drink Gatorade and be like Mike!", "Wear EDEN and rape like Chester." See? That wouldn't be good.'

'So what should we do?'

'We do this: I'm going to show my face a bit, say the EDEN competition's still going strong, say we still got some great guys to choose from including Troy Turnbull blah, blah, then I'll tell them what an asshole Chester is and maybe promise to send a cheque to a women's victim group. Something like that. What I want you to do is go visit the models and make sure they don't mention Chester's name. They could screw it up. They got a free day today, which is good, and tomorrow I'll be in the store with them to deal with the press. OK, Milo?'

'God! I'm sorry I ever got Chester involved, Saul.'

'Don't be. I coulda done without Spencer, but Chester had something. No question. Still, you're right. What have we got? Fabio's had his face beat up, Spencer chickened out, and now Chester's gone and done this. Thank God we still got the Italians. eh? Don't you think? I mean, they're the natural winners anyway.'

'You think so?'

'Didn't I tell you? I saw Bruce Stone last night and he said that Tiziana and Giovanni looked sensational. A match made in heaven, he called it.'

'You mean just like Adam and Eve!' suggested Miles.

'You got it, Milo. Adam and fucking Eve.'

When Weissman hung up, Miles let his head flop back on to the pillow. This was too much for his tired mind to cope with. Chester had raped someone? He couldn't come to terms with it. Rapists were violent people. You recognised them on the street. But Chester? It was terrible.

Except, of course, that Giovanni's route to the contract was free now from obstacles. Unless he was attacked, or arrested, or unless he fled to Italy, he would win, and Miles would become rich. Yet even this prospect of a million dollars couldn't really lift Miles's spirits as he lay alone in bed thinking of Chester and of Poppy, and of what he would give just to get her back.

Jim Woolard was the lawyer Senator Hunt had engaged to fight for his son. It was he who opened the Hunts' apartment door when the Senator arrived in New York. The Senator's handshake was firm and practised – more of a squeeze than a shake, as if he was restraining himself from squeezing too hard and cracking together the bones of his friend.

'Chester's sleeping, Tristan. The doctor gave him some sleeping tablets.'

'I want to look in on him.'

Senator Hunt walked ahead of his old friend and eased open the door to the master bedroom. It was dim inside. He walked lightly to the bed. The sudden sight of Chester's long hair spread across the pillow alarmed Tristan. It looked so much like his ex-wife's. It was even the length she'd had it in the mid-sixties. For a moment the woman shone brightly in her son and there, in the bedroom where Tristan had known the greatest love for his wife, he tripped suddenly into his inner darkness with the jolt of a dreamer's cliff-edge fall. He stood by his son. *Why do you hate me? Why has it been a year? Why is it that I can't control a son while a whole State puts its trust in me?*

The Senator reached out a hand, thinking of touching Chester's face, but he stopped short. They could talk later. He looked down again at his son, so solid and complete and unlike the young Chester his mind foolishly imagined whenever he heard the name. He'd seemed so close to perfection then. But since . . .

I'll stand by him for his sake, not for mine; not for my future but for his. It's time I proved myself again.

Chester woke to the sound of the door shutting behind his father. He hadn't seen him. He opened his eyes, closed them again. He'd glimpsed the slivers of daylight gilding the curtain's edges and guessed it to be mid-afternoon. He could have looked out yet he felt as if trapped beneath an avalanche, unable to move, unable to reach the light. With his eyes closed Chester tried to escape the horrors of the previous hours, but the past seemed more real now than it had when he'd been living it.

Throughout the arrest and interrogation Chester had been living in something of a dream world, unable to believe what he'd known he must. The perversity of his circumstances had been heightened by his familiarity with it. It was not from personal experience that he'd recognised the starkness of the precinct interviewing room, or the holding pens at Central Booking, but from TV shows, books and films. For a while during his ordeal, Chester had imagined himself starring in a made-for-TV drama about a Senator's son unjustly arrested for rape. He'd not been surprised to find himself at a cold table, its legs screwed to the floor, wringing his hands as he pleaded an unbelieved innocence. He had somehow known that unsympathetic sergeants would come and go, their shadows on his face as they bent over him, holding styrofoam coffee cups in their hands. He'd felt he could have written their speeches and his replies.

We know you fucked her. We got it on tape. She made a statement. Now quit with the bullshit! No woman alive would want that shit to be done to her. Burnt while making out? Yeah? Who the fuck did Chester think he was screwing? Joan of screwing Ark?

Oddly, it had been the frequent jokes that had shocked Chester back to reality. Their toy was his future, and his pleas had become more desperate, less hopeful.

It wasn't rape. Believe me, it wasn't. She asked me to do it. She pleaded for me to do it.

Now he wondered what they must have thought. The truth then hadn't sounded absurd; merely true! Yet no one had accepted it. Later, during the terrifying, squalid ordeal of Central Bookings, when for the second time that night they'd handled him with rubber gloves, treated him as HIV positive, Chester had met with Jim Woolard. And even Jim, a man he'd known all his life, the lawyer whose job it was to believe the unbelievable, even *he* had doubted Chester – not with his words, but with every flexed and lying muscle in his face.

Suddenly Chester was frightened with a gust of loneliness. He needed to talk with someone, anyone. He managed to climb out of bed.

Though he hadn't taken the tranquilisers, his body felt weighty and tired. He reached the door, unaware that his father was there. He was surprised by voices. He heard his name spoken. Instead of opening the door, Chester pressed his ear to the wood. His father was talking. 'And you say this tape is damning?'

'I think he's handed them all the demonstrable proof they'll ever need.'

'But surely if Chester's not denying intercourse then the tape won't prove much.'

'I haven't seen it, Tristan, but from what I've heard Chester was quite violent. He handcuffed her, you know.'

There was a silence. Chester's breathing had become so heavy that he feared his father might hear.

The Senator spoke: 'Listen, Jim – forget everything that's possible, just tell me friend-to-friend what you think his chances are.'

'Honestly, I don't think he's got a hope.'

Chester stumbled away from the door. He heard Jim say something about a lenient sentence. But he was going to jail! An innocent man! He felt sick. Not a hope? Chester clasped his head in his hands. I'd rather die than go to jail, he thought. I'd so much rather die. What's the point of living without freedom? The tears now were being almost vomited from his chest. He was hyperventilating, getting dizzy. The whole room was spinning. Not jail! He couldn't survive that!

Oh God, no. Let me die instead of going through that.

* * *

'I'll kill him, I'll fucking kill him. He won't be good for dog meat when I'm through with him.'

Saul Weissman had come as soon as Kristina called. Now he was pacing about her apartment, pummelling his fist like a madman, speaking rapidly. Kristina found Weissman's near-madness reassuring. Not a flicker of doubt had wrinkled his face when she'd recounted her version of the rape. He was nothing if not loyal.

'I hope you got yourself a good lawyer, Kristy. Because these Ivy League bastards are gonna pull every string in the book. That's the thing about those guys.' Weissman loosened his tie, as if preparing to fight. 'They look so fucking clean, but they're dirty. Filthy fucking dirty, the lot of them. But they're not gonna get away with it this time. The Bush days are over, Kristy. We're into a brand new era. Honesty is in, and that jury's gonna hear every last fucking detail about this terrible thing. Right? Chester Hunt is gonna hang by his balls even if I'm the one has to wrap the noose around them. He's not gonna see daylight this side of fifty. OK, sweetheart?' Kristina nodded. 'I just can't imagine a man doing a thing like that. Broke into the office, did he?'

Kristina sipped on the camomile tea Saul had made her. 'Actually, Saul, I'd had dinner with him. Just, you know, a casual thing. We happened to run into each other, and he escorted me up to the office because I'd left my apartment keys there. I'd been . . . working late and . . .'

Saul held up a palm. 'Don't do this to me, Kristy. It's hurting. I'm responsible for you working late.'

'No. No. I suppose I shouldn't have let him come in.'

The couch springs sang as Weissman sat by Kristina. With a characteristically swift swing in temperament, Weissman's voice softened. He picked up her hand, so slender beside his. 'Hey, don't you even think of blaming yourself. He seemed like a nice enough kid. We weren't to know he was a monster inside. There's no telling these things with some people. I mean, they can be just like you and me, but weird and kinky inside.'

Kristina regarded the face of the man who'd been her boss

for almost twenty years. Close to her, its pudginess was cleansed of expression. Unselfconscious and compassionate, Weissman looked back at her with his mouth open and his eyes wide. She could see his tongue, cherry red, squirming as hatching frog's spawn. She looked up into his eyes, and thought he looked mentally defective, autistic or some such thing. Weissman felt he was being unintimidating.

He spoke again, softly still, and yet more slowly. 'You have to listen to me, Kristina. I wanna warn you that these lawyers are gonna keep digging and digging and digging 'til they find something. I don't mean to criticise you or nothing, but they could find out about that naked meditation. You know what I mean? You took classes. People are cruel. They could talk.'

Suddenly, Kristina felt a love for this man. Outside the bedroom, Weissman knew her better than did anyone else alive. He'd seen her every working day for almost twenty years, and this is what he thought: that she was a good person, trustworthy, honest; a woman who deserved his love and support. He could neither see nor hear the warring inside, the bitter turmoil of her constant unease. Good, sweet Saul, who found the idea of meditating naked to be kinky, who had filled her office with Caribbean flowers, who had never denied her anything, was the man she'd been conspiring to cheat. She hadn't simply wanted to bite the hand that had fed her so long. She'd wanted to hack it off, finger by finger, pain guaranteed.

These bastards are gonna keep digging . . .

The idea terrified Kristina. She turned to Weissman and he held out his arms for her and the tears shook her body. It would be the one and only time she would cry about this in another's arms. What had she thought? That she could take a man such as Chester to court and emerge unharmed? In cases of rape even the innocent are never unscathed, and she was as guilty as . . . sin. Weissman rubbed her on the back. Kristina couldn't face it if this man discovered her unending duplicity. And it would all splurge out, her devious, perverted history. Kristina couldn't let that be.

'Saul,' she sniffed, 'I don't want anyone else to know what happened to me. Not Miles, not anyone.'

'I promise, sweetheart.'

'Now I have to call someone.'

'You wanna see Hirschberg?'

She laughed; she actually laughed. 'No thanks, Saul. No.' Kristina walked to the bedroom. 'Someone else.'

She had the number by chance. It rang interminably. *Be there*, she willed. *Please, please be there.*

A woman's voice; a slow, careful voice. '206–2982.'

'Hello, is Steve there please?'

'No, dear. But this is his mother. Can I help at all?'

Kristina found herself shaking her head. 'Do you know where I can reach him? It's important.'

'Oh! He's not in trouble, is he? I worry he gets himself into trouble.'

'He's not.'

'I'm his mother and he doesn't tell me diddly-squat. I worry he gets himself into trouble.'

'So you said. Do you have his number close by?'

'I surely do.'

Kristina took the number wondering where Steve had got the money for a hotel in Manhattan. She thanked Mrs Barefoot.

'Are you a friend of Steven's?'

'Yes. I know him well.'

'Oh.'

'Thanks, then. Goodb . . .'

'A *close* lady friend? I don't mean to pry.'

'He's a friend. Listen, I have to go. Goodbye.' Kristina hung up. Then she dialled Steve's number, and waited for a connection. Steve answered.

'Hello, it's Kristina . . . I know . . . just let me come and talk. I've got something important to say.'

35

Miles had spent half the day tracking down the competitors, breaking the news to them if they hadn't heard, and explaining *Weissmans* policy. Now he was in the Midas talking to the models who were in. The reaction was the same from them all: surprise, sympathy, then concern that the competition might be disrupted. On this Miles could assure them just as he'd assured the journalists to whom he'd spoken. The party on Monday night would go ahead as scheduled, and both winners would be announced. EDEN remained the cologne for the future, and the seven million dollars was still up for grabs.

In the hotel, Miles had talked to Jessica as she sat in the bar, to Jack and Andrea in the hotel gym, and to Fernando as he left for a run through the park to meet Reuben at his home. There was only one other model in the hotel, and it was at her door that Miles was now standing.

Sandy was wearing tight grey leggings and a thick sweater. 'Come in,' she said. 'I just got back.'

'I know. I called by earlier.'

'Sorry!'

Sandy walked first into the room and sat on the edge of her bed. Miles moved to the window. He didn't want to get too close. Perhaps the churning physiological reaction to her beauty was something close to love, but it couldn't compare with what he'd been feeling for Poppy since she'd left. The emotion of the night's lonely hours had been so fervent that Miles had not considered it a threat to his resolve to meet Sandy in her room. But in an instant he'd begun to feel differently. Sandy was rare in being a person whose appeal was greater in life than in fantasy.

'Did you hear about Chester?' he said.

'Yeah. No one can believe it.'

'No. Um, Saul's asked me to ask you not to discuss Chester with the press. Is that OK?' Sandy nodded. 'It's just he's worried about bad publicity.'

'OK.'

Miles had done his bit now. He could go. And yet he didn't want to – not back to the empty apartment. He looked out of the window. The weather was listless, grey, Anglican. It missed the invigorating bite of recent days. From somewhere Miles could hear the sound of a Christmas carol. 'God Rest Ye, Merry Gentlemen.' He smiled to himself. If only! He thought of Poppy, wondered where she was, wondered if she was thinking of him. Maybe she was trying to call the apartment.

'Do you want to get some coffee or tea or something?' Sandy asked.

Miles thought for a moment, and then agreed. Tea. Just tea. Nothing else. It was Poppy he loved.

Sandy rang through with the order. When she hung up she moved beside Miles. He turned to look. Sandy stepped closer and within a second they were kissing as if this was all they'd ever wanted. They fell on the bed together and Poppy was far from Miles's mind as he struggled to unclip the hook of Sandy's bra until they broke their kiss with laughter at his fumbling. Sandy unhooked the bra with ease. They looked at each other, side by side on the bed.

'Let's wait,' said Sandy, 'until after room service has come.'

Miles guided Sandy's hand between his legs. 'Why not the other way around?'

Sandy sat up, 'Because . . .'

So they lay kissing gently, taking it more slowly than Miles thought he'd have had patience for. But the time created a space for his doubts. Hadn't he been awake crying in the night? Hadn't he called Poppy's name into his pillow and willed her, if nothing else, to call? And now he was back with Sandy conspiring to continue his infidelity. If there was a relationship left to dishonour.

The tea was brought by a handsome, sultry waiter whose glances towards the couple Miles found disparaging, as if the man had been sent to remind Miles of his sin. Miles tipped him generously, out of spite, and as soon as the waiter had closed the door Miles came up behind Sandy as she was pouring the tea and linked his arms around her waist. He kissed her neck. Sandy put down the pot, turned to his kiss.

'Wait, Miles!'

But he didn't want to wait, and he pulled her back to the bed. The tea went cold as they made love in the dimming afternoon. Miles feared throughout that this would be their last time. His suspicion imbued the act with an intensity Sandy did not feel herself. While inside her, she above, he closed his eyes and lay perfectly still for a while as if to encourage the sensation to seep through his cells to caves of memory that later he could traverse. And when he came, a sudden sadness spread through him and he drew Sandy close, squeezing her so tightly that she wondered what was happening in his mind.

Later, side by side, she said, 'What do you think's going to happen after Monday?'

'I don't know.'

Sandy leant her head on Miles's shoulder, 'Are you allowed to tell me what my chances are in the competition?'

'No.'

'Will you anyway?'

'We haven't decided yet. Not definitely.'

'But Tiziana's going to win, isn't she? Isn't she?'

'No, not necessarily.'

'Mmm! I can just see it, and then I'll have to go back to Miami and we'll probably never see each other again.'

Miles kissed the top of Sandy's head. 'Don't say that.'

'So what then?'

'I don't know.'

The phone rang. Miles suddenly feared that it might be Poppy, guessing he was there, tracking him down to make the separation final. Yet though it wasn't she, still Miles climbed out of bed and was almost dressed by the time Sandy was through.

'Why are you going?' she asked, sitting up.

'I have to get back.'

'That was Jessica. She said Fernando and Jack are in her room watching the news. You want to come?'

'No, no, I can't.'

Miles laced his shoes and sat by Sandy. He stroked her hair from her forehead. 'I'll try and call later.'

'Can I ring you?'

'Better not.'

He'd wanted to go but he didn't like leaving for it confused him more. And travelling home, Miles thought he'd learnt what he'd always denied: that it was possible to love two people at once; that Poppy and Sandy could live at once in his heart, occupying separate chambers, filling different needs. Was this selfishness on his part, or a heightened awareness of the capacity of his heart? Perhaps both; perhaps, he thought, I'm learning that life becomes worth living only when you start to bend its rules.

Though their reunion had not been easy, Senator Tristan Hunt was surprised by his son's good humour. Chester had emerged from the bedroom calm, as if in mind already of parole for good behaviour. He'd even answered his father's questions with uncharacteristic deference. Of course he'd maintained his innocence, and he had enquired from Jim Woolard of the chances of reasoning directly with Kristina (none), but otherwise he seemed to be accepting defeat with grace. The only conclusion his father could reach was that Chester had been shocked into something approaching maturity.

The Senator had been keen to keep the conversation away from the assault, and now, after an afternoon of claustrophobic tension, he suggested they should all go out for a drink after which Jim Woolard would go home for some much-needed sleep.

'Why don't you two go,' Chester suggested. 'I could do with some time alone.'

'I thought we'd go to get your mind off things, Chester.'

'Dad, how could I do that with people looking at me?'

'But I thought we might go to the club.'

'That's what I meant.'

It was upon opinions such as these that the two had used to argue, so the Senator capitulated, said he'd be back at seven thirty, and reluctantly left his son alone. From one of the penthouse windows Chester watched his father and lawyer as they climbed into a cab. Then he walked through to the study, cleared the desk with a sweep of his arm, and took from the drawer two sheets of paper. He sat, and removed the lid of his pen. Next he telephoned the offices of a reputable courier company.

'I need something taken to midtown, in about thirty minutes,' he said. He gave his address. 'It'll be going to the offices of the *New York Daily Herald*.'

'The *Herald*, please. Larry Meyers.'

A connection was made. 'Meyers.'

'Larry? It's Steve. Steve Barefoot.'

'What's cooking?'

'My ass, Larry. You'll never guess who I just had here.'

'The Long Island Strangler?'

'Close. Kristina.'

Meyers sat up from his slouch. As soon as news of the rape had come through he'd suspected that Kristina was Chester's 'victim', and after a few well-placed calls to the right cops he'd had this suspicion confirmed. So Meyers had told Jakes who'd told William Highton, the *Sunday Herald*'s editor, who'd agreed that Steve's story should be moved to a prominent page in the Sunday edition. Meyers wasn't about to make any direct links between Kristina and the rape, but the public weren't stupid. It would hardly take a genius to find the link between a violent rape involving handcuffs on the executive floor of the *Weissmans* offices, and a story about the *Weissmans* vice president, a Texan rancher, a six-million-dollar scam, and a treasure chest of whips, handcuffs, leather masks and chains.

'She came to your room?' said Meyers. 'Why?'

'I don't know why. She came all in a tizz saying like how she'd forget the two thousand dollars and buy me a ticket home if I never said anything to nobody about what happened between us.'

'What did you tell her?'

Steve laughed. 'I said "too late, Kristy!" I said "Larry Meyers knows it all."'

'And . . .?'

'And she was out of here faster than a bad curry.'

'Did she say where she was going?'

'No. She just ran like hell saying how I'd really fucked things up bad. I tell you,' Steve laughed, 'she didn't look too happy.'

'I bet she didn't.' Meyers was about to hang up when he said, 'Did you notice anything odd about her face?'

'Yeah. She had this big red scar all down one side but she wouldn't tell me why.'

'If I guess right, I think you'll be finding out pretty soon.' Meyers cut Steve's line, punched another, and dialled Brenda at the bar. He'd got into the habit of letting her know of his whereabouts recently.

'It's me. I'm not going to be there when I said. I think this Chester story's about to go up in flames.'

Jessica looked up. 'I mean you think you know someone!'

It was seven p.m., and in her smoke-filled room in the Midas, she, Sandy, Fernando and Jack were smoking spliff and drinking the minibar clean. The TV was turned on to CNN.

'I had to do the test shoot with him,' said Jack. 'He was getting turned on doing that. He even tried to touch my tits, and then in the cab he asked me to come back for a drink at his place.'

'Lucky you didn't,' Sandy said.

There was a murmur of agreement.

Jessica, who was rolling her tenth joint of the afternoon, looked at the others as she ran the glistening tip of her tongue down the edge of a Marlboro Light. Her speech had been slowing all afternoon, down to a London yawn. 'My friend

Neal from London said he worked with Chester in Milan and Chester used to fuck the boys down there.' Jessica split open the cigarette and tipped the tobacco into the open skins. 'I mean I'm not saying that he's gay, I'm just saying that he's sex-crazed. Obviously.'

Sandy was on the floor with legs splayed in a V. She was stretching, her hands on her feet, her back bent over her thighs. Her speech was punctuated by rhythmical grunts as she stretched as far as she could. 'I heard – he went weird – after his mother – died. He had – like a – breakdown – or something – dropped out of – college. I saw it once, on TV. That's when – he started growing – his hair.'

'I don't like his hair,' said Jack. 'Do you?'

Sandy sat up straight, back rigid. She worked on her neck now. 'Yeah, I think it's cool. It's kind of like the new surfer look in Miami. Loads of guys have it.'

'He looks like a girl to me,' said Jessica, tearing more cardboard from her massacred cigarette box. 'I was watching him on the Trudie Love show. I thought he looked like a girl.'

'You think he does it to other men, or that other men do it to him?' Jack wondered aloud.

'I'll ask Neal when I see him,' Jessica promised.

Jack pinched Fernando's arm. 'Do all male models do it with other guys?' she asked him in Spanish.

Fernando pulled his arm away. 'Man, you girls really are nasty.'

Fernando shook his head, and snapped his fingers with a flick of the wrist.

'Don't try to defend him,' said Sandy.

'I'm not! But still, you know? Maybe the woman she was asking for it.' There was a chorus of disagreement from the women. 'I mean,' Fernando argued, 'do you think Chester's like a violent guy?'

'You don't need to be violent, Fernando.' Sandy was standing now, touching her toes. Fernando liked the way her tits were hanging in her top. He could see the slight ridge of her nipples. 'You just got to be a man. All men are capable of rape. They've got one-track minds.'

'This is what I'm saying,' Fernando protested, 'if you listen! I think maybe she was half-naked saying, "Ooh, Chester, I like you Chester, you big boy Chester, kiss me Chester, you touch me Chester . . ." Then when he fuck her she surprised, you know? But come on! He's man! Once you start, heh, it's not easy to stop.'

Fernando whistled. Jessica thought this was funny. She got the giggles. She was trying to light the screwed paper teat of her joint but she couldn't, for as soon as she'd blown one match out with her laughter, she'd light another and with the fierce, cross-eyed concentration of the stoned, she'd follow the match to the joint, giggle again, blow it out and start all over. 'Ooh you big boy Chester!' she said, laughing. 'That's funny, Fernando. Hey, does anyone want to light this thing?'

Jack was leaning across to take the joint (Sandy wasn't smoking – she had a bottle of mineral water and a bag of dried apricots instead) when Fernando said, 'Look! It's him again.'

All but Jessica, who couldn't, focused on the news. They listened as Bobbie Battista did her thing.

'In New York, a startling and bizarre twist to the Chester Hunt story. In the last fifteen minutes the District Attorney's office has announced that all charges against the twenty-two-year-old son of Senator Tristan Hunt have been dropped. Shannon Seal has details.'

Shannon was back at 1 Hogan Place, at the Manhattan DA's office.

This announcement comes only hours after Assistant District Attorney Darryl Jonas told reporters that the city's case against Chester Hunt was, in his words, 'more solid than the White House'. It is believed that the victim, now named by police as thirty-nine-year-old Kristina von Koeler, has admitted to police that she herself

Ego

was partially responsible for the shocking events of last night. Miss von Koeler is the vice president of *Weissmans*, the company which last week flew Chester Hunt here from Paris to compete in a six-million-dollar competition to find a male model to advertise its soon-to-be-launched cologne. In a statement released earlier this afternoon Saul Weissman said that Chester has been disqualified from the competition. However, nothing has been heard from any of the parties involved since the latest development.

In the studio, Bobbie Battista was taking cues from her producer.

Shannon, are we to view this as a date that went too far?

'Bobbie, I think that's exactly it. From what I can gather this may have been a case of rough sexual activity turning into violence. I have already heard one prominent female journalist from the New York *Village Voice* speculating that Miss von Koeler dropped her charges because she didn't want to endure the humiliation of a court case when the law is so heavily slanted against the protection of women. It is very hard to prove rape beyond all reasonable doubt when the female victim has shown some initial willingness.'

'In other words, you can't change your mind if things turn nasty.'

'Exactly, Bobbie. I'm sure this decision by the DA's office is only going to add fuel to the fire already raging over the hot issue of these Date Rapes.'

'Shannon Seal in New York, thank you.'

In the Midas, the models were buzzing with excitement.

'With Kristina? Can you believe it?'

'I knew she was kinky,' said Jessica.

'She tried it on me once,' Fernando claimed.

'Oh, my God,' said Sandy. 'Can you imagine what Chester's feeling like now?'

But Chester didn't know. His 'TV' wasn't on, his telephone

495

was unplugged, his father was still out, about to leave his club having heard the news, wishing that he'd believed his son from the start, but still out all the same. And Chester was in the shower.

He'd just finished the explanations. One was for his father, the other for the world. That, sealed in an envelope, was waiting for collection from the doorman downstairs.

Chester washed thoroughly. Then he dried himself, combed his hair and tied it in a ponytail, picked out fresh underwear, a newly laundered white shirt, his favourite pants, shoes and jacket, and took a long look at himself in the mirror.

There were no tears.

Chester then walked to the window overlooking the street. He looked at his watch. His father was a punctual man. He'd said he'd be back at seven thirty. It was almost twenty to eight.

Chester waited, his mind miraculously free. He thought the Empire State Building looked too gaudy in pink lighting. His apartment was understated in its interiors. It was his mother's way. He preferred that. He looked down again.

A cab pulled up. Was it him? Yes, yes, it was.

Chester moved fast. Taking with him the portrait of his mother that stood on the piano he ran out on to the balcony and screamed at the top of his voice.

'Dad! Dad! Up here. Dad!'

The Senator looked up at his son. His innocent son. He smiled and waved and was glad that Chester must have heard the news. Chester waved back.

And then he jumped.

Kristina wanted to be alone, but Weissman had somehow got inside the building and had surprised her at the door. She slippered her way to the fish-eye lens and was silent, as if she wasn't in, but Saul was leaning on the doorbell. As ever, he was convinced that he was doing the right thing. He'd come, she saw, bearing gifts. A wise man she no longer thought him, but he was sweet, and good, and so she let him inside. It could be their farewell.

'I heard you dropped the case,' he said.

Kristina continued to fold the pale blue cashmere cardigan she had in her hand. 'I couldn't face a trial, Saul.'

'I hate to see the little shit getting away with it, that's all.' Weissman suddenly noticed Kristina's suitcase. 'Hey, what's this?'

'I want to get out of the city for a couple of days.'

'Are you outta your mind? With only two days until the party?'

'Look at my face, Saul! I couldn't go. Think what people would say.'

Weissman held up his hands. 'What are you talking about? It's very hip to be a victim in New York these days. You're gonna be showered with dinner invitations.'

'What?' Truly, Kristina was incredulous.

Weissman sat on the arm of the couch. 'Scars are good, Kristy. Very nineties. They give you minority status and, believe me, that's a department you're lacking in.' As if lost in his thought, Weissman then began to unwrap the chocolates he'd brought. 'I mean, you're not black, you're not a lesbian, you're not even Jewish. Rape victim's good.' He threw a chocolate in his mouth.

Kristina bent to tighten the strap on her case. 'I can't believe you want me to stay in the city because it's trendy to be a rape victim.'

Weissman was struggling with the chocolate in his mouth. A caramel, harder than he'd expected. When he opened his mouth, a string of dribble accidentally slooped out. He wiped at it with his hand. 'All I'm saying is that you don't have to run away. No one's surprised you didn't want to go through with a trial like that.' He held out the chocolates. 'Here, I bought these for you.'

Kristina took the chocolates with a word of thanks. She'd be leaving them here, and they'd go stale and white before she returned. There were so many things Weissman didn't yet know. 'Saul,' she said, 'I'm going out soon and my flight's first thing tomorrow morning.'

'Is that a hint?' Kristina said nothing and looked away, when

Saul stood. He touched her on the arm. 'Some of us are still on your side, sweetheart.'

Kristina offered him a half-smile, and a nod. Anything more would have ended in tears.

'You haven't even told me where you're going.'

'To Florida. Just for a few days.'

Weissman pointed at her. 'Make sure you call if you need anything. Patty says the same. She says you're probably suffering from one of those victim syndromes.'

'Tell her thanks. I'll be fine.'

Saul bunched his fingers into two fists and tapped one on top of the other. 'You sure?'

Kristina nodded. What could she say? No, because when you find out about Steve I won't even have you? A knot as large as one of Saul's fists was lumped in her throat.

'We'll see you back soon, then.' He turned away. 'Oh, what am I doing? I need to know what you think about the models?'

'What models?'

'See? What did I say? You're not with it. The EDEN models, Kristy. The models we've been around the world looking for!'

'What about them?'

'Do you agree the Italians should win?'

'Saul, I . . .'

The ringing of her phone interrupted Kristina. Saul was beside it and, without thinking, he reached down and picked it up. 'Yeah, she's here. Yes, it's me . . . Oh Miles, hi.'

Kristina watched the pupils of Weissman's eyes dart about the room as he listened. Then he hung up. He was silent. Kristina took a step forward. 'What, Saul? What?'

Weissman was shaking his head. 'That stupid, stupid schmuck!'

'Who?'

'Our friend Chester's just thrown himself off of a building.'

Kristina felt her knees weaken. She took hold of the back of a chair. She didn't want to know any more, but she had to ask. 'And . . .?'

'And he died as soon as he hit the sidewalk.'

Miles hung up from Weissman and walked to the fridge to get himself a Rolling Rock. He couldn't believe it. Why? Why had Chester done it? Suicide was something that happened to other people's friends, to soul-torn poets, to cowards. And which of these was Chester? Miles slumped on to the sofa and stared at the ceiling. He remembered the lunch in Paris when Georgina Kemble-Finch had called Chester the least happy man she knew, but Miles had never seen this melancholia. Chester had been a fun-loving man, hadn't he? It wasn't as if his pursuit of happiness had been in vain. He'd always been finding the good times. So why? Why?

And then Miles began to wonder how much he himself was to blame. If he had not invited Chester to join the competition then Chester would have been alive. It was a horrible thought. Hadn't it been he himself who'd introduced Chester to Kristina? Miles began to wonder what had gone on that night. Until the shock of hearing Kristina's name on TV it hadn't occurred to Miles that she was the victim, but now he doubted she had been victimised at all. He decided he'd write to the Senator explaining that Kristina derived pleasure from sexual violence. But if she'd wanted it, why would she have accused Chester of rape? Maybe he raped her from desperation. Miles wondered if he'd ever led Chester to believe he'd win. Maybe after the Trudie Love result he'd bolstered Chester's hopes. He didn't know. He couldn't remember. All he kept seeing was an image of Chester treading water in Paolo Carsagna's swimming pool, a champagne bottle held above his head, a grin splashed over his face. And now he was dead.

Miles wanted to talk to someone. He wished Poppy hadn't gone. She'd always been there when he needed her. He couldn't believe that she'd gone. Maybe, he thought, it'd help to be with Sandy. At least she'd known Chester, and Miles had promised to call. She'd said she was visiting a friend uptown. Miles had written the number down, but he couldn't remember where. He walked to the desk beneath the window to look. He could picture the scrap of paper he'd written the number on, but he couldn't find it. Then he saw an envelope he recognised. From it he took the letter he'd written to Poppy from Miami Beach. He began to read.

It was a love letter, nothing less. In its three pages Miles had written again and again of how much he loved her, of how much he'd miss her while he was away, of how he couldn't imagine ever wanting to be apart. He read it twice to himself, and the memory of how he had felt on the beach became so potent that he began to feel the same again. It was impossible to fall out of love so fast. What had he been thinking? He wanted to call Poppy and tell her. He rang Clare's number, when Poppy was staying, Clare answered.

'It's Miles. Can I speak to Poppy?'

'Hang on.' There was a pause, then Clare was back on the line. 'She says she'll call tomorrow.'

'Can you tell her I just need to say one thing.'

Another pause. Clare again. 'She promises she'll call tomorrow.'

Miles hesitated, said, 'OK,' hung up, checked in his wallet for cash, and put on his coat to take the subway uptown.

Dad

It's six and the sun's gone down and it's weird that I'll never see it again. It looked very beautiful tonight.

I've dreamt up this letter a million times before. I used to think I'd discover some poetry if I knew I was going to die, but it hasn't come. You'd say that was the story of my life, wouldn't you? Me trying to reach horizons that were too far away. But I can't face that any more. I've never understood the point of going on simply to be sad most of the time.

Tristan Hunt was shaking so much that he had to pause before he read on. It was four a.m., the day after Chester's suicide. The first day in a lifetime of painful anniversaries. Virginia had flown up from Washington and was sleeping next door, but he'd woken and got up to read the letter again. Now he laid it flat on the desk Chester had cleared, and tried to focus on the rushed and uneven lettering through his brimming tears.

I wish you'd believed me about the rape. Somehow – after all the hating – that really mattered to me. But you just talked about trying to get me off. We're not all guilty, Dad. How could you think I'd have done something like that? How? We're not all you.

I've got some money in Paris. Give it to my art school. Say sorry and I love you to Grandma. And sorry.

I bet you won't understand this, but I haven't been happy since Mom. Only the hope of something good coming along kept me going. But it can't come now. Not when I go to jail. Everything I want now is out there, wherever there is. The peace of nothing to cry about.

No time! Can't think that's ever meant much until now.

One thing more. You could have stopped it all. Not just me, but Mom as well. She knew about you and Virginia. She drove straight into that car. She said sorry.

Not just her but me – if you'd showed you cared, maybe.

At least now I'll be happy. The blackness has never sounded so good. Can you understand? Nothing is everything I could possibly want.

You'll be back soon and I meant to say lots of things more.

It's much better like this. I swear. Say sorry to Grandma. Tell her I'll be happy now.

Because I will.

Chester

36

Miles kicked closed the front door of his apartment with the back of his foot. The gesture spoke most often of high spirits, but today it came from necessity, his hands being filled with blueberry muffins, milk, and forty dollars worth of flowers. He'd have liked to have stayed in bed, but he was working that Sunday morning, responsible for ensuring that the models showed up for their last *Weissmans* store appearance before the following day's result.

Miles called up to the loft bed. 'I bought muffins. You want one?'

'In a minute,' groaned Poppy. 'Come back to bed!'

Miles glanced at his watch, and then undressed. For the moment, he didn't want to refuse Poppy a thing.

He'd taken the subway to see her as soon as he'd got off the phone. She'd been angry at first, but this had turned to sympathy when he'd talked about Chester and of how much he was missing her. 'You won't learn anything if you don't hurt,' she'd said, but at last she'd agreed to come home for the night. Now she was glad she had.

Miles joined Poppy back in bed. A thought of Sandy crossed his mind, but he didn't equate Sandy with this kind of domesticity. His affair with her belonged in hotel rooms, on beaches, away from a place called home.

Poppy slid her foot over to his. Having trod already on the street it had lost the malleable floppiness Poppy liked about morning bodies. It pleased her that during the night their bodies would find a shared temperature, as if communing. Now Miles was already in an altered state, his body belonged to the new day.

Yet for now it also belonged to her. Poppy didn't consider

it weakness on her part to have returned so soon. She still loved Miles. She couldn't purge herself of desire because of what he'd done behind her back. What if her eye had never seen . . . She would have been happy in her ignorance. She would have been in bed with Miles now. There would not have been the pain.

Yet it was the cause of Miles's infidelity that troubled Poppy. It had never occurred to her to be unfaithful while she remained in love with Miles. Did that mean, then, that he was no longer in love with her? The trial would come during the next few days, when she'd have to decide whether to stay or to go.

Miles drew Poppy close to him. She was resting her head on his upper chest. He too was wondering about what had happened between them, and what was yet to evolve. Of course, splashing about in the whirlpool of his mind were thoughts much different from hers. Miles felt born again, and as with any convert, he'd become blind to the beliefs of those who disagreed. He thought it was stubbornness and prejudice that prevented Poppy from enjoying those things he'd come to appreciate since the trip – nightclubs, models, designer clothes, happening restaurants. Working as an assistant for Legal Aid, Poppy had developed this bullshit holier-than-thou attitude about those kinds of things. Especially about models. As if there was something *wrong* with people making money from their looks! Poppy had had instilled in her this notion that we should all chip in to make the world a better place. But for whom? If, in its screwed-up state, the world was treating you kindly, what was the point in changing it?

And that was what he thought of his relationship with Poppy. No, it wasn't perfect, but in its slightly screwed-up state it worked well enough to survive. And if there were injustices, they were minor and could be swept beneath the carpet. In years to come something might give, but for now what they had was better than having nothing at all.

Miles felt for Poppy's naked breasts. When they made love they did so slowly, with an awareness of each other that had been lacking for months.

Afterwards, Miles brought Poppy the muffins and fresh coffee, the flowers and the papers. The tabloids led on Chester's fall. Miles left the paper with Poppy as he showered. When he was out, Poppy called to him. 'M, you're in the paper.'

'Am I? Where?'

Poppy came down from their bed. Miles had never understood why her hair remained so perfect throughout the night. Was it a reflection, perhaps, of how comfortable she felt within her own skin.

'It's big news,' said Poppy. 'There's this article all about Kristina von Koeler.'

Miles took the paper from her and began to read. The article was headlined **Eden's Snake**, and it was the most shocking thing that Miles Jensen had ever read.

Being a supermodel, Tiziana Ferrari often claimed, was not as easy as it looked.

This was a lie, of course. It *was* as easy; perhaps more so. But it wasn't always fun. As a supermodel, Tiziana did what she'd always done as a model: she posed. She posed in studios, on beaches and catwalks, before mirrors and clients and royalty, in restaurants, with boyfriends, alone. All that stardom had brought was more of what she'd had before – more jobs, more stylists, more admirers, more assistants, more enemies, more money, more early starts, more plane rides, more hangers-on, more people asking interminable questions for themselves, their friends, their magazines, their papers. Did she keep the clothes, they'd ask, drink water, love God, play opera, eat chocolate, want children, respect American Indians, crave junk food? What about exercise, politics, nose-jobs, abortion, moisturiser, AIDS, ordinary friends, the planet? Had she found childhood traumatic, dieting easy, adolescence tense, love a struggle, sushi a joy? Was Clinton right, racism wrong, Buddha a choice, acting an option? Where did she live, shop, eat, breathe, sleep, fuck, hurt? And did she care what she said because they'd write what they wanted irrespective of her replies? For what can you know of yourself, they'd sneer, being such a brazen, coy, unpretentious, vain, shy, brash, generous, mean, haughty, reserved, warm, noble, sensitive, pedestrian, sacrosanct gem? Nothing, except that the world thinks your bone structure sublime, and is making you rich for it.

More money, more questions, less chance of comprehending life.

Tiziana was applying her make-up – natural, she'd told *Seventeen*'s editor the week before, with tinted moisturiser and loose powder, eyebrow pencil (always, always) and lip gloss. Giovanni was dressed downstairs in the silky chicness of a wealthy Italian. He was calling for her to come. They'd been tiffing in Italian, the language of argument.

'Come on, Miles said we should be there at twelve.'

'Giovanni,' Tiziana shouted, 'what's the point of me being famous if I can't be late?'

'I hate that kind of attitude.'

'That's because you're a fascist. Anyway, you told me before that I wouldn't have to do anything for the competition except Bruce Stone's test.'

'I didn't know about this before. Come on, Tiziana! We're going to get seven million dollars for this.'

'You maybe!'

Giovanni was urging his sister to hurry for the gathering of the EDEN models that was about to begin. Weissman had seen the opportunity of eking out some extra publicity from the finalists while they were still in New York at his beck and call. The mere fact of having one of the world's great supermodels in his store on the third Sunday before Christmas – for free – was in itself something of a coup, and certainly ample return for the investment he'd made so far in the models. Tiziana knew this, and there was no way she was going to hurry.

After reading the Meyers article in the *Herald*, Miles had wondered whether there would even be an event for her to hurry to. The astonishing revelations contained within the paper (coming so soon after news of Chester's suicide) had cast in his mind such a shadow over the EDEN competition that Miles had wondered whether Weissman would throw in the towel. He'd telephoned Weissman only to discover that he, as with all life's great achievers, was refusing to be daunted. 'I want them there promptly,' he'd said, 'I want them smiling, I want them looking excited about tomorrow, and I want them talking about the best cologne this world has ever seen.'

With that, he'd hung up the phone.

Tiziana Ferrari came down the stairs. She was wearing an outfit designed by the photographer Fabrizio Ferri.

'Did you see this?' asked Giovanni as he held up a copy of the *Sunday Herald*.

'Yes, I'm not happy!'

Tiziana knew that it was part of her job as a supermodel to stay well clear of the swamps.

'Don't be stupid!' Giovanni said, 'it's only about Chester Hunt and the other men.'

'Exactly!' Tiziana replied. 'That's what I don't like. I'm Tiziana, and I'm being upstaged!'

When Giovanni opened the apartment door he looked for the ironic smile, but was dismayed to see that one had not crossed his sister's famous, glistening lips.

The man sitting in seat 32B on the flight from New York City to Hamburg kept looking up from his *Sunday Herald* at the woman by his side. Her profile, he thought, was strikingly similar to that in the photograph on page two. But it couldn't be! After all that had happened in Manhattan she would surely not be on a flight to Germany. And yet the likeness was bizarre.

The man finished the detailed article about Chester's arrest and suicide. Then he turned the page. On pages four and five there were yet more photographs of Kristina von Koeler – Kristina at a charity function with Saul Weissman; Kristina with the EDEN finalists at Rudy's Fish and Grill; And then, beneath the article by Pulitzer-winning journalist Larry Meyers, a polaroid of Kristina in chains on her bed, a black bar obscuring her pubic hair. The man turned his head. She was looking at him! It was her, he was sure. But he was embarrassed now so he lowered his eyes to read. After all, he was curious to discover how the woman by his side had earned her title as the Snake of Eden.

It's a story worthy of a movie or a book. A tale of sexual perversion, duplicity, greed and deceit.

And now of death.

Only this tale is true.

It began in September of last year. On a balmy autumn evening a young man by the name of Steve Barefoot was assigned the duty of welcoming to the Yee-Haw Adventure Ranch near Dallas the twelve guests for the week. Among them was a tall, beautiful woman called Kristina von Koeler.

Kristina von Koeler had been made the vice-president of *Weissmans Inc.* eight years previously, at the age of thirty-one. She was Saul Weissman's closest confidante and friend.

In time, she would be his Judas.

Steve Barefoot's job on the ranch was to teach the guests the fundamentals of ranching. Although the guests were required to be accomplished riders, as soon as Steve saw Kristina dressed in her designer clothes, with her jewellery and her polished nails, he knew she'd spell trouble. But never in his wildest dreams could he have imagined how much trouble she would bring.

Steve says: 'I was real surprised that Kristina was so good with the horses. It made me respect her.'

In fact, growing up as the privileged daughter of wealthy first generation German immigrants near Greenwich, Connecticut, Kristina was a keen horsewoman by the age of ten. It was a skill that never left her, a skill that caught Steve Barefoot's eye.

Steve: 'I thought something so beautiful riding so well must have been sent from Heaven.'

Or had she come from Hell?

After five days at the ranch, Kristina von Koeler took her young instructor to the stables and seduced him.

Steve Barefoot is a typical young white Texan. He votes Republican. He believes in God. He's none too kind about blacks and gays, feminists, abortions, politicians or city folk. But he's honest. OK, at six foot two and with the face of a Hollywood idol he's much more handsome than your average rancher, but he's still a young man from Texas.

And he was no match for a hardened, cynical New Yorker like Kristina. 'She asked me to show her the stables,' Steve says, 'and as soon as we get there she suggests we make love.'

Steve admits that he was awe-struck and a little intimidated by the elegant Kristina, so when she told him to tie her up with riding tackle he went along with her. What Steve could never have known was that he was tying the knots around himself.

The affair continued for the week Kristina was in Texas. 'We built up a routine, ' he says. 'Always in the stables, always tying her up during sex, always in the daytime when we could easily have been caught.' Why did this handsome young man who'd never been short of admirers fall for a woman of nearly forty? 'Simply,' Steve says, 'because she was far and away the fieriest lover I'd ever known.'

And by the day Kristina was to leave, Steve Barefoot had fallen in love. He thought he'd never see Kristina again. 'But then she asked me to spend the weekend in Dallas.'

Kristina rented the Penthouse Suite in the Five Star Moore Hotel. On the second night, reclining in the jacuzzi after the couple had made steamy love, Kristina made a suggestion that has changed Steve's life. *Weissmans*, she said, was about to launch a cologne called EDEN and she was looking for the model.

Steve: 'It was like something right out of that show *Dallas*. She said she'd persuaded Saul Weissman to pay the model seven million dollars, and that she could get me the job if we split the money fifty-fifty.'

Steve Barefoot was a happy, young man who, in his own words 'had never dreamt of being rich. I already had pretty much everything I'd dreamed of.' But Kristina's offer was too tempting, and he agreed to join her in New York. Steve quit his job without notice and was told he wouldn't be welcome back. He didn't expect to be. Using the ticket Kristina had sent, he left for Manhattan. 'I never much liked the city, but I thought it would all be worth it in the end. Kristina was so sure.'

But Kristina von Koeler was too cunning for her own good. Her boss, Saul Weissman, was happy to entrust the search for the EDEN model to Kristina. But according to Steve, Kristina wanted to distance herself from the process, so she pulled an inexperienced store assistant from *Weissmans* on Madison Avenue and sent him around the world to look for the EDEN model.

'She thought he'd screw up. All the time she was planning on using me. But the first problem came when Miles went to Miami. See . . .'
'Excuse me.'

The man in seat 32B looked up. Kristina was standing, wanting to get out. The man watched her pass. Nice ass! I'd tie her up if she asked, he thought. He twisted his neck and followed her with his eyes. Then he read on.

Steve had told Meyers everything. The article explained how Kristina had plotted to have Steve included in the final line-up. It described in detail their sexual encounters. It revealed how Kristina and Steve had tricked Miles in London, how from that moment on Steve had thought the contract was his. Meyers wrote of Steve's disappointment when he returned to New York to find Reuben chosen, of Steve's subsequent hope when Fabio was attacked, and of how Steve burst in on the Trudie Love show when Troy Turnbull, the Madonna of the modelling world, was drafted in at the last moment. It was then, Meyers wrote, after Kristina had turfed him out without a word or a dime, that Steve decided to sell his story.

Kristina returned to her seat. The man turned to her.
'Do you live in Germany?' he asked.

Kristina pulled out a magazine from the seat pocket as she answered, 'No, I'm visiting.'

'Business?'

'Yes.'

'Oh, what kind?'

'Immigration law.'

Kristina ignored the man and looked down to read. He returned to the article.

The story could have ended there, but Kristina wasn't about to give up without a fight.

Only this time the fight ended in death.

Yesterday evening I received by messenger a note from Chester Hunt. It was written moments before his suicide. It's a short letter written by a desperate young man who thought he was going to jail for a crime he didn't commit. He wanted me to investigate the details and set the record straight. In his note, Chester says Kristina was trying to find a way to share the spoils of the EDEN contract. He thinks she resorted to blackmail, pleading to be tied up with ropes and handcuffs beneath a security camera. Again and again Chester told his story to the police, but they didn't believe him. Why should they? They didn't know about Kristina's past.

If they'd known about Steve Barefoot, then a life might have been saved. I approached the DA's office with this information, but was told to wait until Monday.

But Monday was too late for Chester Hunt.

As the man settled himself into seat 32B to read about the night Kristina had tempted Chester, he glanced briefly to his side and wondered if that was a tear he saw bulging in the corner of Kristina's left eye as she turned her head from him and fixed her eyes on some elusive spot on the horizon.

The star of the show was late. By the time Tiziana arrived at *Weissmans* on Madison, the rest of the models had assembled behind a table and before a heap of jostling lenses on the store's sprawling first floor. She was in time for the photographers. What she'd missed was a rousing pep talk from a belligerent Saul Weissman.

Miles had been impressed by Weissman's tough stance on the phone, but when he'd caught sight of the great man entering the store with his shoulders drooped and his neck sunken, the image had told a different story. Though usually a man who appeared to need his corpulence to sustain his rapacious character, Weissman had arrived at his store with the tramp of someone regretting having eaten too much lunch; for sixty years. There'd been a distressing sluggishness to his movements and language. When he'd spoken to Miles about Kristina's duplicity he'd done so with the hesitant vocabulary of a man who'd suddenly discovered that he'd only six months left to live.

Yet Weissman had dug deep for his speech, and discovered gold. He spoke with great affection of Chester, the man who only the day before he'd threatened to kill. He dismissed Kristina with humorous jibes. And he managed to inject fresh excitement into the competition:

"Just remember that none of this shit flying around ever touched any of you guys. You're the beautiful ones, you're the ones still in the chase, and two of you will be the ones to get the seven million bucks!"

This wasn't strictly true, of course. The two Italian beneficiaries of Saul Weissman's largess hadn't even bothered to show.

But they did at last arrive. By then Weissman had also spoken to the assembled media about Chester and Kristina. He'd been dealing with the vultures long enough to know they'd quit snapping if their stomachs were full, and that they never much cared what they were eating so long as they could crap it out as news. Weissman's great concern was to shift the focus back to EDEN and the competition. And in this respect, Tiziana's arrival was perfectly timed. There was not one camera that didn't turn on her when she arrived, not a shop assistant who didn't raise an eyelash glutinous with mascara, not a child who didn't tug on a sleeve and point and say, 'Tell me, Mummy, who's that?'

Some men would have drowned in the wake, but Giovanni Ferrari rode the crest of this supermodel's wave. Perhaps it was the inner knowledge that for this cologne, for this campaign, he would be the man who'd be making most of the money, all of the waves. He possessed the aura of a winner, and those around accepted this without understanding why.

Yet there was one man who was deeply troubled by Giovanni's cavalier attitude.

Troy Turnbull had rolled the sleeves of his T-shirt back to display his musculature. His only task for the day was to hand out the T-shirts, to look as good as he always thought he did and to sign a few autographs here and there. Up until the arrival of the Italians he'd been enjoying all the attention. Troy wasn't bothered by Chester's death. In fact, the publicity he was getting was great. So too was this chance to meet the public. Only the female models enjoyed the feedback he desired. So what if most people within the business considered him the world's number one male model if he wasn't going to be celebrated by the public? How many grand parties had *he* been invited to because of his career? How many movie stars were waiting to take *his* hand in marriage? It was disgusting the way the male-model stars were treated. Perhaps, just perhaps, the sum to be paid the EDEN model would change that. Six million dollars said a lot about a person's worth.

Troy Turnbull had no doubts that he was the most beautiful man in the store, and as such he was confident he'd win. Not only was Troy inexperienced in losing large campaigns, but also the word in the agencies was that his other competitors were in the final simply for the PR, and that all along *Weissmans* had been intending to use an experienced model. And wasn't Troy the only candidate? The other guys wouldn't even know how to pose. It took some skill. Besides, he'd already worked with Tiziana. They had modelled Donna Karan's show together, and they'd been photographed for

Eugénie in the fall. In Troy's eyes, everything pointed to his success.

But there was one threat, and it was at him that Troy was directing his gaze – Mr Slick-Git Ferrari. Troy despised him. He hated his quiet arrogance, his understated smugness, his unquestionable appeal. But most of all he hated the way Giovanni acted as if he knew *he* would win.

Giovanni shook hands with Weissman who, like many of the models, was wearing an EDEN T-shirt. Fernando had delighted the photographers by stripping to his bare chest to don his. Jack was braless beneath her sweater, and wasn't wearing a Tee, but all the rest were. But when Weissman handed Giovanni his T-shirt, the Italian merely bunched it in his right hand and joined the models behind the table. He stood next to Troy.

'You should put that on, you know,' said Troy as another shopper passed in the line in front to pick up her free shirt.

'I don't want to,' replied Giovanni.

'You think Saul Weissman will appreciate that?'

'I don't care. This T-shirt is very ugly.'

'It's an improvement on yours,' said Troy referring to Giovanni's beige brushed cotton Romeo Gigli shirt.

'I not surprised you think like this. The T-shirt is very American. Very lacking in style.'

'Yeah, well. You'll see about style tomorrow!'

'Oh yes, my friend. We will.'

In Troy's eyes, Giovanni's smile was so cocky and superior that he longed to punch him in the teeth. But of course he held back, and smiled, and relaxed his fist, and wondered if the curvy vein at his temple was bulging to trouble the perfection of his face.

Weissman didn't notice. He was pleased by the way things were going. The models were looking great – Jessica looked a little sick, maybe, but that was part of her kooky appeal. Helima was absolutely devastating. Really she deserved to win, he thought. She was so refined. Andrea looked serene today, Sandy by contrast was vibrant, happy and healthy-looking. Jack was being quiet (mysterious, Weissman hoped they'd call it) and Tiziana, well she was Tiziana. For all her complaints, she knew what she was here to do. If her brother was right, and he swore with his life that he was, she'd already been chosen by Weissman. The knowledge, then, that another million dollars was coming her way made it just a little easier to stand and smile for the cameras, most of which were focused upon her.

When the rabble had left the models began to drift home. Giovanni and Tiziana left first. As agreed on the phone, they didn't speak to Miles. With all the suspicions the Kristina saga had raised, the last thing Miles wanted was to be seen conspiring with the Italians. Miles had no such reservations about talking to Reuben. He was feeling quite sorry for him. If Fernando could keep quiet about Best Burger for a couple more days, he would become a rich man. And Miles was convinced that Fabio was on the verge of success as a model, as soon as his injuries healed. But what was in store for Reuben? Nothing but the fall back to earth. Reuben didn't seem too concerned. 'Any chance of getting a discount for my Christmas shopping?' he asked Miles.

'I don't know, you'd better ask the boss.'

'OK,' he smiled. 'He seems pretty generous. Did you see that TV he gave to Fabio?'

'No.'

'The one he's had there most the week.'

'I . . . I haven't been to see him.'

'Oh! Well it's nice. I'll see ya later, Miles.'

Fabio! Miles felt terrible about him. Miles had been so caught up in the tornado of events over the last few days that Fabio and the attack had gone clear out of his mind. He decided right away to go to visit him at the hospital. He was heading for the exit when he felt a hand on his shoulder.

'Miles.'

Damn! Sandy had been chatting with Helima when Miles had tried to make his escape. She must have eyes in the back of her head, he thought.

'Miles! Where are you going so fast?'

515

'I'm late meeting someone.'

'You said you'd call last night.'

'I know.'

He gazed at her. He couldn't remember having noticed the way her nose turned up at the end before. And she had this annoying way of angling her face down and then looking up with her eyes.

Sandy took a step back, rocked on her heels, glanced around. 'Do you want to come over later?'

'I don't think I can. Not tonight.'

'And probably not tomorrow either, right?'

He paused. 'Probably not!'

'And on Tuesday I'm going back to Miami.'

'Sandy,' Miles paused, lowered his voice, 'what do you want me to do about it?'

'I don't know. I don't know. I guess . . .'

'What?'

'I guess I expected you to care.'

Sandy turned to leave, and though he clasped a hand around her arm Miles said everything by saying nothing. They looked at one another for a moment longer before Sandy turned once more to walk away. Miles watched her go, remembering how he'd longed for her on that first night, and wondering how now he could possibly let her go.

Beneath the draining white of the hospital lights Fabio sat up in bed and smiled his flawed smile when Miles appeared carrying fruit. To Miles's great surprise, Larry Meyers was standing by Fabio's hospital bed. Meyers seemed to be getting everywhere these days. He and Miles had developed a certain friendship since the crustiness of their first meeting, and Miles shook Larry's hand and congratulated him on his startling piece. He asked Fabio how he was.

Fabio nodded. 'I feel fine.'

Fabio's face was very far from being recovered, but he looked much better than he had four days before. His left eye was now open, and though his lips were cut and bruised they were not so swollen. He remained partially toothless, and was still being fed through a drip.

'I dropped by to give Fabio some good news,' said Meyers. 'I just learned that the NYPD know who attacked him.'

'Wow! That's great. I thought these kinds of things usually went unresolved.'

'They do.' Meyers tapped the unlit cigarette he was holding on the back of his left hand. 'Only this time they got a lucky break through another case.'

'Did they make any arrests yet?'

'No, they want to piece it all together first.'

'It'd be great if they arrested them on the day of the result, wouldn't it?'

'You think so?' said Meyers. 'Way I see it, you and your boss don't need any more distractions.'

Fabio spoke up. 'I invited to party. Should I stay or should I go?'

'You have to come,' said Miles. 'Only maybe tomorrow won't be the night for picking up the girls.'

Fabio lifted his hands in exasperation, and smiled again. Miles thought Fabio resembled a character from a movie set in the Dark Ages. The toothless village idiot. He sported the same expression of blissful ignorance. Meyers patted the blanket covering Fabio's foot.

'Don't worry – you'll get the broody ones. Manhattan's full of them. Anyway, I heard you did all your seducing from the waist down.'

The battered smile again. Meyers cocked his head at Miles. 'So, spare us the suspense. Tell us who's won.'

'Are you kidding? Telling you would be like writing it in neon in Times Square!'

Meyers shrugged. 'I know anyway.'

'You do?'

'Yeah! 10–1 on says the Italian playboy and his impover-ished little sister get the pocket money. That's what could go in Times Square.' Meyers spread a palm through the air in front of his face. '"EDEN: For the Way the World Turns!" You think that'd be good?'

'Who says they're going to win?'

Meyers held out his hand. 'I'll bet you ten thousand bucks I'm right.'

'That wouldn't be ethical,' Miles said.

'Sure it would,' Meyers replied. 'But it wouldn't be very smart!'

37

Nothing stood in his way now. Nothing, nothing, nothing. It was seven a.m. and Monday mornings weren't supposed to feel this good. It was like waking up to winning the Lotto. A million dollars! And all because a stunning Italian man had swanned into the right nightclub at the right time.

Miles lay with his hands latticed behind his head. Could anything go wrong now? Weissman was crazy enough to change his mind at the drop of a hat, but who was left to take Giovanni's place? Did any of the others have a realistic chance? Weissman had been making some frightening noises about Fabio (who remained the great man's favourite contestant) but when Miles had seen Fabio the day before he'd been encouraged by the sight. There wasn't a hope in hell that Fabio would be mended by the end of the following month.

Beside him, Poppy groaned and stirred. Miles thought about the party that night. Both Poppy and Sandy would be there. He wondered how easy it would be. The thought further awakened him. He'd had enough of this endless plotting and scheming and deceiving. Now the past he'd had with Poppy was taking on a golden hue. Miles stroked a hand across her cheek.

'Hey,' Poppy said sleepily, without opening her eyes.

Miles surprised her with a kiss on the lips. 'I have to get up,' he said.

'OK.'

'You are coming tonight, aren't you? I think we're going to be on the top table.'

A hum of acquiescence came from Poppy's mouth.

'Pop, talk to me! You promise you're not going to back out on me again.'

Poppy opened her eyes. The sullen early-morning light offered no encouragement to begin a new day. Poppy was thinking of how hard it would be to be enthusiastic and beautiful at the party that night. But by now she did want to meet all the people who'd taken over Miles's life. All but one!

'Is Sandy going to be there?'

Miles propped himself up on an elbow. 'Of course!'

'Is she going to win?'

'No.'

'Promise?'

Miles kissed Poppy again. 'I promise. In fact, that should prove something to you. If I'd wanted her to win I could have made her win easily.'

'So who has won?'

'You'll find out tonight.'

'If it's Sandbag I'm out of here for good, OK?'

Miles laughed. 'OK. And if it isn't?'

She paused. 'Then it isn't.'

Miles took a shower. Poppy was up by the time he dressed. As he was leaving the apartment, she called after him. 'Miles. You didn't dry your hair properly.'

Miles felt the back of his head, returned to give Poppy a kiss, and then left to meet his boss.

The boss was veiled in sunlight as Rona ushered Miles inside. He was seated at his grand office desk, head down, hands woven at the back of his neck. The top of his bald head was a bearded, featureless face welcoming Miles. He didn't look up to address his young employee. 'Remember the day you first walked in here?'

Miles sat. 'Yes, Saul.'

Then he waited for the pearl of Weissman wisdom. And waited. The longest silence Miles had known with Weissman. Two minutes or more before Weissman slowly lifted his head. He looked almost surprised to find Miles with him.

'Yeah,' he said, 'so do I.' Another silence, then: 'And I've been trying to figure out what would've happened if I'd never seen your ugly mug. Huh?'

Miles was getting edgy. What was he supposed to say? Weissman was staring at Miles with such intensity that he felt he had to say something. He opened his mouth, 'I . . .'

'See, Miles, I think you're the guy who took the flame to the fireworks store. One minute everything's fine and dandy, the next . . .' Weissman threw up his arms, '. . . BOOM! Like Naga-fucking-saki. You with me?'

Weissman felt in his drawer, took out a solid silver nutcracker and carefully positioned a walnut in its elbow. A bullet in a gun. Staring at Miles, he squeezed the cracker in his right hand. His face turned red from the exertion. The walnut stayed whole. Weissman's knuckles whitened. He lowered the cracker to his waist and used both hands. Suddenly the nut splintered across the desk and floor. A chip landed in Miles's lap but he didn't like to brush it off. Weissman swore and threw the cracker across the room. Then he picked out a few stray nuggets of nut by pressing down on them with his thumb, and taking his thumb to his mouth. After what seemed to Miles to be an eternity, Weissman once again pointed his finger and said, 'If we'd never met then I'd have never known about Chester, or Spencer, or Fabio, and Kristina's good-looking friend from Texas would have been my EDEN model. Simple, huh? No competition, no fucking rape case, no casualties at the top of the company or from the top of buildings. None of that. And do you think I'd have given a shit whose bank account the money was going to? Do you?'

Miles wanted to defend himself, but the truth was too slippery an adversary. Weissman stood and walked twice around the perimeter of the room. He stopped by a framed front page of *The New York Times*. It showed a photograph of him shaking hands with President Reagan. Miles twisted in his chair to look when Weissman called his name. Weissman tapped the glass frame. 'This shot boosted US sales seven per cent in March 1987, Miles. Seven per cent!'

Weissman returned to the desk, but on Miles's side. Miles felt nervous and frightened for the first time since his initial conference with the great man. His fear came in part from having no idea what Weissman would say or do next. So when he saw Weissman pick up a heavy pile of the day's newspapers, the thought crossed Miles's mind that his boss was about to use them as a weapon to bludgeon Miles for his foolishness. Weissman had that air about him, like a retired general hopelessly pissed off with peace.

'Did you see these, Miles?'

A couple, yes.'

'But you noticed how much my cologne is mentioned?'

'It seems . . . to be in the news. Sir.'

'Damn right! And you know what that means? Huh?'

Weissman was standing right above Miles now, the papers casting a shadow across him. Miles coughed. He was thinking that to fall fifty-three floors to the ground was a more appealing option than to have to answer his boss.

'I'd have thought that was . . . good? Saul.'

Another silence. Then Weissman began to drop the papers on to Miles's lap. As he did so, he read the headlines of each relevant article.

'Sin and controversy in the *Weissmans* Garden of *Eden*.
Genesis Retold.
Eden, American style.
Six-million-dollar Adam chosen today.
Senator's son wanted place in flawed paradise.
And this one, Miles, from our astute friend Mr Larry Meyers: Italians Favoured to Taste Golden Apple.'

Weissman let go the *Herald* and returned to his seat. He leant forward on his forearms as Miles rearranged the papers into a neat pile and placed them on the floor. Miles could feel a sheen of sweat prickling his forehead.

And then Weissman spoke. 'I think you may have taken ten years off my life, Miles, but you've saved me hundreds of thousands of dollars in advertising. This is the best publicity job my company's ever seen.'

Miles wondered if he'd heard right, but Weissman's relaxed expression confirmed that he had. Miles felt like breaking into song. 'Thank you, Saul.'

Weissman leant back in his chair. 'I did think of wringing

your neck, but that would have been stupid, wouldn't it?'
Miles smiled and nodded. See, you did what I asked you to
do, and then some. You should be proud.'

I am, Saul, I am.

Truly it was as if a storm had swept through the room and
cleared the air until it was clean and fresh and invigorating.
The miracle was that the storm itself had never come.

'Now, Miles. I want you to move into Kristina's office for
the moment. You can have her secretary . . . in a manner
of speaking. OK? Cindy's got a list of the don't-knows for
tonight's shindig. I want you on to them. I need a Yes or a
No. A 'maybe' means maybe there won't be a place for them
if they show. OK? Now I'm gonna be making my speech at
the end of the evening, and announcing the winners. That's
something I want to talk to you about. Look what landed on
my desk this morning.'

It was a letter. Three pages of brownish, recycled paper
from Dr P. Gardner, self-appointed head of MAP, the
Movement for African People.

'I read that right through,' Weissman said with pride, as if
he was a schoolboy having, for once, finished his prep.

Miles skimmed his eye over the letter. Certain words
and phrases kept cropping up – melanin deficiency, Adam,
Ice people, Eve, Sun people, Egyptians, African-Americans,
culture, Adam.

'See what he says at the top there? He says I've set a
fine example by including a coloured man like Reuben in
the competition. He says that if I use Reuben I'll go down
in history as . . . how does he put it?'

Miles traced a finger over the page. 'Something other than
a mean-spirited white capitalist Jew.'

'That's it! Now, the guy's out to lunch, Milo, but he does
say that most of the peoples of the world have colour to
their skin. The first man was coloured, Miles. That's what
he says. And who was the first man?'

Oh no, Saul. Not now. Miles could see what was happening.
He himself had used this argument when he'd first introduced
Reuben.

Weissman had little patience. 'Well? Who?'

Miles could hardly bring himself to say it. 'Adam.'

'Adam. Exactly. Adam *was* black, so Adam *should* be black. How do you like that?'

Not at all. Not if you want to make Reuben the EDEN model over Giovanni. Not if you're going to snatch a million dollars from under my nose. Please God, not on the last day!

'I think it's . . . interesting, Saul, but I'm not sure how many people would agree. I think it would be risky to use a black model.'

'Maybe. But I got an idea. I want Reuben as our runner-up.' At once, Miles felt his muscles relax. 'We can pay him a daily rate, say $1500, and take him to Brazil in case Giovanni becomes lunch for a crocodile. What'd'ya think?'

Miles's grin surged from his stomach. 'I think it's a great idea.'

'So do I. Now, what about his Eve? I'm thinking Helima. I mean, that woman's something else.'

'Could be. Or . . .' Miles thought quickly. Would Poppy mind if Sandy came second? She couldn't! Not with Tiziana walking away the EDEN winner. 'How about a contrast, Saul? How about Sandy?'

'Sandy? She's a beautiful girl, no question. Could look good. Could look very good. Black and white. Sun and Ice. Chocolate and vanilla. I like it. United colours. Luciano Benetton can eat his fucking heart out, eh, Miles? I can beat him at his own game.'

'Yes, Saul.'

'The fucking triangle's all broke up, Miles. But you know what we got now?' Weissman paused. 'A circle! There's no sides any more. It's just you and me seeing things in the same way. Wouldn't you say? You're not greedy, Miles. Not like that Kristina. I know you wouldn't screw me around.'

'No, I wouldn't.'

'OK, kid, you're beautiful. But I've gotta write my speech

for tonight. Call me if you need anything. If not, I'll see you at the party. Get there early.'

'Yes, Saul.'

'And make sure you bring your girlfriend along. I'm beginning to get worried that she doesn't even exist.'

38

The sparkling December day ebbed to a winter's tenebrous dusk, and the time had almost arrived. In apartments and houses, from 110th Street to Tribeca, the guests and contestants were wondering what to wear and whether it'd be fun and who would win the prize. Some were more confident than others. In the most luxurious of the houses, the Italians were donning Armani and whistling Puccini and thinking that life was quite fine. Neither Tiziana nor Giovanni had ever imagined wanting to be anyone but themselves, but it was only upon nights such as these that they pondered their good fortune. How many among the world's billions possessed such a balance of culture, breeding, wealth and beauty without any of the disadvantages that marred the lives of movie stars and princesses, presidents and kings? These thoughts filled the minds of brother and sister alike as they smoothed their eyebrows and gorged themselves on their own beauty reflected in each other. This was to be a night of the most glorious self-celebration, and both felt happy to the core.

There were others excited and confident as well, albeit with less reason. In a room in the Midas Hotel, Fabio Nirao, dressed in black tie and bandages, watched Fernando as he clipped on the bow tie that had come with his rented suit. He'd never worn a tuxedo before, there'd been no need, and so seeing himself looking already like someone he was not made Fernando wonder out loud whether he might walk away with the contract. Fabio saw no reason why Fernando shouldn't win, especially when he heard how attentive Weissman had been ever since Fernando and he had met. Miles, too, liked Fernando. That much was obvious. With a smile, Fernando recounted to Fabio the story of Miles appearing in the Sunshine State Park in that monster of a car. Fernando had been keen to send him away, but now he thanked God that he hadn't. So much had come of it already. Miles had been quite right about the Best Burger payout. The guilt had evaporated with the first cheque, and even Fernando's mother had begun to believe: she'd taken a cautious week's holiday from her job. Fernando wondered what more it would take for her to quit. Six million dollars maybe? Well, it was possible. Oh yes, it was certainly that.

Reuben, on the other hand, had no such delusions. He expected to have to return to working part-time in Nuts About You while he finished his degree. The competition hadn't changed him much. Most of his friends teased him about it. Reuben had no idea what Weissman had in store, no idea that he was anything more than the token coloured contestant. It was Marcie who'd been getting excited. She'd read an article in the *Village Voice* that said that Reuben deserved to win, and she had this private hunch that he might. She'd been out and bought herself an expensive dress for the party – a shiny pink number of the type Whitney Houston liked to wear in her videos. Reuben didn't care for it at all (he preferred her in fisherman's sweaters) but when she asked him his opinion, he smiled and said it was the nicest dress he'd ever seen her wear.

Troy, innocently emulating Giovanni, was wearing a new Armani jacket for the bash. He'd booked himself out for the afternoon, and had had a facial and a massage and a swim at the New York Health and Racket so he could look his most vibrant. Though Troy's girlfriend – Sasha, the model – was flying back to Manhattan from Quito that night, Troy was taking his agent Basia as his guest. It was the smartest thing to do. He and Basia had fought recently over a swimwear catalogue Troy had refused to do (he'd developed a recent complex about the size of his anatomy) and he knew he had some making up to do. And anyway, he wanted someone in the agency to witness his moment of triumph. Too many had seen his shame on the Trudie Love show.

Three of the four men thought they might win. Yet, of the six female finalists, only two considered that they had a chance. Tiziana, of course, was one. The other was Sandy. Though she tended to agree with the rest that Tiziana was firmly favoured, Sandy did wonder whether her affair with Miles might have helped. For the others, they viewed the party as a chance to squeeze a little more self-publicity from the competition. The party in Grand Central was to be their biggest-ever casting. Sandy and Helima, Andrea, Jessica and Jack all knew that the only way to get ahead in the modelling world was to make contacts with the important editors, photographers and stylists.

Word had been spreading all week about who was expected at the party. The editors of *Vogue* and *Mademoiselle*, *Elle* and *Harper's Bazaar* were certainly going. So too were some big-name photographers – Sam Emsiel, Brett Iris, B.B. Errucce – and a smattering of the top stylists. For Jessica Warren, the party was to be her big chance to show herself off in a new city. She was the only one of the six without an agent in Manhattan. With luck she hoped to meet one at the party. But failing that, there was a better than good chance that she'd run into someone she knew from London as there'd been a recent invasion of Brits into the New York magazine world. From what she'd heard, there was hardly a magazine left that wasn't run by a vicious bitch with a clipped British accent.

The party itself was being held in the former Waiting Room at New York's Grand Central terminal. Finished in 1913, at about the time Britain passed the Imperial baton to the States, the terminal had been to New Yorkers such as Weissman something more than a train station. In its way, it was a symbol of the city – massive and proud and harmonious, yet always teeming with life. It was more than a beautiful mash of ramps and connecting rail lines and underground passages. It was a triumph over enormity.

Weissman himself had suggested the station as a venue for the party for its grand design mirrored his own dramatic vision. There were venues more showy in the city, but few as magnificent. Weissman might even have fancied himself as a Roman emperor beneath the neoclassical arches of the Waiting Room.

For the party, large banners had been erected featuring the EDEN logo. Beneath two of them, Herb Willis had had painted two ten-foot-high question marks, one in blue, the other in pink. The renowned floral designer Dorrance de Blaby had spared no expense on the flowers. In the middle of each table was a dramatic array of amaryllis, the stems of which blossomed gaudily above a thick glass tank containing pebbles and vines and contorted willow. There were fifty tables in all, ten people at each. The models and their guests were at the tables either side of Saul's top table.

At a little after eight p.m., Miles arrived at the venue to see if he could hurl around his new-found weight. He was the first to arrive. The meticulous elegance of the scene appealed to Miles: the purity of the smooth white tablecloths, the silverware fanning symmetrically about the edge of each table, the polished glasses unused and glinting in the lights. The staff were putting the final touches to the grand scene – straightening a fork, tidying an electrical cable, filling the buckets with ice, taking instructions about when to serve what to whom.

Miles felt like a king, these scurrying people his servants. Hands in pockets, shoulders relaxed, he sauntered up to the head table, his footsteps clicking across the stone floor. Was it his imagination, or was the table bathed in a softer, more sympathetic light? He and Poppy had taken Kristina's places. Miles looked at the twelve names on the largest table: Weissman and Patty, his wife; the mayor and his wife; the *Herald*'s editor, Tony Jakes, plus girlfriend; Bruce Stone and his new wife; Miles and Poppy; Trudie Love and Maury Greenberg. Miles was sandwiched between the bulks of flesh that were Trudie and Weissman's wife. Poppy was seated between the mayor and Maury Greenberg. Miles thought how much she'd like that. Maury would make her feel at ease, and the mayor would praise her for her work with Legal Aid, and listen with a sympathetic tilt of the head to her oft-repeated tales of plea-bargaining injustices. Perhaps, Miles thought, Poppy's placement will help her see me in a better light. It's because of me that she's there.

It's because of me! The sentence lingered in his mind like the vapour trail of a jet in a clear sky. Wasn't most of this because of him? Miles sat at his place and leant back in the chair, pushing it on to its back two legs. He picked up his place card. Mr Miles Jensen, *Weissmans.* Here it was in writing. Mr Miles Jensen, a somebody of importance.

A uniformed waiter approached Miles with a curled lip until he saw the tag on Miles's tuxedo. His demeanour softened. 'Would you care for me to crack open a bottle of champagne for you, sir?'

The waiter spoke as if it was a bottle of his own he'd offered to share.

'That sounds good. Thanks,' Miles said, taking a cigarette from a fresh packet as he spoke.

It was the idea he liked. It smelled of the future. If he invested the million dollars from Giovanni with care he'd be ordering champagne for the rest of his life. Miles thought the whole caring, sharing nineties ethos was pure baloney. Money was as delicious as it had ever been. Maybe more so because it had become valuable again. Miles would be becoming a member of a more exclusive club. A million dollars. It sounded like heaven.

He asked for the whole bottle to be left, and for the next forty minutes he stayed where he was, drinking, smoking, dreaming and watching the room fill with the guests arriving in their finery. Their voices lofted into the high ceiling. Miles cast his eyes about to see if there was anyone he knew. The biggest stars coming were the supermodels Kristina had been smart enough to invite. Perhaps out of loyalty to their friend Tiziana, Candy Hempbell, Dina, and Trish Cuttingham were coming. Tania Fern, the new girl on the block, was also attending along with a few Broadway and television stars, friends of Saul Weissman. Lulu Manette from the soap *Laughter and Tears* would be there, and Kristina had thought it fun to invite Petra, the hottest drag queen Manhattan had ever known. Miles enjoyed searching for their faces among the happy crowd, but soon it became too hard to see people from his chair so Miles broke his promise to wait for Poppy at the table, and began to meander purposefully through the people.

Once or twice he'd been to events such as this, but now, for the first time among the glittering, sparkling faces, Miles felt as if he belonged. Always before he'd looked on and wanted, wanted until it hurt, to be like them, to be among them. Now he felt above them. Wasn't this his show? He ran his fingers through his hair and sucked in his cheeks and thought that this was how it would feel if he made it to the catwalk. He picked up his stride through the people. A man going somewhere. His eyes became like cannons.

You – you – you – you. I see you, and you see me, and I'm what you haven't got. I'm your subliminal desire. You can see me but you can't have me. I hope you like the suit and the hair and the walk and maybe you're wondering who I am. Want to know? I'm Miles Jensen, and this – is – my, show.

Miles made a path to the bar, and came to a stop by it. He had them refill his glass, then he lit a cigarette and began to lighthouse. That was Poppy's expression for the habit Miles had of looking about him at parties. But tonight, thought Miles, everyone is lighthousing. That's what parties such as this are for. On one of the rotations of his head he saw Basia, the agent from Supreme. He joined her at the bar.

'Hi there, Miles. Great to see you. This is fantastic, isn't it?'

Basia was wearing her customary black clothes and bright red lipstick. Looking at her chalky plump skin, Miles suddenly had an urge to poke at her cheek as if pressing a finger into dough. He held back.

'I meant to ask you something,' said Miles.

'Fire away.'

'Do you think I'd have any chance as a model?'

Basia touched Miles's arm. 'Sure you would. Have you ever done any before?'

'I've done some commercials.'

532

'Fabulous. Do you have a headshot?'

'Yeah, but it's not so good.'

'Listen, tell you what. Come in on Monday morning and we'll have a chat.'

'You'll be able to see me this time, will you?'

'Of course,' Basia replied just as Poppy arrived and tugged on the back of Miles's jacket. He spun around.

'Hey you!'

He kissed her.

'You're drunk already.'

'No, I'm not!'

'Why didn't you wait where you said you would?'

'Sorry, babes.'

He kissed her again and slinked an arm around her back. She was wearing a simple black Barneys dress given her by her parents the year before.

'You look nice,' he said.

'You mean that?'

'Yeah! Come and meet the models.'

'Right, now you're not embarrassed by me.'

'Poppy! Come on.'

'I don't really want to.'

'Come on. There's Fernando, you'll like him. Hey,' he said as he led her to Fernando, 'did you see you're sitting by the mayor . . .?'

Miles introduced Poppy to all the models but Troy, Sandy and Tiziana, who was flirting with Paolo Bruni. Reluctantly, Poppy had to admit that she liked them. Especially the bruised and battered Fabio.

Dinner began soon after. Caviar, because Weissman was a man who liked to display his wealth, and then a cold Thai chicken salad with arugula. Patty Weissman was much quieter than her husband. She was a large woman with a mop of grey hair and eyes slightly too close together, but she was friendly to Miles and told him how much Weissman appreciated the work Miles had done. Trudie was less easy. Miles was surprised that a woman nationally famous as an interviewer should find it almost impossible to talk about anything but herself. Miles guessed that Trudie was peeved to be sitting next to him instead of next to the mayor.

Miles had been glad to see Maury Greenberg. 'See, I told you,' he'd said as soon as he'd seen Miles. 'You hit a home run.' Maury's tan seemed to have darkened since Miles had met him. Miles had a picture of Maury relaxing in his pastel and gold Floridian life on the wicker furniture of Miranda's Veranda. He didn't fit the crisply elegant atmosphere of this Manhattan party. But he was all charm with Poppy, and Miles was glad to see her looking so radiant.

Miles tried to avoid glancing at Sandy. She was seated at the table to his right. The desire for her had been so strong that fragments of the emotion remained still, as if carried in his bloodstream, at times passing through his heart in a jolting reminder of what had been. And when their eyes had met for an instant, Miles felt guilty at once, as if his thoughts were visible to Poppy.

After the chicken came a chocolate roulade that Patty and Trudie picked at. Miles was beginning to feel excited about the imminent result. It was all happening as he'd hoped. He hadn't told Poppy about the deal with Giovanni having not only feared that she'd disapprove but that she wouldn't be around to share the spoils. Now Miles felt otherwise. The excitement was almost sexual. He could hardly wait to be alone with Poppy, in bed where he thought he'd share with her the news.

Across the table, Weissman was looking troubled. He was patting the inside pocket of his jacket. Then he stood, felt in his pockets and, looking dismayed, talked to his wife across the table. The rest of the table fell quiet.

'Patty! Sweetheart, do you have my speech?'

'Of course I don't!'

'Well nor do I!'

'Can't you remember who won?' said Maury.

Weissman scratched at his head.

Miles spoke, 'Didn't you think it'd be a good idea to give the campaign to me and Poppy, Saul?'

Weissman laughed. 'Poppy's beautiful enough, Miles – it's you lets the side down!'

Poppy coloured.

'And you weren't on my show!' said Trudie.

'Or in my paper,' added Jakes.

'If they're both New York City taxpayers I think they'd be a fine choice,' said the mayor.

'Well no one's going to know anything if I don't find this speech,' said Weissman.

'You had it out in the car, dear,' said Patty shaking her head. 'He's always losing things,' she added to Miles.

'I heard that Patty. You'll be losing a husband if you don't start being nicer to me!'

'You're the most spoiled man in the city,' the mayor's wife said.

'Ruined's the word, sweetheart. Not spoiled. Ruined!'

'Do you want me to look in the limousine, Saul?' asked Patty.

'I can go,' Miles said.

'Would you Miles? That'd be beautiful.'

Miles liked the attention he received as he stood to walk through the tables. Everyone else was seated. He stopped by one of the models for a moment and leant over.

'Only another ten minutes to go,' he said.

'Is it me?' said Fabio.

'Could be,' Miles said, straightening up and moving to the exit.

Outside it was cold but refreshing. Miles walked briskly through the station concourse towards the limousines, smiling to himself as he went. Beneath the Christmas tree a man was collecting for charity. Miles stopped and gave him five dollars, left, returned and gave him another ten. He thought that Grand Central had never looked so fine before. What a beautiful city Manhattan was!

He found Weissman's limo, and after a little persuasion the driver looked inside and found the speech on the back seat. Miles thanked him, gave him a tip, and opened the speech. It was scratched in Weissman's childish handwriting. Miles smiled at the first joke. And at the bottom of the page, beneath a multitude of references to all things Italian, were two names that made his heart sing. Mr Giovanni and Miss Tiziana Ferrari.

Miles folded the pages again and turned back to the hall. As he did so, four police cars drew up. The first was a detective's car, black and unmarked by anything but the red light clipped above the front passenger door. Ahead of Miles, seven police officers entered the terminal building. He wondered if there was security alert with the mayor. The policemen were heading for the party.

Miles ambled behind and reached the officers as they clustered around the security men at the barrier. He pushed his way to the front, and introduced himself. A tall man with a short haircut stepped forward. There was something about his pinched face and beady eyes that made him seem to belong to another era; to the forties or fifties. He explained why they were there.

'Are you being serious?' said Miles. 'You want to arrest someone in there right now?'

'That's the idea.'

Behind Miles, the photographers were beginning to sense a rat.

'Can I ask you who you're arresting?'

'You can, but I won't tell you.'

Miles felt there was something he should do. The party was going well but he feared an incident such as this would remind the guests of the troubles that had affected the competition.

'Mr Weissman's about to make his speech.' Miles held up the pages. 'Can't you wait until after then?'

'Sorry!'

'Can you at least hang on until I tell Mr Weissman what's happening. I can't believe this person's going anywhere.'

'OK. A couple of minutes, that's all.'

'Thanks.'

As Miles returned inside he saw Larry Meyers stand from his table and approach the detectives at the door.

When Miles reached Weissman, he leant down to whisper

into his ear. Weissman immediately leant over to the mayor. 'Dave, spare me a moment?'

As Weissman and the mayor stood to talk in private, Miles, enjoying the curiosity he was arousing, returned to Meyers and the police. Meyers was in deep conversation with the detective.

'Mr Weissman's talking to the mayor about this,' said Miles. 'I think he might ask you to hold back until after the result announcement.'

'Miles,' said Meyers. 'That's not a good idea.'

'Why?'

As Meyers began to explain, there was a burst of applause from within the party. Miles looked up to see Weissman walking fast to the raised podium in the centre of the hall. The mayor, too, was off his chair, approaching Miles at the entrance.

Saul Weissman had lit a cigar and was now surveying the guests about him.

'Looking at all your faces, I feel like an Oscar winner here, but in fact I'm just the guy opening the envelope.' Weissman picked up a folded piece of paper, and tore at the top. 'And the winner is . . .'

There was a sudden hush. The models at the tables looked shocked, terrified. Weissman was smiling. 'And you thought you were gonna get away that easy? Sorry! Before I do announce the lucky winners I wanna thank you all for coming. You've made it a wonderful evening for me.'

The echo of Weissman's voice through the speakers was drowned by a round of applause. When people stopped clapping, they made themselves comfortable in their chairs, picked up their glasses, and looked at the man who was about to part with seven million dollars.

'There's a couple of people here,' Meyers continued, 'who need special thanks. One is Mr Fabio Nirao, the brave young Brazilian man who was viciously attacked in the West Village. Fabio, where you at?' Fabio raised his hand. 'Stand up so we can see you.'

There was a self-conscious pattering of palms as Fabio

stood. Out of the hospital his face seemed more damaged, and this was not a crowd sympathetic towards ugliness in any form.

'Now there's one other guy whose name you may have heard. Really, this guy's done most of the work for me. He went to Miami and found a wonderful young man called Fernando Padrillas. In Tokyo he found our friend Fabio. He went to Paris, France and met a very special contestant, Mr Giovanni Ferrari. And back here, under our noses in New York, he found Mr Reuben King and then Troy Turnbull. And when he'd done that he suggested Helima, Tiziana, Jackie, Andrea, Sandy, and Jessica, six of the most beautiful women – I'm sure you agree – that this city's ever seen. His name is Miles Jensen. Miles where have you got to?'

Weissman looked towards the head table, but Miles hadn't yet returned. Instead he was by the detectives at the entrance, frantically scribbling a message on a piece of paper.

'Miles!' Weissman called again. 'Come up here!'

There were whistles from Fernando and Jessica, polite applause from the rest. Poppy felt surprisingly proud. Miles, head down now, walked fast through the tables to Weissman. He handed Weissman the note.

'See? The guy never stops working for me,' Weissman said with a grin.

And then he read the message. There was a tremendous silence. Weissman looked across at the entrance. The police were standing there still. The mayor had taken his seat. So too had Miles. Weissman himself looked suddenly uncomfortable. He scratched at his ear lobe, then he looked down. Beside Miles, Patty Weissman was getting concerned. She'd always been terrified that Saul would have a heart attack at a moment like this. Miles didn't notice. He was sitting motionless now, a glazed expression to his face. A murmur of speculation had filled the silence. A few people coughed. Some noticed the waiting police.

Then Weissman lifted his eyes and with great purpose folded the speech he'd planned to make. He slid it into his inside jacket pocket and took a slight step back from the podium. Miles could guess from Weissman's expression – the narrowed eyes, the slight downturn of the mouth – that he was about to launch into a Big Speech. Luke Skywalker and the Force. Triangles and circles and a scent to change the world.

Yet, instead of his customary garrulity, when Weissman began to talk he was struggling with his words. He gave the impression of a man practising a speech in private. He'd taken the microphone out of its clip and was holding it almost against his lips. His breath sounded as punctuation. His eyes didn't seem to be feeding any information to his mind.

'I went to see my son. A few weeks ago. He lives in Upstate New York and, he, he has, he lives in a very beautiful white old house.'

Weissman looked up and around as if suddenly remembering that the audience was there. 'I hadn't been there for quite a while so I was surprised to see he'd put this heavy-duty wire fence up around the front lawn and I said to him, "why'd you do this, Nathan?" and he looked at me and he said, "because it's mine, Dad, why not?"'

Weissman paused, and took a sip of water. The room had fallen quiet. There was something awkward about the situation, as if Weissman was saying something the audience didn't want to hear.

'Now my wife Patty and me, we tried to raise my son to believe that the United States truly is the greatest nation on earth because we *don't* put up fences in our front yards. But looking round me I'm getting the feeling that erecting fences and then shooting down the people who try to climb them is pretty much all we're about these days. And to be honest with you, I'm getting a little sick of it all.'

Now Weissman was rediscovering himself, becoming animated, purposeful, excited by the sound of his own voice. And the tempo and volume of his speech had increased considerably. 'I'm getting sick of people trying to slice up this country for themselves. And *yes* that includes my son, who I love dearly. It includes all Americans who don't think of themselves as Americans first, and ethnic groups second. It includes those guys who attacked Fabio Nirao. It includes those black kids who went on the rampage last week. It includes my ex-vice president. In fact it includes everyone who's responsible for breaking apart this beautiful country because they care too – goddamn – much – about themselves. And what I say is that *we gotta stop doing that*! We got to re-form some community in the States. The United States means something! And it's not the guys at the bottom of the heap who've got to get up off their asses and do something about it but the Nathan Weissmans of this world. The guys who've got front yards. The guys who insist on building their fences and making their rules.

'Now I'm not a politician, and I'm not going to change things that way. But I can do my bit. I can buy *Weissmans* a chunk of the Amazon and say I'm not gonna sit back and watch someone destroy it. And I can be a responsible citizen because if we don't all stand up and start doing something about this land, people, it won't be worth shit in ten, twenty years' time. So that's what I'm trying to do here.'

Weissman wiped at his brow and took a sip of water and began again more slowly, with a softer, more self-deprecating look on his face. 'Now I'm sure some of you guys are saying, "what's he talking about, it's only a cologne!" Right?' There was some laughter. 'Am I right? Well this is the only way I know how to do something.'

Weissman stopped and gestured towards the models' table. Most of the guests turned their heads to look.

'A week ago I met these beautiful people, and I thought, how am I going to choose? They're *all* great. But then I started to understand the characters as well as the faces of these young men and women, and my difficult choice slowly became more easy until I reached the decision I want to share with you now.'

Miles looked across at the models. Giovanni caught his eye, and smiled. He brushed a hair off his face. On the adjacent table, Tiziana was smoking a cigarette and casually stirring her coffee. A million dollars. Pah! Sandy was stirring her coffee.

Reuben was looking surprised, Troy nervous. Fernando was smiling, a glass in his hand. Andrea, Jack and Helima looked uninterested. Jessica, of course, looked stoned.

'The two models we've chosen for the seven million dollars' worth of contracts are . . .'

Weissman, the showman again, drew in on his cigar and then leant very close to the microphone, '. . . maybe I won't tell you.' There was more laughter. Weissman, too, glanced at the models. 'They say it's not over 'til the fat lady sings, so I was going to get my wife to chant out the names. Uh-oh,' Weissman pointed his cigar towards the top table, 'Patty looks like she wants to shoot me!'

'I do,' she said loud enough for Weissman to hear.

Then Weissman stood up straight.

'We got a new President. We got a new feeling. We got a new scent. We gotta stop looking backwards, grab the future and wear EDEN. The models who'll represent this cologne, folks, the Adam and Eve of this new EDEN are both Americans, and proud of it. They are Mr Reuben King and Miss Sandy Gabriel!'

A shriek from somewhere, a spontaneous round of applause. Most of the people in the room were trying to see the models. Marcie had leapt out of her chair and was now standing, her arms flung around Reuben who looked quite dazed. Sandy was staring straight at Miles. So, too, was Poppy.

'Come on you guys. Come on up here.'

Beneath the podium the cameras were flashing ecstatically as Reuben and Sandy joined Weissman. Reuben towered over him. He was grinning so much that he kept closing his eyes with the joy and the surprise. Sandy had tears in her eyes. Weissman stood off the podium, and Reuben put his arm around Sandy.

The photographers were calling out: *Kiss her on the cheek . . . Sandy, over here . . . Reuben, Reuben – smile! . . . Turn this way . . . Hey, Sandy, Sandy, Sandy . . . That's nice . . . Can you get closer? . . . Lovely!*

As soon as the announcement was made, Trudie Love had joined her camera team for some celebrity interviews. Patty

Weissman had gone with the mayor and his wife to talk to Saul. Jakes was talking to Meyers. Bruce Stone looked bemused. And Miles hadn't moved. He was staring into Giovanni's face at the adjacent table. He'd never seen such a look of hatred in a man's face before.

As Miles looked on he saw in the corner of his eye two of the officers approaching Giovanni. The Italian turned around, surprised. They leant down to talk to him. One of the men showed Giovanni his police badge. Another officer arrived when Giovanni refused to stand. Then another. Suddenly the cameras were there too. It was a photo opportunity in a million. Tiziana, so accustomed to the power of her fame, was arguing with the police, but they were not listening. And then, under the scrutiny of twenty or more lenses, Giovanni Ferrari was led from the hall by a couple of uniformed police.

All the while Miles was staring in shock.

'Miles!'

It was Weissman. Miles got to his feet. 'Sir?'

'Come with me.'

Ignoring most people, ignoring the cameras, Weissman led Miles to the police by the entrance. Giovanni was ahead of them, on his way to the precinct house.

'I don't fucking believe this, Miles,' said Weissman under his breath. 'I want to know what the fuck this is all about.'

Larry Meyers stepped forward, dropped his notepad to his side. It was he who told Miles and Weissman the details. Weissman stood to listen with his head down and his hands in his pockets.

'It was almost a freak coincidence,' Meyers said. 'They tracked down Fabio's attackers by the licence plate thinking they were just your regular Jersey Italian bad boys. But then my old friend Brian Reilly recognised one of the attackers from the surveillance he'd been doing on Johnny Fratacci. Apparently Johnny made the mistake of taking this guy to an apartment in Sutton Place.'

'Where Giovanni lives.'

'That's right. That's when they put it together. Johnny was

taking the guy to meet Giovanni Ferrari. They've even got shots of them at the door of Giovanni's place.'

'So you're saying that Giovanni hired these guys to beat up Fabio?' asked Miles.

'Seems so.'

Weissman rubbed at his face with his hand. Miles couldn't remember seeing Weissman look tired like this before. 'This whole competition has been like a launch party on the Titanic, hasn't it?' He looked up sharply at Meyers.' Do me a favour and don't quote me on that. I feel up against it as it is.'

'Don't worry, you'll get a good story tomorrow. I mean, maybe you didn't like the route you had to take, but you should be pretty happy with your destination. You made the best choice, I'm sure.'

'You think so? Yeah, maybe. Maybe I did,' said Weissman as he left.

Miles was about to follow when Meyers said, 'You should have taken me up on that bet last night.'

'I know. I'd be a rich man.'

'Giovanni was going to win, wasn't he? Until this happened.'

'I can't comment on that.'

Meyers smiled. 'I was looking over your shoulder when you wrote that note to Saul Weissman.'

'Then why did you need to ask me?'

'I don't like quoting myself.'

'I can quote you though. When you first interviewed me you said: "no one's going to remember this cologne in six months' time." You still believe that?'

Meyers grinned, said nothing and slapped Miles on the back. Then he left to catch up with Detective Brian Reilly. Miles went to look for Poppy. He found her alone at the table. She was making a pattern on the cloth with torn flower petals.

'Sorry,' he said. 'I got caught up.'

'With Sandy?'

'No, with Saul and Larry Meyers.'

'Mmm.'

Around them most people had stood from their tables, happy to escape from the guests whose tables they'd shared. There was an after-hours party in Club USA to which many were going. The models were grouped together around Reuben and Sandy. Troy had left. Tiziana had followed Giovanni. Jessica was trying to erect a chimney with empty champagne glasses. There was no one but Poppy left at the head table.

Miles drew up a chair close to Poppy's and took a hand in his.

'Can you believe all this?' he said.

Poppy remained curiously expressionless. 'I want to go home,' she said.

'OK, let's go in about ten minutes. I don't much feel like going to the club either.'

'No, Miles. I'm going now.'

'Can't you wait? I'll be ten minutes, I promise.'

Poppy stared at him. Her hands felt cold.

'You made two promises to me recently, Miles. Remember? First you said you'd never sleep with any of the models. Then you promised this morning that Sandy wasn't going to win. How do you expect me to believe anything you say any more?'

'Babes, Giovanni and Tiziana were going to win but he just got arrested! Did you expect me to predict that? I can hardly believe it even now. And I had no idea who Saul was going to choose.'

Poppy stood. 'I want to go.'

'Hang on, please.'

She stood. 'I'll see you later.'

'Poppy!'

Poppy walked straight by Sandy without turning to look. Miles was following when he heard Saul Weissman call his name. Damn! He turned to look. Weissman was calling him over. He turned back to Poppy. She was getting further away. 'Poppy,' Miles called out. 'You are going home to the apartment, aren't you?'

'Miles,' called Weissman. 'Here.'

Poppy turned, shrugged her shoulders, and left the room.

Saul Weissman was standing with his hands on Reuben and Sandy's shoulders. When Sandy saw Miles she stepped forward, took his cheeks in both hands, and gave Miles a kiss on the lips. Reuben shook Miles's hand. Miraculously, Saul Weissman was in a better frame of mind.

'So what do you think of my six-million-dollar man, Milo?'

Miles tapped his foot against Reuben's polished, rented patent leather shoe. 'I think he's just right!'

'That's what I like to hear. They're both beautiful!' A photographer wanting to add to the gold already on his film asked to take a shot of Weissman and the winners. All three grinned into the lens. After a few frames he lifted his eyes and said to Reuben, 'Do you think you're worth so much?'

'I hope so,' Reuben laughed.

'Don't hope,' said Weissman. *'Know!'*

'OK, I know so.'

Weissman clapped together his hands. 'That's better. I know so too. What do you think, Miles? You think Reuben can turn EDEN into the number one seller in the world?'

There'd been a time, so recently before, when Miles would have shaken his head and said that he wasn't sure, didn't know, couldn't guess.

But not any more. Now he knew what to say.

'Of course we can, Saul! And we will.'

'Now that,' Weissman said, 'is what I like to hear. First stop Brazil, Milo . . .'

Miles Jensen smiled. 'And next stop the world!'

39

In a dull but expensive hotel in the centre of Hamburg, Miss Kristina von Koeler read about Giovanni's arrest on the front page of the international edition of *USA TODAY*. It worried her slightly, but not too much. So what if she'd just happened to mention to Giovanni when they'd dined together that Fabio alone was standing between Giovanni and the prize? How was it she'd phrased it? Oh, yes – *He'll have to be hit by a car if you're going to win*. That was it. And when Giovanni had asked where Fabio might be on the night of the party in Rudy's, Kristina had not committed a crime in giving details to Giovanni of the route Fabio would be taking from Stone's studio to the restaurant. She'd simply been passing on harmless information. So maybe by now it was common knowledge that she'd needed someone out of the competition to get Steve in, but even Steve in his interview with Meyers had said that he doubted Kristina was involved with the attack. No, Giovanni wouldn't drag her down. She didn't even think he would go far down himself.

Kristina looked again at the photograph of Reuben and Sandy. It disgusted her. And Saul's speech sounded like the biggest load of schmoozy, sentimental, p.c. hogwash she'd ever heard. What did the man expect? *You have to build the fences to keep the niggers out, Saul! You don't go and give them ladders until they've earned your trust . . .*

Still, he'll come to regret his decision, she thought. EDEN won't sell. Reuben will look ridiculous next to Sandy. There'll be a revolt among customers in Middle America, and Saul will have lost not only the best vice president he's ever likely to have, but millions and millions of dollars as well.

*   *   *

'Miles, what are you doing in there? Let me in.' Again Poppy banged on the bathroom door. 'You're going to make me late for work.'

'Hang on, I'll be two minutes.'

Miles took a step back from the mirror and looked at his face in dismay. How could the most expensive bronzer money could buy have turned his skin orange? Yet it had, and when he'd tried to wash it off, smears of instant tan had streaked his cheeks.

Miles cursed himself for his stupidity. Why had he allowed himself to get so worked up about his meeting at Supreme? Basia knew what he looked like. She hadn't said he was looking pasty. *Everyone* was looking pasty. It was December! Yet all weekend as his moment of judgment neared, Miles had been worrying. And the night before, he hadn't been able to sleep.

Even though Saul Weissman had promised Miles a job, even though Miles would probably be asked to go on the trip to Brazil in January, even though the future held more promise than it had for years, Miles thought he'd be losing a part of his new life unless he became a model.

He imagined benefits only. He'd be able to stay above the fray. He'd be able to stay employed. He wouldn't end up like Jeff Gifford in Tokyo, like Christian in Milan, like Troy Turnbull. He'd do it for the money. For the opportunity to travel the world. For the women!

Poppy banged again at the door. Miles had been too scared to tell her of his intention to become a model. He hadn't mentioned it during the hours they'd spent talking after the party. Instead they'd planned a golden future together – a secure job for him at Weissmans; a new apartment; the start of a new chapter in his life with Poppy.

And not a word about Paris, Miami, Milan or Japan.

Miles emerged from the bathroom.

'At last!' Poppy said, pushing by and closing the door. Miles trudged away. Then he heard the bathroom door open again.

'Miles!' Poppy's tone was inquisitive. Miles turned. 'What's happened?'

'What do you mean?'

'To your face.' Poppy started laughing. 'You look funny.' She came up beside him. Miles wasn't smiling. 'What's on your face?' she asked, touching his cheek with her finger.

'Bronzer.'

'What?'

'It's just bronzer, OK? Bronzer.'

'But why?'

Miles turned to walk away. 'Why do you think? Because I thought I looked sick.'

Poppy followed him. 'I don't believe you. You're going to your first day at work looking like, I don't know what . . . a carrot or something.'

'Thanks!'

'But you do. You look funny.'

'You fucking told me already,' Miles shouted. 'Can't you drop it?'

'Miles! What's wrong with you this morning?'

'Nothing. I just didn't want to look so white, that's all.'

'But you've been to Weissmans a hundred times.'

Miles began to rub at his cheek with the palm of his hand. 'I wasn't going to Weissmans, OK? I was going to Supreme because one of the bookers there told me I should become a model. But then I got worried she'd change her mind if I looked like shit.'

Poppy sat on the arm of the sofa. She looked as if she'd been slapped. Miles walked to the kitchen to refill his coffee. From there he said, 'I didn't tell you because I knew you wouldn't like it.'

Poppy stood. 'I'm going to take my shower.'

'Poppy, please let's not argue about this.'

'Am I arguing?' she asked as she walked by.

'No. But you're not happy about it.'

Poppy reached the bathroom. 'Somehow,' she said, 'I don't think that makes any difference. Do you?'

'Yes, it does. Poppy, Poppy . . .'

But from behind the door he heard the stuttering jets of the shower as Poppy drowned the sound of his voice.

Miles hadn't left when she finished her shower, and he watched in silence as she dressed. When she was collecting together her belongings he said, 'I'm only going to ask them a few things, OK?'

'Whatever, Miles. It's your life. If you really want to be a model, I'm not going to stop you,' Poppy stood tugging at a knot with her hairbrush. 'You can send me nice postcards from Europe.'

'Who said anything about going to Europe?'

'I'm not a complete idiot.'

Miles took her gently by the arm. 'Babes, I don't want to upset you. Do you really not want me to go today?'

When Poppy looked up, she was smiling. 'Miles, if you go in looking like that they won't take you anyway.'

'Oh no! Is it that bad?'

'Mm, it is. Come here.'

Poppy led Miles by the hand into the bathroom and carefully, with cotton wool and cleanser, cleaned his face of the instant tan. Then, complaining about the time, she kissed him, said they'd talk later and ran from the apartment.

Miles walked to Park Avenue South. Ever since he'd been sent on the search he looked differently at people on the streets. What were they wearing? What would they look like on film? Were they more attractive than he? And when he saw beautiful people he couldn't help wondering whether at some time they'd tried to model, and if not, then why?

But he thought too of *Weissmans*. Saul had promised him an office, said he'd figure out a role for Miles doing some of the tasks that had fallen on Kristy's shoulders. He was happy that Miles was coming aboard, completely unaware that his new recruit was intending to jump ship. Already Miles dreaded having to tell Weissman the truth.

Miles arrived at Supreme faster than he'd thought he would. Upstairs he found the reception room crowded with models. It worried Miles that they all seemed more tanned and healthy than he did. He searched their faces for streaks of orange, hoping for the imperfection, but he found none. The receptionist handed Miles a sheet of paper to fill in. What were his measurements, it asked. His sports, particular skills, accomplishments? Was he SAG registered, represented in Europe, willing to go naked? Had he ever advertised condoms before?

The elevator door opened, and another five models joined the crowd. Leather, denim, hair gel, tans.

'How long you been waiting?' one asked Miles.

'I . . . I'm not here for this.'

'About an hour,' another model replied.

'Fuck this, man,' said the first.

But he grabbed a form anyway, and slumped himself in a corner, his portfolio on his knees.

Miles walked through to the main booking room. It too was busy with models waiting for the casting. He heard Scott Farber arguing with one of them.

'Don't blame me, buddy. If you couldn't be fucked to go see Pamela then we can't guarantee the job.'

'They were shooting in Harlem, man.'

'So? There's twenty guys who would have gone, but you said *you* wanted to go.'

Basia interrupted. 'I've got Outline on the phone. They're looking for a gay model for their cover. No fee.'

'Christ! What are we coming to in here?'

Basia looked up and saw Miles. 'Oh, hi, can you wait?'

'Sure.'

'You want a job? No fee but they're using a good photographer.'

Miles reddened, and said no. At the booking table a model whose face Miles recognised from the Bloomingdales ads was looking at his chart, empty for the whole next month. He didn't say anything. He just threw it back in its place and began to walk away. As he was leaving, he said, 'Anyone want to share a cab uptown?'

Miles looked about himself – at the stressed-out bookers snapping insults at whoever came close, at the tens of sullen-faced models hoping for this or any job, at the long wall of composite cards of men for whom beauty was everything. And then he replied, 'Yeah, I do.'

'I'm going to 68th and Broadway. Any use?'

'Great,' said Miles. 'Drop me off at that nut store on Lex. There's something I need for my boss.'